If you loved the exciting new Star Wars® adventures, beginning with *Heir to the Empire*, don't miss the thrilling classics that started it all!

STAR WARS®
by George Lucas

THE EMPIRE STRIKES BACK®
by Donald F. Glut

RETURN OF THE JEDI®
by James Kahn

THE

STAR WARS®

TRILOGY

STAR WARS®
by George Lucas

THE EMPIRE STRIKES BACK®
by Donald F. Glut

RETURN OF THE JEDI®
by James Kahn

A Del Rey Book
Ballantine Books • New York

A Del Rey Book
Published by Ballantine Books
STAR WARS Copyright © 1976 by The Star Wars Corporation
THE EMPIRE STRIKES BACK Copyright © 1980 by Lucasfilm Ltd.
RETURN OF THE JEDI Copyright © 1983 by Lucasfilm Ltd. (LFL)

Library of Congress Catalog Card Number: 87-91126

ISBN: 0-345-38438-5

Manufactured in the United States of America

First Trade Edition: May 1987
First Mass Market Edition: March 1993

Contents

EPISODE IV

STAR WARS:
A New Hope

From the Adventures of Luke Skywalker

A Novel by George Lucas

Prologue

ANOTHER galaxy, another time.

The Old Republic was the Republic of legend, greater than distance or time. No need to note where it was or whence it came, only to know that . . . it was *the* Republic.

Once, under the wise rule of the Senate and the protection of the Jedi Knights, the Republic throve and grew. But as often happens when wealth and power pass beyond the admirable and attain the awesome, then appear those evil ones who have greed to match.

So it was with the Republic at its height. Like the greatest of trees, able to withstand any external attack, the Republic rotted from within though the danger was not visible from outside.

Aided and abetted by restless, power-hungry individuals within the government, and the massive organs of commerce, the ambitious Senator Palpatine caused himself to be elected President of the Republic. He promised to reunite the disaffected among the people and to restore the remembered glory of the Republic.

Once secure in office he declared himself Emperor, shutting himself away from the populace. Soon he was controlled by the very assistants and boot-lickers he had appointed to high office, and the cries of the people for justice did not reach his ears.

Having exterminated through treachery and deception the Jedi Knights, guardians of justice in the galaxy, the Imperial governors and bureaucrats prepared to institute a reign of terror among the disheartened worlds of the galaxy. Many used the imperial forces and the name of the increasingly isolated Emperor to further their own personal ambitions.

But a small number of systems rebelled at these new outrages.

Declaring themselves opposed to the New Order they began the great battle to restore the Old Republic.

From the beginning they were vastly outnumbered by the systems held in thrall by the Emperor. In those first dark days it seemed certain the bright flame of resistance would be extinguished before it could cast the light of new truth across a galaxy of oppressed and beaten peoples . . .

From the First Saga
Journal of the Whills

"They were in the wrong place at the wrong time. Naturally they became heroes."

Leia Organa of Alderaan, Senator

I

IT was a vast, shining globe and it cast a light of lambent topaz into space—but it was not a sun. Thus, the planet had fooled men for a long time. Not until entering close orbit around it did its discoverers realize that this was a world in a binary system and not a third sun itself.

At first it seemed certain nothing could exist on such a planet, least of all humans. Yet both massive G1 and G2 stars orbited a common center with peculiar regularity, and Tatooine circled them far enough out to permit the development of a rather stable, if exquisitely hot, climate. Mostly this was a dry desert of a world, whose unusual starlike yellow glow was the result of double sunlight striking sodium-rich sands and flats. That same sunlight suddenly shone on the thin skin of a metallic shape falling crazily toward the atmosphere.

The erratic course the galactic cruiser was traveling was intentional, not the product of injury but of a desperate desire to avoid it. Long streaks of intense energy slid close past its hull, a multihued storm of destruction like a school of rainbow remoras fighting to attach themselves to a larger, unwilling host.

One of those probing, questing beams succeeded in touching the fleeing ship, striking its principal solar fin. Gemlike fragments of metal and plastic erupted into space as the end of the fin disintegrated. The vessel seemed to shudder.

The source of those multiple energy beams suddenly hove into view—a lumbering Imperial cruiser, its massive outline bristling cactuslike with dozens of heavy weapons emplacements. Light ceased arching from those spines now as the cruiser moved in close. Intermittent explosions and flashes of light could be seen in those portions of the smaller ship which had taken hits. In the absolute cold of space, the cruiser snuggled up alongside its wounded prey.

Another distant explosion shook the ship—but it certainly didn't feel distant to Artoo Detoo or See Threepio. The concussion bounced them around the narrow corridor like bearings in an old motor.

To look at these two, one would have supposed that the tall, human-like machine, Threepio, was the master and the stubby, tripodal robot, Artoo Detoo, an inferior. But while Threepio might have sniffed disdainfully at the suggestion, they were in fact equal in everything save loquacity. Here Threepio was clearly—and necessarily—the superior.

Still another explosion rattled the corridor, throwing Threepio off balance. His shorter companion had the better of it during such moments with his squat, cylindrical body's low center of gravity well balanced on thick, clawed legs

Artoo glanced up at Threepio, who was steadying himself against a corridor wall. Lights blinked enigmatically around a single mechanical eye as the smaller robot studied the battered casing of his friend. A patina of metal and fibrous dust coated the usually gleaming bronze finish, and there were some visible dents all the result of the pounding the rebel ship they were on had been taking.

Accompanying the last attack was a persistent deep hum which even the loudest explosion had not been able to drown out. Then for no apparent reason, the basso thrumming abruptly ceased, and the only sounds in the otherwise deserted corridor came from the eerie dry-twig crackle of shorting relays or the pops of dying circuitry. Explosions began to echo through the ship once more, but they were far away from the corridor.

Threepio turned his smooth, humanlike head to one side. Metallic ears listened intently. The imitation of a human pose was hardly necessary—Threepio's auditory sensors were fully omnidirectional—but the slim robot had been programmed to blend perfectly among human company. This programming extended even to mimicry of human gestures.

"Did you hear that?" he inquired rhetorically of his patient companion, referring to the throbbing sound. "They've shut down the main reactor and the drive." His voice was as full of disbelief and concern as that of any human. One metallic palm rubbed dolefully at a patch of dull gray on his side, where a broken hull brace had fallen and scored the bronze finish. Threepio was a fastidious machine, and such things troubled him.

"Madness, this is madness." He shook his head slowly. "This time we'll be destroyed for sure."

Artoo did not comment immediately. Barrel torso tilted backward, powerful legs gripping the deck, the meter-high robot was engrossed in studying the roof overhead. Though he did not have a head to cock in a listening posture like his friend, Artoo still somehow managed to convey that impression. A series of short beeps and chirps issued from his speaker. To even a sensitive human ear they would have been just so much static, but to Threepio they formed words as clear and pure as direct current.

"Yes, I suppose they did have to shut the drive down," Threepio admitted, "but what are we going to do now? We can't enter atmosphere with our main stablizer fin destroyed. I can't believe we're simply going to surrender."

A small band of armed humans suddenly appeared, rifles held at the ready. Their expressions were as worry-wrinkled as their uniforms, and they carried about them the aura of men prepared to die.

Threepio watched silently until they had vanished around a far bend in the passageway, then looked back at Artoo. The smaller robot hadn't shifted from his position of listening. Threepio's gaze turned upward also though he knew Artoo's senses were slightly sharper than his own.

"What is it, Artoo?" A short burst of beeping came in response. Another moment, and there was no need for highly attuned sensors. For a minute or two more, the corridor remained deathly silent. Then a faint *scrape, scrape* could be heard, like a cat at a door, from somewhere above. That strange noise was produced by heavy footsteps and the movement of bulky equipment somewhere on the ship's hull.

When several muffled explosions sounded, Threepio murmured, "They've broken in somewhere above us. There's no escape for the Captain this time." Turning, he peered down at Artoo. I think we'd better—"

The shriek of overstressed metal filled the air before he could finish, and the far end of the passageway was lit by a blinding actinic flash. Somewhere down there the little cluster of armed crew who had passed by minutes before had encountered the ship's attackers.

Threepio turned his face and delicate photoreceptors away— just in time to avoid the fragments of metal that flew down the corridor. At the far end a gaping hole appeared in the roof, and reflective forms like big metal beads began dropping to the corridor floor. Both robots knew that no machine could match the fluidity with which those shapes moved and instantly assumed fighting postures. The new arrivals were humans in armor, not mechanicals.

One of them looked straight at Threepio—no, not at him, the panicked robot thought frantically, but past him. The figure shifted its big rifle around in armored hands—too late. A beam of intense light struck the head, sending pieces of armor, bone, and flesh flying in all directions.

Half the invading Imperial troops turned and began returning fire up the corridor—aiming past the two robots.

"Quick, this way!" Threepio ordered, intending to retreat from the Imperials. Artoo turned with him. They had taken only a couple of steps when they saw the rebel crewmen in position ahead, firing *down* the corridor. In seconds the passageway was filled with smoke and crisscrossing beams of energy.

Red, green and blue bolts ricocheted off polished sections of wall and floor or ripped long gashes in metal surfaces. Screams of injured and dying humans—a peculiarly unrobotic sound, Threepio thought—echoed piercingly above the inorganic destruction.

One beam struck near the robot's feet at the same time as a second one burst the wall directly behind him, exposing sparking circuitry and rows of conduits. The force of the twin blast tumbled Threepio into the shredded cables, where a dozen different currents turned him into a jerking, twisting display.

Strange sensations coursed through his metal nerve-ends. They caused no pain, only confusion. Every time he moved and tried to free himself there was another violent crackling as a fresh cluster of componentry broke. The noise and man-made lightning remained constant around him as the battle continued to rage.

Smoke began to fill the corridor. Artoo Detoo bustled about trying to help free his friend. The little robot evidenced a phlegmatic indifference to the ravening energies filling the passageway. He was built so low that most of the beams passed over him anyhow.

"Help!" Threepio yelled, suddenly frightened at a new message from an internal sensor. "I think something is melting. Free my left leg—the trouble's near the pelvic servomotor." Typically, his tone turned abruptly from pleading to berating.

"This is all your fault!" he shouted angrily. "I should have known better than to trust the logic of a half-sized thermocapsulary dehousing assister. I don't know why you insisted we leave our assigned stations to come down this stupid access corridor. Not that it matters now. The whole ship must be—" Artoo Detoo cut him off in midspeech with some angry beepings and hoots of his own, though he continued to cut and pull with precision at the tangled high-voltage cables.

"Is that so?" Threepio sneered in reply. "The same to you, you little . . . !"

An exceptionally violent explosion shook the passage, drowning him out. A lung-searing miasma of carbonized component filled the air, obscuring everything.

Two meters tall. Bipedal. Flowing black robes trailing from the figure and a face forever masked by a functional if bizarre black metal breath screen—a Dark Lord of the Sith was an awesome, threatening shape as it strode through the corridors of the rebel ship.

Fear followed the footsteps of all the Dark Lords. The cloud of evil which clung tight about this particular one was intense enough to cause hardened Imperial troops to back away, menacing enough to set them muttering nervously among themselves. Once-resolute rebel crew members ceased resisting, broke and ran in panic at the sight of the black armor—armor which, though black as it was, was not nearly as dark as the thoughts drifting through the mind within.

One purpose, one thought, one obsession dominated that mind now. It burned in the brain of Darth Vader as he turned down another passageway in the broken fighter. There smoke was beginning to clear, though the sounds of faraway fighting still resounded through the hull. The battle here had ended and moved on.

Only a robot was left to stir freely in the wake of the Dark Lord's passing. See Threepio finally stepped clear of the last restraining cable. Somewhere behind him human screams could be heard from where relentless Imperial troops were mopping up the last remnants of rebel resistance.

Threepio glanced down and saw only scarred deck. As he looked around, his voice was full of concern. "Artoo Detoo—where are you?" The smoke seemed to part just a bit more. Threepio found himself staring up the passageway.

Artoo Detoo, it seemed, was there. But he wasn't looking in Threepio's direction. Instead, the little robot appeared frozen in an attitude of attention. Leaning over him was—it was difficult for even Threepio's electronic photoreceptors to penetrate the clinging, acidic smoke—a human figure. It was young, slim, and by abstruse human standards of aesthetics, Threepio mused, of a calm beauty. One small hand seemed to be moving over the front of Artoo's torso.

Threepio started toward them as the haze thickened once more. But when he reached the end of the corridor, only Artoo stood there, waiting. Threepio peered past him, uncertain. Robots were occasionally subject to electronic hallucinations—but why should he hallucinate a human?

He shrugged . . . Then again, why not, especially when one considered the confusing circumstances of the past hour and the dose of raw current he had recently absorbed. He shouldn't be surprised at anything his concatenated internal circuits conjured up.

"Where have you been?" Threepio finally asked. "Hiding, I suppose." He decided not to mention the maybe-human. If it had been a hallucination, he wasn't going to give Artoo the satisfaction of knowing how badly recent events had unsettled his logic circuits.

"They'll be coming back this way," he went on, nodding down the corridor and not giving the small automaton a chance to reply, "looking for human survivors. What are we going to do now? They won't trust the word of rebel-owned machines that we don't know anything of value. We'll be sent to the spice mines of Kessel or taken apart for spare components for other, less deserving robots. That's if they don't consider us potential program traps and blow us apart on sight. If we don't . . . ." But

Artoo had already turned and was ambling quickly back down the passageway.

"Wait, where are you going? Haven't you been listening to me?" Uttering curses in several languages, some purely mechanical, Threepio raced fluidly after his friend. The Artoo unit, he thought to himself, could be downright close-circuited when it wanted to.

Outside the galactic cruiser's control center the corridor was crowded with sullen prisoners gathered by Imperial troops. Some lay wounded, some dying. Several officers had been separated from the enlisted ranks and stood in a small group by themselves, bestowing belligerent looks and threats on the silent knot of troops holding them at bay.

As if on command, everyone—Imperial troops as well as rebels—became silent as a massive caped form came into view from behind a turn in the passage. Two of the heretofore resolute, obstinate rebel officers began to shake. Stopping before one of the men, the towering figure reached out wordlessly. A massive hand closed around the man's neck and lifted him off the deck. The rebel officer's eyes bulged, but he kept his silence.

An Imperial officer, his armored helmet shoved back to reveal a recent scar where an energy beam had penetrated his shielding, scrambled down out of the fighter's control room, shaking his head briskly. "Nothing, sir. Information retrieval system's been wiped clean."

Darth Vader acknowledged this news with a barely perceptible nod. The impenetrable mask turned to regard the officer he was torturing. Metal-clad fingers contracted. Reaching up, the prisoner desperately tried to pry them loose, but to no avail.

"Where is the data you intercepted?" Vader rumbled dangerously. "What have you done with the information tapes?"

"We—intercepted—no information," the dangling officer gurgled, barely able to breathe. From somewhere deep within, he dredged up a squeal of outrage. "This is a . . . councilor vessel . . . Did you not see our . . . exterior markings? We're on a . . . diplomatic . . . mission."

"Chaos take your mission!" Vader growled. "Where are those tapes!" He squeezed harder, the threat in his grip implicit.

When he finally replied, the officer's voice was a bare, choked whisper. "Only . . . the Commander knows."

"This ship carries the system crest of Alderaan," Vader growled, the gargoylelike breath mask leaning close. "Is any of the royal family on board? Who are you carrying?" Thick fingers tightened further, and the officer's struggles became more and more frantic. His last words were muffled and choked past intelligibility.

Vader was not pleased. Even though the figure went limp with an awful, unquestionable finality, that hand continued to tighten, producing a chilling snapping and popping of bone, like a dog padding on plastic. Then with a disgusted wheeze Vader finally threw the doll-form of the dead man against a far wall. Several Imperial troops ducked out of the way just in time to avoid the grisly missile.

The massive form whirled unexpectedly, and Imperial officers shrank under that baleful sculptured stare. "Start tearing this ship apart piece by piece, component by component, until you find those tapes. As for the passengers, if any, I want them alive." He paused a moment, then added, *"Quickly!"*

Officers and men nearly fell over themselves in their haste to leave—not necessarily to carry out Vader's orders, but simply to retreat from that malevolent presence.

Artoo Detoo finally came to a halt in an empty corridor devoid of smoke and the signs of battle. A worried, confused Threepio pulled up behind him.

"You've led us through half the ship, and to what . . . ?" He broke off, staring in disbelief as the squat robot reached up with one clawed limb and snapped the seal on a lifeboat hatch. Immediately a red warning light came on and a low hooting sounded in the corridor.

Threepio looked wildly in all directions, but the passageway remained empty. When he looked back, Artoo was already working his way into the cramped boat pod. It was just large enough to hold several humans, and its design was not laid out to accommodate mechanicals. Artoo had some trouble negotiating the awkward little compartment.

"Hey," a startled Threepio called, admonishing, "you're not permitted in there! It's restricted to humans only. We just might be able to convince the Imperials that we're not robot programmed and are too valuable to break up, but if someone sees you in there we haven't got a chance. Come on out."

Somehow Artoo had succeeded in wedging his body into position in front of the miniature control board. He cocked his body slightly and threw a stream of loud beeps and whistles at his reluctant companion.

Threepio listened. He couldn't frown, but he managed to give a good impression of doing so. "Mission . . . what mission? What are you talking about? You sound like you haven't got an integrated logic terminal left in your brain. No . . . no more adventures. I'll take my chances with the Imperials—and I'm *not* getting in there."

An angry electronic twang came from the Artoo unit.

"Don't call *me* a mindless philosopher." Threepio snapped back, "you overweight, unstreamlined glob of grease!"

Threepio was concocting an additional rejoinder when an explosion blew out the back wall of the corridor. Dust and metal debris whooshed through the narrow subpassageway, followed instantly by a series of secondary explosions. Flames began jumping hungrily from the exposed interior wall, reflecting off Threepio's isolated patches of polished skin.

Muttering the electronic equivalent of consigning his soul to the unknown, the lanky robot jumped into the life pod. "I'm going to regret this," he muttered more audibly as Artoo activated the safety door behind him. The smaller robot flipped a series of switches, snapped back a cover, and pressed three buttons in a certain sequence. With the thunder of explosive latches the life pod ejected from the crippled fighter.

When word came over the communicators that the last pocket of resistance on the rebel ship had been cleaned out, the Captain of the Imperial cruiser relaxed considerably. He was listening with pleasure to the proceedings on the captured vessel when one of his chief gunnery officers called to him. Moving to the man's position, the Captain stared into the circular viewscreen and saw a tiny dot dropping away toward the fiery world below.

"There goes another pod, sir. Instructions?" The officer's hand hovered over a computerized energy battery.

Casually, confident in the firepower and total control under his command, the Captain studied the nearby readouts monitoring the pod. All of them read blank.

"Hold your fire, Lieutenant Hija. Instruments show no life forms aboard. The pod's release mechanism must have short-circuited or received a false instruction. Don't waste your power." He turned away, to listen with satisfaction to the reports of captured men and material coming from the rebel ship.

Glare from exploding panels and erupting circuitry reflected crazily off the armor of the lead storm trooper as he surveyed

the passageway ahead. He was about to turn and call for those
behind to follow him forward when he noticed something moving off to one side. It appeared to be crouching back in a small,
dark alcove. Holding his pistol ready, he moved cautiously forward and peered into the recess.

A small, shivering figure clad in flowing white hugged the
back of the recess and stared up at the man. Now he could see
that he faced a young woman, and her physical description fit
that of the one individual the Dark Lord was most interested in.
The trooper grinned behind his helmet. A lucky encounter for
him. He would be commended.

Within the armor his head turned slightly, directing his voice
to the tiny condenser microphone. "Here she is," he called to
those behind him. "Set for stun forc—"

He never finished the sentence, just as he would never receive
the hoped-for commendation. Once his attention turned from
the girl to his communicator her shivering vanished with startling speed. The energy pistol she had held out of sight behind
her came up and around as she burst from her hiding place.

The trooper who had been unlucky enough to find her fell
first, his head a mass of melted bone and metal. The same fate
met the second armored form coming up fast behind him. Then
a bright green energy pole touched the woman's side and she
slumped instantly to the deck, the pistol still locked in her small
palm.

Metal encased shapes clustered around her. One whose arm
bore the insignia of a lower officer knelt and turned her over.
He studied the paralyzed form with a practiced eye.

"She'll be all right," he finally declared, looking up at his
subordinates. "Report to Lord Vader."

Threepio stared, mesmerized, out the small viewport set in
the front of the tiny escape pod as the hot yellow eye of Tatooine
began to swallow them up. Somewhere behind them, he knew,
the crippled fighter and the Imperial cruiser were receding to
imperceptibility.

That was fine with him. If they landed near a civilized city,
he would seek elegant employment in a halcyon atmosphere,
something more befitting his status and training. These past
months had gifted him with entirely too much excitement and
unpredictability for a mere machine.

Artoo's seemingly random manipulation of the pod controls

promised anything but a smooth landing, however. Threepio regarded his squat companion with concern.

"Are you sure you know how to pilot this thing?"

Artoo replied with a noncommittal whistle that did nothing to alter the taller robot's jangled state of mind.

II

IT was an old settlers' saying that you could burn your eyes out faster by staring straight and hard at the sun-scorched flatlands of Tatooine than by looking directly at its two huge suns themselves, so powerful was the penetrating glare reflected from those endless wastes. Despite the glare, life could and did exist in the flatlands formed by long-evaporated seabeds. One thing made it possible: the reintroduction of water.

For human purposes, however, the water of Tatooine was only marginally accessible. The atmosphere yielded its moisture with reluctance. It had to be coaxed down out of the hard blue sky—coaxed, forced, yanked down to the parched surface.

Two figures whose concern was obtaining that moisture were standing on a slight rise of one of those inhospitable flats. One of the pair was stiff and metallic—a sand-pitted vaporator sunk securely through sand and into deeper rock. The figure next to it was a good deal more animated, though no less sunweathered.

Luke Skywalker was twice the age of the ten-year-old vaporator, but much less secure. At the moment he was swearing softly at a recalcitrant valve adjuster on the temperamental device. From time to time he resorted to some unsubtle pounding in place of using the appropriate tool. Neither method worked very well. Luke was sure that the lubricants used on the vaporators went out of their way to attract sand, beckoning seductively to small abrasive particles with an oily gleam. He wiped sweat from his forehead and leaned back for a moment. The most prepossessing thing about the young man was his name. A light breeze tugged at his shaggy hair and baggy work tunic as he regarded the device. No point in staying angry at it, he counseled himself. It's only an unintelligent machine.

As Luke considered his predicament, a third figure appeared, scooting out from behind the vaporator to fumble awkwardly at the damaged section. Only three of the Treadwell model robot's six arms were functioning, and these had seen more wear than the boots on Luke's feet. The machine moved with unsteady, stop-and-start motions.

Luke gazed at it sadly, then inclined his head to study the sky. Still no sign of a cloud, and he knew there never would be unless he got that vaporator working. He was about to try once again when a small, intense gleam of light caught his eye. Quickly he slipped the carefully cleaned set of macrobinoculars from his utility belt and focused the lenses skyward.

For long moments he stared, wishing all the while that he had a real telescope instead of the binocs. As he stared, vaporators, the heat, and the day's remaining chores were forgotten. Clipping the binoculars back onto his belt, Luke turned and dashed for the landspeeder. Halfway to the vehicle he thought to call behind him.

"Hurry up," he shouted impatiently. "What are you waiting for? Get it in gear."

The Treadwell started toward him, hesitated, and then commenced spinning in a tight circle, smoke belching from every joint. Luke shouted further instructions, then finally gave up in disgust when he realized that it would take more than words to motivate the Treadwell again.

For a moment Luke hesitated at leaving the machine behind—but, he argued to himself, its vital components were obviously shot. So he jumped into the landspeeder, causing the recently repaired repulsion floater to list alarmingly to one side until he was able to equalize weight distribution by sliding behind the controls. Maintaining its altitude slightly above the sandy ground, the light-duty transport vehicle steadied itself like a boat in a heavy sea. Luke gunned the engine, which whined in protest, and sand erupted behind the floater as he aimed the craft toward the distant town of Anchorhead.

Behind him, a pitiful beacon of black smoke from the burning robot continued to rise into the clear desert air. It wouldn't be there when Luke returned. There were scavengers of metal as well as flesh in the wide wastes of Tatooine.

* * *

Metal and stone structures bleached white by the glaze of twin Tatoo I and II huddled together tightly, for company as much as for protection. They formed the nexus of the widespread farming community of Anchorhead.

Presently the dusty, unpaved streets were quiet, deserted. Sandflies buzzed lazily in the cracked eaves of pourstone buildings. A dog barked in the distance, the sole sign of habitation until a lone old woman appeared and started across the street. Her metallic sun shawl was pulled tight around her.

Something made her look up, tired eyes squinting into the distance. The sound suddenly leaped in volume as a shining rectangular shape came roaring around a far corner. Her eyes popped as the vehicle bore down on her, showing no sign of altering its path. She had to scramble to get out of its way.

Panting and waving an angry fist after the landspeeder, she raised her voice over the sound of its passage. "Won't you kids ever learn to slow down!"

Luke might have seen her, but he certainly didn't hear her. In both cases his attention was focused elsewhere as he pulled up behind a low, long concrete station. Various coils and rods jutted from its top and sides. Tatooine's relentless sand waves broke in frozen yellow spume against the station's walls. No one had bothered to clear them away. There was no point. They would only return again the following day.

Luke slammed the front door aside and shouted, "Hey!"

A rugged young man in mechanic's dress sat sprawled in a chair behind the station's unkempt control desk. Sunscreen oil had kept his skin from burning. The skin of the girl on his lap had been equally protected, and there was a great deal more of the protected area in view. Somehow even dried sweat looked good on her.

"Hey, everybody!" Luke yelled again, having elicited something less than an overwhelming response with his first cry. He ran toward the instrument room at the rear of the station while the mechanic, half asleep, ran a hand across his face and mumbled, "Did I hear a young noise blast through here?"

The girl on his lap stretched sensuously, her well-worn clothing tugging in various intriguing directions. Her voice was casually throaty. "Oh," she yawned, "that was just Wormie on one of his rampages."

Deak and Windy looked up from the computer-assisted pool game as Luke burst into the room. They were dressed much like

Luke, although their clothing was of better fit and somewhat less exercised.

All three youths contrasted strikingly with the burly, handsome player at the far side of the table. From neatly clipped hair to his precision-cut uniform he stood out in the room like an Oriental poppy in a sea of oats. Behind the three humans a soft hum came from where a repair robot was working patiently on a broken piece of station equipment.

"Shape it up, you guys," Luke yelled excitedly. Then he noticed the older man in the uniform. The subject of his suddenly startled gaze recognized him simultaneously.

"Biggs!"

The man's face twisted in a half grin. "Hello, Luke." Then they were embracing each other warmly.

Luke finally stood away, openly admiring the other's uniform. "I didn't know you were back. When did you get in?"

The confidence in the other's voice bordered the realm of smugness without quite entering it. "Just a little while ago. I wanted to surprise you, hotshot." He indicated the room. "I thought you'd be here with these other two nightcrawlers." Deak and Windy both smiled. "I certainly didn't expect you to be out working." He laughed easily, a laugh few people found resistible.

"The academy didn't change you much," Luke commented. "But you're back so soon." His expression grew concerned. "Hey, what happened—didn't you get your commission?"

There was something evasive about Biggs as he replied, looking slightly away, "Of course I got it. Signed to serve aboard the freighter *Rand Ecliptic* just last week. First Mate Biggs Darklighter, at your service." He performed a twisting salute, half serious and half humorous, then grinned that overbearing yet ingratiating grin again.

"I just came back to say good-bye to all you unfortunate landlocked simpletons." They all laughed, until Luke suddenly remembered what had brought him here in such a hurry.

"I almost forgot," he told them, his initial excitement returning, "there's a battle going on right here in our system. Come and look."

Deak looked disappointed. "Not another one of your epic battles, Luke. Haven't you dreamed up enough of them? Forget it."

"Forget it, hell—I'm serious. It's a battle, all right."

With words and shoves he managed to cajole the occupants

of the station out into the strong sunlight. Camie in particular looked disgusted.

"This had better be worth it, Luke," she warned him, shading her eyes against the glare.

Luke already had his macrobinoculars out and was searching the heavens. It took only a moment for him to fix on a particular spot. "I told you," he insisted. "There they are."

Biggs moved alongside him and reached for the binoculars as the others strained unaided eyes. A slight readjustment provided just enough magnification for Biggs to make out two silvery specks against the dark blue.

"That's no battle, hotshot," he decided, lowering the binocs and regarding his friend gently. "They're just sitting there. Two ships, all right—probably a barge loading a freighter, since Tatooine hasn't got an orbital station."

"There was a lot of firing—earlier," Luke added. His initial enthusiasm was beginning to falter under the withering assurance of his older friend.

Camie grabbed the binoculars away from Biggs, banging them slightly against a support pillar in the process. Luke took them away from her quickly, inspecting the casing for damage. "Take it easy with those."

"Don't worry so much, Wormie," she sneered. Luke took a step toward her, then halted as the huskier mechanic easily interposed himself between them and favored Luke with a warning smile. Luke considered, shrugged the incident away.

"I keep telling you, Luke," the mechanic said, with the air of a man tired of repeating the same story to no avail, "the rebellion is a long way from here. I doubt if the Empire would fight to keep this system. Believe me, Tatooine is a big hunk of nothing."

His audience began to fade back into the station before Luke could mutter a reply. Fixer had his arm around Camie, and the two of them were chuckling over Luke's ineptitude. Even Deak and Windy were murmuring among themselves—about him, Luke was certain.

He followed them, but not without a last glance back and up to the distant specks. One thing he was sure of were the flashes of light he had seen between the two ships. They hadn't been caused by the suns of Tatooine reflecting off metal.

The binding that locked the girl's hands behind her back was primitive and effective. The constant attention the squad of heavily armed troopers favored her with might have been out of place for one small female, except for the fact that their lives depended on her being delivered safely.

When she deliberately slowed her pace, however, it became apparent that her captors did not mind mistreating her a little. One of the armored figures shoved her brutally in the small of the back, and she nearly fell. Turning, she gave the offending soldier a vicious look. But she could not tell if it had any effect, since the man's face was completely hidden by his armored helmet.

The hallway they eventually emerged into was still smoking around the edges of the smoldering cavity blasted through the hull of the fighter. A portable accessway had been sealed to it and a circlet of light showed at the far end of the tunnel, bridging space between the rebel craft and the cruiser. A shadow moved over her as she turned from inspecting the accessway, startling her despite her usually unshakable self-control.

Above her towered the threatening bulk of Darth Vader, red eyes glaring behind the hideous breath mask. A muscle twitched in one smooth cheek, but other than that the girl didn't react. Nor was there the slightest shake in her voice.

"Darth Vader . . . I should have known. Only you would be so bold—and so stupid. Well, the Imperial Senate will not sit still for this. When they hear that you have attacked a diplomatic miss—"

"Senator Leia Organa," Vader rumbled softly, though strongly enough to override her protests. His pleasure at finding her was evident in the way he savored every syllable.

"Don't play games with me, Your Highness," he continued ominously. "You aren't on any mercy mission this time. You passed directly through a restricted system, ignoring numerous warnings and completely disregarding orders to turn about until it no longer mattered."

The huge metal skull dipped close. "I know that several transmissions were beamed to this vessel by spies within that system. When we traced those transmissions back to the individuals with whom they originated, they had the poor grace to kill themselves before they could be questioned. I want to know what happened to the data they sent you."

Neither Vader's words nor his inimical presence appeared to have any effect on the girl. "I don't know what you're blathering about," she snapped, looking away from him. "I'm a member of the Senate on a diplomatic mission to—"

"To your part of the rebel alliance," Vader declared, cutting her off accusingly. "You're also a traitor." His gaze went to a nearby officer. "Take her away."

She succeeded in reaching him with her spit, which hissed against still-hot battle armor. He wiped the offensive matter away silently, watching her with interest as she was marched through the accessway into the cruiser.

A tall, slim soldier wearing the sign of an Imperial Commander attracted Vader's attention as he came up next to him. "Holding her is dangerous," he ventured, likewise looking after her as she was escorted toward the cruiser. "If word of this does get out, there will be much unrest in the Senate. It will generate sympathy for the rebels." The Commander looked up at the unreadable metal face, then added in an off-handed manner, "She should be destroyed immediately."

"No. My first duty is to locate that hidden fortress of theirs," Vader replied easily. "All the rebel spies have been eliminated—by our hand or by their own. Therefore she is now my only key to discovering its location. I intend to make full use of her. If necessary, I will use her up—but I *will* learn the location of the rebel base."

The Commander pursed his lips, shook his head slightly, perhaps a bit sympathetically, as he considered the woman. "She'll die before she gives you any information." Vader's reply was chilling in its indifference. "Leave that to me." He considered a moment, then went on. "Send out a wide-band distress signal. Indicate that the Senator's ship encountered an unexpected meteorite cluster it could not avoid. Readings indicate that the shift shields were overriden and the ship was hulled to the point of vacating ninety-five percent of its atmosphere. Inform her father and the Senate that all aboard were killed."

A cluster of tired-looking troops marched purposefully up to their Commander and the Dark Lord. Vader eyed them expectantly.

"The data tapes in question are not aboard the ship. There is no valuable information in the ship's storage banks and no evidence of bank erasure," the officer in charge recited mechanically. "Nor were any transmissions directed outward from the ship from the time we made contact. A malfunctioning lifeboat pod was ejected during the fighting, but it was confirmed at the time that no life forms were on board."

Vader appeared thoughtful. "It *could* have been a malfunctioning pod," he mused, "that might also have contained the tapes. Tapes are not life forms. In all probability any native finding them would be ignorant of their importance and would likely clear them for his own use. Still . . .

"Send down a detachment to retrieve them, or to make certain they are not in the pod," he finally ordered the Commander and attentive officer. "Be as subtle as possible; there is no need to attract attention, even on this miserable outpost world."

As the officer and troops departed, Vader turned his gaze back to the Commander. "Vaporize this fighter—we don't want to leave anything. As for the pod, I cannot take the chance it was a simple malfunction. The data it might contain could prove too damaging. See to this personally, Commander. If those data tapes exist, they must be retrieved or destroyed at all costs." Then he added with satisfaction, "With that accomplished and the Senator in our hands, we will see the end of this absurd rebellion."

"It shall be as you direct, Lord Vader," the Commander acknowledged. Both men entered the accessway to the cruiser.

"What a forsaken place this is!"

Threepio turned cautiously to look back at where the pod lay half buried in sand. His internal gyros were still unsteady from the rough landing. Landing! Mere application of the term unduly flattered his dull associate.

On the other hand, he supposed he ought to be grateful they had come down in one piece. Although, he mused as he studied the barren landscape, he still wasn't sure they were better off here than they would have been had they remained on the captured cruiser. High sandstone mesas dominated the skyline to one side. Every other direction showed only endless series of marching dunes like long yellow teeth stretching for kilometer on kilometer into the distance. Sand ocean blended into sky-glare until it was impossible to distinguish where one ended and the other began.

A faint cloud of minute dust particles rose in their wake as the two robots marched away from the pod. That vehicle, its intended function fully discharged, was now quite useless. Neither robot had been designed for pedal locomotion on this kind of terrain, so they had to fight their way across the unstable surface.

"We seem to have been made to suffer," Threepio moaned in self-pity. "It's a rotten existence." Something squeaked in his right leg and he winced. "I've got to rest before I fall apart.

My internals still haven't recovered from that headlong crash you called a landing."

He paused, but Artoo Detoo did not. The little automaton had performed a sharp turn and was now ambling slowly but steadily in the direction of the nearest outjut of mesa.

"Hey," Threepio yelled. Artoo ignored the call and continued striding. "Where do you think you're going?"

Now Artoo paused, emitting a stream of electronic explanation as Threepio exhaustedly walked over to join him.

"Well, I'm not going that way," Threepio declared when Artoo had concluded his explanation. "It's too rocky." He gestured in the direction they had been walking, at an angle away from the cliffs. "This way is much easier." A metal hand waved disparagingly at the high mesas. "What makes you think there are any settlements that way, anyhow?"

A long whistle issued from the depths of Artoo.

"Don't get technical with me," Threepio warned. "I've had just about enough of your decisions."

Artoo beeped once.

"All right, go your way," Threepio announced grandly. "You'll be sandlogged within a day, you nearsighted scrap pile." He gave the Artoo unit a contemptuous shove, sending the smaller robot tumbling down a slight dune. As it struggled at the bottom to regain its feet, Threepio started off toward the blurred, glaring horizon, glancing back over his shoulder. "Don't let me catch you following me, begging for help," he warned, "because you won't get it."

Below the crest of the dune, the Artoo unit righted itself. It paused briefly to clean its single electronic eye with an auxiliary arm. Then it produced an electronic squeal which was almost, though not quite, a human expression of rage. Humming quietly to itself then, it turned and trudged off toward the sandstone ridges as if nothing had happened.

Several hours later a straining Threepio, his internal thermostat overloaded and edging dangerously toward overheat shutdown, struggled up the top of what he hoped was the last towering dune. Nearby, pillars and buttresses of bleached calcium, the bones of some enormous beast, formed an unpromising landmark. Reaching the crest of the dune, Threepio peered anxiously ahead. Instead of the hoped-for greenery of human civilization he saw only several dozen more dunes, identical in form and promise to the one he now stood upon. The farthest rose even higher than the one he presently surmounted.

Threepio turned and looked back toward the now far-off rocky plateau, which was beginning to grow indistinct with distance and heat distortion. "You malfunctioning little twerp," he muttered, unable even now to admit to himself that perhaps, just possibly, the Artoo unit might have been right. "This is all your fault. You tricked me into going this way, but you'll do no better."

Nor would he if he didn't continue on. So he took a step forward and heard something grind dully within a leg joint. Sitting down in an electronic funk, he began picking sand from his encrusted joints.

He could continue on his present course, he told himself. Or he could confess to an error in judgment and try to catch up again with Artoo Detoo. Neither prospect held much appeal for him.

But there was a third choice. He could sit here, shining in the sunlight, until his joints locked, his internals overheated, and the ultraviolet burned out his photoreceptors. He would become another monument to the destructive power of the binary, like the colossal organism whose picked corpse he had just encountered.

Already his receptors were beginning to go, he reflected. It seemed he saw something moving in the distance. Heat distortion, probably. No—no—it was definitely light on metal, and it was moving toward him. His hopes soared. Ignoring the warnings from his damaged leg, he rose and began waving frantically.

It was, he saw now, definitely a vehicle, though of a type unfamiliar to him. But a vehicle it was, and that implied intelligence and technology.

He neglected in his excitement to consider the possibility that it might not be of human origin.

"So I cut off my power, shut down the afterburners, and dropped in low on Deak's tail," Luke finished, waving his arms wildly. He and Biggs were walking in the shade outside the power station. Sounds of metal being worked came from somewhere within, where Fixer had finally joined his robot assistant in performing repairs.

"I was so close to him," Luke continued excitedly, "I thought I was going to fry my instrumentation. As it was, I busted up the skyhopper pretty bad." That recollection inspired a frown.

"Uncle Owen was pretty upset. He grounded me for the rest

of the season.'' Luke's depression was brief. Memory of his feat overrode its immorality.

"You should have been there, Biggs!"

"You ought to take it a little easier," his friend cautioned. "You may be the hottest bush pilot this side of Mos Eisley, Luke, but those little skyhoppers can be dangerous. They move awfully fast for tropospheric craft—faster than they need to. Keep playing engine jockey with one and someday, whammo!'' He slammed one fist violently into his open palm. "You're going to be nothing more than a dark spot on the damp side of a canyon wall.''

"Look who's talking," Luke retorted. "Now that you've been on a few big, automatic starships you're beginning to sound like my uncle. You've gotten soft in the cities.'' He swung spiritedly at Biggs, who blocked the movement easily, making a half-hearted gesture of counterattack.

Biggs's easygoing smugness dissolved into something warmer. "I've missed you, kid.''

Luke looked away, embarrassed. "Things haven't exactly been the same since you left, either, Biggs. It's been so—'' Luke hunted for the right word and finally finished helplessly, "—so *quiet.*'' His gaze traveled across the sandy, deserted streets of Anchorhead. "Its always been quiet, really.''

Biggs grew silent, thinking. He glanced around. They were alone out here. Everyone else was back inside the comparative coolness of the power station. As he leaned close Luke sensed an unaccustomed solemness in his friend's tone.

"Luke, I didn't come back just to say good-bye, or to crow over everyone because I got through the Academy.'' Again he seemed to hesitate, unsure of himself. Then he blurted out rapidly, not giving himself a chance to back down, "But I want somebody to know. I can't tell my parents.''

Gaping at Biggs, Luke could only gulp, "Know what? What are you talking about?''

"I'm talking about the talking that's been going on at the Academy—and other places, Luke. Strong talking. I made some new friends, outsystem friends. We agreed about the way certain things are developing, and—'' his voice dropped conspiratorially—"When we reach one of the peripheral systems, we're going to jump ship and join the Alliance.''

Luke stared back at his friend, tried to picture Biggs—fun-loving, happy-go-lucky, live-for-today Biggs—as a patriot afire with rebellious fervor.

"You're going to join the rebellion?" he started. "You've got to be kidding. How?"

"Damp down, will you?" the bigger man cautioned, glancing furtively back toward the power station. "You've got a mouth like a crater."

"I'm sorry," Luke whispered rapidly. "I'm quiet—listen how quiet I am. You can barely hear me—"

Biggs cut him off and continued. "A friend of mine from the Academy has a friend on Bestine who might enable us to make contact with an armed rebel unit."

"A friend of a—You're crazy," Luke announced with conviction, certain his friend had gone mad. "You could wander around forever trying to find a real rebel outpost. Most of them are only myths. This twice removed friend could be an imperial agent. You'd end up on Kessel, or worse. If rebel outposts were so easy to find, the Empire would have wiped them out years ago."

"I know it's a long shot," Biggs admitted reluctantly. "If I don't contact them, then"—a peculiar light came into Biggs's eyes, a conglomeration of newfound maturity and . . . something else—"I'll do what I can, on my own."

He stared intensely at his friend. "Luke, I'm not going to wait for the Empire to conscript me into its service. In spite of what you hear over the official information channels, the rebellion is growing, spreading. And I want to be on the right side—the side I believe in." His voice altered unpleasantly, and Luke wondered what he saw in his mind's eye.

"You should have heard some of the stories I've heard, Luke, learned of some of the outrages I've learned about. The Empire may have been great and beautiful once, but the people in charge now—" He shook his head sharply. "It's rotten, Luke, rotten."

"And I can't do a damn thing," Luke muttered morosely. "I'm stuck here." He kicked futilely at the ever-present sand of Anchorhead.

"I thought you were going to enter the Academy soon," Biggs observed. "If that's on, then you'll have your chance to get off this sandpile."

Luke snorted derisively. "Not likely. I had to withdraw my application." He looked away, unable to meet his friend's disbelieving stare. "I had to. There's been a lot of unrest among the sandpeople since you left, Biggs. They've even raided the outskirts of Anchorhead."

Biggs shook his head, disregarding the excuse. "Your uncle could hold off a whole colony of raiders with one blaster."

"From the house, sure," Luke agreed, "but Uncle Owen's finally got enough vaporators installed and running to make the farm pay off big. But he can't guard all that land by himself, and he says he needs me for one more season. I can't run out on him now."

Biggs sighed sadly. "I feel for you, Luke. Someday you're going to have to learn to separate what seems to be important from what really is important." He gestured around them.

"What good is all your uncle's work if it's taken over by the Empire? I've heard that they're starting to imperialize commerce in all the outlying systems. It won't be long before your uncle and everyone else on Tatooine are just tenants slaving for the greater glory of the Empire."

"That couldn't happen here," Luke objected with a confidence he didn't quite feel. "You've said it yourself—the Empire won't bother with this rock."

"Things change, Luke. Only the threat of rebellion keeps many in power from doing certain unmentionable things. If that threat is completely removed—well, there are two things men have never been able to satisfy: their curiosity and their greed. There isn't much the high Imperial bureaucrats are curious about."

Both men stood silent. A sandwhirl traversed the street in silent majesty, collapsing against a wall to send newborn baby zephyrs in all directions.

"I wish I was going with you," Luke finally murmured. He glanced up. "Will you be around long?"

"No. As a matter of fact, I'm leaving in the morning to rendezvous with the *Ecliptic*."

"Then I guess . . . I won't be seeing you again."

"Maybe someday," Biggs declared. He brightened, grinning that disarming grin. "I'll keep a look out for you, hotshot. Try not to run into any canyon walls in the meantime."

"I'll be at the Academy the season after," Luke insisted, more to encourage himself than Biggs. "After that, who knows where I'll end up?" He sounded determined. "I won't be drafted into the starfleet, that's for sure. Take care of yourself. You'll . . . always be the best friend I've got." There was no need for a handshake. These two had long since passed beyond that.

"So long, then, Luke," Biggs said simply. He turned and reentered the power station.

Luke watched him disappear through the door, his own thoughts as chaotic and frenetic as one of Tatooine's spontaneous dust storms.

There were any number of extraordinary features unique to Tatooine's surface. Outstanding among them were the mysterious mists which rose regularly from the ground at the points where desert sands washed up against unyielding cliffs and mesas.

Fog in a steaming desert seemed as out of place as cactus on a glacier, but it existed nonetheless. Meteorologists and geologists argued its origin among themselves, muttering hard-to-believe theories about water suspended in sandstone veins beneath the sand and incomprehensible chemical reactions which made water rise when the ground cooled, then fall underground again with the double sunrise. It was all very backward and very real.

Neither the mist nor the alien moans of nocturnal desert dwellers troubled Artoo Detoo, however, as he made his careful way up the rocky arroyo, hunting for the easiest pathway to the mesa top. His squarish, broad footpads made clicking sounds loud in the evening light as sand underfoot gave way gradually to gravel.

For a moment, he paused. He seemed to detect a noise—like metal on rock—ahead of him, instead of rock on rock. The sound wasn't repeated, though, and he quickly resumed his ambling ascent.

Up the arroyo, too far up to be seen from below, a pebble trickled loose from the stone wall. The tiny figure which had accidentally dislodged the pebble retreated mouselike into shadow. Two glowing points of light showed under overlapping folds of brown cape a meter from the narrowing canyon wall.

Only the reaction of the unsuspecting robot indicated the presence of the whining beam as it struck him. For a moment Artoo Detoo fluoresced eerily in the dimming light. There was a single short electronic squeak. Then the tripodal support unbalanced and the tiny automaton toppled over onto its back, the lights on its front blinking on and off erratically from the effects of the paralyzing beam.

Three travesties of men scurried out from behind concealing boulders. Their motions were more indicative of rodent than humankind, and they stood little taller than the Artoo unit. When they saw that the single burst of enervating energy had immobilized the robot, they holstered their peculiar weapons. Nevertheless, they approached the listless machine cautiously, with the trepidation of hereditary cowards.

Their cloaks were thickly coated with dust and sand. Unhealthy red-yellow pupils glowed catlike from the depths of their hoods as they studied their captive. The jawas conversed in low guttural croaks and scrambled analogs of human speech. If, as anthropologists hypothesized, they had ever been human, they had long since degenerated past anything resembling the human race.

Several more jawas appeared. Together they succeeded in alternately hoisting and dragging the robot back down the arroyo.

At the bottom of the canyon—like some monstrous prehistoric beast—was a sandcrawler as enormous as its owners and operators were tiny. Several dozen meters high, the vehicle towered above the ground on multiple treads that were taller than a tall man. Its metal epidermis was battered and pitted from withstanding untold sandstorms.

On reaching the crawler, the jawas resumed jabbering among themselves. Artoo Detoo could hear them but failed to comprehend anything. He need not have been embarrassed at his failure. If they so wished, only jawas could understand other jawas, for they employed a randomly variable language that drove linguists mad.

One of them removed a small disk from a belt pouch and sealed it to the Artoo unit's flank. A large tube protruded from one side of the gargantuan vehicle. They rolled him over to it and then moved clear. There was a brief moan, the *whoosh* of powerful vacuum, and the small robot was sucked into the bowels of the sandcrawler as neatly as a pea up a straw. This part of the job completed, the jawas engaged in another bout of jabbering, following which they scurried into the crawler via tubes and ladders, for all the world like a nest of mice returning to their holes.

None too gently, the suction tube deposited Artoo in a small cubical. In addition to varied piles of broken instruments and outright scrap, a dozen or so robots of differing shapes and sizes populated the prison. A few were locked in electronic conversation. Others muddled aimlessly about. But when Artoo tumbled into the chamber, one voice burst out in surprise.

"Artoo Detoo—it's you, it's you!" called an excited Threepio from the near darkness. He made his way over to the still immobilized repair unit and embraced it most unmechanically.

Spotting the small disk sealed onto Artoo's side, Threepio turned his gaze thoughtfully down to his own chest, where a similar device had likewise been attached.

Massive gears, poorly lubricated, started to move. With a groaning and grinding, the monster sandcrawler turned and lumbered with relentless patience into the desert night.

III

THE burnished conference table was as soulless and unyielding as the mood of the eight Imperial Senators and officers ranged around it. Imperial troopers stood guard at the entrance to the chamber, which was sparse and coldly lit from lights in the table and walls. One of the youngest of the eight was declaiming. He exhibited the attitude of one who had climbed far and fast by methods best not examined too closely. General Tagge did possess a certain twisted genius, but it was only partly that ability which had lifted him to his present exalted position. Other noisome talents had proven equally efficacious.

Though his uniform was as neatly molded and his body as clean as that of anyone else in the room, none of the remaining seven cared to touch him. A certain sliminess clung cloyingly to him, a sensation inferred rather than tactile. Despite this, many respected him. Or feared him.

"I tell you, he's gone too far this time," the General was insisting vehemently. "This Sith Lord inflicted on us at the urging of the Emperor will be our undoing. Until the battle station is fully operational, we remain vulnerable.

"Some of you still don't seem to realize how well equipped and organized the rebel Alliance is. Their vessels are excellent, their pilots better. And they are propelled by something more powerful than mere engines: this perverse, reactionary fanaticism of theirs. They're more dangerous than most of you realize.''

An older officer, with facial scars so deeply engraved that even the best cosmetic surgery could not fully repair them, shifted nervously in his chair. "Dangerous to your starfleet, General Tagge, but not to this battle station." Wizened eyes hopped from man to man, traveling around the table. "I happen to think Lord Vader knows what he's doing. The rebellion will continue only as long as those cowards have a sanctuary, a place where their pilots can relax and their machines can be repaired.''

Tagge objected. "I beg to differ with you, Romodi. I think the construction of this station has more to do with Governor Tarkin's bid for personal power and recognition than with any justifiable military strategy. Within the Senate the rebels will continue to increase their support as long—''

The sound of the single doorway sliding aside and the guards snapping to attention cut him of. His head turned as did everyone else's.

Two individuals as different in appearance as they were united in objectives had entered the chamber. The nearest to Tagge was a thin, hatchet-faced man with hair and form borrowed from an old broom and the expression of a quiescent piranha. The Grand Moff Tarkin, Governor of numerous outlying Imperial territories, was dwarfed by the broad, armored bulk of Lord Darth Vader.

Tagge, unintimidated but subdued, slowly resumed his seat as Tarkin assumed his place at the end of the conference table. Vader stood next to him, a dominating presence behind the Governor's chair. For a minute Tarkin stared directly at Tagge, then glanced away as if he had seen nothing. Tagge fumed but remained silent.

As Tarkin's gaze roved around the table a razor-thin smile of satisfaction remained frozen in his features. "The Imperial Senate will no longer be of any concern to us, gentlemen. I have just received word that the Emperor has permanently dissolved that misguided body.''

A ripple of astonishment ran through the assembly. "The last remnants,'' Tarkin continued, "of the Old Republic have finally been swept away.''

"This is impossible,'' Tagge interjected. "How will the Emperor maintain control of the Imperial bureaucracy?''

"Senatorial representation has not been formally abolished, you must understand,'' Tarkin explained. "It has merely been superseded for the—'' he smiled a bit more—''duration of the emergency. Regional Governors will now have direct control and a free hand in administering their territories. This means that the Imperial presence can at last be brought to bear properly on the vacillating worlds of the Empire. From now on, fear will keep potentially traitorous local governments in line. Fear of the Imperial fleet—and fear of this battle station.''

''And what of the existing rebellion?'' Tagge wanted to know

''If the rebels somehow managed to gain access to a complete technical schema of this battle station, it is remotely possible that they might be able to locate a weakness susceptible to minor exploitation.'' Tarkin's smile shifted to a smirk. ''Of course, we all know how well guarded, how carefully protected, such vital data is. It could not possibly fall into rebel hands.''

''The technical data to which you are obliquely referring,'' rumbled Darth Vader angrily, ''will soon be back in our hands. If—''

Tarkin shook the Dark Lord off, something no one else at the table would have dared to do. ''It is immaterial. Any attack made against this station by the rebels would be a suicidal gesture, suicidal and useless—regardless of any information they managed to obtain. After many long years of secretive construction,'' he declared with evident pleasure, ''this station has become the decisive force in this part of the universe. Events in this region of the galaxy will no longer be determined by fate, by decree, or by any other agency. They will be decided by this station!''

A huge metal-clad hand gestured slightly, and one of the filled cups on the table drifted responsively into it. With a slightly admonishing tone the Dark Lord continued. ''Don't become too proud of this technological terror you've spawned, Tarkin. The ability to destroy a city, a world, a whole system is still insignificant when set against the force.''

'' 'The Force,' '' Tagge sneered. ''Don't try to frighten *us* with your sorcerer's ways, Lord Vader. Your sad devotion to that ancient mythology has not helped you to conjure up those stolen tapes, or gifted you with clairvoyance sufficient to locate the rebels' hidden fortress. Why, it's enough to make one laugh fit to—''

Tagge's eyes abruptly bulged and his hands went to his throat as he began to turn a disconcerting shade of blue.

''I find,'' Vader ventured mildly, ''this lack of faith disturbing.''

"Enough of this," Tarkin snapped, distressed. "Vader, release him. This bickering among ourselves is pointless."

Vader shrugged as if it were of no consequence. Tagge slumped in his seat, rubbing his throat, his wary gaze never leaving the dark giant.

"Lord Vader will provide us with the location of the rebel fortress by the time this station is certified operational," Tarkin declared. "That known, we will proceed to it and destroy it utterly, crushing this pathetic rebellion in one swift stroke."

"As the Emperor wills it," Vader added, not without sarcasm, "so shall it be."

If any of the powerful men seated around the table found this disrespectful tone objectionable, a glance at Tagge was sufficient to dissuade them from mentioning it.

The dim prison reeked of rancid oil and stale lubricants, a veritable metallic charnel house. Threepio endured the discomfiting atmosphere as best he could. It was a constant battle to avoid being thrown by every unexpected bounce into the walls or into a fellow machine.

To conserve power—and also to avoid the steady stream of complaints from his taller companion—Artoo Detoo had shut down all exterior functions. He lay inert among a pile of secondary parts, sublimely unconcerned at the moment as to their fate.

"Will this never end?" Threepio was moaning as another violent jolt roughly jostled the inhabitants of the prison. He had already formulated and discarded half a hundred horrible ends. He was certain only that their eventual disposition was sure to be worse than anything he could imagine.

Then, quite without warning, something more unsettling than even the most battering bump took place. The sandcrawler's whine died, and the vehicle came to a halt—almost as if in response to Threepio's query. A nervous buzz rose from those mechanicals who still retained a semblance of sentience as they speculated on their present location and probable fate.

At least Threepio was no longer ignorant of his captors or of their likely motives. Local captives had explained the nature of the quasi-human mechanic migrants, the jawas. Traveling in their enormous mobile fortress-homes, they scoured the most inhospitable regions of Tatooine in search of valuable minerals—and salvageable machinery. They had never been seen outside of their protective cloaks and sandmasks, so no one knew exactly what they looked like. But they were reputed to be extraordinarily ugly. Threepio did not have to be convinced.

Leaning over his still-motionless companion, he began a steady shaking of the barrellike torso. Epidermal sensors were activated on the Artoo unit, and the lights on the front side of the little robot began a sequential awakening.

"Wake up, wake up," Threepio urged. "We've stopped someplace." Like several of the other, more imaginative robots, his eyes were warily scanning metal walls, expecting a hidden panel to slide aside at any moment and a giant mechanical arm to come probing and fumbling for him.

"No doubt about it, we're doomed," he recited mournfully as Artoo righted himself, returning to full activation. "Do you think they'll melt us down?" He became silent for several minutes, then added, "It's this waiting that gets to me."

Abruptly the far wall of the chamber slid aside and the blinding white glare of a Tatooine morning rushed in on them. Threepio's sensitive photoreceptors were hard pressed to adjust in time to prevent serious damage.

Several of the repulsive-looking Jawas scrambled agilely into the chamber, still dressed in the same swathings and filth Threepio had observed on them before. Using hand weapons of an unknown design, they prodded at the machines. Certain of them, Threepio noted with a mental swallow, did not stir.

Ignoring the immobile ones, the jawas herded those still capable of movement outside, Artoo and Threepio among them. Both robots found themselves part of an uneven mechanical line.

Shielding his eyes against the glare, Threepio saw that five of them were arranged alongside the huge sandcrawler. Thoughts of escape did not enter his mind. Such a concept was utterly alien to a mechanical. The more intelligent a robot was, the more abhorrent and unthinkable the concept. Besides, had he tried to escape, built-in sensors would have detected the critical logic malfunction and melted every circuit in his brain.

Instead, he studied the small domes and vaporators that indicated the presence of a larger underground human homestead. Though he was unfamiliar with this type of construction, all signs pointed to a modest, if isolated, habitation. Thoughts of being dismembered for parts or slaving in some high-temperature mine slowly faded. His spirits rose correspondingly.

"Maybe this won't be so bad after all," he murmured hopefully. "If we can convince these bipedal vermin to unload us here, we may enter into sensible human service again instead of being melted into slag.''

Artoo's sole reply was a noncommittal chirp. Both machines became silent as the jawas commenced scurrying around them, striving to straighten one poor machine with a badly bent spine, to disguise a dent or scrape with liquid and dust.

As two of them bustled about, working on his sandcoated skin, Threepio fought to stifle an expression of disgust. One of his many human-analog functions was the ability to react naturally to offensive odors. Apparently hygiene was unknown among the jawas. But he was certain no good would come of pointing this out to them.

Small insects drifted in clouds about the faces of the jawas, who ignored them. Apparently the tiny individualized plagues were regarded as just a different sort of appendage, like an extra arm or leg.

So intent was Threepio on his observation that he failed to notice the two figures moving toward them from the region of the largest dome. Artoo had to nudge him slightly before he looked up.

The first man wore an air of grim, semiperpetual exhaustion, sandblasted into his face by too many years of arguing with a hostile environment. His graying hair was frozen in tangled twists like gypsum helicites. Dust frosted his face, clothes, hands, and thoughts. But the body, if not the spirit, was still powerful.

Proportionately dwarfed by his uncle's wrestlerlike body, Luke strode slump-shouldered in his shadow, his present attitude one of dejection rather than exhaustion. He had a great deal on his mind, and it had very little to do with farming. Mostly it involved the rest of his life, and the commitment made by his best friend who had recently departed beyond the blue sky above to enter a harsher, yet more rewarding career.

The bigger man stopped before the assembly and entered into a peculiar squeaky dialogue with the jawa in charge. When they wished it, the jawas could be understood.

Luke stood nearby, listening indifferently. Then he shuffled along behind his uncle as the latter began inspecting the five machines, pausing only to mutter an occasional word or two to his nephew. It was hard to pay attention, even though he knew he ought to be learning.

"Luke—oh, Luke!" a voice called.

Turning away from the conversation, which consisted of the

lead jawa extolling the unmatched virtues of all five machines and his uncle countering with derision, Luke walked over to the near edge of the subterranean courtyard and peered down.

A stout woman with the expression of a misplaced sparrow was busy working among decorative plants. She looked up at him. "Be sure and tell Owen that if he buys a translator to make sure it speaks Bocce, Luke."

Turning, Luke looked back over his shoulder and studied the motley collection of tired machines. "It looks like we don't have much of a choice," he called back down to her, "but I'll remind him anyway."

She nodded up at him and he turned to rejoin his uncle.

Apparently Owen Lars had already come to a decision, having settled on a small semi-agricultural robot. This one was similar in shape to Artoo Detoo, save that its multiple subsidiary arms were tipped with different functions. At an order it had stepped out of the line and was wobbling along behind Owen and the temporarily subdued jawa.

Proceeding to the end of the line, the farmer's eyes narrowed as he concentrated on the sand-scoured but still flashy bronze finish of the tall, humanoid Threepio.

"I presume you function," he grumbled at the robot. "Do you know customs and protocol?"

"Do I know protocol?" Threepio echoed as the farmer looked him up and down. Threepio was determined to embarrass the jawa when it came to selling his abilities. "Do I know protocol! Why, it's my primary function. I am also well—"

"Don't need a protocol 'droid," the farmer snapped dryly.

"I don't blame you, sir," Threepio rapidly agreed. "I couldn't be more in agreement. What could be more of a wasteful luxury in a climate like this? For someone of your interests, sir, a protocol 'droid would be a useless waste of money. No, sir—versatility is my middle name. See Vee Threepio—Vee for versatility—at your service. I've been programmed for over thirty secondary functions that require only . . . ."

"I need," the farmer broke in, demonstrating imperious disregard for Threepio's as yet unenumerated secondary functions, "a 'droid that knows something about the binary language of independently programmable moisture vaporators."

"Vaporators! We are both in luck," Threepio countered. "My first post-primary assignment was in programming binary load lifters. Very similar in construction and memory-function to your vaporators. You could almost say . . . ."

Luke tapped his uncle on the shoulder and whispered something in his ear. His uncle nodded, then looked back at the attentive Threepio again.

"Do you speak Bocce?"

"Of course, sir," Threepio replied, confident for a change with a wholly honest answer. "It's like a second language to me. I'm as fluent in Bocce as—"

The farmer appeared determined never to allow him to conclude a sentence. "Shut up." Owen Lars looked down at the jawa. "I'll take this one, too."

"Shutting up, sir," responded Threepio quickly, hard put to conceal his glee at being selected.

"Take them down to the garage, Luke," his uncle instructed him. "I want you to have both of them cleaned up by suppertime."

Luke looked askance at his uncle. "But I was going into Tosche station to pick up some new power converters and . . ."

"Don't lie to me, Luke," his uncle warned him sternly. "I don't mind you wasting time with your idle friends, but only after you've finished your chores. Now hop to it—and before supper, mind."

Downcast, Luke directed his words irritably to Threepio and the small agricultural robot. He knew better than to argue with his uncle.

"Follow me, you two." They started for the garage as Owen entered into price negotiations with the jawa.

Other jawas were leading the three remaining machines back into the sandcrawler when something let out an almost pathetic beep. Luke turned to see an Artoo unit breaking formation and starting toward him. It was immediately restrained by a jawa wielding a control device that activated the disk sealed on the machine's front plate.

Luke studied the rebellious 'droid curiously. Threepio started to say something, considered the circumstances and thought better of it. Instead, he remained silent, staring straight ahead.

A minute later, something pinged sharply nearby. Glancing down, Luke saw that a head plate had popped off the top of the agricultural 'droid. A grinding noise was coming from within. A second later the machine was throwing internal components all over the sandy ground.

Leaning close, Luke peered inside the expectorating mechanical. He called out, "Uncle Owen! The servomotor-central on this cultivator unit is shot. Look . . ." He reached in, tried to adjust the device, and pulled away hurriedly when it began a wild sparking. The odor of crisped insulation and corroded circuitry filled the clear desert air with a pungency redolent of mechanized death.

Owen Lars glared down at the nervous jawa. "What kind of junk are you trying to push on us?"

The jawa responded loudly, indignantly, while simultaneously taking a couple of precautionary steps away from the big human. He was distressed that the man was between him and the soothing safety of the sandcrawler.

Meanwhile, Artoo Detoo had scuttled out of the group of machines being led back toward the mobile fortress. Doing so turned out to be simple enough, since all the jawas had their attention focused on the argument between their leader and Luke's uncle.

Lacking sufficient armature for wild gesticulation, the Artoo unit suddenly let out a high whistle, then broke it off when it was apparent he had gained Threepio's attention.

Tapping Luke gently on the shoulder, the tall 'droid whispered conspiratorially into his ear. "If I might say so, young sir, that Artoo unit is a real bargain. In top condition. I don't believe these creatures have any idea what good shape he's really in. Don't let all the sand and dust deceive you."

Luke was in the habit of making instant decisions—for good or bad—anyway. "Uncle Owen!" he called.

Breaking off the argument without taking his attention from the jawa, his uncle glanced quickly at him. Luke gestured toward Artoo Detoo. "We don't want any trouble. What about swapping this—" he indicated the burned-out agricultural 'droid—"for that one?"

The older man studied the Artoo unit professionally, then considered the jawas. Though inherently cowards, the tiny desert scavengers *could* be pushed too far. The sandcrawler could flatten the homestead—at the risk of inciting the human community to lethal vengeance.

Faced with a no-win situation for either side if he pressed too hard, Owen resumed the argument for show's sake before gruffly assenting. The head jawa consented reluctantly to the trade, and both sides breathed a mental sigh of relief that hostilities had been avoided. While the jawa bowed and whined with impatient greed, Owen paid him off.

Meanwhile, Luke had led the two robots toward an opening

in the dry ground. A few seconds later they were striding down a ramp kept clear of drifting sand by electrostatic repellers.

"Don't you ever forget this," Threepio muttered to Artoo, leaning over the smaller machine. "Why I stick my neck out for you, when all you ever bring me is trouble, is beyond my capacity to comprehend."

The passage widened into the garage proper, which was cluttered with tools and sections of farming machinery. Many looked heavily used, some to the point of collapse. But the lights were comforting to both 'droids, and there was a hominess to the chamber which hinted at a tranquillity not experienced by either machine for a long time. Near the center of the garage was a large tub, and the aroma drifting from it made Threepio's principal olfactory sensors twitch.

Luke grinned, noting the robot's reaction. "Yes, it's a lubrication bath." He eyed the tall bronze robot appraisingly. "And from the looks of it, you could use about a week's submergence. But we can't afford that so you'll have to settle for an afternoon." Then Luke turned his attention to Artoo Detoo, walking up to him and flipping open a panel that shielded numerous gauges.

"As for you," he continued, with a whistle of surprise, "I don't know how you've kept running. Not surprising, knowing the jawas' reluctance to part with any erg-fraction they don't have to. It's recharge time for you." He gestured toward a large power unit.

Artoo Detoo followed Luke's gesture, then beeped once and waddled over to the boxy construction. Finding the proper cord, he automatically flipped open a panel and plugged the triple prongs into his face.

Threepio had walked over to the large cistern, which was filled almost full with aromatic cleansing oil. With a remarkably humanlike sigh he lowered himself slowly into the tank.

"You two behave yourselves," Luke cautioned them as he moved to a small two-man skyhopper. A powerful little suborbital spacecraft, it rested in the hangar section of the garage-workshop. "I've got work of my own to do."

Unfortunately, Luke's energies were still focused on his farewell encounter with Biggs, so that hours later he had finished few of his chores. Thinking about his friend's departure, Luke was running a caressing hand over the damaged port fin of the 'hopper—the fin he had damaged while running down an imaginary Tie fighter in the wrenching twists and turns of a narrow canyon. That was when the projecting ledge had clipped him as effectively as an energy beam.

Abruptly something came to a boil within him. With atypical violence he threw a power wrench across a worktable nearby. "It just isn't fair!" he declared to no one in particular. His voice dropped disconsolately. "Biggs is right. I'll never get out of here. He's planning rebellion against the Empire, and I'm trapped on a blight of a farm."

"I beg your pardon, sir."

Luke spun, startled, but it was only the tall 'droid, Threepio. The contrast in the robot was striking compared with Luke's initial sight of him. Bronze-colored alloy gleamed in the overhead lights of the garage, cleaned of pits and dust by the powerful oils.

"Is there anything I might do to help?" the robot asked solicitously.

Luke studied the machine, and as he did so some of his anger drained away. There was no point in yelling cryptically at a robot.

"I doubt it," he replied, "unless you can alter time and speed up the harvest. Or else teleport me off this sandpile under Uncle Owen's nose."

Sarcasm was difficult for even an extremely sophisticated robot to detect so Threepio considered the question objectively before finally replying, "I don't think so, sir. I'm only a third-degree 'droid and not very knowledgeable about such things as transatomic physics." Suddenly, the events of the past couple of days seemed to catch up with him all at once. "As a matter of fact, young sir," Threepio went on while looking around him with fresh vision, "I'm not even sure which planet I'm on."

Luke chuckled sardonically and assumed a mocking pose. "If there's a bright center to this universe, you're on the world farthest from it."

"Yes, Luke sir."

The youth shook his head irritably. "Never mind the 'sir'— it's just Luke. And this world is called Tatooine."

Threepio nodded slightly. "Thank you, Luke s—Luke. I am See Threepio, human-droid relations specialist." He jerked a casual metal thumb back toward the recharge unit. "That is my companion, Artoo Detoo."

"Pleased to meet you, Threepio," Luke said easily. "You too, Artoo." Walking across the garage, he checked a gauge on the smaller machine's front panel, then gave a grunt of satisfaction. As he began unplugging the charge cord he saw something which made him frown and lean close.

"Something wrong, Luke?" Threepio inquired.

Luke went to a nearby tool wall and selected a small many-armed device. "I don't know yet, Threepio."

Returning to the recharger, Luke bent over Artoo and began scraping at several bumps in the small 'droid's top with a chromed pick. Occasionally he jerked back sharply as bits of corrosion were flicked into the air by the tiny tool.

Threepio watched, interested, as Luke worked. "There's a lot of strange carbon scoring here of a type I'm not familiar with. Looks like you've both seen a lot of action out of the ordinary."

"Indeed, sir," Threepio admitted, forgetting to drop the honorific. This time Luke was too absorbed elsewhere to correct him. "Sometimes I'm amazed we're in as good shape as we are." He added as an afterthought, while still shying away from the thrust of Luke's question, "What with the rebellion and all."

Despite his caution, it seemed to Threepio that he must have given something away, for an almost jawa-like blaze appeared in Luke's eyes. "You know about the rebellion against the Empire?" he demanded.

"In a way," Threepio confessed reluctantly. "The rebellion was responsible for our coming into your service. We are refugees, you see." He did not add from where.

Not that Luke appeared to care. "*Refugees!* Then I *did* see a space battle!" He rambled on rapidly, excited. "Tell me where you've been—in how many encounters. How is the rebellion going? Does the Empire take it seriously? Have you seen many ships destroyed?"

"A bit slower, please, sir," Threepio pleaded. "You misinterpret our status. We were innocent bystanders. Our involvement with the rebellion was of the most marginal nature.

"As to battles, we were in several, I think. It is difficult to tell when one is not directly in contact with the actual battle machinery." He shrugged neatly. "Beyond that, there is not much to say. Remember, sir, I am little more than a cosmeticized interpreter and not very good at telling stories or relating histories, and even less proficient at embellishing them. I am a very literal machine."

Luke turned away, disappointed, and returned to his cleaning of Artoo Detoo. Additional scraping turned up something puzzling enough to demand his full attention. A small metal fragment was tightly lodged between two bar conduits that would normally form a linkage. Setting down the delicate pick, Luke switched to a larger instrument.

"Well, my little friend," he murmured, "you've got something jammed in here real good." As he pushed and pried Luke directed half his attention to Threepio. "Were you on a star freighter or was it—"

Metal gave way with a powerful *crack*, and the recoil sent Luke tumbling head over heels. Getting to his feet, he started to curse—then froze, motionless.

The front of the Artoo unit had begun to glow, exuding a three-dimensional image less than one-third of a meter square but precisely defined. The portrait formed within the box was so exquisite that in a couple of minutes Luke discovered he was out of breath—because he had forgotten to breathe.

Despite a superficial sharpness, the image flickered and jiggled unsteadily, as if the recording had been made and installed with haste. Luke stared at the foreign colors being projected into the prosaic atmosphere of the garage and started to form a question. But it was never finished. The lips on the figure moved, and the girl spoke—or rather, seemed to speak. Luke knew the aural accompaniment was generated somewhere within Artoo Detoo's squat torso.

"Obi-wan Kenobi," the voice implored huskily, "help me! You're my only remaining hope." A burst of static dissolved the face momentarily. Then it coalesced again, and once more the voice repeated, "Obi-wan Kenobi, you're my only remaining hope."

With a raspy hum the hologram continued. Luke sat perfectly still for a long moment, considering what he was seeing, then he blinked and directed his words to the Artoo unit.

"What's this all about, Artoo Detoo?"

The stubby 'droid shifted slightly, the cubish portrait shifting with him, and beeped what sounded vaguely like a sheepish reply.

Threepio appeared as mystified as Luke. "What is that?" he inquired sharply, gesturing at the speaking portrait and then at Luke. "You were asked a question. What and who is that, and how are you originating it—and why?"

The Artoo unit generated a beep of surprise, for all the world as if just noticing the hologram. This was followed by a whistling stream of information.

Threepio digested the data, tried to frown, couldn't and strove to convey his own confusion via the tone of his voice. "He insists it's nothing, sir. Merely a malfunction—old data. A tape that should have been erased but was missed. He insists we pay it no mind."

That was like telling Luke to ignore a cache of Durindfires he might stumble over in the desert. "Who is she?" he demanded, staring enraptured at the hologram. "She's beautiful."

"I really don't know who she is," Threepio confessed honestly. "I think she might have been a passenger on our last voyage. From what I recall, she was a personage of some importance. This might have something to do with the fact that our Captain was attaché to—"

Luke cut him off, savoring the way sensuous lips formed and reformed the sentence fragment. "Is there any more to this recording? It sounds like it's incomplete." Getting to his feet, Luke reached out for the Artoo unit.

The robot moved backward and produced whistles of such frantic concern that Luke hesitated and held off reaching for the internal controls.

Threepio was shocked. "Behave yourself, Artoo," he finally chastised his companion. "You're going to get us into trouble." He had visions of the both of them being packed up as uncooperative and shipped back to the jawas, which was enough to make him imitate a shudder.

"It's all right—he's our master now." Threepio indicated Luke. "You can trust him. I feel that he has our best interests in mind."

Detoo appeared to hesitate, uncertain. Then he whistled and beeped a long complexity at his friend.

"Well?" Luke prompted impatiently.

Threepio paused before replying. "He says that he is the property of one Obi-wan Kenobi, a resident of this world. Of this very region, in fact. The sentence fragment we are hearing is part of a private message intended for this person."

Threepio shook his head slowly. "Quite frankly, sir, I don't know what he's talking about. Our last master was Captain Colton. I never heard Artoo mention a prior master. I've certainly never heard of an Obi-wan Kenobi. But with all we've been through," he concluded apologetically, "I'm afraid his logic circuits have gotten a bit scrambled. He's become decidedly eccentric at times." And while Luke considered this turn of events, Threepio took the opportunity to throw Artoo a furious look of warning.

"Obi-wan Kenobi," Luke recited thoughtfully. His expression suddenly brightened. "Say . . . I wonder if he could be referring to old Ben Kenobi."

"Begging your pardon," Threepio gulped, astonished beyond measure, "but you actually know of such a person?"

"Not exactly," he admitted in a more subdued voice. "I don't know anyone named Obi-wan—but old Ben lives somewhere out on the fringe of the Western Dune Sea. He's kind of a local character—a hermit. Uncle Owen and a few of the other farmers say he's a sorcerer.

"He comes around once in a while to trade things. I hardly ever talk to him, though. My uncle usually runs him off." He paused and glanced across at the small robot again. "But I never heard that old Ben owned a 'droid of any kind. At least, none that I ever heard tell of."

Luke's gaze was drawn irresistibly back to the hologram. "I wonder who she is. She must be important—especially if what you told me just now is true, Threepio. She sounds and looks as if she's in some kind of trouble. Maybe the message *is* important. We ought to hear the rest of it."

He reached again for the Artoo's internal controls, and the robot scurried backward again, squeaking a blue streak.

"He says there's a restraining separator bolt that's circuiting out his self-motivation components," Threepio translated. "He suggests that if you move the bolt he might be able to repeat the entire message," Threepio finished uncertainly. When Luke continued to stare at the portrait, Threepio added, more loudly *"Sir!"*

Luke shook himself. "What . . . ? Oh, yes." He considered the request. Then he moved and peered into the open panel. This time Artoo didn't retreat.

"I see it, I think. Well, I guess you're too small to run away from me if I take this off. I wonder what someone would be sending a message to old Ben for."

Selecting the proper tool, Luke reached down into the exposed circuitry and popped the restraining bolt free. The first noticeable result of this action was that the portrait disappeared.

Luke stood back. "There, now." There was an uncomfortable pause during which the hologram showed no sign of returning. "Where did she go?" Luke finally prompted. "Make her come back. Play the entire message, Artoo Detoo."

An innocent-sounding beep came from the robot. Threepio

appeared embarrassed and nervous as he translated. "He said, 'What message?' "

Threepio's attention turned half angrily to his companion. "What message? You know what message! The one you just played a fragment of for us. The one you're hauling around inside your recalcitrant, rust-ridden innards, you stubborn hunk of junk!"

Artoo sat and hummed softly to himself.

"I'm sorry, sir," Threepio said slowly, "but he shows signs of having developed an alarming flutter in his obedience-rational module. Perhaps if we—"

A voice from down a corridor interrupted him. "Luke . . . oh, Luke—come to dinner!"

Luke hesitated, then rose and turned away from the puzzling little 'droid. "Okay," he called, "I'm coming, Aunt Beru!" He lowered his voice as he spoke to Threepio. "See what you can do with him. I'll be back soon." Tossing the just-removed restraining bolt on the workbench, he hurried from the chamber.

As soon as the human was gone, Threepio whirled on his shorter companion. "You'd better consider playing that whole recording for him," he growled, with a suggestive nod toward a workbench laden with dismembered machine parts. "Otherwise he's liable to take up that cleaning pick again and go digging for it. He might not be too careful what he cuts through if he believes you're deliberately withholding something from him."

A plaintive beep came from Artoo.

"No," Threepio responded, "I don't think he likes you at all."

A second beep failed to alter the stern tone in the taller robot's voice. "No, I don't like you, either."

IV

LUKE'S Aunt Beru was filling a pitcher with blue liquid from a refrigerated container. Behind her, in the dining area, a steady buzz of conversation reached to the kitchen.

She sighed sadly. The mealtime discussions between her husband and Luke had grown steadily more acrimonious as the boy's restlessness pulled him in directions other than farming. Directions for which Owen, a stolid man of the soil if there ever was one, had absolutely no sympathy.

Returning the bulk container to the refrigerator unit, she placed the pitcher on a tray and hurried back to the dining room. Beru was not a brilliant woman, but she possessed an instinctive understanding of her important position in this household. She functioned like the damping rods in a nuclear reactor. As long as she was present, Owen and Luke would continue to generate a lot of heat, but if she was out of their presence for too long— *boom!*

Condenser units built into the bottom of each plate kept the food on the dining-room table hot as she hurried in. Immediately, both men lowered their voices to something civilized and shifted the subject. Beru pretended not to notice the change.

"I think that Artoo unit might have been stolen, Uncle Owen," Luke was saying, as if that had been the topic of conversation all along.

His uncle helped himself to the milk pitcher, mumbling his reply around a mouthful of food. "The jawas have a tendency to pick up anything that's not tied down, Luke, but remember, they're basically afraid of their own shadows. To resort to outright theft, they'd have to have considered the consequences of being pursued and punished. Theoretically, their minds shouldn't be capable of that. What makes you think the 'droid is stolen?"

"For one thing, it's in awfully good shape for a discard. It generated a hologram recording while I was cleaning—" Luke tried to conceal his horror at the slip. He added hastily, "But that's not important. The reason I think it might be stolen is because it claims to be the property of someone it calls Obi-wan Kenobi."

Maybe something in the food, or perhaps the milk, caused Luke's uncle to gag. Then again, it might have been an expression of disgust, which was Owen's way of indicating his opinion of that peculiar personage. In any case, he continued eating without looking up at his nephew.

Luke pretended the display of graphic dislike had never happened. "I thought," he continued determinedly, "it might have meant old Ben. The first name is different, but the last is identical."

When his uncle steadfastly maintained his silence, Luke prompted him directly. "Do *you* know who he's talking about, Uncle Owen?"

Surprisingly, his uncle looked uncomfortable instead of angry. "It's nothing," he mumbled, still not meeting Luke's gaze. "A name from another time." He squirmed nervously in his seat. "A name that can only mean trouble."

Luke refused to heed the implied warning and pressed on. "Is it someone related to old Ben, then? I didn't know he had any relatives."

"You stay away from that old wizard, you hear me!" his uncle exploded, awkwardly substituting threat for reason.

"Owen . . ." Aunt Beru started to interject gently, but the big farmer cut her off sternly.

"Now, this is important, Beru." He turned his attention back to his nephew. "I've told you about Kenobi before. He's a crazy old man; he's dangerous and full of mischief, and he's best left well alone."

Beru's pleading gaze caused him to quiet somewhat. "That 'droid has nothing to do with him. Couldn't have," he grumbled half to himself. "Recording huh! Well, tomorrow I want you to take the unit into Anchorhead and have its memory flushed."

Snorting, Owen bent to his half-eaten meal with determination. "That will be the end of this foolishness. I don't care where that machine thinks it came from. I paid hard credit for it, and it belongs to us now."

"But suppose it *does* belong to someone else," Luke wondered. "What if this Obi-wan person comes looking for his 'droid?"

An expression between sorrow and a sneer crossed his uncle's seamed face at the remembrance. "He won't. I don't think that man exists anymore. He died about the same time as your father." A huge mouthful of hot food was shoveled inward. "Now forget about it."

"Then it *was* a real person," Luke murmured, staring down at his plate. He added slowly, "Did he know my father?"

"I said forget about it," Owen snapped. "Your only worry as far as those two 'droids are concerned is having them ready for work tomorrow. Remember, the last of our savings is tied up in those two. Wouldn't even have bought them if it wasn't so near harvest." He shook a spoon at his nephew. "In the morning I want you to have them working with the irrigation units up on the south ridge.

"You know," Luke replied distantly, "I think these 'droids are going to work out fine. In fact, I—" He hesitated, shooting his uncle a surreptitious glare. "I was thinking about our agreement about me staying on for another season."

His uncle failed to react, so Luke rushed on before his nerve failed. "If these new 'droids do work out, I want to transmit my application to enter the Academy for next year."

Owen scowled, trying to hide his displeasure with food. "You mean, you want to transmit the *application* next year—after the harvest."

"You have more than enough 'droids now, and they're in good condition. They'll last."

" 'Droids, yes," his uncle agreed, "but 'droids can't replace a man, Luke. You know that. The harvest is when I need you the most. It's just for one more season after this one." He looked away, bluster and anger gone now.

Luke toyed with his food, not eating, saying nothing.

"Listen," his uncle told him, "for the first time we've got a chance for a real fortune. We'll make enough to hire some extra hands for next time. Not 'droids—people. Then you can go to the Academy." He fumbled over words, unaccustomed to pleading. "I need you here, Luke. You understand that, don't you?"

"It's another year," his nephew objected sullenly. "Another year."

How many times had he heard that before? How many times had they repeated this identical charade with the same result?

Convinced once more that Luke had come 'round to his way

of thinking, Owen shrugged the objection off. "Time will pass before you know it."

Abruptly Luke rose, shoving his barely touched plate of food aside. "That's what you said last year when Biggs left." He spun and half ran from the room.

"Where are you going, Luke?" his aunt yelled worriedly after him.

Luke's reply was bleak, bitter. "Looks like I'm going nowhere." Then he added, out of consideration for his aunt's sensibilities, "I have to finish cleaning those 'droids if they're going to be ready to work tomorrow."

Silence hung in the air of the dining room after Luke departed. Husband and wife ate mechanically. Eventually Aunt Beru stopped shoving her food around her plate, looked up, and pointed out earnestly, "Owen, you can't keep him here forever. Most of his friends are gone, the people he grew up with. The Academy means so much to him."

Listlessly her husband replied, "I'll make it up to him next year. I promise. We'll have money—or maybe, the year after that."

"Luke's just not a farmer, Owen," she continued firmly. "He never will be, no matter how hard you try to make him one." She shook her head slowly. "He's got too much of his father in him."

For the first time all evening Owen Lars looked thoughtful as well as concerned as he gazed down the passage Luke had taken. "That's what I'm afraid of," he whispered.

Luke had gone topside. He stood on the sand watching the double sunset as first one and then the other of Tatooine's twin suns sank slowly behind the distant range of dunes. In the fading light the sands turned gold, russet, and flaming red-orange before advancing night put the bright colors to sleep for another day. Soon, for the first time, those sands would blossom with food plants. This former wasteland would see an eruption of green.

The thought ought to have sent a thrill of anticipation through Luke. He should have been as flushed with excitement as his uncle was whenever he described the coming harvest. Instead, Luke felt nothing but a vast indifferent emptiness. Not even the prospect of having a lot of money for the first time in his life excited him. What was there to do with money in Anchorhead— anywhere on Tatooine, for that matter?

Part of him, an increasingly large part, was growing more and more restless at remaining unfulfilled. This was not an uncommon feeling in youths his age, but for reasons Luke did not understand it was much stronger in him than in any of his friends.

As the night cold came creeping over the sand and up his legs, he brushed the grit from his trousers and descended into the garage. Maybe working on the 'droids would bury some of the remorse a little deeper in his mind. A quick survey of the chamber showed no movement. Neither of the new machines was in sight. Frowning slightly, Luke took a small control box from his belt and activated a couple of switches set into the plastic.

A low hum came from the box. The caller produced the taller of the two robots, Threepio. In fact, he gave a yell of surprise as he jumped up behind the skyhopper.

Luke started toward him, openly puzzled. "What are you hiding back there for?"

The robot came stumbling around the prow of the craft, his attitude one of desperation. It occurred to Luke then that despite his activating the caller, the Artoo unit was still nowhere to be seen.

The reason for his absence—or something related to it—came pouring unbidden from Threepio. "It wasn't my fault," the robot begged frantically. "Please don't deactivate me! I told him not to go, but he's faulty. He must be malfunctioning. Something has totally boiled his logic circuits. He kept babbling on about some sort of mission, sir. I never heard a robot with delusions of grandeur before. Such things shouldn't even be within the cogitative theory units of one that's as basic as an Artoo unit, and . . ."

"You mean . . . ?" Luke started to gape.

"Yes, sir . . . he's gone."

"And I removed his restraining coupling myself," Luke muttered slowly. Already he could visualize his uncle's face. The last of their savings tied up in these 'droids, he had said.

Racing out of the garage, Luke hunted for non-existent reasons why the Artoo unit should go berserk. Threepio followed on his heels.

From a small ridge which formed the highest point close by the homestead, Luke had a panoramic view of the surrounding desert. Bringing out the precious macrobinoculars, he scanned the rapidly darkening horizons for something small, metallic, three-legged, and out of its mechanical mind.

Threepio fought his way up through the sand to stand beside Luke. "That Artoo unit has always caused nothing but trouble," he groaned. "Astromech 'droids are becoming too iconoclastic even for me to understand, sometimes."

The binoculars finally came down, and Luke commented matter-of-factly, "Well, he's nowhere in sight." He kicked furiously at the ground. "Damn it—how could I have been so stupid, letting it trick me into removing that restrainer! Uncle Owen's going to kill me."

"Begging your pardon, sir," ventured a hopeful Threepio, visions of jawas dancing in his head, "But can't we go after him?"

Luke turned. Studiously he examined the wall of black advancing toward them. "Not at night. It's too dangerous with all the raiders around. I'm not too concerned about the jawas, but sandpeople . . . no, not in the dark. We'll have to wait until morning to try to track him."

A shout rose from the homestead below. "Luke—Luke, are you finished with those 'droids yet? I'm turning down the power for the night."

"All right!" Luke responded, sidestepping the question. "I'll be down in a few minutes, Uncle Owen!" Turning, he took one last look at the vanished horizon. "Boy, am I in for it!" he muttered. "That little 'droid's going to get me in a lot of trouble."

"Oh, he excells at that, sir." Threepio confirmed with mock cheerfulness. Luke threw him a sour look, and together they turned and descended into the garage.

"Luke . . . Luke!" Still rubbing the morning sleep from his eyes, Owen glanced from side to side, loosening his neck muscles. "Where could that boy be loafing now?" he wondered aloud at the lack of response. There was no sign of movement in the homestead, and he had already checked above.

"Luke!" he yelled again. *Luke, Luke, Luke* . . . the name echoed teasingly back at him from the homestead walls. Turning angrily, he stalked back into the kitchen, where Beru was preparing breakfast.

"Have you seen Luke this morning?" he asked as softly as he could manage.

She glanced briefly at him, then returned to her cooking. "Yes. He said he had some things to do before he started out to the south ridge this morning, so he left early."

"Before breakfast?" Owen frowned worriedly. "That's not like him. Did he take the new 'droids with him?"

"I think so. I'm sure I saw at least one of them with him."

"Well," Owen mused, uncomfortable but with nothing to really hang imprecations on, "he'd better have those ridge units repaired by midday or there'll be hell to pay."

An unseen face shielded by smooth white metal emerged from the half-buried life pod that now formed the backbone of a dune slightly higher than its neighbors. The voice sounded efficient, but tired.

"Nothing," the inspecting trooper muttered to his several companions. "No tapes, and no sign of habitation."

Powerful handguns lowered at the information that the pod was deserted. One of the armored men turned, calling out to an officer standing some distance away. "This is definitely the pod that cleared the rebel ship, sir, but there's nothing on board."

"Yet it set down intact," the officer was murmuring to himself. "It *could* have done so on automatics, but if it was a true malfunction, then they shouldn't have been engaged." Something didn't make sense.

"Here's why there's nothing on board and no hint of life, sir," a voice declared.

The officer turned and strode several paces to where another trooper was kneeling in the sand. He held up an object for the officer's inspection. It shone in the sun.

" 'Droid plating," the officer observed after a quick glance at the metal fragment. Superior and underling exchanged a significant glance. Then their eyes turned simultaneously to the high mesas off to the north.

Gravel and fine sand formed a gritty fog beneath the landspeeder as it slid across the rippling wasteland of Tatooine on humming repulsors. Occasionally the craft would jog slightly as it encountered a dip or slight rise, to return to its smooth passage as its pilot compensated for the change in terrain.

Luke leaned back in the seat, luxuriating in unaccustomed relaxation as Threepio skillfully directed the powerful landcraft around dunes and rocky outcrops. "You handle a landspeeder pretty well, for a machine," he noted admiringly.

"Thank you, sir," a gratified Threepio responded, his eyes never moving from the landscape ahead. "I was not lying to your uncle when I claimed versatility as my middle name. In fact, on occasion I have been called upon to perform unexpected functions in circumstances which would have appalled my designers.''

Something pinged behind them, then pinged again.

Luke frowned and popped the speeder canopy. A few moments of digging in the motor casing eliminated the metallic bark.

"How's that?'' he yelled forward.

Threepio signaled that the adjustment was satisfactory. Luke turned back into the cockpit and closed the canopy over them again. Silently he brushed his wind-whipped hair back out of his eyes as his attention returned to the dry desert ahead of them.

"Old Ben Kenobi is supposed to live out in this general direction. Even though nobody knows exactly where, I don't see how that Artoo unit could have come this far so quickly.'' His expression was downcast. "We must have missed him back in the dunes somewhere. He could be anywhere out here. And Uncle Owen must be wondering why I haven't called in from the south ridge by now.''

Threepio considered a moment, then ventured, "Would it help, sir, if you told him that it was my fault?''

Luke appeared to brighten at the suggestion. "Sure . . . he needs you twice as much now. Probably he'll only deactivate you for a day or so, or give you a partial memory flush.''

Deactivate? Memory flush? Threepio added hastily, "On second thought, sir, Artoo would still be around if you hadn't removed his restraining module.''

But something more important than fixing responsibility for the little robot's disappearance was on Luke's mind at the moment. "Wait a minute,'' he advised Threepio as he stared fixedly at the instrument panel. "There's something dead ahead on the metal scanner. Can't distinguish outlines at this distance, but judging by size alone, it *could* be our wandering 'droid. Hit it.''

The landspeeder jumped forward as Threepio engaged the accelerator, but its occupants were totally unaware that other eyes were watching as the craft increased its speed.

Those eyes were not organic, but then, they weren't wholly mechanical, either. No one could say for certain, because no one had ever made that intimate a study of the Tusken Raiders—known less formally to the margin farmers of Tatooine simply as the sandpeople.

The Tuskens didn't permit close study of themselves, discouraging potential observers by methods as effective as they were uncivilized. A few xenologists thought they must be related to the jawas. Even fewer hypothesized that the jawas were actually the mature form of the sandpeople, but this theory was discounted by the majority of serious scientists.

Both races affected tight clothing to shield them from Tatooine's twin dose of solar radiation, but there most comparisons ended. Instead of heavy woven cloaks like the jawas wore, the sandpeople wrapped themselves mummylike in endless swathings and bandages and loose bits of cloth.

Where the jawas feared everything, a Tusken Raider feared little. The sandpeople were larger, stronger, and far more aggressive. Fortunately for the human colonists of Tatooine, they were not very numerous and elected to pursue their nomadic existence in some of Tatooine's most desolate regions. Contact between human and Tusken, therefore, was infrequent and uneasy, and they murdered no more than a handful of humans per year. Since the human population had claimed its share of Tuskens, not always with reason, a peace of a sort existed between the two—as long as neither side gained an advantage.

One of the pair felt that that unstable condition had temporarily shifted in his favor, and he was about to take full advantage of it as he raised his rifle toward the landspeeder. But his companion grabbed the weapon and shoved down on it before it could be fired. This set off a violent argument between the two. And, as they traded vociferous opinions in a language consisting mostly of consonants, the landspeeder sped on its way.

Either because the speeder had passed out of range or because the second Tusken had convinced the other, the two broke off the discussion and scrambled down the back side of the high ridge. Snuffling and a shifting of weight took place at the ridge bottom as the two Banthas stirred at the approach of their masters. Each was as large as a small dinosaur, with bright eyes and long, thick fur. They hissed anxiously as the two sandpeople approached, then mounted them from knee to saddle.

With a kick the Banthas rose. Moving slowly but with enormous strides, the two massive horned creatures swept down the back of the rugged bluff, urged on by their anxious, equally outrageous mahouts.

"It's him, all right," Luke declared with mixed anger and satisfaction as the tiny tripodal form came into view. The speeder banked and swung down onto the floor of a huge sandstone canyon. Luke slipped his rifle out from behind the seat and swung it over his shoulder. "Come round in front of him, Threepio," he instructed.

"With pleasure, sir."

The Artoo unit obviously noted their approach, but made no move to escape; it could hardly have outrun the landspeeder anyway. Artoo simply halted as soon as it detected them and waited until the craft swung around in a smooth arc. Threepio came to a sharp halt, sending up a low cloud of sand on the smaller robot's right. Then the whine from the landspeeder's engine dropped to a low idling hum as Threepio put it in parking mode. A last sigh and the craft stopped completely.

After finishing a cautious survey of the canyon, Luke led his companion out onto the gravelly surface and up to Artoo Detoo. "Just where," he inquired sharply, "did you think you were going?"

A feeble whistle issued from the apologetic robot, but it was Threepio and not the recalcitrant rover who was abruptly doing most of the talking.

"Master Luke here is now your rightful owner, Artoo. How could you just amble away from him like this? Now that he's found you, let's have no more of this 'Obi-wan Kenobi' gibberish. I don't know where you picked that up—or that melodramatic hologram, either."

Artoo started to beep in protest, but Threepio's indignation was too great to permit excuses. "And don't talk to me about your mission. What rot! You're fortunate Master Luke doesn't blast you into a million pieces right here and now."

"Not much chance of that," admitted Luke, a bit overwhelmed by Threepio's casual vindictiveness. "Come on—it's getting late." He eyed the rapidly rising suns. "I just hope we can get back before Uncle Owen really lets go."

"If you don't mind my saying so," Threepio suggested, apparently unwilling that the Artoo unit should get off so easily, "I think you ought to deactivate the little fugitive until you've gotten him safely back in the garage."

"No. He's not going to try anything." Luke studied the softly beeping 'droid sternly. "I hope he's learned his lesson. There's no need to—"

Without warning the Artoo unit suddenly leaped off the ground—no mean feat considering the weakness of the spring mechanisms in his three thick legs. His cylindrical body was twisting and spinning as he let out a frantic symphony of whistles, hoots, and electronic exclamations.

Luke was tired, not alarmed. "What is it? What's wrong with him now?" He was beginning to see how Threepio's patience could be worn thin. He had had about enough of this addled instrument himself.

Undoubtedly the Artoo unit had acquired the holo of the girl by accident, then used it to entice Luke into removing his restraining module. Threepio probably had the right attitude. Still, once Luke got its circuits realigned and its logic couplings cleaned, it would make a perfectly serviceable farm unit. Only . . . if that was the case, then why was Threepio looking around so anxiously?

"Oh my, sir. Artoo claims there are several creatures of unknown type approaching from the southeast."

That *could* be another attempt by Artoo to distract them, but Luke couldn't take the chance. Instantly he had his rifle off his shoulder and had activated the energy cell. He examined the horizon in the indicated direction and saw nothing. But then, sandpeople were experts at making themselves unseeable.

Luke suddenly realized exactly how far out they were, how much ground the landspeeder had covered that morning. "I've never been out in this direction this far from the farm before," he informed Threepio. "There are some awfully strange things living out here. Not all of them have been classified. It's better to treat anything as dangerous until determined otherwise. Of course, if it's something utterly new . . ."

His curiosity prodded him. In any case, this was probably just another ruse of Artoo Detoo's. "Let's take a look," he decided.

Moving cautiously forward and keeping his rifle ready, he led Threepio toward the crest of a nearby high dune. At the same time he took care not to let Artoo out of his sight.

Once at the top he lay flat and traded his rifle for the macrobinoculars. Below, another canyon spread out before them, rising to a wind-weathered wall of rust and ocher. Advancing the binocs slowly across the canyon floor, he settled unexpectedly on two tethered shapes. Banthas and riderlooo!

"Did you say something, sir?" wheezed Threepio, struggling up behind Luke. His locomotors were not designed for such outer climbing and scrambling.

"Banthas, all right," Luke whispered over his shoulder, not considering in the excitement of the moment that Threepio might not know a Bantha from a panda.

He looked back into the eyepieces, refocusing slightly. "Wait . . . it's sandpeople, sure. I see one of them."

Something dark suddenly blocked his sight. For a moment he thought that a rock might have moved in front of him. Irritably he dropped the binoculars and reached out to move the blinding object aside. His hand touched something like soft metal.

It was a bandaged leg about as big around as both of Luke's together. Shocked, he looked up . . . and up. The towering figure glaring down at him was no jawa. It had seemingly erupted straight from the sand.

Threepio took a startled step backward and found no footing. As gyros whined in protest the tall robot tumbled backward down the side of the dune. Frozen in place. Luke heard steadily fading bangs and rattles as Threepio bounced down the steep slope behind him.

As the moment of confrontation passed, the Tusken let out a terrifying grunt of fury and pleasure and brought down his heavy gaderffii. The double-edged ax would have cleaved Luke's skull neatly in two, except that he threw the rifle up in a gesture more instinctive than calculated. His weapon deflected the blow, but would never do so again. Made from cannibalized freighter plating the huge ax shattered the barrel and made metallic confetti of the gun's delicate insides.

Luke scrambled backward and found himself against a steep drop. The Raider stalked him slowly, weapon held high over its rag-enclosed head. It uttered a gruesome, chuckling laugh, the sound made all the more inhuman by the distortion effect of its gridlike sandfilter.

Luke tried to view his situation objectively, as he had been instructed to do in survival school. Trouble was, his mouth was dry, his hands were shaking, and he was paralyzed with fear. With the Raider in front of him and a probably fatal drop behind, something else in his mind took over and opted for the least painful response. He fainted.

None of the Raiders noticed Artoo Detoo as the tiny robot forced himself into a small alcove in the rocks near the landspeeder. One of them was carrying the inert form of Luke. He dumped the unconscious youth in a heap next to the speeder, then joined his fellows as they began swarming over the open craft.

Supplies and spare parts were thrown in all directions. From time to time the plundering would be interrupted as several of them quibbled or fought over a particularly choice bit of booty.

Unexpectedly, distribution of the landspeeder's contents ceased, and with frightening speed the Raiders became part of the desertscape, looking in all directions.

A lost breeze idled absently down the canyon. Far off to the west, something howled. A rolling, booming drone ricocheted off canyon walls and crawled nervously up and down a gorgon scale.

The sandpeople remained poised a moment longer. Then they were uttering loud grunts and moans of fright as they rushed to get away from the highly visible landspeeder.

The shivering howl sounded again, nearer this time. By now the sandpeople were halfway to their waiting Banthas, that were likewise lowing tensely and tugging at their tethers.

Although the sound held no meaning for Artoo Detoo, the little 'droid tried to squeeze himself even deeper into the almost-cave. The booming howl came closer. Judging by the way the sandpeople had reacted, something monstrous beyond imagining had to be behind that rolling cry. Something monstrous and murder-bent which might not have the sense to distinguish between edible organics and inedible machines.

Not even the dust of their passing remained to mark where the Tusken Raiders had only minutes before been dismembering the interior of the landspeeder. Artoo Detoo shut down all but vital functions, trying to minimize noise and light as a swishing sound grew gradually audible. Moving toward the landspeeder, the creature appeared above the top of a nearby dune. . . .

V

IT was tall, but hardly monstrous. Artoo frowned inwardly as he checked ocular circuitry and reactivated his innards.

The monster looked very much like an old man. He was clad in a shabby cloak and loose robes hung with a few small straps, packs, and unrecognizable instruments. Artoo searched the human's wake but detected no evidence of a pursuing nightmare. Nor did the man appear threatened. Actually, Artoo thought, he looked kind of pleased.

It was impossible to tell where the odd arrival's overlapping attire ended and his skin began. That aged visage blended into the sand-stroked cloth, and his beard appeared but an extension of the loose threads covering his upper chest.

Hints of extreme climates other than desert, of ultimate cold and humidity, were etched into that seamed face. A questing beak of nose, like a high rock, protruded outward from a flash-flood of wrinkles and scars. The eyes bordering it were a liquid crystal-azure. The man smiled through sand and dust and beard, squinting at the sight of the crumpled form lying quietly alongside the landspeeder.

Convinced that the sandpeople had been the victims of an auditory delusion of some kind—conveniently ignoring the fact that he had experienced it also—and likewise assured that this stranger meant Luke no harm, Artoo shifted his position slightly, trying to obtain a better view. The sound produced by a tiny pebble he dislodged was barely perceptible to his electronic sensors, but the man whirled as if shot. He stared straight at Artoo's alcove, still smiling gently.

"Hello there," he called in a deep, surprisingly cheerful voice. "Come here, my little friend. No need to be afraid."

Something forthright and reassuring was in that voice. In any case, the association of an unknown human was preferable to remaining isolated in this wasteland. Waddling out into the sunlight, Artoo made his way over to where Luke lay sprawled. The robot's barrellike body inclined forward as he examined the limp form. Whistles and beeps of concern came from within.

Walking over, the old man bent beside Luke and reached out to touch his forehead, then his temple. Shortly, the unconscious youth was stirring and mumbling like a dreaming sleeper.

"Don't worry," the human told Artoo, "he'll be all right."

As if to confirm this opinion, Luke blinked, stared upward uncomprehendingly, and muttered, "What happened?"

"Rest easy, son," the man instructed him as he sat back on his heels. "You've had a busy day." Again the boyish grin. "You're mighty lucky your head's still attached to the rest of you."

Luke looked around, his gaze coming to rest on the elderly

face hovering above him. Recognition did wonders for his condition.

"Ben . . . it's got to be!" A sudden remembrance made him look around fearfully. But there was no sign of sandpeople. Slowly he raised his body to a sitting position. "Ben Kenobi . . . am I glad to see you!"

Rising, the old man surveyed the canyon floor and rolling rimwall above. One foot played with the sand. "The Jundland wastes are not to be traveled lightly. It's the misguided traveler who tempts the Tuskens' hospitality." His gaze went back to his patient. "Tell me, young man, what brings you out this far into nowhere?"

Luke indicated Artoo Detoo. "This little 'droid. For a while I thought he'd gone crazy, claiming he was searching for a former master. Now I don't think so. I've never seen such devotion in a 'droid—misguided or otherwise. There seems to be no stopping him; he even resorted to tricking me."

Luke's gaze shifted upward. "He claims to be the property of someone called Obi-wan Kenobi." Luke watched closely, but the man showed no reaction. "Is that a relative of yours? My uncle thinks he was a real person. Or is it just some unimportant bit of scrambled information that got shifted into his primary performance bank?"

An introspective frown did remarkable things to that sandblasted face. Kenobi appeared to ponder the question, scratching absently at his scruffy beard. "Obi-wan Kenobi!" he recited. "Obi-wan . . . now, that's a name I haven't heard in a long time. A long time. Most curious."

"My uncle said he was dead," Luke supplied helpfully.

"Oh, he's not dead," Kenobi corrected him easily. "Not yet, not yet."

Luke climbed excitedly to his feet, all thoughts of Tusken Raiders forgotten now. "You know him, then?"

A smile of perverse youthfulness split that collage of wrinkled skin and beard. "Of course I know him: he's me. Just as you probably suspected, Luke. I haven't gone by the name *Obi-wan*, though, since before you were born."

"Then," Luke essayed, gesturing at Artoo Detoo, "this 'droid does belong to you, as he claims."

"Now, that's the peculiar part," an openly puzzled Kenobi confessed, regarding the silent robot. "I can't seem to remember owning a 'droid, least of all a modern Artoo unit. Most interesting, most interesting."

Something drew the old man's gaze suddenly to the brow of nearby cliffs. "I think it's best we make use of your landspeeder some. The sandpeople are easily startled, but they'll soon return in greater numbers. A landspeeder's not a prize readily conceded, and after all, jawas they're not."

Placing both hands over his mouth in a peculiar fashion, Kenobi inhaled deeply and let out an unearthly howl that made Luke jump. "That ought to keep any laggards running for a while yet," the old man concluded with satisfaction.

"That's a krayt dragon call!" Luke gaped in astonishment "How did you do that?"

"I'll show you sometime, son. It's not too hard. Just takes the right attitude, a set of well-used vocal cords, and a lot of wind. Now, if you were an imperial bureaucrat, I could teach you right off, but you're not." He scanned the cliff-spine again. "And I don't think this is the time or place for it."

"I won't argue that." Luke was rubbing at the back of his head. "Let's get started."

That was when Artoo let out a pathetic beep and whirled. Luke couldn't interpret the electronic squeal, but he suddenly comprehended the reason behind it. "Threepio." Luke exclaimed, worriedly. Artoo was already moving as fast as possible away from the landspeeder. "Come on, Ben."

The little robot led them to the edge of a large sandpit. It stopped there, pointing downward and squeaking mournfully. Luke saw where Artoo was pointing, then started cautiously down the smooth, shifting slope while Kenobi followed effortlessly.

Threepio lay in the sand at the base of the slope down which he had rolled and tumbled. His casing was dented and badly mangled. One arm lay broken and bent a short distance away.

"Threepio!" Luke called. There was no response. Shaking the 'droid failed to activate anything. Opening a plate on the robot's back, Luke flipped a hidden switch on and off several times in succession. A low hum started, stopped, started again, and then dropped to a normal purr.

Using his remaining arm, Threepio rolled over and sat up. "Where am I," he murmured, as his photoreceptors continued to clear. Then he recognized Luke. "Oh, I'm sorry, sir. I must have taken a bad step."

"You're lucky any of your main circuits are still operational," Luke informed him. He looked significantly toward the top of the hill. "Can you stand? We've got to get out of here before the sandpeople return."

Servomotors whined in protest until Threepio ceased struggling. "I don't think I can make it. You go on, Master Luke. It doesn't make sense to risk yourself on my account. I'm finished."

"No, you're not," Luke shot back, unaccountably affected by this recently encountered machine. But then, Threepio was not the usual uncommunicative, agrifunctional device Luke was accustomed to dealing with. "What kind of talk is that?"

"Logical," Threepio informed him.

Luke shook his head angrily. "Defeatist."

With Luke and Ben Kenobi's aid, the battered 'droid somehow managed to struggle erect. Little Artoo watched from the pit's rim.

Hesitating part way up the slope, Kenobi sniffed the air suspiciously. "Quickly, son. They're on the move again."

Trying to watch the surrounding rocks and his footsteps simultaneously, Luke fought to drag Threepio clear of the pit.

The decor of Ben Kenobi's well-concealed cave was Spartan without appearing uncomfortable. It would not have suited most people, reflecting as it did its owner's peculiarly eclectic tastes. The living area radiated an aura of lean comfort with more importance attached to mental comforts than those of the awkward human body.

They had succeeded in vacating the canyon before the Tusken Raiders could return in force. Under Kenobi's direction, Luke left a trail behind them so confusing that not even a hypernasal jawa could have followed it.

Luke spent several hours ignoring the temptations of Kenobi's cave. Instead he remained in the corner which was equipped as a compact yet complete repair shop, working to fix Threepio's severed arm.

Fortunately, the automatic overload disconnects had given way under the severe strain, sealing electronic nerves and ganglia without real damage. Repair was merely a matter of reattaching the limb to the shoulder, then activating the self-reseals. Had the arm been broken in mid-"bone" instead of at a joint, such repairs would have been impossible save at a factory shop.

While Luke was thus occupied, Kenobi's attention was concentrated on Artoo Detoo. The squat 'droid sat passively on the cool cavern floor while the old man fiddled with its metal insides. Finally the man sat back with a "Humph!" of satisfaction and closed the open panels in the robot's rounded head. "Now let's see if we can figure out what you are, my little friend, and where you came from."

Luke was almost finished anyway, and Kenobi's words were sufficient to pull him away from the repair area. "I saw part of the message," he began, "and I . . ."

Once more the striking portrait was being projected into empty space from the front of the little robot. Luke broke off, enraptured by its enigmatic beauty once again.

"Yes, I think that's got it," Kenobi murmured contemplatively.

The image continued to flicker, indicating a tape hastily prepared. But it was much sharper, better defined now, Luke noted with admiration. One thing was apparent: Kenobi was skilled in subjects more specific than desert scavenging.

"General Obi-wan Kenobi," the mellifluous voice was saying, "I present myself in the name of the world family of Alderaan and of the Alliance to Restore the Republic. I break your solitude at the bidding of my father, Bail Organa, Viceroy and First Chairman of the Alderaan system."

Kenobi absorbed this extraordinary declamation while Luke's eyes bugged big enough to fall from his face.

"Years ago, General," the voice continued, "you served the Old Republic in the Clone Wars. Now my father begs you to aid us again in our most desperate hour. He would have you join him on Alderaan. You *must* go to him.

"I regret that I am unable to present my father's request to you in person. My mission to meet personally with you has failed. Hence I have been forced to resort to this secondary method of communication.

"Information vital to the survival of the Alliance has been secured in the mind of this Detoo 'droid. My father will know how to retrieve it. I plead with you to see this unit safely delivered to Alderaan."

She paused, and when she continued, her words were hurried and less laced with formality. "You *must* help me, Obi-wan Kenobi. You are my last hope. I will be captured by agents of the Empire. They will learn nothing from me. Everything to be learned lies locked in the memory cells of this 'droid. Do not fail us, Obi-wan Kenobi. Do not fail *me*."

A small cloud of tridimensional static replaced the delicate portrait, then it vanished entirely. Artoo Detoo gazed up expectantly at Kenobi.

Luke's mind was as muddy as a pond laced with petroleum. Unanchored, his thoughts and eyes turned for stability to the quiet figure seated nearby.

The old man. The crazy wizard. The desert bum and all-around character whom his uncle and everyone else had known of for as long as Luke could recall.

If the breathless, anxiety-ridden message the unknown woman had just spoken into the cool air of the cave had affected Kenobi in any way he gave no hint of it. Instead, he leaned back against the rock wall and tugged thoughtfully at his beard, puffing slowly on a water pipe of free-form tarnished chrome.

Luke visualized that simple yet lovely portrait. "She's so—so—" His farming background didn't provide him with the requisite words. Suddenly something in the message caused him to stare disbelievingly at the oldster. "General Kenobi, you fought in the Clone Wars? But . . . that was so long ago."

"Um, yes," Kenobi acknowledged, as casually as he might have discussed the recipe for shang stew. "I guess it was a while back. I was a Jedi knight once. Like," he added, watching the youth appraisingly, "your father."

"A Jedi knight," Luke echoed. Then he looked confused. "But my father didn't fight in the Clone Wars. He was no knight—just a navigator on a space freighter."

Kenobi's smile enfolded the pipe's mouthpiece. "Or so your uncle has told you." His attention was suddenly focused elsewhere. "Owen Lars didn't agree with your father's ideas, opinions, or with his philosophy of life. He believed that your father should have stayed here on Tatooine and not gotten involved in . . ." Again the seemingly indifferent shrug. "Well, he thought he should have remained here and minded his farming."

Luke said nothing, his body tense as the old man related bits and pieces of a personal history Luke had viewed only through his uncle's distortions.

"Owen was always afraid that your father's adventurous life might influence you, might pull you away from Anchorhead." He shook his head slowly, regretfully at the remembrance. "I'm afraid there wasn't much of the farmer in your father."

Luke turned away. He returned to cleaning the last particles of sand from Threepio's healing armature. "I wish I'd known him," he finally whispered.

"He was the best pilot I ever knew," Kenobi went on, "and a smart fighter. The force . . . the instinct was strong in him."

For a brief second Kenobi actually appeared old. "He was also a good friend."

Suddenly the boyish twinkle returned to those piercing eyes along with the old man's natural humor. "I understand you're quite a pilot yourself. Piloting and navigation aren't hereditary, but a number of the things that can combine to make a good small-ship pilot are. Those you may have inherited. Still, even a duck has to be taught to swim."

"What's a duck?" Luke asked curiously.

"Never mind. In many ways, you know, you are much like your father." Kenobi's unabashed look of evaluation made Luke nervous. "You've grown up quite a bit since the last time I saw you."

Having no reply for that, Luke waited silently as Kenobi sank back into deep contemplation. After a while the old man stirred, evidently having reached an important decision.

"All this reminds me," he declared with deceptive casualness, "I have something here for you." He rose and walked over to a bulky, old-fashioned chest and started rummaging through it. All sorts of intriguing items were removed and shoved around, only to be placed back in the bin. A few of them Luke recognized. As Kenobi was obviously intent on something important, he forbore inquiring about any of the other tantalizing flotsam.

"When you were old enough," Kenobi was saying, "your father wanted you to have this . . . if I can ever find the blasted device. I tried to give it to you once before, but your uncle wouldn't allow it. He believed you might get some crazy ideas from it and end up following old Obi-wan on some idealistic crusade.

"You see, Luke, that's where your father and your uncle Owen disagreed. Lars is not a man to let idealism interfere with business, whereas your father didn't think the question even worth discussing. His decision on such matters came like his piloting—instinctively."

Luke nodded. He finished picking out the last of the grit and looked around for one remaining component to snap back into Threepio's open chest plate. Locating the restraining module, he opened the receiving latches in the machine and set about locking it back in place. Threepio watched the process and appeared to wince ever so perceptibly.

Luke stared into those metal and plastic photoreceptors for a long moment. Then he set the module pointedly on the work-bench and closed the 'droid up. Threepio said nothing.

A grunt came from behind them, and Luke turned to see a pleased Kenobi walking over. He handed Luke a small, innocuous-looking device, which the youth studied with interest.

It consisted primarily of a short, thick handgrip with a couple of small switches set into the grip. Above this small post was a circular metal disk barely larger in diameter than his spread palm. A number of unfamiliar, jewellike components were built into both handle and disk, including what looked like the smallest power cell Luke had ever seen. The reverse side of the disk was polished to a mirror brightness. But it was the power cell that puzzled Luke the most. Whatever the thing was, it required a great deal of energy, according to the rating form of the cell.

Despite the claim that it had belonged to his father, the gizmo looked newly manufactured. Kenobi had obviously kept it carefully. Only a number of minute scratches on the handgrip hinted at previous usage.

"Sir?" came a familiar voice Luke hadn't heard in a while.

"What?" Luke was startled out of his examination.

"If you'll not be needing me," Threepio declared, "I think I'll shut down for a bit. It will help the armature nerves to knit, and I'm due for some internal self-cleansing anyhow."

"Sure, go ahead," Luke said absently, returning to his fascinated study of the whatever-it-was. Behind him, Threepio became silent, the glow fading temporarily from his eyes. Luke noticed that Kenobi was watching him with interest. "What is it?" he finally asked, unable despite his best efforts to identify the device.

"Your father's lightsaber," Kenobi told him. "At one time they were widely used. Still are, in certain galactic quarters."

Luke examined the controls on the handle, then tentatively touched a brightly colored button up near the mirrored pommel. Instantly the disk put forth a blue-white beam as thick around as his thumb. It was dense to the point of opacity and a little over a meter in length. It did not fade, but remained as brilliant and intense at its far end as it did next to the disk. Strangely, Luke felt no heat from it, though he was very careful not to touch it. He knew what a lightsaber could do, though he had never seen one before. It could drill a hole right through the rock wall of Kenobi's cave—or through a human being.

"This was the formal weapon of a Jedi knight," explained Kenobi. "Not as clumsy or random as a blaster. More skill than simple sight was required for its use. An elegant weapon. It was a symbol as well. Anyone can use a blaster or fusioncutter—but to use a lightsaber *well* was a mark of someone a cut above the ordinary.'' He was pacing the floor of the cave as he spoke.

"For over a thousand generations, Luke, the Jedi knights were the most powerful, most respected force in the galaxy. They served as the guardians and guarantors of peace and justice in the Old Republic.''

When Luke failed to ask what had happened to them since, Kenobi looked up to see that the youth was staring vacantly into space, having absorbed little if any of the oldster's instruction. Some men would have chided Luke for not paying attention. Not Kenobi. More sensitive than most, he waited patiently until the silence weighed strong enough on Luke for him to resume speaking.

"How," he asked slowly, "did my father die?''

Kenobi hesitated, and Luke sensed that the old man had no wish to talk about this particular matter. Unlike Owen Lars, however, Kenobi was unable to take refuge in a comfortable lie.

"He was betrayed and murdered," Kenobi declared solmenly, "by a very young Jedi named Darth Vader.'' He was not looking at Luke. "A boy I was training. One of my brightest disciples . . . one of my greatest failures.''

Kenobi resumed his pacing. "Vader used the training I gave him and the force within him for evil, to help the later corrupt Emperors. With the Jedi knights disbanded, disorganized, or dead, there were few to oppose Vader. Today they are all but extinct.''

An indecipherable expression crossed Kenobi's face. "In many ways they were too good, too trusting for their own health. They put too much trust in the stability of the Republic, failing to realize that while the body might be sound, the head was growing diseased and feeble, leaving it open to manipulation by such as the Emperor.

"I wish I knew what Vader was after. Sometimes I have the feeling he is marking time in preparation for some incomprehensible abomination. Such is the destiny of one who masters the force and is consumed by its dark side.''

Luke's face twisted in confusion. "A force? That's the second time you've mentioned a 'force.' ''

Kenobi nodded. "I forget sometimes in whose presence I babble. Let us say simply that the force is something a Jedi must deal with. While it has never been properly explained, scientists have theorized it is an energy field generated by living things. Early man suspected its existence, yet remained in ignorance of its potential for millennia.

"Only certain individuals could recognize the force for what it was. They were mercilessly labeled: charlatans, fakers, mystics—and worse. Even fewer could make use of it. As it was usually beyond their primitive controls, it frequently was too powerful for them. They were misunderstood by their fellows— and worse."

Kenobi made a wide, all-encompassing gesture with both arms. "The force surrounds each and every one of us. Some men believe it directs our actions, and not the other way around. Knowledge of the force and how to manipulate it was what gave the Jedi his special power."

The arms came down and Kenobi stared at Luke until the youth began to fidget uncomfortably. When he spoke again it was in a tone so crisp and unaged that Luke jumped in spite of himself. "You must learn the ways of the force also, Luke—if you are to come with me to Alderaan."

"Alderaan!" Luke hopped off the repair seat, looking dazed. "I'm not going to Alderaan. I don't even know where Alderaan is." Vaporators, 'droids, harvest—abruptly the surroundings seemed to close in on him, the formerly intriguing furnishings and alien artifacts now just a mite frightening. He looked around wildly, trying to avoid the piercing gaze of Ben Kenobi . . . old Ben . . . crazy Ben . . . General Obi-wan . . .

"I've got to get back home," he found himself muttering thickly. "It's late. I'm in for it as it is." Remembering something, he gestured toward the motionless bulk of Artoo Detoo. "You can keep the 'droid. He seems to want you to. I'll think of something to tell my uncle—I hope," he added forlornly.

"I need your help, Luke," Kenobi explained, his manner a combination of sadness and steel. "I'm getting too old for this kind of thing. Can't trust myself to finish it properly on my own. This mission is far too important." He nodded toward Artoo Detoo. "You heard and saw the message."

"But . . . I can't get involved with anything like that," protested Luke. "I've got work to do; we've got crops to bring in— even though Uncle Owen could always break down and hire a little extra help. I mean, one, I guess. But there's nothing I can do about it. Not now. Besides, that's all such a long way from here. The whole thing is really none of my business."

"That sounds like your uncle talking," Kenobi observed without rancor.

"Oh! My uncle Owen . . . How am I going to explain all this to him?"

The old man suppressed a smile, aware that Luke's destiny had already been determined for him. It had been ordained five minutes before he had learned about the manner of his father's death. It had been ordered before that when he had heard the complete message. It had been fixed in the nature of things when he had first viewed the pleading portrait of the beautiful Senator Organa awkwardly projected by the little 'droid. Kenobi shrugged inwardly. Likely it had been finalized even before the boy was born. Not that Ben believed in predestination, but he did believe in heredity—and in the force.

"Remember, Luke, the suffering of one man is the suffering of all. Distances are irrelevant to injustice. If not stopped soon enough, evil eventually reaches out to engulf all men, whether they have opposed it or ignored it."

"I suppose," Luke confessed nervously, "I *could* take you as far as Anchorhead. You can get transport from there to Mos Eisley, or wherever it is you want to go."

"Very well," agreed Kenobi. "That will do for a beginning. Then you must do what you feel is *right*."

Luke turned away, now thoroughly confused. "Okay. Right now I don't feel too good . . ."

The holding hole was deathly dim, with only the bare minimum of illumination provided. There was barely enough to see the black metal walls and the high ceiling overhead. The cell was designed to maximize a prisoner's feelings of helplessness, and this it achieved well. So much so that the single occupant started tensely as a hum came from one end of the chamber. The metal door which began moving aside was as thick as her body—as if, she mused bitterly, they were afraid she might break through anything less massive with her bare hands.

Straining to see outside, the girl saw several imperial guards assume positions just outside the doorway. Eyeing them defiantly, Leia Organa backed up against the far wall.

Her determined expression collapsed as soon as a monstrous black form entered the room, gliding smoothly as if on treads. Vader's presence crushed her spirit as thoroughly as an elephant would crush an eggshell. That villain was followed by an antiqued whip of a man who was only slightly less terrifying, despite his miniscule appearance alongside the Dark Lord.

Darth Vader made a gesture to someone outside. Something that hummed like a huge bee moved close and slipped inside the doorway. Leia choked on her own breath at the sight of the dark metal globe. It hung suspended on independent repulsors, a farrago of metal arms protruding from its sides. The arms were tipped with a multitude of delicate instruments.

Leia studied the contraption fearfully. She had heard rumors of such machines, but had never really believed that Imperial technicians would construct such a monstrosity. Incorporated into its soulless memory was every barbarity, every substantiated outrage known to mankind—and to several alien races as well.

Vader and Tarkin stood there quietly, giving her plenty of time to study the hovering nightmare. The Governor in particular did not delude himself into thinking that the mere presence of the device would shock her into giving up the information he needed. Not, he reflected, that the ensuing session would be especially unpleasant. There was always enlightenment and knowledge to be gained from such encounters, and the Senator promised to be a most interesting subject.

After a suitable interval had passed, he motioned to the machine. "Now, Senator Organa, Princess Organa, we will discuss the location of the principal rebel base."

The machine moved slowly toward her, traveling on a rising hum. Its indifferent spherical form blocked out Vader, the Governor, the rest of the cell . . . the light . . .

Muffled sounds penetrated the cell walls and thick door, drifting out into the hallway beyond. They barely intruded on the peace and quiet of the walkway running past the sealed chamber. Even so, the guards stationed immediately outside managed to find excuses to edge a sufficient distance away to where those oddly modulated sounds could no longer be heard at all.

VI

"LOOK over there, Luke," Kenobi ordered, pointing to the southwest. The landspeeder continued to race over the gravelly desert floor beneath them. "Smoke, I should think."

Luke spared a glance at the indicated direction. "I don't see anything, sir."

"Let's angle over that way anyhow. Someone may be in trouble."

Luke turned the speeder. Before long the rising wisps of smoke that Kenobi had somehow detected earlier became visible to him also.

Topping a slight rise, the speeder dropped down a gentle slope into a broad, shallow canyon that was filled with twisted, burned shapes, some of them inorganic, some not. Dead in the center of this carnage and looking like a beached metal whale lay the shattered hulk of a jawa sandcrawler.

Luke brought the speeder to a halt. Kenobi followed him onto the sand, and together they began to examine the detritus of destruction.

Several slight depressions in the sand caught Luke's attention. Walking a little faster, he came up next to them and studied them for a moment before calling back to Kenobi.

"Looks like the sandpeople did it, all right. Here's Bantha tracks . . ." Luke noticed a gleam of metal half buried in the sand. "And there's a piece of one of those big double axes of theirs." He shook his head in confusion. "But I never heard of the Raiders hitting something this big." He leaned back, staring up at the towering, burned-out bulk of the sandcrawler.

Kenobi had passed him. He was examining the broad, huge footprints in the sand. "They didn't," he declared casually, "but they intended that we—and anyone else who might happen onto this—should think so." Luke moved up alongside him.

"I don't understand, sir."

"Look at these tracks carefully," the older man directed him, pointing down at the nearest and then up at the others. "Notice anything funny about them?" Luke shook his head. "Whoever left here was riding Banthas side by side. Sandpeople always ride one Bantha behind another, single file, to hide their strength from any distant observers."

Leaving Luke to gape at the parallel sets of tracks, Kenobi turned his attention to the sandcrawler. He pointed out where single weapons' bursts had blasted away portals, treads, and support beams. "Look at the precision with which this firepower was applied. Sandpeople aren't this accurate. In fact, no one on Tatooine fires and destroys with this kind of efficiency." Turning, he examined the horizon. One of those nearby bluffs concealed a secret—and a threat. "Only Imperial troops would mount an attack on a sandcrawler with this kind of cold accuracy."

Luke had walked over to one of the small, crumpled bodies and kicked it over onto its back. His face screwed up in distaste as he saw what remained of the pitiful creature.

"These are the same jawas who sold Uncle Owen and me Artoo and Threepio. I recognize this one's cloak design. Why would Imperial troops be slaughtering jawas and sandpeople? They must have killed some Raiders to get those Banthas." His mind worked furiously, and he found himself growing unnaturally tense as he stared back at the landspeeder, past the rapidly deteriorating corpses of the jawas.

"But . . . if they tracked the 'droids to the jawas, then they had to learn first who they sold them to. That would lead them back to . . ." Luke was sprinting insanely for the landspeeder.

"Luke, wait . . . wait, Luke!" Kenobi called. "It's too dangerous! You'd never . . . !"

Luke heard nothing except the roaring in his ears, felt nothing save the burning in his heart. He jumped into the speeder and was throwing the accelerator full over almost simultaneously. In an explosion of sand and gravel he left Kenobi and the two robots standing alone in the midst of smoldering bodies, framed by the still smoking wreck of the sandcrawler.

The smoke that Luke saw as he drew near the homestead was of a different consistency from that which had boiled out of the jawa machine. He barely remembered to shut down the land-speeder's engine as he popped the cockpit canopy and threw himself out. Dark smoke was drifting steadily from holes in the ground.

Those holes had been his home, the only one he had ever known. They might as well have been throats of small volcanoes now. Again and again he tried to penetrate the surface entrances to the below-ground complex. Again and again the still-intense heat drove him back, coughing and choking.

Weakly he found himself stumbling clear, his eyes watering not entirely from the smoke. Half blinded, he staggered over to the exterior entrance to the garage. It too was burning. But perhaps they managed to escape in the other landspeeder.

"Aunt Beru . . . Uncle Owen!" It was difficult to make out much of anything through the eye-stinging haze. Two smoking shapes showed down the tunnel barely visible through tears and haze. They almost looked like—He squinted harder, wiping angrily at his uncooperative eyes.

No.

Then he was spinning away, falling to his stomach and burying his face in the sand so he wouldn't have to look anymore.

The tridimensional solid screen filled one wall of the vast chamber from floor to ceiling. It showed a million star systems. A tiny portion of the galaxy, but an impressive display nonetheless when exhibited in such a fashion.

Below, far below, the huge shape of Darth Vader stood flanked on one side by Governor Tarkin and on the other by Admiral Motti and General Tagge, their private antagonisms forgotten in the awesomeness of this moment.

"The final checkout is complete," Motti informed them. "All systems are operational." He turned to the others. "What shall be the first course we set?"

Vader appeared not to have heard as he mumbled softly, half to himself, "She has a surprising amount of control. Her resistance to the interrogator is considerable." He glanced down at Tarkin. "It will be some time before we can extract any useful information from her."

"I've always found the methods you recommend rather quaint, Vader."

"They are efficient," the Dark Lord argued softly. "In the interests of accelerating the procedure, however, I am open to your suggestions."

Tarkin looked thoughtful. "Such stubbornness can often be detoured by applying threats to something other than the one involved."

"What do you mean?"

"Only that I think it is time we demonstrated the full power of this station. We may do so in a fashion doubly useful." He instructed the attentive Motti, "Tell your programmers to set course for the Alderaan system."

Kenobi's pride did not prevent him from wrapping an old scarf over nose and mouth to filter out a portion of the bonfire's drifting putrid odor. Though possessed of olfactory sensory apparatus, Artoo Detoo and Threepio had no need of such a screen. Even Threepio, who was equipped to discriminate among aromatic aesthetics, could be artificially selective when he so desired.

Working together, the two 'droids helped Kenobi throw the last of the bodies onto the blazing pyre, then stood back and watched the dead continue to burn. Not that the desert scavengers wouldn't have been equally efficient in picking the burned-out sandcrawler clean of flesh, but Kenobi retained values most modern men would have deemed archaic. He would consign no one to the bone-gnawers and gravel-maggots, not even a filthy jawa.

At a rising thrumming Kenobi turned from the residue of the noisome business to see the landspeeder approaching, now traveling at a sensible pace, far different from when it had left. It slowed and hovered nearby, but showed no signs of life.

Gesturing for the two robots to follow, Ben started toward the waiting craft. The canopy flipped open and up to reveal Luke sitting motionless in the pilot's seat. He didn't look up at Kenobi's inquiring glance. That in itself was enough to tell the old man what had happened.

"I share your sorrow, Luke," he finally ventured softly. "There was nothing you could have done. Had you been there, you'd be dead now, too, and the 'droids would be in the hands of the Imperials. Not even the force—"

"Damn your force!" Luke snarled with sudden violence. Now he turned and glared at Kenobi. There was a set to his jaw that belonged on a much older face.

"I'll take you to the spaceport at Mos Eisley, Ben. I want to go with you—to Alderaan. There's nothing left for me here now." His eyes turned to look out across the desert, to focus on something beyond sand and rock and canyon walls. "I want to learn to be a Jedi, like my father. "I want . . .'' He paused, the words backing up like a logjam in his throat.

Kenobi slid into the cockpit, put a hand gently on the youth's shoulder, then went forward to make room for the two robots. "I'll do my best to see that you get what you want, Luke. For now, let's go to Mos Eisley."

Luke nodded and closed the canopy. The landspeeder moved away to the southeast, leaving behind the still-smoldering sand-crawler, the jawa funeral pyre, and the only life Luke had ever known.

Leaving the speeder parked near the edge of the sandstone bluff, Luke and Ben walked over and peered down at the tiny regularized bumps erupting from the sun-baked plain below. The haphazard collage of low-grade concrete, stone, and plastoid structures spread outward from a central power-and-water-distribution plant like the spokes of a wheel.

Actually the town was considerably larger than it appeared, since a good portion of it lay underground. Looking like bomb craters from this distance, the smooth circular depressions of launch stations pockmarked the cityscape.

A brisk gale was scouring the tired ground. It whipped the sand about Luke's feet and legs as he adjusted his protective goggles.

"There it is," Kenobi murmured, indicating the unimpressive collection of buildings, "Mos Eisley Spaceport—the ideal place for us to lose ourselves while we seek passage offplanet. Not a more wretched collection of villainy and disreputable types exists anywhere on Tatooine. The Empire has been alerted to us, so we must be very cautious, Luke. The population of Mos Eisley should disguise us well."

Luke wore a determined look. "I'm ready for anything, Obi-wan.''

I wonder if you comprehend what that might entail, Luke, Kenobi thought. But he only nodded as he led the way back to the landspeeder.

Unlike Anchorhead, there were enough people in Mos Eisley to require movement in the heat of day. Built from the beginning with commerce in mind, even the oldest of the town's buildings had been designed to provide protection from the twin suns. They looked primitive from the outside, and many were. But oftentimes walls and arches of old stone masked durasteel double walls with circulating coolant flowing freely between.

Luke was maneuvering the landspeeder through the town's outskirts when several tall, gleaming forms appeared from nowhere and began to close a circle around him. For one panicked moment he considered gunning the engine and racing through the pedestrians and other vehicles. A startlingly firm grip on his arm both restrained and relaxed him. He glanced over to see Kenobi smiling, warning him.

So they continued at a normal town cruising speed, Luke hoping that the imperial troops were bent on business elsewhere. No such luck. One of the troopers raised an armored hand. Luke had no choice but to respond. As he pulled the speeder over, he grew aware of the attention they were receiving from curious passersby. Worse yet, it seemed that the trooper's attention was in fact reserved not for Kenobi or himself, but for the two unmoving robots seated in the speeder behind them.

"How long have you had these 'droids?" the trooper who had raised his hand barked. Polite formalities were to be dispensed with, it appeared.

Looking blank for a second, Luke finally came up with "Three or four seasons, I guess."

"They're up for sale, if you want them—and the price is right," Kenobi put in, giving a wonderful impression of a desert finagler out to cajole a few quick credits from ignorant Imperials.

The trooper in charge did not deign to reply. He was absorbed in a thorough examination of the landspeeder's underside.

"Did you come in from the south?" he asked.

"No . . . no," Luke answered quickly, "we live in the west, near Bestine township."

"Bestine?" the trooper murmured, walking around to study the speeder's front. Luke forced himself to stare straight ahead. Finally the armored figure concluded his examination. He moved to stand ominously close to Luke and snapped, "Let me see your identification."

Surely the man sensed his terror and nervousness by now, Luke thought wildly. His resolution of not long before to be ready to take on anything had already disintegrated under the unwinking stare of this professional soldier. He knew what would happen if they got a look at his formal ID, with the location of his homestead and the names of his nearest relatives on it. Something seemed to be buzzing inside his head; he felt faint.

Kenobi had leaned over and was talking easily to the trooper. "You don't need to see his identification," the old man informed the Imperial in an extremely peculiar voice.

Staring blankly back at him, the officer replied, as if it were self-evident. "I don't need to see your identification." His reaction was the opposite of Kenobi's: his voice was normal, but his expression peculiar.

"These aren't the 'droids you're looking for," Kenobi told him pleasantly.

"These aren't the 'droids we're looking for."

"He can go about his business.

"You can go about your business," the metal-masked officer informed Luke.

The expression of relief that spread across Luke's face ought to have been as revealing as his previous nervousness, but the Imperial ignored it.

"Move along," Kenobi whispered.

"Move along," the officer instructed Luke.

Unable to decide whether he should salute, nod, or give thanks to the man, Luke settled for nudging the accelerator. The landspeeder moved forward, drawing away from the circle of troops. As they prepared to round a corner, Luke risked a glance backward. The officer who had inspected them appeared to be arguing with several comrades, though at this distance Luke couldn't be sure.

He peered up at his tall companion and started to say something. Kenobi only shook his head slowly and smiled. Swallowing his curiosity, Luke concentrated on guiding the speeder through steadily narrowing streets.

Kenobi seemed to have some idea where they were headed. Luke studied the run-down structures and equally unwholesome-looking individuals they were passing. They had entered the oldest section of Mos Eisley and consequently the one where the old vices flourished most strongly.

Kenobi pointed and Luke pulled the landspeeder up in front of what appeared to be one of the original spaceport's first blockhouses. It had been converted into a cantina whose clientele was suggested by the diverse nature of transport parked outside. Some of them Luke recognized, others he had only heard rumors of. The cantina itself, he knew from the design of the building, must lie partially underground.

As the dusty but still sleek craft pulled into an open spot, a jawa materialized from nowhere and began running covetous hands over the metal sides. Luke leaned out and barked something harsh at the subhuman which caused it to scurry away.

"I can't abide those jawas," murmured Threepio with lofty disdain. "Disgusting creatures."

Luke's mind was too full of their narrow escape for him to comment on Threepio's sentiments. "I still can't understand how we got by those troops. I thought we were as good as dead."

"The force is in the mind, Luke, and can sometimes be used to influence others. It's a powerful ally. But as you come to know the force, you will discover that it can also be a danger."

Nodding without really understanding, Luke indicated the run-down though obviously popular cantina. "Do you really think we can find a pilot here capable of taking us all the way to Alderaan?"

Kenobi was exiting from the speeder. "Most of the good, independent freighter pilots frequent this place, though many can afford better. They can talk freely here. You should have learned by now, Luke, not to equate ability with appearance." Luke saw the old man's shabby clothing anew and felt ashamed. "Watch yourself, though. This place can be rough."

Luke found himself squinting as they entered the cantina. It was darker inside than he would have liked. Perhaps the regular habitués of this place were unaccustomed to the light of day, or didn't wish to be seen clearly. It didn't occur to Luke that the dim interior in combination with the brilliantly lit entrance permitted everyone inside to see each newcomer before he could see them.

Moving inward, Luke was astonished at the variety of beings making use of the bar. There were one-eyed creatures and thousand-eyed, creatures with scales, creatures with fur, and some with skin that seemed to ripple and change consistency according to their feelings of the moment.

Hovering near the bar itself was a towering insectoid that Luke glimpsed only as a threatening shadow. It contrasted with two of the tallest women Luke had ever seen. They were among the most normal looking of the outrageous assemblage of humans that mixed freely among alien counterparts. Tentacles, claws, and hands were wrapped around drinking utensils of various sizes and shapes. Conversation was a steady babble of human and alien tongues.

Leaning close, Kenobi gestured toward the far end of the bar.

A small knot of rough-looking humans lounged there, drinking, laughing, and trading stories of dubious origin.

"Corellians—pirates, most likely."

"I thought we were looking for an independent freighter captain with his own ship for hire," Luke whispered back.

"So we are, young Luke, so we are," agreed Kenobi. "And there's bound to be one or two adequate for our needs among that group. It's just that in Corellian terminology the distinction between who owns what cargo tends to get a little muddled from time to time. Wait here."

Luke nodded and watched as Kenobi worked his way through the crowd. The Correllians' suspicion at his approach vanished as soon as he engaged them in conversation.

Something grabbed Luke's shoulder and spun him around.

"Hey." Looking around and struggling to regain his composure, he found himself staring up at an enormous, scruffy-looking human. Luke saw by the man's clothing that he must be the bartender, if not the owner of this cantina.

"We don't serve their kind in here," the glaring form growled.

"What?" Luke replied dumbly. He still hadn't recovered from his sudden submergence into the cultures of several dozen races. It was rather different from the poolroom behind the Anchorhead power station. "Your 'droids," the bartender explained impatiently, gesturing with a thick thumb. Luke peered in the indicated direction, to see Artoo and Threepio standing quietly nearby. "They'll have to wait outside. We don't serve them in here. I only carry stuff for organics, not," he concluded with an expression of distaste, "mechanicals."

Luke didn't like the idea of kicking Threepio and Artoo out, but he didn't know how else to deal with the problem. The bartender didn't appear to be the sort who would readily respond to reason, and when he looked around for old Ben, Luke saw that he was locked in deep conversation with one of the Corellians.

Meanwhile, the discussion had attracted the attention of several especially gruesome-looking types who happened to be clustered within hearing range. All were regarding Luke and the two 'droids in a decidedly unfriendly fashion.

"Yes, of course," Luke said, realizing this wasn't the time or place to force the issue of 'droid rights. "I'm sorry." He looked over at Threepio. "You'd better stay outside with the speeder. We don't want any trouble in here."

"I heartily agree with you, sir," Threepio said, his gaze traveling past Luke and the bartender to take in the unfriendly stares at the bar. "I don't feel the need for lubrication at the moment anyway." With Artoo waddling in his wake, the tall robot hastily headed for the exit.

That finished things as far as the bartender was concerned, but Luke now found himself the subject of some unwanted attention. He abruptly became aware of his isolation and felt as if at one time or another every eye in the place rested a moment on him, that things human and otherwise were smirking and making comments about him behind his back.

Trying to maintain an air of quiet confidence, he returned his gaze to old Ben, and started when he saw what the oldster was talking to now. The Corellian was gone. In its place Kenobi was chatting with a towering anthropoid that showed a mouthful of teeth when it smiled.

Luke had heard about Wookiees, but he had never expected to see one, much less meet one. Despite an almost comical quasi-monkey face, the Wookiee was anything but gentle-looking. Only the large, glowing yellow eyes softened its otherwise awesome appearance. The massive torso was covered entirely with soft, thick russet fur. Less appealing cover consisted of a pair of chromed bandoliers which held lethal projectiles of a type unknown to Luke. Other than these, the Wookiees wore little.

Not, Luke knew, that anyone would laugh at the creature's mode of dress. He saw that other denizens of the bar eddied and swirled around the huge form without ever coming too close. All but old Ben—Ben who was talking to the Wookiee in its own language, quarreling and hooting softly like a native.

In the course of the conversation the old man had occasion to gesture in Luke's direction. Once the huge anthropoid stared directly at Luke and let out a horrifying howling laugh.

Disgruntled by the role he was evidently playing in the discussion, Luke turned away and pretended to ignore the whole conversation. He might be acting unfairly toward the creature, but he doubted that spine-quaking laugh was meant in gentle good-fellowship.

For the life of him he couldn't understand what Ben wanted with the monster, or why he was spending his time in guttural conversation with it instead of with the now-vanished Corellians. So he sat and sipped his drink in splendid silence, his eyes roving over the crowd in hopes of meeting a responsive gaze that held no belligerence.

Suddenly, something shoved him roughly from behind, so

hard he almost fell. He turned angrily, but his fury spent itself in astonishment. He found himself confronted by a large squarish monstrosity of multiple eyes and indeterminate origin.

"Negola dewaghi wooldugger?" the apparition bubbled challengingly.

Luke had never seen its like before; he knew neither its species nor its language. The gabbling might have been an invitation to a fight, a request to share a drink, or a marriage proposal. Despite his ignorance, however, Luke could tell by the way the creature bobbed and wove unsteadily on its podal supports that it had imbibed too much of whatever it considered a pleasing intoxicant.

Not knowing what else to do, Luke tried turning back to his own drink while studiously ignoring the creature. As he did so, a thing—a cross between a capybara and a small baboon—bounced over to stand (or squat) next to the quivering many-eye. A short, grubby-looking human also approached and put a companionable arm around the snuffling mass.

"He doesn't like you," the stubby human informed Luke in a surprisingly deep voice.

"I'm sorry about that," Luke admitted, wishing heartily he were somewhere else.

"I don't like you, either," the smiling little man went on with brotherly negativity.

"I said I was sorry about it."

Whether from the conversation it was having with the rodentlike creature or the overdose of booze, the apartment house for wayward eyeballs was obviously growing agitated. It leaned forward, almost toppling into Luke, and spewed a stream of unintelligible gibberish at him. Luke felt the eyes of a crowd on him as he grew increasingly more nervous.

" 'Sorry,' " the human mimicked derisively, clearly deep into his own cups. "Are you insulting us? You just better watch yourself. We're all wanted." He indicated his drunken companions. "I have the death sentence on me in twelve different systems."

"I'll be careful, then," Luke muttered.

The little man was smiling broadly. "You'll be dead."

At this the rodent let out a loud grunt. It was either a signal or a warning, because everything human or otherwise which had been leaning up at the bar immediately backed away, leaving a clear space around Luke and his antagonists.

Trying to salvage the situation, Luke essayed a wan smile.

That faded rapidly when he saw that the three were readying hand weapons. Not only couldn't he have countered all three of them, he had no idea what a couple of the lethal-looking devices did.

"This little one isn't worth the trouble," a calm voice said. Luke looked up, startled. He hadn't heard Kenobi come up alongside him. "Come, let me buy you all something . . ."

By way of reply the bulky monster chittered hideously and swung out a massive limb. It caught an unprepared Luke across the temple and sent him spinning across the room, crashing through tables and shattering a large jug filled with a foul-smelling liquid.

The crowd edged back farther, a few grunts and warning snorts coming from some of them as the drunken monstrosity pulled a wicked-looking pistol from its service pouch. He started to wave it in Kenobi's direction.

That spurred the heretofore neutral bartender to life. He came charging clumsily around the end of the bar, waving his hands frantically but still taking care to stay out of range.

"No blasters, no blasters! Not in my place!"

The rodent thing chattered threateningly at him, while the weapon-wielding many-eye spared him a warning grunt.

In the split second when the gun and its owner's attention was off him, the old man's hand had moved to the disk slung at his side. The short human started to yell as a fiery blue-white light appeared in the dimness of the cantina.

He never finished the yell. It turned into a blink. When the blink was finished, the man found himself lying prone against the bar, moaning and whimpering as he stared at the stump of an arm.

In between the start of his yell and the conclusion of the blink, the rodent-thing had been cleft cleanly in half down the middle, its two halves falling in opposite directions. The giant multi-ocular creature still stood staring, dazed, at the old human who was poised motionless before it, the shining lightsaber held over his head in a peculiar fashion. The creature's chrome pistol fired once, blowing a hole in the door. Then the torso peeled away as neatly as had the body of the rodent, its two cauterized sections falling in opposite directions to lie motionless on the cool stone.

Only then did the suggestion of a sigh escape from Kenobi; only then did his body appear to relax. Bringing the lightsaber down, he flipped it carefully upward in a reflex saluting motion which ended with the deactivated weapon resting innocuously on his hip.

That final movement broke the total quiet which had enshrouded the room. Conversation resumed, as did the movement of bodies in chairs, the scraping of mugs and pitchers and other drinking devices on tabletops. The bartender and several assistants appeared to drag the unsightly corpses out of the room, while the mutilated human vanished wordlessly into the crowd, cradling the stump of his gun arm and counting himself fortunate.

To all appearances the cantina had returned to its former state, with one small exception. Ben Kenobi was given a respectful amount of space at the bar.

Luke barely heard the renewed conversation. He was still shaken by the speed of the fight and by the old man's unimagined abilities. As his mind cleared and he moved to rejoin Kenobi, he could overhear bits and snatches of the talk around him. Much of it centered on admiration for the cleanness and finality of the fight.

"You're hurt, Luke," Kenobi observed solicitously.

Luke felt the bruise where the big creature had struck him. "I . . ." he started to say, but old Ben cut him off. As if nothing had happened, he indicated the great hairy mass which was shouldering its way through the crowd toward them.

"This is Chewbacca," he explained when the anthropoid had joined them at the bar. "He's first mate on a ship that might suit our needs. He'll take us to her captain-owner now."

"This way," the Wookiee grunted—at least, it sounded something like that to Luke. In any case, the huge creature's follow-me gesture was unmistakable. They started to wend their way deeper into the bar, the Wookiee parting the crowd like a gravel storm cutting canyonettes.

Out in front of the cantina, Threepio paced nervously next to the landspeeder. Apparently unconcerned, Artoo Detoo was engaged in animated electronic conversation with a bright red R-2 unit belonging to another of the cantina's patrons.

"What could be taking them so long? They went to hire one ship—not a fleet."

Abruptly Threepio paused, beckoning silently for Artoo to be quiet. Two Imperial troopers had appeared on the scene. They were met by an unkempt human who had emerged almost simultaneously from the depths of the cantina.

"I do not like the looks of this," the tall 'droid murmured.

* * *

Luke had appropriated someone else's drink from a waiter's tray as they made their way to the rear of the cantina. He gulped at it with the giddy air of one who feels himself under divine protection. That safe he was not, but in the company of Kenobi and the giant Wookiee he began to feel confident that no one in the bar would assault him with so much as a dirty look.

In a rear booth they encountered a sharp-featured young man perhaps five years older than Luke, perhaps a dozen—it was difficult to tell. He displayed the openness of the utterly confident—or the insanely reckless. At their approach the man sent the humanoid wench who had been wriggling on his lap on her way with a whispered something which left a wide, if inhuman, grin on her face.

The Wookiee Chewbacca rumbled something at the man, and he nodded in response, glancing up at the newcomers pleasantly.

"You're pretty handy with that saber, old man. Not often does one see that kind of swordplay in this part of the Empire anymore." He downed a prodigious portion of whatever filled his mug. "I'm Han Solo, captain of the *Millennium Falcon*." Suddenly he became all business. "Chewie tells me you're looking for passage to the Alderaan system?"

"That's right, son. If it's on a fast ship," Kenobi told him. Solo didn't bridle at the "son."

"Fast ship? You mean you've never *heard* of the *Millennium Falcon*?"

Kenobi appeared amused. "Should I?"

"It's the ship that made the Kessel run in less than twelve standard timeparts!" Solo told him indignantly. "I've outrun Imperial starships and Corellian cruisers. I think she's fast enough for you, old man." His outrage subsided rapidly. "What's your cargo?"

"Only passengers. Myself, the boy, and two 'droids—no questions asked."

"No questions." Solo regarded his mug, finally looked up. "Is it local trouble?"

"Let's just say we'd like to avoid any Imperial entanglements," Kenobi replied easily.

"These days that can be a real trick. It'll cost you a little extra." He did some mental figuring. "All in all, about ten thousand. In advance." He added with a smile, "And no questions asked."

Luke gaped at the pilot. "Ten thousand! We could almost buy our own ship for that."

Solo shrugged. "Maybe you could and maybe you couldn't. In any case, could you fly it?"

"You bet I could," Luke shot back, rising. "I'm not such a bad pilot myself. I don't—"

Again the firm hand on his arm. "We haven't that much with us," Kenobi explained. "But we could pay you two thousand now, plus another fifteen when we reach Alderaan."

Solo leaned forward uncertainly. "Fifteen . . . You can really get your hands on that kind of money?"

"I promise it—from the government on Alderaan itself. At the worst, you'll have earned an honest fee: two thousand."

But Solo seemed not to hear the last. "Seventeen thousand . . . All right, I'll chance it. You've got yourselves a ship. As for avoiding Imperial entanglements, you'd better twist out of here or even the *Millennium Falcon* won't be any help to you." He nodded toward the cantina entrance, and added quickly, "Docking bay ninety-four, first thing in the morning."

Four Imperial troopers, their eyes darting rapidly from table to booth to bar, had entered the cantina. There was muttering from among the crowd, but whenever the eyes of one of the heavily armed troopers went hunting for the mutterers, the words died with sullen speed.

Moving to the bar, the officer in charge asked the bartender a couple of brief questions. The big man hesitated a moment, then pointed toward a place near the back of the room. As he did so, his eyes widened slightly. Those of the officer were unreadable.

The booth he was pointing to was empty.

VII

LUKE and Ben were securing Artoo Detoo in the back of the speeder while Threepio kept a lookout for any additional troops.

"If Solo's ship is as fast as his boasting, we should be all right," the old man observed with satisfaction.

"But two thousand—and fifteen more when we reach Alderaan!"

"It's not the fifteen that worries me; it's the first two," Kenobi explained. "I'm afraid you'll have to sell your speeder."

Luke let his gaze rove over the landspeeder, but the thrill it had once given him was gone—gone along with other things best not dwelt on.

"It's all right," he assured Kenobi listlessly. "I don't think I'll need it again."

From their vantage point in another booth, Solo and Chewbacca watched as the Imperials strode through the bar. Two of them gave the Corellian a lingering glance. Chewbacca growled once and the two soldiers hurried their pace somewhat.

Solo grinned sardonically, turning to his partner. "Chewie, this charter could save our necks. Seventeen thousand!" He shook his head in amazement. "Those two must really be desperate. I wonder what they're wanted for. But I agreed, no questions. They're paying enough for it. Let's get going—the *Falcon* won't check itself out."

"Going somewhere, Solo?"

The Corellian couldn't identify the voice, coming as it did through an electronic translator. But there was no problem recognizing the speaker or the gun it held stuck in Solo's side.

The creature was roughly man-sized and bipedal, but its head was something out of delirium by way of an upset stomach. It had huge, dull-faceted eyes, bulbous on a pea-green face. A ridge of short spines crested the high skull, while nostrils and mouth were contained in a tapirlike snout.

"As a matter of fact," Solo replied slowly," "I was just on my way to see your boss. You can tell Jabba I've got the money I owe him."

"That's what you said yesterday—and last week—and the week prior to that. It's too late, Solo. I'm not going back to Jabba with another one of your stories."

"But I've really got the money this time!" Solo protested.

"Fine. I'll take it now, please."

Solo sat down slowly. Jabba's minions were apt to be cursed with nervous trigger fingers. The alien took the seat across from him, the muzzle of the ugly little pistol never straying from Solo's chest.

"I haven't got it here with me. Tell Jabba—"

"It's too late, I think. Jabba would rather have your ship."

"Over my dead body," Solo said unamiably.

The alien was not impressed. "If you insist. Will you come outside with me, or must I finish it here?"

"I don't think they'd like another killing in here," Solo pointed out.

Something which might have been a laugh came from the creature's translator. "They'd hardly notice. Get up, Solo. I've been looking forward to this for a long time. You've embarrassed me in front of Jabba with your pious excuses for the last time."

"I think you're right."

Light and noise filled the little corner of the cantina, and when it had faded, all that remained of the unctuous alien was a smoking, slimy spot on the stone floor.

Solo brought his hand and the smoking weapon it held out from beneath the table, drawing bemused stares from several of the cantina's patrons and clucking sounds from its more knowledgeable ones. They had known the creature had committed its fatal mistake in allowing Solo the chance to get his hands under cover.

"It'll take a lot more than the likes of you to finish me off. Jabba the Hut always did skimp when it came to hiring his hands."

Leaving the booth, Solo flipped the bartender a handful of coins as he and Chewbacca moved off. "Sorry for the mess. I always was a rotten host."

* * *

Heavily armed troopers hurried down the narrow alleyway, glowering from time to time at the darkly clad beings who hawked exotic goods from dingy little stalls. Here in Mos Eisley's inner regions the walls were high nd narrow, turning the passageway into a tunnel.

No one stared angrily back at them; no one shouted imprecations or mouthed obscenities. These armored figures moved with the authority of the Empire, their sidearms boldly displayed and activated. All around, men, not-men, and mechanicals were crouched in waste-littered doorways. Among accumulations of garbage and filth they exchanged information and concluded transactions of dubious legality.

A hot wind moaned down the alleyway and the troopers closed their formation. Their precision and order masked a fear of such claustrophobic quarters.

One paused to check a door, only to discover it tightly locked and bolted. A sand-encrusted human shambling nearby visited a half-mad harangue on the trooper. Shrugging inwardly, the soldier gave the crazy human a sour eye before moving on down the alley to join up again with his fellows.

As soon as they were well past, the door slid open a crack and a metallic face peered out. Below Threepio's leg, a squat barrel shape struggled for a view.

"I would rather have gone with Master Luke than stay here with you. Still, orders are orders. I don't quite know what all the trouble is about, but I'm sure it must be your fault."

Artoo responded with a near impossibility: a sniggering beep.

"You watch your language," the taller machine warned.

The number of old landspeeders and other powered transports in the dusty lot which were still capable of motion could be counted on the fingers of one hand. But that was not the concern of Luke and Ben as they stood bargaining with the tall, slightly insectoid owner. They were here not to buy, but to sell.

None of the passersby favored the hagglers with so much as a curious glance. Similar transactions which were the business of no one but the transactors took place half a thousand times daily in Mos Eisley.

Eventually there were no more pleas or threats to be exchanged. As though doling out vials of his own blood, the owner finalized the sale by passing a number of small metal shapes to Luke. Luke and the insectoid traded formal good-byes and then they parted, each convinced he had gotten the better of the deal.

"He says it's the best he can do. Since the XP-38 came out, they just aren't in demand anymore," Luke sighed.

"Don't look so discouraged," Kenobi chided him. "What you've obtained will be sufficient. I've enough to cover the rest."

Leaving the main street, they turned down an alleyway and walked past a small robot herding along a clutch of creatures resembling attenuated anteaters. As they rounded the corner Luke strained for a forlorn glimpse of the old landspeeder—his last link with his former life. Then there was no more time for looking back.

Something short and dark that might have been human underneath all its wrappings stepped out of the shadows as they moved away from the corner. It continued staring after them as they disappeared down a bend in the walkway.

The docking-bay entrance to the small saucer-shaped spacecraft was completely ringed by half a dozen men and aliens, of which the former were by half the most grotesque. A great mobile tub of muscle and suet topped by a shaggy scarred skull surveyed the semicircle of armed assassins with satisfaction. Moving forward from the center of the crescent, he shouted toward the ship.

"Come on out, Solo! We've got you surrounded."

"If so, you're facing the wrong way," came a calm voice.

Jabba the Hut jumped—in itself a remarkable sight. His lackeys likewise whirled—to see Han Solo and Chewbacca standing behind them.

"You see, I've been waiting for you, Jabba."

"I expected you would be," the Hut admitted, at once pleased and alarmed by the fact that neither Solo nor the big Wookiee appeared to be armed.

"I'm not the type to run," Solo said.

"Run? Run from what!" Jabba countered. The absence of visible weapons bothered Jabba more than he cared to admit to himself. There was something peculiar here, and it would be better to make no hasty moves until he discovered what was amiss.

"Han, my boy, there are times when you disappoint me. I merely wish to know why you haven't paid me . . . as you should have long ago. And why did you have to fry poor Greedo like that? After all you and I have been through together."

Solo grinned tightly. "Shove it, Jabba. There isn't enough

sentiment in your body to warm an orphaned bacterium. As for Greedo, you sent him to kill me."

"Why, Han," Jabba protested in surprise. "Why would I do that? You're the best smuggler in the business. You're too valuable to fry. Greedo was only relaying my natural concern at your delays. He wasn't going to kill you."

"I think he thought he was. Next time don't send one of those hired twerps. If you've got something to say, come see me yourself."

Jabba shook his head and his jowls shook—lazy, fleshy echoes of his mock sorrow. "Han, Han—if only you hadn't had to dump that shipment of spice! You understand . . . I just can't make an exception. Where would I be if every pilot who smuggled for me dumped his shipment at the first sign of an Imperial warship? And then simply showed empty pockets when I demanded recompense? It's not good business. I can be generous and forgiving—but not to the point of bankruptcy."

"You know, even I get boarded sometimes, Jabba. Did you think I dumped that spice because I got tired of its smell? I wanted to deliver it as much as you wanted to receive it. I had no choice." Again the sardonic smile. "As you say, I'm too valuable to fry. But I've got a charter now and I can pay you back, plus a little extra. I just need some more time. I can give you a thousand on account, the rest in three weeks."

The gross form seemed to consider, then directed his next words not to Solo but to his hirelings. "Put your blasters away." His gaze and a predatory smile turned to the wary Corellian.

"Han, my boy, I'm only doing this because you're the best and I'll need you again sometime. So, out of the greatness of my soul and a forgiving heart—and for an extra, say, twenty percent—I'll give you a little more time." The voice nearly cracked with restraint. "But this is the last time. If you disappoint me again, if you trample my generosity in your mocking laughter, I'll put a price on your head so large you won't be able to go near a civilized system for the rest of your life, because on every one your name and face will be known to men who'll gladly cut your guts out for one-tenth of what I'll promise them."

"I'm glad we both have my best interests at heart," replied Solo pleasantly as he and Chewbacca started past the staring eyes of the Hut's hired guns. "Don't worry, Jabba, I'll pay you. But not because you threaten me. I'll pay you because . . . it's my pleasure."

* * *

"They're starting to search the spaceport central," the Commander declared, having to alternately run a couple of steps and then walk to keep pace with the long strides of Darth Vader. The Dark Lord was deep in thought as he strode down one of the battle station's main corridors, trailed by several aides.

"The reports are just starting to come in," the Commander went on. "It's only a matter of time before we have those 'droids."

"Send in more men if you have to. Never mind the protests of the planetary Governor—I must have those 'droids. It's her hope of that data being used against us that is the pillar of her resistance to the mind probes."

"I understand, Lord Vader. Until then we must waste our time with Governor Tarkin's foolish plan to break her."

"There's docking bay ninety-four," Luke told Kenobi and the robots who had rejoined them, "and there's Chewbacca. He seems excited about something."

Indeed, the big Wookiee was waving over the heads of the crowd and jabbering loudly in their direction. Speeding their pace, none of the foursome noticed the small, dark-clad thing that had followed them from the transporter lot.

The creature moved into the doorway and pulled a tiny transmitter from a pouch concealed by its multifold robes. The transmitter looked far too new and modern to be in the grasp of so decrepit a specimen, yet its manipulator was speaking into it with steady assurance.

Docking bay ninety-four, Luke noted, was no different in appearance from a host of other grandiosely named docking bays scattered throughout Mos Eisley. It consisted mostly of an entrance rampway and an enormous pit gouged from the rocky soil. This served as clearance radii for the effects of the simple antigrav drive which boosted all spacecraft clear of the gravitational field of the planet.

The mathematics of spacedrive were simple enough even to Luke. Antigrav could operate only when there was a sufficient gravity well to push against—like that of a planet—whereas supralight travel could only take place when a ship was clear of that same gravity. Hence the necessity for the dual-drive system on any extrasystem craft.

The pit which formed docking bay ninety-four was as shabbily cut and run-down as the majority of Mos Eisley. Its sloping sides were crumbling in places instead of being smoothly fash-

ioned as they were on more populous worlds. Luke felt it formed
the perfect setting for the spacecraft Chewbacca was leading
them toward.

That battered ellipsoid which could only loosely be labeled
a ship appeared to have been pieced together out of old hull
fragments and components discarded as unusable by other craft.
The wonder of it, Luke mused, was that the thing actually held
its shape. Trying to picture this vehicle as spaceworthy would
have caused him to collapse in hysteria—were the situation
not so serious. But to think of traveling to Alderaan in this pathetic . . .

"What a piece of junk," he finally murmured, unable to hide
his feelings any longer. They were walking up the rampway
toward the open port. "This thing couldn't possibly make it into
hyperspace."

Kenobi didn't comment, but merely gestured toward the port,
where a figure was coming to meet them.

Either Solo had supernaturally acute hearing, or else he was
used to the reaction the sight of the *Millennium Falcon* produced
in prospective passengers. "She may not look like much," he
confessed as he approached them, "but she's all go. I've added
a few unique modifications to her myself. In addition to piloting,
I like to tinker. She'll make point five factors beyond light-
speed."

Luke scratched his head as he tried to reassess the craft in
view of its owner's claims. Either the Corellian was the biggest
liar this side of the galactic center, or there was more to this
vessel than met the eye. Luke thought back once more to old
Ben's admonition never to trust surface impressions, and decided to reserve judgment on the ship and its pilot until after he
had watched them in operation.

Chewbacca had lingered behind at the docking-bay entrance.
Now he rushed up the ramp, a hairy whirlwind, and blabbered
excitedly at Solo. The pilot regarded him coolly, nodding from
time to time, then barked a brief reply. The Wookiee charged
into the ship, pausing only to urge everyone to follow.

"We seem to be a bit rushed," Solo explained cryptically,
"so if you'll hurry aboard, we'll be off."

Luke was about to venture some questions, but Kenobi was
already prodding him up the ramp. The 'droids followed.

Inside, Luke was slightly startled to see the bulky Chewbacca
squirm and fight his way into a pilot's chair which, despite modifications, was still overwhelmed by his massive form. The

Wookiee flipped several tiny switches with digits seemingly too big for the task. Those great paws drifted with surprising grace over the controls.

A deep throbbing started somewhere within the ship as the engines were activated. Luke and Ben began strapping themselves into the vacant seats in the main passageway.

Outside the docking-bay entrance a long, leathery snout protruded from dark folds of cloth, and somewhere in the depths to either side of that imposing proboscis, eyes stared intently. They turned, along with the rest of the head, as a squad of eight Imperial troops rushed up. Perhaps not surprisingly, they headed straight for the enigmatic figure who whispered something to the lead trooper and gestured to the docking bay.

The information must have been provocative. Activating their weapons and raising them to firing position, the troops charged en masse down the docking-bay entrance.

A glint of light on moving metal caught Solo's eyes as the unwelcome outlines of the first troops showed themselves. Solo thought it unlikely they would pause to engage in casual conversation. His suspicion was confirmed before he could open his mouth to protest their intrusion, as several dropped to their knees and opened fire on him. Solo ducked back inside, turning to yell forward.

"Chewie—deflector shields, quick! Get us out of here!"

A throaty roar of acknowledgment came back to him.

Drawing his own pistol, Solo managed to snap off a couple of bursts from the comparative safety of the hatchway. Seeing that their quarry was neither helpless nor comatose, the exposed troops dove for cover.

The low throbbing rose to a whine, then to a deafening howl as Solo's hand came down on the quick-release button. Immediately the overhead hatchcover slammed shut.

As the retreating troops raced out of the docking-bay entrance, the ground was trembling steadily. They ran smack into a second squad, which had just arrived in response to the rapidly spreading emergency call. One of the soldiers, gesticulating wildly, tried to explain to the newly arrived ranking officer what had happened back in the bay.

As soon as the panting trooper had finished, the officer whipped out a compact communicator and shouted into it,

"Flight deck . . . they're trying to escape! Send everything you've got after this ship."

All across Mos Eisley, alarms began to sound, spreading out from docking bay ninety-four in concentric circles of concern.

Several soldiers scouring one alleyway reacted to the citywide alarm at the same time as they saw the small freighter lift gracefully into the clear blue sky above Mos Eisley. It shrank to a pinpoint before any of them thought to bring a weapon to bear.

Luke and Ben were already undoing their acceleration straps as Solo walked past them, moving toward the cockpit with the easy, loose-limbed stride of the experienced spacer. Once forward, he fell rather than sat in the pilot's seat and immediately began checking readouts and gauges. In the seat next to him Chewbacca was growling and grunting like a poorly tuned speeder engine. He turned from studying his own instruments long enough to jab a massive finger at the tracking screen.

Solo gave it a quick glance, then turned irritably to his own panel. "I know, I know . . . looks like two, maybe three destroyers. Somebody certainly dislikes our passengers. Sure picked ourselves a hot one this time. Try to hold them off somehow until I can finish the programming for the supralight jump. Angle the deflectors for maximum shielding."

With those instructions he ceased conversing with the huge Wookie as his hands flew over the computer input terminals. Solo did not even turn around when a small cylindrical shape appeared in the doorway behind him. Artoo Detoo beeped a few remarks, then scurried away.

Rear scanners showed the baleful lemon eye of Tatooine shrinking rapidly behind them. It wasn't rapid enough to eliminate the three points of light that indicated the presence of the pursuing Imperial warships.

Although Solo had ignored Artoo, he turned to acknowledge the entrance of his human passengers. "We've got two more coming in from different angles," he told them, scrutinizing the remorseless instrumentation. "They're going to try to box up before we can jump. Five ships . . . What did you two do to attract that kind of company?"

"Can't you outrun them?" Luke asked sarcastically, ignoring the pilot's question. "I thought you said this thing was fast."

"Watch your mouth, kid, or you'll find yourself floating home. There's too many of 'em, for one thing. But, we'll be safe enough once we've made the jump into hyperspace." He grinned knowingly. "Can't nobody track another ship accurately at supralight speeds. Plus, I know a few tricks that ought to lose any persistent stick-tights. I wish I'd known you boys were so popular."

"Why?" Luke said challengingly. "Would you have refused to take us?"

"Not necessarily," the Corellian replied, refusing to be baited. "But I sure's hell would've boosted your fare."

Luke had a retort poised on his lips. It was wiped out as he threw up his arms to ward off a brilliant red flash which gave black space outside the viewport the temporary aspect of the surface of a sun. Kenobi, Solo, and even Chewbacca did likewise, since the proximity of the explosion nearly overrode the phototropic shielding.

"Here's where the situation gets interesting," Solo muttered.

"How long before you can make the jump?" Kenobi inquired easily, apparently unconcerned that at any second they all might cease to exist.

"We're still within the gravitational influence of Tatooine," came the cool response. "It will be a few minutes yet before the navigation computer can compensate and effect an accurate jump. I could override its decision, but the hyperdrive would likely shred itself. That would give me a nice hold full of scrap metal in addition to you four."

"A few minutes," Luke blurted, staring at the screens. "At the rate they're gaining . . ."

"Traveling through hyperspace isn't like dusting crops, boy. Ever tried calculating a hyperspace jump?" Luke had to shake his head. "It's no mean trick. Be nice if we rushed it and passed right through a star or some other friendly spatial phenom like a black hole. That would end our trip real quick."

Fresh explosions continued to flare close by despite Chewbacca's best efforts at evasion. On Solo's console a red warning light began to flash for attention.

"What's that?" Luke wondered nervously.

"We're losing a deflector shield," Solo informed him with the air of a man about to have a tooth pulled. "Better strap yourselves back in. We're almost ready to make the jump. It could get bad if we take a near-burst at the wrong moment."

Back in the main hold area Threepio was already locked tightly into his seat by metal arms stronger then any acceleration straps. Artoo swayed back and forth under the concussion produced by increasingly powerful energy bursts against the ships deflectors.

"Was this trip really necessary?" the tall robot muttered in desperation. "I'd forgotten how much I hate space travel." He broke off as Luke and Ben appeared and began strapping themselves back into their chairs.

Oddly, Luke was thinking of a dog he had once owned when an immensely powerful something wrenched at the ship's hull with the strength of a fallen angel.

Admiral Motti entered the quiet conference room, his face streaked by the linear lights lining the walls. His gaze went to the spot where Governor Tarkin stood before the curved viewscreen, and he bowed slightly. Despite the evidence of the small green gem of a world entered in the screen, he formally announced, "We have entered the Alderaan system. We await your order."

The door signaled and Tarkin made a falsely gentle gesture to the admiral. "Wait a moment yet, Motti."

The door slid aside and Leia Organa entered, flanked by two armed guards, followed by Darth Vader.

"I am—," Tarkin began.

"I know who you are," she spat, "Governor Tarkin. I should have expected to find you holding Vader's leash. I thought I recognized your unique stench when I was first brought on board."

"Charming to the last," Tarkin declared in a fashion which suggested he was anything but charmed. "You don't know how hard I found it to sign the order for your termination." His expression changed to one of mock sorrow. "Of course, had you cooperated in our investigation, things might be otherwise. Lord Vader has informed me that your resistance to our traditional methods of inquiry—"

"Torture, you mean," she countered a trifle shakily.

"Let us not bandy semantics," Tarkin smiled.

"I'm surprised you had the courage to take the responsibility for issuing the order on yourself."

Tarkin sighed reluctantly. "I am a dedicated man, and the pleasures I reserve for myself are few. One of them is that before your execution I should like you to be my guest at a small ceremony. It will certify this battle station's operational status while at the same time ushering in a new era of Imperial technical supremacy. This station is the final link in the new-forged Imperial chain which will bind the million systems of the galactic Empire together once and for all. Your petty Alliance will no longer be of any concern to us. After today's demonstration no one will dare to oppose Imperial decree, not even the Senate.''

Organa looked at him with contempt. "Force will not keep the Empire together. Force has never kept anything together for very long. The more you tighten your grip, the more systems will slip through your fingers. You're a foolish man, Governor. Foolish men often choke to death on their own delusions.''

Tarkin smiled a death's-head smile, his face a parchment skull's. "It will be interesting to see what manner of passing Lord Vader has in mind for you. I am certain it will be worthy of you—and of him.

"But before you leave us, we must demonstrate the power of this station once and for all, in a conclusive fashion. In a way, you have determined the choice of subject for this demonstration. Since you have proven reluctant to supply us with the location of the rebel stronghold, I have deemed it appropriate to select as an alternate subject your home planet of Alderaan.''

"No! You can't! Alderaan is a peaceful world, with no standing armies. You can't . . .''

Tarkin's eyes gleamed. "You would prefer another target? A military target, perhaps? We're agreeable . . . name the system.'' He shrugged elaborately. "I grow tired of such games. For the last time, where is the main rebel base?''

A voice announced over a hidden speaker that they had approached within antigrav range of Alderaan—approximately six planetary diameters. That was enough to accomplish what all of Vader's infernal devices had failed to.

"Dantooine,'' she whispered, staring at the deck, all pretense at defiance gone now. "They're on Dantooine.''

Tarkin let out a slow sigh of satisfaction, then turned to the black figure nearby. "There, you see, Lord Vader? She can be reasonable. One needs only frame the question properly to elicit the desired response.'' He directed his attention to the other officers. "After concluding our little test here we shall make haste to move on to Dantooine. You may proceed with the operation, gentlemen.''

It took several seconds for Tarkin's words, so casually uttered, to penetrate. *"What!"* Organa finally gasped.

"Dantooine,'' Tarkin explained, examining his fingers, ''is too far from the centers of Imperial population to serve as the subject of an effective demonstration. You will understand that for reports of our power to spread rapidly through the Empire we require an obstreperous world more centrally located. Have no fear, though. We will deal with your rebel friends on Dantooine as soon as possible."

"But you said . . ." Organa started to protest.

"The only words which have meaning are the last ones spoken," Tarkin declared cuttingly. "We will proceed with the destruction of Alderaan as planned. Then you will enjoy watching with us as we obliterate the Dantooine center of this stupid and futile rebellion."

He gestured to the two soldiers flanking her. "Escort her to the principal observation level and," he smiled, "make certain she is provided with an unobstructed view."

VIII

SOLO was busily checking readouts from gauges and dials in the hold area. Occasionally he would pass a small box across various sensors, study the result, and cluck with pleasure.

"You can stop worrying about your Imperial friends," he told Luke and Ben. "They'll never be able to track us now. Told you I'd lose them."

Kenobi might have nodded briefly in response, but he was engaged in explaining something to Luke.

"Don't everybody thank me at once," Solo grunted, slightly miffed. "Anyway, navigation computer calculates our arrival in Alderaan orbit at oh two hundred. I'm afraid after this little adventure I'll have to forge a new registration."

He returned to his checking, passing in front of a small circular table. The top was covered with small squares lit from beneath, while computer monitors were set into each side. Tiny three-dimensional figures were projected above the tabletop from various squares.

Chewbacca sat hunched over one side of the table, his chin resting in massive hands. His great eyes glowing and facial whiskers wrinkled upward, he gave every sign of being well pleased with himself.

At least, he did until Artoo Detoo reached up with a stubby clawed limb across from him and tapped his own computer monitor. One of the figures walked abruptly across the board to a new square and stopped there.

An expression of puzzlement, then anger crossed the Wookiee's face as he studied the new configuration. Glaring up and over the table, he vented a stream of abusive gibberish on the inoffensive machine. Artoo could only beep in reply, but Threepio soon interceded on behalf of his less eloquent companion and began arguing with the hulking anthropoid.

"He executed a fair move. Screaming about it won't help you."

Attracted by the commotion, Solo looked back over his shoulder, frowning slightly. "Let him have it. Your friend's way ahead anyhow. It's not wise to upset a Wookiee."

"I can sympathize with that opinion, sir," Threepio countered, "but there is principle at stake here. There are certain standards any sentient creature must hold to. If one compromises them for any reason, including intimidation, then one is abrogating his right to be called intelligent."

"I hope you'll both remember that," Solo advised him, "when Chewbacca is pulling the arms off you and your little friend."

"Besides that, however," Threepio continued without missing a beat, "being greedy or taking advantage of someone in a weakened position is a clear sign of poor sportsmanship."

That elicited a beep of outrage from Artoo, and the two robots were soon engaged in violent electronic argument while Chewbacca continued jabbering at each in turn, occasionally waving at them though the translucent pieces waiting patiently on the board.

Oblivious to the altercation, Luke stood frozen in the middle of the hold. He held an activated lightsaber in position over his head. A low hum came from the ancient instrument while Luke lunged and parried under Ben Kenobi's instructive gaze. As Solo glanced from time to time at Luke's awkward movements, his lean features were sprinkled with smugness.

"No, Luke, your cuts should flow, not be so choppy," Kenobi instructed gently. "Remember, the force is omnipresent. It envelops you as it radiates from you. A Jedi warrior can actually feel the force as a physical thing."

"It is an energy field, then?" Luke inquired.

"It is an energy field and something more," Kenobi went on, almost mystically. "An aura that at once controls and obeys. It is a nothingness that can accomplish miracles." He looked thoughtful for a moment.

"No one, not even the Jedi scientists, were able to truly define the force. Possibly no one ever will. Sometimes there is as much magic as science in the explanations of the force. Yet what is a magician but a practicing theorist? Now, let's try again."

The old man was hefting a silvery globe about the size of a man's fist. It was covered with fine antennae, some as delicate as those of a moth. He flipped it toward Luke and watched as it halted a couple of meters away from the boy's face.

Luke readied himself as the ball circled him slowly, turning to face it as it assumed a new position. Abruptly it executed a lightning-swift lunge, only to freeze about a meter away. Luke failed to succumb to the feint, and the ball soon backed off.

Moving slowly to one side in an effort to get around the ball's fore sensors, Luke drew the saber back preparatory to striking. As he did so the ball darted in behind *him*. A thin pencil of red light jumped from one of the antennae to the back of Luke's thigh, knocking him to the deck even as he was bringing his saber around—too late.

Rubbing at his tingling, sleeping leg, Luke tried to ignore the burst of accusing laughter from Solo. "Hocus-pocus religions and archaic weapons are no substitute for a good blaster at your side," the pilot sneered.

"You don't believe in the force?" asked Luke, struggling back to his feet. The numbing effect of the beam wore off quickly.

"I've been from one end of this galaxy to the other," the pilot boasted, "and I've seen a lot of strange things. Too many to believe there couldn't be something like this 'force.' Too many to think that there could be some such controlling one's actions. *I* determine my destiny—not some half-mystical energy field." He gestured toward Kenobi. "I wouldn't follow him so blindly, if I were you. He's a clever old man full of simple tricks and mischief. He might be using you for his own ends."

Kenobi only smiled gently, then turned back to face Luke. "I suggest you try it again, Luke," he said soothingly. "You must try to divorce your actions from conscious control. Try not to focus on anything concrete, visually or mentally. You must let your mind drift, drift; only then can you use the force. You have to enter a state in which you act on what you sense, not on what you think beforehand. You must cease cogitation, relax, stop thinking . . . let yourself drift . . . free . . . free . . .''

The old man's voice had dropped to a mesmerizing buzz. As he finished, the chrome bulb darted at Luke. Dazed by Kenobi's hypnotic tone, Luke didn't see it charge. It's doubtful he saw much of anything with clarity. But as the ball neared, he whirled with amazing speed, the saber arcing up and out in a peculiar fashion. The red beam that the globe emitted was neatly deflected to one side. Its humming stopped and the ball bounced to the deck, all animation gone.

Blinking as if coming awake from a short nap, Luke stared in absolute astonishment at the inert remote.

"You see, you can do it," Kenobi told him. "One can teach only so much. Now you must learn to admit the force when you want it, so that you can learn to control it consciously.''

Moving to one side, Kenobi took a large helmet from behind a locker and walked over to Luke. Placing the helmet over his head effectively eliminated the boy's vision.

"I can't see," Luke muttered, turning around and forcing Kenobi to step back out of range of the dangerously wavering saber. "How can I fight?''

"With the force," old Ben explained. "You didn't really 'see' the seeker when it went for your legs the last time, and yet you parried its beam. Try to let that sensation flow within you again.''

"I *can't* do it," Luke moaned. "I'll get hit again.''

"Not if you let yourself trust *you*," Kenobi insisted, none too convincingly for Luke. "This is the only way to be certain you're relying wholly on the force.''

Noticing that the skeptical Corellian had turned to watch, Kenobi hesitated momentarily. It did Luke no good to have the self-assured pilot laugh every time a mistake was made. But coddling the boy would do him no good either, and there was no time for it anyway. Throw him in and hope he floats, Ben instructed himself firmly.

Bending over the chrome globe, he touched a control at its side. Then he tossed it straight up. It arched toward Luke. Braking in midfall, the ball plummeted stonelike toward the deck. Luke swung the saber at it. While it was a commendable try, it wasn't nearly fast enough. Once again the little antenna glowed. This time the crimson needle hit Luke square on the seat of his pants. Though it wasn't an incapacitating blow, it felt like one; and Luke let out a yelp of pain as he spun, trying to strike his invisible tormentor.

"Relax!" old Ben urged him. "Be free. You're trying to use your eyes and ears. Stop predicting and use the rest of your mind."

Suddenly the youth stopped, wavering slightly. The seeker was still behind him. Changing direction again, it made another dive and fired.

Simultaneously the lightsaber jerked around, as accurate as it was awkward in its motion, to deflect the bolt. This time the ball didn't fall motionless to the deck. Instead it backed up three meters and remained there, hovering.

Aware that the drone of the seeker remote no longer assaulted his ears, a cautious Luke peeked out from under the helmet. Sweat and exhaustion competed for space on his face.

"Did I—?"

"I told you you could," Kenobi informed him with pleasure. "Once you start to trust your inner self there'll be no stopping you. I told you there was much of your father in you."

"I'd call it luck," snorted Solo as he concluded his examination of the readouts.

"In my experience there is no such thing as luck, my young friend—only highly favorable adjustments of multiple factors to incline events in one's favor."

"Call it what you like," the Corellian sniffed indifferently, "but good against a mechanical remote is one thing. Good against a living menace is another."

As he was speaking a small telltale light on the far side of the hold had begun flashing. Chewbacca noticed it and called out to him.

Solo glanced at the board, then informed his passengers, "We're coming up on Alderaan. We'll be slowing down shortly and going back under lightspeed. Come on, Chewie."

Rising from the game table, the Wookiee followed his partner toward the cockpit. Luke watched them depart, but his mind wasn't on their imminent arrival at Alderaan. It was burning with something else, something that seemed to grow and mature at the back of his brain as he dwelt on it.

"You know," he murmured, "I did feel something. I could almost 'see' the outlines of the remote." He gestured at the hovering device behind him.

Kenobi's voice when he replied was solemn. "Luke, you've taken the first step into a larger universe."

Dozens of humming, buzzing instruments lent the freighter's

cockpit the air of a busy hive. Solo and Chewbacca had their attention locked on the most vital of those instruments.

"Steady . . . stand by, Chewie." Solo adjusted several manual compensators. "Ready to go sublight . . . ready . . . cut us in, Chewie."

The Wookiee turned something on the console before him. At the same time Solo pulled back on a comparatively large lever. Abruptly the long streaks of Doppler-distorted starlight slowed to hyphen shapes, then finally to familiar bolts of fire. A gauge on the console registered zero.

Gigantic chunks of glowing stone appeared out of the nothingness, barely shunted aside by the ship's deflectors. The strain caused the *Millennium Falcon* to begin shuddering violently.

"What the—?" a thoroughly startled Solo muttered. Next to him, Chewbacca offered no comment of his own as he flipped off several controls and activated others. Only the fact that the cautious Solo always emerged from supralight travel with his deflectors up—just in case any of many unfriendly folks might be waiting for him—had saved the freighter from instant destruction.

Luke fought to keep his balance as he made his way into the cockpit. "What's going on?"

"We're back in normal space," Solo informed him, "but we've come out in the middle of the worst asteriod storm I've ever seen. It's not on any of our charts." He peered hard at several indicators. "According to the glactic atlas, our position is correct. Only one thing is missing: Alderaan."

"Missing? But—that's crazy!"

"I won't argue with you," the Corellian replied grimly, "but look for yourself." He gestured out the port. "I've triple-checked the coordinates, and there's nothing wrong with the nav 'puter. We ought to be standing out one planetary diameter from the surface. The planet's glow should be filling the cockpit, but—there's nothing out there. Nothing but debris." He paused. "Judging from the level of wild energy outside and the amount of solid waste, I'd guess that Alderaan's been . . . blown away. Totally."

"Destroyed," Luke whispered, overwhelmed at the specter raised by such an unimaginable disaster. "But—how?"

"The Empire," a voice declared firmly. Ben Kenobi had come in behind Luke, and his attention was held by the emptiness ahead as well as the import behind it.

"No." Solo was shaking his head slowly. In his own way

even he was stunned by the enormity of what the old man was suggesting. That a human agency had been responsible for the annihilation of an entire population, of a planet itself . . .

"No . . . the entire Imperial fleet couldn't have done this. It would take a thousand ships massing a lot more firepower than has ever existed."

"I wonder if we should get out of here," Luke was murmuring, trying to see around the rims of the port. "If by some chance it was the Empire . . ."

"I don't know what's happened here," an angry Solo cursed, "but I'll tell you one thing. The Empire isn't—"

Muffled alarms began humming loudly as a synchronous light flashed on the control console. Solo bent to the appropriate instrumentation.

"Another ship," he announced. "Can't judge the type yet."

"A survivor, maybe—someone who might know what happened," Luke ventured hopefully.

Ben Kenobi's next words shattered more than that hope. "That's an Imperial fighter."

Chewbacca suddenly gave an angry bark. A huge flower of destruction blossomed outside the port, battering the freighter violently. A tiny, double-winged ball raced past the cockpit port.

"It followed us!" Luke shouted.

"From Tatooine? It couldn't have," objected a disbelieving Solo. "Not in hyperspace."

Kenobi was studying the configuration the tracking screen displayed. "You're quite right, Han. It's the short-range TIE fighter."

"But where did it come from?" the Corellian wanted to know. "There are no Imperial bases near here. It couldn't have been a TIE job."

"You saw it pass."

"I know. It looked like a TIE fighter—but what about a base?"

"It's leaving in a big hurry," Luke noted, studying the tracker. "No matter where it's going, if it identifies us we're in big trouble."

"Not if I can help it," Solo declared. "Chewie, jam its transmission. Lay in a pursuit course."

"It would be best to let it go," Kenobi ventured thoughtfully. "It's already too far out of range."

"Not for long."

Several minutes followed, during which the cockpit was filled with a tense silence. All eyes were on the tracking screen and viewport.

At first the Imperial fighter tried a complex evasive course, to no avail. The surprisingly maneuverable freighter hung tight on its tail, continuing to make up the distance between them. Seeing that he couldn't shake his pursuers, the fighter pilot had obviously opened up his tiny engine all the way.

Ahead, one of the multitude of stars was becoming steadily brighter. Luke frowned. They were moving fast, but not nearly fast enough for any heavenly object to brighten so rapidly. Something here didn't make sense.

"Impossible for a fighter that small to be this deep in space on its own," Solo observed.

"It must have gotten lost, been part of a convoy or something," Luke hypothesized.

Solo's comment was gleeful. "Well, he won't be around long enough to tell anyone about us. We'll be on top of him in a minute or two."

The star ahead continued to brighten, its glow evidently coming from within. It assumed a circular outline.

"He's heading for that small moon," Luke murmured.

"The Empire must have an outpost there," Solo admitted. "Although, according to the atlas, Alderaan had no moons." He shrugged it off. "Galactic topography was never one of my best subjects. I'm only interested in worlds and moons with customers on them. But I think I can get him before he gets there; he's almost in range."

They drew steadily nearer. Gradually craters and mountains on the moon became visible. Yet there was something extremely odd about them. The craters were far too regular in outline, the mountains far too vertical, canyons and valleys impossibly straight and regularized. Nothing as capricious as volcanic action had formed those features.

"That's no moon," Kenobi breathed softly. "That's a space station."

"But it's too big to be a space station," Solo objected. "The size of it! It can't be artificial—it can't!"

"I have a very strange feeling about this," was Luke's comment.

Abruptly the usually calm Kenobi was shouting. "Turn the ship around! Let's get out of here!"

"Yes, I think you're right, old man. Full reverse, Chewie."

The Wookiee started adjusting controls, and the freighter

seemed to slow, arcing around in a broad curve. The tiny fighter leaped instantly toward the monstrous station until it was swallowed up by its overpowering bulk.

Chewbacca chattered something at Solo as the ship shook and strained against unseen forces.

"Lock in auxiliary power!" Solo ordered.

Gauges began to whine in protest, and by ones and twos every instrument on the control console sequentially went berserk. Try as he might, Solo couldn't keep the surface of the gargantuan station from looming steadily larger, larger—until it became the heavens.

Luke stared wildly at secondary installations as big as mountains, dish antennae larger than all of Mos Eisley. "Why are we still moving toward it?"

"Too late," Kenobi whispered softly. A glance at Solo confirmed his concern.

"We're caught in a tractor beam—strongest one I ever saw It's dragging us in," the pilot muttered

"You mean, there's nothing you can do?" Luke asked, feeling unbelievably helpless.

Solo studied the overloaded sensor readouts and shook his head. "Not against this kind of power. I'm on full power myself, kid, and it's not shifting out of course a fraction of a degree. It's no use. I'm going to have to shut down or we'll melt our engines. But they're not going to suck me up like so much dust without a fight!"

He started to vacate the pilot's chair, but was restrained by an aged yet powerful hand on his shoulder. An expression of concern was on the old man's face—and yet, a suggestion of something somewhat less funereal.

"If it's a fight you cannot win—well, my boy, there are always alternatives to fighting . . ."

The true size of the battle station became apparent as the freighter was pulled closer and closer. Running around the station's equator was an artificial cluster of metal mountains, docking ports stretching beckoning fingers nearly two kilometers above the surface

Now only a miniscule speck against the gray bulk of the station, the *Millennium Falcon* was sucked toward one of those steel pseudopods and finally swallowed by it. A lake of metal closed off the entryway, and the freighter vanished as if it had never existed.

* * *

Vader stared at the motley array of stars displayed on the conference-room map while Tarkin and Admiral Motti conferred nearby. Interestingly, the first use of the most powerful destructive machine ever constructed had seemingly had no influence at all on that map, which in itself represented only a tiny fraction of this section of one modest-sized galaxy.

It would take a microbreakdown of a portion of this map to reveal a slight reduction in spatial mass, caused by the disappearance of Alderaan. Alderaan, with its many cities, farms, factories, and towns—and traitors, Vader reminded himself.

Despite his advances and intricate technological methods of annihilation, the actions of mankind remained unnoticeable to an uncaring, unimaginably vast universe. If Vader's grandest plans ever came to pass, all that would change.

He was well aware that despite all their intelligence and drive, the vastness and wonder were lost on the two men who continued to chatter monkeylike behind him. Tarkin and Motti were talented and ambitious, but they saw things only on the scale of human pettiness. It was a pity, Vader thought, that they did not possess the scope to match their abilities.

Still, neither man was a Dark Lord. As such, little more could be expected of them. These two were useful now, and dangerous, but someday they, like Alderaan, would have to be swept aside. For now he could not afford to ignore them. And while he would have preferred the company of equals, he had to admit reluctantly that at this point, he *had* no equals.

Nonetheless, he turned to them and insinuated himself into their conversation. "The defense systems on Alderaan, despite the Senator's protestations to the contrary, were as strong as any in the Empire. I should conclude that our demonstration was as impressive as it was thorough."

Tarkin turned to him, nodding. "The Senate is being informed of our action at this very moment. Soon we will be able to announce the extermination of the Alliance itself, as soon as we have dealt with their main military base. Now that their main source of munitions, Alderaan, has been eliminated, the rest of those systems with secessionist inclinations will fall in line quickly enough, you'll see."

Tarkin turned as an Imperial officer entered the chamber. "Yes, what is it, Cass?"

The unlucky officer wore the expression of the mouse chosen to bell the cat. "Governor, the advance scouts have reached and circumnavigated Dantooine. They have found the remains of a rebel base . . . which they estimate has been deserted for some time. Years, possibly. They are proceeding with an extensive survey of the remainder of the system."

Tarkin turned apoplectic, his face darkening to a fine pomegranate fury. "She lied! She lied to us!"

No one could see, but it seemed that Vader must have smiled behind his mask. "Then we are even in the first exchange of 'truths'. I told you she would never betray the rebellion—unless she thought her confession could somehow destroy us in the process."

"Terminate her immediately!" The Governor was barely able to form words.

"Calm yourself, Tarkin," Vader advised him. "You would throw away our only link to the real rebel base so casually? She can still be of value to us."

"*Fagh!* You just said it yourself, Vader: we'll get nothing more out of her. I'll find that hidden fortress if I have to destroy every star system in this sector. I'll—"

A quiet yet demanding beep interrupted him.

"Yes, what is it?" he inquired irritably.

A voice reported over an unseen speaker. "Sirs, we've captured a small freighter that was entering the remains of Alderaan. A standard check indicates that its markings apparently match that of the ship which blasted its way out of the quarantine at Mos Eisley, Tatooine system, and went hyper before the imperial blockade craft there could close on it."

Tarkin looked puzzled. "Mos Eisley? Tatooine? What is this? What's this all about, Vader?"

"It means, Tarkin, that the last of our unresolved difficulties is about to be eliminated. Someone apparently received the missing data tapes, learned who transcribed them, and was trying to return them to her. We may be able to facilitate their meeting with the Senator."

Tarkin started to say something, hesitated, then nodded in understanding. "How convenient. I leave this matter in your hands, Vader."

The Dark Lord bowed slightly, a gesture which Tarkin acknowledged with a perfunctory salute. Then he spun and strode from the room, leaving Motti looking from man to man in confusion.

The freighter sat listlessly in the docking hangar of the huge bay. Thirty armed Imperial troopers stood before the lowered

main ramp leading into the ship. They snapped to attention when
Vader and a Commander approached. Vader halted at the base
of the ramp, studying the vessel as an officer and several soldiers
came forward.

"There was no reply to our repeated signals, sir, so we activated the ramp from outside. We've made no contact with anyone aboard either by communicator or in person," the officer
reported.

"Send your men in," Vader ordered.

Turning, the officer relayed the command to a noncom, who
barked orders. A number of the heavily armored soldiers made
their way up the ramp and entered the outer hold. They advanced
with appreciable caution.

Inside, two men covered a third as he advanced. Moving in
groups of three in this fashion, they rapidly spread through the
ship. Corridors rang hollowly under metal-shod feet, and doors
slid aside willingly as they were activated.

"Empty," the Sergeant in charge finally declared in surprise.
"Check the cockpit."

Several troopers made their way forward and slid the portal
aside, only to discover the pilot's chairs as vacant as the rest of
the freighter. The controls were deactivated and all systems shut
down. Only a single light on the console winked on and off
fitfully. The Sergeant moved forward, recognized the source of
the light, and activated the appropriate controls. A printout appeared on a nearby screen. He studied it intently, then turned to
convey the information to his superior, who was waiting by the
main hatch.

That worthy listened carefully before he turned and called
down to the Commander and Vader. "There is no one aboard;
the ship is completely deserted, sirs. According to the ship's
log, her crew abandoned ship immediately after lift-off, then set
her on automatics for Alderaan."

"Possibly a decoy," the Commander ventured aloud. "Then
they should still be on Tatooine!"

"Possibly," Vader admitted reluctantly.

"Several of the escape pods have been jettisoned," the officer
went on.

"Did you find any 'droids on board?" Vader called.

"No, sir—nothing. If there were any, they must have abandoned the ship along with the organic crew."

Vader hesitated before replying. When he did so, uncertainty
was evident in his voice. "This doesn't feel right. Send a fully

equipped scanning team on board. I want every centimeter of that ship checked out. See to it as soon as possible.'' With that, he whirled and stalked from the hangar, pursued by the infuriating feeling that he was overlooking something of vital importance.

The rest of the assembled soldiers were dismissed by the officer. On board the freighter, a last lone figure left off examining the space beneath the cockpit consoles and ran to join his comrades. He was anxious to be off this ghost ship and back in the comfortable surroundings of the barracks. His heavy footsteps echoed through the once more empty freighter.

Below, the muffled sounds of the officer giving final orders faded, leaving the interior in complete quiet. The quivering of a portion of the floor was the only movement on board.

Abruptly the quivering became a sharp upheaval. Two metal panels popped upward, followed by a pair of tousled heads. Han Solo and Luke looked around quickly, then managed to relax a little when it became clear that the ship was as empty as it sounded.

"Lucky you'd built these compartments,'' Luke commented.

Solo was not as cheerily confident. "Where did you think I kept smuggled goods—in the main hold? I admit I never expected to smuggle myself in them.'' He started violently at a sudden sound, but it was only another of the panels shifting aside.

"This is ridiculous. It isn't going to work. Even if I could take off and get past the closed hatch''—he jabbed a thumb upward—"we'd never get past that tractor beam.''

Another panel opened, revealing the face of an elderly imp "You leave that to me.''

"I was afraid you'd say something like that,'' muttered Solo. "You're a damn fool, old man.''

Kenobi grinned at him. "What does that say of the man who allows himself to be hired by a fool?''

Solo muttered something under his breath as they pulled themselves clear of the compartments, Chewbacca doing so with a good deal of grunting and twisting.

Two technicians had arrived at the base of the ramp. They reported to the two bored soldiers guarding it.

"The ship's all yours,'' one of the troopers told them. "If the scanners pick up anything, report it immediately.''

The men nodded, then strained to lug their heavy equipment up the ramp. As soon as they disappeared inside, a loud crash was heard. Both guards whirled, then heard a voice call, "Hey, down there, could you give us a hand with this?"

One trooper looked at his companion, who shrugged. They both started up the ramp, muttering at the inefficiency of mere technicians. A second crashing sound reverberated, but now there was no one left to hear it.

But the absence of the two troopers *was* noticed, soon thereafter. A gantry officer passing the window of a small command office near the freighter entrance glanced out, frowning when he saw no sign of the guards. Concerned but not alarmed, he moved to a comlink and spoke into it as he continued to stare at the ship.

"THX-1138, why aren't you at your post? THX-1138, do you copy?"

The speaker gave back only static.

"THX-1138, why don't you reply?" The officer was beginning to panic when an armored figure descended the ramp and waved toward him. Pointing to the portion of his helmet covering his right ear, the figured tapped it to indicate the comlink inside wasn't working.

Shaking his head in disgust, the gantry officer gave his busy aide an annoyed look as he made for the door. "Take over here. We've got another bad transmitter. I'm going to see what I can do. He activated the door, took a step forward as it slid aside—and stumbled backward in a state of shock.

Filling the door completely was a towering hairy form. Chewbacca leaned inward and with a bone splintering howl flattened the benumbed officer with one swipe of a pan-sized fist.

The aide was already on his feet and reaching for his sidearm when a narrow energy beam passed completely through him, piercing his heart. Solo flipped up the faceplate of his trooper helmet, then slid it back into place as he followed the Wookiee into the room. Kenobi and the 'droids squeezed in behind him, with Luke, also clad in the armor of a luckless Imperial soldier, bringing up the rear.

Luke was looking around nervously as he shut the door behind them. "Between his howling and your blasting everything in sight, it's a wonder the entire station doesn't know we're here."

"Bring 'em on," Solo demanded, unreasonably enthused by their success so far. "I prefer a straight fight to all this sneaking around."

"Maybe you're in a hurry to die," Luke snapped, "but I'm not. All this sneaking around has kept us alive."

The Corellian gave Luke a sour eye but said nothing.

They watched as Kenobi operated an incredibly complex computer console with the ease and confidence of one long accustomed to handling intricate machinery. A screen lit up promptly with a map of sections of the battle station. The old man leaned forward, scrutinizing the display carefully.

Meanwhile, Threepio and Artoo had been going over an equally complicated control panel nearby. Artoo suddenly froze and began whistling wildly at something he had found. Solo and Luke, their momentary disagreement over tactics forgotten, rushed over to where the robots were standing. Chewbacca busied himself hanging the gantry officer up by his toes.

"Plug him in," Kenobi suggested, looking over from his place before the larger readout. "He should be able to draw information from the entire station network. Let's see if he can find out where the tractor-beam power unit is located."

"Why not just disconnect the beam from here, sir?" Luke wanted to know.

It was Solo who replied derisively, "What, and have them lock it right back on us before we can get a ship's length outside the docking bay?"

Luke looked crestfallen. "Oh. I hadn't thought of that."

"We have to break the tractor at its power source in order to execute a clean escape, Luke," old Ben chided gently as Artoo punched a claw arm into the open computer socket he had discovered. Immediately a galaxy of lights came to life on the panel in front of him and the room was filled with the hum of machinery working at high speed.

Several minutes passed while the little 'droid sucked up information like a metal sponge. Then the hum slowed and he turned to beep something back at them.

"He's found it, sir!" Threepio announced excitedly.

"The tractor beam is coupled to the main reactors at seven locations. Most of the pertinent data is restricted, but he'll try to pull the critical information through to the monitor."

Kenobi turned his attention from the larger screen to a small readout near Artoo. Data began to race across it too fast for Luke to see, but apparently Kenobi somehow made something of the schematic blur. "I don't think there's any way you boys can help with this," he told them. "I must go alone."

"That suits me fine," said Solo readily. "I've already done

more than I bargained for on this trip. But I think putting that tractor beam out of commission's going to take more than your magic, old man.''

Luke wasn't put off so easily. ''I want to go with you.''

''Don't be impatient, young Luke. This requires skills you haven't yet mastered. Stay and watch over the 'droids and wait for my signal. They must be delivered to the rebel forces or many more worlds will meet the same fate as Alderaan. Trust in the force, Luke—and wait.''

With a last look at the flow of information on the monitor, Kenobi adjusted the lightsaber at his waist. Stepping to the door, he slid it aside, looked once left, once right, and disappeared down a long, glowing hallway.

As soon as he was gone Chewbacca growled and Solo nodded agreement. ''You said it, Chewie!'' He turned to Luke. ''Where'd you dig up that old fossil?''

''Ben Kenobi—*General* Kenobi—is a great man,'' Luke protested loftily.

''Great at getting us into trouble,'' Solo snorted. '' 'General,' my afterburners! He's not going to get us out of here.''

''You got any better ideas?'' Luke shot back challengingly.

''Anything would be better than just waiting here for them to come and pick us up. If we—''

A hysterical whistling and hooting came from the computer console. Luke hurried over to Artoo Detoo. The little 'droid was all but hopping about on stubby legs.

''What now?'' Luke asked Threepio.

The taller robot looked puzzled himself. ''I'm afraid I don't understand either, sir. He says, 'I found her,' and keeps repeating, 'She's here, she's here!' ''

''Who? Who has he found?''

Artoo turned a flat blinking face toward Luke and whistled frantically.

''Princess Leia,'' Threepio announced after listening carefully. ''Senator Organa—they seem to be one and the same. I believe she may be the person in the message he was carrying.''

That three-dimensional portrait of indescribable beauty coalesced in Luke's mind again. ''The Princess? She's here?''

Attracted by the commotion, Solo wandered over. ''Princess? What's going on?''

''Where? Where is she?'' Luke demanded breathlessly, ignoring Solo completely.

Artoo whistled on while Threepio translated. ''Level five,

detention block AA-23. According to the information, she is scheduled for slow termination."

"No! We've got to do something."

"What are you three blabbering about?" an exasperated Solo demanded.

"She's the one who programmed the message into Artoo Detoo," Luke explained hurriedly, "the one we were trying to deliver to Alderaan. We've got to help her."

"Now, just a minute," Solo cautioned him. "This is going awful fast for me. Don't get any funny ideas. When I said I didn't have any 'better ideas' I meant it. The old man said to wait here. I don't like it, but I'm not going off on some crazy maze through this place."

"But Ben didn't know she was here," Luke half pleaded, half argued. "I'm sure that if he knew he would have changed his plans." Anxiety turned to thougtfulness. "Now, if we could just figure a way to get into that detention block . . ."

Solo shook his head and stepped back. "Huh-uh—I'm not going into any Imperial detention blocks."

"If we don't do something, they're going to execute her. A minute ago you said you didn't just want to sit here and wait to be captured. Now all you want to do is stay. Which is it, Han?"

The Corellian looked troubled—and confused. "Marching into a detention area's not what I had in mind. We're likely to end up there anyway—why rush it?"

"But they're going to execute her!"

"Better her than me."

"Where's your sense of chivalry, Han?"

Solo considered. "Near as I can recall, I traded it for a ten-carat chrysopaz and three bottles of good brandy about five years ago on Commenor."

"I've seen her," Luke pointed desperately. "She's beautiful."

"So's life."

"She's a rich and powerful Senator," Luke pressed, hoping an appeal to Solo's baser instincts might be more effective. "If we could save her, the reward could be substantial."

"Uh . . . rich?" Then Solo looked disdainful. "Wait a minute . . . Reward, from whom? From the government on Alderaan?" He made a sweeping gesture toward the hangar and by implication the space where Alderaan had once orbited.

Luke thought furiously. "If she's being held here and is scheduled to be executed, that means she must be dangerous in some way to whoever destroyed Alderaan, to whoever had this station built. You can bet it had something to do with the Empire instituting a reign of full repression.

"I'll tell you who'll pay for her rescue, and for the information she holds. The Senate, the rebel Alliance, and every concern that did business with Alderaan. She could be the sole surviving heir of the off-world wealth of the entire system! The reward could be more wealth than you can imagine."

"I don't know . . . I can imagine quite a bit." He glanced at Chewbacca, who grunted a terse reply. Solo shrugged back at the big Wookiee. "All right, we'll give it a try. But you'd better be right about that reward. What's your plan, kid?"

Luke was momentarily taken aback. All his energies up till now had been concentrated on persuading Solo and Chewbacca to aid in a rescue attempt. That accomplished, Luke became aware he had no idea how to proceed. He had grown used to old Ben and Solo giving directions. Now the next move was up to him.

His eyes were caught by several metal circlets dangling from the belt of Solo's armor. "Give me those binders and tell Chewbacca to come over here."

Solo handed Luke the thin but quite unbreakable cuffs and relayed the request to Chewbacca. The Wookiee lumbered over and stood waiting next to Luke.

"Now, I'm going to put these on you," Luke began, starting to move behind the Wookiee with the cuffs, "and—"

Chewbacca made a sound low in his throat, and Luke jumped in spite of himself. "Now," he began again, "Han is going to put these on you and . . ." He sheepishly handed the binders to Solo, uncomfortably aware of the enormous anthropoid's glowing eyes on him.

Solo sounded amused as he moved forward. "Don't worry, Chewie. I think I know what he has in mind."

The cuffs barely fit around the thick wrists. Despite his partner's seeming confidence in the plan, the Wookiee wore a worried, frightened look as the restraints were activated.

"Luke, sir." Luke looked over at Threepio. "Pardon me for asking, but, ah—what should Artoo and I do if someone discovers us here in your absence?"

"Hope they don't have blasters," Solo replied.

Threepio's tone indicated he didn't find the answer humorous. "That isn't very reassuring."

Solo and Luke were too engrossed in their coming expedition

to pay much attention to the worried robot. They adjusted their helmets. Then, with Chewbacca wearing a half-real downcast expression, they started off along the corridor where Ben Kenobi had disappeared

IX

AS they traveled farther and deeper into the bowels of the gigantic station, they found it increasingly difficult to maintain an air of casual indifference. Fortunately, those who might have sensed some nervousness on the part of the two armored troopers would regard it as only natural, considering their huge, dangerous Wookiee captive. Chewbacca also made it impossible for the two young men to be as inconspicuous as they would have liked.

The farther they traveled, the heavier the traffic became. Other soldiers, bureaucrats, technicians, and mechanicals bustled around them. Intent on their own assignments, they ignored the trio completely, only a few of the humans sparing the Wookiee a curious glance. Chewbacca's morose expression and the seeming confidence of his captors reassured the inquisitive.

Eventually they reached a wide bank of elevators. Luke breathed a sigh of relief. The computer-controlled transport ought to be capable of taking them just about anywhere on the station in response to a verbal command.

There was a nervous second when a minor official raced to get aboard. Solo gestured sharply, and the other, without voicing a protest, shifted to the next elevator tube in line.

Luke studied the operating panel, then tried to sound at once knowledgeable and important as he spoke into the pickup grid. Instead, he sounded nervous and scared, but the elevator was a pure-response mechanism, not programmed to differentiate the appropriateness of emotions conveyed vocally. So the door slid shut and they were on their way. After what felt like hours but was in reality only minutes, the door opened and they stepped out into the security area.

It had been Luke's hope they would discover something like the old-fashioned barred cells of the kind used on Tatooine in towns like Mos Eisley. Instead, they saw only narrow ramps bordering a bottomless ventilation shaft. These walkways, several levels of them, ran parallel to smooth curving walls which held faceless detention cells. Alert-looking guards and energy gates seemed to be everywhere they looked.

Uncomfortably aware that the longer they stood frozen in place, the sooner someone was bound to come over and ask unanswerable questions, Luke searched frantically for a course of action.

"This isn't going to work," Solo whispered, leaning toward him.

"Why didn't you say so before?" a frustrated, frightened Luke shot back.

"I think I did. I—"

"Shssh!"

Solo shut up as Luke's worst fears were realized. A tall, grim-looking officer approached them. He frowned as he examined the silent Chewbacca.

"Where are you two going with this—thing?"

Chewbacca snarled at the remark, and Solo quieted him with a hasty jab in the ribs. A panicky Luke found himself replying almost instinctively. "Prisoner transfer from block TS-138."

The officer looked puzzled. "I wasn't notified. I'll have to clear it."

Turning, the man walked to a small console nearby and began entering his request. Luke and Han hurriedly surveyed the situation, their gaze traveling from alarms, energy gates, and remote photosensors to the three other guards stationed in the area.

Solo nodded to Luke as he unfastened Chewbacca's cuffs. Then he whispered something to the Wookiee. An ear-splitting howl shook the corridor as Chewbacca threw up both hands, grabbing Solo's rifle from him.

"Look out!" a seemingly terrified Solo shouted. "It's loose. It'll rip us all apart!"

Both he and Luke had darted clear of the rampaging Wookiee, pulled out their pistols, and were blasting away at him. Their reaction was excellent, their enthusiasm undeniable, and their aim execrable. Not a single shot came close to the dodging Wookiee. Instead, they blasted automatic cameras, energy-rate controls, and the three dumbfounded guards.

At this point it occurred to the officer in charge that the abominable aim of the two soldiers was a bit too selectively efficient. He was preparing to jab the general alarm when a burst from Luke's pistol caught him in the midsection and he fell without a word to the gray deck.

Solo rushed to the open comlink speaker, which was screeching anxious questions about what was going on. Apparently there were audio as well as visual links between this detention station and elsewhere.

Ignoring the barrage of alternate threats and queries, he checked the readout set in the panel nearby. "We've got to find out which cell this Princess of yours is in. There must be a dozen levels and— Here it is. Cell 2187. Go on—Chewie and I'll hold them here."

Luke nodded once and was racing down the narrow walkway.

After gesturing for the Wookiee to take up a position where he could cover the elevators, Solo took a deep breath and responded to the unceasing calls from the comlink.

"Everything's under control," he said into the pickup, sounding reasonably official. "Situation normal."

"It didn't sound like that," a voice snapped back in a no-nonsense tone. "What happened?"

"Uh, well, one of the guards experienced a weapon malfunction," Solo stammered, his temporary officialese lapsing into nervousness. "No problem now—we're all fine, thanks. How about you?"

"We're sending a squad up," the voice announced suddenly.

Han could almost smell the suspicion at the other end. What to say? He spoke more eloquently with the business end of a pistol.

"Negative—negative. We have an energy leak. Give us a few minutes to lock it down. Large leak—very dangerous."

"Weapon malfunction, energy leak . . . Who is this? What's your operating ?"

Pointing his pistol at the panels, Solo blew the instrumentation to silent scraps. "It was a dumb conversation anyway," he murmured. Turning, he shouted down the corridor, "Hurry it up, Luke! We're going to have company."

Luke heard, but he was absorbed in running from one cell to the next and studying the numbers glowing above each doorway.

The cell 2187, it appeared, did not exist. But it did, and he found it just as he was about to give up and try the next level down.

For a long moment he examined the featureless convex metal wall. Turning his pistol to maximum and hoping it wouldn't melt in his hand before it broke through, he opened fire on the door. When the weapon became too hot to hold, he tossed it from hand to hand. As he did so the smoke had time to clear, and he saw with some surprise that the door had been blown away.

Peering through the smoke with an uncomprehending look on her face was the young woman whose portrait Artoo Detoo had projected in a garage on Tatooine several centuries ago, or so it seemed.

She was even more beautiful than her image, Luke decided, staring dazedly at her. "You're even—more beautiful—than I—"

Her look of confusion and uncertainty was replaced by first puzzlement and then impatience. "Aren't you a little short for a storm trooper?" she finally commented.

"What? Oh—the uniform." He removed the helmet, regaining a little composure at the same time. "I've come to rescue you. I'm Luke Skywalker."

"I beg your pardon?" she said politely.

"I said, I've come to rescue you. Ben Kenobi is with me. We've got your two 'droids—"

The uncertainty was instantly replaced by hope at the mention of the oldster's name. "Ben Kenobi!" She looked around Luke, ignoring him as she searched for the Jedi. "Where is he? Obi-wan!"

Governor Tarkin watched as Darth Vader paced rapidly back and forth in the otherwise empty conference room. Finally the Dark Lord paused, glancing around as though a great bell only he could hear had rung somewhere close by.

"He is here," Vader stated unemotionally.

Tarkin looked startled. "Obi-wan Kenobi! That's impossible. What makes you think so?"

"A stirring in the force, of a kind I've felt only in the presence of my old master. It is unmistakable."

"Surely—surely he must be dead by now."

Vader hesitated, his assurance suddenly gone. "Perhaps . . . It is gone now. It was only a brief sensation."

"The Jedi are extinct," declared Tarkin positively. "Their

fire was quenched decades ago. You, my friend, are all that's left of their ways."

A comlink buzzed softly for attention. "Yes?" Tarkin acknowledged

"We have an emergency alert in detention block AA-23."

"The Princess!" Tarkin yelped, jumping to his feet. Vader whirled, trying to stare through the walls.

"I knew it—Obi-wan *is* here. I knew I could not mistake a stirring in the force of such power."

"Put all sections on alert," Tarkin ordered through the comlink. Then he turned to stare at Vader. "If you're right, he must not be allowed to escape."

"Escape may not be Obi-wan Kenobi's intention," Vader replied, struggling to control his emotions. "He is the last of the Jedi—and the greatest. The danger he presents to us must not be underestimated—yet only I can deal with him." His head snapped around to stare fixedly at Tarkin. "Alone."

Luke and Leia had started back up the corridor when a series of blinding explosions ripped the walkway ahead of them. Several troopers had tried coming through the elevator, only to be crisped one after another by Chewbacca. Disdaining the elevators, they had blasted a gaping hole through a wall. The opening was too large for Solo and the Wookie to cover completely. In twos and threes, the Imperials were working their way into the detention block.

Retreating down the walkway, Han and Chewbacca encountered Luke and the Princess. "We can't go back that way!" Solo told them, his face flushed with excitement and worry.

"No, it looks like you've managed to cut off our only escape route," Leia agreed readily. "This is a detention area, you know. They don't build them with multiple exits."

Breathing heavily, Solo turned to look her up and down. "Begging your forgiveness, Your Highness," he said sarcastically, "but maybe you'd prefer it back in your cell?" She looked away, her face impassive.

"There's got to be another way out," Luke muttered, pulling a small transmitter unit from his belt and carefully adjusting the frequency: "*See Threepio . . . See Threepio!*"

A familiar voice responded with gratifying speed. "Yes, sir?"

"We've been cut off here. Are there *any* other ways out of the detention area—anything at all?"

Static crackled over the tiny grid as Solo and Chewbacca kept the Imperial troops bottled up at the other end of the walkway.

"What was that . . . ? I didn't copy."

Back in the gantry office Artoo Detoo beeped and whistled frantically as Threepio adjusted controls, fighting to clear the awkward transmission. "I said, all systems have been alerted to your presence, sir. The main entry seems to be the only way in or out of the cell block." He pressed instruments, and the view on the nearby readouts changed steadily. "All other information on your section is restricted."

Someone began banging on the locked door to the office—evenly at first and then, when no response was forthcoming from within, more insistently.

"Oh, no!" Threepio groaned.

The smoke in the cell corridor was now so intense that it was difficult for Solo and Chewbacca to pick their targets. That was fortunate inasmuch as they were now badly outnumbered and the smoke confused the Imperials' fire with equal thoroughness.

Every so often one of the soldiers would attempt to move closer, only to stand exposed as he penetrated the smoke. Under the accurate fire of the two smugglers, he would rapidly join the accumulating mass of motionless figures on the rampway flooring.

Energy bolts continued to ricochet wildly through the block as Luke moved close to Solo.

"There isn't any other way out." he yelled over the deafening roar of concentrated fire.

"Well, they're closing in on us. What do we do now?"

"This is some rescue," an irritated voice complained from behind them. Both men turned to see a thoroughly disgusted Princess eyeing them with regal disapproval. "When you came in here, didn't you have a plan for getting out?"

Solo nodded toward Luke. "He's the brains, sweetheart."

Luke managed an embarrassed grin and shrugged helplessly. He turned to help return fire, but before he could do so, the Princess had snatched the pistol from his hand.

"Hey!"

Luke stared as she moved along the wall, finally locating a small grate nearby. She pointed the pistol at it and fired.

Solo gazed at her in disbelief. "What do you think you're doing?"

"It looks like it's up to me to save our skins. Get into that garbage chute, flyboy!"

While the others looked on in amazement, she jumped feet first into the opening and disappeared. Chewbacca rumbled threateningly, but Solo slowly shook his head.

"No, Chewie, I don't want you to rip her apart. I'm not sure about her yet. Either I'm beginning to like her, or I'm going to kill her myself." The Wookiee snorted something else, and Solo yelled back at him, "Go on in, you furry oaf! I don't care what you smell. This is no time to go dainty on me."

Shoving the reluctant Wookiee toward the tiny opening, Solo helped jam the massive bulk through. As soon as he disappeared, the Corellian followed him in. Luke fired off a last series of blasts, more in the hope of creating a covering smoke than hitting anything, slid into the chute, and was gone.

Not wanting to incur further losses in such a confined space, the pursuing soldiers had momentarily halted to await the arrival of reinforcements and heavier weapons. Besides, they had their quarry trapped, and despite their dedication, none of them were anxious to die needlessly.

The chamber Luke tumbled into was dimly lit. Not that the light was needed to discern its contents. He smelled the decay long before he was dumped into it. Unadorned except for the concealed illuminants, the garbage room was at least a quarter full of slimy muck, much of which had already achieved a state of decomposition sufficient to wrinkle Luke's nose.

Solo was stumbling around the edge of the room, slipping and sinking up to his knees in the uncertain footing in an attempt to locate an exit. All he found was a small, thick hatchway which he grunted and heaved to pry open. The hatchcover refused to budge.

"The garbage chute was a wonderful idea," he told the Princess sardonically, wiping the sweat from his forehead. "What an incredible smell you've discovered. Unfortunately, we can't ride out of here on a drifting odor, and there doesn't seem to be any other exit. Unless I can get this hatch open."

Stepping back, he pulled his pistol and fired at the cover. The bolt promptly went howling around the room as everyone sought cover in the garbage. A last glance and the bolt detonated almost on top of them.

Looking less dignified by the moment, Leia was the first to emerge from the pungent cover. "Put that thing away," she told Solo grimly, "or you're going to get us all killed."

"Yes, Your Worship," Solo muttered in snide supplication. He made no move to reholster his weapon as he glanced back up toward the open chute above. "It won't take long for them to figure out what happened to us. We had things well under control—until you led us down here."

"Sure you did," she shot back, brushing refuse from her hair and shoulders. "Oh, well, it could be worse. . . ."

As if in reply, a piercing, horrible moaning filled the room. It seemed to come from somewhere beneath them. Chewbacca let out a terrified yowl of his own and tried to flatten himself against a wall. Luke drew his own pistol and peered hard at various clumps of debris, but saw nothing.

"What was that?" Solo asked.

"I'm not too sure." Luke suddenly jumped, looking down and behind him. "Something just moved past me, I think. Watch out—"

With shocking suddenness Luke disappeared straight down into the garbage.

"It's got Luke!" the Princess shouted. "It took him under!" Solo looked around frantically for something to shoot at.

As abruptly as he had vanished, Luke reappeared—and so did part of something else. A thick whitish tentacle was wrapped tight around his throat.

"Shoot it, kill it!" Luke screamed.

"Shoot it! I can't even see it," Solo protested.

Once again Luke was sucked under by whatever that gruesome appendage was attached to. Solo stared helplessly around the multicolored surface.

There was a distant rumble of heavy machinery, and two opposing walls of the chamber moved inward several centimeters. The rumble ceased and then it was quiet again. Luke appeared unexpectedly close to Solo, scrabbling his way clear of the suffocating mess and rubbing at the welt on his neck.

"What happened to it?" Leia wondered, eyeing the quiescent garbage warily.

Luke looked genuinely puzzled. "I don't know. It had me— and then I was free. It just let me go and disappeared. Maybe I didn't smell bad enough for it."

"I've got a very bad feeling about this," Solo murmured.

Again the distant rumble filled the room; again the walls began their inward march. Only this time neither sound nor movement showed any sign of stopping.

"Don't just stand there gaping at each other!" the Princess urged them. "Try to brace them with something."

Even with the thick poles and old metal beams Chewbacca

could handle, they were unable to find anything capable of slowing the walls' advance. It seemed as if the stronger the object was that they placed against the walls, the easier it was snapped.

Luke pulled out his comlink, simultaneously trying to talk and will the walls to retreat. "Threepio . . . come in, Threepio!" A decent pause produced no response, causing Luke to look worriedly at his companions.

"I don't know why he doesn't answer." He tried again. "See Threepio, come in. Do you read?"

"See Threepio," the muted voice continued to call, "come in, See Threepio." It was Luke's voice and it issued softly in between buzzings from the small hand comlink resting on the deserted computer console. Save for the intermittent pleading, the gantry office was silent.

A tremendous explosion drowned out the muffled pleadings. It blew the office door clean across the room, sending metal fragments flying in all directions. Several of them struck the comlink, sending it flying to the floor and cutting off Luke's voice in midtransmission.

In the wake of the minor cataclysm four armed and ready troopers entered through the blown portal. Initial study indicated the office was deserted—until a dim, frightened voice was heard coming from one of the tall supply cabinets near the back of the room.

"Help, help! Let us out!"

Several of the troopers bent to inspect the immobile bodies of the gantry officer and his aide while others opened the noisy cabinet. Two robots, one tall and humanoid, the other purely mechanical and three-legged, stepped out into the office. The taller one gave the impression of being half unbalanced with fear.

"They're madmen, I tell you, madmen!" He gestured urgently toward the doorway. "I think they said something about heading for the prison level. They just left. If you hurry, you might catch them. That way, that way!"

Two of the troopers inside joined those waiting in the hallway in hustling off down the corridor. That left two guards to watch over the office. They totally ignored the robots as they discussed what might have taken place.

"All the excitement has overloaded the circuitry in my companion here," Threepio explained carefully. "If you don't mind, I'd like to take him down to Maintenance."

"Hmmm?" One of the guards looked up indifferently and nodded to the robot. Threepio and Artoo hurried out the door without looking back. As they departed it occurred to the guard that the taller of the two 'droids was of a type he had never seen before. He shrugged. That was not surprising on a station of this size.

"That was too close," Threepio muttered as they scurried down an empty corridor. "Now we'll have to find another information-control console and plug you back in, or everything is lost."

The garbage chamber grew remorselessly smaller, the smoothly fitting metal walls moving toward one another with stolid precision. Larger pieces of refuse performed a concerto of snapping and popping that was rising toward a final shuddering crescendo.

Chewbacca whined pitifully as he fought with all his incredible strength and weight to hold back one of the walls, looking like a hirsute Tantalus approaching his final summit.

"One thing's for sure," Solo noted unhappily. "We're all going to be much thinner. This could prove popular for slimming. The only trouble is its permanence."

Luke paused for breath, shaking the innocent comlink angrily. "What could have happened to Threepio?"

"Try the hatch again," advised Leia. "It's our only hope."

Solo shielded his eyes and did so. The ineffectual blast echoed mockingly through the narrowing chamber.

The service bay was unoccupied, everyone apparently having been drawn away by the commotion elsewhere. After a cautious survey of the room Threepio beckoned for Artoo to follow. Together they commenced a hurried search of the many service panels. Artoo let out a beep, and Threepio rushed to him. He waited impatiently as the smaller unit plugged the receptive arm carefully into the open socket.

A superfast flurry of electronics spewed in undisciplined fashion from the grid of the little 'droid. Threepio made cautioning motions.

"Wait a minute, slow down!" The sounds dropped to a crawl. "That's better. They're where? They what? Oh, no! They'll only come out of there as a liquid!"

* * *

Less than a meter of life was left to the trapped occupants of the garbage room. Leia and Solo had been forced to turn sideways, had ended up facing each other. For the first time the haughtiness was gone from the Princess's face. Reaching out, she took Solo's hand, clutching it convulsively as she felt the first touch of the closing walls.

Luke had fallen and was lying on his side, fighting to keep his head above the rising ooze. He nearly choked on a mouthful of compressed sludge when his comlink began buzzing for attention.

"Threepio!"

"Are you there, sir?" the 'droid replied. "We've had some minor problems. You would not believe—"

"Shut up, Threepio!" Luke screamed into the unit. "And shut down all the refuse units on the detention level or immediately below it. Do you copy? Shut down the refuse—"

Moments later Threepio grabbed at his head in pain as a terrific screeching and yelling sounded over the comlink.

"No, shut them *all* down!" he implored Artoo. "Hurry! Oh, listen to them—they're dying, Artoo! I curse this metal body of mine. I was not fast enough. It was my fault. My poor master—all of them . . . no, no *no*!"

The screaming and yelling, however, continued far beyond what seemed like a reasonable interval. In fact, they were shouts of relief. The chamber walls had reversed direction automatically with Artoo's shutdown and were moving apart again.

"Artoo, Threepio," Luke hollered into the comlink, "it's all right, we're all right! Do you read me? We're okay—you did just fine."

Brushing distastefully at the clinging slime, he made his way as rapidly as possible toward the hatchcover. Bending, he scraped accumulated detritus away, noting the number thus revealed.

"Open the pressure-maintenance hatch on unit 366-117891."

"Yes, sir," came Threepio's acknowledgment.

They may have been the happiest words Luke had ever heard.

X

LINED with power cables and circuitry conduits that rose from
the depths and vanished into the heavens, the service trench
appeared to be hundreds of kilometers deep. The narrow catwalk running around one side looked like a starched thread
glued on a glowing ocean. It was barely wide enough for one
man to traverse.

One man edged his way along that treacherous walkway now,
his gaze intent on something ahead of him instead of the awesome metal abyss below. The clacking sounds of enormous
switching devices resounded like captive leviathans in the vast
open space, tireless and never sleeping.

Two thick cables joined beneath an overlay panel. It was
locked, but after careful inspection of sides, top and bottom,
Ben Kenobi pressed the panel cover in a particular fashion
causing it to spring aside. A blinking computer terminal was
revealed beneath.

With equal care he performed several adjustments to the terminal. His actions were rewarded when several indicator lights
on the board changed from red to blue.

Without warning, a secondary door close behind him opened.
Hurriedly reclosing the panel cover, the old man slipped deeper
into the shadows. A detachment of troopers had appeared in the
portal, and the officer in charge moved to within a couple of
meters of the motionless, hidden figure.

"Secure this area until the alert has been cancelled."

As they began to disperse, Kenobi became one with the dark.

Chewbacca grunted and wheezed, and barely succeeded in
forcing his thick torso through the hatchway opening with Luke's

and Solo's help. That accomplished, Luke turned to take stock of their surroundings.

The hallway they had emerged into showed dust on the floor. It gave the impression of not having been used since the station had been built. Probably it was only a repair access corridor. He had no idea where they were.

Something hit the wall behind them with a massive *thunk*, and Luke yelled for everyone to watch out as a long, gelatinous limb worked its way through the hatch and flailed hopefully about in the open corridor. Solo aimed his pistol at it as Leia tried to slip past the half-paralyzed Chewbacca.

"Somebody get this big hairy walking carpet out of my way." Suddenly she noticed what Solo was preparing to do. "No, wait! It'll be heard!"

Solo ignored her and fired at the hatchway. The burst of energy was rewarded with a distant roar as an avalanche of weakened wall and beaming all but buried the creature in the chamber beyond.

Magnified by the narrow corridor, the sounds continued to roll and echo for long minutes afterward. Luke shook his head in disgust, realizing that someone like Solo who spoke with the mouth of a gun might not always act sensibly. Until now he had sort of looked up to the Corellian. But the senseless gesture of firing at the hatchway brought them, for the first time in Luke's mind, to the same level.

The Princess's actions were more surprising than Solo's, however. "Listen," she began, staring up at him, "I don't know where you came from, but I'm grateful." Almost as an afterthought she glanced back at Luke, adding, "To the both of you." Her attention turned back to Solo. "But from now on you do as I tell you."

Solo gaped at her. This time the smug smile wouldn't come. "Look, Your Holiness," he was finally able to stammer, "let's get something straight. I take orders only from one person— me."

"It's a wonder you're still alive," she shot back smoothly. A quick look down the corridor and she had started determinedly off in the other direction.

Solo looked at Luke, started to say something, then hesitated and simply shook his head slowly. "No reward is worth this. I don't know if there's enough credit in the universe to pay for putting up with *her* . . . Hey, slow down!"

Leia had started around a bend in the corridor, and they ran swiftly to catch up with her.

The half dozen troops milling around the entrance to the power trench were more interested in discussing the peculiar disturbance in the detention block than in paying attention to their present boring duty. So engrossed were they in speculation as to the cause of the trouble that they failed to notice the fey wraith behind them. It moved from shadow to shadow like a nightstalking ferret, freezing when one of the troopers seemed to turn slightly in its direction, moving on again as if walking on air.

Several minutes later one of the troopers frowned inside his armor, turning to where he thought he had sensed a movement near the opening to the main passageway. There was nothing but an undefinable something which the ghost-like Kenobi had left behind. Acutely uncomfortable yet understandably unwilling to confess to hallucinations, the trooper turned back to the more prosaic conversation of his fellows.

Someone finally discovered the two unconscious guards tied in the service lockers on board the captured freighter. Both men remained comatose despite all efforts to revive them.

Under the direction of several bickering officers, troopers carried their two armorless comrades down the ramp and toward the nearest hospital bay. On the way they passed two forms hidden by a small open service panel. Threepio and Artoo went unnoticed, despite their proximity to the hangar.

As soon as the troops had passed, Artoo finished removing a socket cover and hurriedly shoved his sensor arm into the opening. Lights commenced a wild flashing on his face and smoke started issuing from several seams in the small 'droid before a frantic Threepio could pull the arm free.

Immediately the smoke vanished, the undisciplined blinking faded to normalcy. Artoo emitted a few wilted beeps, successfully giving the impression of a human who had expected a glass of mild wine and instead unwittingly downed several gulps of something 180 proof.

"Well, next time watch where you stick your sensors," Threepio chastised his companion. "You could have fried your insides." He eyed the socket. "That's a power outlet, stupid, not an information terminal."

Artoo whistled a mournful apology. Together they hunted for the proper outlet.

* * *

Luke, Solo, Chewbacca, and the Princess reached the end of an empty hallway. It dead-ended before a large window which overlooked a hangar, giving them a sweeping, tantalizing view of the freighter just below.

Pulling out his comlink and looking around them with increasing nervousness, Luke spoke into the pickup. "See Threepio . . . do you copy?"

There was a threatening pause, then, "I read you, sir. We had to abandon the region around the office."

"Are you both safe?"

"For the moment, though I'm not sanguine about my old age. We're in the main hangar, across from the ship."

Luke looked toward the bay window in surprise. "I can't see you across the bay—we must be right above you. Stand by. We'll join you as soon as we can." He clicked off, smiling suddenly at Threepio's reference to his "old age." Sometimes the tall 'droid was more human than people.

"Wonder if the old man was able to knock out the tractor," Solo was muttering as he surveyed the scene below. A dozen or so troopers were moving in and out of the freighter.

"Getting back to the ship's going to be like flying through the five Fire Rings of Fornax."

Leia Organa turned long enough to glance in surprise from the ship to Solo. "You came here in that wreck? You're braver than I thought."

At once praised and insulted, Solo wasn't sure how to react. He settled for giving her a dirty look as they started back down the hallway, Chewbacca bringing up the rear.

Rounding a corner, the three humans came to an abrupt halt. So did the twenty Imperial troopers marching toward them. Reacting naturally—which is to say, without thinking—Solo drew his pistol and charged the platoon, yelling and howling in several languages at the top of his lungs.

Startled by the totally unexpected assault and wrongly assuming their attacker knew what he was doing, the troopers started to back away. Several wild shots from the Corellian's pistol initiated complete panic. Ranks and composure shattered, the troopers broke and fled down the passage.

Drunk with his own prowess, Solo continued the chase, turning to shout back at Luke, "Get to the ship. I'll take care of these!"

"Are you out of your mind?" Luke yelled at him. "Where do you think you're going?"

But Solo had already rounded a far bend in the corridor and didn't hear. Not that it would have made any difference.

Upset at his partner's disappearance, Chewbacca let out a thunderous if unsettled howl and rushed down the hallway after him. That left Luke and Leia standing alone in the empty corridor.

"Maybe I was too hard on your friend," she confessed reluctantly. "He certainly is courageous."

"He certainly is an idiot!" a furious Luke countered tightly. "I don't know what good it'll do us if he gets himself killed." Muted alarms suddenly sounded from the bay below and behind them.

"That's done it," Luke growled disgustedly. "Let's go." Together they started off in search of a way down to a hangar-deck level.

Solo continued his rout of all opposition, running at top speed down the long hallway, yelling and brandishing his pistol. Occasionally he got off a shot whose effect was more valuable psychologically than tactically.

Half the troops had already scattered down various subpassages and corridors. The ten troopers he continued to harry still raced headlong away from him, returning his fire only indifferently. Then they came up against a dead end, which forced them to turn and confront their opponents.

Seeing that the ten had halted, Solo likewise slowed. Gradually he came to a complete stop. Corellian and Imperials regarded one another silently. Several of the troopers were staring, not at Han but past him.

It suddenly occurred to Solo that he was very much alone, and the same thought was beginning to seep into the minds of the guards he was confronting. Embarrassment gave way rapidly to anger. Rifles and pistols started to come up. Solo took a step backward, fired one shot, then turned and ran like hell.

Chewbacca heard the whistle and crump of energy weapons firing as he lumbered lightly down the corridor. There was something odd about them, though: they sounded as if they were coming closer instead of moving away.

He was debating what to do when Solo came tearing around a corner and nearly ran him down. Seeing ten troopers in pursuit, the Wookiee decided to reserve his questions for a less confused moment. He turned and followed Solo back up the hallway.

* * *

Luke grabbed the Princess and pulled her back into a recess. She was about to retort angrily at his brusqueness when the sound of marching feet caused her to shrink back into the darkness with him.

A squad of soldiers hurried past, responding to the alarms that continued to ring steadily. Luke looked out at the retreating backs and tried to catch his breath. "Our only hope of reaching the ship is from the other side of the hangar. They already know someone's here." He started back down the corridor, motioning for her to follow.

Two guards appeared at the far end of the passageway, paused, and pointed directly at them. Turning, Luke and Leia began running back the way they had come. A larger squad of troopers rounded the far bend and came racing toward them.

Blocked ahead and behind, they hunted frantically for another way out. Then Leia spotted the cramped subhallway and gestured to it.

Luke fired at the nearest of their pursuers and joined her in running down the narrow passage. It looked like a minor service corridor. Behind them, pursuit sounded deafeningly loud in the confining space. But at least it minimized the amount of fire the troops could concentrate on them.

A thick hatchway appeared ahead. The lighting beyond turned dimmer, raising Luke's hopes. If they could lock the hatch even for a few moments and lose themselves somewhere beyond, they might have a chance of shaking their immediate tormentors.

But the hatch stayed open, showing no inclination to close automatically. Luke was about to let out a shout of triumph when the ground suddenly vanished ahead of him. His toes hanging over nothingness, he flailed to regain his balance, succeeding just in time to nearly go over the edge of the retracted catwalk anyway as the Princess plowed into him from behind.

The catwalk had been reduced to a stub protruding into empty air. A cool draft caressed Luke's face as he studied walls that soared to unseen heights overhead and plunged to fathomless depths below. The service shaft was employed in circulating and recycling the atmosphere of the station.

At the moment Luke was too frightened and concerned to be angry with the Princess for nearly sending them over the edge. Besides, other dangers competed for his attention. A burst of energy exploded above their heads, sending metal slivers flying.

"I think we made a wrong turn," he murmured, firing back

at the advancing troops and illuminating the narrow corridor behind them with destruction.

An open hatchway showed on the other side of the chasm. It might as well have been a light-year away. Hunting along the rim of the doorway, Leia located a switch and hit it quickly. The hatch door behind them slid shut with a resounding boom. At least that cut off fire from the rapidly nearing soldiers. It also left the two fugitives balanced precariously on a small section of catwalk barely a meter square. If the remaining section were to unexpectedly withdraw into the wall, they would see more of the battle station's interior than either wished.

Gesturing for the Princess to move aside as much as possible, Luke shielded his eyes and aimed the pistol at the hatch controls. A brief burst of energy melted them flush with the wall, insuring that no one could open it easily from the other side. Then he turned his attention to the vast cavity blocking their path to the opposite portal. It beckoned invitingly—a small yellow rectangle of freedom.

Only the soft rush of air from below sounded until Luke commented, "This is a shield-rated door, but it won't hold them back very long."

"We've got to get across there somehow," Leia agreed, once more examining the metal bordering the sealed doorway. "Find the controls for extending the bridge."

Some desperate searching produced nothing, while an ominous pounding and hissing sounded from behind the frozen door. A small spot of white appeared in the center of the metal, then began to spread and smoke.

"They're coming through!" Luke groaned.

The Princess turned carefully to stare across the gap. "This must be a single-unit bridge, with the controls only on the other side."

Reaching up to the point at the panel holding the unreachable controls, Luke's hand caught on something at his waist. A frustrated glance downward revealed the cause—and engendered a bit of practical insanity.

The cable coiled tightly in small loops was thin and fragile seeming, but it was general military-issue line and would have supported Chewbacca's weight easily. It certainly ought to hold Leia and himself. Pulling the cable free of the waist catch, he gauged its length, matching it against the width of the abyss. This should span the distance with plenty to spare.

"What now?" the Princess inquired curiously.

Luke didn't reply. Instead, he removed a small but heavy power unit from the utility belt of his armor and tied one end of the cable around it. Making sure the wrapping was secure, he stepped as close to the edge of their uncertain perch as he dared.

Whirling the weighted end of the cord in increasing circles, he let it arc across the gorge. It struck an outcropping of cylindrical conduits on the other side and fell downward. With forced patience he pulled the loose line back in, then recoiled it for another try.

Once again the weighted end orbited in ever greater circles, and again he flung it across the gap. He could feel the rising heat behind him as he let it go, heat from the melting metal doorway.

This time the heavy end looped around an outcropping of pipes above, wrapped itself several times around, and slipped, battery end down, into a crack between them. Leaning backward, he tugged and pulled on the cable, pulling on it at the same time as he tried to rest all his weight on it. The cable showed no sign of parting.

Wrapping the other end of the line several times around his waist and right arm, he reached out and pulled the Princess close to him with the other. The hatch door behind them was now a molten white, and liquid metal was running steadily from its borders.

Something warm and pleasant touched Luke's lips, alerting every nerve in his body. He looked down in shock at the Princess, his mouth still tingling from the kiss.

"Just for luck," she murmured with a slight, almost embarrassed smile as she put her arms around him. "We're going to need it."

Gripping the thin cable as tightly as possible with his left hand, Luke put his right over it, took a deep breath, and jumped out into air. If he had miscalculated the degree of arc in their swing, they would miss the open hatch and slam into the metal wall to either side or below it. If that happened he doubted he could maintain his grip on the rope.

The heart-halting transit was accomplished in less time than that thought. In a moment Luke was on the other side, scrambling on his knees to make sure they didn't fall back into the pit. Leia released her hold on him with admirable timing. She rolled forward and into the open hatchway, climbing gracefully to her feet as Luke fought to untangle himself from the cable.

A distant whine became a loud hiss, then a groan as the hatch door on the other side gave way. It collapsed inward and tumbled into the depths. If it touched bottom, Luke didn't hear it.

A few bolts struck the wall nearby. Luke turned his own weapon on the unsuccessful troopers and returned the fire even as Leia was pulling him into the passageway behind.

Once clear of the door he hit the activating switch. It shut tightly behind them. They would have several minutes, at least, without having to worry about being shot in the back. On the other hand, Luke didn't have the slightest idea where they were, and he found himself wondering what had happened to Han and Chewbacca.

Solo and his Wookiee partner had succeeded in shaking a portion of their pursuers. But it seemed that whenever they slipped free of several soldiers, more appeared to take their place. No question about it: the word was out on them.

Ahead, a series of shield doors was beginning to close.

"Hurry, Chewie!" Solo urged.

Chewbacca grunted once, breathing like an over-used engine. Despite his immense strength, the Wookiee was not built for long-distance sprinting. Only his enormous stride had enabled him to keep pace with the lithe Corellian. Chewbacca left a couple of hairs in one of the doors, but both slipped inside just before the five layers slammed shut.

"That ought to hold them for a while," Solo crowed with delight. The Wookiee growled something at him, but his partner fairly fluoresced with confidence.

"Of course I can find the ship from here—Corellians can't get lost." There came another growl, slightly accusing this time. Solo shrugged. "Tocneppil doesn't count; he wasn't a Corellian. Besides, I was drunk."

Ben Kenobi ducked into the shadows of a narrow passageway, seeming to become part of the metal itself as a large cluster of troopers hurried past him. Pausing to make certain they had all passed, he checked the corridor ahead before starting down it. But he failed to see the dark silhouette which eclipsed the light far behind him.

Kenobi had avoided one patrol after another, slowly working his way back toward the docking bay holding the freighter. Just another two turns and he should be at the hangar. What he would do then would be determined by how inconspicuous his charges had been.

That young Luke, the adventurous Corellian and his partner, and the two robots had been involved in something other than quiet napping he already suspected from the amount of activity he had observed while making his way back from the power trench. Surely all those troops hadn't been out hunting just for him!

But something else was troubling them, judging from the references he had overheard concerning a certain important prisoner, now escaped. That discovery had puzzled him, until he considered the restless natures of both Luke and Han Solo. Undoubtedly they were involved in some fashion.

Ben sensed something directly ahead and slowed cautiously. It had a most familiar feel to it, a half-remembered mental odor he could not quite place.

Then the figure stepped out in front of him, blocking his entry to the hangar not five meters away. The outline and size of the figure completed the momentary puzzle. It was the maturity of the mind he had sensed that had temporarily confused him. His hand moved naturally to the hilt of his deactivated saber.

"I have been waiting a long time, Obi-wan Kenobi," Darth Vader intoned solemnly. "We meet again at last. The circle has been completed." Kenobi sensed satisfaction beneath the hideous mask. "The presence I sensed earlier could only have been you."

Kenobi regarded the great form blocking his retreat and nodded slowly. He gave the impression of being more curious than impressed. "You still have much to learn."

"You were once my teacher," Vader admitted, "and I learned much from you. But the time of learning has long passed, and I am the master now."

The logic that had constituted the missing link in his brilliant pupil remained as absent as before. There would be no reasoning here, Kenobi knew. Igniting his saber, he assumed the pose of warrior-ready, a movement accomplished with the ease and elegance of a dancer.

Rather roughly, Vader imitated the movement. Several minutes followed without motion as the two men remained staring at each other, as if waiting for some proper, as yet unspoken signal.

Kenobi blinked once, shook his head, and tried to clear his

eyes, which had begun to water slightly. Sweat beaded up on his forehead, and his eyelids fluttered again.

"Your powers are weak," Vader noted emotionlessly. "Old man, you should never have come back. It will make your end less peaceful than you might have wished."

"You sense only a part of the force, Darth," Kenobi murmured with the assurance of one to whom death is merely another sensation, like sleeping or making love or touching a candle. "As always, you perceive its reality as little as a utensil perceives the taste of food."

Executing a move of incredible swiftness for one so old, Kenobi lunged at the massive shape. Vader blocked the stab with equal speed, riposting with a counterslash that Kenobi barely parried. Another parry and Kenobi countered again, using this opportunity to move around the towering Dark Lord.

They continued to trade blows, with the old man now backing toward the hangar. Once, his saber and Vader's locked, the interaction of the two energy fields producing a violent sparking and flashing. A low buzzing sound rose from the straining power units as each saber sought to override the other.

Threepio peeked around the entrance to the docking bay, worriedly counting the number of troopers milling around the deserted freighter.

"Where could they be? Oh, oh."

He ducked back out of sight just as one of the guards glanced in his direction. A second, more cautious appraisal was more rewarding. It revealed Han Solo and Chewbacca hugging the wall of another tunnel on the far side of the bay.

Solo also was nonplussed at the number of guards. He muttered, "Didn't we just leave this party?"

Chewbacca grunted, and both turned, only to relax and lower their weapons at the sight of Luke and the Princess.

"What kept you?" Solo quipped mirthlessly.

"We ran into," Leia explained, panting heavily, "some old friends."

Luke was staring at the freighter. "Is the ship all right?"

"Seems okay," was Solo's analysis. "It doesn't look like they've removed anything or disturbed her engines. The problem's going to be getting to it."

Leia suddenly pointed to one of the opposite tunnels. "Look!"

Illuminated by the flare from contacting energy fields, Ben

Kenobi and Darth Vader were backing toward the bay. The fight attracted the attention of others beside the Senator. Every one of the guards moved in for a better view of the Olympian conflict.

"Now's our chance," Solo observed, starting forward.

All seven of the troopers guarding the ship broke and rushed toward the combatants, going to the Dark Lord's aid. Threepio barely ducked aside as they ran past him. Turning back into the alcove, he yelled to his companion.

"Unplug yourself, Artoo. We're leaving." As soon as the Artoo unit slipped his sensor arm free of the socket, the two 'droids began to slowly edge out into the open bay.

Kenobi heard the approaching commotion and spared a glance back into the hangar. The squad of troopers bearing down on him was enough to show that he was trapped.

Vader took immediate advantage of the momentary distraction to bring his saber over and down. Kenobi somehow managed to deflect the sweeping blow, at once parrying and turning a complete circle.

"You still have your skill, but your power fades. Prepare to meet the force, Obi-wan."

Kenobi gauged the shrinking distance between the oncoming troops and himself, then turned a pitying gaze on Vader. "This is a fight you cannot win, Darth. Your power has matured since I taught you, but I too have grown much since our parting. If my blade finds its mark, you will cease to exist. But if you cut me down, I will only become more powerful. Heed my words."

"Your philosophies no longer confuse me, old man," Vader growled contemptuously. "I am the master now."

Once again he lunged forward, feinting, and then slashing in a deadly downward arc with the saber. It struck home, cutting the old man cleanly in half. There was a brief flash as Kenobi's cloak fluttered to the deck in two neat sections.

But Ben Kenobi was not in it. Wary of some tricks, Vader poked at the empty cloak sections with the saber. There was no sign of the old man. He had vanished as though he had never existed.

The guards slowed their approach and joined Vader in examining the place where Kenobi had stood seconds before. Several of them muttered, and even the awesome presence of the Sith Lord couldn't keep a few of them from feeling a little afraid.

* * *

Once the guards had turned and dashed for the far tunnel, Solo and the others started for the starship—until Luke saw Kenobi cut in two. Instantly he shifted direction and was moving toward the guards.

"Ben!" he screamed, firing wildly toward the troops. Solo cursed, but turned to fire in support of Luke.

One of the energy bolts struck the safety release on the tunnel blast door. The emergency hold broken, the heavy door fairly exploded downward. Both the guards and Vader leaped clear—the guards into the bay and Vader backward, to the opposite side of the door.

Solo had turned and started for the entrance to the ship, but he paused as he saw Luke running toward the guards.

"It's too late!" Leia yelled at him. "It's over."

"No!" Luke half shouted, half sobbed.

A familiar, yet different voice rang in his ears—Ben's voice. "Luke . . . listen!" was all it said.

Bewildered, Luke turned to hunt for the source of that admonition. He only saw Leia beckoning to him as she followed Artoo and Threepio up the ramp.

"Come on! There's no time."

Hesitating, his mind still on that imagined voice (or was it imagined?), a confused Luke took aim and felled several soldiers before he, too, whirled and retreated into the freighter.

XI

DAZED, Luke staggered toward the front of the ship. He barely noticed the sound of energy bolts, too weak to penetrate the ship's deflectors, exploding harmlessly outside. His own safety was currently of little concern to him. With misty eyes he stared as Chewbacca and Solo adjusted controls.

"I hope that old man managed to knock out that tractor

beam," the Corellian was saying, "or this is going to be a very short ride."

Ignoring him, Luke returned to the hold area and slumped into a seat, his head falling into his hands. Leia Organa regarded him quietly for a while, then removed her cloak. Moving to him, she placed it gently around his shoulders.

"There wasn't anything you could have done," she whispered comfortingly. "It was all over in an instant."

"I can't believe he's gone," came Luke's reply, his voice a ghost of a whisper. "I can't."

Solo shifted a lever, staring nervously ahead. But the massive bay door was constructed to respond to the approach of any vessel. The safety feature now served to facilitate their escape as the freighter slipped quickly past the still-opening door and out into free space.

"Nothing," Solo sighed, studying several readouts with profound satisfaction. "Not so much as an erg of come-hither. He did it, all right."

Chewbacca rumbled something, and the pilot's attention shifted to another series of gauges. "Right, Chewie. I forgot, for a moment, that there are other ways of persuading us to return." His teeth flashed in a grin of determination. "But the only way they'll get us back in that traveling tomb is in pieces. Take over."

Whirling, he ran out of the cockpit. "Come with me, kid," he shouted at Luke as he entered the hold. "We're not out of this yet."

Luke didn't respond, didn't move, and Leia turned an angry face to Solo. "Leave him alone. Can't you see what the old man meant to him?"

An explosion jarred the ship, nearly tumbling Solo to the deck.

"So what? The old man gave himself to give us a chance to get away. You want to waste that, Luke? You want Kenobi to have wasted himself?"

Luke's head came up and he stared with vacant eyes at the Corellian. No, not quite vacant . . . There was something too old and unpleasant shining blindly in the back of them. Without a word, he threw off the cloak and joined Solo.

Giving him a reassuring smile, Solo gestured down a narrow accessway. Luke looked in the indicated direction, smiled grimly, and rushed down it as Solo started down the opposing passage.

Luke found himself in a large rotating bubble protruding from the side of the ship. A long, wicked-looking tube whose purpose was instantly apparent projected from the apex of the transparent hemisphere. Luke settled himself into the seat and commenced a rapid study of the controls. Activator here, firing grip here . . . He had fired such weapons a thousand times before—in his dreams.

Forward, Chewbacca and Leia were searching the speckled pit outside for the attacking fighters represented by firepricks on several screens. Chewbacca suddenly growled throatily and pulled back on several controls as Leia let out a yelp.

"Here they come."

The starfield wheeled around Luke as an Imperial TIE fighter raced toward him and then swung overhead to vanish into the distance. Within the tiny cockpit its pilot frowned as the supposedly battered freighter darted out of range. Adjusting his own controls, he swung up and over in a high arc intended to take him on a fresh intercept course with the escaping ship.

Solo fired at another fighter, and its pilot nearly slammed his engine through its mountings as he fought to avoid the powerful energy bolts. As he did so, his hurried maneuver brought him under and around to the other side of the freighter. Even as he was lowering the glare reflector over his eyes, Luke opened up on the racing fighter.

Chewbacca was alternating his attention between the instruments and the tracking screens, while Leia strained to separate distant stars from nearby assassins.

Two fighters dove simultaneously on the twisting, spiraling freighter, trying to line their weapons on the unexpectedly flexible craft. Solo fired at the descending globes, and Luke followed with his own weapon a second later. Both fired on the starship and then shot past.

"They're coming in too fast," Luke yelled into his comlink.

Another enemy bolt struck the freighter forward and was barely shunted aside by its deflectors. The cockpit shuddered violently, and gauges whined in protest at the quantity of energy they were being asked to monitor and compensate for.

Chewbacca muttered something to Leia, and she murmured a soft reply as if she almost understood.

Another fighter unloosed a barrage on the freighter, only this time the bolt pierced an overloaded screen and actually struck the side of the ship. Though partially deflected, it still carried enough power to blow out a large control panel in the main passageway, sending a rain of sparks and smoke in all directions. Artoo Detoo started stolidly toward the miniature inferno as the ship lurched crazily, throwing the less stable Threepio into a cabinet full of component chips.

A warning light began to wink for attention in the cockpit. Chewbacca muttered to Leia, who stared at him worriedly and wished for the gift of Wookiee-gab.

Then a fighter floated down on the damaged freighter, right into Luke's sights. His mouth moving silently, Luke fired at it. The incredibly agile little vessel darted out of his range, but as it passed beneath them Solo picked it up instantly, and commenced a steady following fire. Without warning the fighter erupted in an incredible flash of multicolored light, throwing a billion bits of superheated metal to every section of the cosmos.

Solo whirled and gave Luke a victory wave, which the younger man gleefully returned. Then they turned back to their weapons as yet another fighter stormed over the freighter's hull, firing at its transmitter dish.

In the middle of the main passageway, angry flames raged around a stubby cylindrical shape. A fine white powdery spray issued from Artoo Detoo's head. Wherever it touched, the fire retreated sharply.

Luke tried to relax, to become a part of the weapon. Almost without being aware of it, he was firing at a retreating Imperial. When he blinked, it was to see the flaming fragments of the enemy craft forming a perfect ball of light outside the turret. It was his turn to spin and flash the Corellian a grin of triumph.

In the cockpit, Leia paid close attention to scattered readouts as well as searching the sky for additional ships. She directed her voice toward an open mike.

"There are still two more of them out there. Looks like we've lost the lateral monitors and the starboard deflector shield."

"Don't worry," Solo told her, with as much hope as confidence, "she'll hold together." He gave the walls a pleading stare. "You hear me, ship? Hold together! Chewie, try to keep them on our port side. If we—"

He was forced to break off as a TIE fighter seemed to materialize out of nowhere, energy bolts reaching out from it toward him. Its companion craft came up on the freighter's other side and Luke found himself firing steadily at it, ignoring the immensely powerful energy it threw at him. At the last possible instant before it passed out of range, he swung the weapon's nozzle minutely, his finger tightening convulsively on the fire control. The Imperial fighter turned into a rapidly expanding cloud of phosphorescing dust. The other fighter apparently considered the shrunken odds, turned, and retreated at top speed.

"We've made it!" Leia shouted, turning to give the startled Wookiee an unexpected hug. He growled at her—very softly.

Darth Vader strode into the control room where Governor Tarkin stood staring at a huge, brilliantly lit screen. It displayed a sea of stars, but it was not the spectacular view which absorbed the Governor's thoughts at the moment. He barely glanced around as Vader entered.

"Are they away?" the Dark Lord demanded.

"They've just completed the jump to hyperspace. No doubt they are at this very moment congratulating themselves on their daring and success." Now Tarkin turned to face Vader, a hint of warning in his tone.

"I'm taking an awful chance, on your insistence, Vader. This had better work. Are you certain the homing beacon is secure aboard their ship?"

Vader exuded confidence beneath the reflective black mask. "There is nothing to fear. This will be a day long remembered. It already has been witness to the final extinction of the Jedi. Soon it will see the end of the Alliance and the rebellion."

Solo switched places with Chewbacca, the Wookiee grateful for the opportunity to relinquish the controls. As the Corellian moved aft to check the extent of the damage, a determined-looking Leia passed him in the corridor.

"What do you think, sweetheart?" Solo inquired, well pleased with himself. "Not a bad bit of rescuing. You know, sometimes I amaze even myself."

"That doesn't sound too hard," she admitted readily. "The important thing is not my safety, but the fact that the information in the R-2 'droid is still intact."

"What's that 'droid carrying that's so important, anyway?"

Leia considered the blazing starfield forward. "Complete technical schematics of the battle station. I only hope that when the data is analyzed, a weakness can be found. Until then, until the station itself is destroyed, we must go on. This war isn't over yet."

"It is for me," objected the pilot. "I'm not on this mission for your revolution. Economics interest me, not politics. There's business to be done under any government. And I'm not doing it for you, Princess. I expect to be well paid for risking my ship and my hide."

"You needn't worry about your reward," she assured him sadly, turning to leave. "If money is what you love . . . that's what you will receive."

On leaving the cockpit she saw Luke coming forward, and she spoke softly to him in passing. "Your friend is indeed a mercenary. I wonder if he really cares about anything—or anybody."

Luke stared after her until she disappeared into the main hold area, then whispered, "*I* do . . . *I* care." Then he moved into the cockpit and sat in the seat Chewbacca had just vacated.

"What do you think of her, Han?"

Solo didn't hesitate. "I try not to."

Luke probably hadn't intended his response to be audible, but Solo overheard his murmur of "Good" none the less.

"Still," Solo ventured thoughtfully, "she's got a lot of spirit to go with her sass. I don't know, do you think it's possible for a Princess and a guy like me . . . ?"

"No," Luke cut him off sharply. He turned and looked away.

Solo smiled at the younger man's jealousy, uncertain in his own mind whether he had added the comment to bait his naive friend—or because it was the truth.

Yavin was not a habitable world. The huge gas giant was patterned with pastel high-altitude cloud formations. Here and there the softly lambent atmosphere was molded by cyclonic storms composed of six-hundred-kilometer-per-hour winds which boiled rolling gases up from the Yavinesque troposphere. It was a world of lingering beauty and quick death for any who might try to penetrate to its comparatively small core of frozen liquids.

Several of the giant planet's numerous moons, however, were planet-sized themselves, and of these, three could support humanoid life. Particularly inviting was the satellite designated by the system's discoverers as number four. It shone like an emerald in Yavin's necklace of moons, rich with plant and animal life. But it was not listed among those worlds supporting human settlement. Yavin was located too far from the settled regions of the galaxy.

Perhaps the latter reason, or both, or a combination of causes still unknown had been responsible for whatever race had once risen from satellite four's jungles, only to disappear quietly long before the first human explorer set foot on the tiny world. Little was known of them save that they left a number of impressive monuments, and that they were one of the many races which had aspired to the stars only to have their desperate reach fall short.

Now all that remained were the mounds and foliage-clad clumps formed by jungle-covered buildings. But though they had sunk back into the dust, their artifacts and their world continued to serve an important purpose.

Strange cries and barely perceptible moans sounded from every tree and copse; hoots and growls and strange mutterings issued from creatures content to remain concealed in the dense undergrowth. Whenever dawn broke over moon the fourth, heralding one of its long days, an especially feral chorus of shrieks and weirdly modulated screams would resound through the thick mist.

Even stranger sounds surged continually from one particular place. Here lay the most impressive of those edifices which a vanished race had raised toward the heavens. It was a temple, a roughly pyramidal structure so colossal that it seemed impossible it could have been built without the aid of modern gravitonic construction techniques. Yet all evidence pointed only to simple machines, hand technology—and, perhaps, devices alien and long lost.

While the science of this moon's inhabitants had led them to a dead end as far as offworld travel was concerned, they had produced several discoveries which in certain ways surpassed similar Imperial accomplishments—one of which involved a still unexplained method of cutting and transporting gargantuan blocks of stone from the crust of the moon.

From these monstrous blocks of solid rock, the massive temple had been constructed. The jungle had scaled even its soaring crest, clothing it in rich green and brown. Only near its base, in the temple front, did the jungle slide away completely, to reveal a long, dark entrance cut by its builders and enlarged to suit the needs of the structure's present occupants.

A tiny machine, its smooth metal sides and silvery hue incongruous amidst the all-pervasive green, appeared in the forest. It hummed like a fat, swollen beetle as it conveyed its cluster of passengers toward the open temple base. Crossing a considerable clearing, it was soon swallowed up by the dark maw in the front of the massive structure, leaving the jungle once more in the paws and claws of invisible squallers and screechers.

The original builders would never have recognized the interior of their temple. Seamed metal had replaced rock, and poured paneling did service for chamber division in place of wood. Nor would they have been able to see the buried layers excavated into the rock below, layers which contained hangar upon hangar linked by powerful elevators.

A landspeeder came to a gradual stop within the temple, whose first level was the uppermost of those ship-filled hangars. Its engine died obediently as the vehicle settled to the ground. A noisy cluster of humans waiting nearby ceased their conversation and rushed toward the craft.

Fortunately Leia Organa quickly emerged from the speeder, or the man who reached it first might have pulled her bodily from it, so great was his delight at the sight of her. He settled for giving her a smothering hug as his companions called their own greetings.

"Your're safe! We'd feared you'd been killed." Abruptly he composed himself, stepped away from her, and executed a formal bow. "When we heard about Alderaan, we were afraid that you were . . . lost along with the rest of the population."

"All that is past history, Commander Willard," she said. "We have a future to live for. Alderaan and its people are gone." Her voice turned bitter cold, frightening in so delicate-looking a person. "We must see that such does not happen again.

"We don't have time for our sorrows, Commander," she continued briskly. "The battle station has surely tracked us here."

Solo started to protest, but she shut him up with logic and a stern look.

"That's the only explanation for the ease of our escape. They sent only four TIE fighters after us. They could as easily have launched a hundred."

Solo had no reply for that, but continued to fume silently. Then Leia gestured at Artoo Detoo.

"You must use the information locked in this R-2 'droid to form a plan of attack. It's our only hope. The station itself is more powerful than anyone suspected." Her voice dropped. "If the data does not yield a weakness, there will be no stopping them."

Luke was then treated to a sight unique in his experience, unique in most men's. Several rebel technicians walked up to Artoo Detoo, positioned themselves around him, and gently hoisted him in their arms. This was the first, and probably the last time he would ever see a robot being carried respectfully by men.

Theoretically, no weapon could penetrate the exceptionally dense stone of the ancient temple, but Luke had seen the shattered remains of Alderaan and knew that for those in the incredible battle station the entire moon would present simply another abstract problem in mass-energy conversion.

Little Artoo Detoo rested comfortably in a place of honor, his body radiating computer and data-bank hookups like a metal hairdo. On an array of screens and readouts nearby the technical information stored on the submicroscopic record tape within the robot's brain was being played out. Hours of it—diagrams, charts, statistics.

First the rush of material was slowed and digested by more sophisticated computer minds. Then the most critical information was turned over to human analysts for detailed evaluation.

All the while See Threepio stood close to Artoo, marveling at how so much complex data could be stored in the mind of so simple a 'droid.

The central briefing room was located deep within the bowels of the temple. The long, low-ceiling auditorium was dominated by a raised dais and huge electronic display screen at its far end. Pilots, navigators, and a sprinkling of Artoo units filled the seats. Impatient, and feeling very out of place, Han Solo and Chewbacca stood as far away from the stage, with its assemblage of officers and Senators, as possible. Solo scanned the crowd, searching for Luke. Despite some common sense entreaties, the crazy kid had gone and joined the regular pilots. He didn't see Luke, but he recognized the Princess as she talked somberly with some bemedaled oldster.

When a tall, dignified gentleman with too many deaths on his soul moved to stand by the far side of the screen, Solo turned his attention to him, as did everyone else in the room. As soon as an expectant silence had gripped the crowd, General Jan Dodonna adjusted the tiny mike on his chest and indicated the small group seated close to him.

"You all know these people," he intoned with quiet power. "They are the Senators and Generals whose worlds have given us support, whether open or covert. They have come to be with us in what may well prove to be the decisive moment." He let his gaze touch many in the crowd, and none who were so favored remained unmoved.

"The Imperial battle station you now all have heard of is approaching from the far side of Yavin and its sun. That gives us a little extra time, but it must be stopped—once and for all—before it can reach this moon, before it can bring its weaponry to bear on us as it did on Alderaan." A murmur ran through the crowd at the mention of that world, so callously obliterated.

"The station," Dodonna went on, "is heavily shielded and mounts more firepower than half the Imperial fleet. But its defenses were designed to fend off large-scale, capital ship assaults. A small, one- or two-man fighter should be able to slip through its defensive screens."

A slim, supple man who resembled an older version of Han Solo rose. Dodonna acknowledged his presence. "What is it, Red Leader?"

The man gestured toward the display screen, which showed a computer portrait of the battle station. "Pardon me for asking, sir, but what good are our *snub* fighters going to be against *that*?"

Dodonna considered. "Well, the Empire doesn't think a one-man fighter is any threat to anything except another small ship, like a TIE fighter, or they would have provided tighter screens. Apparently they're convinced that their defensive weaponry can fend off any light attacks.

"But an analysis of the plans provided by Princess Leia has revealed what we think is a weakness in the station's design. A big ship couldn't get near it, but an X- or Y-wing fighter might.

"It's a small thermal exhaust port. Its size belies its importance, as it appears to be an unshielded shaft that runs directly into the main reactor system powering the station. Since this serves as an emergency outlet for waste heat in the event of reactor overproduction, its usefulness would be eliminated by particle shielding. A direct hit would initiate a chain reaction that would destroy the station."

Mutterings of disbelief ran through the room. The more experienced the pilot, the greater his expressed disbelief.

"I didn't say your approach would be easy," Dodonna admonished them. He gestured at the screen. "You must maneuver straight in down this shaft, level off in the trench, and skim the surface to—this point. The target is only two meters across. It will take a precise hit at exactly ninety degrees to reach the reactor systematization. And only a direct hit will start the complete reaction.

"I said the port wasn't particle-shielded. However, it is completely ray-shielded. That means no energy beams. You'll have to use proton torpedoes."

A few of the pilots laughed humorlessly. One of them was a teenaged fighter jockey seated next to Luke who bore the unlikely name of Wedge Antilles. Artoo Detoo was there also, seated next to another Artoo unit who emitted a long whistle of hopelessness.

"A two-meter target at maximum speed—with a torpedo, yet," Antilles snorted. "That's impossible even for the computer."

"But it's not impossible," protested Luke. "I used to bullseye womp-rats in my T-16 back home. They're not much bigger than two meters."

"Is that so?" the rakishly uniformed youth noted derisively. "Tell me, when you were going after your particular varmint, were there a thousand other, what did you call it, 'womp-rats' armed with power rifles firing up at you?" He shook his head sadly.

"With all that firepower on the station directed at us, this will take a little more than barnyard marksmanship, believe me."

As if to confirm Antilles' pessimism, Dodonna indicated a string of lights on the ever-changing schematic. "Take special note of these emplacements. There's a heavy concentration of firepower on the latitudinal axes, as well as several dense circum-polar clusters.

"Also, their field generators will probably create a lot of distortion, especially in and around the trench. I figure that maneuverability in that sector will be less than point three." This produced more murmurs and a few groans from the assembly.

"Remember," the General went on, "you must achieve a direct hit. Yellow squadron will cover for Red on the first run. Green will cover Blue on the second. Any questions?"

A muted buzz filled the room. One man stood, lean and handsome—too much so, it seemed, to be ready to throw away his life for something as abstract as freedom.

"What if both runs fail? What happens after that?"

Dodonna smiled tightly. "There won't be any 'after that.' " The man nodded slowly, understandingly, and sat down. "Anyone else?" Silence now, pregnant with expectation.

"Then man your ships, and may the force be with you."

Like oil draining from a shallow pot, the seated ranks of men, women, and machines rose and flowed toward the exits.

Elevators hummed busily, lifting more and more deadly shapes from buried depths to the staging area in the primary temple hangar as Luke, Threepio, and Artoo Detoo walked toward the hangar entrance.

Neither the bustling flight crews, nor the pilots performing final checkouts, nor the massive sparks thrown off as power couplings were disconnected captured Luke's attention at the moment. Instead, it was held by the activity of two far more familiar figures.

Solo and Chewbacca were loading a pile of small strongboxes onto an armored landspeeder. They were completely absorbed with this activity, ignoring the preparations going on all around them.

Solo glanced up briefly as Luke and the robots approached, then returned to his loading. Luke simply watched sadly, conflicting emotions careening confusedly off one another inside him. Solo was cocky, reckless, intolerant, and smug. He was also brave to a fault, instructive, and unfailingly cheery. The combination made for a confusing friend—but a friend nonetheless.

"You got your reward," Luke finally observed, indicating the boxes. Solo nodded once. "And you're leaving, then?"

"That's right, kid. I've got some old debts to pay off, and even if I didn't, I don't think I'd be fool enough to stick around here." He eyed Luke appraisingly. "You're pretty good in a scrap, kid. Why don't you come with us? I could use you."

The mercenary gleam in Solo's eyes only made Luke mad. "Why don't you look around and see something besides yourself for a change? You know what's going to happen here, what they're up against. They could use a good pilot. But you're turning your back on them."

Solo didn't appear upset at Luke's tirade. "What good's a reward if you're not around to spend it? Attacking that battle station isn't my idea of courage—more like suicide."

"Yeah . . . Take care of yourself, Han," Luke said quietly, turning to leave. "But I guess that's what you're best at, isn't it?" He started back into the hangar depths, flanked by the two 'droids.

Solo stared after him, hesitated, then called, "Hey, Luke . . . may the force be with you." Luke looked back to see Solo wink at him. He waved—sort of. Then he was swallowed up by moving mechanics and machinery.

Solo returned to his work, lifted a box—and stopped, to see Chewbacca gazing fixedly at him.

"What are you staring at, gruesome? I know what I'm doing. Get back to work!"

Slowly, still eyeing his partner, the Wookiee returned to the task of loading the heavy crates.

Sorrowful thoughts of Solo vanished when Luke saw the petite, slim figure standing by his ship—the ship he had been granted.

"Are you sure this is what you want?" Princess Leia asked him. "It could be a deadly reward."

Luke's eyes were filled with the sleek, venomous metal shape. "More than anything."

"Then what's wrong?"

Luke looked back at her and shrugged. "It's Han. I thought he'd change his mind. I thought he'd join us."

"A man must follow his own path," she told him, sounding now like a Senator. "No one can choose it for him. Han Solo's priorities differ from ours. I wish it were otherwise, but I can't find it in my heart to condemn him." She stood on tiptoes, gave him a quick, almost embarrassed kiss, and turned to go. "May the force be with you."

"I only wish," Luke murmured to himself as he started back to his ship, "Ben were here."

So intent was he on thoughts of Kenobi, the Princess, and Han that he didn't notice the larger figure which tightly locked on to his arm. He turned, his initial anger gone instantly in astonishment as he recognized the figure.

"Luke!" the slightly older man exclaimed. "I don't believe it! How'd you get here? Are you going out with us?"

"Biggs!" Luke embraced his friend warmly. "Of course I'll be up there with you." His smile faded slightly. "I haven't got a choice, anymore." Then he brightened again. "Listen, have I got some stories to tell you . . ."

The steady whooping and laughing the two made was in marked contrast to the solemnity with which the other men and women in the hangar went about their business. The commotion attracted the attention of an older, war-worn man known to the younger pilots only as Blue Leader.

His face wrinkled with curiosity as he approached the two younger men. It was a face scorched by the same fire that flickered in his eyes, a blaze kindled not by revolutionary fervor but by years of living through and witnessing far too much injustice. Behind that fatherly visage a raging demon fought to escape. Soon, very soon, he would be free to let it loose.

Now he was interested in these two young men, who in a few hours were likely to be particles of frozen meat floating about Yavin. One of them he recognized.

"Aren't you Luke Skywalker? Have you been checked out on the Incom T-65?"

"Sir," Biggs put in before his friend could reply, "Luke's the best bush pilot in the outer-rim territories."

The older man patted Luke reassuringly on the back as they studied his waiting ship. "Something to be proud of. I've got over a thousand hours in an Incom skyhopper myself." He paused a moment before going on.

"I met your father once when I was just a boy, Luke. He was a great pilot. You'll do all right out there. If you've got half your father's skill, you'll do a damn sight better than all right."

"Thank you, sir. I'll try."

"There's not much difference control-wise between an X-wing T-65," Blue Leader went on, "and a skyhopper." His smile turned ferocious. "Except the payload's of a somewhat different nature."

He left them and hurried toward his own ship. Luke had a hundred questions to ask him, and no time for even one.

"I've got to get aboard my own boat, Luke. Listen, you'll tell me your stories when we come back. All right?"

"All right. I told you I'd make it here someday, Biggs."

"You did." His friend was moving toward a cluster of waiting fighters, adjusting his flight suit. "It's going to be like old times, Luke. We're a couple of shooting stars that can't be stopped!"

Luke laughed. They used to reassure themselves with that cry when they piloted starships of sandhills and dead logs behind the flaking, pitted buildings of Anchorhead . . . years and years ago.

Once more Luke turned toward his ship, admiring its deadly lines. Despite Blue Leader's assurances, he had to admit that it didn't look much like an Incom skyhopper. Artoo Detoo was being snuggled into the R-2 socket behind the fighter cockpit. A forlorn metal figure stood below, watching the operation and shuffling nervously about.

"Hold on tight," See Threepio was cautioning the smaller robot. "You've got to come back. If you don't come back, who am I going to have to yell at?'' For Threepio, that query amounted to an overwhelming outburst of emotion.

Artoo beeped confidently down at his friend, however, as Luke mounted the cockpit entry. Farther down the hangar he saw Blue Leader already set in his acceleration chair and signaling to his ground crew. Another roar was added to the monstrous din filling the hangar area as ship after ship activated its engines. In that enclosed rectangle of temple the steady thunder was overpowering.

Slipping into the cockpit seat, Luke studied the various controls as ground attendants began wiring him via cords and umbilicals into the ship. His confidence increased steadily. The instrumentation was necessarily simplified and, as Blue Leader had indicated, much like his old skyhopper.

Something patted his helmet, and he glanced left to see the crew chief leaning close. He had to shout to be heard above the deafening howl of multiple engines. "That R-2 unit of yours seems a little beat up. Do you want a new one?"

Luke glanced briefly back at the secured 'droid before replying. Artoo Detoo looked like a permanent piece of the fighter.

"Not on your life. That 'droid and I have been through a lot together. All secure, Artoo?" The 'droid replied with a reassuring beep.

As the ground chief jumped clear, Luke commenced the final checkout of all instruments. It slowly occurred to him what he and the others were about to attempt. Not that his personal feelings could override his decision to join them. He was no longer an individual, functioning solely to satisfy his personal needs. Something now bound him to every other man and woman in this hangar.

All around him, scattered scenes of good-bye were taking place—some serious, some kidding, all with the true emotion of the moment masked by efficiency. Luke turned away from where one pilot left a mechanic, possibly a sister or wife, or just a friend, with a sharp, passionate kiss.

He wondered how many of them had their own little debts to settle with the Empire. Something crackled in his helmet. In response, he touched a small lever. The ship began to roll forward, slowly but with increasing speed, toward the gaping mouth of the temple.

XII

LEIA Organa sat silently before the huge display screen on which Yavin and its moons were displayed. A large red dot moved steadily toward the fourth of those satellites. Dodonna and several other field commanders of the Alliance stood behind her, their eyes also intent on the screen. Tiny green flecks began to appear around the fourth moon, to coalesce into small clouds like hovering emerald gnats.

Dodonna put a hand on her shoulder. It was comforting. "The red represents the progress of the Imperial battle station as it moves deeper into Yavin's system."

"Our ships are all away," a Commander behind him declared.

A single man stood alone in the cylindrical hold, secured to the top of a rapier-thin tower. Staring through fixed-mount electrobinoculars, he was the sole visible representative of the vast technology buried in the green purgatory below.

Muted cries, moans, and primeval gurglings drifted up to him from the highest treetops. Some were frightening, some less so, but none were as indicative of power held in check as the four silvery starships which burst into view above the observer. Keeping a tight formation, they exploded through humid air to vanish in seconds into the morning cloud cover far above. Sound-shadows rattled the trees moments later, in a forlorn attempt to catch up to the engines which had produced them.

Slowly assuming attack formations combining X- and Y-wing ships, the various fighters began to move outward from the moon, out past the oceanic atmosphere of giant Yavin, out to meet the technologic executioner.

The man who had observed the byplay between Biggs and Luke now lowered his glare visor and adjusted his half-automatic, half-manual gunsights as he checked the ships to either side of him.

"Blue boys," he addressed his intership pickup, "this is Blue Leader. Adjust your selectors and check in. Approaching target at one point three . . ."

Ahead, the bright sphere of what looked like one of Yavin's moons but wasn't began to glow with increasing brightness. It shone with an eerie metallic glow utterly unlike that of any natural satellite. As he watched the giant battle station make its way around the rim of Yavin, Blue Leader's thoughts traveled back over the years. Over the uncountable injustices, the innocents taken away for interrogation and never heard from again—the whole multitude of evils incurred by an increasingly corrupt and indifferent Imperial government. All those terrors and agonies were concentrated, magnified, represented by the single bloated feat of engineering they were approaching now.

"This is it, boys," he said to the mike. "Blue Two, you're too far out. Close it up, Wedge."

The young pilot Luke had encountered in the temple briefing room glanced to starboard, then back to his instruments. He executed a slight adjustment, frowning. "Sorry, boss. My ranger seems to be a few points off. I'll have to go on manual."

"Check, Blue Two. Watch yourself. All ships, stand by to lock S-foils in attack mode."

One after another, from Luke and Biggs, Wedge and the other members of Blue assault squadron, the replies came back. "Standing by . . ."

"Execute," Blue Leader commanded, when John D. and Piggy had indicated they were in readiness.

The double wings on the X-wing fighters split apart, like narrow seeds. Each fighter now displayed four wings, its wing-mounted armament and quadruple engines now deployed for maximum firepower and maneuverability.

Ahead, the Imperial station continued to grow. Surface features became visible as each pilot recognized docking bays, broadcast antennae, and other man-made mountains and canyons.

As he neared that threatening black sphere for the second time, Luke's breathing grew faster. Automatic life-support machinery detected the respiratory shift and compensated properly.

Something began to buffet his ship, almost as if he were back in his skyhopper again, wrestling with the unpredictable winds of Tatooine. He experienced a bad moment of uncertainty until the calming voice of Blue Leader sounded in his ears.

"We're passing through their outer shields. Hold tight. Lock down freeze-floating controls and switch your own deflectors on, double front."

The shaking and buffeting continued, worsened. Not knowing how to compensate, Luke did exactly what he should have: remained in control and followed orders. Then the turbulence was gone and the deathly cold peacefulness of space had returned.

"That's it, we're through," Blue Leader told them quietly. "Keep all channels silent until we're on top of them. It doesn't look like they're expecting much resistance."

Though half the great station remained in shadow, they were now near enough for Luke to be able to discern individual lights on its surface. A ship that could show phases matching a moon . . . once again he marveled at the misplaced ingenuity and effort which had gone into its construction. Thousands of lights scattered across its curving expanse gave it the appearance of a floating city.

Some of Luke's comrades, since this was their first sight of the station, were even more impressed. "Look at the size of that thing!" Wedge Antilles gasped over his open pickup.

"Cut the chatter, Blue Two," Blue Leader ordered. "Accelerate to attack velocity."

Grim determination showed in Luke's expression as he flipped several switches above his head and began adjusting his computer target readout. Artoo Detoo reexamined the nearing station and thought untranslatable electronic thoughts.

Blue Leader compared the station with the location of their proposed target area. "Red Leader," he called toward the pickup, "this is Blue Leader. We're in position; you can go right in. The exhaust shaft is farther to the north. We'll keep 'em busy down here."

Red Leader was the physical opposite of Luke's squadron commander. He resembled the popular notion of a credit accountant—short, slim, shy of face. His skills and dedication, however, easily matched those of his counterpart and old friend.

"We're starting for the target shaft now, Dutch. Stand by to take over if anything happens."

"Check, Red Leader," came the other's reply. "We're going to cross their equatorial axis and try to draw their main fire. May the force be with you."

From the approaching swarm, two squads of fighters broke

clear. The X-wing ships dove directly for the bulge of the station, far below, while the Y-ships curved down and northward over its surface.

Within the station, alarm sirens began a mournful, clangorous wail as slow-to-react personnel realized that the impregnable fortress was actually under organized attack. Admiral Motti and his tacticians had expected the rebels' resistance to be centered around a massive defense of the moon itself. They were completely unprepared for an offensive response consisting of dozens of tiny snub ships.

Imperial efficiency was in the process of compensating for this strategic oversight. Soldiers scrambled to man enormous defensive-weapons emplacements. Servodrivers thrummed as powerful motors aligned the huge devices for firing. Soon a web of annihilation began to envelop the station as energy weapons, electrical bolts, and explosive solids ripped out at the oncoming rebel craft.

"This is Blue Five," Luke announced to his mike as he nose dived his ship in a radical attempt to confuse any electronic predictors below. The gray surface of the battle station streaked past his ports. "I'm going in."

"I'm right behind you, Blue Five," a voice recognizable as Biggs's sounded in his ears.

The target in Luke's sights was as stable as that of the Imperial defenders was evasive. Bolts flew from the tiny vessel's weapons. One started a huge fire on the dim surface below, which would burn until the crew of the station could shut off the flow of air to the damaged section.

Luke's glee turned to terror as he realized he couldn't swerve his craft in time to avoid passing through the fireball of unknown composition. "Pull out, Luke, pull out!" Biggs was screaming at him.

But despite commands to shift course, the automatic pressors wouldn't allow the necessary centrifugal force. His fighter plunged into the expanding ball of superheated gases.

Then he was through and clear, on the other side. A rapid check of his controls enabled him to relax. Passage through the intense heat had been insufficient to damage anything vital—though all four wings bore streaks of black, carbonized testimony to the nearness of his escape.

Hell-flowers bloomed outside his ship as he swung it up and around in a sharp curve. "You all right, Luke?" came Biggs's concerned query.

"I got a little toasted, but I'm okay."

A different, stern voice sounded. "Blue Five," warned the squadron leader, "you'd better give yourself more lead time or you're going to destroy yourself as well as the Imperial construction."

"Yes, sir. I've got the hang of it now. Like you said, it's not *exactly* like flying a skyhopper."

Energy bolts and sun-bright beams continued to create a chromatic maze in the space above the station as the rebel fighters crisscrossed back and forth over its surface, firing at whatever looked like a decent target. Two of the tiny craft concentrated on a power terminal. It blew up, throwing lightning-sized electric arcs from the station's innards.

Inside, troopers, mechanicals, and equipment were blown in all directions by subsidiary explosions as the effects of the blast traveled back down various conduits and cables. Where the explosion had hulled the station, escaping atmosphere sucked helpless soldiers and 'droids out into a bottomless black tomb.

Moving from position to position, a figure of dark calm amid the chaos, was Darth Vader. A harried Commander rushed up to him and reported breathlessly.

"Lord Vader, we count at least thirty of them, of two types. They are so small and quick the fixed guns cannot follow them accurately. They continuously evade the predictors."

"Get all TIE crews to their fighters. We'll have to go out after them and destroy them ship by ship."

Within numerous hangars red lights began flashing and an insistent alarm started to ring. Ground crews worked frantically to ready ships as flight-suited Imperial pilots grabbed for helmets and packs.

"Luke," requested Blue Leader as he skimmed smoothly through a rain of fire, "let me know when you're off the block."

"I'm on my way now."

"Watch yourself," the voice urged over the cockpit speaker. "There's a lot of fire coming from the starboard side of that deflection tower."

"I'm on it, don't worry," Luke responded confidently. Putting his fighter into a twisting dive, he sliced once more across metal horizons. Antennae and small protruding emplacements burst into transitory flame as bolts from his wing tips struck with deadly accuracy.

He grinned as he pulled up and away from the surface as intense lines of energy passed through space recently vacated.

Darned if it *wasn't* like hunting womp-rats back home in the crumbling canyons of Tatooine's wastes.

Biggs followed Luke on a similar run, even as Imperial pilots prepared to lift clear of the station. Within the many docking bays technical crews rushed hurriedly to unlock power cables and conclude desperate final checks.

More care was taken in preparing a particular craft nearest one of the bay ports, the one into which Darth Vader barely succeeded in squeezing his huge frame. Once set in the seat he slid a second set of eye shields across his face.

The atmosphere of the war room back in the temple was one of nervous expectancy. Occasional blinks and buzzes from the main battle screen sounded louder than the soft sussuration of hopeful people trying to reassure one another. Near a far corner of the mass of flickering lights a technician leaned a little closer to his own readouts before speaking into the pickup suspended near his mouth.

"Squad leaders—attention; squad leaders—attention! We've picked up a new set of signals from the other side of the station. Enemy fighters coming your way."

Luke received the report at the same time as everyone else. He began hunting the sky for the predicted Imperial craft, his gaze dropping to his instrumentation. "My scope's negative. I don't see anything."

"Maintain visual scanning," Blue Leader directed. "With all this energy flying, they'll be on top of you before your scope can pick them up. Remember, they can jam every instrument on your ship except your eyes."

Luke turned again, and this time saw an Imperial already pursuing an X-wing—an X-wing with a number Luke quickly recognized.

"Biggs!" he shouted. "You've picked one up. On your tail . . . watch it!"

"I can't see it," came his friend's panicked response. "Where is he? I can't see it."

Luke watched helplessly as Biggs's ship shot away from the station surface and out into clear space, closely followed by the Imperial. The enemy vessel fired steadily at him, each successive bolt seeming to pass a little closer to Biggs's hull.

"He's on me tight," the voice sounded in Luke's cockpit. "I can't shake him."

Twisting, spinning, Biggs looped back toward the battle station, but the pilot trailing him was persistent and showed no sign of relinquishing pursuit.

"Hang on, Biggs," Luke called, wrenching his ship around so steeply that straining gyros whined. "I'm coming in."

So absorbed in his pursuit of Biggs was the Imperial pilot that he didn't seee Luke, who rotated his own ship, flipped out of the concealing gray below and dropped in behind him.

Electronic crosshairs lined up according to the computer-readout instructions, and Luke fired repeatedly. There was a small explosion in space—tiny compared with the enormous energies being put out by the emplacements on the surface of the battle station. But the explosion was of particular significance to three people: Luke, Biggs, and, most particularly, to the pilot of the TIE fighter, who was vaporized with his ship.

"Got him!" Luke murmured.

"I've got one! I've got one!" came a less restrained cry of triumph over the open intercom. Luke identified the voice as belonging to a young pilot known as John D. Yes, that was Blue Six chasing another Imperial fighter across the metal landscape. Bolts jumped from the X-wing in steady succession until the TIE fighter blew in half, sending leaflike glittering metal fragments flying in all directions.

"Good shooting, Blue Six," the squadron leader commented. Then he added quickly, "Watch out, you've got one on your tail."

Within the fighter's cockpit the gleeful smile on the young man's face vanished instantly as he looked around, unable to spot his pursuer. Something flared brightly nearby, so close that his starboard port burst. Then something hit even closer and the interior of the now open cockpit became a mass of flames.

"I'm hit, I'm hit!

That was all he had time to scream before oblivion took him from behind. Far above and to one side Blue Leader saw John D.'s ship expand in a fiery ball. His lips may have whitened slightly. Otherwise he might as well never have seen the X-wing explode, for all the reaction he displayed. He had more important things to do.

On the fourth moon of Yavin a spacious screen chose that moment to flicker and die, much as John D. had. Worried technicians began rushing in all directions. One turned a drawn face to Leia, the expectant Commanders, and one tall, bronzed robot.

"The high-band receiver has failed. It will take some time to fix . . ."

"Do the best you can," Leia snapped. "Switch to audio only."

Someone overheard, and in seconds the room was filled with the sounds of distant battle, interspersed with the voices of those involved.

"Tighten it up, Blue Two, tighten it up," Blue Leader was saying. "Watch those towers."

"Heavy fire, Boss," came the voice of Wedge Antilles, "twenty-three degrees."

"I see it. Pull in, pull in. We're picking up some interference."

"I can't believe it," Biggs was stammering. "I've never seen such firepower!"

"Pull in, Blue Five. Pull in." A pause, then, "Luke, do you read me? Luke?"

"I'm all right, Chief," came Luke's reply. "I've got a target. I'm going to check it out."

"There's too much action down there, Luke," Biggs told him. "Get out. Do you read me, Luke? Pull out."

"Break off, Luke," ordered the deeper tones of Blue Leader. "We've hit too much interference here. Luke, I repeat, break off! I can't see him. Blue Two, can you see Blue Five?"

"Negative," Wedge replied quickly. "There's a fire zone here you wouldn't believe. My scanner's jammed. Blue Five, where are you? Luke, are you all right?"

"He's gone," Biggs started to report solemnly. Then his voice rose. "No, wait . . . there he is! Looks like a little fin damage, but the kid's fine."

Relief swept the war room, and it was most noticeable in the face of the slightest, most beautiful Senator present.

On the battle station, troopers worn half to death or deafened by the concussion of the big guns were replaced by fresh crews. None of them had time to wonder how the battle was going, and at the moment none of them much cared, a malady shared by common soldiers since the dawn of history.

Luke skimmed daringly low over the station's surface, his attention riveted on a distant metal projection.

"Stick close, Blue Five," the squadron commander directed him. "Where are you going?"

"I've picked up what looks like a lateral stabilizer," Luke replied. "I'm going to try for it."

"Watch yourself, Blue Five. Heavy fire in your area."

Luke ignored the warning as he headed the fighter straight toward the oddly shaped protuberance. His determination was rewarded when, after saturating it with fire, he saw it erupt in a spectacular ball of superhot gas.

"Got it!" he exclaimed. "Continuing south for another one."

Within the rebel temple-fortress, Leia listened intently. She seemed simultaneously angry and frightened. Finally she turned to Threepio and muttered, "Why is Luke taking so many chances?" The tall 'droid didn't reply.

"Watch your back, Luke," Biggs's voice sounded over the speakers, "watch your back! Fighters above you, coming in."

Leia strained to see what she could only hear. She wasn't alone. "Help him, Artoo," Threepio was whispering to himself, "and keep holding on."

Luke continued his dive even as he looked back and spotted the object of Biggs's concern close on his tail. Reluctantly he pulled up and away from the station surface, abandoning his target. His tormentor was good, however, and continued closing on him.

"I can't shake him," he reported.

Something cut across the sky toward both ships. "I'm on him, Luke," shouted Wedge Antilles. "Hold on."

Luke didn't have to for very long. Wedge's gunnery was precise, and the Tie fighter vanished brightly shortly thereafter.

"Thanks, Wedge," Luke murmured, breathing a little more easily.

"Good shooting, Wedge." That was Biggs again. "Blue Four, I'm going in. Cover me, Porkins."

"I'm right with you, Blue Three," came the other pilot's assurance.

Biggs leveled them off, then let go with full weaponry. No one ever decided exactly what it was he hit, but the small tower that blew up under his energy bolts was obviously more important than it looked.

A series of sequential explosions hopscotched across a large section of the battle station's surface, leaping from one terminal to the next. Biggs had already shot past the area of disturbance, but his companion, following slightly behind, received a full dose of whatever energy was running wild down there.

"I've got a problem," Porkins announced. "My converter's running wild." That was an understatement. Every instrument on his control panels had abruptly gone berserk.

"Eject—eject, Blue Four," advised Biggs. "Blue Four, do you read?"

"I'm okay," Porkins replied. "I can hold her. Give me a little room to run, Biggs."

"You're too low," his companion yelled. "Pull up, pull up!"

With his instrumentation not providing proper information, and at the altitude he was traveling, Porkins's ship was simple for one of the big, clumsy gun emplacements to track. It did as its designers had intended it should. Porkins's demise was as glorious as it was abrupt.

It was comparatively quiet near the pole of the battle station. So intense and vicious had been Blue and Green squadron's assault on the equator that Imperial resistance had concentrated there. Red Leader surveyed the false peace with mournful satisfaction, knowing it wouldn't last for long.

"Blue Leader, this is Red Leader," he announced into his mike. "We're starting our attack run. The exhaust port is located and marked. No flak, no enemy fighters up here—yet. Looks like we'll get at least one smooth run at it."

"I copy, Red Leader," the voice of his counterpart responded. "We'll try to keep them busy down here."

Three Y-wing fighters dropped out of the stars, diving toward the battle-station surface. At the last possible minute they swerved to dip into a deep artificial canyon, one of many streaking the northern pole of the Death Star. Metal ramparts raced past on three sides of them.

Red Leader hunted around, noticed the temporary absence of Imperial fighters. He adjusted a control and addressed his squadron.

"This is it, boys. Remember, when you think you're close, go in closer before you drop that rock. Switch all power to front deflector screens—never mind what they throw at you from the side. We can't worry about that now."

Imperial crews lining the trench rudely awoke to the fact that their heretofore ignored section of the station was coming under attack. They reacted speedily, and soon energy bolts were racing at the attacking ships in a steadily increasing volume. Occasionally one would explode near one of the onrushing Y-wings, jostling it without real damage.

"A little aggressive, aren't they," Red Two reported over his mike.

Red Leader reacted quietly. "How many guns do you think, Red Five?"

Red Five, known casually to most of the rebel pilots as Pops, somehow managed to make an estimate of the trench's defenses while simultaneously piloting his fighter through the growing hail of fire. His helmet was battered almost to the point of uselessness from the effects of more battles than anyone had a right to survive.

"I'd say about twenty emplacements," he finally decided, "some in the surface and some on the towers."

Red Leader acknowledged the information with a grunt as he pulled his computer-targeting visor down in front of his face. Explosions continued to rock the fighter. "Switch to targeting computers," he declared.

"Red Two," came one reply, "computer locked in and I'm getting a signal." The young pilot's rising excitement marked his reply.

But the senior pilot among all the rebels, Red Five, was expectantly cool and confident—though it didn't sound like it from what he murmured half to himself: "No doubt about it, this is going to be some trick."

Unexpectedly, all defensive fire from the surrounding emplacements ceased. An eerie quiet clung to the trench as the surface continued to blur past the skimming Y-wings.

"What's this?" Red Two blurted, looking around worriedly. "They stopped. Why?"

"I don't like it," growled Red Leader. But there was nothing to confuse their approach now, no energy bolts to avoid.

It was Pops who was first to properly evaluate this seeming aberration on the enemy's part. "Stabilize your rear deflectors now. Watch for enemy fighters."

"You pinned it, Pops," Red Leader admitted, studying a readout. "Here they come. Three marks at two-ten."

A mechanical voice continued to recite the shrinking distance to their target, but it wasn't shrinking fast enough. "We're sitting ducks down here," he observed nervously.

"We'll just have to ride it out," the old man told them all. "We can't defend ourselves and go for the target at the same time." He fought down old reflexes as his own screen revealed three TIE fighters in precision formation diving almost vertically down toward them.

"Three-eight-one-oh-four," Darth Vader announced as he calmly adjusted his controls. The stars whipped past behind him. "I'll take them myself. Cover me."

Red Two was the first to die, the young pilot never knowing

what hit him, never seeing his executioner. Despite his experience, Red Leader was on the verge of panic when he saw his wingman dissolve in flame.

"We're trapped down here. No way to maneuver—trench walls are too close. We've got to loosen it up somehow. Got—"

"Stay on target," admonished an older voice. "Stay on target."

Red Leader took Pops's words like tonic, but it was all he could do to ignore the closing TIE fighters as the two remaining Y-wings continued to streak toward the target.

Above them, Vader permitted himself a moment of undisciplined pleasure as he readjusted his targeting 'puter. The rebel craft continued to travel a straight, unevasive course. Again Vader touched finger to fire control.

Something screeched in Red Leader's helmet, and fire started to consume his instrumentation. "It's no good," he yelled into his pickup, "I'm hit. I'm hit . . . !"

A second Y-wing exploded in a ball of vaporized metal, scattering a few solid shards of debris across the trench. This second loss proved too much even for Red Five to take. He manipulated controls, and his ship commenced rising in a slow curve out of the trench. Behind him, the lead Imperial fighter moved to follow.

"Red Five to Blue Leader," he reported. "Aborting run under heavy fire. TIE fighters dropped on us out of nowhere. I can't— wait—"

Astern, a silent, remorseless enemy was touching a deadly button once more. The first bolts struck just as Pops had risen high enough to commence evasive action. But he had pulled clear a few seconds too late.

One energy beam seared his port engine, igniting gas within. The engine blew apart, taking controls and stabilizing elements with it. Unable to compensate, the out-of-control Y-wing began a long, graceful plunge toward the station surface.

"Are you all right, Red Five?" a troubled voice called over the intership system.

"Lost Tiree . . . lost Dutch," Pops explained slowly, tiredly. "They drop in behind you, and you can't maneuver in the trench. Sorry . . . it's your baby now. So long, Dave. . . ."

It was the last message of many from a veteran.

Blue Leader forced a crispness he didn't feel into his voice as he tried to shunt aside the death of his old friend. "Blue boys, this is Blue Leader. Rendezvous at mark six point one. All wings report in."

"Blue Leader, this is Blue Ten. I copy."

"Blue Two here," Wedge acknowledged. "Coming toward you, Blue Leader."

Luke was also waiting his turn to report when something beeped on his control board. A glance backward confirmed the electronic warning as he spotted an Imperial fighter slipping in behind him.

"This is Blue Five," he declared, his ship wobbling as he tried to lose the TIE fighter. "I have a problem here. Be right with you."

He sent his ship into a steep dive toward the metal surface, then cut sharply up to avoid a burst of defensive fire from emplacements below. Neither maneuver shook his pursuit.

"I see you, Luke," came a reassuring call from Biggs. "Stay with it."

Luke looked above, below, and to the sides, but there was no sign of his friend. Meanwhile, energy bolts from his trailing assailant were passing uncomfortably close.

"Blast it, Biggs, where are you?"

Something appeared, not to the sides or behind, but almost directly in front of him. It was bright and moving incredibly fast, and then it was firing just above him. Taken completely by surprise, the Imperial fighter came apart just as its pilot realized what had happened.

Luke turned for the rendezvous mark as Biggs shot past overhead. "Good move, Biggs. Fooled me, too."

"I'm just getting started," his friend announced as he twisted his ship violently to avoid the fire from below. He hove into view over Luke's shoulder and executed a victory roll. "Just point me at the target."

Back alongside Yavin's indifferent bulk, Dodonna finished an intense discussion with several of his principal advisors, then moved to the long-range transmitter.

"Blue Leader, this is Base One. Double-check your own attack prior to commencement. Have your wingmen hold back and cover for you. Keep half your group out of range to make the next run."

"Copy, Base One," the response came. "Blue Ten, Blue Twelve, join with me."

Two ships leveled off to flank the squadron commander. Blue Leader checked them out. Satisfied that they were positioned properly for the attack run, he set the group to follow in case they should fail.

"Blue Five, this is Blue Leader, Luke, take Blue Two and Three with you. Hold up here out of their fire and wait for my signal to start your own run."

"Copy, Blue Leader," Luke acknowledged, trying to slow his heart slightly. "May the force be with you. Biggs, Wedge, let's close it up." Together, the three fighters assumed a tight formation high above the firefight still raging between other rebel craft of Green and Yellow squadrons and the imperial gunners below.

The horizon flip-flopped ahead of Blue Leader as he commenced his approach to the station surface. "Blue Ten, Blue Twelve, stay back until we spot those fighters, then cover me."

All three X-wings reached the surface, leveled off, then arced into the trench. His wingmen dropped farther and farther behind until Blue Leader was seemingly alone in the vast gray chasm.

No defensive fire greeted him as he raced toward the distant target. He found himself looking around nervously, checking and rechecking the same instruments.

"This doesn't look right," he found himself muttering.

Blue Ten sounded equally concerned. "You should be able to pick up the target by now."

"I know. The disruption down here is unbelievable. I think my instruments are off. Is this the right trench?"

Suddenly, intense streaks of light began to shoot close by as the trench defenses opened up. Near misses shook the attackers. At the far end of the trench a huge tower dominated the metal ridge, vomiting enormous amounts of energy at the nearing ships.

"It's not going to be easy with that tower up there," Blue Leader declared grimly. "Stand by to close up a little when I tell you."

Abruptly the energy bolts ceased and all was silent and dark in the trench once again. "This is it," Blue Leader announced, trying to locate the attack from above that had to be coming. "Keep your eyes open for those fighters."

"All short- and long-range scopes are blank," Blue Ten reported tensely. "Too much interference here. Blue Five, can you see them from where you are?"

Luke's attention was riveted to the surface of the station. "No sign of—Wait!" Three rapidly moving points of light caught his eye. "There they are. Coming in point three five."

Blue Ten turned and looked in the indicated direction. Sun bounced off stabilizing fins as the TIE fighters looped downward. "I see them."

"It's the right trench, all right," Blue Leader exclaimed as his tracking scope suddenly began a steady beeping. He adjusted his targeting instrumentation, pulling his visor down over his eyes. "I'm almost in range. Targets ready . . . coming up. Just hold them off me for a few seconds—keep 'em busy."

But Darth Vader was already setting his own fire control as he dropped like a stone toward the trench. "Close up the formation. I'll take them myself."

Blue Twelve went first, both engines blown. A slight deviation in flight path and his ship slammed into the trench wall. Blue Ten slowed and accelerated, bobbed drunkenly, but could do little within the confines of those metal walls.

"I can't hold them long. You'd better fire while you can, Blue Leader—we're closing on you."

The squadron commander was wholly absorbed in lining up two circles within his targeting visor. "We're almost home. Steady, steady . . ."

Blue Ten glanced around frantically. "They're right behind me!"

Blue Leader was amazed at how calm he was. The targeting device was partly responsible, enabling him to concentrate on tiny, abstract images to the exclusion of all else, helping him to shut out the rest of the inimical universe.

"Almost there, almost there . . ." he whispered. Then the two circles matched, turned red, and a steady buzzing sounded in his helmet. "Torpedoes away, torpedoes away."

Immediately after, Blue Ten let his own missiles loose. Both fighters pulled up sharply, just clearing the end of the trench as several explosions billowed in their wake.

"It's a hit! We've done it!" Blue Ten shouted hysterically.

Blue Leader's reply was thick with disappointment. "No, we haven't. They didn't go in. They just exploded on the surface outside the shaft."

Disappointment killed them, too, as they neglected to watch behind them. Three pursuing Imperial fighters continued up out of the fading light from the torpedo explosions. Blue Ten fell to Vader's precision fire, then the Dark Lord changed course slightly to fall in behind the squadron commander.

"I'll take the last one," he announced coldly. "You two go back."

Luke was trying to pick the assault team out of the glowing gases below when Blue Leader's voice sounded over the communicator.

"Blue Five, this is Blue Leader. Move into position, Luke. Start your attack run—stay low and wait until you're right on top of it. It's not going to be easy."

"Are you all right?"

"They're on top of me—but I'll shake them."

"Blue Five to Blue pack," Luke ordered, "let's go!" The three ships peeled off and plunged toward the trench sector.

Meanwhile Vader finally succeeded in hitting his quarry, a glancing bolt that nonetheless started small, intense explosions in one engine. Its R-2 unit scrambled back toward the damaged wing and struggled to repair the crippled power plant.

"R-2, shut off the main feed to number-one starboard engine," Blue Leader directed quietly, staring resignedly at instruments which were running impossibilities. "Hang on tight, this could get rough."

Luke saw that Blue Leader was in trouble. "We're right above you, Blue Leader," he declared. "Turn to point oh five, and we'll cover for you."

"I've lost my upper starboard engine," came the reply.

"We'll come down for you."

"Negative, negative. Stay there and get set up for your attack run."

"You're sure you're all right?"

"I think so . . . Stand by for a minute."

Actually, it was somewhat less than a minute before Blue Leader's gyrating X-wing plowed into the surface of the station.

Luke watched the huge explosion dissipate below him, knowing without question its cause, sensing fully for the first time the helplessness of his situaton. "We just lost Blue Leader," he murmured absently, not particularly caring if his mike picked up the somber announcement.

On Yavin Four, Leia Organa rose from her chair and nervously began pacing the room. Normally perfect nails were now jagged and uneven from nervous chewing. It was the only indication of physical unease. The anxiety visible in her expression was far more revealing of her feelings, an anxiety and worry that filled the war room on the announcement of Blue Leader's death.

"Can they go on?" she finally asked Dodonna.

The general replied with gentle resolve. "They must."

"But we've lost so *many*. Without Blue or Red Leader, how will they regroup?"

Dodonna was about to reply, but held his words as more critical ones sounded over the speakers.

"Close it up, Wedge," Luke was saying, thousands of kilometers away. "Biggs, where are you?"

"Coming in right behind you."

Wedge replied soon after. "Okay, Boss, we're in position."

Dodonna's gaze went to Leia. He looked concerned.

The three X-wings moved close together high above the battle station's surface. Luke studied his instruments and fought irritably with one control that appeared to be malfunctioning.

Someone's voice sounded in his ears. It was a young-old voice, a familiar voice: calm, content, confident, and reassuring—a voice he had listened to intently on the desert of Tatooine and in the guts of the station below, once upon a time.

"Trust your feelings, Luke," was all the Kenobi-like voice said.

Luke tapped his helmet, unsure whether he had heard anything or not. This was no time for introspection. The steely horizon of the station tilted behind him.

"Wedge, Biggs, we're going in," he told his wingmen. "We'll go in full speed. Never mind finding the trench and then accelerating. Maybe that will keep those fighters far enough behind us."

"We'll stay far enough back to cover you," Biggs declared. "At that speed will you be able to pull out in time?"

"Are you kidding?" Luke sneered playfully as they began their dive toward the surface. "It'll be just like Beggar's Canyon back home."

"I'm right with you, *boss*," noted Wedge, emphasizing the title for the first time. "Let's go . . ."

At high speed the three slim fighters charged the glowing surface, pulling out *after* the last moment. Luke skimmed so close over the station hull that the tip of one wing grazed a protruding antenna, sending metal splinters flying. Instantly they were enveloped in a meshwork of energy bolts and explosive projectiles. It intensified as they dropped down into the trench.

"We seem to have upset them," Biggs chortled, treating the deadly display of energy as though it were all a show being put on for their amusement.

"This is fine," Luke commented, surprised at the clear view ahead. "I can see everything."

Wedge wasn't quite as confident as he studied his own readouts. "My scope shows the tower, but I can't make out the exhaust port. It must be awfully small. Are you sure the computer can target it?"

"It better," Biggs muttered.

Luke didn't offer an evaluation—he was too busy holding a course through the turbulence produced by exploding bolts. Then, as if on command, the defensive fire ceased. He glanced around and up for signs of the expected TIE fighters, but saw nothing.

His hand went to drop the targeting visor into position, and for just a moment he hesitated. Then he swung it down in front of his eyes. "Watch yourselves," he ordered his companions.

"What about the tower?" Wedge asked worriedly.

"You worry about those fighters," Luke snapped. "I'll worry about the tower."

They rushed on, closing on the target every second. Wedge stared upward, and his gaze suddenly froze. "Here they come—oh point three."

Vader was setting his controls when one of his wingmen broke attack silence. "They're making their approach too fast—they'll never get out in time."

"Stay with them," Vader commanded.

"They're going too fast to get a fix," his other pilot announced with certainty.

Vader studied several readouts and found that his sensors confirmed the other estimates. "They'll still have to slow down before they reach that tower."

Luke contemplated the view in his targeting visor. "Almost home." Seconds passed and the twin circlets achieved congruence. His finger convulsed on the firing control. "Torpedoes away! Pull up, pull up."

Two powerful explosions rocked the trench, striking harmlessly far to one side of the minute opening. Three Tie fighters shot out of the rapidly dissipating fireball, closing on the retreating rebels. "Take them," Vader ordered softly.

Luke detected the pursuit at the same time as his companions. "Wedge, Biggs, split up—it's the only way we'll shake them."

The three ships dropped toward the station, then abruptly raced off in three different directions. All three TIE fighters turned and followed Luke.

Vader fired on the crazily dodging ship, missed, and frowned to himself. "The force is strong with this one. Strange. I'll take him myself."

Luke darted between defensive towers and wove a tight path around projecting docking bays, all to no avail. A single remaining TIE fighter stayed close behind. An energy bolt nicked one wing, close by an engine. It started to spark irregularly, threateningly. Luke fought to compensate and retain full control.

Still trying to shake his persistent assailant, he dropped back into a trench again. "I'm hit," he announced, "but not bad. Artoo, see what you can do with it."

The tiny 'droid unlocked himself and moved to work on the damaged engine as energy bolts flashed by dangerously close. "Hang on back there," Luke counseled the Artoo unit as he worked a path around projecting towers, the fighter spinning and twisting tightly through the topography of the station.

Fire remained intense as Luke randomly changed direction and speed. A series of indicators on the control panel slowly changed color; three vital gauges relaxed and returned to where they belonged.

"I think you've got it, Artoo," Luke told him gratefully. "I think—there, that's it. Just try to lock it down so it can't work loose again."

Artoo beeped in reply while Luke studied the whirling panorama behind and above them. "I think we've lost those fighters, too. Blue group, this is Blue Five. Are you clear?" He manipulated several controls and the X-wing shot out of the trench, still followed by emplacement fire.

"I'm up here waiting, Boss," Wedge announced from his position high above the station. "I can't see you."

"I'm on my way. Blue Three, are you clear? Biggs?"

"I've had some trouble," his friend explained, "but I think I lost him."

Something showed again, damnably, on Biggs's screen. A glance behind showed the TIE fighter that had been chasing him for the past several minutes dropping in once more behind him. He swung down toward the station again.

"Nope, not yet," Biggs told the others. "Hold on, Luke. I'll be right there."

A thin, mechanical voice sounded over the speakers. "Hang on, Artoo, hang on!" Back at the temple headquarters, Threepio turned away from the curious human faces which had turned to stare at him.

As Luke soared high above the station another X-wing swung in close to him. He recognized Wedge's ship and began hunting around anxiously for his friend.

"We're goin' in, Biggs—join up. Biggs, are you all right? Biggs!" There was no sign of the other fighter. "Wedge, do you see him anywhere?"

Within the transparent canopy of the fighter bobbing close by, a helmeted head shook slowly. "Nothing," Wedge told him over the communicator. "Wait a little longer. He'll show."

Luke looked around, worried, studied several instruments, then came to a decision. "We can't wait; we've got to go now. I don't think he made it."

"Hey, you guys," a cheerful voice demanded to know, "what are you waiting for?"

Luke turned sharply to his right, in time to see another ship racing past and slowing slightly ahead of him. "Don't ever give up on old Biggs," the intercom directed as the figure in the X-wing ahead looked back at them.

Within the central control room of the battle station, a harried officer rushed up to a figure studying the great battle screen and waved a handful of printouts at him.

"Sir, we've completed an analysis of their attack plan. There is a danger. Should we break off the engagement or make plans to evacuate? Your ship is standing by."

Governor Tarkin turned an incredulous gaze on the officer, who shrank back. "Evacuate!" he roared. "At our moment of triumph? We are about to destroy the last remnants of the Alliance, and you call for evacuation? You overestimate their chances badly . . . Now, get out!"

Overwhelmed by the Governor's fury, the subdued officer turned and retreated from the room.

"We're going in," Luke declared as he commenced his dive toward the surface. Wedge and Biggs followed just aft.

"Let's go—Luke," a voice he had heard before sounded inside his head. Again he tapped his helmet and looked around. It sounded as if the speaker were standing just behind him. But there was nothing, only silent metal and nonverbal instrumentation. Puzzled, Luke turned back to his controls.

Once more, energy bolts reached out for them, passing harmlessly on both sides as the surface of the battle station charged up into his face. But the defensive fire wasn't the cause of the renewed trembling Luke suddenly experienced. Several critical gauges were beginning their swing back into the danger zone again.

He leaned toward the pickup. "Artoo, those stabilizing elements must have broken loose again. See if you can't lock it back down—I've got to have full control."

Ignoring the bumpy ride, the energy beams and explosions lighting space around him, the little robot moved to repair the damage.

Additional, tireless explosions continued to buffet the three fighters as they dropped into the trench. Biggs and Wedge dropped behind to cover for Luke as he reached to pull down the targeting visor.

For the second time a peculiar hesitation swept through him. His hand was slower yet as he finally pulled the device down in front of his eyes, almost as if the nerves were in conflict with one another. As expected, the energy beams stopped as if on signal and he was barreling down the trench unchallenged.

"Here we go again," Wedge declared as he spotted three Imperial fighters dropping down on them.

Biggs and Wedge began crossing behind Luke, trying to draw the coming fire away from him and confuse their pursuers. One TIE fighter ignored the maneuvers, continuing to gain inexorably on the rebel ships.

Luke stared into the targeting device—then reached up slowly to move it aside. For a long minute he pondered the deactivated instrument, staring at it as if hypnotized. Then he slid it sharply back in front of his face and studied the tiny screen as it displayed the shifting relationship of the X-wing to the nearing exhaust port.

"Hurry, Luke," Biggs called out as he wrenched his ship in time to narrowly avoid a powerful beam. "They're coming in faster this time. We can't hold them much longer."

With inhuman precision, Darth Vader depressed the fire control of his fighter again. A loud, desperate shout sounded over the speakers, blending into a final agonized scream of flesh and metal as Biggs's fighter burst into a billion glowing splinters that rained down on the bottom of the trench.

Wedge heard the explosion over his speakers and hunted frantically behind him for the trailing enemy ships. "We lost Biggs," he yelled toward his own pickup.

Luke didn't reply immediately. His eyes were watering, and

he angrily wiped them clear. They were blurring his view of the targeting readout.

"We're a couple of shooting stars, Biggs," he whispered huskily, "and we'll never be stopped." His ship rocked slightly from a near miss and he directed his words to his remaining wingman, biting down hard on the end of each sentence.

"Close it up, Wedge. You can't do any more good back there. Artoo, try to give me a little more power on our rear reflectors."

The Artoo unit hurried to comply as Wedge pulled up alongside Luke's ship. The trailing TIE fighters also increased their speed.

"I'm on the leader," Vader informed his soldiers. "Take the other one."

Luke flew just in front of Wedge, slightly to port side. Energy bolts from the pursuing Imperials began to streak close about them. Both men crossed each other's path repeatedly, striving to present as confusing a target as possible.

Wedge was fighting with his controls when several small flashes and sparks lit his control board. One small panel exploded, leaving molten slag behind. Somehow he managed to retain control of the ship.

"I've got a bad malfunction, Luke. I can't stay with you."

"Okay, Wedge, get clear."

Wedge mumbled a heartfelt "Sorry" and peeled up out of the trench.

Vader, concentrating his attention on the one ship remaining before him, fired.

Luke didn't see the near-lethal explosion which burst close behind him. Nor did he have time to examine the smoking shell of twisted metal which now rode alongside one engine. The arms went limp on the little 'droid.

All three TIE fighters continued to chase the remaining X-wing down the trench. It was only a matter of moments before one of them caught the bobbing fighter with a crippling burst. Except now there were only two Imperials pursuing. The third had become an expanding cylinder of decomposing debris, bits and pieces of which slammed into the walls of the canyon.

Vader's remaining wingman looked around in panic for the source of the attack. The same distortion fields that confused rebel instrumentation now did likewise to the two TIE fighters.

Only when the freighter fully eclipsed the sun forward did the new threat become visible. It was a Corellian transport, far larger than any fighter, and it was diving directly at the trench. But it didn't move precisely like a freighter, somehow.

Whoever was piloting that vehicle must have been unconscious or out of his mind, the wingman decided. Wildly he adjusted controls in an attempt to avoid the anticipated collision. The freighter swept by just overhead, but in missing it the wingman slid too far to one side.

A small explosion followed as two huge fins of the paralleling TIE fighters intersected. Screaming uselessly into his pickup, the wingman fluttered toward the near trench wall. He never touched it, his ship erupting in flame before contact.

To the other side, Darth Vader's fighter began spinning helplessly. Unimpressed by the Dark Lord's desperate glower, various controls and instruments gave back readings which were brutally truthful. Completely out of control, the tiny ship continued spinning in the opposite direction from the destroyed wingman—out into the endless reaches of deep space.

Whoever was at the controls of the supple freighter was neither unconscious nor insane—well, perhaps slightly touched, but fully in command nonetheless. It soared high above the trench, turning to run protectively above Luke.

"You're all clear now, kid," a familiar voice informed him. "Now blow this thing so we can all go home."

This pep talk was followed by a reinforcing grunt which could only have been produced by a particularly large Wookiee.

Luke looked up through the canopy and smiled. But his smile faded as he turned back to the targeting visor. There was a tickling inside his head.

"Luke . . . trust me," the tickle requested, forming words for the third time. He stared into the targeter. The emergency exhaust port was sliding toward the firing circle again, as it had once before—when he'd missed. He hesitated, but only briefly this time, then shoved the targeting screen aside. Closing his eyes, he appeared to mumble to himself, as if in internal conversation with something unseen. With the confidence of a blind man in familiar surroundings, Luke moved a thumb over several controls, then touched one. Soon after, a concerned voice filled the cockpit from the open speakers.

"Base One to Blue Five, your targeting device is switched off. What's wrong?"

"Nothing," Luke murmured, barely audible. "Nothing."

He blinked and cleared his eyes. Had he been asleep? Looking around, he saw that he was out of the trench and shooting back into open space. A glance outside showed the familiar shape of Han Solo's ship shadowing him. Another, at the control board, indicated that he had released his remaining torpedoes, although he couldn't remember touching the firing stud. Still, he must have.

The cockpit speakers were alive with excitment. "You did it! You did it!" Wedge was shouting over and over. "I think they went right in."

"Good shot kid." Solo complimented him, having to raise his voice to be heard over Chewbacca's unrestrained howling.

Distant, muted rumblings shook Luke's ship, an omen of incipient success. He must have fired the torpedoes, mustn't he? Gradually he regained his composure.

"Glad . . . you were here to see it. Now let's get some distance between us and that thing before it goes. I hope Wedge was right."

Several X-wings, Y-wings, and one battered-looking freighter accelerated away from the battle station, racing toward the distant curve of Yavin.

Behind them small flashes of fading light marked the receding station. Without warning, something appeared in the sky in place of it which was brighter than the glowing gas giant, brighter than its far-off sun. For a few seconds the eternal night became day. No one dared look directly at it. Not even multiple shields set on high could dim that awesome flare.

Space filled temporarily with trillions of microscopic metal fragments, propelled past the retreating ships by the liberated energy of a small artificial sun. The collapsed residue of the battle station would continue to consume itself for several days, forming for that brief span of time the most impressive tombstone in this corner of the cosmos.

XIII

A CHEERING, gleeful throng of technicians, mechanics, and other inhabitants of the Alliance headquarters swarmed around each fighter as it touched down and taxied into the temple hangar. Several of the other surviving pilots had already vacated their ships and were waiting to greet Luke.

On the opposite side of the fighter, the crowd was far smaller and more restrained. It consisted of a couple of technicians and one tall, humanoid 'droid who watched worriedly as the humans mounted the scorched fighter and lifted a badly burned metal hulk from its back.

"Oh, my! Artoo?" Threepio pleaded, bending close to the carbonized robot. "Can you hear me? Say something." His unwinking gaze turned to one of the techs. "You can repair him, can't you?"

"We'll do our best." The man studied the vaporized metal, the dangling components. "He's taken a terrible beating."

"You must repair him! Sir, if any of my circuits or modules will help, I'll gladly donate them . . ."

They moved slowly away, oblivious to the noise and excitement around them. Between robots and the humans who repaired them there existed a very special relationship. Each partook a little of the other and sometimes the dividing line between man and machine was more blurred than many would admit.

The center of the carnival atmosphere was formed by three figures who battled to see who could compliment the others the most. When it came to congratulatory back-slapping, however, Chewbacca won by default. There was laughter as the Wookiee looked embarrassed at having nearly flattened Luke in his eagerness to greet him.

"I knew you'd come back," Luke was shouting, "I just knew it! I would've been nothing but dust if you hadn't sailed in like that, Han!"

Solo had lost none of his smug self-assurance. "Well, I couldn't very well let a flying farm boy go up against that station all by himself. Besides, I was beginning to realize what could happen, and I felt terrible about it, Luke—leaving you to maybe take all the credit and get all the reward."

As they laughed, a lithe figure, robes flowing, rushed up to Luke in a very unsenatorial fashion. "You did it, Luke, you did it!" Leia was shouting.

She fell into his arms and hugged him as he spun her around. Then she moved to Solo and repeated the embrace. Expectantly, the Corellian was not quite as embarrassed.

Suddenly awed by the adulation of the crowd, Luke turned away. He gave the tired fighter a look of approval, then found his gaze traveling upward, up to the ceiling high overhead. For a second he thought he heard something faintly like a gratified sigh, a relaxing of muscles a crazy old man had once performed in moments of pleasure. Of course, it was probably the intruding hot wind of a steaming jungle world, but Luke smiled anyway at what he thought he saw up there.

There were many rooms in the vast expanse of the temple which had been converted for modern service by the technicians of the Alliance. Even in their desperate need, however, there was something too clean and classically beautiful about the ruins of the ancient throne room for the architects to modify. They had left it as it was, save for scouring it clear of creeping jungle growth and debris.

For the first time in thousands of years that spacious chamber was full. Hundreds of rebel troops and technicians stood assembled on the old stone floor, gathered together for one last time before dispersing to new posts and distant homes. For the first time ever the massed ranks of pressed uniforms and polished semi-armor stood arrayed together in a fitting show of Alliance might.

The banners of the many worlds which had lent support to the rebellion fluttered in the gentle breeze formed inside. At the far end of a long open aisle stood a vision gowned in formal white, barred with chalcedony waves—Leia Organa's signet of office.

Several figures appeared at the far end of the aisle. One, massive and hirsute, showed signs of running for cover, but was urged on down the open row by his companion. It took several minutes for Luke, Han, Chewie, and Threepio to cover the distance to the other end.

They stopped before Leia, and Luke recognized General Dodonna among the other dignitaries seated nearby. There was a pause and a gleaming, familiar Artoo unit joined the group, moving to stand next to a thoroughly awestruck Threepio.

Chewbacca shuffled nervously, giving every indication of wishing he were someplace else. Solo silenced him as Leia rose and came forward. At the same time banners tilted in unison and all those gathered in the great hall turned to face the dais.

She placed something heavy and golden around Solo's neck, then Chewbacca's—having to strain to do so—and finally around Luke's. Then she made a signal to the crowd, and the rigid discipline dissolved as every man, woman, and mechanical present was permitted to give full vent to their feelings.

As he stood awash in the cheers and shouts, Luke found that his mind was neither on his possible future with the Alliance nor on the chance of traveling adventurously with Han Solo and Chewbacca. Instead, unlikely as Solo had claimed it might be, he found his full attention occupied by the radiant Leia Organa.

She noticed his unabashed stare, but this time she only smiled.

EPISODE V

STAR WARS:
The Empire Strikes Back

by Donald F. Glut

Based on a story by George Lucas

I

"NOW this is what I call cold!" Luke Skywalker's voice broke the silence he had observed since leaving the newly established Rebel base hours earlier. He was astride a Tauntaun, the only other living being as far as the eye could see. He felt tired and alone, and the sound of his own voice startled him.

Luke as well as his fellow members of the Rebel Alliance took turns exploring the white wastelands of Hoth, gathering information about their new home. They all returned to base with mixed feelings of comfort and loneliness. There was nothing to contradict their earliest findings that no intelligent life-forms existed on this cold planet. All that Luke had seen on his solitary expeditions were barren white plains and ranges of blue-tinged mountains that seemed to vanish in the mists of the distant horizons.

Luke smiled behind the masklike gray bandana that protected him against Hoth's frigid winds. Peering out at the icy wastes through his goggles, he pulled his fur-lined cap down more snugly about his head.

One corner of his mouth curled upward as he tried to visualize the official researchers in the service of the Imperial government. "The galaxy is peppered with settlements of colonizers who care little about the affairs of the Empire or its opposition, the Rebel Alliance," he thought. "But a settler would have to be crazy to stake his claims on Hoth. This planet doesn't have a thing to offer anyone—except *us*."

The Rebel Alliance had established an outpost on the ice world little more than a month before. Luke was well-known on the base and, although barely twenty-three years old, he was addressed as *Commander* Skywalker by other Rebel warriors. The title made him feel a bit uncomfortable. Nonetheless, he was already in the position of giving orders to a band of seasoned soldiers. So much had happened to Luke and he had changed a great deal. Luke, himself, found it hard to believe that only three years ago he was a wide-eyed farm boy on his home world of Tatooine.

The youthful commander spurred his Tauntaun. "Come on, girl," he urged.

The snow-lizard's gray body was insulated from the cold by a covering of thick fur. It galloped on muscular hind legs, its tridactyl feet terminating in large hooked claws that dug up great plumes of snow. The Tauntaun's llamalike head thrust forward and its serpentine tail coiled out behind as the beast ran up the ice slope. The animal's horned head turned from side to side buffeting the winds that assaulted its shaggy muzzle.

Luke wished his mission were finished. His body felt nearly frozen in spite of his heavily padded Rebel-issue clothing. But he knew that it was his choice to be there; he had volunteered to ride across the ice fields looking for other lifeforms. He shivered as he looked at the long shadow he and the beast cast on the snow. "The winds are picking up," he thought. "And these chilling winds bring unendurable temperatures to the plains after nightfall." He was tempted to return to the base a little early, but he knew the importance of establishing the certainty that the Rebels were alone on Hoth.

The Tauntaun quickly turned to the right, almost throwing Luke off-balance. He was still getting used to riding the unpredictable creatures. "No offense," he said to his mount, "but I'd feel a lot more at ease in the cockpit of my old reliable landspeeder." But for this mission, a Tauntaun—despite its disadvantages—was the most efficient and practical form of transportation available on Hoth.

When the beast reached the top of another ice slope, Luke brought the animal to halt. He pulled off his dark-lensed goggles and squinted for a few moments, just long enough for his eyes to adjust to the blinding glare of the snow.

Suddenly his attention was diverted by the appearance of an object streaking across the sky, leaving behind a lingering trail of smoke as it dipped toward the misty horizon. Luke flashed his gloved hand to his utility belt and clutched his pair of electrobinoculars. Apprehensive, he felt a chill that competed with the coldness of the Hoth atmosphere. What he had seen could have been man-made, perhaps even something launched by the Empire. The young commander, still focused on the object, followed its fiery course and watched intently as it crashed on the white ground and was consumed in its own explosive brilliance.

At the sound of the explosion, Luke's Tauntaun shuddered. A fearful growl escaped its muzzle and it began to claw nervously at the snow. Luke patted the animal's head, trying to reassure the beast. He found it difficult to hear himself over the blustering wind. "Easy, girl, it's just another meteorite!" he shouted. The animal calmed and Luke brought the communicator to his mouth. "Echo Three to Echo Seven. Han ol' buddy, do you read me?"

Static crackled from the receiver. Then a familiar voice cut through the interference. "Is that you, kid? What's up?"

The voice sounded a little older and somewhat sharper than Luke's. For a moment Luke fondly recalled first meeting the Corellian space smuggler in that dark, alien-packed cantina at a spaceport on Tatooine. And now he was one of Luke's only friends who was not an official member of the Rebel Alliance.

"I've finished my circle and I haven't picked up any life readings," Luke spoke into his comlink, pressing his mouth close to the transmitter.

"There isn't enough life on this ice cube to fill a space cruiser," Han answered, fighting to make his voice heard above the whistling winds. "My sentry markers are placed. I'm heading back to base."

"See you shortly," Luke replied. He still had his eye on the twisting column of dark smoke rising from a black spot in the distance. "A meteorite just hit the ground near here and I want to check it out. I won't be long."

Clicking off his comlink, Luke turned his attention to his Tauntaun. The reptilian creature was pacing, shifting its weight from one foot to the other. It gave out a deep-throated roar that seemed to signal fear.

"Whoa, girl!" he said, patting the Tauntaun's head. "What's the matter . . . you smell something? There's nothing out there."

But Luke, too, was beginning to feel uneasy, for the first time since he had set out from the hidden Rebel base. If he knew anything about these snowlizards, it was that their senses were keen. Without question the animal was trying to tell Luke that something, some danger, was near.

Not wasting a moment, Luke removed a small object from his utility belt and adjusted its miniature controls. The device was sensitive enough to zero in on even the most minute life readings by detecting body temperature and internal life systems. But as Luke began to scan the readings, he realized there was no need—or time—to continue.

A shadow crossed over him, towering above by a good meter and a half. Luke spun around and suddenly it seemed as if the terrain itself had come to life. A great white-furred bulk, perfectly camouflaged against the sprawling mounds of snow, rushed savagely at him.

"Son of a jumpin' . . ."

Luke's hand blaster never cleared its holster. The huge claw of the Wampa Ice Creature struck him hard and flat against his face, knocking him off the Tauntaun and into the freezing snow.

Unconsciousness came swiftly to Luke, so swiftly that he never even heard the pitiful screams of the Tauntaun nor the abrupt silence following the sound of a snapping neck. And he never felt his own ankle savagely gripped by his giant, hairy attacker, or felt his body dragged like a lifeless doll across the snow-covered plain.

Black smoke was still rising from the depression in the hillside where the air-borne thing had fallen. The smoky clouds had thinned considerably since the object had crashed to the ground and formed a smoldering crater, the dark fumes being dispersed over the plains by the icy Hoth winds.

Something stirred within the crater.

First there was only a sound, a droning mechanical sound swelling in intensity as if to compete with the howling wind. Then the thing moved—something that glinted in the bright afternoon light as it slowly began to rise from the crater.

The object appeared to be some form of alien organic life, its head a multiorbed, skull-like horror, its dark-lensed blister eyes training their cold gaze across the even colder reaches of wilderness. But as the thing rose higher from the crater, its form showed it clearly to be a machine of some sort, possessing a large cylindrical "body" connected to a circular head, and equipped with cameras, sensors, and metal appendages, some of which terminated in crablike grasping pincers.

The machine hovered over the smoking crater and extended its appendages in various directions. Then a signal was set off within its internal mechanical systems, and the machine began to float across the icy plain.

The dark probe droid soon vanished over the distant horizon.

* * *

Another rider, bundled in winter clothing and mounted on a spotted gray Tauntaun, raced across the slopes of Hoth toward the Rebel base of operations.

The man's eyes, like points of cold metal, glanced without interest at the domes of dull gray, the myriad gun turrets and the colossal power generators that were the only indications of civilized life on this world. Han Solo gradually slowed his snow-lizard, guiding the reins so the creature trotted through the entrance of the enormous ice cave.

Han welcomed the relative warmth of the vast complex of caverns, warmed by Rebel heating units that obtained their power from the huge generators outside. This subterranean base was both a natural ice cave and a maze of angular tunnels blasted from a solid mountain of ice by Rebel lasers. The Corellian had been in more desolate hell-holes in the galaxy, but for the moment he couldn't remember the exact location of any one of them.

He dismounted his Tauntaun, then glanced around to watch the activity taking place inside the mammoth cave. Wherever he looked he saw things being carried, assembled, or repaired. Rebels in gray uniforms rushed to unload supplies and adjust equipment. And there were robots, mostly R2 units and power droids, that seemed to be everywhere, rolling or walking through the ice corridors, efficiently performing their innumerable tasks.

Han was beginning to wonder if he were mellowing with age. At first he had had no personal interest in or loyalty to this whole Rebel affair. His ultimate involvement in the conflict between Empire and Rebel Alliance began as a mere business transaction, selling his services and the use of his ship, the *Millennium Falcon*. The job had seemed simple enough. Just pilot Ben Kenobi, plus young Luke and two droids, to the Alderaan system. How could Han have known at the time that he would also be called on to rescue a princess from the Empire's most feared battle station, the Death Star?

Princess Leia Organa . . .

The more Solo thought about her, the more he realized how much trouble he eventually bought himself by accepting Ben Kenobi's money. All Han had wanted originally was to collect his fee and rocket off to pay back some bad debts that hung over his head like a meteor ready to fall. Never had he intended to become a hero.

And yet, something had kept him around to join Luke and his crazy Rebel friends as they launched the now-legendary space attack on the Death Star. Something. For the present, Han couldn't decide just what that something was.

Now, long after the Death Star's destruction, Han was still with the Rebel Alliance, lending his assistance to establish this base on Hoth, probably the bleakest of all planets in the galaxy. But all that was about to change, he told himself. As far as he was concerned, Han Solo and the Rebels were about to blast off on divergent courses.

He walked rapidly through the underground hangar deck where several Rebel fighter ships were docked and being serviced by men in gray assisted by droids of various designs. Of greatest concern to Han was the saucer-shaped freighter ship resting on its newly installed landing pods. This, the largest ship in the hangar, had garnered a few new dents in its metal hull since Han first hooked up with Skywalker and Kenobi. Yet the *Millennium Falcon* was famous not for its outward appearance but for its speed: This freighter was still the fastest ship ever to make the Kessel Run or to outrun an Imperial TIE fighter.

Much of the *Falcon*'s success could be attributed to its maintenance, now entrusted to the shaggy hands of a two-meter-tall mountain of brown hair, whose face was at the moment hidden behind a welder's mask.

Chewbacca, Han Solo's giant Wookiee copilot, was repairing the *Millennium Falcon*'s central lifter when he noticed Solo approaching. The Wookiee stopped his work and raised his face shield, exposing his furry countenance. A growl that few non-Wookiees in the universe could translate roared from his toothy mouth.

Han Solo was one of those few. "*Cold* isn't the word for it, Chewie," the Corellian replied. "I'll take a good fight any day over all this hiding and freezing!" He noticed the smoky wisps rising from the newly welded section of metal. "How are you coming with those lifters?"

Chewbacca replied with a typical Wookiee grumble.

"All right," Han said, fully agreeing with his friend's desire to return to space, to some other planet—anywhere but Hoth. "I'll go report. Then I'll give you a hand. Soon as those lifters are fixed, we're out of here."

The Wookiee barked, a joyful chuckle, and returned to his work as Han continued through the artificial ice cavern.

The command center was alive with electronic equipment and monitoring devices reaching toward the icy ceiling. As in the hangar, Rebel personnel filled the command center. The room was full of controllers, troopers, maintenance men—along with droids of varying models and sizes, all of whom were diligently involved in converting the chamber into a workable base to replace the one on Yavin.

The man Han Solo had come to see was busily engaged behind a great console, his attention riveted to a computer screen flashing brilliantly colored readouts. Rieekan, wearing the uniform of a Rebel general, straightened his tall frame to face Solo as he approached.

"General, there isn't a hint of life in the area," Han reported. "But all the perimeter markings are set, so you'll know if anyone comes calling."

As usual, General Rieekan did not smile at Solo's flippancy. But he admired the young man's taking a kind of unofficial membership in the Rebellion. So impressed was Rieekan by Solo's qualities that he often considered giving him an honorary officer's commission.

"Has Commander Skywalker reported in yet?" the general inquired.

"He's checking out a meteorite that hit near him," Han answered. "He'll be in soon.' "

Rieekan quickly glanced at a newly installed radar screen and studied the flashing images. "With all the meteor activity in this system, it's going to be difficult to spot approaching ships."

"General, I . . ." Han hesitated. "I think it's time for me to move on."

Han's attention was drawn from General Rieekan to a steadily approaching figure. Her walk was both graceful and determined, and somehow the young woman's feminine features seemed incongruous with her white combat uniform. Even at this distance, Han could tell Princess Leia was upset.

"You're good in a fight," the general remarked to Han, adding, "I hate to lose you."

"Thank you, General. But there's a price on my head. If I don't pay off Jabba the Hut, I'm a walking dead man."

"A death mark is not an easy thing to live with—" the officer began as Han turned to Princess Leia. Solo was not a sentimental sort, but he was aware that he was very emotional now. "I guess this is it, Your Highness." He paused, not knowing what response to expect from the princess.

"That's right," Leia replied coldly. Her sudden aloofness was quickly evolving into genuine anger.

Han shook his head. Long ago he had told himself that females—mammalian, reptilian, or some biological class yet to be discovered—were beyond his meager powers of comprehension. Better leave them to mystery, he'd often advised himself.

But for a while, at least, Han had begun to believe that there was at least one female in all the cosmos that he *was* beginning to understand. And yet, he had been wrong before.

"Well," Han said, "don't go all mushy on me. So long, Princess."

Abruptly turning his back to her, Han strode into the quiet corridor that connected with the command center. His destination was the hangar deck, where a giant Wookiee and a smuggler's freighter—two realities he did understand—were waiting for him. He was not about to stop walking.

"Han!" Leia was rushing after him, slightly out of breath.

Coolly, he stopped and turned toward her. "Yes, Your Highness?"

"I thought you had decided to stay."

There seemed to be real concern in Leia's voice, but Han could not be certain.

"That bounty hunter we ran into on Ord Mantell changed my mind."

"Does Luke know?" she asked.

"He'll know when he gets back," Han replied gruffly.

Princess Leia's eyes narrowed, her gaze judging him with a look he knew well. For a moment Han felt like one of the icicles on the surface of the planet.

"Don't give me that look," he said sternly. "Every day more bounty hunters are searching for me. I'm going to pay off Jabba before he sends any more of his remotes, Gank killers, and who knows what else. I've got to get this price off my head while I still *have* a head."

Leia was obviously affected by his words, and Han could see that she was concerned for him as well as, perhaps, feeling something more.

"But we still need you," she said.

"We?" he asked.

"Yes."

"What about *you*?" Han was careful to emphasize the last word, but really wasn't certain why. Maybe it was something he had for some time wanted to say but had lacked the courage— no, he amended, the *stupidity*—to expose his feelings. At the moment there seemed to be little to lose, and he was ready for whatever she might say.

"Me?" she said bluntly. "I don't know what you mean."

Incredulous, Han Solo shook his head. "No, you probably don't."

"And what precisely *am* I supposed to know?" Anger was growing in her voice again, probably because, Han thought, she was finally beginning to understand.

He smiled. "You want me to stay because of the way you feel about me."

Again the princess mellowed. "Well, yes, you've been a great help," she said, pausing before going on, " . . . to us. You're a natural leader—"

But Han refused to let her finish, cutting her off in midsentence. "No, Your Worship. That's not it."

Suddenly Leia was staring directly into Han's face, with eyes that were, at last, fully understanding. She started to laugh. "You're imagining things."

"Am I? I think you were afraid I was going to leave you without even a   " Han's eyes focused on her lips, " . . . kiss."

She began to laugh harder now. "I'd just as soon kiss a Wookiee."

"I can arrange that." He moved closer to her, and she looked radiant even in the cold light of the ice chamber. "Believe me, you could use a good kiss. You've been so busy giving orders, you've forgotten how to be a woman. If you'd have let go for a moment, I could have helped you. But it's too late now, sweetheart. Your big opportunity is flying out of here."

"I think I can survive," she said, obviously irked.

"Good luck!"

"You don't even care if the—"

He knew what she was going to say and didn't let her finish. "Spare me, please!" he interrupted. "Don't tell me about the Rebellion again. It's all you think about. You're as cold as this planet."

"And you think you're the one to apply some heat?"

"Sure, if I were interested. But I don't think it'd be much fun." With that, Han stepped back and looked at her again, appraising her coolly. "We'll meet again," he said. "Maybe by then you'll have warmed up a little." Her expression had changed again. Han had seen killers with kinder eyes.

"You have all the breeding of a Bantha," she snarled, "but not as much class. Enjoy your trip, hot shot!" Princess Leia quickly turned away from Han and hurried down the corridor.

II

THE temperature on the surface of Hoth had dropped. But despite the frigid air, the Imperial Probe Droid continued its leisurely drift above the snow-swept fields and hills, its extended sensors still reaching in all directions for life signs.

The robot's heat sensors suddenly reacted. It had found a heat source in the vicinity, and warmth was a good indication of life. The head swiveled on its axis, the sensitive eyelike blisters noting the direction from which the heat source originated. Automatically the probe robot adjusted its speed and began to move at maximum velocity over the icy fields.

The insectlike machine slowed only when it neared a mound of snow bigger than the probe droid itself. The robot's scanners made note of the mound's size—nearly one-point-eight meters in height and an enormous six meters long. But the mound's size was of only secondary importance. What was truly astounding, if a surveillance machine could ever be astounded, was the amount of heat radiating from beneath the mound. The creature under that snowy hill must surely be well protected against the cold.

A thin blue-white beam of light shot from one of the probe robot's appendages, its intense heat boring into the white mound and scattering gleaming snow flecks in all directions.

The mound began to shiver, then to quake. Whatever existed beneath it was deeply irritated by the robot's probing laser beam. Snow began to fall away from the mound in sizable clumps when, at one end, two eyes showed through the mass of white.

Huge yellow eyes peered like twin points of fire at the mechanical creature that continued to blast away with its painful beams. The eyes burned with primeval hatred for the thing that had interrupted its slumber.

The mound shook again, with a roar that nearly destroyed the probe droid's auditory sensors. It zoomed back several meters, widening the space between it and the creature. The droid had never before encountered a Wampa Ice Creature; its computers advised that the beast be dealt with expeditiously.

The droid made an internal adjustment to regulate the potency of its laser beam. Less than a moment later the beam was at maximum intensity. The machine aimed the laser at the creature, enveloping it in a great flaming and smoking cloud. Seconds later the few remaining particles of the Wampa were swept away by the icy winds.

The smoke disappeared, leaving behind no physical evidence—save for a large depression in the snow—that an Ice Creature had ever been there.

But its existence had been properly recorded in the memory of the probe droid, which was already continuing on its programmed mission.

The roars of another Wampa Ice Creature finally awakened the battered young Rebel commander.

Luke's head was spinning, aching, perhaps exploding for all he could tell. With painstaking effort he brought his vision into focus, discerning that he was in an ice gorge, its jagged walls reflecting the fading twilight.

He suddenly realized he was hanging upside down, arms dangling and fingertips some thirty centimeters from the snowy floor. His ankles were numb. He craned his neck and saw that his feet were frozen in ice hanging from the ceiling and that the ice was forming on his legs like stalactites. He could feel the frozen mask of his own blood caked on his face where the Wampa Ice Creature had viciously slashed him.

Again Luke heard the bestial moans, louder now as they resounded through the deep and narrow passageway of ice. The roars of the monster were deafening. He wondered which would kill him first, the cold or the fangs and claws of the thing that inhabited the gorge.

I've got to free myself, he thought, get free of this ice. His strength had not yet returned fully, but with a determined effort, he pulled himself up and reached for the confining bonds. Still too weak, Luke could not break the ice and fell back into his hanging position, the white floor rushing up at him.

"Relax," he said to himself. "Relax."

The ice walls creaked with the ever-louder bellows of the

approaching creature. Its feet crunched on the frigid ground, coming frighteningly nearer. It would not be long before the shaggy white horror would be back and possibly warming the cold young warrior in the darkness of its belly.

Luke's eyes darted about the gorge, finally spotting the pile of gear he had brought with him on his mission, now lying in a useless, crumpled heap on the floor. The equipment was nearly a full, unattainable meter beyond his grasp. And with that gear was a device that entirely captured his attention—a stout hand-grip unit with a pair of small switches and a surmounting metal disk. The object had once belonged to his father, a former Jedi Knight who had been betrayed and murdered by the young Darth Vader. But now it was Luke's, given him by Ben Kenobi to be wielded with honor against Imperial tyranny.

In desperation Luke tried twisting his aching body, just enough to reach the discarded lightsaber. But the freezing cold coursing through his body slowed him down and weakened him. Luke was beginning to resign himself to his fate as he heard the snarling Wampa Ice Creature approaching. His last feelings of hope were nearly gone when he sensed the presence.

But it was not the presence of the white giant that dominated this gorge.

Rather, it was that soothing spiritual presence which occasionally visited Luke in moments of stress or danger. The presence that had first come to him only after old Ben, once again in his Jedi role of Obi-Wan Kenobi, vanished into a crumple of his own dark robes after being cut down by Darth Vader's lightsaber. The presence that was sometimes like a familiar voice, an almost silent whisper that spoke directly to Luke's mind.

"Luke." The whisper was there again, hauntingly. "Think of the lightsaber in your hand."

The words made Luke's already aching head throb. Then he felt a sudden resurgence of strength, a feeling of confidence that urged him to continue fighting despite his apparently hopeless situation. His eyes fixed upon the lightsaber. His hand reached out painfully, the freezing in his limbs already taking its toll. He squeezed his eyes shut in concentration. But the weapon was still beyond his reach. He knew that the lightsaber would require more than just struggling to reach.

"Gotta relax," Luke told himself, "relax . . ."

Luke's mind whirled as he heard the words of his disembodied guardian. "Let the Force flow, Luke."

The Force!

Luke saw the inverted gorillalike image of the Wampa Ice Creature looming, its raised arms ending in enormous gleaming claws. He could see the apish face for the first time now, and shivered at the sight of the beast's ramlike horns, the quivering lower jaw with its protruding fangs.

But then the warrior divorced the creature from his thoughts. He stopped struggling for his weapon, his body relaxed and went limp, allowing his spirit to be receptive to his teacher's suggestion. Already he could feel coursing through him that energy field generated by all living beings, that bound the very universe together.

As Kenobi had taught him, the Force was within Luke to use as he saw fit.

The Wampa Ice Creature spread its black, hooked claws and lumbered toward the hanging youth. Suddenly the lightsaber, as if by magic, sprang to Luke's hand. Instantly, he depressed a colored button on the weapon, releasing a bladelike beam that quickly severed his icy bonds.

As Luke, weapon in hand, dropped to the floor, the monstrous figure towering over him took a cautious step backward. The beast's sulfurous eyes blinked incredulously at the humming lightshaft, a sight baffling to its primitive brain.

Though it was difficult to move, Luke jumped to his feet and waved his lightsaber at the snow-white mass of muscle and hair, forcing it back a step, another step. Bringing the weapon down, Luke cut through the monster's hide with the blade of light. The Wampa Ice Creature shrieked, its hideous roar of agony shaking the gorge walls. It turned and hastily lumbered out of the gorge, its white bulk blending with the distant terrain.

The sky was already noticeably darker, and with the encroaching darkness came the colder winds. The Force was with Luke, but even that mysterious power could not warm him now. Every step he took as he stumbled out of the gorge was more difficult than the last. Finally, his vision dimming as rapidly as the daylight, Luke stumbled down an embankment of snow and was unconscious before he even reached the bottom.

In the subsurface main hangar dock, Chewie was getting the *Millennium Falcon* ready for takeoff. He looked up from his work to see a rather curious pair of figures that had just appeared from around a nearby corner to mingle with the usual Rebel activity in the hangar.

Neither of these figures was human, although one of them had a humanoid shape and gave the impression of a man in knightly golden armor. His movements were precise, almost too precise to be human, as he clanked stiffly through the corridor. His companion required no manlike legs for locomotion, for he was doing quite well rolling his shorter, barrellike body along on miniature wheels.

The shorter of the two droids was beeping and whistling excitedly.

"It is *not* my fault, you malfunctioning tin can," the tall, anthropomorphic droid stated, gesturing with a metallic hand. "I did not ask you to turn on the thermal heater. I merely commented that it was freezing in her chamber. But it's *supposed* to be freezing. How are we going to get all her things dried out? . . . Ah! Here we are."

See-Threepio, the golden droid in human shape, paused to focus his optical sensors on the docked *Millennium Falcon.*

The other robot, Artoo-Detoo, retracted his wheels and frontal leg, and rested his stout metal body on the ground. The smaller droid's sensors were reading the familiar figures of Han Solo and his Wookiee companion as those two continued the work of replacing the freighter's central lifters.

"Master Solo, sir," Threepio called, the only one of the robotic twosome equipped with an imitation human voice. "Might I have a word with you?"

Han was not particularly in a mood to be disturbed, especially by this fastidious droid. "What is it?"

"Mistress Leia has been trying to reach you on the communicator," Threepio informed him. "It must be malfunctioning."

But Han knew that it was not. "I shut it off," he said sharply as he continued to work on his ship. "What does her royal holiness want?"

Threepio's auditory sensors identified the disdain in Han's voice but did not understand it. The robot mimicked a human gesture as he added, "She is looking for Master Luke and assumed he would be here with you. No one seems to know—"

"Luke's not back yet?" Immediately Han became concerned. He could see that the sky beyond the ice cavern entrance had grown considerably darker since he and Chewbacca had begun to repair the *Millennium Falcon.* Han knew just how severely the temperatures dropped on the surface after nightfall and how deadly the winds could be.

In a flash he jumped off the *Falcon*'s lift, not even looking back toward the Wookiee. "Bolt it down, Chewie. Officer of the Deck!" Han yelled, then brought his comlink to his mouth and asked, "Security Control, has Commander Skywalker reported in yet?" A negative reply brought a scowl to Han's face.

The deck sergeant and his aide hurried up to Solo in response to his summons.

"Is Commander Skywalker back yet?" Han asked, tension in his voice.

"I haven't seen him," the deck sergeant replied. "It's possible he came in through the south entrance."

"Check on it!" Solo snapped, though he was not in an official position to give commands. "It's urgent."

As the deck sergeant and his aide turned and rushed down the corridor, Artoo emitted a concerned whistle that rose inquiringly in pitch.

"I don't know, Artoo," Threepio answered, stiffly turning his upper torso and head in Han's direction. "Sir, might I inquire what's going on?"

Anger welled up inside Han as he grunted back at the robot, "Go tell your precious princess that Luke is dead unless he shows up soon."

Artoo began to whistle hysterically at Solo's grim prediction and his now-frightened golden partner exclaimed, "Oh, no!"

The main tunnel was filled with activity when Han Solo rushed in. He saw a pair of Rebel troopers employing all their physical strength to restrain a nervous Tauntaun that was trying to break free.

From the opposite end, the deck officer rushed into the corridor, his eyes darting around the chamber until he had spotted Han. "Oh," he said frantically, "Commander Skywalker hasn't come through the south entrance. He might have forgotten to check in."

"Not likely," Han snapped. "Are the speeders ready?"

"Not yet," the deck officer answered. "Adapting them to the cold is proving difficult. Maybe by morning—"

Han cut him off. There wasn't any time to waste on machines that could and probably would break down. "We'll have to go out on Tauntauns. I'll take sector four."

"The temperature is falling too rapidly."

"You bet it is," Han growled, "and Luke's out in it."

The other officer volunteered, "I'll cover sector twelve. Have control set screen alpha."

But Han knew there was not time for control to get its surveillance cameras operating, not with Luke probably dying somewhere on the desolate plains above. He pushed his way through the assemblage of Rebel troops and took the reins of one of the trained Tauntauns, leaping onto the creature's back.

"The night storms will start before any of you can reach the first marker," the deck officer warned.

"Then I'll see you in hell," grunted Han, tugging the reins of his mount and maneuvering the animal out of the cave.

Snow was falling heavily as Han Solo raced his Tauntaun through the wilderness. Night was near and the winds were howling fiercely, piercing his heavy clothes. He knew that he would be as useless as an icicle to Luke unless he found the young warrior soon.

The Tauntaun was already feeling the effects of the temperature drop. Not even its layers of insulating fat or the matted gray fur could protect it from the elements after nightfall. Already the beast was wheezing, its breathing becoming increasingly labored.

Han prayed that the snow-lizard wouldn't drop, at least not until he had located Luke.

He drove his mount harder, forcing it on across the icy plains.

Another figure was moving across the snow, its metal body hovering above the frozen ground.

The Imperial Probe Droid paused briefly in midflight, its sensors twitching.

Then, satisfied with its findings, the robot gently lowered itself, coming to rest on the ground. Like spider legs, several probes separated from the metal hull, dislodging some of the snow that had settled there.

Something began to take shape around the robot, a pulsating glow that gradually covered the machine as if with a transparent dome. Quickly this force field solidified, repelling the blowing snow that brushed over the droid's hull.

After a moment the glow faded, and the blowing snow soon formed a perfect dome of white, completely concealing the droid and its protective force field.

The Tauntaun was racing at maximum speed, certainly too fast considering the distance it had traveled and the unbearable frigid air. No longer wheezing, it had begun moaning pitifully, and its legs were becoming more and more unsteady. Han felt sorry about the Tauntaun's pain, but at present the creature's life was only secondary to that of his friend Luke.

It was becoming difficult for Han to see through the thickening snowfall. Desperate, he searched for some interruption in the eternal plains, some distant spot that might actually be Luke. But there was nothing to see other than the darkening expanses of snow and ice.

Yet there was a sound.

Han drew the reins in, bringing the Tauntaun to an abrupt halt on the plain. Solo could not be certain, but there seemed to be some sound other than the howling of the winds that whipped past him. He strained to look in the direction of the sound.

Then he spurred his Tauntaun, forcing it to gallop across the snow-swept field.

Luke could have been a corpse, food for the scavengers, by the time the light of dawn returned. But somehow he was still alive, though barely, and struggling to stay that way even with the night storms violently assaulting him. Luke painfully pulled himself upright from the snow, only to be blasted back down by the freezing gale. As he fell he considered the irony of it all—a farm boy from Tatooine maturing to battle the Death Star, now perishing alone in a frozen alien wasteland.

It took all of Luke's remaining strength to drag himself a half meter before finally collapsing, sinking into the ever-deepening drifts. "I can't . . ." he said, though no one could hear his words.

But someone, though still unseen, had heard.

"You must." The words vibrated in Luke's mind. "Luke, look at me!"

Luke could not ignore that command; the power of those softly spoken words was too great.

With a great effort, Luke lifted his head and saw what he thought was a hallucination. In front of him, apparently unaffected by the cold and still clad only in the shabby robes he had worn in the hot desert of Tatooine, stood Ben Kenobi.

Luke wanted to call out to him, but he was speechless.

The apparition spoke with the same gentle authority Ben had always used with the young man. "You must survive, Luke."

The young commander found the strength to move his lips again. "I'm cold . . . so cold . . ."

"You must go to the Dagobah system," the spectral figure of

Ben Kenobi instructed. "You will learn from Yoda, the Jedi Master, the one who taught me."

Luke listened, then reached to touch the ghostly figure. "Ben . . . Ben . . ." he groaned.

The figure remained unmoved by Luke's efforts to reach it. "Luke," it spoke again, "you're our only hope."

Our only hope.

Luke was confused. Yet before he could gather the strength to ask for an explanation, the figure began to fade. And when every trace of the apparition had passed from his sight, Luke thought he saw the approach of a Tauntaun with a human rider on its back. The snow-lizard was approaching, its gait unsteady. The rider was still too far away, too obscured by the storm for identification.

In desperation the young Rebel commander called out, "Ben?!" before again dropping off into unconsciousness.

The snow-lizard was barely able to stand on its saurian hind legs when Han Solo reined it to a stop and dismounted.

Han looked with horror at the snow-covered, almost frozen form lying as if dead at his feet.

"Come on, buddy," he appealed to Luke's inert figure, immediately forgetting his own nearly frozen body, "you aren't dead yet. Give me a signal here."

Han could detect no sign of life, and noticed that Luke's face, nearly covered with snow, was savagely torn. He rubbed at the youth's face, being careful not to touch the drying wounds. "Don't do this, Luke. It's not your time."

Finally a slight response. A low moan, barely audible over the winds, was strong enough to send a warm glow through Han's own shivering body. He grinned with relief. "I knew you wouldn't leave me out here all alone! We've got to get you out of here."

Knowing that Luke's salvation—and his own—lay in the speed of the Tauntaun, Han moved toward the beast, carrying the young warrior limply in his arms. But before he could drape the unconscious form over the animal's back, the snow-lizard gave an agonized roar, then fell into a shaggy gray heap on the snow. Laying his companion down, Han rushed to the side of the fallen creature. The Tauntaun made one final sound, not a roar or bellow but only a sickly rasp. Then the beast was silent.

Solo gripped the Tauntaun's hide, his numbed fingers searching for even the slightest indication of life. "Deader than a Triton moon," he said, knowing that Luke did not hear a word. "We haven't got much time."

Resting Luke's motionless form against the belly of the dead snow-lizard, Han proceeded to work. It might be something of a sacrilege, he mused, using a Jedi Knight's favorite weapon like this, but right now Luke's lightsaber was the most efficient and precise tool to cut through the thick skin of a Tauntaun.

At first the weapon felt strange in his hand, but momentarily he was cutting the animal's carcass from hairy head to scaly hind paws. Han winced at the foul odor that rose from the steaming incision. There were few things he could remember that stank like a snow-lizard's innards. Without deliberation he tossed the slippery entrails into the snow.

When the animal's corpse had been entirely eviscerated, Han shoved his friend inside the warm, hair-covered skin. "I know this doesn't smell so good, Luke, but it'll keep you from freezing. I'm sure this Tauntaun wouldn't hesitate if it were the other way around."

From the body of the snow-lizard, another blast of entrail-stench rose out of the disemboweled cavity. "Whew!" Han almost gagged. "It's just as well you're out cold, pal."

There wasn't much time left to do what had to be done. Han's freezing hands went to the supply pack strapped to the Tauntaun's back and rummaged through the Rebel-issue items until he located the shelter container.

Before unpacking it, he spoke into his comlink. "Echo Base, do you copy?"

No response.

"This comlink is useless!"

The sky had darkened ominously and the winds blew violently, making even breathing close to impossible. Han fought to open the shelter container and stiffly began to construct the one piece of Rebel equipment that might protect them both—if only for a short while longer.

"If I don't get this shelter up fast," he grumbled to himself, "Jabba won't need those bounty hunters."

III

ARTOO-DETOO stood just outside the entrance to the secret Rebel ice hangar, dusted with a layer of snow that had settled over his plug-shaped body. His inner timing mechanisms knew he had waited here a long time and his optical sensors told him that the sky was dark.

But the R2 unit was concerned only with his built-in probe-sensors that were still sending signals across the ice fields. His long and earnest sensorsearch for the missing Luke Skywalker and Han Solo had not turned up a thing.

The stout droid began beeping nervously when Threepio approached him, plodding stiffly through the snow.

"Artoo," the gold-colored robot inclined the upper half of his form at the hip joints, "there's nothing more you can do. You must come inside." Threepio straightened to his full height again, simulating a human shiver as the night winds howled past his gleaming hull. "Artoo, my joints are freezing up. Will you hurry . . . please? . . ." But before he could finish his own sentence, Threepio was hurrying back toward the hangar entrance.

Hoth's sky was then entirely black with night, and Princess Leia Organa stood inside the Rebel base entrance, maintaining a worried vigil. She shivered in the night wind as she tried to see into the Hoth darkness. Waiting near a deeply concerned Major Derlin, her mind was somewhere out on the ice fields.

The giant Wookiee sat nearby, his maned head lifting quickly from his hairy hands as the two droids Threepio and Artoo reentered the hangar.

Threepio was humanly distraught. "Artoo has not been able to pick up any signals," he reported, fretting, "although he feels his range is probably too limited to cause us to give up hope." Still, very little confidence could be detected in Three-pio's artificial voice.

Leia gave the taller droid a nod of acknowledgment, but did not speak. Her thoughts were occupied with the pair of missing heroes. Most disturbing to her was that she found her mind focused on one of the two: a dark-haired Corellian whose words were not always to be taken literally.

As the princess kept watch, Major Derlin turned to acknowledge a Rebel lieutenant reporting in. "All patrols are now in except Solo and Skywalker, sir."

The major looked over at Princess Leia. "Your Highness," he said, his voice weighty with regret, "nothing more can be done tonight. The temperature is dropping fast. The shield doors must be closed. "I'm sorry." Derlin waited a moment then addressed the lieutenant. "Close the doors."

The Rebel officer turned to carry out Derlin's order and immediately the chamber of ice seemed to drop even more in temperature as the mournful Wookiee howled his grief.

"The speeders should be ready in the morning," the major said to Leia. "They'll make the search easier."

Not really expecting an affirmative reply, Leia asked, "Is there any chance of their surviving until morning?"

"Slim," Major Derlin answered with grim honesty. "But yes, there's a chance."

In response to the major's words, Artoo began to operate the miniature computers inside his barrellike metal body, taking only moments to juggle numerous sets of mathematical computations, and climaxing his figurings with a series of triumphant beeps.

"Ma'am," Threepio interpreted, "Artoo says the chances against survival are seven hundred twenty-five to one." Then, tilting toward the shorter robot, the protocol droid grumbled, "Actually, I don't think we needed to know that."

No one responded to Threepio's translation. For several prolonged moments there was a solemn silence, broken only by the echoing clang of metal slamming against metal: the huge doors of the Rebel base were closed for the night. It was as if some heartless deity had officially severed the assembled group from the two men out on the ice plains and had, with a metallic bang, announced their deaths.

Chewbacca let out another suffering howl.

And a silent prayer, often spoken on an erst-while world called Alderaan, crept into Leia's thoughts.

* * *

The sun that was creeping over Hoth's northern horizon was relatively dim, but its light was enough to shed some warmth on the planet's icy surface. The light crawled across the rolling hills of snow, fought to reach the darker recesses of the icy gorges, then finally came to rest on what must have been the only perfect white mound on the entire world.

So perfect was the snow-covered mound that it must have owed its existence to some power other than Nature. Then, as the sky grew steadily brighter, this mound began to hum. Anyone observing the mound now would have been startled as the snow dome seemed to erupt, sending its snowy outer covering skyward in a great burst of white particles. A droning machine began pulling back its retractable sensor arms, and its awesome bulk slowly rose from its frozen white bed.

The probe robot paused briefly in the windy air, then continued on its morning mission across the snow-covered plains.

Something else had invaded the morning air of the ice world—a relatively small, snub-nosed craft, with dark cockpit windows and laser guns mounted on each side. The Rebel snowspeeder was heavily armored and designed for warfare near the planet's surface. But this morning the small craft was on a reconnaissance mission, racing above the expansive white landscape and arcing over the contours of the snowdrifts.

Although the snowspeeder was designed for a two-man crew, Zev was the ship's only occupant. His eyes took in a panoramic scan of the desolate stretches below, and he prayed that he would find the objects of his search before he went snowblind.

Presently he heard a low beeping signal.

"Echo Base," he shouted jubilantly into his cockpit comlink, "I've got something! Not much, but it could be a sign of life. Sector four-six-one-four by eight-eight-two. I'm closing in."

Frantically working the controls of his ship, Zev reduced its speed slightly and banked the craft over a snowdrift. He welcomed the sudden G-force pressing him against his seat and headed the snowspeeder in the direction of the faint signal.

As the white infinity of Hoth's terrain streaked under him, the Rebel pilot switched his comlink to a new frequency. "Echo Three, this is Rogue Two. Do you copy? Commander Skywalker, this is Rogue Two."

The only reply that came through his comlink receiver was static.

But then he heard a voice, a very distant-sounding voice, fighting its way through the crackling noise. "Nice of you guys to drop by. Hope we didn't get you up too early."

Zev welcomed the characteristic cynicism in Han Solo's voice. He switched his transmitter back to the hidden Rebel base. "Echo Base, this is Rogue Two," he reported, his voice suddenly rising in pitch. "I found them. Repeat . . ."

As he spoke, the pilot pulled in a fine-tune fix on the signals winking on his cockpit monitor screens. Then he further reduced the speed of his craft, bringing it down close enough to the planet's surface so that he could better see a small object standing out against the fleecy plains.

The object, a portable Rebel-Issue shelter, sat atop a snowdrift. On the shelter's windward side was a hard-packed layer of white. And resting gingerly against the upper part of the snowdrift was a makeshift radio antenna.

But a more welcome sight than any of this was the familiar human figure standing in front of the snow shelter, frantically waving his arms at the snowspeeder.

As Zev dipped his craft for a landing, he felt overwhelmingly grateful that at least one of the warriors he had been sent out to find was still alive.

Only a thick glass window separated the battered, near-frozen body of Luke Skywalker from four of his watchful friends.

Han Solo, who appreciated the relative warmth of the Rebel medical center, was standing beside Leia, his Wookiee copilot, Artoo-Detoo, and See-Threepio. Han exhaled with relief. He knew that, despite the grim atmosphere of the chamber enclosing him, the young commander was finally out of danger and in the best of mechanical hands.

Clad only in white shorts, Luke hung in a vertical position inside a transparent cylinder with a combination breath mask and microphone covering his nose and mouth. The surgeon droid, Too-Onebee, was attending to the youth with the skill of the finest humanoid doctors. He was aided by his medical assistant droid, FX-7, which looked like nothing more than a metal-capped set of cylinders, wires, and appendages. Gracefully, the surgeon droid worked a switch that brought a gelatinous red fluid pouring down over his human patient. This bacta, Han knew, could work miracles, even with patients in such dire shape as Luke.

As the bubbling slime encapsulated his body, Luke began to

thrash about and rave deliriously. "Watch out," he moaned. ". . . snow creatures. Dangerous . . . Yoda . . . go to Yoda . . . only hope."

Han had not the slightest idea what his friend was raving about. Chewbacca, also perplexed by the youth's babbling, expressed himself with an interrogative Wookiee bark.

"He doesn't make sense to me either, Chewie," Han replied.

Threepio commented hopefully, "I do hope he's all there, if you take my meaning. It would be most unfortunate if Master Luke were to develop a short circuit."

"The kid ran into something," Han observed matter-of-factly, "and it wasn't just the cold."

"It's those creatures he keeps talking about," Leia said, looking at the grimly staring Solo. "We've doubled the security, Han," she began, tentatively trying to thank him, "I don't know how—"

"Forget it," he said brusquely. Right now he was concerned only with his friend in the red bacta fluid.

Luke's body sloshed through the brightly colored substance, the bacta's healing properties by now taking effect. For a while it appeared as if Luke were trying to resist the curative flow of the translucent muck. Then, at last, he gave up his mumbling and relaxed, succumbing to the bacta's powers.

Too-Onebee turned away from the human who had been entrusted to his care. He angled his skull-shaped head to gaze at Han and the others through the window. "Commander Skywalker has been in dormo-shock but is responding well to the bacta," the robot announced, his commanding, authoritative voice heard distinctly through the glass. "He is now out of danger."

The surgeon robot's words immediately wiped away the tension that had seized the group on the other side of the window. Leia sighed in relief, and Chewbacca grunted his approval of Too-Onebee's treatment.

Luke had no way of estimating how long he had been delirious. But now he was in full command of his mind and senses. He sat up on his bed in the Rebel medical center. What a relief, he thought, to be breathing real air again, however cold it might be.

A medical droid was removing the protective pad from his healing face. His eyes were uncovered and he was beginning to perceive the face of someone standing by his bed. Gradually the smiling image of Princess Leia came into focus. She gracefully moved toward him and gently brushed his hair out of his eyes.

"The bacta are growing well," she said as she looked at his healing wounds. "The scars should be gone in a day or so. Does it still hurt you?"

Across the room, the door banged open. Artoo beeped a cheerful greeting as he rolled toward Luke, and Threepio clanked noisily toward Luke's bed. "Master Luke, it's good to see you functional again."

"Thanks, Threepio."

Artoo emitted a series of happy beeps and whistles.

"Artoo expresses his relief also," Threepio translated helpfully.

Luke was certainly grateful for the robots' concern. But before he could reply to either of the droids, he met with yet another interruption.

"Hi, kid," Han Solo greeted him boisterously as he and Chewbacca burst into the medical center.

The Wookiee growled a friendly greeting.

"You look strong enough to wrestle a Gundark," Han observed.

Luke felt that strong, and felt grateful to his friend. "Thanks to you."

"That's two you owe me, junior." Han gave the princess a wide, devilish grin. "Well, Your Worship," he said mockingly, "it looks like you arranged to keep me close by for a while longer."

"I had nothing to do with it," Leia said hotly, annoyed at Han's vanity. "General Rieekan thinks it's dangerous for any ships to leave the system until the generators are operational."

"That makes a good story. But *I* think you just can't bear to let me out of your sight."

"I don't know where you get your delusions, laser brains," she retorted.

Chewbacca, amused by this verbal battle between two of the strongest human wills he had ever encountered, let out a roaring Wookiee laugh.

"Laugh it up, fuzz ball," Han said goodnaturedly. "You didn't see us alone in the south passage."

Until now, Luke had scarcely listened to this lively exchange. Han and the princess had argued frequently enough in the past. But that reference to the south passage sparked his curiosity, and he looked at Leia for an explanation.

"She expressed her true feeling for me," Han continued,

delighting in the rosy flush that appeared on the princess's cheeks. "Come on, Your Highness, you've already forgotten?"

"Why, you low-down, stuck-up, half-witted, scruffy-looking nerf-herder . . ." she sputtered in fury.

"Who's scruffy-looking?" he grinned. "I tell ya, sweetheart, I must've hit pretty close to the mark to get you hoppin' like this. Doesn't it look that way to you, Luke?"

"Yeah," he said, staring at the princess incredulously, "it does . . . kind of."

Leia looked over at Luke with a strange mixture of emotions showing on her flushed face. Something vulnerable, almost childlike, was reflected in her eyes for a moment. And then the tough mask fell again.

"Oh, it does, does it?" she said. "Well, I guess you don't understand everything about women, do you?"

Luke agreed silently. He agreed even more when in the next moment Leia leaned over and kissed him firmly on the lips. Then she turned on her heel and marched across the room, slamming the door behind her. Everyone in the room—human, Wookiee, and droid—looked at one another, speechless.

In the distance, a warning alarm blared through the subterranean corridors.

General Rieekan and his head controller were conferring in the Rebel command center when Han Solo and Chewbacca burst into the room. Princess Leia and Threepio, who had been listening to the general and his officer, turned in anticipation at their approach.

A warning signal blared across the chamber from the huge console located behind Rieekan and monitored by Rebel control officers.

"General," the sensor controller called.

Grimly attentive, General Rieekan watched the console screens. Suddenly he saw a flashing signal that had not been there a moment before. "Princess," he said, "I think we have a visitor."

Leia, Han, Chewbacca, and Threepio gathered around the general and watched the beeping monitor screens.

"We've picked up something outside the base in Zone Twelve. It's moving east," said Rieekan.

"Whatever it is, it's metal," the sensor controller observed.

Leia's eyes widened in surprise. "Then it can't be one of those creatures that attacked Luke?"

"Could it be ours?" Han asked. "A speeder?"

The sensor controller shook his head. "No, there's no signal." Then came a sound from another monitor. "Wait, something very weak . . ."

Walking as rapidly as his stiff joints allowed, Threepio approached the console. His auditory sensors tuned in the strange signals. "I must say, sir, I'm fluent in over sixty million forms of communication, but this is something new. Must be in a code or—"

Just then the voice of a Rebel trooper cut in through the console's comlink speaker. "This is Echo Station Three-Eight. Unidentified object is in our scope. It's just over the ridge. We should have visual contact in about—" Without warning the voice filled with fear. "What the—? Oh, no!"

A burst of radio static followed, then the transmission broke off completely.

Han frowned. "Whatever it is," he said, "it isn't friendly. Let's have a look. Come on, Chewie."

Even before Han and Chewbacca were out of the chamber, General Rieekan had dispatched Rogues Ten and Eleven to Station Three-Eight.

The mammoth Imperial Star Destroyer occupied a position of deadly prominence in the Emperor's fleet. The sleekly elongated ship was larger and even more ominous than the five wedge-shaped Imperial Star Destroyers guarding it. Together these six cruisers were the most dreaded and devastating warships in the galaxy, capable of reducing to cosmic scrap anything that strayed too close to their weapons.

Flanking the Star Destroyers were a number of smaller fighter ships and, darting about this great space armada, were the infamous TIE fighters.

Supreme confidence reigned in the heart of every crew member in this Imperial death squadron, especially among the personnel on the monstrous central Star Destroyer. But something also blazed within their souls. Fear—fear of merely the sound of the familiar heavy footsteps as they echoed through the enormous ship. Crew members dreaded these footfalls and shuddered whenever they were heard approaching, bringing their much feared, but much respected leader.

Towering above them in his black cloak and concealing black headgear, Darth Vader, Dark Lord of the Sith, entered the main control deck, and the men around him fell silent. In what seemed to be an endless moment, no sounds except those from the ship's control boards and the loud wheezes coming from the ebony figure's metal breath screen were to be heard.

As Darth Vader watched the endless array of stars, Captain Piett rushed across the wide bridge of the ship, carrying a message for the squat, evil-looking Admiral Ozzel, who was stationed on the bridge. "I think we've found something, Admiral," he announced nervously, looking from Ozzel to the Dark Lord.

"Yes, Captain?" The admiral was a supremely confident man who felt relaxed in the presence of his cloaked superior.

"The report we have is only a fragment, from a probe droid in the Hoth system. But it's the best lead we've had in—"

"We have had thousands of probe droids searching the galaxy," Ozzel broke in angrily. "I want proof, not leads. I don't intend to continue to chase around from one side of—"

Abruptly the figure in black approached the two and interrupted. "You found something?" he asked, his voice somewhat distorted by the breath mask.

Captain Piett respectfully gazed at his master, who loomed above him like a black-robed, omnipotent god. "Yes, sir," Piett said slowly, choosing his words with caution. "We have visuals. The system is supposed to be devoid of human forms . . ."

But Vader was no longer listening to the captain. His masked face turned toward an image beamed on one of the viewscreens—an image of a small squadron of Rebel snowspeeders streaking above the white fields.

"That's it," Darth Vader boomed without further deliberation.

"My lord," Admiral Ozzel protested, "there are so many uncharted settlements. It could be smugglers—"

"That is the one!" the former Jedi Knight insisted, clenching a black-gloved fist. "And Skywalker is with them. Bring in the patrol ships, Admiral, and set your course for the Hoth system." Vader looked toward an officer wearing a green uniform with matching cap. "General Veers," the Dark Lord addressed him, "prepare your men."

As soon as Darth Vader had spoken, his men set about to launch his fearful plan.

The Imperial Probe Droid raised a large antenna from its buglike head and sent out a piercing, high-frequency signal. The robot's scanners had reacted to a lifeform hidden behind a great dune of snow and noted the appearance of a brown Wookiee head and the sound of a deep-throated growl. The blasters that had been built into the probe robot took aim at the furry giant. But before the robot had a chance to fire, a red beam from a hand blaster exploded from behind the Imperial Probe Droid and nicked its darkly finished hull.

As he ducked behind a large snow dune, Han Solo noticed Chewbacca still hidden, and then watched as the robot spun around in midair to face him. So far the ruse was working and now *he* was the target. Han had barely moved out of range as the floating machine fired, blasting chunks of snow from the edge of his dune. He fired again, hitting it square on with the beam of his weapon. Then he heard a high-pitched whine coming from the deadly machine, and in an instant the Imperial Probe Droid burst into a billion or more flaming pieces.

". . . I'm afraid there's not much left," Han said over the comlink as he concluded his report to the underground base.

Princess Leia and General Rieekan were still manning the console where they had maintained constant communication with Han. "What is it?" Leia asked.

"Droid of some kind," he answered. "I didn't hit it that hard. It must have had a self-destruct."

Leia paused as she considered this unwelcome piece of information. "An Imperial droid," she said, betraying some trepidation.

"If it was," Han warned, "the Empire surely knows we're here."

General Rieekan shook his head slowly. "We'd better start to evacuate the planet."

IV

SIX ominous shapes appeared in the black space of the Hoth system and loomed like vast demons of destruction, ready to unleash the furies of their Imperial weapons. Inside the largest of the six Imperial Star Destroyers, Darth Vader sat alone in a small spherical room. A single shaft of light gleamed on his black helmet as he sat motionless in his raised meditation chamber.

As General Veers approached, the sphere opened slowly, the upper half lifting like a jagged-toothed mechanical jaw. To Veers, the dark figure seated inside the mouthlike cocoon hardly seemed alive, though a powerful aura of sheer evil emanated from him, sending a chilling fear through the officer.

Uncertain of his own courage, Veers took a step forward. He had a message to deliver but felt prepared to wait for hours if necessary rather than disturb Vader's meditation.

But Vader spoke immediately. "What is it, Veers?"

"My lord," the general replied, choosing each word with care, "the fleet has moved out of light-speed. Com-Scan has detected an energy field protecting an area of the sixth planet in the Hoth system. The field is strong enough to deflect any bombardment."

Vader stood, rising to his full two-meter height, his cloak swaying against the floor. "So, the Rebel scum are alerted to our presence." Furious, he clenched his black-gloved hands into fists. "Admiral Ozzel came out of light-speed too close to the system."

"He felt surprise was a wiser—"

"He's as clumsy as he is stupid," Vader cut in, breathing heavily. "A clean bombardment is impossible through their energy field. Prepare your troops for a surface attack."

With military precision, General Veers turned and marched out of the meditation room, leaving behind an enraged Darth Vader. Alone in the chamber, Vader activated a large viewscreen that showed a brightly lit image of his Star Destroyer's vast bridge.

Admiral Ozzel, responding to Vader's summons, stepped forward, his face almost filling the Dark Lord's monitor screen. There was trepidation in Ozzel's voice when he announced, "Lord Vader, the fleet has moved out of light-speed—"

But Vader's reply was addressed to the officer standing slightly behind Ozzel. "Captain Piett."

Knowing better than to delay, Captain Piett stepped forward instantly as the admiral staggered back a step, his hand automatically reaching for his throat.

"Yes, my lord," Piett answered respectfully.

Ozzel began to gag now as his throat, as if in the grip of invisible talons, began to constrict.

"Make ready to land assault troops beyond the energy field," Vader ordered. "Then deploy the fleet so that nothing can get off that planet. You're in command now, Admiral Piett."

Piett was simultaneously pleased and unsettled by this news. As he turned to carry out the orders, he saw a figure that might someday be himself. Ozzel's face was hideously contorted as he fought for one final breath of air; then he dropped into a dead heap on the floor.

The Empire had entered the system of Hoth.

Rebel troops rushed to their alert stations as the warning alarms wailed through the ice tunnels. Ground crews and droids of all sizes and makes hurried to perform their assigned duties, responding efficiently to the impending Imperial threat.

The armored snowspeeders were fueled as they waited in attack formation to blast out of the main cavern entranceway. Meanwhile, in the hangar, Princess Leia was addressing a small band of Rebel fighter pilots. "The large transport ships will leave as soon as they're loaded. Only two fighter escorts per ship. The energy shield can only be opened for a split second, so you'll have to stay very close to the transports."

Hobbie, a Rebel veteran of many battles, looked at the princess with concern. "Two fighters against a Star Destroyer?"

"The ion cannon will fire several blasts which should destroy any ships in your flight path," Leia explained. "When you clear the energy shield, you will proceed to the rendezvous point. Good luck."

Somewhat reassured, Hobbie and the other pilots raced toward their fighter cockpits.

Meanwhile, Han was working frantically to complete welding a lifter on the *Millennium Falcon*. Finishing quickly, he hopped to the hangar floor and switched on his comlink. "All right, Chewie," he said to the hairy figure seated at the *Falcon*'s controls, "give it a try."

Just then Leia walked past, throwing him an angry look. Han looked at her smugly while the freighter's lifters began to rise off the floor, whereupon the right lifter began to shake erratically, then broke partially loose to swing back down again with an embarrassing crash.

He turned away from Leia, catching only a glimpse of her face as she mockingly raised an eyebrow.

"Hold it, Chewie," Han grunted into his small transmitter.

The *Avenger*, one of the Imperial armada's wedgelike Star Destroyers, hovered like a mechanized death angel in the sea of stars outside the Hoth system. As the colossal ship began to move closer to the ice world, the planet became clearly visible through the windows which stretched 100 meters or more across the huge bridge of the warship.

Captain Needa, commander of the *Avenger*'s crew, gazed out a main port, looking at the planet when a controller came up to him. "Sir, Rebel ship coming into our sector."

"Good," Needa replied with a gleam in his eyes. "Our first catch of the day."

"Their first target will be the power generators," General Rieekan told the princess.

"First transport Three Zone approaching shield," one of the Rebel controllers said, tracking a bright image that could only be an Imperial Star Destroyer.

"Prepare to open shield," a radarman ordered.

"Stand by, Ion Control," another controller said.

A giant metal globe on Hoth's icy surface rotated into position and angled its great turret gun upward.

"Fire!" came the order from General Rieekan.

Suddenly two red beams of destructive energy were released into the cold skies. The beams almost immediately overtook the first of the racing Rebel transport craft, and sped on a direct course toward the huge Star Destroyer.

The twin red bolts struck the enormous ship and blasted its conning tower. Explosions set off by the blast began to rock the great flying fortress, spinning it out of control. The Star Destroyer plunged into deep space as the Rebel transport and its two fighter escorts streaked off to safety.

Luke Skywalker, preparing to depart, pulled on his heavy-weather gear and watched the pilots, gunners, and R2 units hurrying to complete their tasks. He started toward the row of snowspeeders that awaited him. On his way, the young commander paused at the tail section of the *Millennium Falcon*, where Han Solo and Chewbacca were working frenetically on the right lifter.

"Chewie," Luke called, "take care of yourself. And watch over this guy, will ya?"

The Wookiee barked a farewell, gave Luke a big hug, then turned back to his work on the lifters.

The two friends, Luke and Han, stood looking at each other, perhaps for the last time.

"I hope you make your peace with Jabba," Luke said at last.

"Give 'em hell, kid," the Corellian responded lightly.

The young commander began to walk away as memories of exploits shared with Han rushed to his mind. He stopped and looked back at the *Falcon*, and saw his friend still staring after him. As they gazed at each other for a brief moment, Chewbacca looked up and knew that each was wishing the other the best, wherever their individual fates might take them.

The public address system broke in on their thoughts. "First transport is clear," a Rebel announcer proclaimed the good news.

At the announcement, a cheer burst from those gathered in the hangar. Luke turned and hurried over to his snowspeeder. When he reached it, Dack, his fresh-faced young gunner, was standing outside the ship waiting for him.

"How are you feeling, sir?" Dack asked enthusiastically.

"Like new, Dack. How about you?"

Dack beamed. "Right now I feel like I could take on the whole Empire myself."

"Yeah," Luke said quietly, "I know what you mean." Though there were only a few years between them, at that moment Luke felt centuries older.

Princess Leia's voice came over the address system: "Attention, speeder pilots . . . on the withdrawal signal assemble at South Slope. Your fighters are being prepared for takeoff. Code One Five will be transmitted when evacuation is complete."

Threepio and Artoo stood amid the rapidly moving personnel as the pilots readied for departure. The golden droid tilted slightly as he turned his sensors on the little R2 robot. The shadows playing over Threepio's face gave the illusion that his faceplate had lengthened into a frown. "Why is it," he asked, "when things seem to get settled, everything falls apart?" Leaning forward, he gently patted the other droid's hull. "Take good care of Master Luke. And take good care of yourself."

Artoo whistled and tooted a good-bye, then turned to roll down the ice corridor. Waving stiffly, Threepio watched as his stout and faithful friend moved away.

To an observer, it may have seemed that Threepio grew misty-eyed, but then it wasn't the first time he had gotten a drop of oil clogged before his optical sensors.

Finally turning, the human-shaped robot moved off in the opposite direction.

V

NO one on Hoth heard the sound. At first, it was simply too distant to carry above the whining winds. Besides, the Rebel troopers, fighting the cold as they prepared for battle, were too busy to really listen.

In the snow trenches, Rebel officers screamed out their orders to make themselves heard above the gale-force winds. Troopers hurried to carry out their commands, running through the snow with heavy bazookalike weapons on their shoulders, and lodging those death rays along the icy rims of the trenches.

The Rebel power generators near the gun towers began popping, buzzing, and crackling with deafening bursts of electrical power—enough to supply the vast underground complex. But above all this activity and noise a strange sound could be heard, an ominous thumping that was coming nearer and was beginning to shake the frozen ground. When it was close enough to attract the attention of an officer, he strained to see through the storm, looking for the source of the heavy, rhythmic pounding. Other men looked up from their work and saw what looked like a number of moving specks. Through the blizzard, the small dots seemed to be advancing at a slow yet steady pace, churning up clouds of snow as they moved toward the Rebel base.

The officer raised his electrobinoculars and focused on the approaching objects. There must have been a dozen of them resolutely advancing through the snow, looking like creatures out of some uncharted past. But they were machines, each of them stalking like enormous ungulates on four jointed legs.

Walkers!

With a shock of recognition, the officer identified the Empire's All Terrain Armored Transports. Each machine was formidably armed with cannons placed on its foreside like the horns of some prehistoric beast. Moving like mechanized pachyderms, the walkers emitted deadly fire from their turnstile guns and cannons.

The officer grabbed his comlink. "Rogue Leader . . . Incoming! Point Zero Three."

"Echo Station Five-Seven, we're on our way."

Even as Luke Skywalker replied, an explosion sprayed ice and snow around the officer and his terror-struck men. The walkers already had them within range. The troopers knew their job was to divert attention while the transport ships were launched, but none of the Rebel soldiers was prepared to die under the feet or weapons of these horrible machines.

Brilliant billows of orange and yellow flames exploded from the walker guns. Nervously the Rebel troopers aimed their weapons at the walkers, each soldier feeling icy, unseen fingers pierce his body.

Of the twelve snowspeeders, four took the lead, soaring at full throttle as they moved toward the enemy. One All Terrain Armored Transport machine fired, barely missing the banking craft. A burst of gunfire blew another speeder into a ball of flaming oblivion that lit up the sky.

Luke saw the explosion of his squadron's first casualty as he looked from his cockpit window. Angrily, Luke fired his ship's guns at a walker, only to receive a hail of Imperial fire power that shook his speeder in a barrage of flak.

Regaining control of his ship, Luke was joined by another snowspeeder, Rogue Three. They swarmed like insects around the relentlessly stomping walkers, as other speeders continued to exchange fire with the Imperial assault machines. Rogue Leader and Rogue Three flitted alongside the lead walker, then moved away from each other, both banking to the right.

Luke saw the horizon tilt as he maneuvered his speeder between the walker's jointed legs and soared out from under the monster machine. Bringing his speeder back to horizontal flight, the young commander contacted his companion ship. "Rogue Leader to Rogue Three."

"Copy, Rogue Leader," acknowledge Wedge, the pilot of Rogue Three.

"Wedge," Luke called into his comlink, "split your squad into pairs." Luke's snowspeeder then banked and turned, while Wedge's ship moved off in the opposite direction with another Rebel craft.

The walkers, firing all cannons, continued their march across the snow. Inside one of the assault machines two Imperial pilots had spotted the Rebel guns, conspicuous against the white field. The pilots began to maneuver the walker toward the guns when they noticed a lone snowspeeder making a reckless charge directly toward their main viewport, guns blazing. A huge explosion flashed outside the impenetrable window and dissipated as the snowspeeder, roaring through the smoke, disappeared overhead.

As Luke soared up and away from the walker, he looked back. That armor is too strong for blasters, he thought. There *must* be some other way of attacking these horrors; something other than fire power. For a moment Luke thought of some of the simple tactics a farm boy might employ against a wild beast. Then, turning his snowspeeder for yet another run against the walkers, he made a decision.

"Rogue group," he called into his comlink, "use your harpoons and tow cables. Go for the legs. It's our only hope of stopping them. Hobbie, are you still with me?"

The reassuring voice immediately responded. "Yes, sir."

"Well, stick close now."

As he leveled his ship, Luke was grimly determined to glide in tight formation with Hobbie. Together they veered, dropping nearer Hoth's surface.

In Luke's cockpit, his gunner, Dack, was jostled by the abrupt movement of the craft. Trying to keep his grip on the Rebel harpoon gun in his hand, he shouted, "Whoea! Luke, I can't seem to find my restraints."

Explosions rocked Luke's ship, tossing it about violently in the enveloping flak. Through the window he could see another walker that appeared to be unaffected by the full fire power of the Rebel attack speeders. This lumbering machine now became Luke's target as he flew, moving in a descending arc. The walker was firing directly at him, creating a wall of laser bolts and flak.

"Just hang on, Dack," he yelled over the explosions, "and get ready to fire that tow cable!"

Another great blast shook Luke's snowspeeder. He fought to regain control as the ship wobbled in its flight. Luke began to sweat profusely, despite the cold, as he desperately attempted to right his plunging ship. But the horizon still spun in front of him.

"Stand by, Dack. We're almost there. Are you okay?"

Dack didn't answer. Luke managed to turn and saw that Hobbie's speeder was maintaining its course next to him as they evaded the explosions bursting around them. He craned his head around and saw Dack, blood streaming from his forehead, slumped against the controls.

"Dack!"

On the ground, the gun towers near the Rebel power generators blasted away at the walking Imperial machines, but with no apparent effect. Imperial weapons bombarded the area all around them, blasting the snow skyward, almost blinding their human targets with the continuous onslaught. The officer who had first seen the incredible machines and fought alongside his men, was one of the first to be cut down by a walker's body-ripping rays. Troops rushed to his aid, but couldn't save him; too much of his blood had already spilled, making a scarlet stain against the snow.

More Rebel fire power blasted from one of the dishlike guns that had been erected near the power generators. Despite these tremendous explosions, the walkers continued to march. Another speeder made a heroic dive between a pair of the walkers, only to be caught by fire from one of the machines that exploded it into a great ball of rippling flames.

The surface explosions made the walls of the ice hangar tremble, causing deep cracks to spread.

Han Solo and Chewbacca were working frantically to complete their welding job. As they worked, it became obvious that the widening cracks would soon bring the entire ice ceiling smashing down upon them.

"First chance we get," Han said, "we're giving this crate a complete overhaul." But he knew that first he would have to get the *Millennium Falcon* out of this white hell.

Even as he and the Wookiee labored on the ship, enormous pieces of ice, broken loose by the explosions, came tumbling down throughout the underground base. Princess Leia moved quickly, trying to avoid the falling frozen chunks, as she sought shelter in the Rebel command center.

"I'm not sure we can protect two transports at a time," General Rieekan told her as she entered the chamber.

"It's risky," she answered, "but our holding action is faltering." Leia realized that the transport launchings were taking too much time and that the procedure had to be hastened.

Rieekan issued a command through his comlink. "Launch patrol, proceed with accelerated departures . . ."

As the general gave his order, Leia looked toward an aide and said, "Begin clearing the remaining ground staff." But she knew that their escape depended completely on Rebel success in the on-going battle above.

Inside the cold and cramped cockpit of the lead Imperial walker, General Veers moved between his snow-suited pilots. "What is the distance to the power generators?"

Without looking away from the control panel, one of the pilots replied, "Six-four-one."

Satisfied, General Veers reached for an electrotelescope and peered through the viewfinder to focus on the bullet-shaped power generators and the Rebel soldiers fighting to save them. Suddenly the walker began to rock violently under a barrage of Rebel gunfire. As he was propelled backward, Veers saw his pilots scrambling over the controls to keep the machine from toppling over.

The Rogue Three snowspeeder had just attacked the lead walker. Its pilot, Wedge, hooted with a loud Rebel shout of victory as he saw the damage his guns had caused.

Other snowspeeders passed Wedge, racing in the opposite direction. He steered his craft on a direct course toward another walking death machine. As he approached the monster, Wedge shouted to his gunner, "Activate harpoon!"

The gunner pressed the firing switch as his pilot daringly maneuvered their craft through the walker's legs. Immediately the harpoon whooshed from the rear of the speeder, a long length of cable unwinding behind it.

"Cable out!" the gunner yelled. "Let her go!"

Wedge saw the harpoon plunge into one of the metal legs, the cable still connected to his snowspeeder. He checked his controls, then brought the speeder around in front of the Imperial machine. Making an abrupt turn, Wedge guided his ship around one of the hind legs, the cable banding around it like a metallic lariat.

So far, thought Wedge, Luke's plan was working. Now all he had to do was fly his speeder around to the tail end of the walker. Wedge caught a glimpse of Rogue Leader as he carried out the maneuver.

"Cable out!" shouted the speeder's gunner again as Wedge flew their craft alongside the cable-entangled walker, close to the metal hull. Wedge's gunner depressed another switch and released the cable from the rear of the snowspeeder.

The speeder zoomed away and Wedge laughed as he looked down at the results of their efforts. The walker was awkwardly struggling to continue on its way, but the Rebel cable had completely entangled its legs. Finally it leaned to one side and crashed against the ground, its impact stirring up a cloud of ice and snow.

"Rogue Leader . . . One down, Luke," Wedge announced to the pilot of his companion speeder.

"I see it, Wedge," Commander Skywalker answered. "Good work."

In the trenches, Rebel troops cheered in triumph when they saw the assault machine topple. An officer leaped from his snow trench and signaled his men. Bolting out of the trench, he led his troopers in a boisterous charge against the fallen walker, reaching the great metallic hulk before a single Imperial soldier could pull himself free.

The Rebels were about to enter the walker when it suddenly exploded from within, hurtling great jagged chunks of torn metal at them, the impact of the blast flinging the stunned troops back against the snow.

Luke and Zev could see the destruction of the walker as they flew overhead, banking from right to left to avoid the flak bursting around them. When they finally leveled off, their craft were shaken by explosions from the walkers' cannons.

"Steady, Rogue Two," Luke said, looking over at the snowspeeder flying parallel to his own ship. "Set harpoon. I'll cover for you."

But there was another explosion, this one damaging the front section of Zev's ship. The pilot could barely see through the engulfing cloud of smoke that fogged his windshield. He fought to keep his ship on a horizontal path, but more blasts by the enemy made it rock violently.

His view had become so obscured that it wasn't until Zev was directly in the line of fire that he saw the massive image of another Imperial walker. Rogue Two's pilot felt an instant of pain; then his snub-nosed craft, spewing smoke and hurtling on a collision course with the walker, suddenly erupted in flames amid a burst of cannon fire. Very little of Zev or his ship remained to hit the ground.

Luke saw the disintegration and was sickened by the loss of yet another friend. But he couldn't let himself dwell on his grief, especially now when so many other lives depended on his steady leadership.

He looked around desperately, then spoke into his comlink. "Wedge . . . Wedge . . . Rogue Three. Set your harpoon and follow me on the next pass."

As he spoke, Luke was hit hard by a terrific explosion that ripped through his speeder. He struggled with the controls in a futile attempt to keep the small craft under control. A chill of fear swept over him when he noticed the dense twisting funnel of black smoke pouring from his ship's aft section. He realized then that there was no way his damaged speeder could remain aloft. And, to make matters even worse, a walker loomed directly in his path.

Luke struggled with the controls as his ship plunged toward the ground, leaving a trail of smoke and flames behind. By then the heat in the cockpit was nearly unbearable. Flames were beginning to leap about inside the speeder and were coming uncomfortably close to Luke. He finally brought his ship down to skid and crash into the snow just a few meters away from one of the walking Imperial machines.

After impact, Luke struggled to pull himself from the cockpit and looked with horror at the looming figure of the approaching walker.

Gathering all his strength, Luke quickly squeezed himself from under the twisted metal of the control board and moved up against the top of his cockpit. Somehow he managed to open the hatch halfway and climbed out of the ship. With each elephantine step of the oncoming walker, the speeder shook violently. Luke had not realized just how enormous these four-legged horrors were until, unprotected by the shelter of his craft, he saw one up close.

Then he remembered Dack and returned to try and pull his friend's lifeless form from the wrecked speeder. But Luke had to give up. The body was too tightly wedged in the cockpit, and the walker was now almost upon him. Braving the flames, Luke reached into his speeder and grabbed the harpoon gun.

He gazed at the advancing mechanical behemoth and suddenly had an idea. He reached back inside the cockpit of the speeder and groped for a land mine attached to the ship's interior. With a great effort he stretched his fingers and firmly grasped the mine.

Luke leaped away from his vehicle just as the towering machine lifted a massive foot and planted it firmly on the snowspeeder, crushing it flat.

Luke crouched underneath the walker, moving with it to avoid its slow steps. Raising his head, he felt the cold wind slap against his face as he studied the monster's vast underbelly.

As he ran along under the machine, Luke aimed his harpoon gun and fired. A powerful magnet attached to a long thin cable was ejected from the gun and firmly attached itself to the machine's underbelly.

Still running, Luke yanked on the cable, testing to make sure its strength was sufficient to sustain his weight. Then he attached the cable drum to the buckle of his utility belt, allowing its mechanism to pull him up off the ground. Now, dangling from the monster's underbelly, Luke could see the remaining walkers and two Rebel snowspeeders continuing the battle as they soared through fiery explosions.

He climbed up to the machine's hull where he had observed a small hatch. Quickly cutting it open with his laser sword, Luke pulled open the hatch, threw in the land mine, and made a rapid descent along the cable. As he reached the end, Luke dropped hard onto the snow and became unconscious; his inert body was nearly crushed by one of the walker's hind feet.

As the walker passed over and away from him, a muffled explosion tore at its insides. Suddenly the tremendous bulk of the mechanical beast exploded at the seams, machinery and pieces of hull flying in every direction. The Imperial assault machine crumbled into a smoking, motionless heap coming to rest upon what remained of its four stiltlike legs.

VI

THE Rebel command center, its walls and ceiling still shaking and cracking under the force of the battle on the surface, was attempting to operate amid the destruction. Pipes, torn apart by the blasting, belched sprays of scalding steam. The white floors were littered with broken pieces of machinery and chunks of ice were scattered everywhere. Except for the distant rumblings of laser fire, the command center was forebodingly quiet.

There were still Rebel personnel on duty, including Princess Leia, who watched the images on the few still-functioning console screens. She wanted to be certain that the last of the transport ships had slipped past the Imperial armada and were approaching their rendezvous point in space.

Han Solo rushed into the command center, dodging great sections of the ice ceiling that came plunging down at him. One great chunk was followed by an avalanche of ice that poured onto the floor near the entrance to the chamber. Undaunted, Han hurried to the control board where Leia stood beside See-Threepio.

"I heard the command center was hit." Han appeared concerned. "Are you all right?"

The princess nodded. She was surprised to see him there where the danger was severest.

"Come on," he urged before she could reply. "You've got to get to your ship."

Leia looked exhausted. She had been standing at the console viewscreens for hours and had participated in dispatching Rebel personnel to their posts. Taking her hand, Han led her from the chamber, with the protocol droid clacking after them.

As they left, Leia gave one final order to the controller. "Give the evacuation code signal . . . and get to the transport."

224

Then, as Leia, Han, and Threepio made their hasty exit from the command center, a voice blared from the public address speakers, echoing in the nearby deserted ice corridors. "Disengage, disengage! Begin retreat action!"

"Come on," Han urged, grimacing. "If you don't get there fast, your ship won't be able to take off."

The walls quaked even more violently than before. Ice chunks continued to fall throughout the underground base as the three hurried toward the transport ships. They had nearly reached the hangar where Leia's transport ship was waiting, ready for departure. But as they neared the corner they found the entrance to the hangar completely blocked by ice and snow.

Han knew they would have to find some other route to Leia's escape ship—and quickly. He began to lead them back down the corridor, careful to avoid falling ice, and snapped on his comlink as they hurried toward the ship. "Transport C One Seven!" he yelled into the small microphone. "We're coming! Hold on!"

They were close enough to the hangar to hear Leia's escape vessel preparing for lift-off from the Rebel ice base. If he could lead them safely just a few meters more, the princess would be safe and—

The chamber suddenly quaked with a terrible noise that thundered through the underground base. In an instant the entire ceiling had crashed down in front of them, creating a solid barrier of ice between them and the hangar docks. They stared in shock at the dense white mass.

"We're cut off," Han yelled into his comlink, knowing that if the transport were to make good its escape there could be no time wasted in melting down or blasting through the barricade. "You'll have to take off without Princess Organa." He turned to her. "If we're lucky we can still make it to the Falcon."

The princess and See-Threepio followed as Han dashed toward another chamber, hoping that the Millennium Falcon and his Wookiee copilot had not already been buried under an avalanche of ice.

Looking out across the white battlefield, the Rebel officer watched the remaining snowspeeders whisking through the air and the last of the Imperial vehicles as they passed the wreckage of the exploded walker. He flipped on his comlink and heard the order to retreat: "Disengage, disengage. Begin retreat action." As he signaled his men to move back inside the ice cavern, he noticed that the lead walker was still treading heavily in the direction of the power generators.

In the cockpit of that assault machine, General Veers stepped close to the port. From this position he could clearly see the target below. He studied the crackling power generators and observed the Rebel troops defending them.

"Point-three-point-three-point-five . . . coming within range, sir," reported his pilot.

The general turned to his assault officer. "All troops will debark for ground assault," Veers said. "Prepare to target the main generator."

The lead walker, flanked by two of the hulking machines, lurched forward, its guns blazing to scatter the retreating Rebel troops.

As more laser fire came from the oncoming walkers, Rebel bodies and parts of Rebel bodies were flung through the air. Many of the soldiers who had managed to avoid the obliterating laser beams were crushed into unrecognizable pulp beneath the walkers' stomping feet. The air was charged with the stink of blood and burning flesh, and thundering with the explosive noises of battle.

As they fled, the few surviving Rebel soldiers glimpsed a lone snowspeeder as it retreated in the distance, a black trail of smoke escaping its burning hull.

Although the smoke rising from his crippled speeder obstructed his view, Hobbie could still see some of the carnage that raged on the ground. His wounds from a walker's laser fire made it torture even to move, let alone operate the controls of his craft. But if he could manage to work them just long enough to return to the base, he might be able to find a medical robot and . . .

No, he doubted he would survive even that long. He was dying—of that he was now certain—and the men in the trench would soon be dead, too, unless something were done to save them.

General Veers, proudly transmitting his report to Imperial headquarters, was totally unaware of Rogue Four's approach. "Yes, Lord Vader, I've reached the main power generators. The shield will be down in moments. You may commence your landing."

As he ended his transmission, General Veers reached for the electrorangefinder and looked through the eyepiece to line up the main power generators. Electronic crosshairs aligned according to the information from the walker's computers. Then suddenly the readouts on the small monitor screens mysteriously vanished.

Confounded, General Veers moved away from the eyepiece of the electrorangefinder and turned instinctively toward a cockpit window. He flinched in terror at seeing a smoking projectile heading on a direct course toward his walker's cockpit.

The other pilots also saw the hurtling speeder, and knew that there was no time to turn the massive assault machine. "He's going to—" one of the pilots began.

At that instant, Hobbie's burning ship crashed through the walker cockpit like a manned bomb, its fuel igniting into a cascade of flame and debris. For a second there were human screams, then fragments, and the entire machine crashed to the ground.

Perhaps it was the sound of this nearby blast that jarred Luke Skywalker back to consciousness. Dazed, he slowly lifted his head from the snow. He felt very weak and was achingly stiff with cold. The thought crossed his mind that frostbite might already have damaged his tissues. He hoped not; he had no desire to spend any more time in that sticky bacta fluid.

He tried to stand, but fell back against the snow, hoping he would not be spotted by any of the walker pilots. His comlink whistled, and somehow he found the strength to flick on its receiver.

"Forward units' withdrawal complete," the broadcast voice reported.

Withdrawal? Luke thought a moment. Then Leia and the others must have escaped! Luke suddenly felt that all the fighting and the deaths of loyal Rebel personnel had not been for nothing. A warmth rushed through his body, and he gathered his strength to rise and begin making the long trek back toward a distant formation of ice.

Another explosion rocked the Rebel hangar deck, cracking the ceiling and almost burying the docked *Millennium Falcon* in a mound of ice. At any moment the entire ceiling might cave in. The only safe place in the hangar seemed to be underneath the ship itself where Chewbacca was impatiently awaiting the return of his captain. The Wookiee had begun to worry. If Han did not return soon, the *Falcon* would surely be buried in a tomb of ice. But loyalty to his partner kept Chewie from taking off in the freighter alone.

As the hangar started to tremble more violently, Chewbacca detected movement in the adjoining chamber. Throwing back his head, the shaggy giant filled the hangar with his loudest roar as he saw Han Solo climb over hills of ice and snow and enter the chamber, followed closely by Princess Leia and an obviously nervous See-Threepio.

Not far from the hangar, Imperial stormtroopers, their faces shielded by white helmets and white snowscreens, had begun moving down deserted corridors. With them strode their leader, the dark-robed figure who surveyed the shambles that had been the Rebel base at Hoth. Darth Vader's black image stood out starkly against the white walls, ceiling, and floor. As he moved through the white catacombs, he regally stepped aside to avoid a falling section of the ice ceiling. Then he continued on his way with such quick strides that his troops had to hurry to keep up.

A low whine, rising in pitch, began to issue from the saucer-shaped freighter. Han Solo stood at the controls in the *Millennium Falcon*'s cockpit, at last feeling at home. He quickly flipped one switch after another, expecting to see the board flash its familiar mosaic of light; but only some of the lights were working.

Chewbacca had also noticed something amiss and barked with concern as Leia examined a gauge that seemed to be malfunctioning.

"How's that, Chewie?" asked Han anxiously.

The Wookiee's bark was distinctly negative.

"Would it help if I got out and pushed?" snapped Princess Leia, who was beginning to wonder if it were the Corellian's spit that held the ship together.

"Don't worry, Your Holiness. I'll get it started."

See-Threepio clanked into the hold and, gesturing, tried to get Han's attention. "Sir," the robot volunteered, "I was wondering if I might—" But his scanners read the scowl on the face staring at him. "It can wait," he concluded.

Imperial stormtroopers, accompanied by the rapidly moving Darth Vader, thundered through the ice corridors of the Rebel base. Their pace quickened as they rushed in the direction of the low whine coming from the ion engines. Vader's body tensed slightly as, entering the hangar, he perceived the familiar saucer-shaped form of the *Millennium Falcon*.

Within the battered freighter ship, Han Solo and Chewbacca were trying desperately to get the craft moving.

"This bucket of bolts is never going to get us past that blockade," Princess Leia complained.

Han pretended that he didn't hear her. Instead, he checked the *Falcon*'s controls and struggled to keep his patience even though his companion had so obviously lost hers. He flipped switches on the control console, ignoring the princess's look of disdain. Clearly, she doubted that this assemblage of spare parts and welded hunks of scrap metal would hold together even if they *did* manage to get beyond the blockade.

Han pushed a button on the intercom. "Chewie . . . come on!" Then, winking at Leia, he said, "This baby's still got a few surprises left in her."

"I'll be surprised if we start moving."

Before Han could make a carefully honed retort, the *Falcon* was jolted by a blast of Imperial laser fire that flashed outside the cockpit window. They could all see the squad of Imperial stormtroopers rushing with drawn weapons into the far end of the ice hangar. Han knew that the *Falcon*'s dented hull might resist the force of those hand weapons, but would be destroyed by the more powerful bazooka-shaped weapon that two of the Imperial troopers were hurriedly setting up.

"Chewie!" Han yelled as he quickly strapped himself into his pilot's chair. Meanwhile, a somewhat subdued young woman seated herself in the navigator's chair.

Outside the *Millennium Falcon*, stormtroopers worked with military efficiency to set up their enormous gun. Behind them the hangar doors began to open. One of the *Falcon*'s powerful laser weapons appeared from the hull and swung about, aiming directly at the stormtroopers.

Han moved urgently to block the Imperial soldiers' efforts. Without hesitation he released a deadly blast from the powerful laser weapon he had aimed at the stormtroopers. The explosion scattered their armored bodies all over the hangar.

Chewbacca dashed into the cockpit.

"We'll just have to switch over," Han announced, "and hope for the best."

The Wookiee hurled his hairy bulk into the copilot's seat as yet another laser blast erupted outside the window next to him.

He yelled indignantly, then yanked back on the controls to bring the welcome roar of engine fire from deep inside the *Falcon*.

The Corellian grinned at the princess, a gleeful I-told-you-so gleam in his eyes.

"Someday," she said with mild disgust, "you're going to be wrong, and I just hope I'm there to see it."

Han just smiled then turned to his copilot. "Punch it!" he shouted.

The huge freighter's engines roared. And everything behind the craft instantly melted in the fiery exhaust billowing from its tailpiece. Chewbacca furiously worked the controls, watching out of the corner of his eyes the ice walls rushing past as the freighter blasted away.

At the last moment, just before takeoff, Han caught a glimpse of additional stormtroopers running into the hangar. In their wake strode a foreboding giant clad entirely in black. Then there was only the blue and the beckoning of billions of stars.

As the *Millennium Falcon* soared from the hangar, its flight was detected by Commander Luke Skywalker, who turned to smile at Wedge and his gunner. "At least Han got away." The three then trudged along to their waiting X-wing fighter ships. When they finally reached them, they shook hands and moved off toward their separate vehicles.

"Good luck, Luke," Wedge said as they parted. "See you at the rendezvous."

Luke waved and began to walk toward his X-wing. Standing there amid the mountains of ice and snow, he was overcome by a surge of loneliness. He felt desperately alone now that even Han was gone. Worse than that, Princess Leia was also somewhere else; she might just as well be an entire universe away . . .

Then out of nowhere a familiar whistle greeted Luke.

"Artoo!" he exclaimed. "Is that you?"

Sitting snugly in the socket that had been installed for these helpful R2 units was the little barrel-shaped droid, his head peeking from the top of the ship. Artoo had scanned the approaching figure and had whistled with relief when his computers informed him it was Luke. The young commander was equally relieved to reencounter the robot that had accompanied him on so many of his previous adventures.

As he climbed into the cockpit and seated himself behind the controls, Luke could hear the sound of Wedge's fighter roaring into the sky toward the Rebel rendezvous point. "Activate the power and stop worrying. We'll soon be airborne," Luke said in response to Artoo's nervous beeping.

His was the last Rebel ship to abandon what had, for a very brief time, been a secret outpost in the revolution against the tyranny of the Empire.

Darth Vader, a raven specter, quickly strode through the ruins of the Rebel ice fortress, forcing his accompanying men into a brisk jog to keep up. As they moved through the corridors, Admiral Piett rushed up to overtake his master.

"Seventeen ships destroyed," he reported to the Dark Lord. "We don't know how many got away."

Without turning his head, Vader snarled through his mask, "The *Millennium Falcon*?"

Piett paused a moment before replying. He would have preferred to avoid *that* issue. "Our tracking scanners are on it now," he responded a bit fearfully.

Vader turned to face the admiral, his towering figure looming over the frightened officer. Piett felt a chill course through his veins, and when the Dark Lord spoke again his voice conveyed an image of the dreadful fate that would be inflicted if his commands were not executed.

"I want that ship," he hissed.

The ice planet was rapidly shrinking to a point of dim light as the *Millennium Falcon* sped into space. Soon that planet seemed nothing more than one of the billions of light specks scattered throughout the black void.

But the *Falcon* was not alone in its escape into deep space. Rather, it was followed by an Imperial fleet that included the *Avenger* Star Destroyer and a half-dozen TIE fighters. The fighters moved ahead of the huge, slower-moving Destroyer, and closed in on the fleeing *Millennium Falcon*.

Chewbacca howled over the roar of the *Falcon*'s engines. The ship was beginning to lurch with the buffeting flak blasted at it by the fighters.

"I know, I know, I see them," Han shouted. It was taking everything he had to maintain control of the ship.

"See what?" Leia asked.

Han pointed out the window at two very bright objects.

"Two more Star Destroyers, and they're heading right at us."

"I'm glad you said there was going to be no problem," she

commented with more than a touch of sarcasm, "or I'd be worried."

The ship rocked under the steady fire from the TIE fighters, making it difficult for Threepio to maintain his balance as he returned to the cockpit. His metal skin bumped and banged against the walls as he approached Han. "Sir," he began tentatively, "I was wondering . . ."

Han Solo shot him a threatening glance. "Either shut up or shut down," Han warned the robot, who immediately did the former.

Still struggling with the controls to keep the *Millennium Falcon* on course, the pilot turned to the Wookiee. "Chewie, how's the deflector shield holding up?"

The copilot adjusted an overhead switch and barked a reply that Solo interpreted as positive.

"Good," said Han. "At sublight, they may be faster, but we can still out-maneuver them. Hold on!" Suddenly the Corellian shifted his ship's course.

The two Imperial Star Destroyers had come almost within firing range of the *Falcon* as they loomed ahead; the pursuing TIE fighters and the *Avenger* were also dangerously close. Han felt he had no choice but to take the *Falcon* into a ninety-degree dive.

Leia and Chewbacca felt their stomachs leap into their throats as the *Falcon* executed its steep dive. Poor Threepio quickly had to alter his inner mechanisms if he wanted to remain on his metallic feet.

Han realized that his crew might think he was some kind of lunatic star jockey, pushing his ship on this madman's course. But he had a strategy in mind. With the *Falcon* no longer between them, the two Star Destroyers were now on a direct collision course with the *Avenger*. All he had to do was sit back and watch.

Alarms blared through the interiors of all three Star Destroyers. These ponderously massive ships could not respond quickly enough to such emergencies. Sluggishly one of the Destroyers began to move to the left in its effort to avoid collision with the *Avenger*. Unfortunately, as it veered, it brushed its companion ship, violently shaking up both spaceborne fortresses. The damaged Destroyers began to drift through space, while the *Avenger* continued in pursuit of the *Millennium Falcon* and its obviously insane pilot.

Two down, Han thought. But there was still a quartet of TIE fighters tailing the *Falcon*, blasting at its stern with full laser fire, but Han thought he could outstrip them. The ship was buffeted violently by the fighters' laser blasts, forcing Leia to hold on in a desperate attempt to keep her seat.

"That slowed them down a bit!" Han exulted. "Chewie, stand by to make the jump to lightspeed." There was not a moment to waste—the laser attack was intense now, and the TIE fighters were almost on top of them.

"They're very close," Leia warned, finally able to speak.

Han looked at her with a wicked glint in his eyes. "Oh, yeah? Watch this."

He threw the hyperspace throttle forward, desperate to escape, but also eager to impress the princess with both his own cleverness and his ship's fantastic power. Nothing happened! The stars that should by then have been mere blurs of light were still. Something was definitely wrong.

"Watch what?" Leia asked impatiently.

Instead of responding, Han worked the lightspeed controls a second time. Again, nothing. "I think we're in trouble," he muttered. His throat tightened. He knew "trouble" was a gross understatement.

"If I may say so, sir," Threepio volunteered, "I noticed earlier that the entire main para-light system seemed to have been damaged."

Chewbacca threw back his head and let out a loud and miserable wail.

"We're in trouble!" Han repeated.

All around them, the laser attack had increased violently. The *Millennium Falcon* could only continue at its maximum sublight velocity as it moved deeper into space, closely followed by a swarm of TIE fighters and one gigantic Imperial Star Destroyer.

VII

THE double sets of wings on Luke Skywalker's X-wing fighter were pulled together to form one wing as the small, sleek craft streaked away from the planet of snow and ice.

During his flight, the young commander had time to reflect on the events of the past few days. He now had time to ponder the enigmatic words of the ghostly Ben Kenobi and think about his friendship with Han Solo, and also consider his tenuous relationship with Leia Organa. As he thought of the people he cared most about, he arrived at a sudden decision. Gazing back one last time at the small icy planet, he told himself there was no longer any turning back.

Luke flipped a number of switches on his control board and took the X-wing into a steep turn. He watched the heavens shift as he rocketed off in a new direction, flying at top velocity. He was bringing his craft back onto an even course when Artoo, still snug in his specially designed socket, began to whistle and beep.

The miniature computer installed in Luke's ship for translating the droid's language flashed the small droid's message onto a control panel viewscreen.

"There's nothing wrong, Artoo," Luke replied after reading the translation. "I'm just setting a new course."

The small droid beeped excitedly, and Luke turned to read the updated printout on the viewscreen.

"No," Luke replied, "we're not going to regroup with the others."

This news startled Artoo, who immediately emitted a series of galvanic noises.

"We're going to the Dagobah system," answered Luke.

Again the robot beeped, calculating the amount of fuel carried by the X-wing.

"We have enough power."

Artoo gave vent to a longer, singsong series of toots and whistles.

"They don't need us there," said Luke to the droid's question about the planned Rebel rendezvous.

Artoo then gently beeped a reminder about Princess Leia's order. Exasperated, the young pilot exclaimed, "I'm countermanding that order! Now, be still."

The little droid fell silent. Luke was, after all, a commander in the Rebel Alliance and, as such, could countermand orders. He was making a few minor adjustments on the controls when Artoo chirped up again.

"Yes, Artoo," sighed Luke.

This time the droid made a series of soft noises, selecting each beep and whistle carefully. He did not want to annoy Luke, but the findings on his computer were important enough to report.

"Yes, Artoo, I know the Dagobah system doesn't appear on any of our navigational charts. But don't worry. It's there."

Another worried beep from the R2 unit.

"I'm very sure," the youth said, trying to reassure his mechanical companion. "Trust me."

Whether or not Artoo did trust the human being at the X-wing's controls, he only vented a meek little sigh. For a moment he was completely silent, as if thinking. Then he beeped again.

"Yes, Artoo?"

This communication from the robot was even more carefully put forth than before—one might even call the whistle-sentences tactful. It seemed Artoo had no intention of offending the human to whom he had entrusted himself. But wasn't it possible, the robot calculated, that the human's brain was slightly malfunctioning? After all, he had lain a long time in the snowdrifts of Hoth. Or, another possibility computed by Artoo, perhaps the Wampa Ice Creature had struck him more seriously than Too-Onebee had diagnosed? . . .

"No," Luke answered, "no headache. I feel fine. Why?"

Artoo's chirp was coyly innocent.

"No dizziness, no drowsiness. Even the scars are gone."

The next whistle rose questioningly in pitch.

"No, that's all right, Artoo. I'd rather keep it on manual control for a while."

Then the stout robot delivered a final whimper that sounded to Luke like a noise of defeat. Luke was amused by the droid's concern for his health. "Trust me, Artoo," Luke said with a gentle smile. "I know where I'm going and I'll get us there safely. It's not far."

Han Solo was desperate now. The *Falcon* had still not been able to shrug off the four TIE fighters or the enormous Star Destroyer that pursued it.

Solo raced down to the ship's hold and began to work frantically on repairing the malfunctioning hyperdrive unit. It was all but impossible to carry out the delicate repair work necessary while the *Falcon* shook with each blast of flak from the fighters.

Han snapped orders at his copilot, who checked the mechanisms as he was commanded. "Horizontal booster."

The Wookiee barked. It looked fine to him.

"Alluvial damper."

Another bark. That part was also in place.

"Chewie, get me the hydrospanners."

Chewbacca rushed over to the pit with the tools. Han grabbed the spanners, then paused and looked at his faithful Wookiee friend.

"I don't know how we're going to get out of this one," he confided.

Just then a resounding *thump* hit the *Falcon*'s side, making the ship pitch and turn radically.

Chewbacca barked anxiously.

Han braced himself at the impact, the hydrospanners flew from his hand. When he managed to regain his balance, he shouted at Chewbacca over the noise, "That was no laser blast! Something hit us!"

"Han . . . Han . . ." Princess Leia called to him from the cockpit. She was frantic. "Get up here!"

Like a shot, he lurched out of the hold and raced back to the cockpit with Chewbacca. They were stunned by what they saw through the windows.

"Asteroids!"

Enormous chunks of flying rock hurtled through space as far as they could see. As if those damn Imperial pursuit ships weren't trouble enough!

Han instantly returned to his pilot's seat, once more taking over the *Falcon*'s controls. His copilot settled himself back into his own seat just as a particularly large asteroid sped by the prow of the ship.

Han felt he had to stay as calm as possible; otherwise they might not last more than a few moments. "Chewie," he ordered, "set two-seven-one."

Leia gasped. She knew what Han's order meant and was stunned by so reckless a plan. "You're not thinking of heading into the asteroid field?" she asked, hoping she had misunderstood his command.

"Don't worry, they won't follow us through this!" he shouted with glee.

"If I might remind you, sir," Threepio offered, trying to be a rational influence, "the possibility of successfully navigating through an asteroid field is approximately two thousand four hundred and sixty-seven to one."

No one seemed to hear him.

Princess Leia scowled. "You don't have to do this to impress me," she said, as the *Falcon* was pummeled hard by another asteroid.

Han was enjoying himself enormously and chose to ignore her insinuations. "Hang on, sweetheart," he laughed, grasping the controls more tightly. "We're gonna do some *flyin'*."

Leia winced and, resigned, buckled herself firmly into her seat.

See-Threepio, still muttering calculations, shut down his synthesized human voice when the Wookiee turned and growled at him.

But Han concentrated only on carrying out his plan. He knew it would work; it had to . . . there was no other choice. Flying more on instinct than on instruments, he steered his ship through the relentless rain of stone. Glancing quickly at his scanner screens, he saw that the TIE fighters and the *Avenger* had not yet abandoned the chase. It would be an Imperial funeral, he thought, as he maneuvered the *Falcon* through the asteroid hail.

He looked at another viewscreen and smiled as it showed a collision between an asteroid and a TIE fighter. The explosion registered on the screen with a burst of light. No survivors in *that* one, Han thought.

The TIE fighter pilots chasing the *Falcon* were among the best in the Empire. But they couldn't compete with Han Solo. Either they weren't good enough, or they weren't crazy enough. Only a lunatic would have plunged his ship into a suicidal journey through these asteroids. Crazy or not, these pilots had no choice but to follow in hot pursuit. They undoubtedly would be better off perishing in this bombardment of rocks than reporting failure to their dark master.

The greatest of all the Imperial Star Destroyers regally moved out of Hoth's orbit. It was flanked by two other Star Destroyers and the entire group was accompanied by a protective squadron of smaller warships. In the central Destroyer, Admiral Piett stood outside Darth Vader's private meditation chamber. The upper jaw slowly opened until Piett was able to glimpse his robed master standing in the shadows. "My lord," Piett said with reverence.

"Come in, Admiral."

Admiral Piett felt great awe as he stepped into the dimly lit room and approached the Dark Lord of the Sith. His master stood silhouetted so that Piett could just barely make out the lines of a set of mechanical appendages as they retracted a respirator tube from Vader's head. He shuddered when he realized that he might be the first ever to have seen his master unmasked.

The sight was horrifying. Vader, his back turned to Piett, was entirely clothed in black; but above his studded black neck band gleamed his naked head. Though the admiral tried to avert his eyes, morbid fascination forced him to look at that hairless, skull-like head. It was covered with a maze of thick scar tissue that twisted around against Vader's corpse-pale skin. The thought crossed Piett's mind that there might be a heavy price for viewing what no one else had seen. Just then, the robot hands grasped the black helmet and gently lowered it over the Dark Lord's head.

His helmet back in place, Darth Vader turned to hear his admiral's report.

"Our pursuit ships have sighted the *Millennium Falcon*, my lord. It has entered an asteroid field."

"Asteroids don't concern me, Admiral," Vader said as he slowly clenched his fist. "I want that ship, not excuses. How long until you will have Skywalker and the others in the *Millennium Falcon*?"

"Soon, Lord Vader," the admiral answered, trembling in fear.

"Yes, Admiral . . ." Darth Vader said slowly, ". . . soon."

* * *

Two gigantic asteroids hurtled toward the *Millennium Falcon*. Its pilot quickly made a daring banking maneuver that brought it skirring out of the path of those two asteroids, nearly to collide with a third.

As the *Falcon* darted in and out of the asteroid field, it was followed closely by three Imperial TIE fighters that veered through the rocks in hot pursuit. Suddenly one of the three was fatally scraped by a shapeless chunk of rock and spun off in another direction, hopelessly out of control. The other two TIE fighters continued their chase, accompanied by the Star Destroyer *Avenger*, which was blasting speeding asteroids in its path.

Han Solo glimpsed the pursuing ships through the windows of his cockpit as he spun his craft around, speeding under yet another oncoming asteroid, then bringing the freighter back to its right-side-up position. But the *Millennium Falcon* was not yet out of danger. Asteroids were still streaking past the freighter. A small one bounced off the ship with a loud, reverberating *clang*, terrifying Chewbacca and causing See-Threepio to cover his eye lenses with a bronzed hand.

Han glanced at Leia and saw that she was sitting stone-faced as she stared at the swarm of asteroids. It looked to him as if she wished she were thousands of miles away.

"Well," he remarked, "you said you wanted to be around when I was wrong."

She didn't look at him. "I take it back."

"That Star Destroyer is slowing down," Han announced, checking his computer readings.

"Good," she replied shortly.

The view outside the cockpit was still thick with racing asteroids. "We're going to get pulverized if we stay out here much longer," he observed.

"I'm against that," Leia remarked dryly.

"We've got to get out of this shower."

"That makes sense."

"I'm going to get in closer to one of the big ones," Han added.

That did *not* make sense.

"Closer!" Threepio exclaimed, throwing up his metal arms. His artificial brain could scarcely register what his auditory sensors had just perceived.

"Closer!" Leia repeated in disbelief.

Chewbacca stared at his pilot in amazement and barked.

None of the three could understand why their captain, who

had risked his life to save them all, would now try to get them killed! Making a few simple adjustments on the cockpit controls, Han swerved the *Millennium Falcon* between a few larger asteroids, then aimed the craft directly at one the size of a moon.

A flashing shower of smaller rocks exploded against the enormous asteroid's craggy surface as the *Millennium Falcon*, with the Emperior's TIE fighters still in pursuit, flew directly above the asteroid. It was like skimming over the surface of a small planet, barren and devoid of all life.

With expert precision, Han Solo steered his ship toward still another giant asteroid, the largest one they had yet encountered. Summoning all the skill that had made his reputation known throughout the galaxy, he maneuvered the *Falcon* so that the only object between it and the TIE fighters was the deadly floating rock.

There was only a brief, brilliant flare of light, then nothing. The shattered remains of the two TIE fighters drifted away into the darkness and the tremendous asteroid—undeflected in its course—continued on its way.

Han felt an inner glow as bright as the spectacle that had just lighted up the view. He smiled to himself in quiet triumph.

Then he noticed an image on the main scope of his control console and nudged his hairy copilot. "There." Han pointed to the image. "Chewie, get a reading on that. Looks pretty good."

"What is it?" Leia asked.

The *Falcon*'s pilot ignored her question. "That should do nicely," he said.

As they flew near the asteroid's surface, Han looked down at the craggy terrain, his eye caught by a shadowy area that looked like a crater of mammoth proportions. He lowered the *Falcon* to surface level and flew it directly into the crater, its bowllike walls suddenly rising up around his ship.

And still two TIE fighters chased after him, firing their laser cannons and attempting to mimic his every maneuver.

Han Solo knew he had to be trickier and more daring if he was to lose the deadly pursuit ships. Spotting a narrow chasm through his windscreen, he banked the *Millennium Falcon* to one side. The ship soared sideways through the high-walled rocky trench.

Unexpectedly the two TIE fighters followed. One of them even sparked as it grazed the walls with its metal hull.

Twisting, banking, and turning his ship, Han pressed through the narrow gorge. From behind, the black sky flared as the two

TIE fighters crashed against one another, then exploded against the rocky ground.

Han reduced his speed. He still wasn't safe from the Imperial hunters. Searching about the canyon, he spotted something dark, a gaping cave mouth at the very bottom of the crater, large enough to hold the *Millennium Falcon*—perhaps. If not, he and his crew would know soon enough.

Slowing his ship, Han coursed into the cave entrance and through a large tunnel, which he hoped would make the ideal hiding place. He took a deep breath as his ship was promptly devoured by the cave's shadows.

A tiny X-wing was approaching the atmosphere of the Dagobah planet.

As he neared the planet, Luke Skywalker was able to glimpse a portion of its curved surface through a heavy cover of thick clouds. The planet was uncharted and virtually unknown. Somehow Luke had made his way there, though he wasn't certain whether it was his hand alone that had guided his ship into this unexplored sector of space.

Artoo-Detoo, riding in the back of Luke's X-wing, scanned the passing stars, then addressed his remarks to Luke via the computer scope.

Luke read the viewscreen interpreter. "Yes, that's Dagobah, Artoo," he answered the little robot, then glanced out the cockpit window as the fighter ship began to descend toward the planet's surface. "Looks a little grim, doesn't it?"

Artoo beeped, attempting for one last time to get his master back on a more sensible course.

"No," Luke replied, "I don't want to change my mind about this." He checked the ship's monitors and began to feel a bit nervous. "I'm not picking up any cities or technology. Massive life-form readings, though. There's something alive down there."

Artoo was worried, too, and that was translated as an apprehensive inquiry.

"Yes, I'm sure it's perfectly safe for droids. Will you take it easy?" Luke was beginning to get annoyed. "We'll just have to see what happens."

He heard a pathetic electronic whimper from the rear of the cockpit.

"Don't worry!"

The X-wing sailed through the twilight halo separating pitch black space from the planet's surface. Luke took a deep breath, then plunged his craft into the white blanket of mists.

He couldn't see a thing. His vision was entirely obstructed by the dense whiteness pressing against the canopy windows of his ship. His only choice was to control his X-wing solely by instruments. But the scopes weren't registering anything, even as Luke flew ever nearer to the planet. Desperately he worked his controls, no longer able to discern even so much as his altitude.

When an alarm began to buzz, Artoo joined its clarion call with his own frantic series of whistles and beeps.

"I know, I know!" Luke shouted, still fighting the controls of his ship. "All the scopes are dead! I can't see a thing. Hang on, I'm going to start the landing cycle. Let's just hope there's something underneath us."

Artoo squealed again, but his sounds were effectively drowned by the ear-splitting blast of the X-wing's retrorockets. Luke felt his stomach plunge as the ship began to drop rapidly. He braced against his pilot's seat, steeling himself for any possible impact. Then the ship lunged and Luke heard an awful sound as if the limbs of trees were being snapped off by his speeding craft.

When the X-wing finally screeched to a halt, it was with a tremendous jolt that nearly flung its pilot through the cockpit window. Certain, at last, that he was on the ground, Luke slumped back in his chair and sighed with relief. He then pulled a switch that lifted his ship's canopy. When he raised his head outside the ship to get his first look at the alien world, Luke Skywalker gasped.

The X-wing was completely surrounded by mists, its bright landing lights not illuminating more than a few feet in front of it. Luke's eyes gradually began to grow accustomed to the gloom all around him so that he could just barely see the twisted trunks and roots of grotesque-looking trees. He pulled himself out of the cockpit as Artoo detached his stout body from its cubbyhole plug.

"Artoo," Luke said, "you stay put while I look around."

The enormous gray trees had gnarled and intertwining roots that rose far above Luke before they joined to form trunks. He tilted back his head and could see the branches, high above, that seemed to form a canopy with the low-hanging clouds. Luke cautiously climbed out onto the long nose of his ship and saw that he had crash-landed in a small, fog-shrouded body of water.

Artoo emitted a short beep—then there was a loud splash, followed by silence. Luke turned just in time to glimpse the droid's domed topside as it disappeared beneath the water's foggy surface.

"Artoo! Artoo!" Luke called. He kneeled down on the smooth hull of the ship and leaned forward, anxiously searching for his mechanical friend.

But the black waters were serene, revealing not a sign of the little R2 unit. Luke could not tell how deep this still, murky pond might be; but it looked *extremely* deep. He was suddenly gripped by the realization that he might never see his droid friend again. Just then, a tiny periscope broke through the surface of the water and Luke could hear a faint gurgling beep.

What a relief! Luke thought, as he watched the periscope make its way toward shore. He ran along the nose of his X-wing fighter, and when the shore line was less than three meters away, the young commander jumped into the water and scrambled up the shore. He looked back and saw that Artoo was still making his way toward the beach.

"Hurry, Artoo!" Luke shouted.

Whatever it was that suddenly moved through the water behind Artoo moved too quickly and was too obscured by the mist for Luke to clearly identify it. All he could see was a massive dark form. This creature rose up for a moment, then dove beneath the surface, making a loud bang against the little droid's metal hull. Luke heard the robot's pathetic electronic scream for help. Then, nothing . . .

Luke stood there, horror-struck, as he continued to stare at the black waters, still as death itself. As he watched, a few telltale bubbles began to erupt at the surface. Luke's heart began to pound in fear as he realized he was standing too near the pool. But before he could move, the runt-size robot was spit out by the thing lurking beneath the black surface. Artoo made a graceful arc through the air and came crashing down onto a soft patch of gray moss.

"Artoo," Luke yelled, running to him, "are you okay?" Luke was grateful that the shadowy swamp lurker apparently found metal droids neither palatable nor digestible.

Feebly the robot replied with a series of faint whistles and beeps.

"If you're saying coming here was a bad idea, I'm beginning to agree with you," Luke admitted, looking around at their dismal surroundings. At least, he thought, there was human companionship on the ice world. Here, except for Artoo, there seemed to be nothing but this murky bog—and creatures, as yet unseen, that might lurk in the falling darkness.

Dusk was quickly approaching. Luke shivered in the thickening fog that closed in on him like something alive. He helped Artoo-Detoo back onto his feet, then wiped away the swamp muck that covered the droid's cylindrical body. As he worked, Luke heard eerie and inhuman cries that emanated from the distant jungle and shuddered as he imagined the beasts that might be making them.

By the time he finished cleaning off Artoo, Luke observed that the sky had grown noticeably darker. Shadows loomed ominously all around him and the distant cries didn't seem quite so far away anymore. He and Artoo glanced around at the spooky swamp-jungle surrounding them, then huddled a bit closer. Suddenly, Luke noticed a pair of tiny but vicious eyes winking at them through the shadowy underbrush, then vanishing with a scutter of diminutive feet.

He hesitated to doubt the advice of Ben Kenobi, but now he was beginning to wonder if that robed specter had somehow made a mistake leading him to this planet with its mysterious Jedi teacher.

He looked over at his X-wing and groaned when he saw that the entire bottom section was completely submerged in the dark waters. "How are we going to get that thing flying again?" The whole set of circumstances seemed hopeless and somewhat ridiculous. "What are we doing here?" he moaned.

It was beyond the computerized abilities of Artoo to provide an answer for either of those questions, but he made a little comforting beep anyway.

"It's like part of a dream," Luke said. He shook his head, feeling cold and frightened. "Or maybe I'm going crazy."

At least, he knew for certain, he couldn't have gotten himself into a crazier situation.

VIII

DARTH Vader looked like a great silent god as he stood on the main control deck of his mammoth Star Destroyer.

He was staring through the large rectangular window above the deck at the raging field of asteroids that was pelting his ship as it glided through space. Hundreds of rocks streaked past the windows. Some collided with one another and exploded in brilliant displays of vivid light.

As Vader watched, one of his smaller ships disintegrated under the impact of an enormous asteroid. Seemingly unmoved, he turned to look at a series of twenty holographic images. These twenty holograms re-created in three dimensions the features of twenty Imperial battleship commanders. The image of the commander whose ship had just been obliterated was fading rapidly, almost as quickly as the glowing particles of his exploded ship were being flung to oblivion.

Admiral Piett and an aide quietly moved to stand behind their black-garbed master as he turned to an image in the center of the twenty holograms which was continually interrupted by static and faded in and out as Captain Needa of the Star Destroyer *Avenger* made his report. His first words had already been drowned by static.

". . . which was the last time they appeared in any of our scopes," Captain Needa continued, "Considering the amount of damage we've sustained, they also must have been destroyed."

Vader disagreed. He knew of the *Millennium Falcon*'s power and was quite familiar with the skills of her cocky pilot. "No, Captain," he snarled angrily, "they're alive. I want every ship available to sweep the asteroid field until they're found."

As soon as Vader had given his command, Captain Needa's

image and those of the other nineteen captains faded completely. When the last hologram vanished, the Dark Lord, having sensed the two men standing behind him, turned. "Now what is so important it couldn't wait, Admiral?" he asked imperiously. "Speak up!"

The admiral's face turned pale with fear, his trembling voice shaking almost as much as his body. "It was . . . the Emperor."

"The Emperor?" the voice behind the black breath mask repeated.

"Yes," the admiral replied. "He commands you make contact with him."

"Move this ship out of the asteroid field," Vader ordered, "into a position where we can send a clear transmission."

"Yes, my lord."

"And code the signal to my private chamber."

The *Millennium Falcon* had come to rest hidden in the small cave which was pitch black and dripping with moisture. The *Falcon*'s crew turned down its engines until no sound at all was emitted from the small craft.

Inside the cockpit, Han Solo and his shaggy copilot were just completing shutting down the ship's electronic systems. As they did so, all the service lights dimmed and the interior of the ship became nearly as dark as its sheltering cave.

Han glanced over at Leia and flashed her a quick grin. "Getting kind of romantic in here."

Chewbacca growled. There was work to be done in here and the Wookiee needed Han's undivided attention if they were going to repair the malfunctioning hyperdrive.

Irritated, Han returned to his work. "What are you so grouchy about?" he snapped.

Before the Wookiee could respond, the protocol droid timidly approached Han and posed a question of burning importance. "Sir, I'm almost afraid to ask, but does shutting down all except emergency power systems include me?"

Chewbacca expressed his opinion with a resounding bark of affirmation, but Han disagreed. "No," he said, "we're going to need you to talk to the old *Falcon* here and find out what happened to our hyperdrive." He looked over at the princess and added, "How are you with a macrofuser, Your Holiness?"

Before Leia could get off a suitable retort, the *Millennium Falcon* lurched forward as a sudden impact struck its hull. Everything that was not bolted down flew through the cockpit;

even the giant Wookiee, howling boisterously, had to struggle to stay in his chair.

"Hang on!" Han yelled. "Watch out!"

See-Threepio clattered against a wall, then collected himself. "Sir, it's very possible this asteroid is not stable."

Han glared at him. "I'm glad you're here to tell us these things."

The ship rocked once more, even more violently than before.

The Wookiee howled again; Threepio stumbled backward, and Leia was hurled across the cabin directly into the waiting arms of Captain Solo.

The ship's rocking stopped as suddenly as it had started. But Leia still stood in Han's embrace. For once she did not draw away, and he could almost swear she was willingly embracing him. "Why, Princess," he said, pleasantly surprised, "this is so sudden."

At that, she began to pull back. "Let go," she insisted, trying to move out of his arms. "I'm getting angry."

Han saw the old familiar expression of arrogance beginning to return to her face. "You don't look angry," he lied.

"How do I look?"

"Beautiful," he answered truthfully, with an emotion that surprised him.

Leia felt suddenly, unexpectedly shy. Her cheeks flushed pink and, when she realized she was blushing, she averted her eyes. But she still did not really try to get free.

Han somehow couldn't let the tender moment last. "And excited," he had to add.

Leia became infuriated. Once again the angry princess and haughty senator, she quickly moved away from him and drew herself up to her most regal bearing. "Sorry, Captain," she said, her cheeks now reddened in anger, "being held by you isn't enough to get me excited."

"Well, I hope you don't expect more," he grunted, angrier at himself than at her stinging words.

"I don't expect anything," Leia said indignantly, "except to be left alone."

"If you'll just get out of my way, I'll leave you alone."

Embarrassed to realize that she was, indeed, still standing rather close, Leia stepped aside and made an effort to change the subject. "Don't you think it's time we got to work on your ship?"

Han frowned. "Fine with me," he said coldly, not looking at her.

Leia quickly turned on her heel and left the cockpit.

For a moment Han stood there quietly, just gathering his composure. Sheepishly he looked at the now quiet Wookiee and droid, both of whom had witnessed the entire incident.

"Come on, Chewie, let's tear into this flying short circuit," he said quickly to end the awkward moment.

The copilot barked in agreement, then joined his captain as they began to leave the cockpit. As they walked out, Han looked back at Threepio, who was still standing in the dim chamber looking dumbfounded. "You too, goldenrod!"

"I must admit," the robot muttered to himself as he began to shuffle out of the cockpit, "there are times I don't understand human behavior."

The lights of Luke Skywalker's X-wing fighter pierced the darkness of the bog planet. The ship had sunk deeper into the scummy waters, but there was still enough of it above the surface to let Luke carry needed supplies from the storage compartments. He knew it could not be much longer before his ship sank deeper—possibly all the way—beneath the water. He thought that his chance of survival might be increased if he gathered as many supplies as he could.

It was now so dark that Luke could scarcely see in front of him. Out in the dense jungle he heard a sharp snapping noise and felt a chill run through him. Grabbing his pistol, he prepared to blast anything that leaped from the jungle to attack him. But nothing did, and he clipped his weapon back onto its holster and continued to unpack his gear.

"You ready for some power?" Luke asked Artoo, who was patiently waiting for his own form of nourishment. Luke took a small fusion furnace from an equipment box and ignited it, welcoming even the tiny glow thrown off by the small heating device, then took a power cable and attached it to Artoo through a protuberance that roughly resembled a nose. As power radiated through Artoo's electronic innards, the stout robot whistled his appreciation.

Luke sat down and opened a container of processed food. As he began to eat, he talked to the robot. "Now all I have to do is find this Yoda, if he even exists."

He looked around nervously at the shadows in the jungle and felt frightened, miserable, and increasingly in doubt about his quest. "This certainly seems like a strange place to find a Jedi Master," he said to the little robot. "Gives me the creeps."

From the sound of his beep, it was clear Artoo shared Luke's opinion of the swamp world.

"Although," Luke continued as he reluctantly tasted more of the food, "there's something familiar about this place. I feel like—"

"You feel like what?"

That wasn't Artoo's voice! Luke leaped up, grabbed his pistol, then spun around, peering into the gloom to try to find the source of those words.

As he turned he saw a tiny creature standing directly in front of him. Luke immediately stepped back in surprise; this little being seemed to have materialized out of nowhere! It stood no more than half a meter in height, fearlessly holding its ground in front of the towering youth who wielded an awesome laser pistol.

The little wizened thing could have been any age. Its face was deeply lined, but was framed with elfin, pointed ears that gave it a look of eternal youth. Long white hair was parted down the middle and hung down on either side of the blue-skinned head. The being was bipedal, and stood on short legs that terminated in tridactyl, almost reptilian feet. It wore rags as gray as the mists of the swamp, and in such tatters that they must have approximated the creature's very age.

For the moment, Luke could not decide whether to be frightened or to laugh. But when he gazed into those bulbous eyes and sensed the being's kindly nature, he relaxed. At last the creature motioned toward the pistol in Luke's hand.

"Away put your weapon. I mean you no harm," it said.

After some hesitation, Luke quietly put his pistol back into his belt. As he did so, he wondered why he felt impelled to obey this little creature.

"I am wondering," the creature spoke again, "why are you here?"

"I'm looking for someone," Luke answered.

"Looking? Looking?" the creature repeated curiously with a wide smile beginning to crease his already-lined face. "You've found someone I'd say. Hch? Yes!"

Luke had to force himself not to smile. "Yeah."

"Help you I can . . . yes . . . yes."

Inexplicably Luke found himself trusting the odd creature, but wasn't at all sure that such a tiny individual could be of help on his important quest. "I don't think so," he replied gently. "You see, I'm looking for a great warrior."

"A *great* warrior?" The creature shook his head, the whitish hair flopping about his pointed ears. "Wars don't make one great."

A strange phrase, Luke thought. But before he could answer, Luke saw the tiny hominid hobble over to the top of the salvaged supply cases. Shocked, he watched as the creature began to rummage through the articles Luke had brought with him from Hoth.

"Get away from there," he said, surprised at this sudden strange behavior.

Moving across the ground, Artoo waddled toward the pile of cases, standing just about at optical sensor level with the creature. The droid squealed his disapproval as he scanned the creature that was carelessly digging through the supplies.

The strange being grabbed the container holding the remains of Luke's food and took a bite.

"Hey, that's my dinner!" Luke exclaimed.

But no sooner had the creature taken his first bite than he spat out what he had tasted, his deeply lined face wrinkling like a prune. *"Peewh!"* he said, spitting. "Thank you, no. How get you so big eating food of this kind?" He looked Luke up and down.

Before the astounded youth could reply, the creature flipped the food container in Luke's direction, then dipped one of his small and delicate hands into another supply case.

"Listen, friend," Luke said, watching this bizarre scavenger, "we didn't mean to land here. And if I could get my fighter out of this puddle I would, but I can't. So—"

"Can't get your ship out? Have you tried? Have you tried?" the creature goaded.

Luke had to admit to himself that he had not, but then the whole idea was patently ludicrous. He didn't have the proper equipment to—

Something in Luke's case had attracted the creature's interest. Luke finally reached the end of his patience when he saw the crazy little being snatch something out of the supply case. Knowing that survival depended on those supplies, he grabbed for the case. But the creature held on to his prize—a miniature power lamp that he gripped tightly in his blue-skinned hand. The little light came alive in the creature's hand, throwing its radiance up into his delighted face, and he immediately began to examine his treasure.

"Give me that!" Luke cried.

The creature retreated from the approaching youth like a petulant child. "Mine! Mine! Or I'll help you not."

Still clutching the lamp to his breast, the creature stepped backward, inadvertently bumping into Artoo-Detoo. Not remembering that the robot was at all animate, the being stood next to it as Luke approached.

"I don't want your help," Luke said indignantly. "I want my lamp back. I'll need it in this slimy mudhole."

Luke instantly realized he had issued an insult.

"Mudhole? Slimy? My home this is!"

As they argued, Artoo slowly reached out a mechanical arm. Suddenly his appendage grabbed the pilfered lamp and immediately the two little figures were engaged in a tug-of-war over the stolen prize. As they spun about in battle, Artoo beeped a few electronic, "give me that's."

"Mine, mine. Give it back," the creature cried. Abruptly, though, he seemed to give up the bizarre struggle and lightly poked the droid with one bluish finger.

Artoo emitted a loud, startled squeal and immediately released the power lamp.

The victor grinned at the glowing object in his tiny hands, gleefully repeating, "Mine, mine."

Luke was about fed up with these antics and advised the robot that the battle was over. "Okay, Artoo," he said with a sigh, "let him have it. Now get out of here, little fellow. We've got things to do."

"No, no!" the creature pleaded excitedly. "I'll stay and help you find your friend."

"I'm not looking for a friend," Luke said. "I'm looking for a Jedi Master."

"Oh," the creature's eyes widened as he spoke, "a Jedi Master. Different altogether. Yoda, you seek, Yoda."

Mention of that name surprised Luke, but he felt skeptical. How could an elf like this know anything about a great teacher of the Jedi Knights? "You know him?"

"Of course, yes," the creature said proudly. "I'll take you to him. But first we must eat. Good food. Come, come."

With that, the creature scurried out of Luke's camp and into the shadows of the swamp. The tiny power lamp he carried was gradually dimming in the distance as Luke stood feeling baffled.

At first he had no intention of pursuing the creature, but all at once he found himself diving into the fog after him.

As Luke started off into the jungle, he heard Artoo whistling and beeping as if he would blow his circuits. Luke turned around to see the little droid standing forlornly next to the miniature fission furnace.

"You'd better stay here and watch over the camp," Luke instructed the robot.

But Artoo only intensified his noisy output, running through the entire gamut of his electronic articulations.

"Artoo, now settle down," Luke called as he ran into the jungle. "I can take care of myself. I'll be safe, okay?"

Artoo's electronic grumblings grew fainter as Luke hurried to catch up with the little guide. I must really be out of my mind, Luke thought, following this weird being into who-knows-what. But the creature *had* mentioned Yoda's name, and Luke felt compelled to accept any help he could get to find the Jedi Master. He stumbled in the dark over thick weeds and twisting roots as he pursued the flickering light ahead.

The creature was chattering gaily as he led the way through the swamp. "Heh . . . safe . . . heh . . . quite safe . . . yes, of course." Then, in his odd little way, this mysterious being started to laugh.

Two Imperial cruisers slowly moved across the surface of the great asteroid. The *Millennium Falcon* had to be hidden somewhere within—but where?

As the ships skimmed the surface of the asteroid, they dropped bombs on its pock-marked terrain, trying to scare out the freighter. The shock waves from the explosives violently shook the spheroid, but still there was no sign of the *Falcon*. As it drifted above the asteroid, one of the Imperial Star Destroyers cast an eclipsing shadow across the tunnel entrance. Yet the ship's scanners failed to note the curious hole in the bowllike wall. Within that hole, in a winding tunnel not detected by the minions of the powerful Empire, sat the freighter. It rattled and vibrated with every explosion that pounded the surface above.

Inside, Chewbacca worked feverishly to repair the complex powertrain. He had scrambled into an overhead compartment to get at the wires that operated the hyperdrive system. But when he felt the first of the explosions, he popped his head out through the mass of wires and gave out a worried yelp.

Princess Leia, who was welding a damaged valve, stopped her work and looked up. The bombs sounded very close.

See Threepio glanced up at Leia and nervously tilted his head. "Oh, my," he said, "they've found us."

Everyone became quiet, as if fearing that the sound of their voices might somehow carry and betray their exact position. Again the ship was shaken by a blast, less intense than the last.

"They're moving away," Leia said.

Han saw through their tactic. "They're just trying to see if they can stir up something," he told her. "We're safe if we stay put."

"Where have I heard that line before?" Leia said with an innocent air.

Ignoring her sarcasm, Han moved past her as he went back to work. The passageway in the hold was so narrow that he couldn't avoid brushing against her as he passed by—or could he?

With mixed emotions the princess watched him for a moment as he continued to work on his ship. And then she turned back to her welding.

See Threepio ignored all this odd human behavior. He was too busy trying to communicate with the *Falcon*, trying to find out what was wrong with its hyperdrive. Standing at the central control panel, Threepio was making uncharacteristic whistle and beep sounds. A moment later, the control panel whistled back.

"Where is Artoo when I need him?" sighed the golden robot. The control panel's response had been difficult for him to interpret. "I don't know where your ship learned to communicate," Threepio announced to Han, "but its dialect leaves something to be desired. I believe, sir, it says the power coupling on the negative axis has been polarized. I'm afraid you'll have to replace it."

"Of course I'll have to replace it," Han snapped, then called up to Chewbacca, who was peering from the ceiling compartment. "Replace it!" he whispered.

He noticed that Leia had finished her welding but was having trouble reengaging the valve, struggling with a lever that simply would not budge. He moved toward her and began offering to help, but she coldly turned her back to him and continued her battle with the valve.

"Easy, Your Worship," he said. "Only trying to help."

Still struggling with the lever, Leia asked quietly, "Would you please stop calling me that?"

Han was surprised at the princess's simple tone. He had expected a stinging retort or, at best, a cold silence. But her words were missing the mocking tone that he was accustomed to hearing. Was she finally bringing their relentless battle of wills to an end? "Sure," he said gently.

"You make things difficult sometimes," Leia said as she shyly glanced at him.

He had to agree. "I do, I really do." But he added, "You could be a little nicer, too. Come on, admit it, sometimes you think I'm all right."

She let go of the lever and rubbed her sore hand. "Sometimes," she said with a little smile, "maybe . . . occasionally, when you aren't acting the scoundrel."

"Scoundrel?" he laughed, finding her choice of words endearing. "I like the sound of that."

Without another word, he reached for Leia's hand and began to massage it.

"Stop it," Leia protested.

Han continued to hold her hand. "Stop what?" he asked softly.

Leia felt flustered, confused, embarrassed—a hundred things in that moment. But her sense of dignity prevailed. "Stop that!" she said regally. "My hands are dirty."

Han smiled at her feeble excuse, but held on to her hand and looked right into her eyes. "My hands are dirty, too. What are you afraid of?"

"Afraid?" She returned his direct gaze. "Of getting my hands dirty."

"That's why you're trembling?" he asked. He could see that she was affected by his closeness and by his touch, and her expression softened. Whereupon he reached out and took her other hand.

"I think you like me *because* I'm a scoundrel," he said. "I think you haven't had *enough* scoundrels in your life." As he spoke he slowly drew her near.

Leia didn't resist his gentle pull. Now, as she looked at him, she thought he had never seemed more handsome, but she was still the princess. "I happen to *like* nice men," she chided in a whisper.

"And I'm not nice?" Han asked, teasing.

Chewbacca stuck his head out from the overhead compartment and watched the proceedings unnoticed.

"Yes," she whispered, "but you . . ."

Before she could finish, Han Solo drew her to him and felt her body tremble as he pressed his lips to hers. It seemed forever, it seemed an eternity to share between them, as he gently bent her body back. This time she didn't resist at all.

When they parted, Leia needed a moment to catch her breath. She tried to regain her composure and work up a measure of indignation, but she found it difficult to talk.

"Okay, hot shot," she began. "I—"

But then she stopped, and suddenly found herself kissing him, pulling him even closer than before.

When their lips finally parted, Han held Leia in his arms as they looked at each other. For a long moment there was a peaceful kind of emotion between them. Then Leia began to draw away, her thoughts and feelings a turmoil. She averted her eyes and began to disengage herself from Han's embrace. In the next second she turned and rushed from the cabin.

Han silently looked after her as she left the room. He then became acutely aware of the very curious Wookiee whose head was poking from the ceiling.

"Okay, Chewie!" he bellowed. "Give me a hand with this valve."

The fog, dispersed by a torrent of rain, snaked around the swamp in diaphanous swirls. Scooting along amid the pounding rain was a single R2 droid looking for his master.

Artoo-Detoo's sensing devices were busily sending impulses to his electronic nerve ends. At the slightest sound, his auditory systems reacted—perhaps overreacted—and sent information to the robot's nervous computer brain.

It was too wet for Artoo in this murky jungle. He aimed his optical sensors in the direction of a strange little mud house on the edge of a dark lake. The robot, overtaken by an almost-human perception of loneliness, moved closer to the window of the tiny abode. Artoo extended his utility feet toward the window and peeked inside. He hoped no one inside noticed the slight shiver of his barrel-shaped form or heard his nervous little electronic whimper.

Somehow Luke Skywalker managed to squeeze inside the miniature house, where everything within was perfectly scaled to its tiny resident. Luke sat cross-legged on the dried mud floor in the living room, careful not to bang his skull against the low ceiling. There was a table in front of him and he could see a few containers holding what appeared to be hand-written scrolls.

The wrinkle-faced creature was in his kitchen, next to the living room, busily concocting an incredible meal. From where Luke sat he could see the little cook stirring steaming pots, chopping this, shredding that, scattering herbs over all, and scurrying back and forth to put platters on the table in front of the youth.

Fascinated as he was by this bustling activity, Luke was growing very impatient. As the creature made one of his frantic runs into the living room area, Luke reminded his host, "I told you, I'm not hungry."

"Patience," the creature said, as he scuttled back into the steamy kitchen. "It's time to eat."

Luke tried to be polite. "Look," he said, "it smells good. I'm sure it's delicious. But I don't know why we can't see Yoda now."

"It's the Jedi's time to eat, too," the creature answered.

But Luke was eager to be on his way. "Will it take long to get there? How far is he?"

"Not far, not far. Be patient. Soon you will see him. Why wish you become a Jedi?"

"Because of my father, I guess," Luke answered, as he reflected that he never really knew his father that well. In truth his deepest kinship with his father was through the lightsaber Ben had entrusted to him.

Luke noticed the curious look in the creature's eyes as he mentioned his father. "Oh, your father," the being said, sitting down to begin his vast meal. "A powerful Jedi was he. Powerful Jedi."

The youth wondered if the creature were mocking him. "How could you know my father?" he asked a little angrily. "You don't even know who I am." He glanced around at the bizarre room and shook his head. "I don't know what I'm doing here . . ."

Then he noticed that the creature had turned away from him and was talking to a corner of the room. This really is the final straw, Luke thought. Now this impossible creature is talking to thin air!

"No good is this," the creature was saying irritably. "This will not do. I cannot teach him. The boy has no patience!"

Luke's head spun in the direction the creature was facing. *Cannot teach. No patience.* Bewildered, he still saw no one there. Then the truth of the situation gradually became as plain to him as the deep lines on the little creature's face. Already he was being tested—and by none other than Yoda himself!

From the empty corner of the room, Luke heard the gentle, wise voice of Ben Kenobi responding to Yoda. "He will learn patience," Ben said.

"Much anger in him," the dwarfish Jedi teacher persisted. "Like in his father."

"We've discussed this before," Kenobi said.

Luke could no longer wait. "I *can* be a Jedi," he interrupted. It meant more than anything else to him to become a part of the noble band that had championed the causes of justice and peace. "I'm ready, Ben . . . Ben . . ." The youth called to his invisible mentor, looking about the room in hopes of finding him. But all he saw was Yoda sitting across from him at the table.

"Ready are you?" the skeptical Yoda asked. "What know you of ready? I have trained Jedi for eight hundred years. My own counsel I'll keep on who is to be trained."

"Why not me?" Luke asked, insulted by Yoda's insinuation.

"To become a Jedi," Yoda said gravely, "takes the deepest commitment, the most serious mind."

"He can do it," Ben's voice said in defense of the youth.

Looking toward the invisible Kenobi, Yoda pointed at Luke. "This one I have watched a long time. All his life has he looked away . . . to the horizon, to the sky, to the future. Never his mind on where he was, on what he was doing. Adventure, excitement." Yoda shot a glaring look at Luke. "A Jedi craves not these things!"

Luke tried to defend his past. "I have followed my feelings."

"You are reckless!" the Jedi Master shouted.

"He will learn," came the soothing voice of Kenobi.

"He's too old," Yoda argued. "Yes. Too old, too set in his ways to start the training."

Luke thought he heard a subtle softening in Yoda's voice. Perhaps there was still a chance to sway him. "I've learned much," Luke said. He couldn't give up now. He had come too far, endured too much, *lost* too much for that.

Yoda seemed to look right through Luke as he spoke those words, as if trying to determine how much he *had* learned. He turned to the invisible Kenobi again. "Will he finish what he begins?" Yoda asked.

"We've come this far," was the answer. "He is our only hope."

"I will not fail you," Luke said to both Yoda and Ben. "I'm not afraid." And, indeed, at that moment, the young Skywalker felt he could face anyone without fear.

But Yoda was not so optimistic. "You will be, my young one," he warned. The Jedi Master turned slowly to face Luke as a strange little smile appeared on his blue face. "Heh. You will be."

IX

ONLY one being in the entire universe could instill fear in the dark spirit of Darth Vader. As he stood, silent and alone in his dim chamber, the Dark Lord of the Sith waited for a visit from his own dreaded master.

As he waited, his Imperial Star Destroyer floated through a vast ocean of stars. No one on his ship would have dared disturb Darth Vader in his private cubicle. But if they had, they might have detected a slight trembling in that black-cloaked frame. And there might even have been a hint of terror to be seen upon his visage, had anyone been able to see through his concealing black breath mask.

But no one approached, and Vader remained motionless as he kept his lonely, patient vigil. Soon a strange electronic whine broke the dead silence of the room and a flickering light began to glimmer on the Dark Lord's cloak. Vader immediately bowed deeply in homage to his royal master.

The visitor arrived in the form of a hologram that materialized before Vader and towered above him. The three-dimensional figure was clad in simple robes and its face was concealed behind an enormous hood.

When the hologram of the Galactic Emperor finally spoke, it did so with a voice even deeper than Vader's. The Emperor's presence was awesome enough, but the sound of his voice sent a thrill of terror coursing through Vader's powerful frame. "You may rise, my servant," the Emperor commanded.

Immediately Vader straightened up. But he did not dare gaze

into his master's face, and instead cast his eyes down at his own black boots.

"What is thy bidding, my master?" Vader asked with all the solemnity of a priest attending his god.

"There is a grave disturbance in the Force," the Emperor said.

"I have felt it," the Dark Lord replied solemnly.

The Emperor emphasized the danger as he continued. "Our situation is most precarious. We have a new enemy who could bring about our destruction."

"Our destruction? Who?"

"The son of Skywalker. You must destroy him, or he will be our undoing."

Skywalker!

The thought was impossible. How could the Emperor be concerned with this insignificant youth?

"He's not a Jedi," Vader reasoned. "He's just a boy. Obi-Wan could not have taught him so much that—"

The Emperor broke in. "The Force is strong in him," he insisted. "He must be destroyed."

The Dark Lord reflected a moment. Perhaps there was another way to deal with the boy, a way that might benefit the imperial cause. "If he could be turned, he would be a powerful ally," Vader suggested.

Silently the Emperor considered the possibility.

After a moment, he spoke again. "Yes . . . yes," he said thoughtfully. "He would be a great asset. Can it be done?"

For the first time in their meeting, Vader lifted his head to face his master directly. "He will join us," he answered firmly, "or die, my master."

With that, the encounter had come to an end. Vader kneeled before the Galactic Emperor, who passed his hand over his obedient servant. In the next moment, the holographic image had completely disappeared, leaving Darth Vader alone to formulate what would be, perhaps, his most subtle plan of attack.

The indicator lights on the control panel cast an eerie glow through the quiet cockpit of the *Millennium Falcon*. They softly lit Princess Leia's face as she sat in the pilot's chair, thinking about Han. Deep in thought, she ran her hand along the control panel in front of her. She knew something was churning up within her, but wasn't certain that she was willing to acknowledge it. And yet, could she deny it?

Suddenly her attention was attracted by a flurry of movement outside the cockpit window. A dark shape, at first too swift and too shadowy to identify, streaked toward the *Millennium Falcon*. In an instant it had attached itself to the ship's front window with something that looked like a soft suction cup. Cautiously Leia moved forward for a closer look at the black smudgelike shape. As she peered out the window, a set of large yellow eyes suddenly popped open and stared right at her.

Leia started in shock and stumbled backward into the pilot's seat. As she tried to compose herself, she heard the scurry of feet and an inhuman screech. Suddenly the black shape and its yellow eyes disappeared into the darkness of the asteroid cave.

She caught her breath, leaped up out of the chair, and raced to the ship's hold.

The *Falcon*'s crew was finishing its work on the ship's power system. As they worked, the lights flickered weakly, then came on and stayed on brightly. Han finished reconnecting the wires, and began setting a floor panel back in place while the Wookiee watched See Threepio complete his work at the control panel.

"Everything checks out here," Threepio reported. "If I might say so, I believe that should do it."

Just then, the princess rushed breathlessly into the hold.

"There's something out there!" Leia cried.

Han looked up from his work. "Where?"

"Outside," she said, "in the cave."

As she spoke, they heard a sharp banging against the ship's hull. Chewbacca looked up and let out a loud bark of concern.

"Whatever it is sounds like it's trying to get in," Threepio observed worriedly.

The captain began to move out of the hold. "I'm going to see what it is," he announced.

"Are you crazy?" Leia looked at him in astonishment.

The banging was getting louder.

"Look, we just got this bucket going again," Han explained. "I'm not about to let some varmint tear it apart."

Before Leia could protest, he had grabbed a breath mask off a supply rack and pulled it down over his head. As Han walked out, the Wookiee hurried up behind him and grabbed his own face mask. Leia realized that, as part of the crew, she was duty-bound to join them.

"If there's more than one," she told the captain, "you're going to need help."

Han looked at her affectionately as she removed a third breath mask and placed it over her lovely, but determined, face.

Then the three of them rushed out, leaving the protocol droid to complain pitifully to the empty hold: "But that leaves me here all alone!"

The darkness outside the *Millennium Falcon* was thick and dank. It surrounded the three figures as they carefully moved around their ship. With each step they heard unsettling noises, *squishing* sounds, that echoed through the dripping cavern.

It was too dark to tell where the creature might be hiding. They moved cautiously, peering as well as they could into the deep gloom. Suddenly Chewbacca, who could see better in the dark than either his captain or the princess, emitted a muffled bark and pointed toward the thing that moved along the *Falcon*'s hull.

A shapeless leathery mass scurried over the top of the ship, apparently startled by the Wookiee's yelp. Han leveled his blaster at the creature and blasted the thing with a laser bolt. The black shape screeched, stumbled, then fell off the spaceship, landing with a *thud* at the princess's feet.

She leaned over to get a better look at the black mass. "Looks like some kind of Mynock," she told Han and Chewbacca.

Han glanced quickly around the dark tunnel. "There will be more of them," he predicted. "They always travel in groups. And there's nothing they like better than to attach themselves to ships. Just what we need right now!"

But Leia was more distracted by the consistency of the tunnel floor. The tunnel itself struck her as peculiar; the smell of the place was unlike that of any cave she had ever known. The floor was especially cold and seemed to cling to her feet.

As she stamped her foot against the floor, she felt the ground give a bit beneath her heel. "This asteroid has the strangest consistency," she said. "Look at the ground. It's not like rock at all."

Han knelt to inspect the floor more closely and noted how pliable it was. As he studied the floor, he tried to make out how far it reached and to see the contours of the cave.

"There's an awful lot of moisture in here," he said. He looked up and aimed his hand blaster at the far side of the cave, then fired toward the sound of a screeching Mynock in the distance; as soon as he shot the bolt, the entire cavern began to shake and the ground to buckle. "I was afraid of that," he shouted. "Let's get out of here!"

Chewbacca barked in agreement, and bolted toward the *Millennium Falcon*. Close behind him, Leia and Han rushed toward the ship, covering their faces as a swarm of Mynocks flew past them. They reached the *Falcon* and ran up the platform into the ship. As soon as they were on board, Chewbacca closed the hatch after them, careful that none of the Mynocks could slip inside.

"Chewie, fire her up!" Han yelled as he and Leia darted through the ship's hold. "We're getting out of here!"

Chewbacca hurriedly lumbered to his seat in the cockpit, while Han rushed to check the scopes on the hold control panel.

Leia, running to keep up, warned, "They would spot us long before we could get up to speed."

Han didn't seem to hear her. He checked the controls, then turned to rush back to the cockpit. But as he passed her, his comment made it clear he had heard every word. "There's no time to discuss this in committee."

And with that he was gone, racing to his pilot's chair, where he began working the engine throttles. The next minute the whine of the main engines resounded through the ship.

But Leia hurried after him. "I am not a committee," she shouted indignantly.

It didn't appear that he heard her. The sudden cave-quake was beginning to subside, but Han was determined to get his ship out—and out fast.

"You can't make the jump to light-speed in this asteroid field," she called over the engine roar.

Solo grinned at her over his shoulder. "Strap yourself in, sweetheart," he said, "we're taking off!"

"But the tremors have stopped!"

Han was not about to stop his ship now. Already the craft moved forward, quickly passing the craggy walls of the tunnel. Suddenly Chewbacca barked in horror as he stared out the front windscreen.

Directly in front of them stood a jagged white row of stalactites and stalagmites completely surrounding the cave's entrance.

"I see it, Chewie," Han shouted. He pulled hard on the throttle, and the *Millennium Falcon* surged forward. "Hang on!"

"The cave is collapsing," Leia screamed as she saw the entrance ahead grow smaller.

"This is no cave."

"What?!"

Threepio began jabbering in terror. "Oh, my, no! We're doomed. Good-bye, Mistress Leia. Good-bye, Captain."

Leia's mouth dropped open as she stared at the rapidly approaching tunnel opening.

Han was right; they were not in a cave. As they came nearer the opening, it was apparent that the white mineral formations were giant teeth. And it was very apparent that, as they soared out of this giant mouth, those teeth were beginning to close!

Chewbacca roared.

"Bank, Chewie!"

It was an impossible maneuver, but Chewbacca responded immediately and once again accomplished the impossible. He rolled the *Millennium Falcon* steeply on its side, tilting the ship as he accelerated it between two of those gleaming white fangs. And not a second too soon, for just as the *Falcon* flew from that living tunnel, the jaws clamped shut.

The *Falcon* sped through the rocky crevice of the asteroid, pursued by a titanic space slug. The enormous pink bulk didn't intend to lose its tasty meal and pushed itself out of its crater to swallow the escaping ship. But the monster was too slow. Within another moment the freighter had soared out, away from the slimy pursuer and into space. As it did so, the ship plunged into yet another danger: The *Millennium Falcon* had re-entered the deadly asteroid field.

Luke was panting, nearly out of breath in this, the latest of his endurance tests. His Jedi taskmaster had ordered him out on a marathon run through the dense growth of his planet's jungle. Not only had Yoda sent Luke on the exhausting run, but he had invited himself along for the ride. As the Jedi-in-training puffed and sweated his way on his rugged race, the little Jedi Master observed his progress from a pouch strapped to Luke's back.

Yoda shook his head and muttered to himself disparagingly about the youth's lack of endurance.

By the time they returned to the clearing where Artoo-Detoo was patiently waiting, Luke's exhaustion had nearly overcome him. As he stumbled into the clearing, Yoda had yet another test planned for him

Before Luke had caught his breath, the little Jedi on his back tossed a metal bar in front of Luke's eyes. In an instant Luke ignited his laser sword and swung frantically at the bar. But he was not fast enough, and the bar fell—untouched—onto the ground with a thud. Luke collapsed on the wet earth in complete exhaustion. "I can't," he moaned, ". . . too tired."

Yoda, who showed no sign of sympathy, retorted, "It would be in seven pieces, were you a Jedi."

But Luke knew that he was not a Jedi—not yet, anyway. And the rigorous training program devised by Yoda had left him nearly out of breath. "I thought I was in good shape," he gasped.

"Yes, but by what standard, ask I?" the little instructor quizzed. "Forget your old measures. Unlearn, unlearn!"

Luke truly felt ready to unlearn all his old ways and willing to free himself to learn all this Jedi Master had to teach. It was rigorous training, but as time passed, Luke's strength and abilities increased and even his skeptical little master began to see hope. But it was not easy.

Yoda spent long hours lecturing his student about the ways of the Jedi. As they sat under the trees near Yoda's little house, Luke listened intently to all the master's tales and lessons. And as Luke listened, Yoda chewed on his Gimer Stick, a short twig with three small branches at the far end.

And there were physical tests of all kinds. In particular, Luke was working hard to perfect his leap. Once he felt ready to show Yoda his improvement. As the master sat on a log next to a wide pond, he heard the loud rustling of someone approaching through the vegetation.

Suddenly Luke appeared on the other side of the pond, coming toward the water at a run. As he approached the shore, he made a running leap toward Yoda, rising high above the water as he hurtled himself through the air. But he fell short of the other side and landed in the water with a loud splash, completely soaking Yoda.

Yoda's blue lips turned down in disappointment.

But Luke was not about to give up. He was determined to become a Jedi and, no matter how foolish he might feel in the attempt, would pass every test Yoda set for him. So he didn't complain when Yoda told him to stand on his head. A bit awkwardly at first, Luke inverted his body and, after a few wobbly moments, was standing firmly on his hands. It seemed he had been in this position for hours, but it was less difficult than it would have been before his training. His concentration had improved so much that he was able to maintain a perfect balance—even with Yoda perched on the soles of his feet.

But that was only part of the test. Yoda signaled Luke by tapping on his leg with his Gimer Stick. Slowly, carefully, and with full concentration, Luke raised one hand off the ground. His body wavered slightly with the weight shift—but Luke kept his balance, and, concentrating, started to lift a small rock in front of him. But suddenly a whistling and beeping R2 unit came rushing up to his youthful master.

Luke collapsed, and Yoda jumped clear of his falling body. Annoyed, the young Jedi student asked, "Oh, Artoo, what is it?"

Artoo-Detoo rolled about in frantic circles as he tried to communicate his message through a series of electronic chirps. Luke watched as the droid scooted to the edge of the swamp. He hurried to follow and then saw what it was the little robot was trying to tell him.

Standing at the water's edge, Luke saw that all but the tip of the X-wing's nose had disappeared beneath the water's surface.

"Oh, no," moaned Luke. "We'll never get it out now."

Yoda had joined them, and stamped his foot in irritation at Luke's remark. "So sure are you?" Yoda scolded. "Tried have you? Always with you it can't be done. Hear you nothing that I say?" His little wrinkled face puckered with a furious scowl.

Luke glanced at his master, then looked doubtfully toward the sunken ship.

"Master," he said skeptically, "lifting rocks is one thing, but this is a little different."

Yoda was really angry now. "No! No different!" he shouted. "The differences are in your mind. Throw them out! No longer of use are they to you."

Luke trusted his master. If Yoda said this could be done, then maybe he should try. He looked at the downed X-wing and readied himself for maximum concentration. "Okay," he said at last, "I'll give it a try."

Again he had spoken the wrong words. "No," Yoda said impatiently. "Try not. Do, do. Or do not. There is no try."

Luke closed his eyes. He tried to envision the contours, the shape, to feel the weight of his X-wing fighter. And he concentrated on the movement it would make as it rose from the murky waters.

As he concentrated, he began to hear the waters churn and gurgle, and then begin to bubble with the emerging nose of the X-wing. The tip of the fighter was slowly lifting from the water, and it hovered there for a moment, then sank back beneath the surface with a loud splash.

Luke was drained and had to gasp for breath. "I can't," he said dejectedly. "It's too big."

"Size has no meaning," Yoda insisted. "It matters not. Look at *me*. Judge me by my *size*, do you?"

Luke, chastened, just shook his head.

"And well you shouldn't," the Jedi Master advised. "For my ally is the Force. And a powerful ally it is. Life creates it and makes it grow. Its energy surrounds us and binds us. Luminous beings we are, not this crude matter," he said as he pinched Luke's skin.

Yoda made a grand sweeping gesture to indicate the vastness of the universe about him. "Feel it you must. Feel the flow. Feel the Force around you. Here," he said, as he pointed, "between you and me and that tree and that rock."

While Yoda gave his explanation of the Force, Artoo spun his domed head around, trying without success to register this "Force" on his scanners. He whistled and beeped in bafflement.

"Yes, everywhere," Yoda continued, ignoring the little droid, "waiting to be felt and used. Yes, even between this land and that ship!"

Then Yoda turned and looked at the swamp, and as he did the water began to swirl. Slowly, from the gently bubbling waters, the nose of the fighter appeared again.

Luke gasped in astonishment as the X-wing gracefully rose from its watery tomb and moved majestically toward the shore.

He silently vowed never to use the word "impossible" again. For there, standing on his tree root pedestal, was tiny Yoda, effortlessly gliding the ship from the water onto the shore. It was a sight that Luke could scarcely believe. But he knew that it was a potent example of Jedi mastery over the Force.

Artoo, equally astounded but not so philosophical, issued a series of loud whistles, then bolted off to hide behind some giant roots.

The X-wing seemed to float onto the beach, and then gently came to a stop.

Luke was humbled by the feat he had witnessed and approached Yoda in awe. "I . . ." he began, dazzled. "I don't believe it."

"That," Yoda stated emphatically, "is why you fail."

Bewildered, Luke shook his head, wondering if he would ever rise to the station of a Jedi.

* * *

Bounty hunters! Among the most reviled of the galaxy's inhabitants, this class of amoral money-grubbers included members of every species. It was a repellent occupation, and it often attracted repellent creatures to its fold. Some of these creatures had been summoned by Darth Vader and now stood with him on the bridge of his Imperial Star Destroyer.

Admiral Piett observed this motley group from a distance as he stood with one of Vader's captains. They saw that the Dark Lord had invited a particularly bizarre assortment of fortune hunters, including Bossk, whose soft, baggy face gawked at Vader with huge bloodshot orbs. Next to Bossk stood Zuckuss and Dengar, two human types, battle-scarred by innumerable, unspeakable adventures. A battered and tarnished chrome-colored droid named IG-88 was also with the group, standing next to the notorious Boba Fett. A human bounty hunter, Fett was known for his extremely ruthless methods. He was dressed in a weapon-covered, armored spacesuit, the kind worn by a group of evil warriors defeated by the Jedi Knights during the Clone Wars. A few braided scalps completed his unsavory image. The very sight of Boba Fett sent a shudder of revulsion through the admiral.

"Bounty hunters!" Piett said with disdain. "Why should he bring them into this? The Rebels won't escape us."

Before the captain could reply, a ship's controller rushed up to the admiral. "Sir," he said urgently, "we have a priority signal from the Star Destroyer *Avenger*."

Admiral Piett read the signal, then hurried to inform Darth Vader. As he approached the group, Piett heard the last of Vader's instructions to them. "There will be a substantial reward for the one who finds the *Millennium Falcon*," he was saying. "You are free to use any methods necessary, but I want proof. No disintegrations."

The Sith Lord stopped his briefing as Admiral Piett hurried to his side.

"My lord," the admiral whispered ecstatically, "we have them!"

X

THE *Avenger* had spotted the *Millennium Falcon* the moment the freighter shot out of the enormous asteroid.

From that moment, the Imperial ship renewed its pursuit of the freighter with a blinding barrage of fire. Undaunted by the steady rain of asteroids on its massive hull, the Star Destroyer relentlessly followed the smaller ship.

The *Millennium Falcon*, far more maneuverable than the other ship, darted around the larger asteroids as they came rocketing toward it. The *Falcon* was succeeding in holding its lead in front of the *Avenger*, but it was clear that the steadily pursuing ship was not about to abandon the chase.

Suddenly a gigantic asteroid appeared in the *Millennium Falcon*'s path, rushing toward the freighter at incredible speed. The ship quickly banked out of the way, and the asteroid hurtled past it, only to explode harmlessly against the *Avenger*'s hull.

Han Solo glimpsed the explosion's flare through the front window of his ship's cockpit. The craft that followed them seemed absolutely invulnerable; but he had no time to reflect on the differences between the ships. It took everything in his power to maintain control of the *Falcon* as it was pelted by Imperial cannon fire.

Princess Leia tensely watched the asteroids and cannon fire flaring in the blackness of space outside the cockpit windows. Her fingers had tightened on the arms of her chair. Silently she hoped against hope that they would emerge from this chase alive.

Carefully following the bleeping images on a tracking scope, See Threepio turned to Han. "I can see the edge of the asteroid field, sir," he reported.

"Good," Han replied. "Soon as we're clear, we'll kick this baby into hyperdrive." He was confident that within moments the pursuing Star Destroyer would be left light-years behind. The repairs in the freighter's light-speed systems had been completed, and there was nothing left to do now but get the ship free of the asteroid field and into space, where it could blast away to safety.

There was an excited Wookiee bark as Chewbacca, looking out a cockpit window, saw that the asteroid density was already decreasing. But their escape could not yet be completed, for the *Avenger* was closing in, and the bolts from its laser cannons bombarded the *Falcon*, making it lurch and carom to one side.

Han rapidly adjusted the controls and brought his ship back on an even keel. And in the next instant, the *Falcon* zoomed out of the asteroid field and entered the peaceful, star-dotted silence of deep space. Chewbacca whined, joyful that they were at last out of the deadly field—but eager to leave the Star Destroyer far behind.

"I'm with you, Chewie," Han responded. "Let's vacate the area. Stand by for light-speed. This time *they* get the surprise. Hang on . . ."

Everyone braced himself as Han pulled back on the light-speed throttle. But it was the crew of the *Millennium Falcon*, and mostly the captain himself, that got the surprise, once again—

—nothing happened.

Nothing!

Han frantically pulled back the throttle again.

The ship maintained its sublight speed.

"This isn't fair!" he exclaimed, beginning to panic.

Chewbacca was furious. It was rare that he lost his temper with his friend and captain. But now he was exasperated and roared his fury in angry Wookiee growls and barks.

"Couldn't be," Han replied defensively, as he looked at his computer screens and quickly noted their readings. "I checked the transfer circuits."

Chewbacca barked again.

"I tell you, this time it's not my fault. I'm *sure* I checked it."

Leia sighed deeply. "No light-speed?" in a tone that indicated she had expected *this* catastrophe, too.

"Sir," See Threepio interjected, "we've lost the rear deflector shield. One more direct hit on the back quarter and we're done for."

"Well," Leia said, as she glared at the captain of the *Millennium Falcon*, "what now?"

Han realized he had only one choice. There was no time to plan or to check computer readouts, not with the *Avenger* already out of the asteroid field and rapidly gaining on them. He had to make a decision based on instinct and hope. They really had no alternative.

"Sharp bank, Chewie," he ordered and pulled back a lever as he looked at his copilot. "Let's turn this bucket around."

Not even Chewbacca could fathom what Han had in mind. He barked in bewilderment—perhaps he hadn't heard the order quite right.

"You heard me!" Han yelled. "Turn around! Full power front shield!" This time there was no mistaking his command and, though Chewbacca couldn't comprehend the suicidal maneuver, he obeyed.

The princess was flabbergasted. "You're going to attack them!" she stammered in disbelief. There wasn't a *chance* of survival now, she thought. Was it possible that Han really was crazy?

Threepio, after running some calculations through his computer brain, turned to Han Solo. "Sir, if I might point out, the odds of surviving a direct assault on an Imperial Star Destroyer are—"

Chewbacca snarled at the golden droid, and Threepio immediately shut up. No one on board really wanted to hear the statistics, especially since the *Falcon* was already banking into a steep turn to begin its course into the erupting storm of Imperial cannon fire.

Solo concentrated intently on his flying. It was all he could do to avoid the barrage of flak bursts rocketing toward the *Falcon* from the Imperial ship. The freighter bobbed and weaved as Han, still heading directly for the Star Destroyer, steered to avoid the bolts.

No one on his tiny ship had the slightest idea what his plan might be.

"He's coming in too low!" the Imperial deck officer shouted, though he scarcely believed what he was seeing.

Captain Needa and the Star Destroyer crew rushed to the *Avenger*'s bridge to watch the suicidal approach of the *Millennium Falcon*, while alarms blared all over the vast Imperial ship. A small freighter could not do much damage if it collided against a Star Destroyer's hull; but if it smashed through the bridge windows, the control deck would be littered with corpses.

The panicked tracking officer reported his sighting. "We're going to collide!"

"Shields up?" Captain Needa asked. "He must be insane!"

"Look out!" the deck officer yelled.

The *Falcon* was headed straight for the bridge window and the *Avenger* crew and officers fell to the floor in terror. But at the last instant, the freighter veered up sharply. Then—

Captain Needa and his men slowly lifted their heads. All they saw outside the bridge windows was a peaceful ocean of stars.

"Track them," Captain Needa ordered. "They may come around for another pass."

The tracking officer attempted to find the freighter on his scopes. But there was nothing to find.

"That's strange," he muttered.

"What is it?" Needa asked, walking over to look at the tracking monitors for himself.

"The ship doesn't appear on any of our scopes."

The captain was perplexed. "It couldn't have disappeared. Could a ship that small have a cloaking device?"

"No, sir," the deck officer answered. "Maybe they went into light-speed at the last minute."

Captain Needa felt his anger mounting at about the same rate as his befuddlement. "Then why did they attack? They could have gone into hyperspace when they cleared the asteroid field."

"Well, there's no trace of them, sir, no matter how they did it," the tracking officer replied, still unable to locate the *Millennium Falcon* on his viewers. "The only logical explanation is that they went into light-speed."

The captain was staggered. How had that crate of a ship eluded him?

An aide approached. "Sir, Lord Vader demands an update on the pursuit," he reported. "What should he be told?"

Needa braced himself. Letting the *Millennium Falcon* get away when it was so close was an unforgiveable error, and he knew he had to face Vader and report his failure. He felt resigned to whatever punishment waited in store for him.

"I am responsible for this," he said. "Get the shuttle ready. When we rendezvous with Lord Vader, I will apologize to him myself. Turn around and scan the area one more time."

Then, like a living behemoth, the great *Avenger* slowly began to turn; but there was still no sign of the *Millennium Falcon*.

* * *

The two glowing balls hovered like alien fireflies above Luke's body lying motionless in the mud. Standing protectively next to his fallen master, a little barrel-shaped droid periodically extended a mechanical appendage to swat at the dancing objects as if they were mosquitoes. But the hovering balls of light leaped just out of the robot's reach.

Artoo-Detoo leaned over Luke's inert body and whistled in an effort to revive him. But Luke, stunned unconscious by the charges of these energy balls, did not respond. The robot turned to Yoda, who was sitting calmly on a tree stump, and angrily began to beep and scold the little Jedi Master.

Getting no sympathy from him, Artoo turned back to Luke. His electronic circuits told him there was no use trying to wake Luke with his little noises. An emergency rescue system was activated within his metal hull and Artoo extended a small metal electrode and rested it on Luke's chest. Uttering a quiet beep of concern, Artoo generated a mild electrical charge, just strong enough to jolt Luke back to consciousness. The youth's chest heaved, and he awoke with a start.

Looking dazed, the young Jedi student shook his head clear. He looked around him, rubbing his shoulders to ease the ache from Yoda's seeker balls' attack. Glimpsing the seekers still suspended over him, Luke scowled. Then he heard Yoda chuckling merrily nearby, and turned his glare on him.

"Concentration, heh?" Yoda laughed, his lined face creased with enjoyment. "Concentration!"

Luke was in no mood to return his smile. "I thought those seekers were set for stun!" he exclaimed angrily.

"That they are," the amused Yoda answered.

"They're a lot stronger than I'm used to." Luke's shoulder ached painfully.

"That would not matter were the Force flowing through you," Yoda reasoned. "Higher you'd jump! Faster you'd move!" he exclaimed. "Open yourself to the Force you must."

The youth was beginning to feel exasperated with his arduous training, although he had only been at it a short time. He had felt very close to knowing the Force—but so many times he had failed and had realized how very far away it was from him still. But now Yoda's goading words made him spring to his feet. He was tired of waiting so long for this power, weary at his lack of success, and increasingly infuriated by Yoda's cryptic teachings.

Luke grabbed his laser sword from the mud and quickly ignited it.

Terrified, Artoo-Detoo scurried away to safety.

"I'm open to it now!" Luke shouted. "I feel it. Come on, you little flying blasters!" With fire in his eyes, Luke poised his weapon and moved toward the seekers. Immediately they zipped away and retreated to hover over Yoda.

"No, no," the Jedi Master scolded, shaking his hoary head. "This will not do. *Anger* is what you feel."

"But I feel the Force!" Luke protested vehemently.

"Anger, anger, fear, aggression!" Yoda warned. "The dark side of the Force are they. Easily *they* flow . . . quick to join in a fight. Beware, beware, beware of them. A heavy price is paid for the power they bring."

Luke lowered his sword and stared at Yoda in confusion. "Price?" he asked. "What do you mean?"

"The dark side beckons," Yoda said dramatically. "But if once start you down the dark path, forever will it dominate your destiny. Consume you it will . . . as it did Obi-Wan's apprentice."

Luke nodded. He knew who Yoda meant. "Lord Vader," he said. After he thought for a moment, Luke asked, "Is the dark side stronger?"

"No, no. Easier, quicker, more seductive."

"But how am I to know the good side from the bad?" he asked, puzzled.

"You will know," Yoda answered. "When you are at peace . . . calm, passive. A Jedi uses the Force for knowledge. Never for attack."

"But tell me why—" Luke began.

"No! There is no why. Nothing more will I tell you. Clear your mind of questions. Quiet now be—at peace . . ." Yoda's voice trailed off, but his words had a hypnotic effect on Luke. The young student stopped protesting and began to feel peaceful, his body and mind relaxing.

"Yes . . ." Yoda murmured, "calm."

Slowly Luke's eyes closed as he let his mind clear of distracting thoughts.

"Passive . . ."

Luke heard Yoda's soothing voice as it entered the receptive darkness of his mind. He willed himself to travel along with the master's words to wherever they might lead.

"Let yourself go . . ."

When Yoda perceived that Luke was as relaxed as the young student could be at this stage, he made the tiniest of gestures.

As he did, the two seeker balls above his head shot toward Luke, firing stun bolts as they moved.

In that instant Luke sprang to life and ignited his laser sword. He leaped to his feet and, with pure concentration, began deflecting the bolts as they spun toward him. Fearlessly he faced the attack, and moved and dodged with extreme grace. His leaps into the air, as he jumped to meet the bolts, were higher than any he had achieved before. Luke wasted not a single motion as he concentrated only on every bolt as it sped his way.

Then, as suddenly as it had begun, the seeker attack was over. The glowing balls returned to hover on either side of their master's head.

Artoo-Detoo, the ever-patient observer, let out an electronic sigh and shook his metal dome-head.

Grinning proudly, Luke looked toward Yoda.

"Much progress do you make, young one," the Jedi Master confirmed. "Stronger do you grow." But the little instructor would not compliment him more than that.

Luke was full of pride at his marvelous achievement. He watched Yoda, expectantly waiting for further praise from him. But Yoda did not move or speak. He sat calmly—and then two more seeker balls floated up behind him and moved into formation with the first two.

Luke Skywalker's grin began to melt away.

A pair of white-armored stormtroopers lifted Captain Needa's lifeless form from the floor of Darth Vader's Imperial Star Destroyer.

Needa had known that death was the likely consequence of his failure to capture the *Millennium Falcon*. He had known, too, that he had to report the situation to Vader and make his formal apology. But there was no mercy for failure among the Imperial military. And Vader, in disgust, had signaled for the captain's death.

The Dark Lord turned, and Admiral Piett and two of his captains came to report their findings. "Lord Vader," Piett said, "our ships have completed their scan of the area and found nothing. The *Millennium Falcon* definitely went into light-speed. It's probably somewhere on the other side of the galaxy by now."

Vader hissed through his breath mask. "Alert all commands," he ordered. "Calculate every possible destination along their last known trajectory and disburse the fleet to search for them. Don't fail me again, Admiral, I've had quite enough!"

Admiral Piett thought of the *Avenger*'s captain, whom he had just seen carried out of the room like a sack of grain. And he remembered the excruciating demise of Admiral Ozzel. "Yes, my lord," he answered, trying to hide his fear. "We'll find them."

Then the admiral turned to an aide. "Deploy the fleet," he instructed. As the aide moved to carry out his orders, a shadow of worry crossed the admiral's face. He was not at all certain that his luck would be any better than that of Ozzel or Needa.

Lord Vader's Imperial Star Destroyer regally moved off into space. Its protecting fleet of smaller craft hovered nearby as the Imperial armada left the Star Destroyer *Avenger* behind.

No one on the *Avenger* or in Vader's entire fleet had any idea how near they were to their prey. As the *Avenger* glided off into space to continue its search, it carried with it, clinging unnoticed to one side of the huge bridge tower, a saucer-shaped freighter ship—the *Millennium Falcon*.

Inside the *Falcon*'s cockpit all was quiet. Han Solo had stopped his ship and shut down all systems so quickly that even the customarily talkative See Threepio was silent. Threepio stood, not moving a rivet, a look of wonder frozen on his golden face.

"You could have warned him before you shut him off," Princess Leia said, looking at the droid that stood motionless like a bronzed statue.

"Oh, so sorry!" Han said in mock concern. "Didn't mean to offend your droid. You think braking and shutting everything down in that amount of time is easy?"

Leia was dubious about Han's entire strategy. "I'm still not sure what you've accomplished."

He shrugged off her doubt. She'll find out soon enough, he thought; there just wasn't any other choice. He turned to his copilot. "Chewie, check the manual release on the landing claws."

The Wookiee barked, then pulled himself out of his chair and moved toward the rear of the ship.

Leia watched as Chewbacca proceeded to disengage the landing claws so that the ship could take off without mechanical delay.

Shaking her head incredulously, she turned to Han. "What do you have in mind for your *next* move?"

"The fleet is finally breaking up," he answered as he pointed out a port window. "I'm *hoping* they follow standard Imperial procedure and dump their garbage before they go into light-speed.''

The princess reflected on this strategy for a moment, and then began to smile. This crazy man might know what he was doing after all. Impressed, she patted him on the head. ''Not bad, hot shot, not bad. Then what?''

''Then,'' Han said, ''we have to find a safe port around here. Got any ideas?''

''That depends. Where are we?''

''Here,'' Han said, pointing to a configuration of small light points, ''near the Anoat system.''

Slipping out of her chair, Leia moved next to him for a better look at the screen.

''Funny,'' Han said after thinking for a moment, ''I have the feeling I've been in this area before. Let me check my logs.''

''You keep logs?'' Leia was more impressed by the minute. ''My, how organized,'' she teased.

''Well, sometimes,'' he answered as he hunted through the computer readout. ''Ah-ha, I knew it! Lando—now this should be interesting.''

''I never heard of that system,'' said Leia.

''It's not a system. He's a man, Lando Calrissian. A gambler, con artist, all-around scoundrel,'' he paused long enough for the last word to sink in, and gave the princess a wink, ''. . . your kind of guy. The Bespin system. It's a fair distance but reachable.''

Leia looked at one of the computer monitor screens and read the data. ''A mining colony,'' she noted.

''A Tibanna gas mine,'' Han added. ''Lando won it in a sabacc match, or so he claims. Lando and I go way back.''

''Can you trust him?'' Leia asked.

''No. But he has no love for the Empire, that much I know.''
The Wookiee barked over the intercom.

Quickly responding, Han flicked some switches to bring new information to the computer screens, and then stretched to look out the cockpit window. ''I see it, Chewie, I see it,'' he said. ''Prepare for manual release.'' Then, turning to the princess, Han said, ''Here goes nothing, sweetheart.'' He leaned back in his chair and smiled invitingly at her.

Leia shook her head, then grinned shyly and gave him a quick kiss. ''You do have your moments,'' she reluctantly admitted. ''Not many, but you have them.''

Han was getting used to the princess's left-handed compliments, and he couldn't say that he really minded them. More and more he was enjoying the fact that she shared his own sarcastic sense of humor. And he was fairly sure that she was enjoying it, too.

"Let'er go, Chewie," he shouted gleefully.

The hatch on the underbelly of the *Avenger* yawned open. And as the Imperial galactic cruiser zoomed into hyperspace, it spewed out its own belt of artificial asteroids—garbage and sections of irreparable machinery that scattered out into the black void of space. Hidden among that trail of refuse, the *Millennium Falcon* tumbled undetected off the side of the larger ship, and was left far behind as the *Avenger* streaked away.

Safe at last, Han Solo thought.

The *Millennium Falcon* ignited its ion engines, and raced off through the train of drifting space junk toward another system.

But concealed among that scattered debris was another ship.

And as the *Falcon* roared off to seek the Bespin system, this other ship ignited its own engines. Boba Fett, the most notorious and dreaded bounty hunter in the galaxy, turned his small, elephant's head-shaped craft, *Slave I*, to begin its pursuit. For Boba Fett had no intention of losing sight of the *Millennium Falcon*. Its pilot had too high a price on his head. And this was one reward that the fearsome bounty hunter was quite determined to collect.

Luke felt that he was definitely progressing.

He ran through the jungle—with Yoda perched on his neck—and leaped with gazellelike grace over the profusion of foliage and tree roots growing throughout the bog.

Luke had at last begun to detach himself from the emotion of pride. He felt unburdened, and was finally open to experience fully the flow of the Force.

When his diminutive instructor threw a silver bar above Luke's head, the young Jedi student reacted instantly. In a flash he turned to slice the bar into four shiny segments before it fell to the ground.

Yoda was pleased and smiled at Luke's accomplishment. "Four this time! The Force you feel."

But Luke was suddenly distracted. He sensed something dangerous, something evil. "Something's not right," he said to Yoda. "I feel danger . . . death."

He looked around him, trying to see what it was that emitted so powerful an aura. As he turned he saw a huge, tangled tree, its blackened bark dry and crumbling. The base of the tree was surrounded by a small pond of water, where the gigantic roots had grown to form the opening to a darkly sinister cave.

Luke gently lifted Yoda from his neck and set him on the ground. Transfixed, the Jedi student stared at the dark monstrosity. Breathing hard, he found himself unable to speak.

"You brought me here purposely," Luke said at last.

Yoda sat on a tangled root and put his Gimer Stick in his mouth. Calmly looking at Luke, he said nothing.

Luke shivered. "I feel cold," he said, still gazing at the tree.

"This tree is strong with the dark side of the Force. A servant of evil it is. Into it you must go."

Luke felt a tremor of apprehension. "What's in there?"

"Only what you take with you," Yoda said cryptically.

Luke looked warily at Yoda, and then at the tree. He silently resolved to take his courage, his willingness to learn, and step within that darkness to face whatever it was that awaited him. He would take nothing more than—

No. He would also bring his lightsaber.

Lighting his weapon, Luke stepped through the shallow waters of the pond and toward the dark opening between those great and foreboding roots.

But the Jedi Master's voice stopped him.

"Your weapon," Yoda reproved. "You won't need it."

Luke paused and looked again at the tree. Go into that evil cave completely unarmed? As skilled as Luke was becoming, he did not feel quite equal to that test. He gripped his saber tighter and shook his head.

Yoda shrugged and placidly gnawed his Gimer Stick.

Taking a deep breath, Luke cautiously stepped into the grotesque tree cave.

The dark inside the cave was so thick that Luke could feel it against his skin, so black that the light thrown by his laser sword was quickly absorbed and illuminated scarcely more than a meter in front of him. As he slowly moved forward, slimy, dripping things brushed against his face and the moisture from the soggy cave floor began to seep into his boots.

As he pushed through the blackness, his eyes began to grow accustomed to the dark. He saw a corridor before him, but as he moved toward it, he was surprised by a thick, sticky membrane that completely enveloped him. Like the web of some gigantic spider, the mass clung tightly to Luke's body. Thrashing at it with his lightsaber, Luke finally managed to disentangle himself and clear a path ahead.

He held his glowing sword in front of him and noticed an object on the cave floor. Pointing his lightsaber downward, Luke illuminated a black, shiny beetle the size of his hand. In an instant, the thing scurried up the slimy wall to join a cluster of its mates.

Luke caught his breath and stepped back. At that moment he considered hunting for the exit—but he braced himself and ventured still deeper into the dark chamber.

He felt the space about him widen as he moved forward, using his lightsaber as a dim beacon. He strained to see in the darkness, trying his best to hear. But there was no sound at all. Nothing.

Then, a very loud *hiss*.

The sound was familiar. He froze where he stood. He had heard that hiss even in his nightmares; it was the labored breath of a thing that had once been a man.

Out of the darkness a light appeared—the blue flame of a just-ignited laser sword. In its illumination Luke saw the looming figure of Darth Vader raise his lighted weapon to attack, and then lunge.

Prepared by his disciplined Jedi training, Luke was ready. He raised his own lightsaber and perfectly side-stepped Vader's attack. In the same movement, Luke turned to Vader and, with his mind and body completely focused, the youth summoned the Force. Feeling its power within him, Luke raised his laser weapon and brought it crashing down on Vader's head.

With one powerful stroke, the Dark Lord's head was severed from his body. Head and helmet crashed to the ground and rolled about the cave floor with a loud metallic bang. As Luke watched in astonishment, Vader's body was completely swallowed up by the darkness. Then Luke looked down at the helmet that had come to rest directly in front of him. For a moment it was completely still. Then the helmet cracked in half and split open.

As Luke watched in shocked disbelief, the broken helmet fell aside to reveal, not the unknown, imagined face of Darth Vader, but Luke's own face, looking up at him.

He gasped, horrified at the sight. And then, as suddenly as it had appeared, the decapitated head faded away as if in a ghostly vision.

Luke stared at the dark space where the head and pieces of

helmet had lain. His mind reeled, the emotions that raged inside of him were almost too much to bear.

The tree! he told himself. It was all some trick of this ugly cave, some charade of Yoda's, arranged because he had come into the tree carrying a weapon.

He wondered if he were really fighting himself, or if he had fallen prey to the temptations of the dark side of the Force. He might himself become a figure as evil as Darth Vader. And he wondered if there might be some even darker meaning behind the unsettling vision.

It was a long while before Luke Skywalker was able to move from that deep, dark cave.

Meanwhile, sitting on the root, the little Jedi Master calmly gnawed his Gimer Stick.

XI

IT was dawn on the gaseous Bespin planet.

As the *Millennium Falcon* began its approach through the planet's atmosphere, it soared past several of Bespin's many moons. The planet itself glowed with the same soft pink hue of dawn that tinted the hull of the powerful pirate starship. As the ship neared, it swerved to avoid a billowing canyon of clouds that swirled up around the planet.

When Han Solo finally lowered his ship through the clouds, he and his crew got their first glimpse of the gaseous world of Bespin. And as they maneuvered through the clouds, they noticed that they were being followed by some kind of flying vehicle. Han recognized the craft as a twin-pod cloud car but was surprised when the car began to bank close to his freighter. The *Falcon* suddenly lurched as a round of laser fire struck its hull. No one on the *Falcon* had expected *this* kind of greeting.

The other craft transmitted a static-obscured message over the *Falcon*'s radio system.

"No," Han snarled in reply, "I do not have a landing permit. My registration is—"

But his words were drowned out by a loud crackle of radio static.

The twin-pod car was apparently not willing to accept static for a reply. Again it opened up fire on the *Falcon*, shaking and rattling the ship with each strike.

A clear warning voice came over the freighter's speakers: "Stand by. Any aggressive move will bring about your destruction."

At this point Han had no intention of making any aggressive moves. Bespin was their only hope of sanctuary, and he didn't plan to alienate his prospective hosts.

"Rather touchy, aren't they?" the reactivated See Threepio asked.

"I thought you knew these people," Leia chided, casting a suspicious look at Han.

"Well," the Corellian hedged, "it's been a while."

Chewbacca growled and barked, shaking his head meaningfully at Han.

"That was a long time ago," he answered sharply. "I'm sure he's forgotten all about it." But he began to wonder if Lando had forgotten the past . . .

"Permission granted to land on Platform 327. Any deviation of flight pattern will bring about your—"

Angrily, Han switched off the radio. Why was he being put through this harrassment? He was coming here peacefully; wasn't Lando going to let bygones be bygones? Chewbacca grunted and glanced at Solo, who turned to Leia and her worried robot. "He'll help us," he said, trying to reassure them all. "We go way back . . . really. Don't worry."

"Who's worried?" she lied unconvincingly.

By then they could clearly see the Cloud City of Bespin through the cockpit window. The city was immense and seemed to float in the clouds as it emerged through the white atmosphere. As the *Millennium Falcon* approached the city, it became evident that the expansive city structure was supported from below by a thin unipod. The base of this supporting stalk was a large round reactor that floated through its billowing sea of clouds.

The *Millennium Falcon* dipped closer to the huge city and

veered in the direction of its landing platforms, flying past the rising towers and spires that dotted the city's landscape. In and about these structures cruised more of the twin-pod cloud cars, gliding effortlessly through the mists.

Han gently brought the *Falcon* in to land on Platform 327; and as the ship's ion engines whined to a stop, the captain and his crew could see the welcoming party moving toward the landing platform with weapons drawn. Like any cross-section of the citizenry of Cloud City, this group included aliens, droids, and humans of all races and descriptions. One of these humans was the group's leader, Lando Calrissian.

Lando, a handsome black man perhaps the same age as Solo, was clad in elegant gray pants, blue shirt, and a flowing blue cape. He stood, unsmiling, on Landing Platform 327, waiting for the *Falcon*'s crew to disembark.

Han Solo and Princess Leia appeared at the open door of their ship, with blasters drawn. Standing behind them was the giant Wookiee, his gun in hand and a bandoleer of ammunition packs slung over his left shoulder.

Han didn't speak but quietly surveyed the menacing welcoming party that was marching across the platform toward them. An early morning wind began to sweep along the ground, making Lando's cloak fly up behind him like enormous deep blue wings.

"I don't like this," Leia whispered to Han.

He didn't much like it either, but he wasn't going to let the princess know that. "It'll be all right," he said quietly. "Trust me." Then, cautioning her, he added, "But keep your eyes open. Wait here."

Han and Chewbacca left Leia guarding the *Falcon* and they walked down the ramp to face Calrissian and his motley army. The two parties moved toward each other until Han and Calrissian stopped, three meters apart, to face each other. For a long moment, each one eyed the other silently.

Finally Calrissian spoke, shaking his head and squinting at Han. "Why, you slimy, double-crossing, no-good swindler," he said grimly.

"I can explain everything, ol' buddy," Han said quickly, "if you'll just listen."

Still unsmiling, Lando surprised alien and human alike when he said, "Glad to see you."

Han lifted an eyebrow skeptically. "No hard feelings?"

"Are you kidding?" Lando asked coolly.

Han was becoming nervous. Had he been forgiven or not? The guards and aides still had not lowered their weapons, and Lando's attitude was mystifying. Trying to conceal his worry, Han remarked gallantly, "I always said you were a gentleman."

With that, the other man broke into a grin. "I'll bet," he chuckled.

Han laughed in relief, as the two old friends at last embraced each other like the long-lost accomplices they were.

Lando waved at the Wookiee, standing behind his boss. "How you doing, Chewbacca?" he asked amiably. "Still wasting your time with this clown, eh?"

The Wookiee growled a reserved greeting.

Calrissian was not certain what to make of that growl. "Right," he half-smiled, looking uncomfortable. But his attention was distracted from this shaggy mass of muscle and hair when he saw Leia beginning to walk down the ramp. This lovely vision was followed closely by her protocol droid, who cautiously glanced around as they walked toward Lando and Han.

"Hello! What have we here?" Calrissian welcomed her admiringly. "I am Lando Calrissian, administrator of this facility. And who might you be?"

The princess remained coolly polite. "You may call me Leia," she replied.

Lando bowed formally and gently kissed the princess's hand.

"And I," her robot companion said, introducing himself to the administrator, "am See Threepio, human-cyborg relations, at your—"

But before Threepio could finish his little speech, Han draped one arm about Lando's shoulder and steered him away from the princess. "She's travelling with me, Lando," he advised his old friend, "and I don't intend to gamble her away. So you might as well forget she exists."

Lando looked longingly over his shoulder as he and Han began to walk across the landing platform, followed by Leia, Threepio, and Chewbacca. "That won't be easy, my friend," Lando said regretfully.

Then he turned to Han. "What brings you here anyway?"

"Repairs."

Mock panic spread across Lando's face. "What have you done to my ship?"

Grinning, Han glanced back at Leia. "Lando used to own the *Falcon*," he explained. "And he sometimes forgets that he lost her fair and square."

Lando shrugged as he conceded to Han's boastful claim. "That ship saved my life more than a few times. It's the fastest hunk of junk in the galaxy. What's wrong with her?"

"Hyperdrive."

"I'll have my people get to work on it right away," Lando said. "I hate the thought of the *Millennium Falcon* without her heart."

The group crossed the narrow bridge that joined the landing area to the city—and were instantly dazzled by its beauty. They saw numerous small plazas ringed by smooth-edged towers and spires and buildings. The structures that constituted Cloud City's business and residential sections were gleaming white, shining brightly in the morning sun. Numerous alien races made up the city's populace and many of these citizens leisurely walked through the spacious streets alongside the *Falcon* visitors.

"How's your mining operation going?" Han asked Lando.

"Not as well as I'd like," Calrissian answered. "We're a small outpost and not very self-sufficient. I've had supply problems of every kind and . . ." The administrator noticed Han's amused grin. "What's so funny?"

"Nothing." Then Han chuckled. "I never would have guessed that underneath that wild schemer I knew was a responsible leader and businessman." Grudgingly, Han had to admit that he was impressed. "You wear it well."

Lando looked at his old friend reflectively. "Seeing you sure brings back a few memories." He shook his head, smiling. "Yes, I'm *responsible* these days. It's the price of success. And you know what, Han? You were right all along. It's overrated."

Both burst out laughing, causing a head or two to turn as the group moved through the city walkways.

See Threepio lagged a bit behind, fascinated by the bustling alien crowds in the Cloud City streets, the floating cars, the fabulous, fanciful buildings. He turned his head back and forth, trying to register it all in his computer circuits.

As the golden droid gawked at the new sights, he passed a door facing the walkway. Hearing it open, he turned to see a silver Threepio unit emerging and stopped to watch the other robot move away. While Threepio paused there, he heard a muffled beeping and whistling coming from behind the door.

He peeked in and saw a familiar-looking droid sitting in the anteroom. "Oh, an R2 unit!" he chirped in delight. "I'd almost forgotten what they sound like."

Threepio moved through the doorway and walked into the

room. Instantly he sensed that he and the R2 unit were not alone. He threw his golden arms up in surprise, the expression of wonder on his gilded faceplate frozen in place. "Oh, my!" he exclaimed. "Those look like—"

As he spoke, a rocketing laser bolt crashed into his metal chest, sending him flying in twenty directions around the room. His bronzed arms and legs crashed against the walls and settled in a smoldering heap with the rest of his mechanical body.

Behind him, the door slammed shut.

Some distance away, Lando guided the small group into his hall of offices, pointing out objects of interest as they moved through the white corridors. None of them had noticed Threepio's absence as they walked along, discussing life in Bespin.

But Chewbacca suddenly stopped and curiously sniffed the air as he looked behind him. Then he shrugged his huge shoulders and continued to follow the others.

Luke was perfectly calm. Even his present position did not make him feel tense or strained or unsure, or any of the negative things he used to feel when he first attempted this feat. He stood, perfectly balanced on one hand. He knew the Force was with him.

His patient master, Yoda, sat calmly on the soles of Luke's upturned feet. Luke concentrated serenely on his task and all at once he lifted four fingers from the ground. His balance undisturbed, he held his upside-down position—on one thumb.

Luke's determination had made him a quick study. He was eager to learn and was undaunted by the tests Yoda had devised for him. And now he felt confident that when he finally left this planet, it would be as a full fledged Jedi Knight prepared to fight only for the noblest of causes.

Luke was rapidly growing stronger with the Force and, indeed, was accomplishing miracles. Yoda grew more pleased with his apprentice's progress. Once, while Yoda stood watching nearby, Luke used the Force to lift two large equipment cases and suspend them in midair. Yoda was pleased, but no ticed Artoo-Detoo observing this apparent impossibility and emitting electronic beeps of disbelief. The Jedi Master raised his hand and, with the Force, lifted the little droid off the ground.

Artoo hovered, his baffled internal circuits and sensors trying to detect the unseen power that held him suspended in the air. And suddenly the invisible hand played still another joke on him: While hanging in midair, the little robot was abruptly turned upside down. His white legs kicked desperately and his dome head spun helplessly around. When Yoda finally lowered his hand, the droid, along with two supply cases, began to drop. But only the boxes smashed against the ground. Artoo remained suspended in space.

Turning his head, Artoo perceived his young master, standing with hand extended, preventing Artoo from a fatal tumble.

Yoda shook his head, impressed by his student's quick thinking and by his control.

Yoda sprang onto Luke's arm and the two of them turned back toward the house. But they had forgotten something: Artoo-Detoo was still hanging in the air, beeping and whistling frantically, trying to get their attention. Yoda was merely playing another joke on the fretful droid, and as Yoda and Luke strolled away, Artoo heard the Jedi Master's bell-like laugh float in gay peals behind him as the droid slowly lowered to the ground.

Some time later, as dusk crept through the dense foliage of the bog, Artoo was cleaning the X-wing's hull. Through a hose that ran from the pond to an orifice in his side, the robot sprayed down the ship with a powerful stream of water. And while he worked, Luke and Yoda sat in the clearing, Luke's eyes closed in concentration.

"Be calm," Yoda told him. "Through the Force things you will see: other places, other thoughts, the future, the past, old friends long gone."

Luke was losing himself as he concentrated on Yoda's words. He was becoming unaware of his body and let his consciousness drift with the words of his master.

"My mind fills with so many images."

"Control, control you must learn of what you see," the Jedi Master instructed. "Not easy, not fast."

Luke closed his eyes, relaxed, and began to free his mind, began to control the images. At last there was something, not clear at first, but something white, amorphous. Gradually the image cleared. It seemed to be that of a city, a city that perhaps floated in a billowing white sea.

"I see a city in the clouds," he finally said.

"Bespin," Yoda identified it. "I see it, too. Friends you have there, heh? Concentrate and see them you will."

Luke's concentration intensified. And the city in the clouds became clearer. As he concentrated he was able to see forms, familiar forms of people he knew.

"I see them!" Luke exclaimed, his eyes still shut. Then a sudden agony, of body and spirit, took hold of him. "They're in pain. They're suffering."

"It is the future you see," the voice of Yoda explained.

The future, Luke thought. Then the pain he had felt had not yet been inflicted on his friends. So perhaps the future was not unchangeable.

"Will they die?" he asked his master.

Yoda shook his head and shrugged gently. "Difficult to see. Always in motion is the future."

Luke opened his eyes again. He stood up and quickly began to gather his equipment. "They're my friends," he said, guessing that the Jedi Master might try to dissuade him from doing what he knew he must.

"And therefore," Yoda added, "decide you must how to serve them best. If you leave now, help them you would. But you would destroy all for which they have fought and suffered."

His words stopped Luke cold. The youth sank to the ground, feeling a shroud of gloom envelop him. Could he really destroy everything he had worked for and possibly also destroy his friends? But how could he *not* try to save them?

Artoo perceived his master's despair and rolled over to stand by him and provide what comfort he could.

Chewbacca, who had grown concerned about See Threepio, slipped away from Han Solo and the others and began hunting for the missing droid. All he had to follow were his keen Wookiee instincts as he wandered through the unfamiliar white passageways and corridors of Bespin.

Following his senses, Chewbacca finally came upon an enormous room in a corridor on the outside of the Cloud City. He approached the entrance to the room and heard the clamor of metallic objects clattering together. Along with the clanging, he heard the low grunting of creatures he had never encountered before.

The room he had found was a Cloud City junk room—the repository of all the city's broken machines and other discarded metal junk.

Standing amid the scattered pieces of metal and tangled wire were four hoglike creatures. White hair grew thickly on their heads and partially covered their wrinkled piggish faces. The humanoid beasts—called Ugnaughts on this planet—were busy separating the junked pieces of metal and casting them into a pit of molten metal.

Chewbacca entered the room and saw that one of the Ugnaughts held a familiar-looking piece of golden metal.

The piglike creature was already raising his arm to toss the severed metal leg into the sizzling pit when Chewbacca roared at him, barking desperately. The Ugnaught dropped the leg and ran, to cower in terror with his fellows.

The Wookiee grabbed the metal leg and inspected it closely. He hadn't been mistaken. And as he growled angrily at the huddled Ugnaughts, they shivered and grunted like a pack of frightened pigs.

Sunlight streamed into the circular lounge of the apartments assigned to Han Solo and his group. The lounge was white and furnished simply, with a couch and a table and little of anything else. Each of the four sliding doors, placed along the circular wall, led to an adjoining apartment.

Han leaned out the lounge's large bay window to take in the panoramic view of Cloud City. The sight was breathtaking, even to such a jaded star jockey. He watched the flying cloud cars weave between the towering buildings, then looked down to see the people moving through the networks of streets below. The cool, clean air swept against his face, and, at least for the present, he felt as if he didn't have a care in all the universe.

A door behind him opened, and he turned to see Princess Leia standing in the entranceway to her apartment. She was stunning. Dressed in red with a cloud-white cloak flowing to the floor, Leia looked more beautiful than Han had ever seen her. Her long, dark hair was tied with ribbons and it softly framed her oval face. And she was looking at him, smiling at his astounded expression.

"What are you staring at?" she asked, beginning to blush.

"Who's staring?"

"You look silly," she said, laughing.

"You look great."

Leia looked away in embarrassment. "Has Threepio turned up yet?" she asked, trying to change the subject.

Solo was taken off guard. "Huh? Oh. Chewie went to look for him. He's been gone too long just to be lost." He patted the softly cushioned sofa. "Come over here," he beckoned. "I want to check this out."

She thought about his invitation for a moment, then walked

over and sat next to him on the couch. Han was overjoyed at her apparent compliance and leaned over to put his arm around her. But just before he had quite succeeded, she spoke again. "I hope Luke made it to the fleet all right."

"Luke!" He was becoming exasperated. How hard did he have to play at this game of hard-to-get? It was her game, and her rules—but he *had* chosen to play. She was too lovely to resist. "I'm sure he's fine," Han said, soothingly. "Probably sitting around wondering what we're doing right now."

He moved closer and put his arm around her shoulders, pulling her closer to him. She gazed at him invitingly, and he moved to kiss her—

Just then one of the doors zapped open. Chewbacca lumbered in carrying a large packing case filled with disturbingly familiar metal parts—the remains, in bronzed bits and pieces, of See-Threepio. The Wookiee dropped the case on the table. Gesturing toward Han, he barked and growled in distress.

"What happened?" Leia asked, moving closer to inspect the pile of disjointed parts.

"He found Threepio in a junk room."

Leia gasped. "What a mess! Chewie, do you think you can repair him?"

Chewbacca studied the collection of robot parts, then, looking back at the princess, shrugged his shoulders and howled. It looked to him like an impossible job.

"Why don't we just turn him over to Lando to fix?" Han suggested.

"No thanks," Leia answered, with a cold look in her eyes. "Something's wrong here. Your friend Lando is very charming, but I don't trust him."

"Well, I do trust him," Han argued, defending his host. "Listen, sweetheart, I'm not going to have you accusing my friend of—"

But he was interrupted by a buzz as a door slid open, and Lando Calrissian entered the lounge. Smiling cordially, he walked toward the small group. "Sorry, am I interrupting anything?"

"Not really," the princess said distantly.

"My dear," Lando said, ignoring her coldness toward him, "your beauty is unparalleled. Truly you belong here with us among the clouds."

She smiled icily. "Thanks."

"Would you care to join me for a little refreshment?"

Han had to admit that he was a bit hungry. But for some reason he could not quite name, he felt a wave of suspicion about his friend flood over him. He didn't remember Calrissian being quite so polite, quite so smooth. Perhaps Leia was correct in her suspicions . . .

His thoughts were interrupted by Chewbacca's enthusiastic bark at the mention of food. The big Wookiee was licking his lips at the prospect of a hearty meal.

"Everyone's invited, of course," Lando said.

Leia took Lando's proffered arm and, as the group moved toward the door, Calrissian glimpsed the box of golden robot parts. "Having problems with your droid?" he asked.

Han and Leia exchanged a quick glance. If Han was going to ask for Lando's help in repairing the droid, now was the moment. "An accident," he grunted. "Nothing we can't handle."

They left the lounge, leaving behind them the shattered remains of the protocol droid.

The group strolled through the long white corridors and Leia walked between Han and Lando. Han wasn't at all certain he liked the prospect of competing with Lando for Leia's affections—especially under the circumstances. But they were dependent on Lando's good graces now. They had no other choice.

Joining them as they walked was Lando's personal aide, a tall bald man dressed in a gray jacket with ballooning yellow sleeves. The aide wore a radio device that wrapped around the back of his head and covered both his ears. He walked along with Chewbacca a short distance behind Han, Leia, and Lando, and as they walked toward Lando's dining hall, the administrator described the status of his planet's government.

"So you see," Lando explained, "we are a free station and do not fall under the jurisdiction of the Empire."

"You're part of the mining guild then?" Leia asked.

"Not actually. Our operation is small enough not to be noticed. Much of our trade is, well . . . unofficial."

They stepped onto a veranda that overlooked the spiraled top of Cloud City. From here they saw several flying cloud cars gracefully swooping around the beautiful spired buildings of the city. It was a spectacular view, and the visitors were very impressed.

"It's a lovely outpost," Leia marveled.

"Yes, we're proud of it," Lando replied. "You'll find the air quite special here . . . very stimulating." He smiled at Leia meaningfully. "You could grow to like it."

Hans didn't miss Lando's flirtatious glance—and he didn't like it, either. "We don't plan on staying that long," he said brusquely.

Leia raised an eyebrow and glanced mischievously at the now fuming Han Solo. "I find it most relaxing."

Lando chuckled, and led them from the veranda. They approached the dining hall with its massive closed doors and, as they paused in front of them, Chewbacca lifted his head and sniffed the air curiously. He turned and barked urgently at Han.

"Not now, Chewie," Han reproved, turning to Calrissian. "Lando, aren't you afraid the Empire might eventually discover this little operation and shut you down?"

"That's always been the danger," the administrator replied. "It's loomed like a shadow over everything we've built here. But circumstances have developed which will insure security. You see, I've made a deal that will keep the Empire out of here forever."

With that the mighty doors slid open—and immediately Han understood just what that "deal" must have involved. At the far end of the huge banquet table stood the bounty hunter Boba Fett.

Fett stood next to a chair that held the black essence of evil itself—Darth Vader. Slowly the Dark Lord rose to his full, menacing two-meter height.

Han shot his meanest look at Lando.

"Sorry, friend," Lando said, sounding mildly apologetic. "I had no choice. They arrived right before you did."

"I'm sorry, too," Han snapped. In that instant, he cleared his blaster from its holster, aimed it directly at the figure in black, and began to pump laser bolts Vader's way.

But the man who may have been the fastest draw in the galaxy was not fast enough to surprise Vader. Before those bolts zipped halfway across the table, the Dark Lord had lifted a gauntlet-protected hand and effortlessly deflected them so they exploded against the wall in a harmless spray of flying white shards.

Astounded by what he had just seen, Han tried firing again. But before he could discharge another laser blast, something—something unseen yet incredibly strong—yanked the weapon from his hand and sent it flying into Vader's grip. The raven figure calmly placed the weapon on top of the dining table.

Hissing through his obsidian mask, the Dark Lord addressed his would-be assailant. "We would be honored if you joined us."

* * *

Artoo Detoo felt the rain plunking on top of his metal dome as he trudged through the muddy puddles of the bog. He was headed for the sanctuary of Yoda's little hut, and soon his optical sensors picked up the golden glow shining through its windows. As he neared the inviting house, he felt a robot's relief that at last he would get out of this annoying, persistent rain.

But when he tried to pass through the entrance he discovered that his inflexible droid body just could not get in; he tried from one angle, then from another. At last the perception that he was simply the wrong shape to get in seeped into his computer mind.

He could scarcely believe his sensors. As he peered into the house, he scanned a busy figure, bustling about the kitchen, stirring steaming pots, chopping this and that, running back and forth. But the figure in Yoda's tiny kitchen, doing Yoda's kitchen tasks, was not the Jedi Master—but his apprentice.

Yoda, it appeared from Artoo's scan, was simply sitting back observing his young pupil from the adjacent room, and quietly smiling. Then suddenly, in the midst of all his kitchen activity, Luke paused, as if a painful vision had appeared before him.

Yoda noticed Luke's troubled look. As he watched his student, three glow-ball seekers appeared from behind Yoda and noiselessly shot through the air to attack the young Jedi from behind. Instantly Luke turned to face them, a pot lid in one hand and a spoon in the other.

The seekers sent one rocketing bolt after another directly at Luke. But, with astounding skill, he warded off every one. He knocked one of the seekers toward the open door where Artoo stood watching his master's performance. But the faithful droid saw the shining ball too late to avoid the bolt it shot at him. The impact knocked the shrieking robot onto the ground with a *clunk* that nearly shook loose his electronic insides.

Later that evening, after the student had successfully passed a number of his teacher's tests, a weary Luke Skywalker finally fell asleep on the ground outside Yoda's house. He slept fitfully, tossing and softly moaning. His concerned droid stood by him, reaching out an extension arm and covering Luke with the blanket that had slipped halfway off. But when Artoo started to roll away, Luke began to groan and shudder as if in the grip of some horrible nightmare.

Inside the house, Yoda heard the groans and hurried to his doorway.

Luke awoke from his sleep with a start. Dazed, he looked

about him, then saw his teacher worriedly watching him from his house. "I can't keep the vision out of my head," Luke told Yoda. "My friends . . . they're in trouble . . . and I feel that—"

"Luke, you must not go," Yoda warned.

"But Han and Leia will die if I don't."

"You don't know that." It was the whispered voice of Ben, who was beginning to materialize before them. The dark-robed figure stood, a shimmering image, and told Luke, "Even Yoda cannot see their fate."

But Luke was deeply worried about his friends and was determined to do something. "I can help them!" he insisted.

"You're not ready yet," Ben said gently. "You still have much to learn."

"I feel the Force," Luke said.

"But you cannot control it. This is a dangerous stage for you, Luke. You are now most susceptible to the temptations of the dark side."

"Yes, yes," Yoda added. "To Obi-Wan you listen, young one. The tree. Remember your failure at the tree! Heh?"

Painfully, Luke remembered, though he felt he had gained a great deal of strength and understanding in that experience. "I've learned much since then. And I'll return to finish. I promise that, master."

"You underestimate the Emperor," Ben told him gravely. "It is you he wants. That is why your friends suffer."

"And that," Luke said, "is why I must go."

Kenobi was firm. "I will not lose you to the Emperor as I once lost Vader."

"You won't."

"Only a fully trained Jedi Knight, with the Force as his ally, will conquer Vader and his Emperor," Ben emphasized. "If you end your training now, if you choose the quick and easy path—as Vader did—you will become an agent of evil, and the galaxy will be plunged deeper into the abyss of hate and despair."

"Stopped they must be," Yoda interjected. "Do you hear? On this *all* depends."

"You are the last Jedi, Luke. You are our only hope. Be patient."

"And sacrifice Han and Leia?" the youth asked incredulously.

"If you honor what they fight for," Yoda said, pausing for a long moment, ". . . yes!"

Great anguish overcame Luke. He wasn't certain that he could reconcile the advice of these two great mentors with his own feelings. His friends were in terrible danger, and of course he must save them. But his teachers thought he was not ready, that he might be too vulnerable to the powerful Vader and his Emperor, that he might bring harm to his friends and himself—and possibly be lost forever on the path of evil.

Yet how could he fear these abstract things when Han and Leia were real and were suffering? How could he permit himself to fear possible danger to himself when his friends were presently in real danger of death?

There was no longer any question in his mind as to what he had to do.

It was dusk the next day on the bog planet when Artoo-Detoo settled himself into his nook behind the cockpit of Luke's X-wing fighter.

Yoda stood on one of the storage cases, watching Luke load the cases one by one into the fighter's underbelly as he worked in the glow of the X-wing's lights.

"I cannot protect you, Luke," the voice of Ben Kenobi came, as his robed figure took solid form. "If you choose to face Vader, you will do it alone. Once you've made this decision, I cannot interfere."

"I understand," Luke replied calmly. Then, turning to his droid, he said, "Artoo, fire up the power converters."

Artoo, who had already unfastened the power couplings on the ship, whistled happily, grateful to be leaving this dismal bog world, which was certainly no place for a droid.

"Luke," Ben advised, "use the Force only for knowledge and for defense, not as a weapon. Don't give in to hate or anger. They lead the way to the dark side."

Luke nodded, only half-listening. His mind was on the long journey and on the difficult tasks ahead of him. He must save his friends, whose lives were in danger because of him. He climbed into the cockpit, then looked at his little Jedi Master.

Yoda was deeply concerned about his apprentice. "Strong is Vader," he warned ominously. "Clouded is your fate. Mind what you have learned. Notice *everything*, everything! It can save you."

"I will, Master Yoda," Luke assured him. "I will and I'll be back to finish what I have begun. I give you my word!"

Artoo closed the cockpit and Luke started the engines.

Yoda and Obi-Wan Kenobi watched the X-wing gear its engines and begin to move away for take-off.

"Told you, I did," Yoda said sorrowfully, as the sleek fighter craft began to lift into the misty heavens. "Reckless is he. Now things are going to worse."

"That boy is our last hope," Ben Kenobi said, his voice heavy with emotion.

"No," Kenobi's former teacher corrected with a knowing gleam in his large eyes, "there is another."

Yoda lifted his head toward the darkening sky where Luke's ship was already a barely distinguishable point of light among the flickering stars.

XII

CHEWBACCA thought he was going mad!

The prison cell was flooded with hot, blinding light that seared his sensitive Wookiee eyes. Not even his huge hands and hairy arms, thrust up over his face, could entirely protect him from the glare. And to add to his misery, a high pitched whistle blared into the cubicle, tormenting his keen sense of hearing. He roared in agony, but his guttural roars were drowned out by the piercing, screeching noise.

The Wookiee paced back and forth within the confines of the cell. Moaning pitifully, he pounded at the thick walls in desperation, wanting someone, anyone, to come and free him. While he pounded, the whistle that had nearly exploded his eardrums suddenly stopped and the deluge of light flickered and went out.

Chewbacca staggered back a step with the sudden absence of torture, and then moved to one of the cell walls to try to detect whether anyone was approaching to release him. But the thick walls revealed nothing and, maddened to a fury, Chewbacca slammed a giant fist against the wall.

But the wall stood undamaged and as impenetrable as before, and Chewbacca realized it would take more than Wookiee brute strength to topple it. Despairing of his chances of breaking through the cell to freedom, Chewbacca shuffled toward the bed, where the box of 3PO parts had been placed.

Idly at first, and then with more interest, the Wookiee began poking through the box. It dawned on him that it might be possible to repair the disjointed droid. Not only would doing so pass the time, but it might be helpful to have Threepio back in working condition.

He picked up the golden head and gazed into its darkened eyes. He held the head and barked a few soliloquizing words as if to prepare the robot for the joy of re-entry into activity—or for the disappointment of Chewbacca's possible failure to reconstruct him properly.

Then, quite delicately for a creature of his size and strength, the giant Wookiee placed the staring head atop the bronzed torso. Tentatively he began experimenting with Threepio's tangle of wires and circuits. His mechanical skills had previously only been tested in repairs on the *Millennium Falcon*, so he wasn't at all certain he could complete the delicate task. Chewbacca jiggled and fiddled with the wires, baffled by this intricate mechanism, when suddenly Threepio's eyes lit up.

A whine came from inside the robot. It sounded vaguely like Threepio's normal voice, but was so low and so slow that the words were unintelligible.

"Imm-peeeeer-eee-all-storr-mmm-trppp . . ."

Bewildered, Chewbacca scratched his furry head and studied the broken robot intently. An idea came to him and he tried switching one wire to another plug. Instantly Threepio began speaking in his normal voice. What he had to say sounded like words from a bad dream.

"Chewbacca!" the head of See Threepio cried. "Watch out, there are Imperial stormtroopers hidden in—" He paused, as if reliving the whole traumatic experience, and then he cried, "Oh, no! I've been shot!"

Chewbacca shook his head in sympathy. All he could do at this point was try to put the rest of See Threepio back together again.

* * *

Quite possibly it was the first time Han Solo had ever screamed. Never had he endured such excruciating torment. He was strapped to a platform that angled away from the floor at approximately forty-five degrees. While he was strapped there, electric currents of searing power shot through his body at short intervals, each jolt more painfully powerful than the last. He squirmed to free himself but his agony was so severe that it was all he could do just to remain conscious.

Standing near the torture rack, Darth Vader silently watched Han Solo's ordeal. Seeming neither pleased nor displeased, he watched until he had seen enough, and then the Dark Lord turned his back on the writhing figure and left the cell, the door sliding behind him to muffle Solo's anguished screams.

Outside the torture chamber, Boba Fett waited for Lord Vader with Lando Calrissian and the administrator's aide.

With obvious disdain, Vader turned to Fett. "Bounty hunter," Vader addressed the man in the black-marked silver helmet, "if you are waiting for your reward, you will wait until I have Skywalker."

The self-assured Boba Fett appeared unruffled by this news. "I am in no hurry, Lord Vader. My concern is that Captain Solo not be damaged. The reward from Jabba the Hut is double if he's alive."

"His pain is considerable, bounty hunter," Vader hissed, "but he will not be harmed."

"What about Leia and the Wookiee?" Lando asked with some concern.

"You will find them well enough," Vader answered. "But," he added with unmistakable finality, "they must never again leave this city."

"That was never a condition of our agreement," Calrissian urged, "Nor was giving Han to this bounty hunter."

"Perhaps you think you're being treated unfairly," Vader said sarcastically.

"No," Lando said, glancing at his aide.

"Good," Vader continued, adding a veiled threat. "It would be most unfortunate if I had to leave a permanent garrison here."

Bowing his head reverently, Lando Calrissian waited until Darth Vader had turned and swept into a waiting elevator with the silver-armored bounty hunter. Then, taking his aide with him, the administrator of Cloud City strode swiftly down a white-walled corridor.

"This deal's becoming worse all the time," Lando complained.

"Maybe you should have tried to negotiate with him," the aide suggested.

Lando looked at his aide grimly. He was beginning to realize that the deal with Darth Vader was giving nothing to him. And, beyond that, it was bringing harm to people he might have called friends. Finally, he said, low enough not to be heard by any of Vader's spies, "I've got a bad feeling about this."

See Threepio was at last beginning to feel something like his old self.

The Wookiee had been busily working on reconnecting the droid's many wires and internal circuits, and just now was beginning to figure out how to attach the limbs. So far he had reattached the head to the torso and had successfully completed connecting an arm. The rest of Threepio's parts still lay on the table with wires and circuits hanging out of the severed joints.

But, though the Wookiee was diligently working to complete his task, the golden droid began to complain vociferously. "Well, something's not right," he fussed, "because now I can't see."

The patient Wookiee barked, and adjusted a wire in Threepio's neck. At last the robot could see again and he breathed a little mechanical sigh of relief. "There now, that's better."

But it wasn't *much* better. When he cast his newly activated sensor gaze toward where his chest should be he saw—his back! "Wait—Oh, my. What have you done? I'm backwards!" Threepio sputtered. "You flea-bitten furball! Only an overgrown mophead like you would be stupid enough to put my head—"

The Wookiee growled menacingly. He had forgotten what a complainer this droid was. And this cell was too small for him to listen to any more of that! Before Threepio knew what was happening to him, the Wookiee lumbered over and pulled a wire. Instantly the grumbling ceased, and the room became quiet again.

Then there was a familiar scent nearing the cell.

The Wookiee sniffed the air and hurried to the door.

The cell door buzzed open and a ragged, exhausted Han Solo was shoved in by two Imperial stormtroopers. The troopers left and Chewbacca quickly moved to his friend, embracing him with relief. Han's face was pale, with dark circles under his eyes. It seemed that he was on the verge of collapse, and Chewbacca barked his concern to his long-time companion.

"No," Han said wearily, "I'm all right. I'm all right."

The door opened once again, and Princess Leia was thrown into the cell by the stormtroopers. She was still dressed in her elegant cloak but, like Han, she looked tired and disheveled.

When the stormtroopers left and the door slid shut behind them, Chewbacca helped Leia over to Han. The two gazed at one another with great emotion, then reached out and tightly embraced. After a moment they kissed tenderly.

While Han still held her, Leia weakly asked him, "Why are they doing this? I can't understand what they're up to."

Han was as puzzled as she. "They had me howling on the scan grid, but they never asked me any questions."

Then the door slid open again, admitting Lando and two of his Cloud City guards.

"Get out of here, Lando!" Han snarled. If he had felt stronger, he would have leaped up to attack his traitorous friend.

"Shut up a minute and listen," Lando snapped. "I'm doing what I can to make this easier for you."

"This ought to be good," Han remarked caustically.

"Vader has agreed to turn Leia and Chewie over to me," explained Lando. "They'll have to stay here, but at least they'll be safe."

Leia gasped. "What about Han?"

Lando looked solemnly at his friend. "I didn't know you had a price on your head. Vader has given you to the bounty hunter."

The princess quickly looked at Han, concern flooding her eyes.

"You don't know much about much," Han said to Calrissian, "if you think Vader won't want us dead before all this is over."

"He doesn't want you at all," Lando said. "He's after someone called Skywalker."

The two prisoners caught their breath at the casual mention of that name.

Han seemed puzzled. "Luke? I don't get it."

The princess's mind was racing. All the facts were beginning to fit together into a terrible mosaic. In the past, Vader had wanted Leia because of her political importance in the war between Empire and Rebel Alliance. Now she was almost beneath his notice, useful only for one possible function.

"Lord Vader has set a trap for him," Lando added, "and—"

Leia finished his statement. "We're the bait."

"All this just to get the kid?" Han asked. "What's so important about him?"

"Don't ask me, but he's on his way."

"Luke's coming here?"

Lando Calrissian nodded.

"You fixed us all pretty good," Han growled, spitting his words at Lando, "—friend!"

As he snarled that last, accusing word, Han Solo's strength returned in a rush. He put all of his might into a punch that sent Lando reeling. Instantly the two former friends were engaged in a furious, close-quarters battle. Lando's two guards moved closer to the two grappling opponents and began striking at Han with the butts of their laser rifles. One powerful blow struck Han on the chin and sent him flying across the room, blood streaming from his jaw.

Chewbacca began to growl savagely and started for the guards. As they raised their laser weapons, Lando shouted, "Don't shoot!"

Bruised and winded, the administrator turned to Han. "I've done what I can for you," he said. "I'm sorry it's not better, but I've got my own problems." Then turning to leave the cell, Lando Calrissian added, "I've already stuck my neck out farther than I should."

"Yeah," Han Solo retorted, regaining his composure, "you're a real hero."

When Lando had left with his guards, Leia and Chewbacca helped Han back to his feet and led him to one of the bunks. He eased his weary, battered body onto the bunk, and Leia took a piece of her cloak and began gently dabbing at his chin, cleaning off the oozing blood.

As she did so, she started to chuckle softly. "You certainly have a way with people," she teased.

Artoo Detoo's head swiveled atop his barrellike body as his scanners perceived the star-studded void of the Bespin system.

The speeding X-wing had just entered the system, and was swooping through black space like a great white bird.

The R2 unit had a lot to communicate to his pilot. His electronic thoughts were tumbling out, one on top of the other, and were translated on the cockpit scope.

The grim-faced Luke quickly responded to the first of Artoo's urgent questions. "Yes," Luke replied. "I'm sure Threepio is with them."

The little robot whistled an excited exclamation.

"Just hold on," Luke said patiently, "we'll be there soon."

Artoo's turning head perceived the regal clusters of stars, his innards warm and cheerful, as the X-wing continued like a celestial arrow toward a planet with a city in the clouds.

Lando Calrissian and Darth Vader stood near the hydraulic platform that dominated the huge carbon-freezing chamber. The Dark Lord was quiet while aides hurried to prepare the room.

The hydraulic platform was housed within a deep pit in the center of the chamber and was surrounded by countless steam pipes and enormous chemical tanks of varying shapes.

Standing guard with laser rifles clutched in their hands were four armor-suited Imperial stormtroopers.

Darth Vader turned to Calrissian after appraising the chamber. "The facility is crude," he remarked, "but it should suit our needs."

One of Vader's officers rushed to the Sith Lord's side. "Lord Vader," he reported, "ship approaching—X-wing class."

"Good," Vader said coldly. "Monitor Skywalker's progress and allow him to land. We'll have the chamber ready for him shortly."

"We only use this facility for carbon-freezing," the administrator of Cloud City said nervously. "If you put him in there, it might kill him."

But Vader had already considered that possibility. He knew a way to find out just how powerful this freezing unit was. "I don't wish the Emperor's prize to be damaged. We'll test it first." He caught the attention of one of his stormtroopers. "Bring in Solo," the Dark Lord commanded.

Lando quickly glanced at Vader. He hadn't been prepared for the pure evil that was manifested in this terrifying being.

The X-wing speedily made its descent, and began to pierce the dense cloud blanket enveloping the planet.

Luke checked his monitor screens with growing concern. Maybe Artoo had more information than he was getting on his own panel. He tapped out a question to the robot.

"You haven't picked up any patrol ships?"

Artoo Detoo's reply was negative.

And so Luke, thoroughly convinced that his arrival was thus far undetected, pressed his ship onward, toward the city of his troubled vision.

* * *

Six of the piglike Ugnaughts frantically prepared the carbon-freezing chamber for use, while Lando Calrissian and Darth Vader—now the true master of Cloud City—observed the hasty activity.

As they scurried about the carbon-freezing platform, the Ugnaughts lowered a network of pipes—resembling some alien giant's circulatory system—into the pit. They raised the carbonite hoses and hammered them into place. Then the six humanoids lifted the heavy coffinlike container and set it securely onto the platform.

Boba Fett rushed in, leading a squad of six Imperial stormtroopers. The troopers shoved and pulled Han, Leia, and the Wookiee in front of them, forcing them to hurry into the chamber. Strapped to the Wookiee's broad back was the partially reassembled See Threepio, whose unattached arm and legs were roughly bundled against his gilded torso. The droid's head, facing the opposite direction from Chewbacca's, frantically turned around to try to see where they were going and what lay in store for them.

Vader turned to the bounty hunter. "Put him in the carbon-freezing chamber."

"What if he doesn't survive?" the calculating Boba Fett asked. "He is worth a lot to me."

"The Empire will compensate you for the loss," Vader said succinctly.

Anguished, Leia protested, "No!"

Chewbacca threw back his maned head and gave out a bellowing Wookiee howl. Then he charged directly at the line of stormtroopers guarding Han.

Screaming in panic, See Threepio raised his one functioning arm to protect his face.

"Wait!" the robot yelled. "What are you doing?"

But the Wookiee wrestled and grappled with the troopers, undaunted by their number or by Threepio's frightened shrieks.

"Oh, no . . . Don't hit me!" the droid begged, trying to protect his disassembled parts with his arm. "No! He doesn't mean it! Calm down, you hairy fool!"

More stormtroopers had come into the room and joined the fight. Some of the troopers began to club the Wookiee with the butts of their rifles, banging against Threepio in the process.

"Ouch!" the droid screamed. "*I* didn't do anything!"

The stormtroopers had begun to overpower Chewbacca, and

were about to smash him in the face with their weapons when, over the sounds of the fray, Han shouted, "Chewie, no! Stop it, Chewbacca!"

Only Han Solo could deflect the maddened Wookiee from his battle. Straining against the hold of his guards, Han broke away from them and rushed over to break up the fight.

Vader signaled his guards to let Han go and signaled the battling stormtroopers to stop the fight.

Han gripped the massive forearms of his hairy friend to calm him down, then gave him a stern look.

The flustered Threepio was still fussing and fuming. "Oh, yes . . . stop, stop." Then, with a robotic sigh of relief, he said, "Thank heavens!"

Han and Chewbacca faced each other, the former looking grimly into his friend's eyes. For a moment they embraced tightly, then Han told the Wookiee, "Save your strength for another time, pal, when the odds are better." He mustered a reassuring wink, but the Wookiee was grief-stricken and barked a mournful wail.

"Yeah," Han said, trying his best to crack a grin, "I know. I feel the same way. Keep well." Han Solo turned to one of the guards. "You'd better chain him until it's over."

The subdued Chewbacca did not resist as the stormtrooper guards placed restraining bands around his wrists. Han gave his partner a final farewell hug, then turned to Princess Leia. He took her in his arms and they embraced as if they would never let go.

Then Leia pressed her lips to his in a lingering kiss of passion. When their kiss ended, tears were in her eyes. "I love you," she said softly. "I couldn't tell you before, but it's true."

He smiled his familiar cocky smile. "Just remember that, because I'll be back." Then his face grew tender and he kissed her gently on the forehead.

Tears began to roll down her cheeks as Han turned away from her and walked quietly and fearlessly toward the waiting hydraulic platform.

The Ugnaughts rushed to his side and positioned him on the platform, binding his arms and legs tightly onto the hydraulic deck. He stood alone and helpless, and gazed one last time at his friends. Chewbacca looked at his friend mournfully, Threepio's head peeking over the Wookiee's shoulder to get one last look at the brave man. The administrator, Calrissian, watched this ordeal, a solemn look of regret etched deeply into his face.

And then there was Leia. Her face was contorted with the pain of her grief as she stood regally trying to be strong.

Leia's was the last face Han saw when he felt the hydraulic platform suddenly drop. As it dropped, the Wookiee bellowed a final, baleful farewell.

In that terrible moment, the grieving Leia turned away, and Lando grimaced in sorrow.

Instantly fiery liquid began to pour down into the pit in a great cascading shower of fluid and sparks.

Chewbacca half-turned from the horrifying spectacle, giving Threepio a better view of the process.

"They're encasing him in carbonite," the droid reported. "It's high-quality alloy. Much better than my own. He should be quite well protected . . . That is, if he survived the freezing process."

Chewbacca quickly glanced over his shoulder at Threepio, silencing his technical description with an angry bark.

When the liquid finally solidified, huge metal tongs lifted the smoldering figure from the pit. The figure, which was cooling rapidly, had a recognizably human shape, but was featureless and rocky like an unfinished sculpture.

Some of the hogmen, their hands protected by thick black gloves, approached the metal-encased body of Han Solo and shoved the block over. After the figure crashed to the platform with a loud, metallic *clang*, the Ugnaughts hoisted it into the casket-shaped container. They then attached a boxlike electronic device to its side and stepped away.

Kneeling, Lando turned some knobs on the device and checked the gauge measuring the temperature of Han's body. He sighed with relief and nodded his head. "He's alive," he informed Han Solo's anxious friends, "and in perfect hibernation."

Darth Vader turned to Boba Fett. "He's all yours, bounty hunter," he hissed. "Reset the chamber for Skywalker."

"He's just landed, my lord," an aide informed him.

"See to it that he finds his way here."

Indicating Leia and Chewbacca, Lando told Vader, "I'll take what is mine now." He was determined to whisk them out of Vader's clutches before the Dark Lord reneged on their contract.

"Take them," Vader said, "but I'm keeping a detachment of troops here to watch over them."

"That wasn't part of the bargain," Lando protested hotly. "You said the Empire wouldn't interfere in—"

"I'm altering the bargain. Pray I don't alter it any further."

A sudden tightness grasped Lando's throat, a threatening sign of what would happen to him if he gave Vader any difficulty. Lando's hand automatically went to his neck, but in the next moment the unseen hold was released and the administrator turned to face Leia and Chewbacca. The look in his eyes might have expressed despair, but neither of them cared to look at him at all.

Luke and Artoo moved cautiously through a deserted corridor.

It concerned Luke that thus far they had not been stopped for questioning. No one had asked them for landing permits, identification papers, purpose of visit. No one in Cloud City seemed at all curious about who this young man and his little droid might be—or what they were doing there. It all seemed rather ominous, and Luke was beginning to feel very uneasy.

Suddenly he heard a sound at the far end of the corridor. Luke halted, pressing himself close against the corridor wall. Artoo, thrilled to think that they might be back among familiar droids and humans, began to whistle and beep excitedly. Luke glanced at him to be still, and the little robot emitted one last, feeble squeak. Luke then peered around a corner and saw a group approaching from a side hallway. Leading the group was an imposing figure in battered armor and helmet. Behind him, two Cloud City armed guards pushed a transparent case down the corridor. From where Luke stood it appeared the case contained a floating, statuelike human figure. Following the case were two Imperial stormtroopers, who spotted Luke.

Instantly, the troopers took aim and began to fire.

But Luke dodged their laser bolts and, before they could shoot another round, the youth fired his blaster, ripping two sizzling holes into the stormtroopers' armored chests.

As the troopers fell, the two guards quickly whisked the encased figure into another hallway and the armor-clad figure leveled his laser blaster at Luke, sending a deadly bolt at him. The beam just missed the youth, and nicked a large chunk out of the wall next to him, shattering it into a shower of dustlike particles. When the particles had cleared, Luke peeked back around the corner and saw that the nameless attacker, the guards, and the case had all disappeared behind a thick metal door.

Hearing sounds behind him, Luke turned to see Leia, Chewbacca, See Threepio, and an unfamiliar man in a cloak moving down yet another hallway, and guarded by a small band of Imperial stormtroopers.

He gestured to catch the princess's attention.

"Leia!" he shouted.

"Luke, no!" she exclaimed, her voice charged with fear. "It's a trap!"

Leaving Artoo trailing behind, Luke ran off to follow them. But when he reached a small anteroom, Leia and the others had disappeared. Luke heard Artoo whistling frantically as he scooted toward the anteroom. Yet, as the youth swiftly turned, he saw a mammoth metal door crash down in front of the startled robot with a thundering *clang*.

With the slamming of that door, Luke was cut off from the main corridor. And, when he turned to find another way out, he saw more metal doors bang shut in the other doorways of the chamber.

Meanwhile, Artoo stood somewhat dazed by the shock of his close call. If he had rolled just a tiny bit farther into the anteroom, that door would have squashed him into scrap metal. He pressed his metal nose against the door, then gave out a whistle of relief and wandered off in the opposite direction.

The anteroom was full of hissing pipes and steam that belched from the floor. Luke began to explore the room and noticed an opening above his head, leading to a place he could not even imagine. He moved forward to get a better look, and as he did, the section of floor he stood on began to rise slowly upward. Luke rode up with the lifting platform, determined to face the foe he had traveled so far to meet.

Keeping his blaster clutched in his hand, Luke rose into the carbon-freezing chamber. The room was deathly quiet, except for the hissing of steam escaping some of the pipes in the room. It appeared to Luke that he was the only living creature in this chamber of strange machinery and chemical containers, but he sensed that he was not alone.

"Vader . . ."

He spoke the name to himself as he looked around the chamber.

"Lord Vader. I feel your presence. Show yourself," Luke taunted his unseen enemy, "or do you fear me?"

While Luke spoke, the escaping steam began to billow out in great clouds. Then, unaffected by the searing heat, Vader appeared and strode through the hissing vapors, stepping onto the narrow walkway above the chamber, his black cloak trailing behind him.

Luke took a cautious step toward the demonic figure in black and holstered his blaster. He experienced a surge of confidence and felt completely ready to face the Dark Lord as one Jedi against another. There was no need for his blaster. He sensed that the Force was with him and that, at last, he was ready for this inevitable battle. Slowly he began to mount the stairs toward Vader.

"The Force is with you, young Skywalker," Darth Vader said from above, "but you are not a Jedi yet."

Vader's words had a chilling effect. Briefly Luke hesitated, recalling the words of another former Jedi Knight; *"Luke, use the Force only for knowledge and for defense, not as a weapon. Don't give in to hate or anger. They lead the way to the dark side."*

But throwing aside any fragment of doubt, Luke gripped the smoothly finished handle of his lightsaber and quickly ignited the laser blade.

At the same instant, Vader ignited his own laser sword and quietly waited for the young Skywalker to attack.

His great hatred for Vader impelled Luke to lunge at him savagely, bringing his sizzling blade down upon Vader's. But effortlessly, the Dark Lord deflected the blow with a defensive turn of his own weapon.

Again Luke attacked. Once again their energy blades clashed.

And then they stood, staring at one another for an endless moment through their crossed lightsabers.

XIII

SIX Imperial stormtroopers guarded Lando, Leia, and Chewbacca as they marched through the inner corridor of Cloud City. They reached an intersection when twelve of Lando's guards, and his aide, arrived to block their path.

"Code Force Seven," Lando commanded as he stopped in front of his aide.

At that moment the twelve guards aimed their laser weapons at the startled stormtroopers, and Lando's aide calmly took the six troopers' weapons from them. He handed one of the guns to Leia and one to Lando, then waited for the next order.

"Hold them in the security tower," the Cloud City administrator said. "Quietly! No one must know."

The guards and Lando's aide, carrying the extra weapons, marched the stormtroopers away to the tower.

Leia had watched this rapid turn of events in confusion. But her confusion turned to astonishment when Lando, the man who had betrayed Han Solo, began removing Chewbacca's bonds.

"Come on," he urged. "We're getting out of here."

The Wookiee's giant hands were freed at last. Not caring to wait for explanations, Chewbacca turned toward the man who had freed him, and with a blood-curdling roar, lunged at Lando and began to throttle him.

"After what you did to Han," Leia said, "I wouldn't trust you to—"

Lando, desperately trying to free himself from Chewbacca's ferocious grip, tried to explain. "I had no choice," he began—but the Wookiee interrupted him with an angry bark.

"There's still a chance to save Han," Lando gasped. "They're at the East Platform."

"Chewie," Leia said at last, "let go!"

Still fuming, Chewbacca released Lando and glared at him as Calrissian fought to regain his breath.

"Keep your eyes on him, Chewie," Leia cautioned as the Wookiee growled threateningly.

"I have a feeling," Lando muttered under his breath, "that I'm making another big mistake."

The stout little R2 unit meandered up and down the corridor, sending his scanners in every possible direction as he tried to detect some sign of his master—or of *any* kind of life. He realized he was dreadfully turned around and had lost track of how many meters he had traveled.

As Artoo Detoo turned a corner he spotted a number of forms moving up the corridor. Beeping and whistling droid greetings, he hoped that these were friendly sorts.

His tooting was detected by one of the creatures, who began to call out to him.

"Artoo . . . Artoo . . ." It was Threepio!

Chewbacca, still carrying the semiassembled See Threepio, quickly turned around to see the stubby R2 droid rolling their way. But as the Wookiee turned, Threepio was spun out of sight of his friend.

"Wait!" the aggravated Threepio demanded. "Turn around, you woolly . . . Artoo, hurry! We're trying to save Han from the bounty hunter."

Artoo scooted forward, beeping all the way, and Threepio patiently replied to his frantic questions.

"I know. But Master Luke can take care of himself." At least that was what See Threepio kept telling himself as the group continued its search for Han.

On the East Landing Platform of Cloud City, two guards shoved the frozen body of Han Solo through a side hatchway of the *Slave I*. Boba Fett climbed up a ladder next to the opening and boarded his ship, ordering it sealed as soon as he entered the cockpit.

Fett ignited his ship's engines and the craft began rolling across the platform for takeoff.

Lando, Leia, and Chewbacca raced onto the platform in time only to see the *Slave I* lifting off and soaring into the orange and purple of the Cloud City sunset. Raising his blaster, Chewbacca howled and fired the weapon at the departing spaceship.

"It's no use," Lando told him. "They're out of range."

All but Threepio gazed at the departing craft. Still strapped to Chewbacca's back, he saw something that the others had not yet noticed.

"Oh, my, no!" he exclaimed.

Charging the group was a squad of Imperial stormtroopers, blasts already issuing from their drawn blasters. The first bolt narrowly missed Princess Leia. Lando responded quickly in returning the enemy fire, and the air was ablaze with a brilliant criss-cross of red and green laser bolts.

Artoo scooted over to the platform's elevator and hid inside, peeking out to see the fury of the battle from a safe distance.

Lando shouted above the sounds of the blasters. "Come on, let's move!" he called, breaking for the open elevator and blasting at the stormtroopers as he ran.

But Leia and Chewbacca did not move. They stood their ground and kept up a steady fire against the assault of the stormtroopers. Troopers groaned and dropped as their chests, arms, and stomachs erupted under the fatally accurate aim of this one female human and one male Wookiee.

Lando, sticking his head out of the elevator, tried to get their attention, motioning them to run. But the two seemed possessed as they blasted away, getting retaliation for all of their anger and captivity and the loss of one they both loved. They were determined to extinguish the lives of these minions of the Galactic Empire.

Threepio would gladly have been *anywhere* else. Unable to get away, all he could do was frantically yell for help. "Artoo, help me!" he screamed. "How did I get into this? What a fate worse than death it is to be strapped to the back of a Wookiee!"

"Get in here!" Lando shouted again. "Hurry up! Hurry up!"

Leia and Chewbacca began to move toward him, evading the erupting rain of laser fire as they rushed inside the waiting elevator. As the elevator doors closed, they glimpsed the remaining troopers racing at them.

Lightsabers clashed in Luke Skywalker and Darth Vader's battle on the platform above the carbon-freezing chamber.

Luke felt the shaking platform shudder with every blow and parry and thrust of their weapons. But he was undaunted, for with every thrust of his sword he drove the evil Darth Vader back.

Vader, using his lightsaber to ward off Luke's aggressive lunges, spoke calmly as they fought. "The fear does not reach you. You have learned more than I anticipated."

"You'll find I'm full of surprises," the confident youth retorted, threatening Vader with yet another thrust.

"And I, too," was the calm, portentous reply.

With two graceful moves, the Dark Lord hooked Luke's weapon out of his hands and sent it flying away. A slash of Vader's energy blade at Luke's feet made the youth jump back in an effort to protect himself. But he stumbled backward, and tumbled down the stairs.

Sprawled on the platform, Luke gazed up and saw the ominous dark figure looming above him at the top of the stairs. Then the figure flew right at him, its sable cloak billowing out in the air like the wings of a monstrous bat.

Quickly Luke rolled to one side, not taking his eyes off Vader, as the vast black figure landed soundlessly next to him.

"Your future lies with me, Skywalker," Vader hissed, looming over the crouching youth. "Now you will embrace the dark side. Obi-Wan knew this to be true."

"No!" Luke yelled, trying to fight off the evil presence.

"There is much Obi-Wan did not tell you," Vader continued. "Come, I will complete your training."

Vader's influence was incredibly strong; it seemed to Luke like a thing alive.

Don't listen to him, Luke told himself. *He is trying to trick me, to lead me astray, to lead me to the dark side of the Force, just like Ben warned me!*

Luke began to back away from the advancing Sith Lord. Behind the youth, the hydraulic elevator cover silently opened, ready to receive him.

"I'll die first," Luke proclaimed.

"That won't be necessary." The Dark Lord suddenly lunged at Luke with his lightsaber, so forcefully that the youth lost his balance and tumbled into the gaping opening.

Vader turned away from the freezing-pit and casually deactivated his lightsaber. "All too easy," he shrugged. "Perhaps you are not as strong as the Emperor thought."

As he spoke, molten metal began to pour into the opening behind him. And, while his back was still turned, something rose in a blur upward.

"Time will tell," Luke quietly replied to Vader's remark.

The Dark Lord spun around. At this point in the freezing process, the subject certainly shouldn't be able to speak! Vader glanced around the room and then turned his helmeted head up toward the ceiling.

Hanging from some hoses draped across the ceiling, Luke was suspended, having leaped some five meters into the air to escape the carbonite.

"Impressive," Vader admitted. "your agility is impressive."

Luke dropped back to the platform on the other side of the steaming pit. He reached his hand out and his sword, lying on another part of the platform, flew back into his grip. Immediately the lightsaber ignited.

Vader's sword sprang to life at the very same moment. "Ben has taught you well. You have controlled your fear. Now release your anger. I destroyed your family. Take your revenge."

But this time Luke was cautious and more controlled. If he could subdue his anger, as he had finally controlled his fear, he would not be swayed.

Remember the training, Luke cautioned himself. *Remember what Yoda taught! Cast out all hatred and anger and receive the Force!*

Gaining control over his negative feelings, Luke began to advance, ignoring Vader's goading. He lunged at Vader and, after a quick exchange, began to force him back.

"Your hatred can give you the power to destroy me," Vader tempted. "Use it."

Luke began to realize just how awesomely powerful his dark enemy was, and softly told himself, "I will not become a slave to the dark side of the Force," and moved cautiously toward Vader.

As Luke approached, Vader slowly moved backward in retreat. Luke lunged at him with a powerful swing. But when Vader blocked it, he lost his balance and fell into the outer rim of steaming pipes.

Luke's knees nearly buckled with the exhaustion of battling his fearsome opponent. He gathered his strength and cautiously moved to the edge and looked down. But he saw no sign of Vader. Switching off his lightsaber and hooking it into his belt, Luke lowered himself into the pit.

He dropped to the floor of the pit and found himself in a large control and maintenance room that overlooked the reactor powering the entire city. Looking around the chamber, he noticed a large window; standing silhouetted in front of it was the unmoving figure of Darth Vader.

Luke slowly moved closer to the window and reignited his lightsaber.

But Vader did not light his own sword, nor did he make any effort to defend himself as Luke drew nearer. The Dark Lord's only weapon, in fact, was his tempting voice. "Attack," he goaded the young Jedi. "Destroy me."

Confused by Vader's ploy, Luke hesitated.

"Only by taking your revenge can you save yourself . . ."

Luke stood locked in place. Should he act on Vader's words and thus use the Force as a tool of revenge? Or should he step away from this battle now, hoping for another chance to fight Vader when he had gained better control?

No, how could he delay the opportunity to destroy this evil being? Here was his chance, now, and he must not delay . . .

There might never again be such an opportunity!

Luke grasped his deadly lightsaber in both hands, tightly gripping the smooth handle like an ancient broadsword and raising the weapon to deliver the blow that would slay this masked horror.

But before he could swing, a large piece of machinery detached itself from the wall behind him and came hurtling at his back. Turning instantly, Luke flashed his lightsaber and cut the thing in half, and the two massive pieces crashed to the floor.

A second piece of machinery sped toward the youth, and he again used the Force to deflect it. The weighty object bounced away as if it had struck an unseen shield. Then a large pipe came tumbling toward him through the air. But even as Luke repelled that enormous object, tools and pieces of machinery came flying at him from all directions. Then wires, that pulled themselves out of the walls, came twisting and sparking and whipping at him.

Bombarded on all sides, Luke did what he could to deflect the assault; but he was beginning to get bloodied and bruised in the attempt.

Another large piece of machinery glanced off Luke's body and crashed out the large window, letting in the screaming wind. Suddenly everything in the room was blown about, and the fierce wind lashed Luke's body and filled the room with a bansheelike howl.

And in the very center of the room, standing still and triumphant, was Darth Vader.

"You are beaten," the Dark Lord of the Sith gloated. "It is useless to resist. You will join me or you will join Obi-Wan in death!"

As Vader spoke those words, a final piece of heavy machinery soared through the air, striking the young Jedi and knocking him through the broken window. Everything became a great blur as the wind carried him, tossing and rolling, until he managed to grab hold of a beam with one hand.

When the wind subsided a bit and his vision cleared, Luke realized that he was hanging from the gantry of the reactor shaft outside the control room. When he gazed down he saw what appeared to be an endless abyss. A wave of dizziness swept over him and he squeezed his eyes closed in an effort to keep from panicking.

Compared to the podlike reactor from which he hung, Luke was no more than a speck of squirming matter, while the pod itself—just one of many jutting from the circular, light-dotted inner wall—was no more than a speck itself in comparison with the rest of the immense chamber.

Grasping the beam firmly with only one hand, Luke managed to hook his lightsaber on to his belt and then grab the beam with both hands. Hoisting himself up, he scrambled onto the gantry

and stood on it, just in time to see Darth Vader walking toward
him down the shaft.

As Vader approached Luke, the public address system began
to blare, echoing through the cavernous rooms: "Fugitives
heading toward Platform 327. Secure all transports. All security
forces on alert."

Walking menacingly toward Luke, Vader predicted, "Your
friends will never escape and neither will you."

Vader took another step, and Luke immediately raised his
sword, ready to renew the battle.

"You are beaten," Vader stated with horrifying certainty and
finality. "It is useless to resist."

But Luke did resist. He lunged at the Dark Lord with a vicious
blow, bringing his sizzling laser blade to crash onto Vader's
armor and sear through to the flesh. Vader staggered from the
blow, and it seemed to Luke that he was in pain. But only for a
moment. Then, once again, Vader began to move toward him.

Taking another step, the Dark Lord warned, "Don't let yourself be destroyed as Obi-Wan was."

Luke was breathing hard, cold sweat dropping from his forehead. But the sound of Ben's name instilled a sudden resolve in
him.

"Calm—" he reminded himself. "Be calm."

But the grimly cloaked specter stalked toward him along the
narrow gantry, and it seemed he wanted the young Jedi's life.

Or worse, his fragile soul.

Lando, Leia, Chewbacca, and the droids hurried down a corridor. They turned a corner and saw the door to the landing
platform standing open. Through it they glimpsed the *Millennium Falcon* waiting for their escape. But suddenly the door
slammed shut. Ducking into an alcove, the group saw a squad
of stormtroopers charging them, their laser guns blasting as they
ran. Chunks of wall and floor shattered and flew into the air
with the impact of the ricocheting energy beams.

Chewbacca growled, returning the stormtroopers' fire with
savage Wookiee rage. He covered Leia, who punched desperately at the door's control panel. But the door failed to budge.

"Artoo!" Threepio called. "The control panel. You can override the alert system.'

Threepio gestured at the panel, urging the little robot to hurry,
and pointing out a computer socket on the control board.

Artoo Detoo scooted toward the control panel, beeping and whistling as he scurried to help.

Twisting his body to avoid the burning laser bolts, Lando feverishly worked to connect his com-link to the panel's intercom.

"This is Calrissian," he broadcast over the system. "The Empire is taking control of the city. I advise you to leave before more Imperial troops arrive."

He switched off the communicator. Lando knew that he had done what he could to warn his people; his job now was to get his friends safely off the planet.

Meanwhile, Artoo removed a connector cover and inserted an extended computer arm into the waiting socket. The droid issued a short beep that suddenly turned into a wild robot scream. He began to quiver, his circuits lighting up in a mad display of flashing brilliance, and every orifice in his hull spewing smoke. Lando quickly pulled Artoo away from the power socket. As the droid began to cool off, he directed a few wilted beeps Threepio's way.

"Well, next time *you* pay more attention," Threepio replied defensively. "I'm not supposed to know power sockets from computer feeds. I'm an interpreter—"

"Anybody else got any ideas?" Leia shouted as she stood firing at the attacking stormtroopers.

"Come on," Lando answered over the din of the battle, "we'll try another way."

The wind that shrieked though the reactor shaft entirely absorbed the sounds of the clashing lightsabers.

Luke moved agilely across the gantry and took refuge beneath a huge instrument panel to evade his pursuing foe. But Vader was there in an instant, his lightsaber thrashing down like a pulsating guillotine blade, cutting the instrument complex loose. The complex began to fall, but was abruptly caught by the wind and blown upward.

An instant of distraction was all Vader needed. As the instrument panel floated away, Luke involuntarily glanced at it. At that second, the Dark Lord's laser blade came slashing down across Luke's hand, cutting it, and sending the youth's lightsaber flying.

The pain was excruciating. Luke smelled the terrible odor of his own seared flesh and squeezed his forearm beneath his armpit to try to stop the agony. He stepped backward along the gantry until he reached its extreme end, stalked all the while by the black-garbed apparition.

Abruptly, ominously, the wind subsided. And Luke realized he had nowhere else to go.

"There is no escape," the Dark Lord of the Sith warned, looming over Luke like a black angel of death. "Don't make me destroy you. You are strong with the Force. Now you must learn to use the dark side. Join me and together we will be more powerful than the Emperor. Come, I will complete your training and we will rule the galaxy together."

Luke refused to give in to Vader's taunts. "I will never join you!"

"If you only knew the power of the dark side," Vader continued. "Obi-Wan never told you what happened to your father, did he?"

Mention of his father aroused Luke's anger. "He told me enough!" he yelled. "He told me you killed him."

"No," Vader replied calmly. "I am your father."

Stunned, Luke stared with disbelief at the black-clad warrior and then pulled away at this revelation. The two warriors stood staring at one another, father and son.

"No, no! That's not true . . ." Luke said, refusing to believe what he had just heard. "That's impossible."

"Search your feelings," Vader said, sounding like an evil version of Yoda, "you know it to be true."

Then Vader turned off the blade of his lightsaber and extended a steady and inviting hand.

Bewildered and horror-stricken at Vader's words, Luke shouted, "No! No!"

Vader continued persuasively. "Luke, you can destroy the Emperor. He has foreseen this. It is your destiny. Join me and together we can rule the galaxy as father and son. Come with me. It is the only way."

Luke's mind whirled with those words. Everything was finally beginning to coalesce in his brain. Or was it? He wondered if Vader were telling him the truth—if the training of Yoda, the teaching of saintly old Ben, his own strivings for good and his abhorrence of evil, if everything he had fought for were no more than a lie.

He didn't want to believe Vader, tried convincing himself that it was Vader who lied to him—but somehow he could *feel* the truth in the Dark Lord's words. But, if Darth Vader did speak the truth, why, he wondered, had Ben Kenobi lied to him? *Why?*

His mind screamed louder than any wind the Dark Lord could ever summon against him.

The answers no longer seemed to matter.

His Father.

With the calmness that Ben himself and Yoda, the Jedi Master, had taught him, Luke Skywalker made, perhaps, what might be his final decision of all. "Never," Luke shouted as he stepped out into the empty abyss beneath him. For all its unperceived depth, Luke might have been falling to another galaxy.

Darth Vader moved to the end of the gantry to watch as Luke tumbled away. A strong wind began to blow, billowing Vader's black cloak out behind him as he stood looking over the edge.

Skywalker's body quickly plunged downward. Toppling head over foot, the wounded Jedi desperately reached out to grab at something to stop his fall.

The Dark Lord watched until he saw the youth's body sucked into a large exhaust pipe in the side of the reactor shaft. When Luke vanished, Vader quickly turned and hurried off the platform.

Luke sped through the exhaust shaft trying to grab the sides to slow his fall. But the smooth, shiny sides of the pipe had no hand-holes or ridges for Luke to grasp.

At last he came to the end of the tunnellike pipe, his feet striking hard against a circular grill. The grill, which opened over an apparently bottomless drop, was knocked out by the impact of Luke's momentum, and he felt his body start to slide out through the opening. Frantically clawing at the smooth interior of the pipe, Luke began to call out for assistance.

"Ben . . . Ben, help me," he pleaded desperately.

Even at he called out, he felt his fingers slip along the inside of the pipe, while his body inched ever closer to the yawning opening.

Cloud City was in chaos.

As soon as Lando Calrissian's broadcast was heard throughout the city, its residents began to panic. Some of them packed a few belongings, others just rushed out into the streets seeking escape. Soon the streets were filled with running humans and aliens, rushing chaotically through the city. Imperial stormtroopers charged after the fleeing inhabitants, exchanging laser fire with them in a raging, clamorous battle.

In one of the city's central corridors, Lando, Leia, and Chewbacca held off a squad of stormtroopers by blasting heavy rounds of laser bolts at the Imperial warriors. It was urgent that Lando and the others hold their ground, for they had come upon another entrance that would lead them to the landing platform. If only Artoo succeeded in opening the door.

Artoo was trying to remove the plate from this door's control panel. But because of the noise and distraction of the laser fire blasting around him, it was difficult for the little droid to concentrate on his work. He beeped to himself as he worked, sounding a bit befuddled to Threepio.

"What are you talking about?" Threepio called to him. "We're not interested in the hyperdrive on the *Millennium Falcon*. It's fixed. Just tell the computer to open the door."

Then, as Lando, Leia, and the Wookiee edged toward the door, dodging heavy Imperial laser fire, Artoo beeped triumphantly and the door snapped open.

"Artoo, you did it!" Threepio exclaimed. The droid would have applauded had his other arm been attached. "I never doubted you for a second."

"Hurry," Lando shouted, "or we'll never make it."

The helpful R2 unit came through once again. As the others dashed through the entrance, the stout robot sprayed out a thick fog—as dense as the clouds surrounding this world—that obscured his friends from the encroaching stormtroopers. Before the cloud had cleared, Lando and the others were racing toward Platform 327.

The stormtroopers followed, blasting at the small band of fugitives bolting toward the *Millennium Falcon*. Chewbacca and the robots boarded the freighter while Lando and Leia covered them with their blasters, cutting down still more of the Emperor's warriors.

When the low-pitched roar of the *Falcon*'s engines started and then rose to an ear-battering whine, Lando and Leia discharged a few more bolts of brilliant energy. Then they sprinted up the ramp. They entered the pirate ship and the main hatchway closed behind them. And as the ship began to move, they heard a barrage of Imperial laser fire that sounded as if the entire planet were splitting apart at its foundations.

Luke could no longer slow his inexorable slide out the exhaust pipe.

He slid the final few centimeters and then dropped through

the cloudy atmosphere, his body spinning and his arms flailing to grip on to something solid.

After what seemed like forever, he caught hold of an electronic weather vane that jutted out from the bowllike underside of Cloud City. Winds buffeted him and clouds swirled around him as he held on tightly to the weather vane. But his strength was beginning to fail; he didn't think he could hang like this— suspended above the gaseous surface—for very much longer.

All was very quiet in the *Millennium Falcon* cockpit.

Leia, just catching her breath from their close escape, sat in Han Solo's chair. Thoughts of him rushed to her mind, but she tried not to worry about him, tried not to miss him.

Behind the princess, looking over her shoulder out the front windscreen, stood a silent and exhausted Lando Calrissian.

Slowly the ship began to move, picking up speed as it coursed along the landing platform.

The giant Wookiee, in his old copilot's chair, threw a series of switches that brought a dancing array of lights across the ship's main control panel. Pulling the throttle, Chewbacca began to guide the ship upward, to freedom.

Clouds rushed by the cockpit windows and everyone finally breathed with relief as the *Millennium Falcon* soared into a red-orange twilight sky.

Luke managed to hook one of his legs over the electronic weather vane, which continued to support his weight. But air from the exhaust pipe rushed at him, making it difficult for him to keep from slipping off the vane.

"Ben . . ." he moaned in agony. ". . . Ben."

Darth Vader strode onto the empty landing platform and watched the speck that was the *Millennium Falcon* disappear in the far distance.

He turned to his two aides. "Bring my ship in!" he commanded. And then he left, black robes flowing behind him, to prepare for his journey.

Somewhere near the supporting stalk of Cloud City, Luke spoke again. Concentrating his mind on one whom he thought cared for him and might somehow come to his aid, he called, "Leia, hear me." Pitifully he cried out once again. "Leia."

Just then, a large piece of the weather vane broke off and went hurtling off into the clouds far below. Luke tightened his grip on what remained of the vane, and strained to hold on in the blast of air rushing at him from the pipe above.

"It looks like three fighters," Lando said to Chewbacca as they watched the computer-screen configurations. "We can outdistance them easily," he added, knowing the capabilities of the freighter as well as Han Solo did.

Looking at Leia, he mourned the passing of his administratorship. "I knew that setup was too good to last," he moaned. "I'm going to miss it."

But Leia seemed to be in a daze. She didn't acknowledge Lando's comments, but stared straight ahead of her as if transfixed. Then, out of her dreamlike trance, she spoke. "Luke," she said, as if responding to something she heard.

"What?" Lando asked.

"We've got to go back," she said urgently. "Chewie, head for the bottom of the city."

Lando looked at her in astonishment. "Wait a minute. We're not going back there!"

The Wookiee barked, for once in agreement with Lando.

"No argument," Leia said firmly, assuming the dignity of one accustomed to having her orders obeyed. "Just do it. That's a command!"

"What about those fighters?' Lando argued as he pointed to the three TIE fighters closing in on them. He looked to Chewbacca for support.

But, growling menacingly, Chewbacca conveyed that he knew who was in command now.

"Okay, okay," Lando quietly acquiesced.

With all the grace and speed for which the *Millennium Falcon* was famed, the ship banked through the clouds and turned back toward the city. And, as the freighter continued on what could become a suicide run, the three pursuing TIE fighters matched its turn.

Luke Skywalker was unaware of the *Millennium Falcon*'s approach. Barely conscious, he somehow maintained his hold on the creaking and swaying weather vane. The device bent under the weight of his body, then completely broke off from its foundation, and sent Luke tumbling helplessly through the sky. And this time, he knew, there would be nothing for him to cling to as he fell.

"Look!" Lando exclaimed, indicating a figure plunging in the distance. "Someone's falling . . ."

Leia managed to remain calm; she knew that panic now would doom them all. "Get under him, Chewie," she told the pilot. "It's Luke."

Chewbacca immediately responded and carefully eased the *Millennium Falcon* on a descent trajectory.

"Lando," Leia called, turning to him, "open the top hatch."

As he rushed out of the cockpit, Lando thought it a strategy worthy of Solo himself.

Chewbacca and Leia could see Luke's plunging body more clearly, and the Wookiee guided the ship toward him. As Chewie retarded the ship's speed drastically, the plummeting form skimmed the windscreen and then landed with a *thud* against the outer hull.

Lando opened the upper hatch. In the distance he glimpsed the three TIE fighters approaching the *Falcon,* their laser guns brightening the twilight sky with streaks of hot destruction. Lando stretched his body out of the hatch and reached to grasp the battered warrior and pull him inside the ship. Just then the *Falcon* lurched as a bolt exploded near it, and almost threw Luke's body overboard. But Lando caught his hand and held on tightly.

The *Millennium Falcon* veered away from Cloud City and soared through the thick billowing cloud cover. Swerving to avoid the blinding flak from the TIE fighters, Princess Leia and the Wookiee pilot struggled to keep their ship skyborne. But explosions burst all around the cockpit, the din competing with Chewbacca's howl as he frantically worked the controls.

Leia switched on the intercom. "Lando, is he all right?" she shouted over the noise in the cockpit. "Lando, do you hear me?"

From the rear of the cockpit, she heard a voice that wasn't Lando's. "He'll survive," Luke replied faintly.

Leia and Chewbacca turned to see Luke, battered and bloodied and wrapped in a blanket, being helped into the cockpit by Lando. The princess jumped up from her chair and hugged him ecstatically. Chewbacca, still trying to guide the ship out of the TIE fighters' range of fire, threw back his head and barked in jubilation.

Behind the *Millennium Falcon,* the planet of clouds was receding farther in the distance. But the TIE fighters kept up their close pursuit, firing their laser weapons and rocking the pirate craft with each on-target hit.

Working diligently in the *Falcon*'s hold, Artoo Detoo struggled against the constant lunging and tossing to reassemble his golden friend. Meticulously trying to undo the mistakes of the well-intentioned Wookiee, the little droid beeped as he performed the intricate task.

"Very good," the protocol droid praised. His head was on properly and his second arm was nearly completely reattached. "Good as new."

Artoo beeped apprehensively.

"No, Artoo, don't worry. I'm sure we'll make it this time."

But in the cockpit, Lando was not so optimistic. He saw the warning lights on the control panel begin to flash; suddenly alarms all over the ship went on. "The deflector shields are going," he reported to Leia and Chewbacca.

Leia looked over Lando's shoulder and noticed another blip, ominously large, that had appeared on the radarscope. "There's another ship," she said, "much bigger, trying to cut us off."

Luke quietly gazed out the cockpit window toward the starry void. Almost to himself, he said, "It's Vader."

Admiral Piett approached Vader, who stood on the bridge of this, the greatest of all Imperial Star Destroyers, and stared out the windows.

"They'll be in range of the tractor beam in moments," the admiral reported confidently.

"And their hyperdrive has been deactivated?" Vader asked.

"Right after they were captured, sir."

"Good," the giant black-robed figure said. "Prepare for the boarding and set your weapons for stun."

The *Millennium Falcon* so far had managed to evade its TIE fighter pursuers. But could it escape attack from the ominous Star Destroyer that pressed toward it, ever closer?

"We don't have any room for mistakes," Leia said tensely, watching the large blip on the monitors.

"If my men said they fixed this baby, they fixed it," Lando assured her. "We've got nothing to worry about."

"Sounds familiar," Leia mused to herself.

The ship was rocked again by the concussion of another laser explosion, but at that moment a green light began flashing on the control panel.

"The coordinates are set, Chewie," Leia said. "It's now or never."

The Wookiee barked in agreement. He was ready for the hyperdrive escape.

"Punch it!" Lando yelled.

Chewbacca shrugged as if to say it was worth a try. He pulled back on the light-speed throttle, suddenly altering the sound of the ion engines. All on board were praying in human and droid fashion that the system would work; they had no other hope of escape. But abruptly the sound choked and died and Chewbacca roared a howl of desperate frustration.

Again the hyperdrive system had failed them.

And still the *Millennium Falcon* lurched with the TIE fighters' fire.

From his Imperial Star Destroyer, Darth Vader watched in fascination as the TIE fighters relentlessly fired at the *Millennium Falcon*. Vader's ship was closing in on the fleeing *Falcon*—it would not be long before the Dark Lord had Skywalker completely in his power.

And Luke sensed it, too. Quietly he gazed out, knowing that Vader was near, that his victory over the weakened Jedi would soon be complete. His body was battered, was exhausted; his spirit was prepared to succumb to his fate. There was no reason to fight any more—there was nothing left to believe in.

"Ben," he whispered in utter despair, "why didn't you tell me?"

Lando tried to adjust some controls, and Chewbacca leaped from his chair to race to the hold. Leia took Chewbacca's seat and helped Lando as they flew the *Falcon* through the exploding flak.

As the Wookiee ran into the hold, he passed Artoo, who was still working on Threepio. The R2 unit began to beep in great consternation as he scanned the Wookiee frantically trying to fix the hyperdrive system.

"I said we're doomed!" the panicked Threepio told Artoo. "The light-speed engines are malfunctioning again."

Artoo beeped as he connected a leg.

"How could you know what's wrong?" the golden droid scoffed. "Ouch! Mind my foot! And stop chattering on so."

Lando's voice sounded in the hold through the intercom. "Chewie, check the secondary deviation controls."

Chewbacca dropped into the hold's pit. He fought to loosen a section of the paneling with an enormous wrench. But it failed to budge. Roaring in frustration, he gripped the tool like a club and bashed the panel with all his strength.

Suddenly the cockpit control panel sprayed Lando and the princess with a shower of sparks. They jumped back in their seats in surprise, but Luke didn't seem to notice anything happening around him. His head hung in discouragement and deep pain.

"I won't be able to resist him," he muttered softly.

Again Lando banked the *Millennium Falcon*, trying to shed the pursuers. But the distance between freighter and TIE fighters was narrowing by the moment.

In the *Millennium Falcon*'s hold, Artoo raced to a control panel, leaving an outraged Threepio to stand sputtering in place on his one attached leg. Artoo worked swiftly, relying only on mechanical instinct to reprogram the circuit board. Lights flashed brightly with each of Artoo's adjustments, when suddenly, from deep within the *Falcon*'s hyperspeed engines, a new and powerful hum resonated throughout the ship.

The freighter tilted suddenly, sending the whistling R2 droid rolling across the floor into the pit to land on the startled Chewbacca.

Lando, who had been standing near the control panel, tumbled back against the cockpit wall. But as he fell back, he saw the stars outside become blinding, infinite streaks of light.

"We did it!" Lando yelled triumphantly.

The *Millennium Falcon* had shot victoriously into hyperdrive.

Darth Vader stood silently. He gazed at the black void where, a moment before, the *Millennium Falcon* had been. His deep, black silence brought terror to the two men standing near him. Admiral Piett and his captain waited, chills of fear coursing through their bodies, and wondered how soon they would feel the invisible, viselike talons around their throats.

But the Dark Lord did not move. He stood silently contemplative, with his hands behind his back. Then he turned and slowly walked off the bridge, his ebony cloak billowing behind him.

XIV

THE *Millennium Falcon* was at last safely docked on a huge Rebel cruiser. Gleaming in the distance was a glorious red glow that radiated from a large red star—a glow that shed its crimson light on the battered hull of the small freighter craft.

Luke Skywalker rested in the medical center of the Rebel Star Cruiser, where he was attended by the surgeon droid called Too-Onebee. The youth sat quietly, thoughtfully, while Too-Onebee gently began to look at his wounded hand.

Gazing up, Luke saw Leia, followed by See Threepio and Artoo Detoo, entering the medical center to check his progress, and, perhaps, bring him a little cheer. But Luke knew that the best therapy he had received yet aboard this cruiser was in the radiant image before him.

Princess Leia was smiling. Her eyes were wide and sparkling with a wondrous glow. She looked just as she had that first time he saw her—a lifetime ago, it seemed—when Artoo Detoo first projected her holographic image. And, in her floor length, high-necked gown of purest white, she looked angelic.

Raising his hand, Luke offered it to the expert service of Too-Onebee. The surgeon droid examined the bionic hand that was skillfully fused to Luke's arm. Then the robot wrapped a soft metalized strip about the hand and attached a small electronic unit to the strip, tightening it slightly. Luke made a fist with his new hand and felt the healing pulsations imparted by Too-Onebee's apparatus. Then he let his hand and arm relax.

Leia and the two droids moved closer to Luke as a voice came over an intercom loudspeaker. It was Lando: "Luke . . ," the voice blared, "we're ready for takeoff."

Lando Calrissian sat in the *Millennium Falcon*'s pilot's chair. He had missed his old freighter, but now that he was once again its captain, he felt quite uncomfortable. In his copilot's chair, the great Wookiee Chewbacca noticed his new captain's discomfort while he began to throw the switches to ready the ship for takeoff.

Luke's voice came over Lando's comlink speaker: "I'll meet you on Tatooine."

Again Lando spoke into his comlink microphone, but this time he spoke to Leia: "Don't worry, Leia," he said with emotion, "we'll find Han."

And leaning over, Chewbacca barked his farewell into the microphone—a bark that may have transcended the limits of time and space to be heard by Han Solo, wherever the bounty hunter had taken him.

It was Luke who spoke the final farewell, though he refused to say good-bye. "Take care, my friends," he said with a new maturity in his voice. "May The Force Be With You."

Leia stood alone at the great circular window of the Rebel Star Cruiser, her slim white-draped form dwarfed by the vast canopy of stars and the drifting ships of the fleet. She watched the majestic scarlet star that burned in the infinite black sea.

Luke, with Threepio and Artoo tagging along, moved to stand next to her. He understood what she was feeling for he knew how terrible such a loss could be.

Standing together, the group faced the inviting heavens and saw the *Millennium Falcon* moving into view, then veering off in another direction to soar with great dignity through the Rebel fleet. Soon the *Millennium Falcon* had left the fleet in its wake.

They needed no words in this moment. Luke knew that Leia's mind and heart were with Han, no matter where he was or what his fate might be. As to his own destiny, he was now more uncertain about himself than he had ever been—even before this simple farm boy on a distant world first learned of the intangible something called the Force. He only knew he had to return to Yoda and finish his training before he set off to rescue Han.

Slowly he put his arm around Leia and together with Threepio and Artoo, they faced the heavens bravely, each of them gazing at the same crimson star.

EPISODE VI

STAR WARS:
Return of the Jedi

by James Kahn
Screenplay by
Lawrence Kasdan and George Lucas

Story by George Lucas

A long time ago, in a galaxy far, far away . . .

Prologue

THE very depth of space. There was the length, and width, and height; and then these dimensions curved over on themselves into a bending blackness measurable only by the glinting stars that tumbled through the chasm, receding to infinity. To the very depth.

These stars marked the moments of the universe. There were aging orange embers, blue dwarfs, twin yellow giants. There were collapsing neutron stars, and angry supernovae that hissed into the icy emptiness. There were borning stars, breathing stars, pulsing stars, and dying stars. There was the Death Star.

At the feathered edge of the galaxy, the Death Star floated in stationary orbit above the green moon Endor—a moon whose mother planet had long since died of unknown cataclysm and disappeared into unknown realms. The Death Star was the Empire's armored battle station, nearly twice as big as its predecessor, which Rebel forces had destroyed so many years before—nearly twice as big, but more than twice as powerful. Yet it was only half complete.

Half a steely dark orb, it hung above the green world of Endor, tentacles of unfinished superstructure curling away toward its living companion like the groping legs of a deadly spider.

An Imperial Star Destroyer approached the giant space station at cruising speed. It was massive—a city itself—yet it moved with deliberate grace, like some great sea dragon. It was accompanied by dozens of Twin Ion Engine fighters—black insectlike combat flyers that zipped back and forth around the battleship's perimeter: scouting, sounding, docking, regrouping.

Soundlessly the main bay of the ship opened. There was a brief ignition-flash, as an Imperial shuttle emerged from the darkness of the hold, into the darkness of space. It sped toward the half-completed Death Star with quiet purpose.

In the cockpit the shuttle captain and his copilot made final readings, monitored descent functions. It was a sequence they'd each performed a thousand times, yet there was an unusual tension in the air now. The captain flipped the transmitter switch, and spoke into his mouthpiece.

"Command Station, this is ST321. Code Clearance Blue. We're starting our approach. Deactivate the security shield."

Static filtered over the receiver; then the voice of the port controller: "The security deflector shield will be deactivated when we have confirmation of your code transmission. Stand by . . ."

Once more silence filled the cockpit. The shuttle captain bit the inside of his cheek, smiled nervously at his copilot, and muttered, "Quick as you can, please—this better not take long. He's in no mood to wait . . ."

They refrained from glancing back into the passenger section of the shuttle, now under lights-out for landing. The unmistakable sound of the mechanical breathing coming from the chamber's shadow filled the cabin with a terrible impatience.

In the control room of the Death Star below, operators moved along the bank of panels, monitoring all the space traffic in the area, authorizing flight patterns, accessing certain areas to certain vehicles. The shield operator suddenly checked his monitor with alarm; the view-screen depicted the battle station itself, the moon Endor, and a web of energy—the deflector shield— emanating from the green moon, encompassing the Death Star. Only now, the security web was beginning to separate, to retract and form a clear channel—a channel through which the dot that was the Imperial shuttle sailed, unimpeded, toward the massive space station.

The shield operator quickly called his control officer over to the view-screen, uncertain how to proceed.

"What is it?" the officer demanded.

"That shuttle has a class-one priority ranking." He tried to replace the fear in his voice with disbelief.

The officer glanced at the view-screen for only a moment before realizing who was on the shuttle and spoke to himself: "Vader!"

He strode past the view port, where the shuttle could be seen already making its final approach, and headed toward the docking bay. He turned to the controller.

"Inform the commander that Lord Vader's shuttle has arrived."

The shuttle sat quietly, dwarfed by the cavernous reaches of the huge docking bay. Hundreds of troops stood assembled in formation, flanking the base of the shuttle ramp—white-armored Imperial stormtroopers, gray-suited officers, and the elite, red-robed Imperial Guard. They snapped to attention as Moff Jerjerrod entered.

Jerjerrod—tall, thin, arrogant—was the Death Star commander. He walked without hurry up the ranks of soldiers, to the ramp of the shuttle. Hurry was not in Jerjerrod, for hurry implied a wanting to be elsewhere, and he was a man who distinctively *was* exactly where he wanted to be. Great men never hurried (he was fond of saying); great men caused *others* to hurry.

Yet Jerjerrod was not blind to ambition; and a visit by such a one as this great Dark Lord could not be taken too lightly. He stood at the shuttle mouth, therefore, waiting—with respect, but not hurry.

Suddenly the exit hatch of the shuttle opened, pulling the troops in formation to even tauter attention. Only darkness glowed from the exit at first; then footsteps; then the characteristic electrical respirations, like the breathing of a machine; and finally Darth Vader, Lord of the Sith, emerged from the void.

Vader strode down the ramp, looking over the assemblage. He stopped when he came to Jerjerrod. The commander bowed from the neck, and smiled.

"Lord Vader, this is an unexpected pleasure. We are honored by your presence."

"We can dispense with the pleasantries, Commander." Vader's words echoed as from the bottom of a well. "The Emperor is concerned with your progress, I am here to put you back on schedule."

Jerjerrod turned pale. This was news he'd not expected. "I assure you, Lord Vader, my men are working as fast as they can."

"Perhaps I can encourage their progress in ways you have not considered," Vader growled. He had ways, of course; this was known. Ways, and ways again.

Jerjerrod kept his tone even, though deep inside, the ghost of hurry began to scrabble at his throat. "That won't be necessary, my Lord. I tell you, without question this station will be operational as planned."

"I'm afraid the Emperor does not share your optimistic appraisal of the situation."

"I fear he asks the impossible," the commander suggested.

"Perhaps you could explain that to him when he arrives." Vader's face remained invisible behind the deathly black mask that protected him; but the malice was clear in the electronically modified voice.

Jerjerrod's pallor intensified. "The Emperor is coming here?"

"Yes, Commander. And he will be quite displeased if you are still behind schedule when he arrives." He spoke loudly, to spread the threat over all who could hear.

"We shall double our efforts, Lord Vader." And he meant it. For sometimes didn't even great men hurry, in time of great need?

Vader lowered his voice again. "I hope so, Commander, for your sake. The Emperor will tolerate no further delay in the final destruction of the outlaw Rebellion. And we have secret news now"—he included Jerjerrod, only, in this intimate detail—"The Rebel fleet has gathered all its forces into a single giant armada. The time is at hand when we can crush them, without mercy, in a single blow."

For the briefest second, Vader's breathing seemed to quicken, then resumed its measured pace, like the rising of a hollow wind.

I

OUTSIDE the small adobe hut, the sandstorm wailed like a beast in agony, refusing to die. Inside, the sounds were muted.

It was cooler in this shelter, more hushed, and darker. While the beast without howled, in this place of nuance and shadow a shrouded figure worked.

Tanned hands, holding arcane tools, extended from the sleeves of a caftanlike robe. The figure crouched on the ground, working. Before him lay a discoid device of strange design, wires trailing from it at one end, symbols etched into its flat surface. He connected the wired end to a tubular, smooth handle, pulled through an organic-looking connector, locked it in place with another tool. He motioned to a shadow in the corner; the shadow moved toward him.

Tentatively, the obscure form rolled closer to the robed figure. "Vrrrr-dit dweet?" the little R2 unit questioned timidly as it approached, pausing when it was just a foot from the shrouded man with the strange device.

The shrouded man motioned the droid nearer still. Artoo Detoo scooted the last distance, blinking; and the hands raised toward his domed little head.

The fine sand blew hard over the dunes of Tatooine. The wind seemed to come from everywhere at once, typhooning in spots, swirling in devil-winds here, hovering in stillness there, without pattern or meaning.

A road wound across the desert plain. Its nature changed constantly, at one moment obscured by drifts of ochre sand, the next moment swept clean, or distorted by the heat of the shimmering air above it. A road more ephemeral than navigable; yet a road to be followed, all the same. For it was the only way to reach the palace of Jabba the Hutt.

Jabba was the vilest gangster in the galaxy. He had his fingers in smuggling, slave-trading, murder; his minions scattered across the stars. He both collected and invented atrocities, and his court was a den of unparalleled decay. It was said by some that Jabba had chosen Tatooine as his place of residence because only in this arid crucible of a planet could he hope to keep his soul from rotting away altogether—here the parched sun might bake his humor to a festering brine.

In any case, it was a place few of kind spirit even knew of, let alone approached. It was a place of evil, where even the most courageous felt their powers wilt under the foul gaze of Jabba's corruption.

"Poot-wEEt beDOO gung ooble DEEp!" vocalized Artoo Detoo.

"Of course I'm worried," See Threepio fussed. "And you should be too. Poor Lando Calrissian never returned from this place. Can you imagine what they've done to him?"

Artoo whistled timidly.

The golden droid waded stiffly through a shifting sand hill, then stopped short, as Jabba's palace suddenly loomed, suddenly dark, in the near distance. Artoo almost bumped into him, quickly skidding to the side of the road.

"Watch where you're going, Artoo." See Threepio resumed walking, but more slowly, his little friend rolling along at his side. And as they went, he chattered on. "Why couldn't Chewbacca have delivered this message? No, whenever there's an impossible mission, they turn to us. No one worries about droids. Sometimes I wonder why we put up with it all."

On and on he rambled, over the desolate final stretch of road, until at last they reached the gates to the palace: massive iron doors, taller than Threepio could see—part of a series of stone and iron walls, forming several gigantic cylindrical towers that seemed to rise out of a mountain of packed sand.

The two droids fearfully looked around the ominous door for signs of life, or welcome, or some sort of signaling device with which to make their presence known. Seeing nothing in any of those categories, See Threepio mustered his resolve (which function had been programmed into him quite a long time earlier), knocked softly three times on the thick metal grate, then quickly turned around and announced to Artoo, "There doesn't seem to be anyone here. Let's go back and tell Master Luke."

Suddenly a small hatch opened in the center of the door. A spindly mechanical arm popped out, affixed to which a large electronic eyeball peered unabashedly at the two droids. The eyeball spoke.

"Tee chuta hhat yudd!"

Threepio stood erect, proud though his circuits quivered a bit. He faced the eye, pointed to Artoo, and then to himself. "Artoo Detoowha bo Seethreepiosha ey toota odd mischka Jabba du Hutt."

The eye looked quickly from one robot to the other, then retracted back through the little window and slammed the hatch shut.

"Boo-dEEp gaNOOng," whispered Artoo with concern.

Threepio nodded. "I don't think they're going to let us in, Artoo. We'd better go." He turned to leave, as Artoo beeped a reluctant four-tone.

At that, a horrific, grinding screech erupted, and the massive iron door slowly began to rise. The two droids looked at each other skeptically, and then into the yawning black cavity that faced them. They waited, afraid to enter, afraid to retreat.

From the shadows, the strange voice of the eye screamed at them: "Nudd chaa!"

Artoo beeped and rolled forward into the gloom. Threepio hesitated, then rushed after his stubby companion with a start. "Artoo wait for me!" They stopped together in the gaping passageway, as Threepio scolded: "You'll get lost."

The great door slammed shut behind them with a monumental crash that echoed through the dark cavern. For a moment the two frightened robots stood there without moving; then, haltingly, they stepped forward.

They were immediately joined by three large Gamorrean guards—powerful piglike brutes whose racial hatred of robots was well known. The guards ushered the two droids down the dark corridor without so much as a nod. When they reached the first half-lit hallway, one of them grunted an order. Artoo beeped a nervous query at Threepio.

"You don't want to know," the golden droid responded apprehensively. "Just deliver Master Luke's message and get us out of here quick."

Before they could take another step, a form approached them from the obscurity of a cross-corridor: Bib Fortuna, the inelegant major-domo of Jabba's degenerate court. He was a tall, humanoid creature with eyes that saw only what was necessary, and a robe that hid all. Protruding from the back of his skull were two fat, tentacular appendages that exhibited prehensile, sensual, and cognitive functions at various times—which he wore either draped over his shoulders for decorative effect or, when the situation called for balance, hanging straight down behind him as if they were twin tails.

He smiled thinly as he stopped before the two robots. "Die wanna wanga."

Threepio spoke up officially "Die wanna wanaga. We bring a message to your master, Jabba the Hutt." Artoo beeped a postscript, upon which Threepio nodded and added: "And a gift." He thought about this a moment, looked as puzzled as it was possible for a droid to look, and whispered loudly to Artoo, "Gift, what gift?"

Bib shook his head emphatically. "Nee Jabba no badda. Me chaade su goodie." He held out his hand toward Artoo.

The small droid backed up meekly, but his protest was lengthy. "bDooo EE NGrwrrr Op dbooDEEop!"

"Artoo, give it to him!" Threepio insisted. Sometimes Artoo could be *so* binary.

At this, though, Artoo became positively defiant, beeping and tooting at Fortuna and Threepio as if they'd *both* had their programs erased.

Threepio nodded finally, hardly happy with Artoo's answer. He smiled apologetically at Bib. "He says our master's instructions are to give it only to Jabba himself." Bib considered the problem a moment, as Threepio went on explaining. "I'm terribly sorry. I'm afraid he's ever so stubborn about these things." He managed to throw a disparaging yet loving tone into his voice, as he tilted his head toward his small associate.

Bib gestured for them to follow. "Nudd chaa." He walked back into the darkness, the droids following close behind, the three Gamorrean guards lumbering along at the rear.

As See Threepio descended into the belly of the shadow, he muttered quietly to the silent R2 unit, "Artoo, I have a bad feeling about this."

See Threepio and Artoo Detoo stood at the entrance of the throne room, looking in. "We're doomed," whimpered Threepio, wishing for the thousandth time that he could close his eyes.

The room was filled, wall to cavernous wall, with the animate dregs of the universe. Grotesque creatures from the lowest star systems, drunk on spiced liquor and their own fetid vapors. Gamorreans, twisted humans, jawas—all reveling in base pleasures, or raucously comparing mean feats. And in the front of the room, reclining on a daïs that overlooked the debauchery, was Jabba the Hutt.

His head was three times human size, perhaps four. His eyes were yellow, reptilian—his skin was like a snake's, as well, except covered with a fine layer of grease. He had no neck, but only a series of chins that expanded finally into a great bloated body, engorged to bursting with stolen morsels. Stunted, almost useless arms sprouted from his upper torso, the sticky fingers of his left hand languidly wrapped around the smoking-end of his water-pipe. He had no hair—it had fallen out from a combination of diseases. He had no legs—his trunk simply tapered gradually to a long, plump snake-tail that stretched along the length of the platform like a tube of yeasty dough. His lipless mouth was wide, almost ear to ear, and he drooled continuously. He was quite thoroughly disgusting.

Chained to him, chained at the neck, was a sad, pretty dancing-girl, a member of Fortuna's species, with two dry, shapely tentacles sprouting from the back of her head, hanging suggestively down her bare, muscled back. Her name was Oola. Looking forlorn, she sat as far away as her chain would allow, at the other end of the daïs.

And sitting near Jabba's belly was a small monkey-like reptile named Salacious Crumb, who caught all the food and ooze that spilled out of Jabba's hands or mouth and ate it with a nauseating cackle.

Shafts of light from above partially illuminated the drunken courtiers as Bib Fortuna crossed the floor to the daïs. The room was composed of an endless series of alcoves within alcoves, so that much of what went on was, in any case, visible only as shadow and movement. When Fortuna reached the throne, he delicately leaned forward and whispered into the slobbering monarch's ear. Jabba's eyes became slits . . . then with a maniacal laugh he motioned for the two terrified droids to be brought in.

"Bo shuda," wheezed the Hutt, and lapsed into a fit of coughing. Although he understood several languages, as a point of honor he only spoke Huttese. His only such point.

The quaking robots scooted forward to stand before the repulsive ruler, though he grossly violated their most deeply programmed sensibilities. "The message, Artoo, the message," Threepio urged.

Artoo whistled once, and a beam of light projected from his domed head, creating a hologram of Luke Skywalker that stood before them on the floor. Quickly the image grew to over ten feet tall, until the young Jedi warrior towered over the assembled throng. All at once the room grew quiet, as Luke's giant presence made itself felt.

"Greetings, Exalted One," the hologram said to Jabba. "Allow me to introduce myself. I am Luke Skywalker, Jedi Knight and friend of Captain Solo. I seek an audience with Your Greatness, to bargain for his life." At this, the entire room burst into laughter which Jabba instantly stopped with a hand motion. Luke didn't pause long. "I know that you are powerful, mighty Jabba, and that your anger with Solo must be equally powerful. But I'm sure we can work out an arrangement which will be mutually beneficial. As a token of my good will, I present to you a gift—these two droids."

Threepio jumped back as if stung. "What! What did he say?"

Luke continued. ". . . Both are hardworking and will serve you well." With that, the hologram disappeared.

Threepio wagged his head in despair. "Oh no, this can't be. Artoo, you must have played the wrong message."

Jabba laughed and drooled.

Bib spoke in Huttese. "Bargain rather than fight? He is no Jedi."

Jabba nodded in agreement. Still grinning, he rasped at Threepio, "There will be no bargain. I have no intention of giving up my favorite decoration." With a hideous chuckle he looked toward the dimly lit alcove beside the throne; there, hanging flat against the wall, was the carbonized form of Han Solo, his face and hands emerging out of the cold hard slab, like a statue reaching from a sea of stone.

Artoo and Threepio marched dismally through the dank passageway at the prodding of a Gamorrean guard. Dungeon cells lined both walls. The unspeakable cries of anguish that emanated from within as the droids passed echoed off the stone and down the endless catacombs. Periodically a hand or claw or tentacle would reach through the bars of a door to grab at the hapless robots.

Artoo beeped pitifully. Threepio only shook his head. "What could have possibly come over Master Luke? Was it something I did? He never expressed any unhappiness with my work . . ."

They approached a door at the end of the corridor. It slid open automatically, and the Gamorrean shoved them forward. Inside, their ears were assaulted by deafening machine sounds—wheels creaking, piston-heads slamming, water-hammers, engine hums—and a continuously shifting haze of steam made visibility short. This was either the boiler room, or programmed hell.

An agonized electronic scream, like the sound of stripping gears, drew their attention to the corner of the room. From out of the mist walked EV-9D9, a thin humanlike robot with some disturbingly human appetites. In the dimness behind Ninedenine, Threepio could see the legs being pulled off a droid on a torture rack, while a second droid, hanging upside down, was having red-hot irons applied to its feet; it had emitted the electronic scream Threepio heard a few moments earlier, as the sensor circuits in its metal skin melted in agony. Threepio cringed at the sound, his own wiring sympathetically crackling with static electricity.

Ninedenine stopped in front of Threepio, raising her pincer hands expansively. "Ah, new acquisitions," she said with great satisfaction. "I am Eve-Ninedenine, Chief of Cyborg Operations. You're a protocol droid, aren't you?"

"I am See Threepio, human-cyborg re—"

"Yes or no will do," Ninedenine said icily.

"Well, yes," Threepio replied. This robot was going to be trouble, that much was obvious—one of those droids who always had to prove she was more-droid-than-thou.

"How many languages do you speak?" Ninedenine continued.

Well, two can play at that game, thought Threepio. He ran his most dignified, official introductory tape. "I am fluent in over six million forms of communication, and can—"

"Splendid!" Ninedenine interrupted gleefully. "We have been without an interpreter since the master got angry with something our last protocol droid said and disintegrated him."

"Disintegrated!" Threepio wailed. Any semblance of protocol left him.

Ninedenine spoke to a pig guard who suddenly appeared. "This one will be quite useful. Fit him with a restraining bolt, then take him back up to the main audience chamber.

The guard grunted and roughly shoved Threepio toward the door.

"Artoo, don't leave me!" Threepio called out, but the guard grabbed him and pulled him away; and he was gone.

Artoo let out a long, plaintive cry as Threepio was removed. Then he turned to Ninedenine and beeped in outrage, and at length.

Ninedenine laughed. "You're a feisty little one, but you'll soon learn some respect. I have need for you on the master's Sail Barge. Several of our astrodroids have been disappearing recently—stolen for spare parts, most likely. I think you'll fill in nicely."

The droid on the torture rack emitted a high-frequency wail, then sparked briefly and was silent.

The court of Jabba the Hutt roiled in malignant ecstasy. Oola, the beautiful creature chained to Jabba, danced in the center of the floor, as the inebriated monsters cheered and heckled. Threepio hovered warily near the back of the throne, trying to keep the lowest profile possible. Periodically he had to duck to avoid a fruit hurled in his direction or to sidestep a rolling body. Mostly, he just laid low. What else was a protocol droid to do, in a place of so little protocol?

Jabba leered through the smoke of his hooka and beckoned the creature Oola to come sit beside him. She stopped dancing instantly, a fearful look in her eye, and backed up, shaking her head. Apparently she had suffered such invitations before.

Jabba became angry. He pointed unmistakably to a spot beside him on the daïs. "Da eitha!" he growled.

Oola shook her head more violently, her face a mask of terror. "Na chuba negatorie. Na! Na! Natoota . . ."

Jabba became livid. Furiously he motioned to Oola. "Boscka!"

Jabba pushed a button as he released Oola's chain. Before she could flee, a grating trap door in the floor dropped open, and she tumbled into the pit below. The door snapped shut instantly. A moment of silence, followed by a low, rumbling roar, followed by a terrified shriek was followed once more by silence.

Jabba laughed until he slobbered. A dozen revelers hurried over to peer through the grate, to observe the demise of the nubile dancer.

Threepio shrank even lower and looked for support to the carbonite form of Han Solo, suspended in bas relief above the floor. Now *there* was a human without a sense of protocol, thought Threepio wistfully.

His reverie was interrupted by an unnatural quiet that suddenly fell over the room. He looked up to see Bib Fortuna making his way through the crowd, accompanied by two Gamorrean guards, and followed by a fierce-looking cloaked-and-helmeted bounty hunter who led his captive prize on a leash: Chewbacca, the Wookiee.

Threepio gasped, stunned. "Oh, no! Chewbacca!" The future was looking very bleak indeed.

Bib muttered a few words into Jabba's ear, pointing to the bounty hunter and his captive. Jabba listened intently. The bounty hunter was humanoid, small and mean: a belt of cartridges was slung across his jerkin and an eye-slit in his helmet-mask gave the impression of his being able to see through things. He bowed low, then spoke in fluent Ubese. "Greetings, Majestic One. I am Boushh." It was a metallic language, well-adapted to the rarefied atmosphere of the home planet from which this nomadic species arose.

Jabba answered in the same tongue, though his Ubese was stilted and slow. "At last someone has brought me the mighty Chewbacca . . ." He tried to continue, but stuttered on the word he wanted. With a roaring laugh, he turned toward Threepio.

"Where's my talkdroid?" he boomed, motioning Threepio to come closer. Reluctantly, the courtly robot obeyed.

Jabba ordered him congenially. "Welcome our mercenary friend and ask his price for the Wookiee."

Threepio translated the message to the bounty hunter. Boushh listened carefully, simultaneously studying the feral creatures around the room, possible exits, possible hostages, vulnerable points. He particularly noticed Boba Fett—standing near the door—the steel-masked mercenary who had caught Han Solo.

Boushh assessed this all in a moment's moment, then spoke evenly in his native tongue to Threepio. "I will take fifty thousand, no less."

Threepio quietly translated for Jabba, who immediately became enraged and knocked the golden droid off the raised throne with a sweep of his massive tail. Threepio clattered in a heap on the floor, where he rested momentarily, uncertain of the correct protocol in this situation.

Jabba raved on in guttural Huttese, Boushh shifted his weapon to a more usable position. Threepio sighed, struggled back onto the throne, composed himself, and translated for Boushh—loosely—what Jabba was saying.

"Twenty-five thousand is all he'll pay . . ." Threepio instructed.

Jabba motioned his pig guards to take Chewbacca, as two jawas covered Boushh. Boba Fett, also raised his weapon. Jabba added, to Threepio's translation: "Twenty five thousand, plus his life."

Threepio translated. The room was silent, tense, uncertain. Finally Boushh spoke, softly, to Threepio.

"Tell that swollen garbage bag he'll have to do better than that, or they'll be picking his smelly hide out of every crack in this room. I'm holding a thermal detonator."

Threepio suddenly focused on the small silver ball Boushh held partially concealed in his left hand. It could be heard humming a quiet, ominous hum. Threepio looked nervously at Jabba, then back at Boushh.

Jabba barked at the droid. "Well? What did he say?"

Threepio cleared his throat. "Your Grandness, he, uh . . . He—"

"Out with it, droid!" Jabba roared.

"Oh, dear," Threepio fretted. He inwardly prepared himself for the worst, then spoke to Jabba in flawless Huttese. "Boushh respectfully disagrees with Your Exaltedness, and begs you to reconsider the amount . . . or he will release the thermal detonator he is holding.''

Instantly a disturbed murmuring circled in the room. Everyone backed up several feet, as if that would help. Jabba stared at the ball clenched in the bounty hunter's hand. It was beginning to glow. Another tense hush came over the onlookers.

Jabba stared malevolently at the bounty hunter for several long seconds. Then, slowly, a satisfied grin crept over his vast, ugly mouth. From the bilious pit of his belly, a laugh rose like gas in a mire. ''This bounty hunter is my kind of scum. Fearless and inventive. Tell him thirty-five, no more—and warn him not to press his luck.''

Threepio felt greatly relieved by this turn of events. He translated for Boushh. Everyone studied the bounty hunter closely for his reaction; guns were readied.

Then Boushh released a switch on the thermal detonator, and it went dead. ''Zeebuss,'' he nodded.

''He agrees,'' Threepio said to Jabba.

The crowd cheered; Jabba relaxed. ''Come, my friend, join our celebration. I may find other work for you.'' Threepio translated, as the party resumed its depraved revelry.

Chewbacca growled under his breath, as he was led away by the Gamorreans. He might have cracked their heads just for being so ugly, or to remind everyone present what a Wookiee was made of—but near the door he spotted a familiar face. Hidden behind a half-mask of pit-boar teeth was a human in the uniform of a skiff guard—Lando Calrissian. Chewbacca gave no sign of recognition; nor did he resist the guard who now escorted him from the room.

Lando had managed to infiltrate this nest of maggots months earlier to see if it was possible to free Solo from Jabba's imprisonment. He'd done this for several reasons.

First, because he felt (correctly) that it was his fault Han was in this predicament, and he wanted to make amends—provided, of course, he could do so without getting hurt. Blending in here, like just one of the pirates, was no problem for Lando, though—mistaken identity was a way of life with him.

Second, he wanted to join forces with Han's buddies at the top of the Rebel Alliance. They were out to beat the Empire, and he wanted nothing more in his life now than to do just that. The Imperial police had moved in on his action once too often; so this was a grudge match, now. Besides, Lando liked being part of Solo's crowd, since they seemed to be right up at the business end of all the action against the Empire.

Third, Princess Leia had asked him to help, and he just never could refuse a princess asking for help. Besides, you never knew how she might thank you some day.

Finally, Lando would have bet anything that Han simply could not be rescued from this place—and Lando just plain couldn't resist a bet.

So he spent his days watching a lot. Watching and calculating. That's what he did now, as Chewie was led away—he watched, and then he faded into the stonework.

The band started playing, led by a blue, flop-eared jizz-wailer named Max Rebo. Dancers flooded the floor. The courtiers hooted, and brewed their brains a bit more.

Boushh leaned against a column, surveying the scene. His gaze swept coolly over the court, taking in the dancers, the smokers, the rollers, the gamblers . . . until it came to rest squarely on an equally unflappable stare from across the room. Boba Fett was watching him.

Boushh shifted slightly, posturing with his weapon cradled like a loving child. Boba Fett remained motionless, an arrogant sneer all but visible behind his ominous mask.

Pig guards led Chewbacca through the unlit dungeon corridor. A tentacle coiled out one of the doors to touch the brooding Wookiee.

"Rheeaaahhr!" he screamed, and the tentacle shot back into its cell.

The next door was open. Before Chewie fully realized what was happening, he was hurled forcefully into the cell by all the guards. The door slammed shut, locking him in darkness.

He raised his head and let out a long, pitiful howl that carried through the entire mountain of iron and sand up to the infinitely patient sky.

The throne room was quiet, dark, and empty as night filled its littered corners. Blood, wine, and saliva stained the floor, shreds of tattered clothing hung from the fixtures, unconscious bodies curled under broken furniture. The party was over.

A dark figure moved silently among the shadows, pausing behind a column here, a statue there. He made his way stealthily along the perimeter of the room, stepping once over a snoring

Yak Face. He never made a sound. This was Boushh, the bounty
hunter.

He reached the curtained alcove beside which the slab that
was Han Solo hung suspended by a force field on the wall.
Boushh looked around furtively, then flipped a switch near the
side of the carbonite coffin. The humming of the force field
wound down, and the heavy monolith slowly lowered to the
floor.

Boushh stepped up and studied the frozen face of the space
pirate. He touched Solo's carbonized cheek, curiously, as if it
were a rare, precious stone. Cold and hard as diamond.

For a few seconds he examined the controls at the side of the
slab, then activated a series of switches. Finally, after one last,
hesitant glance at the living statue before him, he slid the decarbonization lever into place.

The casing began to emit a high-pitched sound. Anxiously
Boushh peered all around again, making certain no one heard.
Slowly, the hard shell that was covering the contours of Solo's
face started to melt away. Soon, the coating was gone from the
entire front of Solo's body, freeing his upraised hands—so long
frozen in protest—to fall slackly to his sides. His face relaxed
into what looked like nothing so much as a death-mask. Boushh
extracted the lifeless body from its casing and lowered it gently
to the floor.

He leaned his gruesome helmet close to Solo's face, listening
closely for signs of life. No breath. No pulse. With a start, Han's
eyes suddenly snapped open, and he began to cough. Boushh
steadied him, tried to quiet him—there were still guards who
might hear.

"Quiet!" he whispered. "Just relax."

Han squinted up at the dim form above him. "I can't see . . .
What's happening?" He was, understandably, disoriented, after
having been in suspended animation for six of this desert planet's months—a period that was, to him, timeless. It had been a
grim sensation—as if for an eternity he'd been trying to draw
breath, to move, to scream, every moment in conscious, painful
asphyxiation—and now suddenly he was dumped into a loud,
black, cold pit.

His senses assaulted him all at once. The air bit at his skin
with a thousand icy teeth; the opacity of his sight was impenetrable; wind seemed to rush around his ears at hurricane vol-
umes; he couldn't feel which way was up; the myriad smells

filling his nose made him nauseous, he couldn't stop salivating, all his bones hurt—and then came the visions.

Visions from his childhood, from his last breakfast, from twenty-seven piracies . . . as if all the images and memories of his life had been crammed into a balloon, and the balloon popped and they all came bursting out now, randomly, in a single moment. It was nearly overwhelming, it was sensory overload; or more precisely, memory overload. Men had gone mad, in these first minutes following decarbonization, hopelessly, utterly mad—unable ever again to reorganize the ten-billion individual images that comprised a lifespan into any kind of coherent, selective order.

Solo wasn't that susceptible. He rode the surge of this tide of impressions until it settle down to a churning backwash, submerging the bulk of his memories, leaving only the most recent flotsam to foam on the surface; his betrayal by Lando Calrissian, whom he'd once called friend; his ailing ship; his last view of Leia; his capture by Boba Fett, the iron-masked bounty hunter who . . .

Where was he now? What had happened? His last image was of Boba Fett watching him turn into carbonite. Was this Fett again now, come to thaw him for more abuse? The air roared in his ears, his breathing felt irregular, unnatural. He batted his hand in front of his face.

Boushh tried to reassure him. "You're free of the carbonite and have hibernation sickness. Your eyesight will return in time. Come, we must hurry if we're to leave this place."

Reflexively Han grabbed the bounty hunter, felt at the grated face-mask, then drew back. "I'm not going anywhere—I don't even know where I am." He began sweating profusely as his heart once again churned blood, and his mind groped for answers. "Who are you, anyway?" he demanded suspiciously. Perhaps it was Fett after all.

The bounty hunter reached up and pulled the helmet away from his head revealing, underneath, the beautiful face of Princess Leia.

"One who loves you," she whispered, taking his face tenderly in her still-gloved hands and kissing him long on the lips.

II

HAN strained to see her, though he had the eyes of a newborn. "Leia! Where are we?"

"Jabba's palace. I've got to get you out of here quick."

He sat up shakily. "Everything's a blur . . . I'm not going to be much help . . ."

She looked at him a long moment, her blinded love—she'd traveled light-years to find him, risked her life, lost hard-won time needed sorely by the Rebellion, time she couldn't really afford to throw away on personal quests and private desires . . . but she loved him.

Tears filled her eyes. "We'll make it," she whispered.

Impulsively, she embraced him and kissed him again. He, too, was flooded with emotion all at once—back from the dead, the beautiful princess filling his arms, snatching him from the teeth of the void. He felt overwhelmed. Unable to move, even to speak, he held her tightly, his blind eyes closed fast against all the sordid realities that would come rushing in soon enough.

Sooner than that, as it happened. A repulsive squishing sound suddenly became all too obvious behind them. Han opened his eyes, but could still see nothing. Leia looked up to the alcove beyond, and her gaze turned to an expression of horror. For the curtain had been drawn away, and the entire area, floor to ceiling, was composed of a gallery of the most disgusting miscreants of Jabba's court—gawking, salivating, wheezing.

Leia's hand shot up to her mouth.

"What is it?" Han pressed her. Something obviously was terribly wrong. He stared into his own blackness.

An obscene cackle rose from the other side of the alcove. A Huttese cackle.

Han held his head, closed his eyes again, as if to keep away the inevitable for just one more moment. "I know that laugh."

The curtain on the far side was suddenly drawn open. There sat Jabba, Ishi Tib, Bib, Boba, and several guards. They all laughed, kept laughing, laughed to punish.

"My, my, what a touching sight," Jabba purred. "Han, my boy, your taste in companions has improved, even if your luck has not."

Even blind, Solo could slide into smooth talk easier than a spice-eater. "Listen, Jabba, I was on my way back to pay you when I got a little side-tracked. Now I know we've had our differences, but I'm sure we can work this out . . ."

This time Jabba genuinely chuckled. "It's too late for that, Solo. You may have been the best smuggler in the business, but now you're Bantha fodder." He cut short his smile and gestured to his guards. "Take him."

Guards grabbed Leia and Han. They dragged the Corellian pirate off, while Leia continued struggling where she was.

"I will decide how to kill him later," Jabba muttered.

"I'll pay you triple," Solo called out. "Jabba, you're throwing away a fortune. Don't be a fool." Then he was gone.

From the rank of guards, Lando quickly moved forward, took hold of Leia, and attempted to lead her away.

Jabba stopped them. "Wait! Bring her to me."

Lando and Leia halted in mid-stride. Lando looked tense, uncertain what to do. It wasn't quite time to move yet. The odds still weren't just right. He knew he was the ace-in-the-hole, and an ace-in-the-hole was something you had to know how to play to win.

"I'll be all right," Leia whispered.

"I'm not so sure," he replied. But the moment was past; there was nothing else to be done now. He and Ishi Tib, the Birdlizard, dragged the young princess to Jabba.

Threepio, who'd been watching everything from his place behind Jabba, could watch no more. He turned away in dread.

Leia, on the other hand, stood tall before the loathsome monarch. Her anger ran high. With all the galaxy at war, for her to be detained on this dustball of a planet by this petty scumdealer was more outrageous than she could tolerate. Still, she kept her voice calm; for she was, in the end, a princess. "We have powerful friends Jabba. You will soon regret this . . ."

"I'm sure, I'm sure," the old gangster rumbled with glee,

"but in the meantime, I will thoroughly enjoy the pleasure of your company."

He pulled her eagerly to him until their faces were mere inches apart, her belly pressed to his oily snake skin. She thought about killing him outright, then and there. But she held her ire in check, since the rest of these vermin might have killed her before she could escape with Han. Better odds were sure to come later. So she swallowed hard and, for the time being, put up with this slimepot as best she could.

Threepio peeked out momentarily, then immediately withdrew again. "Oh no, I can't watch."

Foul beast that he was, Jabba poked his fat, dripping tongue out to the princess, and slopped a beastly kiss squarely on her mouth.

Han was thrown roughly into the dungeon cell; the door crashed shut behind him. He fell to the floor in the darkness, then picked himself up and sat against the wall. After a few moments of pounding the ground with his fist, he quieted down and tried to organize his thoughts.

Darkness. Well, blast it, blind is blind. No use wishing for moondew on a meteorite. Only it was so frustrating, coming out of deep-freeze like that, saved by the one person who . . .

Leia! The star captain's stomach dropped at the thought of what must be happening to her now. If only he knew where he was. Tentatively he knocked on the wall behind him. Solid rock.

What could he do? Bargain, maybe. But what did he have to bargain with? Dumb question, he thought—when did I ever have to *have* something before I could *bargain* with it?

What, though? Money? Jabba had more than he could ever count. Pleasures? Nothing could give Jabba more pleasure than to defile the princess and kill Solo. No, things were bad—in fact, it didn't look like they could get much worse.

Then he heard the growl. A low, formidable snarl from out of the dense blackness at the far corner of the cell, the growl of a large and angry beast.

The hair on Solo's arms stood on end. Quickly he rose, his back to the wall. "Looks like I've got company," he muttered.

The wild creature bellowed out an insane *"Groawwwwr!"* and raced straight at Solo, grabbing him ferociously around the chest, lifting him several feet into the air, squeezing off his breathing.

Han was totally motionless for several long seconds—he couldn't believe his ears. "Chewie, is that you!?"

The giant Wookiee barked with joy.

For the second time in an hour, Solo was overcome with happiness; but this was an entirely different matter. "All right, all right, wait a second, you're crushing me."

Chewbacca put his friend down. Han reached up and scratched his partner's chest; Chewie cooed like a pup.

"Okay, what's going on around here, anyway?" Han was instantly back on track. Here was unbelievably good fortune— here was someone he could make a plan *with*. And not only someone, but his most loyal friend in the galaxy.

Chewie filled him in at length. "Arh arhaghh shpahrgh rahr aurowwwrahrah grop rahp rah."

"Lando's plan? What is *he* doing here?"

Chewie barked extensively.

Han shook his head. "Is Luke crazy? Why'd you listen to him? That kid can't even take care of himself, let alone rescue anyone."

"Rowr ahrgh awf ahraroww rowh rohngr grgrff rf rf."

"A Jedi Knight? Come on. I'm out of it for a little while and everybody gets delusions . . ."

Chewbacca growled insistently.

Han nodded dubiously in the blackness. "I'll believe it when I see it—" he commented, walking stoutly into the wall. "If you'll excuse the expression."

The iron main gate of Jabba's palace scraped open harshly, oiled only with sand and time. Standing outside in the dusty gale, staring into the black cavernous entranceway, was Luke Skywalker.

He was clad in the robe of the Jedi Knight—a cassock, really—but bore neither gun nor lightsaber. He stood loosely, without bravado, taking a measure of the place before entering. He was a man now. Wiser, like a man—older more from loss than from years. Loss of illusions, loss of dependency. Loss of friends, of war. Loss of sleep, of stress. Loss of laughter. Loss of his hand.

But of all his losses, the greatest was that which came from knowledge, and from the deep recognition that he could never un-know what he knew. So many things he wished he'd never learned. He had aged with the weight of this knowledge.

Knowledge brought benefits, of course. He was less impulsive now. Manhood had given him perspective, a framework in which to fit the events of his life—that is, a lattice of spatial and time coordinated spanning his existence, back to earliest memories, ahead to a hundred alternative futures. A lattice of depths, and conundrums, and interstices, through which Luke could peer at any new event in his life, peer at it with perspective. A lattice of shadows and corners, rolling back to the vanishing point on the horizon of Luke's mind. And all these shadow boxes that lent such *perspective* to things . . . well, this lattice gave his life a certain darkness.

Nothing of substance, of course—and in any case, some would have said this shading gave a depth to his personality, where before it had been thin, without dimension—though such a suggestion probably would have come from jaded critics, reflecting a jaded time. Nonetheless, there was a certain darkness, now.

There were other advantages to knowledge: rationality, etiquette, choice. Choice, of them all, was a true double-edged sword; but it did have its advantages.

Furthermore he was skilled in the craft of the Jedi now, where before he'd been merely precocious.

He was more aware now.

These were all desirable attributes, to be sure; and Luke knew as well as anyone that all things alive must grow. Still, it carried a certain sadness, the sum of all this knowledge. A certain sense of regret. But who could afford to be a boy in times such as these?

Resolutely, Luke strode into the arching hallway.

Almost immediately two Gamorreans stepped up, blocking his path. One spoke in a voice that did not invite debate. "No chuba!"

Luke raised his hand and pointed at the guards. Before either could draw a weapon, they were both clutching their own throats, choking, gasping. They fell to their knees.

Luke lowered his hand and walked on. The guards, suddenly able to breathe again, slumped to the sanddrifted steps. They didn't follow.

Around the next corner Luke was met by Bib Fortuna. Fortuna began speaking as he approached the young Jedi, but Luke never broke stride, so Bib had to reverse his direction in midsentence and hurry along with Skywalker in order to carry on a conversation.

"You must be the one called Skywalker. His Excellency will not see you."

"I will speak to Jabba, now," Luke spoke evenly, never slowing. They passed several more guards at the next crossing, who fell in behind them.

"The great Jabba is asleep," Bib explained. "He has instructed me to tell you there will be no bargains—"

Luke stopped suddenly, and stared at Bib. He locked eyes with the major-domo, raised his hand slightly, took a minutely inward turn. "You will take me to Jabba, now."

Bib paused, tilted his head a fraction. What were his instructions? Oh, yes, now he remembered. "I will take you to Jabba now."

He turned and walked down the twisting corridor that led to the throne chamber. Luke followed him into the gloom.

"You serve your master well," he whispered in Bib's ear.

"I serve my master well," Bib nodded with conviction.

"You are sure to be rewarded," Luke added.

Bib smiled smugly. "I am sure to be rewarded."

As Luke and Bib entered Jabba's court, the level of tumult dropped precipitously as if Luke's presence had a cooling effect. Everyone felt the change.

The lieutenant and the Jedi Knight approached the throne. Luke saw Leia seated there, now, by Jabba's belly. She was chained at the neck and dressed in the skimpy costume of a dancing girl. He could feel her pain immediately, from across the room—but he said nothing, didn't even look at her, shut her anguish completely out of his mind. For he needed to focus his attention entirely on Jabba.

Leia, for her part, sensed this at once. She closed her mind to Luke, to keep herself from distracting him; yet at the same time she kept it open, ready to receive any sliver of information she might need to act. She felt charged with possibilities.

Threepio peeked out from behind the throne as Bib walked up. For the first time in many days, he scanned his hope program. "Ah! At last Master Luke's come to take me away from all this," he beamed.

Bib stood proudly before Jabba. "Master, I present Luke Skywalker, Jedi Knight."

"I told you not to admit him," the gangster-slug growled in Huttese.

"I must be allowed to speak," Luke spoke quietly, though his words were heard throughout the hall.

"He must be allowed to speak," Bib concurred thoughtfully. Jabba, furious, bashed Bib across the face and sent him reeling to the floor. "You weak-minded fool! He's using an old Jedi mind trick!"

Luke let all the rest of the motley horde that surrounded him melt into the recesses of his consciousness, to let Jabba fill his mind totally. "You will bring Captain Solo and the Wookiee to me."

Jabba smiled grimly. "Your mind powers will not work on me, boy. I am not affected by your human thought pattern." Then, as an after thought: "I was killing your kind when being a Jedi meant something."

Luke altered his stance somewhat, internally and externally. "Nevertheless, I am taking Captain Solo and his friends. You can either profit from this . . . or be destroyed. It's your choice, but I warn you not to underestimate my powers." He spoke in his own language, which Jabba well understood.

Jabba laughed the laugh of a lion cautioned by a mouse.

Threepio, who had been observing this interplay intently, leaned forward to whisper to Luke: "Master, you're standing—" A guard abruptly restrained the concerned droid, though, and pulled him back to his place.

Jabba cut short his laugh with a scowl. "There will be no bargain, young Jedi. I shall enjoy watching you die."

Luke raised his hand. A pistol jumped out of the holster of a nearby guard and landed snugly in the Jedi's palm. Luke pointed the weapon at Jabba.

Jabba spat. "Boscka!"

The floor suddenly dropped away, sending Luke and his guard crashing into the pit below. The trap door immediately closed again. All the beasts of the court rushed to the floor-grating and looked down.

"Luke!" yelled Leia. She felt part of her self torn away, pulled down into the pit with him. She started forward, but was held in check by the manacle around her throat. Raucous laughter crowded in from everywhere at once, set her on edge. She poised to flee.

A human guard touched her shoulder. She looked. It was Lando. Imperceptibly, he shook his head. No. Imperceptibly, her muscles relaxed. This wasn't the right moment, he knew— but it was the right hand. All the cards were here, now—Luke, Han, Leia, Chewbacca . . . and old Wild Card Lando. He just didn't want Leia revealing the hand before all the bets were out. The stakes were just too high.

In the pit below, Luke picked himself up off the floor. He

found he was now in a large cavelike dungeon, the walls formed of craggy boulders pocked with lightless crevices. The half-chewed bones of countless animals were strewn over the floor, smelling of decayed flesh and twisted fear.

Twenty-five feet above him, in the ceiling, he saw the iron grating through which Jabba's repugnant courtiers peered.

The guard beside him suddenly began to scream uncontrollably, as a door in the side of the cave slowly rumbled open. With infinite calm, Luke surveyed his surroundings as he removed his long robe down to his Jedi tunic, to give him more freedom of movement. He backed quickly to the wall and crouched there, watching.

Out of the side passage emerged the giant Rancor. The size of an elephant, it was somehow reptilian, somehow as unformed as a nightmare. Its huge screeching mouth was asymmetrical in its head, its fangs and claws set all out of proportion. It was clearly a mutant, and wild as all unreason.

The guard picked up the pistol from the dirt where it had fallen and began firing laser bursts at the hideous monster. This only made the beast angrier. It lumbered toward the guard.

The guard kept firing. Ignoring the laser blasts, the beast grabbed the hysterical guard, popped him into its slavering jaws, and swallowed him in a gulp. The audience above cheered, laughed, and threw coins.

The monster then turned and started for Luke. But the Jedi Knight leaped eight meters straight up and grabbed onto the overhead grate. The crowd began to boo. Hand over hand, Luke traversed the grating toward the corner of the cave, struggling to maintain his grip as the audience jeered his efforts. One hand slipped on the oily grid, and he dangled precariously over the baying mutant.

Two Jawas ran across the top of the grate. They mashed Luke's fingers with their rifle butts; once again, the crowd roared its approval.

The Rancor pawed at Luke from below, but the Jedi dangled just out of reach. Suddenly Luke released his hold and dropped directly onto the eye of the howling monster; he then tumbled to the floor.

The Rancor screamed in pain and stumbled, swatting its own face to knock away the agony. It ran in circles a few times, then spotted Luke again and came at him. Luke stooped down to pick up the long bone of an earlier victim. He brandished it before him. The gallery above thought this was hilarious and hooted in delight.

The monster grabbed Luke and brought him up to its salivating mouth. At the last moment, though, Luke wedged the bone deep in the Rancor's mouth and jumped to the floor as the beast began to gag. The Rancor bellowed and flailed about, running headlong into a wall. Several rocks were dislodged, starting an avalanche that nearly buried Luke, as he crouched deep in a crevice near the floor. The crowd clapped in unison.

Luke tried to clear his mind. Fear is a great cloud, Ben used to tell him. It makes the cold colder and the dark darker; but let it rise and it will dissolve. So Luke let it rise past the clamor of the beast above him, and examined ways he might turn the sad creature's rantings on itself.

It was not an evil beast, that much was clear. Had it been purely malicious, its wickedness could easily have been turned on itself—for pure evil, Ben had said, was always self-destructive in the end. But this monster wasn't bad—merely dumb and mistreated. Hungry and in pain, it lashed out at whatever came near. For Luke to have looked on that as evil would only have been a projection of Luke's own darker aspects—it would have been false, and it certainly wouldn't have helped him out of this situation.

No, he was going to have to keep his mind clear—that was all—and just outwit the savage brute, to put it out of its misery.

Most preferable would have been to set it loose in Jabba's court, but that seemed unlikely. He considered, next, giving the creature the means to do itself in—to end its own pain. Unfortunately, the creature was far too angered to comprehend the solace of the void. Luke finally began studying the specific contours of the cave, to try to come up with a specific plan.

The Rancor, meanwhile, had knocked the bone from its mouth and, enraged, was scrabbling through the rubble of fallen rocks, searching for Luke. Luke, though his vision was partially obscured by the pile that still sheltered him, could see now past the monster, to a holding cave beyond—and beyond that, to a utility door. If only he could get to it.

The Rancor knocked away a boulder and spotted Luke recoiling in the crevice. Voraciously, it reached in to pluck the boy out. Luke grabbed a large rock and smashed it down on the creature's finger as hard as he could. As the Rancor jumped, howling in pain once more, Luke ran for the holding cave.

He reached the doorway and ran in. Before him, a heavy

barred gate blocked the way. Beyond this gate, the Rancor's two
keepers sat eating dinner. They looked up as Luke entered, then
stood and walked toward the gate.

Luke turned around to see the monster coming angrily after
him. He turned back to the gate and tried to open it. The keepers
poked at him with their two-pronged spears, jabbed at him
through the bars, laughing and chewing their food, as the Rancor drew closer to the young Jedi.

Luke backed against the side wall, as the Rancor reached in
the room for him. Suddenly he saw the restraining-door control
panel halfway up the opposite wall. The Rancor began to enter
the holding room, closing for the kill, when all at once Luke
picked up a skull off the floor and hurled it at the panel.

The panel exploded in a shower of sparks, and the giant iron
overhead restraining door came crashing down on the Rancor's
head, crushing it like an axe smashing through a ripe water-
melon.

Those in the audience above gasped as one, then were silent.
They were all truly stunned at this bizarre turn of events. They
all looked to Jabba, who was apoplectic with rage. Never had
he felt such fury. Leia tried to hide her delight, but was unable
to keep from smiling, and this increased Jabba's anger even
further. Harshly he snapped at his guards: "Get him out of
there. Bring me Solo and the Wookiee. They will all suffer for
this outrage."

In the pit below, Luke stood calmly as several of Jabba's
henchmen ran in, clapped him in bonds, and ushered him out.

The Rancor keeper wept openly and threw himself down on
the body of his dead pet. Life would be a lonely proposition for
him from that day.

Han and Chewie were led before the steaming Jabba. Han
still squinted and stumbled every few feet. Threepio stood behind the Hutt, unbearably apprehensive. Jabba kept Leia on a
short tether, stroking her hair to try to calm himself. A constant
murmuring filled the room, as the rabble speculated on what
was going to happen to whom.

With a flurry, several guards—including Lando Calrissian—
dragged Luke in across the room. To give them passage, the
courtiers parted like an unruly sea. When Luke, too, was standing before the throne, he nudged Solo with a smile. "Good to
see you again, old buddy."

Solo's face lit up. There seemed to be no end to the number

of friends he kept bumping into. "Luke! Are you in this mess now, too?"

"Wouldn't miss it," Skywalker smiled. For just a moment, he almost felt like a boy again.

"Well, how we doing?" Han raised his eyebrows.

"Same as always," said Luke.

"Oh-oh," Solo replied under his breath. He felt one hundred percent relaxed. Just like old times—but a second later, a bleak thought chilled him.

"Where's Leia? Is she . . ."

Her eyes had been fixed on him from the moment he'd entered the room, though—guarding his spirit with her own. When he spoke of her now, she responded instantly, calling from her place on Jabba's throne. "I'm all right, but I don't know how much longer I can hold off your slobbering friend, here." She was intentionally cavalier, to put Solo at ease. Besides, the sight of all of her friends there at once made her feel nearly invincible. Han, Luke, Chewie, Lando—even Threepio was skulking around somewhere, trying to be forgotten. Leia almost laughed out loud, almost punched Jabba in the nose. She could barely restrain herself. She wanted to hug them all.

Suddenly Jabba shouted; the entire room was immediately silent. "Talkdroid!"

Timidly, Threepio stepped forward and with an embarrassed, self-effacing head gesture, addressed the captives. "His High Exaltedness, the great Jabba the Hutt, has decreed that you are to be terminated immediately."

Solo said loudly, "That's good, I hate long waits . . ."

"Your extreme offense against His Majesty," Threepio went on, "demands the most torturous form of death . . ."

"No sense in doing things halfway," Solo cracked. Jabba could be so pompous, sometimes, and now with old Goldenrod, there, making his pronouncements . . .

No matter what else, Threepio simply *hated* being interrupted. He collected himself, nonetheless, and continued. "You will be taken to the Dune Sea, where you will be thrown into the Great Pit of Carkoon—"

Han shrugged, then turned to Luke. "That doesn't sound too bad."

Threepio ignored the interruption. ". . . the resting place of the all-powerful Sarlacc. In his belly you will find a new definition of pain and suffering, as you slowly digest for a thousand years."

"On second thought we could pass on that," Solo reconsidered. A thousand years was a bit much.

Chewie barked his whole-hearted agreement.

Luke only smiled. "You should have bargained, Jabba. This is the last mistake you'll ever make." Luke was unable to suppress the satisfaction in his voice. He found Jabba despicable—a leech of the galaxy, sucking the life from whatever he touched. Luke wanted to burn the villain, and so was actually rather glad Jabba had refused to bargain—for now Luke would get his wish precisely. Of course, his primary objective was to free his friends, whom he loved dearly; it was this concern that guided him now, above all else. But in the process, to free the universe of this gangster slug—this was a prospect that tinted Luke's purpose with an ever-so-slightly dark satisfaction.

Jabba chortled evilly. "Take them away." At last, a bit of pure pleasure on an otherwise dreary day—feeding the Sarlacc was the only thing he enjoyed as much as feeding the Rancor. Poor Rancor.

A loud cheer rose from the crowd as the prisoners were carried off. Leia looked after them with great concern; but when she caught a glimpse of Luke's face she was stirred to see it still fixed in a broad, genuine smile. She sighed deeply, to expel her doubts.

Jabba's giant antigravity Sail Barge glided slowly over the endless Dune Sea. Its sand-blasted iron hull creaked in the slight breeze, each puff of wind coughing into the two huge sails as if even nature suffered some terminal malaise wherever it came near Jabba. He was belowdecks, now, with most of his court, hiding the decay of his spirit from the cleansing sun.

Alongside the barge, two small skiffs floated in formation one an escort craft, bearing six scruffy soldiers; the other, a gun skiff, containing the prisoners. Han, Chewie, Luke. They were all in bonds, and surrounded by armed guards—Barada, two Weequays. And Lando Calrissian.

Barada was the no-nonsense sort, and not likely to let anything get out of hand. He carried a long-gun as if he wanted nothing more than to hear it speak.

The Weequays were an odd sort. They were brothers, leathery and bald save for a tribal top-knot, braided and worn to the side. No one was certain whether Weequay was the name of their tribe, or their species; or whether all in their tribe were brothers, or all were named Weequays. It was known only that these two were called by this name, and that they treated all other creatures indifferently. With each other they were gentle, even tender; but like Barada, they seemed anxious for the prisoners to misbehave.

And Lando, of course, remained silent, ready—waiting for an opportunity. This reminded him of the lithium scam he'd run on Pesmenben IV—they'd salted the dunes there with lithium carbonate, to con this Imperial governor into leasing the planet. Lando, posing as a nonunion mine guard, had made the governor lie face down in the bottom of the boat and throw his bribe overboard when the "union officials" raided them. They'd gotten away scot-free on that one; Lando expected this job would go much the same, except they might have to throw the guards overboard as well.

Han kept his ear tuned, for his eyes were still useless. He spoke with reckless disregard, to put the guards at ease—to get them used to his talking and moving, so when the time came for him *really* to move, they'd be a critical fraction behind his mark. And, of course—as always—he spoke just to hear himself speak.

"I think my sight is getting better," he said, squinting over the sand. "Instead of a big dark blur, I see a big bright blur."

"Believe me, you're not missing anything." Luke smiled. "I grew up here."

Luke thought of his youth on Tatooine, living on his uncle's farm, cruising in his souped-up landspeeder with his few friends—sons of other settlers, sitting their own lonely outposts. Nothing ever to do here, really, for man or boy, but cruise the monotonous dunes and try to avoid the peevish Tusken Raiders who guarded the sand as if it were gold-dust. Luke knew this place.

He'd met Obi-Wan Kenobi, here—old Ben Kenobi, the hermit who'd lived in the wilderness since nobody knew when. The man who'd first shown Luke the way of the Jedi.

Luke thought of him now with great love, and great sorrow. For Ben was, more than anyone, the agent of Luke's discoveries and losses—and discoveries *of* losses.

Ben had taken Luke to Mos Eisley, the pirate city on the western face of Tatooine, to the cantina where they'd first met Han Solo, and Chewbacca the Wookiee. Taken him there after Imperial stormtroopers had murdered Uncle Owen and Aunt Beru, searching for the fugitive droids, Artoo and Threepio.

That's how it had all started for Luke, here on Tatooine. Like a recurring dream he knew this place; and he had sworn then that he would never return.

"I grew up here," he repeated softly.

"And now we're going to die here," Solo replied.

"I wasn't planning on it," Luke shook himself out of his reverie.

"If this is your big plan, so far I'm not crazy about it."

"Jabba's palace was too well guarded. I had to get you out of there. Just stay close to Chewie and Lando. We'll take care of everything."

"I can hardly wait." Solo had a sinking feeling this grand escape depended on Luke's thinking he was a Jedi—a questionable premise at best, considering it was an extinct brotherhood that had used a Force he didn't really believe in anyway. A fast ship and a good blaster are what Han believed in, and he wished he had them now.

Jabba sat in the main cabin of the Sail Barge, surrounded by his entire retinue. The party at the palace was simply continuing, in motion—the result being a slightly wobblier brand of carousing—more in the nature of a prelynching celebration. So blood lust and belligerence were testing new levels.

Threepio was way out of his depth. At the moment, he was being forced to translate an argument between Ephant Mon and Ree-Yees, concerning a point of quark warfare that was marginally beyond him. Ephant Mon, a bulky upright pachydermoid with an ugly, betusked snout, was taking (to Threepio's way of thinking) an untenable position. However, on his shoulder sat Salacious Crumb, the insane little reptilian monkey who had the habit of repeating verbatim everything Ephant said, thereby effectively doubling the weight of Ephant's argument.

Ephant concluded the oration with a typically bellicose avowal. "Woossie jawamba boog!"

To which Salacious nodded, then added, "Woossie jawamba boog!"

Threepio didn't really want to translate this to Ree-Yees, the three-eyed goat-face who was already drunk as a spigot, but he did.

All three eyes dilated in fury. "Backawa! Backawa!" Without further preamble, he punched Ephant Mon in the snout, sending him flying into a school of Squid Heads.

See Threepio felt this response needed no translation, and took the opportunity to slip to the rear—where he promptly bumped into a small droid serving drinks. The drinks spilled everywhere.

The stubby little droid let out a fluent series of irate beeps, toots, and whistles—recognizable to Threepio instantly. He looked down in utter relief. "Artoo! What are you doing here?"

"dooo WEEp chWHRrrrree bedzhng."

"I can see you're serving drinks. But this place is dangerous. They're going to execute Master Luke, and if we're not careful, us too!"

Artoo whistled—a bit nonchalantly, as far as Threepio was concerned. "I wish I had your confidence," he replied glumly.

Jabba chuckled to see Ephant Mon go down—he loved a good beating. He especially loved to see strength crumble, to see the proud fall.

He tugged, with his swollen fingers, on the chain attached to Princess Leia's neck. The more resistance he met with, the more he drooled—until he'd drawn the struggling, scantily-clad princess close to him once more.

"Don't stray too far, my lovely. Soon you will begin to appreciate me." He pulled her very near and forced her to drink from his glass.

Leia opened her mouth and she closed her mind. It was disgusting, of course; but there were worse things, and in any case, this wouldn't last.

The worse things she knew well. Her standard of comparison was the night she'd been tortured by Darth Vader. She had almost broken. The Dark Lord never knew how close he'd come to extracting the information he wanted from her, the location of the Rebel base. He had captured her just after she'd managed to send Artoo and Threepio for help—captured her, taken her to the Death Star, injected her with mind-weakening chemicals . . . and tortured her.

Tortured her body first, with his efficient pain-droids. Needles, pressure points, fire-knives, electrojabbers. She'd endured these pains, as she now endured Jabba's loathsome touch—with a natural, inner strength.

She slid a few feet away from Jabba, now, as his attention was distracted—moved to peer out the slats in the louvered windows, to squint through the dusty sunlight at the skiff on which her rescuers were being carried.

It was stopping.

The whole convoy was stopping, in fact, over a huge sand pit. The Sail Barge moved to one side of the giant depression, with the escort skiff. The prisoners' skiff hovered directly over the pit, though, perhaps twenty feet in the air.

At the bottom of the deep cone of sand, a repulsive, mucus-lined, pink, membranous hole puckered, almost unmoving. The hole was eight feet in diameter, its perimeter clustered with three rows of inwardly-directed needle-sharp teeth. Sand stuck to the mucus that lined the sides of the opening, occasionally sliding into the black cavity at the center.

This was the mouth of the Sarlacc.

An iron plank was extended over the side of the prisoners' skiff. Two guards untied Luke's bonds and shoved him gruffly out onto the plank, straight above the orifice in the sand, now beginning to undulate in peristaltic movement and salivate with increased mucus secretion as it smelled the meat it was about to receive.

Jabba moved his party up to the observation deck.

Luke rubbed his wrists to restore circulation. The heat shimmering off the desert warmed his soul—for finally, this would always be his home. Born and bred in a Bantha patch. He saw Leia standing at the rail of the big barge, and winked. She winked back.

Jabba motioned Threepio to his side, then mumbled orders to the golden droid. Threepio stepped up to the comlink. Jabba raised his arm, and the whole motley array of intergalactic pirates fell silent. Threepio's voice arose, amplified by the loudspeaker.

"His Excellency hopes you will die honorably," Threepio announced. This did not scan at all. Someone had obviously mislaid the correct program. Nonetheless, *he* was only a *droid*, his functions well delineated. Translation only, no free will *please*. He shook his head and continued. "But should any of you wish to beg for mercy, Jabba will now listen to your pleas."

Han stepped forward to give the bloated slime pot his last thoughts, in case all else failed. "You tell that slimy piece of worm-ridden filth—"

Unfortunately, Han was facing into the desert, away from the Sail Barge. Chewie reached over and turned Solo around, so he was now properly facing the piece of worm-ridden filth he was addressing.

Han nodded, without stopping. "—worm-ridden filth he'll get no such pleasure from us."

Chewie made a few growly noises of general agreement.

Luke was ready. "Jabba, this is your last chance," he shouted.

"Free us or die." He shot a quick look to Lando, who moved unobtrusively toward the back of the skiff. This was it, Lando figured—they'd just toss the guards overboard and take off under everyone's nose.

The monsters on the barge roared with laughter. Artoo, during this commotion, rolled silently up the ramp to the side of the upper deck.

Jabba raised his hand, and his minions were quiet. "I'm sure you're right, my young Jedi friend," he smiled. Then he turned his thumb down. "Put him in."

The spectators cheered, as Luke was prodded to the edge of the plank by Weequay. Luke looked up at Artoo, standing alone by the rail, and flipped the little droid a jaunty salute. At that prearranged signal, a flap slid open in Artoo's domed head, and a projectile shot high into the air and curved in a gentle arc over the desert.

Luke jumped off the plank; another bloodthirsty cheer went up. In less than a second, though, Luke had spun around in freefall, and caught the end of the plank with his fingertips. The thin metal bent wildly from his weight, paused near to snapping, then catapulted him up. In mid-air he did a complete flip and dropped down in the middle of the plank—the spot he'd just left, only now behind the confused guards. Casually, he extended his arm to his side, palm up—and suddenly, his lightsaber, which Artoo had shot sailing toward him, dropped neatly into his open hand.

With Jedi speed, Luke ignited his sword and attacked the guard at the skiff-edge of the plank, sending him, screaming, overboard into the twitching mouth of the Sarlacc.

The other guards swarmed toward Luke. Grimly he waded into them, lightsaber flashing.

His own lightsaber—not his father's. He had lost his father's in the duel with Darth Vader in which he'd lost his hand as well. Darth Vader, who had told Luke *he* was his father.

But this lightsaber Luke had fashioned himself, in Obi-Wan Kenobi's abandoned hut on the other side of Tatooine—made with the old Master Jedi's tools and parts, made with love and craft and dire need. He wielded it now as it it were fused to his hand; as if it were an extension of his own arm. This lightsaber, truly, was Luke's.

He cut through the onslaught like a light dissolving shadows.

Lando grappled with the helmsman, trying to seize the controls of the skiff. The helmsman's laser pistol fired, blasting the nearby panel; and the skiff lurched to the side, throwing another guard into the pit, knocking everyone else into a pile on the deck. Luke picked himself up and ran toward the helmsman, lightsaber raised. The creature retreated at the overpowering sight, stumbled . . . and he, too, went over the edge, into the maw.

The bewildered guard landed in the soft, sandy slope of the pit and began an inexorable slide down toward the toothy, viscous opening. He clawed desperately at the sand, screaming. Suddenly a muscled tentacle oozed out of the Sarlacc's mouth, slithered up the caked sand, coiled tightly around the helmsman's ankle, and pulled him into the hole with a grotesque slurp.

All this happened in a matter of seconds. When he saw what was happening, Jabba exploded in a rage, and yelled furious commands at those around him. In a moment, there was general uproar, with creatures running through every door. It was during this directionless confusion that Leia acted.

She jumped onto Jabba's throne, grabbed the chain which enslaved her, and wrapped it around his bulbous throat. Then she dove off the other side of the support, pulling the chain violently in her grasp. The small metal rings buried themselves in the loose folds of the Hutt's neck, like a garrote.

With a strength beyond her own strength, she pulled. He bucked with his huge torso, nearly breaking her fingers, nearly yanking her arms from their sockets. He could get no leverage, his bulk was too unwieldy. But just his sheer mass was almost enough to break any mere physical restraint.

Yet Leia's hold was not merely physical. She closed her eyes, closed out the pain in her hands, focused all of her life-force—and all it was able to channel—into squeezing the breath from the horrid creature.

She pulled, she sweated, she visualized the chain digging millimeter by millimeter deeper into Jabba's windpipe—as Jabba wildly thrashed, frantically twisted from this least expected of foes.

With a last gasping effort, Jabba tensed every muscle and lurched forward. His reptilian eyes began to bulge from their sockets as the chain tightened; his oily tongue flopped from his mouth. His thick tail twitched in spasms of effort, until he finally lay still—deadweight.

Leia set about trying to free herself from the chain at her neck, while outside, the battle began to rage.

Boba Fett ignited his rocket pack, leaped into the air, and

with a single effort flew down from the barge to the skiff just as Luke finished freeing Han and Chewie from their bonds. Boba aimed his laser gun at Luke, but before he could fire, the young Jedi spun around, sweeping his lightsword in an arc that sliced the bounty hunter's gun in half.

A series of blasts suddenly erupted from the large cannon on the upper deck of the barge, hitting the skiff broadside, and rocking it forty degrees askew. Lando was tossed from the deck, but at the last moment he grabbed a broken strut and dangled desperately above the Sarlacc. This development was definitely not in his game plan, and he vowed to himself never again to get involved in a con that he didn't run from start to finish.

The skiff took another direct hit from the barge's deck gun, throwing Chewie and Han against the rail. Wounded, the Wookiee howled in pain. Luke looked over at his hairy friend; whereupon Boba Fett, taking advantage of that moment of distraction, fired a cable from out of his armored sleeve.

The cable wrapped itself several times around Luke, pinning his arms to his sides, his sword arm now free only from the wrist down. He bent his wrist, so the lightsaber pointed straight up . . . and then spun toward Boba along the cable. In a moment, the lightsaber touched the end of the wire lasso, cutting through it instantly. Luke shrugged the cable away, just as another blast hit the skiff, knocking Boba unconscious to the deck. Unfortunately this explosion also dislodged the strut from which Lando was hanging, sending him careening into the Sarlacc pit.

Luke was shaken by the explosion, but unhurt. Lando hit the sandy slope, shouted for help, and tried to scramble out. The loose sand only tumbled him deeper toward the gaping hole. Lando closed his eyes and tried to think of all the ways he might give the Sarlacc a thousand years of indigestion. He bet himself three to two he could outlast anybody else in the creature's stomach. Maybe if he talked that last guard out of his uniform . . .

"Don't move!" Luke screamed, but his attention was immediately diverted by the incoming second skiff, full of guards firing their weapons.

It was a Jedi rule-of-thumb, but it took the soldiers in the second skiff by surprise: when outnumbered, attack. This drives the force of the enemy in toward himself. Luke jumped directly into the center of the skiff and immediately began decimating them in their midst with lightning sweeps of his lightsaber.

Back in the other boat, Chewie tried to untangle himself from the wreckage, as Han struggled blindly to his feet. Chewie barked at him, trying to direct him toward a spear lying loose on the deck.

Lando screamed, starting to slide closer to the glistening jaws. He was a gambling man, but he wouldn't have taken long odds on his chances of escape right now.

"Don't move, Lando!" Han called out. "I'm coming!" Then, to Chewie: "Where is it, Chewie?" He swung his hands frantically over the deck as Chewie growled directions, guiding Solo's movements. At last, Han locked onto the spear.

Boba Fett stumbled up just then, still a little dizzy from the exploding shell. He looked over at the other skiff, where Luke was in a pitched battle with six guards. With one hand Boba steadied himself on the rail; with the other he aimed his weapon at Luke.

Chewie barked at Han.

"Which way?" shouted Solo. Chewie barked.

The blinded space pirate swung his long spear in Boba's direction. Instinctively, Fett blocked the blow with his forearm; again, he aimed at Luke. "Get out of my way, you blind fool," he cursed Solo.

Chewie barked frantically. Han swung his spear again, this time in the opposite direction, landing the hit squarely in the middle of Boba's rocket pack.

The impact caused the rocket to ignite. Boba blasted off unexpectedly, shooting over the second skiff like a missile and ricocheting straight down into the pit. His armored body slid quickly past Lando and rolled without pause into the Sarlacc's mouth.

"Rrgrrowrrbroo fro bo," Chewie growled.

"He did?" Solo smiled. "I wish I could have seen that—"

A major hit from the barge deck gun flipped the skiff on its side, sending Han and almost everything else overboard. His foot caught on the railing, though, leaving him swinging precariously above the Sarlacc. The wounded Wookiee tenaciously held on to the twisted debris astern.

Luke finished going through his adversaries on the second skiff, assessed the problem quickly, and leaped across the chasm of sand to the sheer metal side of the huge barge. Slowly, he began a hand-over-hand climb up the hull, toward the deck gun.

Meanwhile, on the observation deck, Leia had been intermittently struggling to break the chain which bound her to the dead gangster, and hiding behind his massive carcass whenever some guard ran by. She stretched her full length, now, trying to retrieve a discarded laser pistol—to no avail. Fortunately, Artoo at last came to her rescue, after having first lost his bearings and rolled down the wrong plank.

He zipped up to her finally, extended a cutting appendage from the side of his casing, and sliced through her bonds.

"Thanks, Artoo, good work. Now let's get out of here."

They raced for the door. On the way, they passed Threepio, lying on the floor, screaming, as a giant, tuberous hulk named Hermi Odle sat on him. Salacious Crumb, the reptilian monkey-monster, crouched by Threepio's head, picking out the golden droid's right eye.

"No! No! Not my eyes!" Threepio screamed.

Artoo sent a bolt of charge into Hermi Odle's backside, sending him wailing through a window. A similar flash blasted Salacious to the ceiling, from which he didn't come down. Threepio quickly rose, his eye dangling from a sheaf of wires; then he and Artoo hurriedly followed Leia out the back door.

The deck gun blasted the tilting skiff once more, shaking out virtually everything that remained inside except Chewbacca. Desperately holding on with his injured arm, he was stretching over the rail, grasping the ankle of the dangling Solo, who was, in turn, sightlessly reaching down for the terrified Calrissian. Lando had managed to stop his slippage by lying very still. Now, every time he reached up for Solo's outstretched arm, the loose sand slid him a fraction closer to the hungry hole. He sure hoped Solo wasn't still holding that silly business back on Bespin against him.

Chewie barked another direction at Han.

"Yeah, I know, I can see a lot better now—it must be all the blood rushing to my head."

"Great," Lando called up. "Now could you just grow a few inches taller?"

The deck gunners on the barge were lining up this human chain in their sights for the coup de grace, when Luke stepped in front of them, laughing like a pirate king. He lit his lightsaber before they could squeeze off a shot; a moment later they were smoking corpses.

A company of guards suddenly rushed up the steps from the lower decks, firing. One of the blasts shot Luke's lightsaber from his hand. He ran down the deck, but was quickly surrounded. Two of the soldiers manned the deck gun again. Luke looked at his hand; the mechanism was exposed—the complex steel-and-circuit construction that replaced his real hand, which Vader had cut off in their last encounter.

He flexed the mechanism; it still worked.

The deck gunners fired at the skiff below. It hit to the side of the small boat. The shock wave almost knocked Chewie loose, but in tipping the boat further, Han was able to grab onto Lando's wrist.

"Pull!" Solo yelled at the Wookiee.

"I'm caught!" screamed Calrissian. He looked down in panic to see one of the Sarlacc's tentacles slowly wrap around his ankle. Talk about a wild card—they kept changing the rules every five minutes in this game. Tentacles! What kind of odds was anybody gonna give on tentacles? Very long, he decided with a fatalistic grunt; long, and sticky.

The deck gunners realigned their sights for the final kill, but it was all over for them before they could fire—Leia had commandeered the second deck gun, at the other end of the ship. With her first shot she blasted the rigging that stood between the two deck guns. With her second shot she wiped out the first deck gun.

The explosions rocked the great barge, momentarily distracting the five guards who surrounded Luke. In that moment he reached out his hand, and the lightsaber, lying on the deck ten feet away, flew into it. He leaped straight up as two guards fired at him—their laser bolts killed each other. He ignited his blade in the air and, swinging it as he came down, mortally wounded the others.

He yelled to Leia across the deck. "Point it down!"

She tilted the second deck gun into the deck and nodded to Threepio at the rail.

Artoo, beside him, beeped wildly.

"I can't, Artoo!" Threepio cried. "It's too far to jump . . . aaahhh!"

Artoo butted the golden droid over the edge, and then stepped off himself, tumbling head over wheels toward the sand.

Meanwhile, the tug-of-war was continuing between the Sarlacc and Solo, with Baron Calrissian as the rope and the prize. Chewbacca held Han's leg, braced himself on the rail, and succeeded in pulling a laser pistol out of the wreckage with his other hand. He aimed the gun toward Lando, then lowered it, barking his concern.

"He's right!" Lando called out. "It's too far!"

Solo looked up. "Chewie, give me the gun."

Chewbacca gave it to him. He took it with one hand, still holding on to Lando with the other.

"Now, wait a second, pal," Lando protested, "I thought you were blind."

"I'm better, trust me," Solo assured him.

"Do I have a choice? Hey! A little higher, please." He lowered his head.

Han squinted . . . pulled the trigger . . . and scored a direct hit on the tentacle. The wormy thing instantly released its grip, slithering back into its own mouth.

Chewbacca pulled mightily, drawing first Solo back into the boat—and then Lando.

Luke, meantime, gathered Leia up in his left arm; with his right he grabbed a hold of a rope from the rigging of the half blown-down mast, and with his foot kicked the trigger of the second deck gun—and jumped into the air as the cannon exploded into the deck.

The two of them swung on the swaying rope, all the way down to the empty, hovering escort skiff. Once there, Luke steered it over to the still-listing prison skiff, where he helped Chewbacca, Han, and Lando on board.

The Sail Barge continued exploding behind them. Half of it was now on fire.

Luke guided the skiff around beside the barge, where See Threepio's legs could be seen sticking straight up out of the sand. Beside them, Artoo Detoo's periscope was the only part of his anatomy visible above the dune. The skiff stopped just above them and lowered a large electromagnet from its compartment in the boat's helm. With a loud clang, the two droids shot out of the sand and locked to the magnet's plate.

"Ow," groaned Threepio.

"beeeDOO dwEET!" Artoo agreed.

In a few minutes, they were all in the skiff together, more or less in one piece; and for the first time, they looked at one another and realized they were all in the skiff together, more or less in one piece. There was a great, long moment of hugging, laughing, crying, and beeping. Then someone accidentally squeezed Chewbacca's wounded arm, and he bellowed; and then they all ran about, securing the boat, checking the perimeters, looking for supplies—and sailing away.

The great Sail Barge settled slowly in a chain of explosions and violent fires, and—as the little skiff flew quietly off across the desert—disappeared finally in a brilliant conflagration that was only partially diminished by the scorching afternoon light of Tatooine's twin suns.

III

THE sandstorm obscured everything—sight, breath, thought, motion. The roar of it alone was disorienting, sounding like it came from everywhere at once, as if the universe were composed of noise, and this was its chaotic center.

The seven heroes walked step by step through the murky gale, holding on to one another so as not to get lost. Artoo was first, following the signal of the homing device which sang to him in a language not garbled by the wind. Threepio came next, then Leia guiding Han, and finally Luke and Lando, supporting the hobbling Wookiee.

Artoo beeped loudly, and they all looked up: vague, dark shapes could be seen through the typhoon.

"I don't know," shouted Han. "All I can see is a lot of blowing sand."

"That's all any of us can see," Leia shouted back.

"Then I guess I'm getting better."

For a few steps, the dark shapes grew darker; and then out of the darkness, the *Millennium Falcon* appeared, flanked by Luke's X-wing and a two-seater Y-wing. As soon as the group huddled under the bulk of the *Falcon*, the wind died down to something more describable as a severe weather condition. Threepio hit a switch, and the gangplank lowered with a hum.

Solo turned to Skywalker. "I've got to hand it to you, kid, you were pretty good out there."

Luke shrugged it off. "I had a lot of help." He started toward his X-wing.

Han stopped him, his manner suddenly quieter, even serious. "Thanks for coming after me, Luke."

Luke felt embarrassed for some reason. He didn't know how to respond to anything but a wisecrack from the old pirate. "Think nothing of it," he finally said.

"No, I'm thinkin' a lot about it. That carbon freeze was the closest thing to dead there is. And it wasn't just sleepin', it was a big, wide awake Nothin'."

A Nothing from which Luke and the others had saved him—put their own lives in great peril at his expense, for no other reason than that . . . he was their friend. This was a new idea for the cocky Solo—at once terrible and wonderful. There was jeopardy in this turn of events. It made him feel somehow blinder than before, but visionary as well. It was confusing. Once, he was alone; now he was a part.

That realization made him feel indebted, a feeling he'd always abhorred; only now the debt was somehow a new kind of bond, a bond of brotherhood. It was even freeing, in a strange way.

He was no longer so alone.

No longer alone.

Luke saw a difference had come over his friend, like a sea change. It was a gentle moment; he didn't want to disturb it. So he only nodded.

Chewie growled affectionately at the young Jedi warrior, mussing his hair like a proud uncle. And Leia warmly hugged him.

They all had great love for Solo, but somehow it was easier to show it by being demonstrative to Luke.

"I'll see you back at the fleet," Luke called, moving toward his ship.

"Why don't you leave that crate and come with us?" Solo nudged.

"I have a promise I have to keep first . . . to an old friend." A *very* old friend, he smiled to himself in afterthought.

"Well, hurry back," Leia urged. "The entire Alliance should be assembled by now." She saw something in Luke's face; she couldn't put a name to it, but it scared her, and simultaneously made her feel closer to him. "Hurry back," she repeated.

"I will," he promised. "Come on, Artoo."

Artoo rolled toward the X-wing, beeping a farewell to Three-pio.

"Good-bye, Artoo," Threepio called out fondly. "May the maker bless you. You will watch out for him, won't you, Master Luke?"

But Luke and the little droid were already gone, on the far side of the flyer.

The others stood without moving for a moment, trying to see their futures in the swirling sand.

Lando jarred them awake. "Come on, let's get off this miserable dirt ball." His luck here had been abominable; he hoped to fare better in the next game. It would be house rules for a while, he knew; but he might be able to load a few dice along the way.

Solo clapped him on the back. "Guess I owe you some thanks too, Lando."

"Figured if I left you frozen like that you'd just give me bad luck the rest of my life, so I might as well get you unfrozen sooner, as later."

"He means 'you're welcome.' " Leia smiled. "We all mean you're welcome." She kissed Han on the cheek to say it personally one more time.

They all headed up the ramp of the *Falcon*. Solo paused just before going inside and gave the ship a little pat. "You're lookin' good, old girl. I never thought I'd live to see you again."

He entered at last, closing the hatch behind him.

Luke did the same in the X-wing. He strapped himself into the cockpit, started up the engines, felt the comfortable roar. He looked at his damaged hand: wires crossed aluminum bones like spokes in a puzzle. He wondered what the solution was. Or the puzzle, for that matter. He pulled a black glove over the exposed infrastructure, set the X-wing's controls, and for the second time in his life, he rocketed off his home planet, into the stars.

The Super Star Destroyer rested in space above the half-completed Death Star battle station and its green neighbor, Endor. The Destroyer was a massive ship, attended by numerous smaller warships of various kinds, which hovered or darted around the great mother ship like children of different ages and temperaments: medium range fleet cruisers, bulky cargo vessels, TIE fighter escorts.

The main bay of the Destroyer opened, space-silent. An Imperial shuttle emerged and accelerated toward the Death Star, accompanied by four squads of fighters.

Darth Vader watched their approach on the view-screen in the control room of the Death Star. When docking was imminent, he marched out of the command center, followed by Commander Jerjerrod and a phalanx of Imperial stormtroopers, and headed toward the docking bay. He was about to welcome his master.

Vader's pulse and breathing were machine-regulated, so they could not quicken; but something in his chest became more electric around his meetings with the Emperor; he could not say how. A feeling of fullness, of power, of dark and demon mastery—of secret lusts, unrestrained passion, wild submission—all these things were in Vader's heart as he neared his Emperor. These things and more.

When he entered the docking bay, thousands of Imperial troops snapped to attention with a momentous clap. The shuttle came to rest on the pod. Its ramp lowered like a dragon jaw, and the Emperor's royal guard ran down, red robes flapping, as if they were licks of flame shooting out the mouth to herald the angry roar. They poised themselves at watchful guard in two lethal rows beside the ramp. Silence filled the great hall. At the top of the ramp, the Emperor appeared.

Slowly, he walked down. A small man was he, shriveled with age and evil. He supported his bent frame on a gnarled cane and covered himself with a long, hooded robe—much like the robe of the Jedi, only black. His shrouded face was so thin of flesh it was nearly a skull; his piercing yellow eyes seemed to burn through all at which they stared.

When the Emperor reached the bottom of the ramp, Commander Jerjerrod, his generals, and Lord Vader all kneeled before him. The Supreme Dark Ruler beckoned to Vader, and began walking down the row of troops.

"Rise, my friend, I would talk with you."

Vader rose, and accompanied his master. They were followed in procession by the Emperor's courtiers, the royal guard, Jerjerrod, and the Death Star elite guard, with mixed reverence and fear.

Vader felt complete at the Emperor's side. Though the emptiness at his core never left him, it became a glorious emptiness in the glare of the Emperor's cold light, an exalted void that could encompass the universe. And someday *would* encompass the universe . . . when the Emperor was dead.

For that was Vader's final dream. When he'd learned all he could of the dark power from this evil genius, to take that power from him, seize it and keep its cold light at his own core—kill the Emperor and devour his darkness, and rule the universe. Rule with his son at his side.

For that was his other dream—to reclaim his boy, to show Luke the majesty of this shadow force: why it was so potent, why he'd chosen rightly to follow its path. And Luke would come with him, he knew. That seed was sown. They would rule together, father and son.

His dream was very close to realization, he could feel it; it was near. Each event fell into place, as he'd nudged it, with Jedi subtlety; as he'd pressed, with delicate dark strength.

"The Death Star will be completed on schedule, my master," Vader breathed.

"Yes, I know," replied the Emperor. "You have done well, Lord Vader . . . and now I sense you wish to continue your search for the young Skywalker."

Vader smiled beneath his armored mask. The Emperor always knew the sense of what was in his heart; even if he didn't know the specifics. "Yes, my master."

"Patience, my friend," the Supreme Ruler cautioned. "You always had difficulty showing patience. In time, *he* will seek *you* out . . . and when he does, you must bring him before me. He has grown strong. Only together can we turn him to the dark side of the Force."

"Yes, my master." Together, they would corrupt the boy—the child of the father. Great, dark glory. For soon, the old Emperor would die—and though the galaxy would bend from the horror of that loss, Vader would remain to rule, with young Skywalker at his side. As it was always meant to be.

The Emperor raised his head a degree, scanning all the possible futures. "Everything is proceeding as I have foreseen."

He, like Vader, had plans of his own—plans of spiritual violation, the manipulation of lives and destinies. He chuckled to himself, savoring the nearness of his conquest: the final seduction of the young Skywalker.

Luke left his X wing parked at the edge of the water and carefully picked his way through the adjoining swamp. A heavy mist hung in layers about him. Jungle steam. A strange insect flew at him from out of a cluster of hanging vines, fluttered madly about his head, and vanished. In the undergrowth, something snarled. Luke concentrated momentarily. The snarling stopped. Luke walked on.

He had terribly ambivalent feelings about this place. Dagobah. His place of tests, of training to be a Jedi. This was where he'd truly learned to use the Force, to let it flow through him to whatever end he directed it. So he'd learned how caretaking he must be in order to use the Force well. It was walking on light; but to a Jedi it was as stable as an earthen floor.

Dangerous creatures lurked in this swamp; but to a Jedi, none were evil. Voracious quicksand mires waited, still as pools; tentacles mingled with the hanging vines. Luke knew them all, now, they were all part of the living planet, each integral to the Force of which he, too, was a pulsing aspect.

Yet there were dark things here, as well—unimaginably dark, reflections of the dark corners of his soul. He'd seen these things here. He'd run from them, he'd struggled with them; he'd even faced them. He'd vanquished some of them.

But some still cowered here. These dark things.

He climbed around a barricade of gnarled roots, slippery with moss. On the other side, a smooth, unimpeded path led straight in the direction he wanted to go; but he did not take it. Instead, he plunged once more into the undergrowth.

High overhead, something black and flapping approached, then veered away. Luke paid no attention. He just kept walking.

The jungle thinned a bit. Beyond the next bog, Luke saw it—the small, strangely-shaped dwelling, its odd little windows shedding a warm yellow light in the damp rain-forest. He skirted the mire, and crouching low, entered the cottage.

Yoda stood smiling inside, his small green hand clutching his walking stick for support. "Waiting for you I was," he nodded.

He motioned Luke to sit in a corner. The boy was struck by how much more frail Yoda's manner seemed—a tremor to the hand, a weakness to the voice. It made Luke afraid to speak, to betray his shock at the old master's condition.

"That face you make," Yoda crinkled his tired brow cheerfully. "Look I so bad to young eyes?"

He tried to conceal his woeful countenance, shifting his position in the cramped space. "No, Master . . . of course not."

"I do, yes, I do!" the tiny Jedi Master chuckled gleefully. "Sick I've become. Yes. Old and weak." He pointed a crooked finger at his young pupil. "When nine hundred years old you reach, look as good you will not."

The creature hobbled over to his bed, still chuckling and, with great effort, lay down. "Soon will I rest. Yes, forever sleep. Earned it, I have."

Luke shook his head. "You can't die, Master Yoda—I won't let you."

"Trained well, and strong with the Force are you—but not

that strong! Twilight is upon me, and soon night must fall. That is the way of things . . . the way of the Force."

"But I need your help," Luke insisted. "I want to complete my training." The great teacher couldn't leave him now—there was too much, still, to understand. And he'd taken so much from Yoda already, and as yet given back nothing. He had much he wanted to share with the old creature.

"No more training do you require," Yoda assured him. "Already know you that which you need."

"Then I am a Jedi?" Luke pressed. No. He knew he was not, quite. Something still lacked.

Yoda wrinkled up his wizened features. "Not yet. One thing remains. Vader . . . Vader you must confront. Then, only then, a full Jedi you'll be. And confront him you will, sooner or later."

Luke knew this would be his test, it could not be otherwise. Every quest had its focus, and Vader was inextricably at the core of Luke's struggle. It was agonizing for him to put the question to words; but after a long silence, he again spoke to the old Jedi. "Master Yoda—is Darth Vader my father?"

Yoda's eyes filled with a weary compassion. This boy was not yet a man complete. A sad smile creased his face, he seemed almost to grow smaller in his bed. "A rest I need. Yes. A rest."

Luke stared at the dwindling teacher, trying to give the old one strength, just by the force of his love and will. "Yoda, I must know," he whispered.

"Your father he is," Yoda said simply.

Luke closed his eyes, his mouth, his heart, to keep away the truth of what he knew was true.

"Told you, did he?" Yoda asked.

Luke nodded, but did not speak. He wanted to keep the moment frozen, to shelter it here, to lock time and space in this room, so it could never escape into the rest of the universe with this terrible knowledge, this unrelenting truth.

A look of concern filled Yoda's face. "Unexpected this is, and unfortunate—"

"Unfortunate that I know the truth?" A bitterness crept into Luke's voice, but he couldn't decide if it was directed at Vader, Yoda, himself, or the universe at large.

Yoda gathered himself up with an effort that seemed to take all his strength. "Unfortunate that you rushed to face him—that incomplete your training was . . . that not ready for the burden were you. Obi-Wan would have told you long ago, had I let him

. . . now a great weakness you carry. Fear for you, I do. Fear for you, yes.'' A great tension seemed to pass out of him and he closed his eyes.

"Master Yoda, I'm sorry." Luke trembled to see the potent Jedi so weak.

"I know, but face Vader again you must, and sorry will not help." He leaned forward, and beckoned Luke close to him. Luke crawled over to sit beside his master. Yoda continued, his voice increasingly frail. "Remember, a Jedi's strength flows from the Force. When you rescued your friends, you had revenge in your heart. Beware of anger, fear, and aggression. The dark side are they. Easily they flow, quick to join you in a fight. Once you start down the dark path, forever will it dominate your destiny."

He lay back in bed, his breathing became shallow. Luke waited quietly, afraid to move, afraid to distract the old one an iota, lest it jar his attention even a fraction from the business of just keeping the void at bay.

After a few minutes, Yoda looked at the boy once more, and with a maximum effort, smiled gently, the greatness of his spirit the only thing keeping his decrepit body alive. "Luke—of the Emperor beware. Do not underestimate his powers, or suffer your father's fate you will. When gone I am . . . last of the Jedi will you be. Luke, the Force is strong in your family. Pass on what you . . . have . . . learned . . ." He began to falter, he closed his eyes. "There . . . is . . . another . . . sky . . ."

He caught his breath, and exhaled, his spirit passing from him like a sunny wind blowing to another sky. His body shivered once; and he disappeared.

Luke sat beside the small, empty bed for over an hour, trying to fathom the depth of this loss. It was unfathomable.

His first feeling was one of boundless grief. For himself, for the universe. How could such a one as Yoda be gone forever? It felt like a black, bottomless hole had filled his heart, where the part that was Yoda had lived.

Luke had known the passing of old mentors before. It was helplessly sad; and inexorably, a part of his own growing. Is this what coming of age was, then? Watching beloved friends grow old and die? Gaining a new measure of strength or maturity from their powerful passages?

A great weight of hopelessness settled upon him, just as all the lights in the little cottage flickered out. For several more minutes he sat there, feeling it was the end of everything, that all the lights in the universe had flickered out. The last Jedi, sitting in a swamp, while the entire galaxy plotted the last war.

A chill came over him, though, disturbing the nothingness into which his consciousness had lapsed. He shivered, looked around. The gloom was impenetrable.

He crawled outside and stood up. Here in the swamp, nothing had changed. Vapor congealed, to drip from dangling roots back into the mire, in a cycle it had repeated a million times, would repeat forever. Perhaps *there* was his lesson. If so, it cut his sadness not a whit.

Aimlessly he made his way back to where his ship rested. Artoo rushed up, beeping his excited greeting; but Luke was disconsolate, and could only ignore the faithful little droid. Artoo whistled a brief condolence, then remained respectfully silent.

Luke sat dejectedly on a log, put his head in his hands, and spoke softly to himself. "I can't do it. I can't go on alone."

A voice floated down to him on the dim mist. "Yoda and I will be with you always." It was Ben's voice.

Luke turned around swiftly to see the shimmering image of Obi-Wan Kenobi standing behind him. "Ben!" he whispered. There were so many things he wanted to say, they rushed through his mind all in a whirl, like the churning, puffed cargo of a ship in a maelstrom. But one question rose quickly to the surface above all the others. "Why, Ben? Why didn't you tell me?"

It was not an empty question. "I was going to tell you when you had completed your training," the vision of Ben answered. "But you found it necessary to rush off unprepared. I warned you about your impatience." His voice was unchanged, a hint of scolding, a hint of love.

"You told me Darth Vader betrayed and murdered my father." The bitterness he'd felt earlier, with Yoda, had found its focus now on Ben.

Ben absorbed the vitriol undefensively, then padded it with instruction. "Your father, Anakin, was seduced by the dark side of the Force—He ceased to be Anakin Skywalker, and became Darth Vader. When that happened, he betrayed everything that Anakin Skywalker believed in. The good man who was your father was destroyed. So what I told you was true . . . from a certain point of view."

"A certain point of view!" Luke rasped derisively. He felt betrayed—by life more than anything else, though only poor Ben was available to take the brunt of his conflict.

"Luke," Ben spoke gently, "you're going to find that many of the truths we cling to depend greatly on our point of view."

Luke turned unresponsive. He wanted to hold onto his fury, to guard it like a treasure. It was all he had, he would not let it be stolen from him, as everything else had been stolen. But already he felt it slipping, softened by Ben's compassionate touch.

"I don't blame you for being angry," Ben coaxed. "If I was wrong in what I did, it certainly wouldn't have been for the first time. You see, what happened to your father was my fault . . ."

Luke looked up with sudden acute interest. He'd never heard this and was rapidly losing his anger to fascination and curiosity—for knowledge was an addictive drug, and the more he had the more he wanted.

As he sat on his stump, increasingly mesmerized, Artoo pedaled over, silent, just to offer a comforting presence.

"When I first encountered your father," Ben continued, "he was already a great pilot. But what amazed me was how strongly the Force was with him. I took it upon myself to train Anakin in the ways of the Jedi. My mistake was thinking I could be as good a teacher as Yoda. I was not. Such was my foolish pride. The Emperor sensed Anakin's power, and he lured him to the dark side." He paused sadly and looked directly into Luke's eyes, as if he were asking for the boy's forgiveness. "My pride had terrible consequences for the galaxy."

Luke was entranced. That Obi-Wan's hubris could have caused his father's fall was horrible. Horrible because of what his father had needlessly become, horrible because Obi-Wan wasn't perfect, wasn't even a perfect Jedi, horrible because the dark side could strike so close to home, could turn such right so wrong. Darth Vader must yet have a spark of Anakin Skywalker deep inside. "There is still good in him," he declared.

Ben shook his head remorsefully. "I also thought he could be turned back to the good side. It couldn't be done. He is more machine, now, than man—twisted, and evil."

Luke sensed the underlying meaning in Kenobi's statement, he heard the words as a command. He shook his head back at the vision. "I can't kill my own father."

"You should not think of that machine as your father." It was the teacher speaking again. "When I saw what had become of him, I tried to dissuade him, to draw him back from the dark side. We fought . . . your father fell into a molten pit. When your father clawed his way out of that fiery pool, the change had been burned into him forever—he was Darth Vader, without a trace of Anakin Skywalker. Irredeemably dark. Scarred. Kept alive only by machinery and his own black will . . .''

Luke looked down at his own mechanical right hand. "I tried to stop him once. I couldn't do it." He would not challenge his father again. He could not.

"Vader humbled you when first you met him, Luke—but that experience was *part* of your training. It taught you, among other things, the value of patience. Had you not been so impatient to defeat Vader *then*, you could have finished your training here with Yoda. You would have been prepared."

"But I had to help my friends."

"And did you help them? It was *they* who had to save *you*. You achieved little by rushing back prematurely, I fear."

Luke's indignation melted, leaving only sadness in its wake. "I found out Darth Vader was my father," he whispered.

"To be a Jedi, Luke, you must confront and then go beyond the dark side—the side your father couldn't get past. Impatience is the easiest door—for you, like your father. Only, your father was seduced by what he found on the other side of the door, and you have held firm. You're no longer so reckless now, Luke. You are strong and patient. And you are ready for your final confrontation."

Luke shook his head again, as the implications of the old Jedi's speech became clear. "I can't do it, Ben."

Obi-Wan Kenobi's shoulders slumped in defeat. "Then the Emperor has already won. You were our only hope."

Luke reached for alternatives. "Yoda said I could train another to . . .''

"The other he spoke of is your twin sister," the old man offered a dry smile. "She will find it no easier than you to destroy Darth Vader."

Luke was visibly jolted by this information. He stood up to face this spirit. "Sister? I don't have a sister."

Once again Obi-Wan put a gentle inflection in his voice, to soothe the turmoil brewing in his young friend's soul. "To protect you both against the Emperor, you were separated when you were born. The Emperor knew, as I did, that one day, with the Force on their side, Skywalker's offspring would be a threat to him. For that reason, your sister has remained safely anonymous."

Luke resisted this knowledge at first. He neither needed nor wanted a twin. He was unique! He had no missing parts—save the hand whose mechanical replacement he now flexed tightly. Pawn in a castle conspiracy? Cribs mixed, siblings switched and parted and whisked away to different secret lives? Impossible. He knew who he was! He was Luke Skywalker, born to a Jedi-turned-Sithlord, raised on a Tatooine sandfarm by Uncle Owen and Aunt Beru, raised in a life without frills, a hardworking honest pauper—because his mother . . . his mother . . . What was it about his mother? What had she said, who was she? What had she told him? He turned his mind inward, to a place and time far from the damp soil of Dagobah, to his mother's chamber, his mother and his . . . sister. His sister . . .

"Leia! Leia is my sister," he exclaimed, nearly falling over the stump.

"Your insight serves you well," Ben nodded. He quickly became stern, though. "Bury your feelings deep down, Luke. They do you credit, but they could be made to serve the Emperor."

Luke tried to comprehend what his old teacher was saying. So much information, so fast, so vital . . . it almost made him swoon.

Ben continued his narrative. "When your father left, he didn't know your mother was pregnant. Your mother and I knew he would find out eventually, but we wanted to keep you both as safe as possible, for as long as possible. So I took you to live with my brother Owen, on Tatooine . . . and your mother took Leia to live as the daughter of Senator Organa, on Alderaan."

Luke settled down to hear this tale, as Artoo nestled up beside him, humming in a subaudible register to comfort.

Ben, too, kept his voice even, so that the sounds could give solace when the words did not. "The Organa family was highborn and politically quite powerful in that system. Leia became a princess by virtue of lineage—no one knew she'd been adopted, of course. But it was a title without real power, since Alderaan had long been a democracy. Even so, the family continued to be politically powerful, and Leia, following in her foster father's path, became a senator as well. That's not all she became, of course—she became the leader of her cell in the Alliance against the corrupt Empire. And because she had diplomatic immunity, she was a vital link for getting information to the Rebel cause.

"That's what she was doing when her path crossed yours—for her foster parents had always told her to contact *me* on Tatooine, if her troubles became desperate."

Luke tried sorting through his multiplicity of feelings—the love he'd always felt for Leia, even from afar, now had a clear basis. But suddenly he was feeling protective toward her as well, like an older brother—even though, for all he knew, she might have been his elder by several minutes.

"But you can't let her get involved now, Ben," he insisted "Vader will destroy her." Vader. Their father. Perhaps Leia *could* resurrect the good in him.

"She hasn't been trained in the ways of the Jedi the way you have, Luke—but the Force is strong with her, as it is with all of your family. That is why her path crossed mine—because the Force in her must be nourished by a Jedi. You're the last Jedi, now, Luke . . . but she returned to us—to me—to learn, and grow. Because it was her destiny to learn and grow; and mine to teach."

He went on more slowly, each word deliberate, each pause emphatic. "You cannot escape your destiny, Luke." He locked his eyes on Luke's eyes, and put as much of his spirit as he could into the gaze, to leave it forever imprinted on Luke's mind. "Keep your sister's identity secret, for if you fail she is truly our last hope. Gaze on me now, Luke—the coming fight is yours alone, but much will depend on its outcome, and it may be that you can draw some strength from my memory. There is no avoiding the battle, though—you can't escape your destiny. You will have to face Darth Vader again . . ."

IV

DARTH Vader stepped out of the long, cylindrical chamber into what had been the Death Star control room, and now was the Emperor's throne room. Two royal guards stood either side of the door, red robes from neck to toe, red helmets covering all but eyeslits that were actually electrically modified view-screens. Their weapons were always drawn.

The room was dim except for the light cables running either

side of the elevator shaft, carrying power and information through the space station. Vader walked across the sleek black steel floor, past the humming giant converter engines, up the short flight of steps to the platform level upon which sat the Emperor's throne. Beneath this platform, off to the right, was the mouth of the shaft that delved deeply into the pit of the battle station, down to the very core of the power unit. The chasm was black, and reeked of ozone, and echoed continuously in a low, hollow rumble.

At the end of the overhanging platform was a wall, in the wall, a huge, circular observation window. Sitting in an elaborate control-chair before the window, staring out into space, was the Emperor.

The uncompleted half of the Death Star could be seen immediately beyond the window, shuttles and transports buzzing around it, men with tight-suits and rocket-packs doing exterior construction or surface work. In the near-distance beyond all this activity was the jade green moon Endor, resting like a jewel on the black velvet of space—and scattered to infinity, the gleaming diamonds that were the stars.

The Emperor sat, regarding this view, as Vader approached from behind. The Lord of the Sith kneeled and waited. The Emperor let him wait. He perused the vista before him with a sense of glory beyond all reckoning: this was all his. And more glorious still, all his by his own hand.

For it wasn't always so. Back in the days when he was merely Senator Palpatine, the galaxy had been a Republic of stars, cared for and protected by the Jedi Knighthood that had watched over it for centuries. But inevitably it had grown too large—too massive a bureaucracy had been required, over too many years, in order to maintain the Republic. Corruption had set in.

A few greedy senators had started the chain reaction of malaise, some said; but who could know? A few perverted bureaucrats, arrogant, self-serving—and suddenly a fever was in the stars. Governor turned on governor, values eroded, trusts were broken—fear had spread like an epidemic in those early years, rapidly and without visible cause, and no one knew what was happening, or why.

And so Senator Palpatine had seized the moment. Through fraud, clever promises, and astute political maneuvering, he'd managed to get himself elected head of the Council. And then through subterfuge, bribery and terror, he'd named himself Emperor.

Emperor. It had a certain ring to it. The Republic had crumbled, the Empire was resplendent with its own fires, and would always be so—for the Emperor knew what others refused to believe: the dark forces were the strongest.

He'd known this all along, in his heart of hearts—but relearned it every day: from traitorous lieutenants who betrayed their superiors for favors; from weak-principled functionaries who gave him the secrets of local star systems' governments; from greedy landlords, and sadistic gangsters, and power-hungry politicians. No one was immune, they all craved the dark energy at their core. The Emperor had simply recognized this truth, and utilized it—for his own aggrandizement, of course.

For his soul was the black center of the Empire.

He contemplated the dense impenetrability of the deep space beyond the window. Densely black as his soul—as if he *were*, in some real way, this blackness; as if his inner spirit was itself this void over which he reigned. He smiled at the thought: he *was* the Empire; he *was* the Universe.

Behind him, he sensed Vader still waiting in genuflection. How long had the Dark Lord been there? Five minutes? Ten? The Emperor was uncertain. No matter. The Emperor had not quite finished his meditation.

Lord Vader did not mind waiting, though, nor was he even aware of it. For it was an honor, and a noble activity, to kneel at his ruler's feet. He kept his eyes inward, seeking reflection in his own bottomless core. His power was great, now, greater than it had ever been. It shimmered from within, and resonated with the waves of darkness that flowed from the Emperor. He felt engorged with this power, it surged like black fire, demon electrons looking for ground . . . but he would wait. For his Emperor was not ready; and his son was not ready, and the time was not yet. So he waited.

Finally the chair slowly rotated until the Emperor faced Vader.

Vader spoke first. "What is thy bidding, my master?"

"Send the fleet to the far side of Endor. There it will stay until called for."

"And what of the reports of the Rebel fleet massing near Sullust?"

"It is of no concern. Soon the Rebellion will be crushed and young Skywalker will be one of us. Your work here is finished, my friend. Go out to the command ship and await my orders."

"Yes, my master." He hoped he would be given command

over the destruction of the Rebel Alliance. He hoped it would
be soon.

He rose and exited, as the Emperor turned back to the galactic
panorama beyond the window, to view his domain.

In a remote and midnight vacuum beyond the edge of the
galaxy, the vast Rebel fleet stretched, from its vanguard to its
rear echelon, past the range of human vision. Corellian battle
ships, cruisers, destroyers, carriers, bombers, Sullustian cargo
freighters, Calamarian tankers, Alderaanian gunships, Kesse-
lian blockade runners, Bestinian skyhoppers, X-wing, Y-wing,
and A-wing fighters, shuttles, transport vehicles, manowars.
Every Rebel in the galaxy, soldier and civilian alike, waited
tensely in these ships for instructions. They were led by the
largest of the Rebel Star Cruisers, the *Headquarters Frigate*.

Hundreds of Rebel commanders, of all species and lifeforms,
assembled in the war room of the giant Star Cruiser, awaiting
orders from the High Command. Rumors were everywhere, and
an air of excitement spread from squadron to squadron.

At the center of the briefing room was a large, circular light-
table, projected above which a holographic image of the unfinished Imperial Death Star hovered beside the Moon of Endor,
whose scintillating protective deflector shield encompassed them
both.

Mon Mothma entered the room. A stately, beautiful woman
of middle age, she seemed to walk above the murmurs of the
crowd. She wore white robes with gold braiding, and her sever-
ity was not without cause—for she was the elected leader of the
Rebel Alliance.

Like Leia's adopted father—like Palpatine the Emperor himself—Mon Mothma had been a senior senator of the Republic,
a member of the High Council. When the Republic had begun
to crumble, Mon Mothma had remained a senator until the
end, organizing dissent, stabilizing the increasingly ineffectual
government.

She had organized cells, too, toward the end. Pockets of
resistance, each of which was unaware of the identity of the
others—each of which was responsible for inciting revolt against
the Empire when it finally made itself manifest.

There had been other leaders, but many were killed when the
Empire's first Death Star annihilated the planet Alderaan. Leia's
adopted father died in that calamity.

Mon Mothma went underground. She joined her political cells

with the thousands of guerrillas and insurgents the Empire's cruel dictatorship had spawned. Thousands more joined this Rebel Alliance. Mon Mothma became the acknowledged leader of all the galaxy's creatures who had been left homeless by the Emperor. Homeless, but not without hope.

She traversed the room, now, to the holographic display where she conferred with her two chief advisors, General Madine and Admiral Ackbar. Madine was Corellian—tough, resourceful, if a bit of a martinet. Ackbar was pure Calamarian—a gentle, salmon-colored creature, with huge, sad eyes set in a high-domed head, and webbed hands that made him more at home in water or free space than on board a ship. But if the humans were the arm of the Rebellion, the Calamarians were the soul—which isn't to say they couldn't fight with the best, when pushed to the limit. And the evil Empire had reached that limit.

Lando Calrissian made his way through the crowd, now, scanning faces. He saw Wedge, who was to be his wing pilot—they nodded at each other, gave the thumbs-up sign; but then Lando moved on. Wedge wasn't the one he was looking for. He made it to a clearing near the center, peered around, finally saw his friends standing by a side door. He smiled and wandered over.

Han, Chewie, Leia, and the two droids greeted Lando's appearance with a cacophony of cheers, laughs, beeps, and barks.

"Well, look at you," Solo chided, straightening the lapel of Calrissian's new uniform and pulling on the insignias: "A general!"

Lando laughed affectionately. "I'm a man of many faces and many costumes. Someone must have told them about my little maneuver at the battle of Taanab." Taanab was an agrarian planet raided seasonally by bandits from Norulac. Calrissian—before his stint as governor of Cloud City—had wiped out the bandits against all odds, using legendary flying and unheard of strategies. And he'd done it on a bet.

Han opened his eyes wide with sarcasm. "Hey, don't look at me. I just told them you were a 'fair' pilot. I had no idea they were looking for someone to lead this crazy attack."

"That's all right, I asked for it. I *want* to lead this attack." For one thing, he *liked* dressing up like a general. People gave him the respect he deserved, and he didn't have to give up flying circles around some pompous Imperial military policeman. And that was the other thing—he was finally going to stick it to this Imperial navy, stick it so it hurt, for all the times he'd been stuck.

Stick it and leave his signature on it. *General* Calrissian, thank you.

Solo looked at his old friend, admiration combined with disbelief. "Have you ever seen one of those Death Stars? You're in for a very short generalship, old buddy."

"I'm surprised they didn't ask you to do it," Lando smiled.

"Maybe they did," Han intimated. "But I'm not crazy. You're the respectable one, remember? Baron-Administrator of the Bespin Cloud City?"

Leia moved closer to Solo and took his arm protectively. "Han is going to stay on the command ship with me . . . we're both very grateful for what you're doing, Lando. And proud."

Suddenly, at the center of the room, Mon Mothma signaled for attention. The room fell silent. Anticipation was keen.

"The data brought to us by the Bothan spies have been confirmed," the supreme leader announced. "The Emperor has made a critical error, and the time for our attack has come."

This caused a great stir in the room. As if her message had been a valve letting off pressure, the air hissed with comment. She turned to the hologram of the Death Star, and went on. "We now have the exact location of the Emperor's new battle station. The weapon systems on this Death Star are not yet operational. With the Imperial fleet spread throughout the galaxy in a vain effort to engage us, it is relatively unprotected." She paused here, to let her next statement register its full effect. "Most important, we have learned the Emperor himself is personally overseeing the construction."

A volley of spirited chatter erupted from the assembly. This was it. The chance. The hope no one could hope to hope for. A shot at the Emperor.

Mon Mothma continued when the hubbub died down slightly. "His trip was undertaken in the utmost secrecy, but he underestimated our spy network. Many Bothans died to bring us this information." Her voice turned suddenly stern again to remind them of the price of this enterprise.

Admiral Ackbar stepped forward. His specialty was Imperial defense procedures. He raised his fin and pointed at the holographic model of the force field emanating from Endor. "Although uncompleted, the Death Star is not entirely without a defense mechanism," he instructed in soothing Calamarian tones. "It is protected by an energy shield which is generated by the nearby Moon of Endor, here. No ship can fly through it, no weapon can penetrate it." He stopped for a long moment.

He wanted the information to sink in. When he thought it had, he spoke more slowly. "The shield must be deactivated if *any* attack is to be attempted. Once the shield is down, the cruisers will create a perimeter while the fighters fly into the superstructure, here . . . and attempt to hit the main reactor . . ." he pointed to the unfinished portion of the Death Star ". . . somewhere in here."

Another murmur swept over the room of commanders, like a swell in a heavy sea.

Ackbar concluded. "General Calrissian will lead the fighter attack."

Han turned to Lando, his doubts gilded with respect. "Good luck, buddy."

"Thanks," said Lando simply.

"You're gonna need it."

Admiral Ackbar yielded the floor to General Madine, who was in charge of covert operations. "We have acquired a small Imperial shuttle," Madine declared smugly. "Under this guise, a strike team will land on the moon and deactivate the shield generator. The control bunker is well guarded, but a small squad should be able to penetrate its security."

This news stimulated another round of general mumbling.

Leia turned to Han and said under her breath, "I wonder who they found to pull that one off?"

Madine called out: "General Solo, is your strike team assembled?"

Leia looked up at Han, shock quickly melting to joyous admiration. She knew there was a reason she loved him—in spite of his usual crass insensitivity and oafish bravado. Beneath it all, he had heart.

Moreover, a change *had* come over him since he emerged from carbonization. He wasn't just a loner anymore, only in this for the money. He had lost his solitary edge and had somehow, subtly, become part of the whole. He was actually doing something for someone else, now, and that fact moved Leia greatly. Madine had called him *General*; that meant Han had let himself officially become a member of the army. A part of the whole.

Solo responded to Madine. "My squad is ready, sir, but I need a command crew for the shuttle." He looked questioningly at Chewbacca, and spoke in a lower voice. "It's gonna be rough, old pal. I didn't want to speak for you."

"Roo roowfl," Chewie shook his head with gruff love, and raised his hairy paw.

"That's one," Han called.

"Here's two!" Leia shouted, sticking her arm in the air. Then softly, to Solo: "I'm not letting you out of my sight again, Your Generalship."

"And I'm with you, too!" a voice was raised from the back of the room.

They all turned their heads to see Luke standing at the top of the stairs.

Cheers went up for the last of the Jedi.

And though it wasn't his style, Han was unable to conceal his joy. "That's three," he smiled.

Leia ran up to Luke and hugged him warmly. She felt a special closeness to him all of a sudden, which she attributed to the gravity of the moment, the import of their mission. But then she sensed a change in him, too, a difference of substance that seemed to radiate from his very core—something that she alone could see.

"What is it, Luke?" she whispered. She suddenly wanted to hold him; she could not have said why.

"Nothing. I'll tell you someday," he murmured quietly. It was distinctly not nothing, though.

"All right," she answered, not pushing. "I'll wait." She wondered. Maybe he was just dressed differently—that was probably it. Suited up all in black now—it made him look older. Older, that was it.

Han, Chewie, Lando, Wedge, and several others crowded around Luke all at once, with greetings and diverse sorts of hubbub. The assembly as a whole broke up into multiple such small groups. It was a time for last farewells and good graces.

Artoo beeped a singsong little observation to a somewhat less sanguine Threepio.

"I don't think 'exciting' is the right word," the golden droid answered. Being a translator in his master program, of course, Threepio was most concerned with locating the right word to describe the present situation.

The *Millennium Falcon* rested in the main docking bay of the Rebel Star Cruiser, getting loaded and serviced. Just beyond it sat the stolen Imperial shuttle, looking anomalous in the midst of all the Rebel X-wing fighters.

Chewie supervised the final transfer of weapons and supplies to the shuttle and oversaw the placement of the strike team. Han stood with Lando between the two ships, saying good-bye—for all they knew, forever.

"I mean it, take her!" Solo insisted, indicating the *Falcon*. "She'll bring you luck. You *know* she's the fastest ship in the whole fleet, now." Han had really souped her up after winning her from Lando. She'd always been fast, but now she was much faster. And the modifications Solo added had really made the *Falcon* a part of him—he'd put his love and sweat into it. His spirit. So giving her to Lando now was truly Solo's final transformation—as selfless a gift as he'd ever given.

And Lando understood. "Thanks, old buddy. I'll take good care of her. *You* know I always flew her better than you did, anyway. She won't get a scratch on her, with me at the stick."

Solo looked warmly at the endearing rogue. "I've got your word—not a scratch."

"Take off, you pirate—next thing you'll have me putting down a security deposit."

"See you soon, pal."

They parted without their true feelings expressed aloud, as was the way between men of deeds in those times; each walked up the ramp into a different ship.

Han entered the cockpit of the Imperial shuttle as Luke was doing some fine tuning on a rear navigator panel. Chewbacca, in the copilot's seat, was trying to figure out the Imperial controls. Han took the pilot's chair, and Chewie growled grumpily about the design.

"Yeah, yeah," Solo answered, "I don't think the Empire designed it with a Wookiee in mind."

Leia walked in from the hold, taking her seat near Luke. "We're all set back there."

"Rrrwfr," said Chewie, hitting the first sequence of switches. He looked over at Solo, but Han was motionless, staring out the window at something. Chewie and Leia both followed his gaze to the object of his unyielding attention—the *Millennium Falcon*.

Leia gently nudged the pilot. "Hey, you awake up there?"

"I just got a funny feeling," Han mused. "Like I'm not going to see her again." He thought of the times she'd saved him with her speed, of the times he'd saved her with his cunning, or his touch. He thought of the universe they'd seen together, of the shelter she'd given him; of the way he knew her, inside and out. Of the times they'd slept in each other's embrace, floating still as a quiet dream in the black silence of deep space.

Chewbacca, hearing this, took his own longing look at the

Falcon. Leia put her hand on Solo's shoulder, She knew he had special love for his ship and was reluctant to interrupt this last communion. But time was dear, and becoming dearer. "Come on, Captain," she whispered. "Let's move."

Han snapped back to the moment. "Right. Okay, Chewie, let's find out what this baby can do."

They fired up the engines in the stolen shuttle, eased out of the docking bay, and banked off into the endless night.

Construction on the Death Star proceeded. Traffic in the area was thick with transport ships, TIE fighters and equipment shuttles. Periodically, the Super Star Destroyer orbited the area, surveying progress on the space station from every angle.

The bridge of the Star Destroyer was a hive of activity. Messengers ran back and forth along a string of controllers studying their tracking screens, monitoring ingress and egress of vehicles through the deflector shield. Codes were sent and received, orders given, diagrams plotted. It was an operation involving a thousand scurrying ships, and everything was proceeding with maximum efficiency, until Controller Jhoff made contact with a shuttle of the Lambda class, approaching the shield from Sector Seven.

"Shuttle to Control, please come in," the voice broke into Jhoff's headset with the normal amount of static.

"We have you on our screen now," the controller replied into his comlink. "Please identify."

"This is Shuttle *Tydirium*, requesting deactivation of the deflector shield." "Shuttle *Tydirium*, transmit the clearance code for shield passage."

Up in the shuttle, Han threw a worried look at the others and said into his comlink, "Transmission commencing."

Chewie flipped a bank of switches, producing a syncopated series of high-frequency transmission noises.

Leia bit her lip, bracing herself for fight or flight. "Now we find out if that code was worth the price we paid."

Chewie whined nervously.

Luke stared at the huge Super Star Destroyer that loomed everywhere in front of them. It fixed his eye with its glittering darkness, filled his vision like a malignant cataract—but it made more than his vision opaque. It filled his mind with blackness, too; and his heart. Black fear, and a special knowing. "Vader is on that ship," he whispered.

"You're just jittery, Luke," Han reassured them all. "There

are lots of command ships. But, Chewie," he cautioned, "let's keep our distance, without looking like we're keeping our distance."

"Awroff rwrgh rrfrough?"

"I don't know—fly casual," Han barked back.

"They're taking a long time with that code clearance," Leia said tightly. What if it didn't work? The Alliance could do nothing if the Empire's deflector shield remained functioning. Leia tried to clear her mind, tried to focus on the shield generator she wanted to reach, tried to weed away all feelings of doubt or fear she may have been giving off.

"I'm endangering the mission," Luke spoke now, in a kind of emotional resonance with his secret sister. His thoughts were of Vader, though: their father. "I shouldn't have come."

Han tried to buoy things up. "Hey, why don't we try to be optimistic about this?" He felt beleaguered by negativity.

"He knows I'm here," Luke avowed. He kept staring at the command ship out the view-window. It seemed to taunt him. It awaited.

"Come on, kid, you're imagining things."

"Ararh gragh," Chewie mumbled. Even he was grim.

Lord Vader stood quite still, staring out a large view-screen at the Death Star. He thrilled to the sight of this monument to the dark side of the Force. Icily he caressed it with his gaze.

Like a floating ornament, it sparkled for him. A magic globe. Tiny specks of light raced across its surface, mesmerizing the Dark Lord as if he were a small child entranced by a special toy. It was a transcendent state he was in, a moment of heightened perceptions.

And then, all at once, in the midst of the stillness of his contemplation, he grew absolutely motionless: not a breath, not even a heartbeat stirred to mar his concentration. He strained his every sense into the ether. What had he felt? His spirit tilted its head to listen. Some echo, some vibration apprehended only by him, had passed—no, had not passed. Had swirled the moment and altered the very shape of things. Things were no longer the same.

He walked down the row of controllers until he came to the spot where Admiral Piett was leaning over the tracking screen of Controller Jhoff. Piett straightened at Vader's approach, then bowed stiffly, at the neck.

"Where is that shuttle going?" Vader demanded quietly, without preliminary.

Piett turned back to the view-screen and spoke into the comlink. "Shuttle *Tydirium*, what is your cargo and destination?"

The filtered voice of the shuttle pilot came back over the receiver. "Parts and technical personnel for the Sanctuary Moon."

The bridge commander looked to Vader for a reaction. He hoped nothing was amiss. Lord Vader did not take mistakes lightly.

"Do they have a code clearance?" Vader questioned.

"It's an older code, but it checks out," Piett replied immediately. "I was about to clear them." There was no point in lying to the Lord of the Sith. He always knew if you lied; lies sang out to the Dark Lord.

"I have a strange feeling about that ship," Vader said more to himself than to anyone else.

"Should I hold them?" Piett hurried, anxious to please his master.

"No, let them pass, I will deal with this myself."

"As you wish, my Lord." Piett bowed, partly to hide his surprise. He nodded at Controller Jhoff, who spoke into the comlink, to the Shuttle *Tydirium*.

In the Shuttle *Tydirium*, the group waited tensely. The more questions they were asked about things like cargo and destination, the more likely it seemed they were going to blow their cover.

Han looked fondly at his old Wookiee partner. "Chewie, if they don't go for this, we're gonna have to beat it quick." It was a good-bye speech, really; they all knew this pokey shuttle wasn't about to outrun anything in the neighborhood.

The static voice of the controller broke up, and then came in clearly over the comlink. "Shuttle *Tydirium*, deactivation of the shield will commence immediately. Follow your present course."

Everyone but Luke exhaled in simultaneous relief; as if the trouble were all over now, instead of just beginning. Luke continued to stare at the command ship, as if engaged in some silent, complex dialogue.

Chewie barked loudly.

"Hey, what did I tell you?" Han grinned. "No sweat."

Leia smiled affectionately. "Is that what you told us?"

Solo pushed the throttle forward, and the stolen shuttle moved smoothly toward the green Sanctuary Moon.

Vader, Piett, and Jhoff watched the view-screen in the control room, as the weblike deflector grid read-out parted to admit the Shuttle *Tydirium*, which moved slowly toward the center of the web—to Endor.

Vader turned to the deck officer and spoke with more urgency in his voice than was usually heard. "Ready my shuttle. I must go to the Emperor."

Without waiting for response, the Dark Lord strode off, clearly in the thrall of a dark thought.

V

THE trees of Endor stood a thousand feet tall. Their trunks, covered with shaggy, rust bark, rose straight as a pillar, some of them as big around as a house, some thin as a leg. Their foliage was spindly, but lush in color, scattering the sunlight in delicate blue-green patterns over the forest floor.

Distributed thickly among these ancient giants was the usual array of woodsy flora—pines of several species, various deciduous forms, variously gnarled and leafy. The groundcover was primarily fern, but so dense in spots as to resemble a gentle green sea that rippled softly in the forest breeze.

This was the entire moon: verdant, primeval, silent. Light filtered through the sheltering branches like golden ichor, as if the very air were alive. It was warm, and it was cool. This was Endor.

The stolen Imperial shuttle sat in a clearing many miles from the Imperial landing port, camouflaged with a blanket of dead branches, leaves, and mulch. In addition the little ship was thoroughly dwarfed by the towering trees. Its steely hull might have looked incongruous here, had it not been so totally inconspicuous.

On the hill adjacent to the clearing, the Rebel contingent was just beginning to make its way up a steep trail. Leia, Chewie, Han, and Luke led the way, followed in single file by the raggedy, helmeted squad of the strike team. This unit was composed of the elite groundfighters of the Rebel Alliance. A scruffy bunch in some ways, they'd each been hand-picked for initiative, cunning, and ferocity. Some were trained commandos, some paroled criminals—but they all hated the Empire with a passion that exceeded self-preservation. And they all knew this was the crucial raid. If they failed to destroy the shield generator here, the Rebellion was doomed. No second chances.

Consequently, no one had to tell them to be alert as they made their way silently up the forest path. They were, every one, more alert than they had ever been.

Artoo Detoo and See Threepio brought up the rear of the brigade. Artoo's domed pate swiveled 'round and 'round as he went, blinking his sensor lights at the infinitely tall trees which surrounded them.

"Beee-doop!" he commented to Threepio.

"No, I don't think it's pretty here," his golden companion replied testily. "With our luck, it's inhabited solely by droid-eating monsters."

The trooper just ahead of Threepio turned around and gave them a harsh "Shush!"

Threepio turned back to Artoo, and whispered, "Quiet, Artoo."

They were all a bit nervous.

Up ahead, Chewie and Leia reached the crest of the hill. They dropped to the ground, crawled the last few feet, and peered over the edge. Chewbacca raised his great paw, signaling the rest of the group to stop. All at once, the forest seemed to become much more silent.

Luke and Han crawled forward on their bellies, to view what the others were observing. Pointing through the ferns, Chewie and Leia cautioned stealth. Not far below, in a glen beside a clear pool, two Imperial scouts had set up temporary camp. They were fixing a meal of rations and were preoccupied warming it over a portable cooker. Two speeder bikes were parked nearby.

"Should we try to go around?" whispered Leia.

"It'll take time," Luke shook his head.

Han peeked from behind a rock. "Yeah, and if they catch sight of us and report, this whole party's for nothing."

"Is it just the two of them?" Leia still sounded skeptical.

"Let's take a look," smiled Luke, with a sigh of tension about to be released; they all responded with a similar grin. It was beginning.

Leia motioned the rest of the squad to remain where they were; then she, Luke, Han, and Chewbacca quietly edged closer to the scout camp.

When they were quite near the clearing, but still covered by underbrush, Solo slid quickly to the lead position. "Stay here," he rasped, "Chewie and I will take care of this." He flashed them his most roguish smile.

"Quietly," warned Luke, "there might be—"

But before he could finish, Han jumped up with his furry partner and rushed into the clearing.

"—more out there," Luke finished speaking to himself. He looked over at Leia.

She shrugged. "What'd you expect?" Some things never changed.

Before Luke could respond, though, they were distracted by a loud commotion in the glen. They flattened to the ground and watched.

Han was engaged in a rousing fist fight with one of the scouts—he hadn't looked so happy in days. The other scout jumped on his speeder bike to escape. But by the time he'd ignited the engines, Chewie was able to get off a few shots from his crossbow laser. The ill-fated scout crashed instantly against an enormous tree; a brief, muffled explosion followed.

Leia drew her laser pistol and raced into the battle zone, followed closely by Luke. As soon as they were running clear, though, several large laser blasts went off all around them, tumbling them to the ground. Leia lost her gun.

Dazed, they both looked up to see two more Imperial scouts emerge from the far side of the clearing, heading for their speeder bikes hidden in the peripheral foliage. The scouts holstered their pistols as they mounted the bikes and fired up the engines.

Leia staggered to her feet, "Over there, two more of them!"

"I see 'em," answered Luke, rising. "Stay here."

But Leia had ideas of her own. She ran to the remaining rocket speeder, charged it up, and took off in pursuit of the fleeing scouts. As she tore past Luke, he jumped up behind her on the bike, and off they flew.

"Quick, center switch," he shouted to her over her shoulder, over the roar of the rocket engines. "Jam their comlinks!"

As Luke and Leia soared out of the clearing after the Imperials, Han and Chewie were just subduing the last scout. "Hey, wait!" Solo shouted; but they were gone. He threw his weapon to the ground in frustration, and the rest of the Rebel commando squad poured over the rise into the clearing.

Luke and Leia sped through the dense foliage, a few feet off the ground, Leia at the controls, Luke grabbing on behind her. The two escaping Imperial scouts had a good lead, but at two hundred miles per hour, Leia was the better pilot—the talent ran in her family.

She let off a burst from the speeder's laser cannon periodically, but was still too far behind to be very accurate. The explosions hit away from the moving targets, splintering trees and setting the shrubbery afire, as the bikes weaved in and out between massive, imposing branches.

"Move closer!" Luke shouted.

Leia opened the throttle, closed the gap. The two scouts sensed their pursuer gaining and recklessly veered this way and that, skimming through a narrow opening between two trees. One of the bikes scraped the bark, tipping the scout almost out of control, slowing him significantly.

"Get alongside!" Luke yelled into Leia's ear.

She pulled her speeder so close to the scout's, their steering vanes scraped hideously against each other. Luke suddenly leaped from the back of Leia's bike to the back of the scout's, grabbed the Imperial warrior around the neck, and flipped him off. The white-armored trooper smashed into a thick trunk with a bone-shattering crunch, and settled forever into the sea of ferns.

Luke scooted forward to the driver's seat of the speeder bike, played with the controls a few seconds, and lurched forward, following Leia, who'd pulled ahead. The two of them now tore after the remaining scout.

Over hill and under stonebridge they flew, narrowly avoiding collision, flaming dry vines in their afterburn. The chase swung north and passed a gully where two more Imperial scouts were resting. A moment later, *they* swung into pursuit, now hot on Luke and Leia's tail, blasting away with laser cannon. Luke, still behind Leia took a glancing blow.

"Keep on that one!" he shouted up at her, indicating the scout in the lead. "I'll take the two behind us!"

Leia shot ahead. Luke, at the same instant, flared up his retrorockets, slamming the bike into rapid deceleration. The two scouts on his tail zipped past him in a blur on either side, unable to slow their momentum. Luke immediately roared into high velocity again, firing with his blasters, suddenly in pursuit of his pursuers.

His third round hit its mark: one of the scouts, blown out of control, went spinning against a boulder in a rumble of flame.

The scout's cohort took a single glance at the flash, and put his bike into supercharge mode, speeding even faster. Luke kept pace.

Far ahead, Leia and the first scout continued their own high-speed slalom through the barricades of impassive trunks and low-slung branches. She had to brake through so many turns, in fact, Leia seemed unable to draw any closer to her quarry. Suddenly she shot into the air, at an unbelievably steep incline, and quickly vanished from sight.

The scout turned in confusion, uncertain whether to relax or cringe at his pursuer's sudden disappearance. Her whereabouts became clear soon enough. Out of the tree-tops, Leia dove down on him, cannon blasting from above. The scout's bike took the shock wave from a near hit. Her speed was even greater than she'd anticipated, and in a moment she was racing alongside him. But before she knew what was happening, he reached down and drew a handgun from his holster—and before she could react, he fired.

Her bike spun out of control. She jumped free just in time—the speeder exploded on a giant tree, as Leia rolled clear into a tangle of matted vines, rotting logs, shallow water. The last thing she saw was the orange fireball through a cloud of smoking greenery; and then blackness.

The scout looked behind him at the explosion, with a satisfied sneer. When he faced forward again, though, the smug look faded, for he was on a collision course with a fallen tree. In a moment it was all over but the flaming.

Meanwhile, Luke was closing fast on the last scout. As they wove from tree to tree, Luke eased up behind and then drew even with the Imperial rider. The fleeing soldier suddenly swerved, slamming his bike into Luke's—they both tipped precariously, barely missing a large fallen trunk in their path. The scout zoomed under it, Luke over it—and when he came down on the other side, he crashed directly on top of the scout's vehicle. Their steering vanes locked.

The bikes were shaped more or less like one-man sleds, with long thin rods extending from their snouts, and fluttery ailerons for guidance at the tip of the rods. With these vanes locked, the bikes flew as one, though either rider could steer.

The scout banked hard right, to try to smash Luke into an onrushing grove of saplings on the right. But at the last second Luke leaned all his weight left, turning the locked speeders actually horizontal, with Luke on top, the scout on the bottom.

The biker scout suddenly stopped resisting Luke's leftward leaning and threw his own weight in the same direction, resulting in the bikes flipping over three hundred sixty degrees and coming to rest exactly upright once more . . . but with an enormous tree looming immediately in front of Luke.

Without thinking, he leaped from his bike. A fraction of a second later, the scout veered steeply left—the steering vanes separated—and Luke's riderless speeder crashed explosively into the redwood.

Luke rolled, decelerating, up a moss-covered slope. The scout swooped high, circled around, and came looking for him.

Luke stumbled out of the bushes as the speeder was bearing down on him full throttle, laser cannon firing. Luke ignited his lightsaber and stood his ground. His weapon deflected every bolt the scout fired at Luke; but the bike kept coming. In a few moments, the two would meet; the bike accelerated even more, intent on bodily slicing the young Jedi in half. At the last moment, though, Luke stepped aside—with perfect timing, like a master matador facing a rocket-powered bull—and chopped off the bike's steering vanes with a single mighty slash of his lightsaber.

The bike quickly began to shudder; then pitch and roll. In a second it was out of control entirely, and in another second it was a rumbling billow of fire on the forest floor.

Luke snuffed out his lightsaber and headed back to join the others.

Vader's shuttle swung around the unfinished portion of the Death Star and settled fluidly into the main docking bay. Soundless bearings lowered the Dark Lord's ramp; soundless were his feet as they glided down the chilly steel. Chill with purpose were his strides, and swift.

The main corridor was filled with courtiers, all awaiting an audience with the Emperor. Vader curled his lip at them—fools, all. Pompous toadys in their velvet robes and painted faces;

perfumed bishops passing notes and passing judgments among themselves—for who else cared; oily favor-merchants, bent low from the weight of jewelry still warm from a previous owner's dying flesh; easy, violent men and women, lusting to be tampered with.

Vader had no patience for such petty filth. He passed them without a nod, though many of them would have paid dearly for a felicitous glance from the high Dark Lord.

When he reached the elevator to the Emperor's tower, he found the door closed. Red-robed, heavily armed royal guards flanked the shaft, seemingly unaware of Vader's presence. Out of the shadow, an officer stepped forward, directly in Lord Vader's path, preventing his further approach.

"You may not enter," the officer said evenly.

Vader did not waste words. He raised his hand, fingers outstretched, toward the officer's throat. Ineffably, the officer began to choke. His knees started buckling, his face turned ashen.

Gasping for air, he spoke again. "It is the . . . Emperor's . . . command."

Like a spring, Vader released the man from his remote grip. The officer, breathing again, sank to the floor, trembling. He rubbed his neck gently.

"I will await his convenience," Vader said. He turned and looked out the view window. Leaf-green Endor glowed there, floating in black space, almost as if it were radiant from some internal source of energy. He felt its pull like a magnet, like a vacuum, like a torch in the dead night.

Han and Chewie crouched opposite each other in the forest clearing, being quiet, being near. The rest of the strike squad relaxed—as much as was possible—spread out around them in groups of twos and threes. They all waited.

Even Threepio was silent. He sat beside Artoo, polishing his fingers for lack of anything better to do. The others checked their watches, or their weapons, as the afternoon sunlight ticked away.

Artoo sat, unmoving except for the little radar screen that stuck out the top of his blue and silver dome, revolving, scanning the forest. He exuded the calm patience of a utilized function, a program being run.

Suddenly, he beeped.

Threepio ceased his obsessive polishing and looked apprehensively into the forest. "Someone's coming," he translated.

The rest of the squad faced out; weapons were raised. A twig cracked beyond the western perimeter. No one breathed.

With a weary stride, Luke stepped out of the foliage, into the clearing. All relaxed, lowered their guns. Luke was too tired to care. He plopped down on the hard dirt beside Solo and lay back with an exhausted groan.

"Hard day, huh kid?" Han commented.

Luke sat up on one elbow, smiling. It seemed like an awful lot of effort and noise just to nail a couple of Imperial scouts; and they hadn't even gotten to the really tough part yet. But Han could still maintain his light tone. It was a state of grace, his particular brand of charm. Luke hoped it never vanished from the universe. "Wait'll we get to that generator," he retorted in kind.

Solo looked around, into the forest Luke had just come from. "Where's Leia?"

Luke's face suddenly turned to one of concern. "She didn't come back?"

"I thought she was with you," Han's voice marginally rose in pitch and volume.

"We got split up," Luke explained. He exchanged a grim look with Solo, then both of them slowly stood. "We better look for her."

"Don't you want to rest a while?" Han suggested. He could see the fatigue in Luke's face and wanted to spare him for the coming confrontation, which would surely take more strength than any of them had.

"I want to find Leia," he said softly.

Han nodded, without argument. He signaled to the Rebel officer who was second in command of the strike squad. The officer ran up and saluted.

"Take the squad ahead," ordered Solo. "We'll rendezvous at the shield generator at 0-30."

The officer saluted again and immediately organized the troops. Within a minute they were filing silently into the forest, greatly relieved to be moving at last.

Luke, Chewbacca, General Solo, and the two droids faced in the opposite direction. Artoo led the way, his revolving scanner sensing for all the parameters that described his mistress; and the others followed him into the woods.

The first thing Leia was aware of was her left elbow. It was wet. It was lying in a pool of water, getting quite soaked.

She moved the elbow out of the water with a little splash, revealing something else: pain—pain in her entire arm when it moved. For the time being, she decided to keep it still.

The next thing to enter her consciousness were sounds. The splash her elbow had made, the rustle of leaves, an occasional bird chirp. Forest sounds. With a grunt, she took a short breath and noted the grunting sound.

Smells began to fill her nostrils next: humid mossy smells, leafy oxygen smells, the odor of a distant honey, the vapor of rare flowers.

Taste came with smell—the taste of blood on her tongue. She opened and closed her mouth a few times, to localize where the blood was coming from; but she couldn't. Instead, the attempt only brought the recognition of new pains—in her head, in her neck, in her back. She started to move her arms again, but this entailed a whole catalogue of new pains; so once again, she rested.

Next she allowed temperature to waft into her sensorium. Sun warmed the fingers of her right hand, while the palm, in shadow, stayed cool. A breeze drafted the back of her legs. Her left hand, pressed against the skin of her belly, was warm.

She felt . . . awake.

Slowly—reticent actually to witness the damage, since seeing things made them real, and seeing her own broken body was not a reality she wanted to acknowledge—slowly, she opened her eyes. Things were blurry here at ground level. Hazy browns and grays in the foreground, becoming progressively brighter and greener in the distance. Slowly, things came into focus.

Slowly, she saw the Ewok.

A strange, small, furry creature, he stood three feet from Leia's face and no more than three feet tall. He had large, dark, curious, brownish eyes, and stubby little finger-paws. Completely covered, head to foot, with soft, brown fur, he looked like nothing so much as the stuffed baby Wookiee doll Leia remembered playing with as a child. In fact, when she first saw the creature standing before her, she thought it merely a dream, a childhood memory rising out of her addled brain.

But this wasn't a dream. It was an Ewok. And his name was Wicket.

Nor was he exclusively cute—for as Leia focused further, she could see a knife strapped to his waist. It was all he wore, save for a thin leather mantle only covering his head.

They watched each other, unmoving, for a long minute. The

Ewok seemed puzzled by the princess; uncertain of what she was, or what she intended. At the moment, Leia intended to see if she could sit up.

She sat up, with a groan.

The sound apparently frightened the little fluffball; he rapidly stumbled backward, tripped, and fell. "Eeeeep!" he squeaked.

Leia scrutinized herself closely, looking for signs of serious damage. Her clothes were torn; she had cuts, bruises, and scrapes everywhere—but nothing seemed to be broken or irreparable. On the other hand, she had no idea where she was. She groaned again.

That did it for the Ewok. He jumped up, grabbed a four-foot-long spear, and held it defensively in her direction. Warily, he circled, poking the pointed javelin at her, clearly more fearful than aggressive.

"Hey, cut that out," Leia brushed the weapon away with annoyance. That was all she needed now—to be skewered by a teddy bear. More gently, she added: "I'm not going to hurt you."

Gingerly, she stood up, testing her legs. The Ewok backed away with caution.

"Don't be afraid," Leia tried to put reassurance into her voice. "I just want to see what happened to my bike here." She knew the more she talked in this tone, the more at ease it would put the little creature. Moreover, she knew if she was talking, she was doing okay.

Her legs were a little unsteady, but she was able to walk slowly over to the charred remains of the speeder, now lying in a half-melted pile at the base of the partially blackened tree.

Her movement was away from the Ewok, who, like a skittish puppy, took this as a safe sign and followed her to the wreckage. Leia picked the Imperial scout's laser pistol off the ground; it was all that was left of him.

"I think I got off at the right time," she muttered.

The Ewok appraised the scene with his big, shiny eyes, nodded, shook his head, and squeaked vociferously for several seconds.

Leia looked all around her at the dense forest, then sat down, with a sigh, on a fallen log. She was at eyelevel with the Ewok, now, and they once again regarded each other, a little bewildered, a little concerned. "Trouble is, I'm sort of stuck here," she confided. "And I don't even know where here is."

She put her head in her hands, partly to mull over the situation, partly to rub some of the soreness from her temples. Wicket sat down beside her and mimicked her posture exactly—head in paws, elbows on knees—then let out a little sympathetic Ewok sigh.

Leia laughed appreciatively and scratched the small creature's furry head, between the ears. He purred like a kitten.

"You wouldn't happen to have a comlink on you by any chance?" Big joke—but she hoped maybe talking about it would give her an idea. The Ewok blinked a few times—but he only gave her a mystified look. Leia smiled. "No, I guess not."

Suddenly Wicket froze; his ears twitched, and he sniffed the air. He tilted his head in an attitude of keen attention.

"What is it?" Leia whispered. Something was obviously amiss. Then she heard it: a quiet snap in the bushes beyond, a tentative rustling.

All at once the Ewok let out a loud, terrified screech. Leia drew her pistol, jumping behind the log; Wicket scurried beside her and squeezed under it. A long silence followed. Tense, uncertain, Leia trained her senses on the near underbrush. Ready to fight.

For all her readiness, she hadn't expected the laser bolt to come from where it did—high, off to the right. It exploded in front of the log with a shower of light and pine needles. She returned the fire quickly—two short blasts—then just as quickly sensed something behind her. Slowly she swiveled, to find an Imperial scout standing over her, his weapon leveled at her head. He reached out his hand for the pistol she held.

"I'll take that," he ordered.

Without warning, a furry hand came out from under the log and jabbed the scout in the leg with a knife. The man howled in pain, began jumping about on one foot.

Leia dove for his fallen laser pistol. She rolled, fired and hit the scout squarely in the chest, flash-burning his heart.

Quickly the forest was quiet once more, the noise and light swallowed up as if they had never been. Leia lay still where she was, panting softly, waiting for another attack. None came.

Wicket poked his fuzzy head up from under the log, and looked around. "Eeep rrp scrp ooooh," he mumbled in a tone of awe.

Leia hopped up, ran all about the area, crouched, turned her head from side to side. It seemed safe for the time being. She motioned to her chubby new friend. "Come on, we'd better get out of here."

As they moved into the thick flora, Wicket took the lead. Leia was unsure at first, but he shrieked urgently at her and tugged her sleeve. So she relinquished control to the odd little beast and followed him.

She cast her mind adrift for a while, letting her feet carry her nimbly along among the gargantuan trees. She was struck, suddenly, not by the smallness of the Ewok who guided her, but by her own smallness next to these trees. They were ten thousand years old, some of them, and tall beyond sight. They were temples to the life-force she championed; they reached out to the rest of the universe. She felt herself part of their greatness, but also dwarfed by it.

And lonely. She felt lonely here, in this forest of giants. All her life she'd lived among giants of her own people: her father, the great Senator Organa; her mother, then Minister of Education; her peers and friends, giants all . . .

But these trees. They were like mighty exclamation points, announcing their own preeminence. They were here! They were older than time! They would be here long after Leia was gone, after the Rebellion, after the Empire . . .

And then she didn't feel lonely again, but felt a part again, of these magnificent, poised beings. A part of them across time, and space, connected by the vibrant, vital force, of which . . .

It was confusing. A part, and apart. She couldn't grasp it. She felt large and small, brave and timid. She felt like a tiny, creative spark, dancing about in the fires of life . . . dancing behind a furtive, pudgy midget bear, who kept beckoning her deeper into the woods.

It was this, then, that the Alliance was fighting to preserve—furry creatures in mammoth forests helping scared, brave princesses to safety. Leia wished her parents were alive, so she could tell them.

Lord Vader stepped out of the elevator and stood at the entrance to the throne room. The light-cables hummed either side of the shaft, casting an eerie glow on the royal guards who waited there. He marched resolutely down the walkway, up the stairs, and paused subserviently behind the throne. He kneeled, motionless.

Almost immediately, he heard the Emperor's voice. "Rise. Rise and speak, my friend."

Vader rose, as the throne swiveled around, and the Emperor faced him.

They made eye contact from light-years and a soul's breath away. Across that abyss, Vader responded. "My master, a small Rebel force has penetrated the shield and landed on Endor."

"Yes, I know." There was no hint of surprise in his tone; rather, fulfillment.

Vader noted this, then went on. "My son is with them."

The Emperor's brow furrowed less than a millimeter. His voice remained cool, unruffled, slightly curious. "Are you sure?"

"I felt him, my master." It was almost a taunt. He knew the Emperor was frightened of young Skywalker, afraid of his power. Only together could Vader and the Emperor hope to pull the Jedi Knight over to the dark side. He said it again, emphasizing his own singularity. "*I* felt him."

"Strange, that *I* have not," the Emperor murmured, his eyes becoming slits. They both knew the Force wasn't all-powerful—and no one was infallible with its use. It had everything to do with awareness, with vision. Certainly, Vader and his son were more closely linked than was the Emperor with young Skywalker—but, in addition, the Emperor was now aware of a crosscurrent he hadn't read before, a buckle in the Force he couldn't quite understand. "I wonder if your feelings on this matter are clear, Lord Vader."

"They are clear, my master." He knew his son's presence, it galled him and fueled him and lured him and howled in a voice of its own.

"Then you must go to the Sanctuary Moon and wait for him," Emperor Palpatine said simply. As long as things were clear, things were clear.

"He will come to me?" Vader asked eloquently. This was not what he felt. He felt drawn.

"Of his own free will," the Emperor assured him. It must be of his own free will, else all was lost. A spirit could not be coerced into corruption, it had to be seduced. It had to participate actively. It had to crave. Luke Skywalker knew these things, and still he circled the black fire, like a cat. Destinies could never be read with absolute certainty—but Skywalker would come, that was clear. "I have foreseen it. His compassion for you will be his undoing." Compassion had always been the weak belly of the Jedi, and forever would be. It was the ultimate vulnerability. The Emperor had none. "The boy will come to you, and you will then bring him before me."

Vader bowed low. "As you wish."

With casual malice, the Emperor dismissed the Dark Lord. With grim anticipation, Vader strode out of the throne room, to board the shuttle for Endor.

Luke, Chewie, Han, and Threepio picked their way methodically through the undergrowth behind Artoo, whose antenna continued to revolve. It was remarkable the way the little droid was able to blaze a trail over jungle terrain like this, but he did it without fuss, the miniature cutting tools on his walkers and dome slicing neatly through anything too dense to push out of the way.

Artoo suddenly stopped, causing some consternation on the part of his followers. His radar screen spun faster, he clicked and whirred to himself, then darted forward with an excited announcement. "Vrrr dEEP dWP booooo dWEE op!"

Threepio raced behind him. "Artoo says the rocket bikes are right up—oh, dear."

They broke into the clearing just ahead of the others, but all stopped in a clump on entering. The charred debris of three speeder bikes was strewn around the area—not to mention the remains of some Imperial scouts.

They spread out to inspect the rubble. Little of note was evident, except a torn piece of Leia's jacket. Han held it soberly, thinking.

Threepio spoke quietly. "Artoo's sensors find no other trace of Princess Leia."

"I hope she's nowhere near here, now," Han said to the trees. He didn't want to imagine her loss. After all that had happened, he simply couldn't believe it would end this way for her.

"Looks like she ran into two of them," Luke said, just to say something. None of them wanted to draw any conclusions.

"She seems to have done all right," Han responded somewhat tersely. He was addressing Luke, but speaking to himself.

Only Chewbacca seemed uninterested in the clearing in which they were standing. He stood facing the dense foliage beyond, then wrinkled his nose, sniffing.

"Rahrr!" he shouted, plunging into the thicket. The others rushed after him.

Artoo whistled softly, nervously.

"Picking up what?" Threepio snapped. "Try to be more specific, would you?"

The trees became significantly taller as the group pushed on. Not that it was possible to see any higher, but the girth of the trunks was increasingly massive. The rest of the forest was thinning a bit in the process, making passage easier, but giving them the distinct sense that they were shrinking. It was an ominous feeling.

All at once the undergrowth gave way again, to yet another open space. At the center of this clearing, a single tall stake was planted in the ground, from which hung several shanks of raw meat. The searchers stared, then cautiously walked to the stake.

"What's this?" Threepio voiced the collective question.

Chewbacca's nose was going wild, in some kind of olfactory delirium. He held himself back as long as he could, but was finally unable to resist: he reached out for one of the slabs of meat.

"No wait!" shouted Luke. "Don't—"

But it was too late. The moment the meat was pulled from the stake, a huge net sprang up all around the adventurers, instantly hoisting them high above the ground, in a twisting jumble of arms and legs.

Artoo whistled wildly—he was programmed to hate being upside-down—as the Wookiee bayed his regret.

Han peeled a hairy paw away from his mouth, spitting fur. "Great, Chewie. Nice work. Always thinking with your stomach—"

"Take it easy," called Luke. "Let's just figure out how to get out of this thing." He tried, but was unable, to free his arms; one locked behind him through the net, one pinned to Threepio's leg. "Can anyone reach my lightsaber?"

Artoo was bottommost. He extended his cutting appendage and began clipping the loops of the viney net.

Solo, meantime, was trying to squeeze his arm past Threepio, trying to stretch to reach the lightsaber hanging at Luke's waist. They settled, jerkily, as Artoo cut through another piece of mesh, leaving Han pressed face to face with the protocol droid.

"Out of the way, Goldenrod—unh—get off of—"

"How do you think *I* feel?" Threepio charged. There *was* no protocol in a situation like this.

"I don't really—" Han began, but suddenly Artoo cut through the last link, and the entire group crashed out of the net, to the ground. As they gradually regained their senses, sat up, checked to make certain the others were all safe, one by one they realized they were surrounded by twenty furry little creatures, all wearing soft leather hoods, or caps; all brandishing spears.

One came close to Han, pushing a long spear in his face, screeching "eeee wk!"

Solo knocked the weapon aside, with a curt directive. "Point that thing somewhere else."

A second Ewok became alarmed, and lunged at Han. Again, he deflected the spear, but in the process got cut on the arm.

Luke reached for his lightsaber, but just then a third Ewok ran forward, pushing the more aggressive ones out of the way, and shrieked a long string of seeming invective at them, in a decidedly scolding tone. At this, Luke decided to hold off on his lightsaber.

Han was wounded and angry, though. He started to draw his pistol. Luke stopped him before he cleared his holster, with a look. "Don't—it'll be all right," he added. Never confuse ability with appearance, Ben used to tell him—or actions with motivations. Luke was uncertain of these little furries, but he had a feeling.

Han held his arm, and held his peace, as the Ewoks swarmed around, confiscating all their weapons. Luke even relinquished his lightsaber. Chewie growled suspiciously.

Artoo and Threepio were just extracting themselves from the collapsed net, as the Ewoks chattered excitedly to each other.

Luke turned to the golden droid. "Threepio, can you understand what they're saying?"

Threepio rose from the mesh trap, feeling himself for dents or rattles. "Oh, my head," he complained.

At the sight of his fully upright body, the Ewoks began squeaking among themselves, pointing and gesticulating.

Threepio spoke to the one who appeared to be the leader. "Chree breeb a shurr du."

"Bloh wreee dbleeop weeschhreee!" answered the fuzzy beast.

"Du wee sheess?"

"Reeop glwah wrrripsh."

"Shreee?"

Suddenly one of the Ewoks dropped his spear with a little gasp and prostrated himself before the shiny droid. In another moment, all the Ewoks followed suit. Threepio looked at his friends with a slightly embarrassed shrug.

Chewie let out a puzzled bark. Artoo whirred speculatively. Luke and Han regarded the battalion of kow-towing Ewoks in wonder.

Then, at some invisible signal from one of their group, the

small creatures began to chant in unison: "Eekee whoh, eekee whoh, Rheakee rheekee whoh . . ."

Han looked at Threepio with total disbelief. "What'd you *say* to them?"

" 'Hello,' I think," Threepio replied almost apologetically. He hastened to add, "I could be mistaken, they're using a very primitive dialect . . . I believe they think I'm some sort of god."

Chewbacca and Artoo thought that was very funny. They spent several seconds hysterically barking and whistling before they finally managed to quiet down. Chewbacca had to wipe a tear from his eye.

Han just shook his head with a galaxy-weary look of patience. "Well how about using your divine influence to get us out of this?" he suggested solicitously.

Threepio pulled himself up to his full height, and spoke with unrelenting decorum. "I beg your pardon, Captain Solo, but that wouldn't be proper."

"Proper!?" Solo roared. He always knew this pompous droid was going to go too far with him one day—and this might well be the day.

"It's against my programming to impersonate a deity," he replied to Solo, as if nothing so obvious needed explanation.

Han moved threateningly toward the protocol droid, his fingers itching to pull a plug. "Listen, you pile of bolts, if you don't—" He got no farther, as fifteen Ewok spears were thrust menacingly in his face. "Just kidding," he smiled affably.

The procession of Ewoks wound its way slowly into the ever-darkening forest—tiny, somber creatures, inching through a giant's maze. The sun had nearly set, now, and the long criss-crossing shadows made the cavernous domain even more imposing than before. Yet the Ewoks seemed well at home, turning down each dense corridor of vines with precision.

On their shoulders they carried their four prisoners—Han, Chewbacca, Luke, Artoo—tied to long poles, wrapped around and around with vines, immobilizing them as if they were wriggling larvae in some leafy cocoons.

Behind the captives, Threepio, borne on a litter—rough-hewn of branches in the shape of a chair—was carried high upon the shoulders of the lowly Ewoks. Like a royal potentate, he perused the mighty forest through which they carried him—the magnificent lavender sunset glowing between the vinery, the exotic flowers starting to close, the ageless trees, the glistening ferns—and knew that no one before him had ever appreciated these things in just precisely the manner he was now. No one else had his sensors, his circuits, his programs, his memory banks—and so in some real way, he *was* the creator of this little universe, its images, and colors.

And it was good.

VI

THE starry sky seemed very near the treetops to Luke as he and his friends were carried into the Ewok village. He wasn't even aware it was a village at first—the tiny orange sparks of light in the distance he thought initially to be stars. This was particularly true when—dangling on his back, strapped to the pole as he was—the fiery bright points flickered directly above him, between the trees.

But then he found himself being hoisted up intricate stairways and hidden ramps *around* the immense trunks; and gradually, the higher they went, the bigger and cracklier the lights became. When the group was hundreds of feet up in the trees, Luke finally realized the lights were bonfires—*among* the treetops.

They were finally taken out onto a rickety wooden walkway, far too far off the ground to be able to see anything below them but the abysmal drop. For one bleak moment Luke was afraid they were simply going to be pitched over the brink to test their knowledge of forest lore. But the Ewoks had something else in mind.

The narrow platform ended midway between two trees. The first creature in line grabbed hold of a long vine and swung across to the far trunk—which Luke could see, by twisting his head around, had a large cavelike opening carved into its titanic surface. Vines were quickly tossed back and forth across the chasm, until soon a kind of lattice was constructed—and Luke found himself being pulled across it, on his back, still tied to the wooden poles. He looked down once, into nothingness. It was an unwelcome sensation.

On the other side they rested on a shaky, narrow platform until everyone was across. Then the diminutive monkey-bears dismantled the webbing of vines and proceeded into the tree with their captives. It was totally black inside, but Luke had the impression it was more of a tunnel through the wood than an actual cavern. The impression of dense, solid walls was everywhere, like a burrow in a mountain. When they emerged, fifty yards beyond, they were in the village square.

It was a series of wooden platforms, planks, and walkways connecting an extensive cluster of enormous trees. Supported by this scaffolding was a village of huts, constructed of an odd combination of stiffened leather, daub and wattle, thatched roofs, mud floors. Small campfires burned before many of the huts—the sparks were caught by an elaborate system of hanging vines, which funneled them to a smothering point. And everywhere, were hundreds of Ewoks.

Cooks, tanners, guards, grandfathers. Mother Ewoks gathered up squealing babies at the sight of the prisoners and scurried into their huts or pointed or murmured. Dinner smoke filled the air; children played games; minstrels played strange, resonant music on hollow logs, windy reeds.

There was vast blackness below, vaster still, above; but here in this tiny village suspended between the two, Luke felt warmth and light, and special peace.

The entourage of captors and captives stopped before the largest hut. Luke, Chewie, and Artoo were leaned, on their poles, against a nearby tree. Han was tied to a spit, and balanced above a pile of kindling that looked suspiciously like a barbecue pit. Dozens of Ewoks gathered around, chattering curiously in animated squeals.

Teebo emerged from the large structure. He was slightly bigger than most of the others, and undeniably fiercer. His fur was a pattern of light and dark gray stripes. Instead of the usual leathery hood, he wore a horned animal half-skull atop his head, which he'd further adorned with feathers. He carried a stone hatchet, and even for someone as small as an Ewok, he walked with a definite swagger.

He examined the group cursorily, then seemed to make some kind of pronouncement. At that, a member of the hunting party stepped forward—Paploo, the mantled Ewok who seemed to have taken a more protective view toward the prisoners.

Teebo conferred with Paploo for a short time. The discussion soon turned into a heated disagreement, however, with Paploo apparently taking the Rebels' side, and Teebo seemingly dismissing whatever considerations arose. The rest of the tribe stood around watching the debate with great interest, occasionally shouting comments or squeaking excitedly.

Threepio, whose litter/throne had been set down in a place of honor near the stake to which Solo was tied, followed the ongoing argument with rapt fascination. He began to translate once or twice for Luke and the others—but stopped after only a few words, since the debaters were talking so fast, he didn't want to lose the gist of what was being said. Consequently, he didn't transmit any more information than the names of the Ewoks involved.

Han looked over at Luke with a dubious frown. "I don't like the looks of this."

Chewie growled his wholehearted agreement.

Suddenly Logray exited from the large hut, silencing everyone with his presence. Shorter than Teebo, he was nonetheless clearly the object of greater general respect. He, too, wore a half-skull on his head—some kind of great bird skull, a single feather tied to its crest. His fur was striped tan, though, and his face wise. He carried no weapon; only a pouch at his side, and a staff topped by the spine of a once-powerful enemy.

One by one, he carefully appraised the captives, smelling Han, testing the fabric of Luke's clothing between his fingers. Teebo and Paploo babbled their opposing points of view at him, but he seemed supremely uninterested, so they soon stopped.

When Logray came to Chewbacca, he became fascinated, and poked at the Wookiee with his staff of bones. Chewie took exception to this, though: he growled dangerously at the tiny bear-man. Logray needed no further coaching and did a quick back-step—at the same time reaching into his pouch and sprinkling some herbs in Chewie's direction.

"Careful, Chewie," Han cautioned from across the square. "He must be the head honcho."

"No," Threepio corrected, "actually I believe he's their Medicine Man."

Luke was about to intervene, then decided to wait. It would be better if this serious little community came to its own conclusions about them, in its own way. The Ewoks seemed curiously grounded for a people so airborne.

Logray wandered over to examine Artoo Detoo, a most wondrous creature. He sniffed, tapped, and stroked the droid's metal shell, then scrunched up his face in a look of consternation. After a few moments of thought, he ordered the small robot cut down.

The crowd murmured excitedly and backed off a few feet. Artoo's vine binders were slashed by two knife-wielding guards, causing the droid to slide down his pole and crash unceremoniously to the ground.

The guards set him upright. Artoo was instantly furious. He zeroed in on Teebo as the source of his ignominy, and beeping a blue streak, began to chase the terrified Ewok in circles. The crowd roared—some cheering on Teebo, some squeaking encouragement to the deranged droid.

Finally Artoo got close enough to Teebo to zing him with an electric charge. The shocked Ewok jumped into the air, squealed raucously, and ran away as fast as his stubby little legs could carry him. Wicket slipped surreptitiously into the big hut, as the onlookers screeched their indignation or delight.

Threepio was incensed. "Artoo, stop that! You're only going to make matters worse."

Artoo scooted over directly in front of the golden droid, and began beeping a vehement tirade. "Wreee op doo rhee vrrr gk gdk dk whoo dop dhop vree doo dweet . . ."

This outburst miffed Threepio substantially. With a haughty tilt he sat up straight in his throne. "That's no way to speak to someone in my position."

Luke was afraid the situation was well on its way to getting out of control. He called with the barest hint of impatience to his faithful droid. "Threepio, I think it's time you spoke on our behalf."

Threepio—rather ungraciously, actually—turned to the assemblage of fuzzy creatures and made a short speech, pointing from time to time to his friends tied to the stakes.

Logray became visibly upset by this. He waved his staff, stamped his feet, shrieked at the golden droid for a full minute. At the conclusion of his statement, he nodded to several attentive fellows, who nodded back and began filling the pit under Han with firewood.

"Well, what did he say?" Han shouted with some concern.

Threepio wilted with chagrin. "I'm rather embarrassed, Captain Solo, but it appears you are to be the main course at a banquet in my honor. He is quite offended that I should suggest otherwise.''

Before another word could be said, log-drums began beating in ominous syncopation. As one, all the furry heads turned toward the mouth of the large hut. Out of it came Wicket; and behind him, Chief Chirpa.

Chirpa was gray of fur, strong of will. On his head he bore a garland woven of leaves, teeth, and the horns of great animals he'd bested in the hunt. In his right hand he carried a staff fashioned from the longbone of a flying reptile, in his left he held an iguana, who was his pet and advisor.

He surveyed the scene in the square at a glance, then turned to wait for the guest who was only now emerging from the large hut behind him.

The guest was the beautiful young Princess of Alderaan.

"Leia!" Luke and Han shouted together.

"Rahrhah!"

"Boo dEEdwee!"

"Your Highness!"

With a gasp she rushed toward her friends, but a phalanx of Ewoks blocked her way with spears. She turned to Chief Chirpa, then to her robot interpreter.

"Threepio, tell them these are my friends. They must be set free."

Threepio looked at Chirpa and Logray. "Eep sqee rheeow," he said with much civility. "Sqeeow roah meep meeb eerah."

Chirpa and Logray shook their heads with a motion that was unequivocally negative. Logray chattered an order at his helpers, who resumed vigorously piling wood under Solo.

Han exchanged helpless looks with Leia. "Somehow I have a feeling that didn't do us much good."

"Luke, what can we do?" Leia urged. She hadn't expected this at all. She'd expected a guide back to her ship, or at worst a short supper and lodging for the night. She definitely didn't understand these creatures. "Luke?" she questioned.

Han was about to offer a suggestion when he paused, briefly taken aback by Leia's sudden intense faith in Luke. It was something he hadn't really noted before; he merely noted it now.

Before he could speak up with his plan, though, Luke chimed in. "Threepio, tell them if they don't do as you wish, you'll become angry and use your magic."

"But Master Luke, what magic?" the droid protested. "I couldn't—"

"Tell them!" Luke ordered, uncharacteristically raising his voice. There were times when Threepio could test even the patience of a Jedi.

The interpreter-droid turned to the large audience, and spoke with great dignity. "Eemeeblee screesh oahr aish sh sheestee meep eep eep."

The Ewoks seemed greatly disturbed by this proclamation. They all backed up several steps, except for Logray, who took two steps forward. He shouted something at Threepio—something that sounded very in the nature of a challenge.

Luke closed his eyes with absolute concentration. Threepio began rattling on in a terribly unsettled manner, as if he'd been caught falsifying his own program. "They don't believe me, Master Luke, just as I told you . . ."

Luke wasn't listening to the droid, though; he was visualizing him. Seeing him sitting shiny and golden on his throne of twigs, nodding this way and that, prattling on about the most inconsequential of matters, sitting there in the black void of Luke's consciousness . . . and slowly beginning to rise.

Slowly, Threepio began to rise.

At first, he didn't notice; at first, nobody did. Threepio just went right on talking, as his entire litter steadily elevated off the ground. ". . . told you, I told you, I told you they wouldn't. I don't know why you—wha—wait a minute . . . what's happening here? . . ."

Threepio and the Ewoks all realized what was happening at just about the same moment. The Ewoks silently fell back in terror from the floating throne. Threepio now began to spin, as if he were on a revolving stool. Graceful, majestic spinning.

"Help," he whispered. "Artoo, help me."

Chief Chirpa shouted orders to his cowering minions. Quickly they ran forward and released the bound prisoners. Leia, Han, and Luke enfolded each other in a long, powerful embrace. It seemed, to all of them, a strange setting in which to gain the first victory of this campaign against the Empire.

Luke was aware of a plaintive beeping behind him, and turned to see Artoo staring up at a still-spinning Threepio. Luke lowered the golden droid slowly to the ground.

"Thanks, Threepio," the young Jedi patted him gratefully on the shoulder.

Threepio, still a bit shaken, stood with a wobbly, amazed smile. "Why—why—I didn't know I had it in me."

The hut of Chief Chirpa was large, by Ewok standards—though Chewbacca, sitting cross-legged, nearly scraped the ceiling with his head. The Wookiee hunched along one side of the dwelling with his Rebel comrades, while the Chief and ten Elders sat on the other side facing them. In the center, between the two groups, a small fire warmed the night air, casting ephemeral shadows on the earthen walls.

Outside, the entire village awaited the decisions this council would arrive at. It was a pensive, clear night, charged with high moment. Though it was quite late, not an Ewok slept.

Inside, Threepio was speaking. Positive and negative feedback loops had already substantially increased his fluency in this squeaky language; he was now in the midst of an animated history of the Galactic Civil War—replete with pantomime, elocution, explosive sound effects, and editorial commentary. He even mimicked an Imperial walker at one point.

The Ewok Elders listened carefully, occasionally murmuring comments to each other. It was a fascinating story, and they were thoroughly absorbed—at times, horrified; at times, outraged. Logray conferred with Chief Chirpa once or twice, and several times asked Threepio questions, to which the golden droid responded quite movingly—once Artoo even whistled, probably for emphasis.

In the end, though, after a rather brief discussion among the Elders, the Chief shook his head negatively, with an expression of rueful dissatisfaction. He spoke finally to Threepio, and Threepio interpreted for his friends.

"Chief Chirpa says it's a very moving story," the droid explained. "But it really has nothing to do with Ewoks."

A deep and pressing silence filled the small chamber. Only the fire softly crackled its bright but darkling soliloquy.

It was finally Solo—of all people—who opened his mouth to speak for the group. For the Alliance.

"Tell them this, Goldenrod—" he smiled at the droid, with conscious affection for the first time. "Tell them it's hard to translate a rebellion, so maybe a translator shouldn't tell the story. So *I'll* tell 'em.

"They shouldn't help us 'cause we're asking 'em to. They shouldn't even help us 'cause it's in their own interest to—even though it *is*, you know—just for one example, the Empire's tap-pin' a *lot* of energy out of this moon to generate its deflector shield, and that's a lot of energy you guys are gonna be *without* come winter, and I mean you're gonna be hurtin' . . . but never mind that. Tell 'em, Threepio.''

Threepio told them. Han went on.

''But that's not why they should help us. That's why *I* used to do stuff, because it was in my interest. But not anymore. Well, not so much, anyway. Mostly I do things for my *friends*, now—'cause what else is so important? Money? Power? Jabba had that, and you know what happened to him. Okay, okay, the point is—your friends are . . . your *friends*. You know?''

This was one of the most inarticulate pleas Leia had ever heard, but it made her eyes fill with tears. The Ewoks, on the other hand, remained silent, impassive. Teebo and the stoic little fellow named Paploo traded a few muttered words; the rest were motionless, their expressions unreadable.

After another protracted pause, Luke cleared his throat. ''I realize this concept may be abstract—may be difficult to draw these connections,'' he started slowly, ''but it's terribly important for the entire galaxy, for our Rebel force to destroy the Imperial presence here on Endor. Look up, there, through the smoke hole in the roof. Just through that tiny hole, you can count a hundred stars. In the whole sky there are millions, and billions more you can't even see. And they all have planets, and moons, and happy people just like you. And the Empire is destroying all that. You can . . . you could get dizzy just lying on your back and staring up at all the starshine. You could almost . . . explode, it's so beautiful sometimes. And you're part of the beauty, it's all part of the same Force. And the Empire is trying to turn out the lights.''

It took a while for Threepio to finish translating this—he wanted to get all the words just right. When he did eventually stop talking, there was an extensive squeaking among the Elders, rising and falling in volume, ceasing and then resuming again.

Leia knew what Luke was trying to say, but she feared greatly that the Ewoks wouldn't see the connection. It was connected intimately, though, if she could only bridge the gap for them. She thought of her experience in the forest earlier—her sense of oneness with the trees, whose outstretched limbs seemed to touch the very stars; the stars, whose light filtered down like cascading magic. She felt the power of the magic within her, and it resonated around the hut, from being to being, flowing through her again, making her stronger, still; until she felt one with these Ewoks, nearly—felt as if she understood them, knew them; conspired with them, in the primary sense of the word: they breathed together.

The debate wound down, leaving finally another quiet moment in the hut. Leia's respirations quieted, too, in resonance; and with an air of confident serenity, she made her appeal to the council.

"Do it because of the trees," she said.

That's all she said. Everyone expected more, but there was no more; only this short, oblique outburst.

Wicket had been observing these proceedings with increasing concern, from the sidelines. On several occasions it was apparent he was restraining himself with great difficulty from entering the council's discourse—but now he jumped to his feet, paced the width of the hut several times, finally faced the Elders, and began his own impassioned speech.

"Eep eep, meep eek squee . . ."

Threepio translated for his friends: "Honorable Elders, we have this night received a perilous, wondrous gift. The gift of freedom. This golden god . . ."—here Threepio paused in his translation just long enough to savor the moment; then went on—" . . . This golden god, whose return to us has been prophesied since the First Tree, tells us now he will not be our Master, tells us we are free to choose as we will—that we *must* choose; as all living things must choose their own destiny. He has come, Honorable Elders, and he will go; no longer may we be slaves to his divine guidance. We are free.

"Yet how must we comport ourselves? Is an Ewok's love of the wood any less because he can leave it? No—his love is more, because he can leave it, yet he stays. So is it with the voice of the Golden One: we can close our eyes; yet we listen.

"His friends tell us of a Force, a great living spirit, of which we are all part, even as the leaves are things separate yet part of the tree. We know this spirit, Honorable Elders, though we call it not the Force. The friends of the Golden One tell us this Force is in great jeopardy, here and everywhere. When the fire reaches the forest, who is safe? Not even the Great Tree of which all things are part; nor its leaves, nor its roots, nor its birds. All are in peril, forever and ever.

"It is a brave thing to confront such a fire, Honorable Elders. Many will die, that the forest lives on.

"But the Ewoks are brave."

The little bear-creature fixed his gaze on the others in the hut. Not a word was spoken; nonetheless, the communication was intense. After a minute like this, he concluded his statement.

"Honorable Elders, we must aid this noble party not less for the trees, but more for the sake of the *leaves* on the trees. These Rebels are like the Ewoks, who are like the leaves. Battered by the wind, eaten without thought by the tumult of locusts that inhabit the world—yet do we throw ourselves on smoldering fires, that another may know the warmth of light; yet do we make a soft bed of ourselves, that another may know rest; yet do we swirl in the wind that assails us, to send the fear of chaos into the hearts of our enemies; yet do we change color, even as the season calls upon us to change. So must we help our Leaf-brothers, these Rebels—for so has come a season of change upon us."

He stood, still, before them, the small fire dancing in his eye. For a timeless moment, all the world seemed still.

The Elders were moved. Without saying another word, they nodded in agreement. Perhaps they were telepathic.

In any case, Chief Chirpa stood and, without preface, made a brief pronouncement.

All at once drums began to beat throughout the entire village. The Elders jumped up—no longer at all so serious—and ran across the tent to hug the Rebels. Teebo even began to hug Artoo, but thought better of it as the little droid backed off with a low warning whistle. Teebo scurried over to hop playfully on the Wookiee's back instead.

Han smiled uncertainly. "What's going on?"

"I'm not sure," Leia answered out the side of her mouth, "But it doesn't look too bad."

Luke, like the others, was sharing the joyous occasion—whatever it meant—with a pleasant smile and diffuse good will, when suddenly a dark cloud filled his heart, hovered there, nestled a clammy chill into the corners of his soul. He wiped its traces from his visage, made his face a mask. Nobody noticed.

Threepio finally nodded his understanding to Wicket, who was explaining the situation to him. He turned, with an expansive gesture, to the Rebels. "We are now part of the tribe."

"Just what I've always wanted," said Solo.

Threepio continued talking to the others, trying to ignore the sarcastic Star Captain. "The Chief has vowed to help us in any way to rid their land of the evil ones."

"Well, short help is better than no help, I always say," Solo chuckled.

Threepio was once again rapidly overheating his circuits toward the Corellian ingrate. "Teebo says his chief scouts, Wicket and Paploo, will show us the fastest way to the shield generator."

"Tell him thanks, Goldenrod." He just loved irking Threepio. He couldn't help himself.

Chewie let out a righteous bark, happy to be on the move again. One of the Ewoks thought he was asking for food, though, and brought the Wookiee a large slab of meat. Chewbacca didn't refuse. He downed the meat in a single gulp, as several Ewoks gathered, watching in amazement. They were so incredulous at this feat, in fact, they began giggling furiously; and the laughter was so infectious, it started the Wookiee chortling. His gruff guffaws were *really* hilarious to the chuckling Ewoks, so—as was their custom—they jumped on him in a frenzy of tickling, which he returned threefold, until they all lay in a puddle, quite exhausted. Chewie wiped his eyes and grabbed another piece of meat, which he gnawed at a more leisurely pace.

Solo, meanwhile, began organizing the expedition. "How far is it? We'll need some fresh supplies. There's not much time, you know. Give me some of that, Chewie . . ."

Chewie snarled.

Luke drifted to the back of the hut and then slipped outside during the commotion. Out in the square, a great party was going on—dancing, squealing, tickling—but Luke avoided this, too. He wandered away from the bonfires, away from the gaiety, to a secluded walkway on the dark side of a colossal tree.

Leia followed him.

The sounds of the forest filled the soft night air, here. Crickets, skittering rodents, desolate breezes, anguished owls. The perfumes were a mixture of night-blooming jasmine, and pine; the harmonies were strictly ethereal. The sky was crystal black.

Luke stared at the brightest star in the heavens. It looked to be fired from deep within its core by raging elemental vapors. It was the Death Star.

He couldn't take his eyes from it. Leia found him like that.

"What's wrong?" she whispered.

He smiled wearily. "Everything, I'm afraid. Or nothing, maybe. Maybe things are finally going to be as they were meant to be."

He felt the presence of Darth Vader very near.

Leia took his hand. She felt so close to Luke, yet . . . she couldn't say how. He seemed so lost now, so alone. So distant. She almost couldn't feel his hand in hers. "What is it, Luke?"

He looked down at their intertwined fingers. "Leia . . . do you remember your mother? Your real mother?"

The question took her totally by surprise. She'd always felt so close to her adopted parents, it was as if they *were* her real parents. She almost never thought of her *real* mother—that was like a dream.

Yet now Luke's question made her start. Flashes from her infancy assaulted her—distorted visions of running . . . a beautiful woman . . . hiding in a trunk. The fragments suddenly threatened to flood her with emotion.

"Yes," she said, pausing to regain her composure. "Just a little bit. She died when I was very young."

"What do you remember?" he pressed. "Tell me."

"Just feelings, really . . . images." She wanted to let it slide, it was so out of the blue, so far from her immediate concerns . . . but somehow so loud inside, all of a sudden.

"Tell me," Luke repeated.

She felt surprised by his insistence, but decided to follow him with it, at least for the time being. She trusted him, even when he frightened her. "She was very beautiful," Leia remembered aloud. "Gentle and kind—but sad." She looked deeply into his eyes, seeking his intentions. "Why are you asking me this?"

He turned away, peering back up at the Death Star, as if he'd been on the verge of opening up; then something scared him, and he pulled it all in once more. "I have no memory of my mother," he claimed. "I never knew her."

"Luke, tell me what's troubling you." She wanted to help, she knew she could help.

He stared at her a long moment, estimating her abilities, gauging her need to know, her desire to know. She was strong. He felt it, unwaveringly. He could depend on her. They all could. "Vader is here . . . now. On this moon."

She felt a chill, like a physical sensation, as if her blood had actually congealed. "How do you know?"

"I can feel his presence. He's come for me."

"But how could he know we were here? Was it the code, did we leave out some password?" She knew it was none of these things.

"No, it's me. He can feel it when I'm near." He held her by the shoulders. He wanted to tell her everything, but now as he tried, his will was starting to fail. "I must leave you, Leia. As long as I'm here, I endanger the whole group and our mission here." His hands trembled. "I have to face Vader."

Leia was fast becoming distraught, confused. Intimations were rushing at her like wild owls out of the night, their wings brushing her cheek, their talons catching her hair, their harsh whispers thrilling her ear: "Who? Who? Who?"

She shook her head hard. "I don't understand, Luke. What do you mean, you have to face Vader?"

He pulled her to him, his manner suddenly gentle; abidingly calm. To say it, just to say it, in some basic way released him. "He's my father, Leia."

"Your father!?" She couldn't believe it; yet of course it was true.

He held her steady, to be a rock for her. "Leia, I've found something else out. It's not going to be easy for you to hear it, but you have to. You have to know before I leave here because I might not be back. And if I don't make it, you're the only hope for the Alliance."

She looked away, she shook her head, she wouldn't look at him. It was terribly disturbing, what Luke was saying, though she couldn't imagine why. It was nonsense, of course; *that* was why. To call her the only hope for the Alliance if he should die— why, it was absurd. absurd to think of Luke dying, and to think of her being the only hope.

Both thoughts were out of the question. She moved away from him, to deny his words; at least to give them distance, to let her breathe. Flashes of her mother came again, in this breathing space. Parting embraces, flesh torn from flesh . . .

"Don't talk that way, Luke. You have to survive. I do what I can—we all do—but I'm of no importance. Without you . . . I can do nothing. It's you, Luke. I've seen it. You have a power I don't understand . . . and could never have."

"You're wrong, Leia." He held her at arm's length. "You have that power, too. The Force is strong in you. In time you'll learn to use it as I have."

She shook her head. She couldn't hear this. He was lying. She had no power, the power was elsewhere, she could only help and succor and support. What was he saying? Was it possible?

He brought her closer still, held her face in his hands.

He looked so tender now, so giving. Was he giving her the

power? Could she truly hold it? What was he saying? "Luke, what's come over you?"

"Leia, the Force is strong in my family. My father has it, I have it, and . . . my sister has it."

Leia stared full into his eyes again. Darkness whirled there. And truth. What she saw frightened her . . . but now, this time, she didn't draw away. She stood close to him. She started to understand.

"Yes," he whispered, seeing her comprehension. "Yes. It's you, Leia." He held her in his arms.

Leia closed her eyes tightly against his words, against her tears. To no avail. It all washed over her, now, and through her. "I know," she nodded. Openly she wept.

"Then you know I must go to him."

She stood back, her face hot, her mind swimming in a storm. "No, Luke, no. Run away, far away. If he can feel your presence, go away from this place." She held his hands, put her cheek on his chest. "I wish I could go with you."

He stroked the back of her head. "No, you don't. You've never faltered. When Han and I and the others have doubted, you've always been strong. You've never turned away from your responsibility. I can't say the same." He thought of his premature flight from Dagobah, racing to risk everything before his training had been completed, almost destroying everything because of it. He looked down at the black, mechanical hand he had to show for it. How much more would be lost to his weakness? "Well," he choked, "now we're both going to fulfill our destinies."

"Luke, why? Why must you confront him?"

He thought of all the reasons—to win, to lose, to join, to struggle, to kill, to weep, to walk away, to accuse, to ask why, to forgive, to not forgive, to die—but knew, in the end, there was only one reason, now and always. Only one reason that could ever matter. "There's good in him, I've felt it. He won't give me over to the Emperor. I can save him, I can turn him back to the good side." His eyes became wild for just a moment, torn by doubts and passions. "I have to try, Leia. He's our father."

They held each other close. Tears streamed silently down her face.

"Goodbye, dear sister lost, and found. Goodbye, sweet, sweet Leia."

She cried openly, now—they both did—as Luke held her away

and moved slowly back along the planking. He disappeared into the darkness of the tree-cave that led out of the village.

Leia watched him go, quietly weeping. She gave free vent to her feelings, did not try to stop the tears—tried, instead, to feel them, to feel the source they came from, the path they took, the murky corners they cleansed.

Memories poured through her, now, clues, suspicions, half-heard mutterings when they'd thought she was asleep. Luke, her brother! And Vader, her father. This was too much to assimilate all at once, it was information overload.

She was crying and trembling and whimpering all at once, when suddenly Han stepped up and embraced her from behind. He'd gone looking for her, and heard her voice, and came around just in time to see Luke leaving—but only now, when Leia jumped at his touch and he turned her around, did he realize she was sobbing.

His quizzical smile turned to concern, tempered by the heart-fear of the would-be lover. "Hey, what's going on here?"

She stifled her sobs, wiped her eyes. "It's nothing, Han. I just want to be alone for a while."

She was hiding something, that much was plain, and that much was unacceptable. "It's not nothing!" he said angrily. "I want to know what's going on. Now you tell me what it is." He shook her. He'd never felt like this before. He wanted to know, but he didn't want to know what he thought he knew. It made him sick at heart to think of Leia . . . with Luke . . . he couldn't even bring himself to imagine what it was he didn't want to imagine.

He'd never been out of control like this, he didn't like it, he couldn't stop it. He realized he was still shaking her, and stopped.

"I can't, Han . . ." Her lip began to tremble again.

"You can't! You can't tell *me*? I thought we were closer than that, but I guess I was wrong. Maybe you'd rather tell Luke. Sometimes I—"

"Oh, Han!" she cried, and burst into tears once more. She buried herself in his embrace.

His anger turned slowly to confusion and dismay, as he found himself wrapping his arms around her, caressing her shoulders, comforting her. "I'm sorry," he whispered into her hair. "I'm sorry." He didn't understand, not an iota—didn't understand her, or himself, or his topsy-turvy feelings, or women, or the universe. All he knew was that he'd just been furious, and now he was affectionate, protective, tender. Made no sense.

"Please . . . just hold me," she whispered. She didn't want to talk. She just wanted to be held.

He just held her.

Morning mist rose off dewy vegetation as the sun broke the horizon over Endor. The lush foliage of the forest's edge had a moist, green odor; in that dawning moment the world was silent, as if holding its breath.

In violent contrast, the Imperial landing platform squatted over the ground. Harsh, metallic, octagonal, it seemed to cut like an insult into the verdant beauty of the place. The bushes at its perimeter were singed black from repeated shuttle landings; the flora beyond that was wilting—dying from refuse disposal, trampling feet, chemical exhaust fumes. Like a blight was this outpost.

Uniformed troops walked continuously on the platform and in the area—loading, unloading, surveilling, guarding. Imperial walkers were parked off to one side—square, armored, two-legged war machines, big enough for a squad of soldiers to stand inside, firing laser cannons in all directions. An Imperial shuttle took off for the Death Star, with a roar that made the trees cringe. Another walker emerged from the timber on the far side of the platform, returning from a patrol mission. Step by lumbering step, it approached the loading dock.

Darth Vader stood at the rail of the lower deck, staring mutely into the depths of the lovely forest. Soon. It was coming soon; he could feel it. Like a drum getting louder, his destiny approached. Dread was all around, but fear like this excited him, so he let it bubble quietly within. Dread was a tonic, it heightened his senses, honed a raw edge to his passions. Closer, it came.

Victory, too he sensed. Mastery. But laced with something else . . . what was it? He couldn't see it, quite. Always in motion, the future; difficult to see. Its apparitions tantalized him, swirling specters, always changing. Smoky was his future, thunderous with conquest and destruction.

Very close, now. Almost here.

He purred, in the pit of his throat, like a wild cat smelling game on the air.

Almost here.

The Imperial walker docked at the opposite end of the deck,

and opened its doors. A phalanx of stormtroopers marched out in tight circular formation. They lock-stepped toward Vader.

He turned around to face the oncoming troopers, his breathing even, his black robes hanging still in the windless morning. The stormtroopers stopped when they reached him, and at a word from their captain, parted to reveal a bound prisoner in their midst. It was Luke Skywalker.

The young Jedi gazed at Vader with complete calm, with many layers of vision.

The stormtrooper captain spoke to Lord Vader. "This is the Rebel that surrendered to us. Although he denies it, I believe there may be more of them, and I request permission to conduct a wider search of the area." He extended his hand to the Dark Lord; in it, he held Luke's lightsaber. "He was armed only with this."

Vader looked at the lightsaber a moment, then slowly took it from the captain's hand. "Leave us. Conduct your search, and bring his companions to me."

The officer and his troops withdrew back to the walker.

Luke and Vader were left standing alone facing each other, in the emerald tranquillity of the ageless forest. The mist was beginning to burn off. Long day ahead.

VII

"SO," the Dark Lord rumbled. "You have come to me."

"And you to me."

"The Emperor is expecting you. He believes you will turn to the dark side."

"I know . . . Father." It was a momentous act for Luke—to address his father, as his father. But he'd done it, now, and kept himself under control, and the moment was past. It was done. He felt stronger for it. He felt potent.

"So, you have finally accepted the truth," Vader gloated.

"I have accepted the truth that you were once Anakin Skywalker, my father."

"That name no longer has meaning for me." It was a name from long ago. A different life, a different universe. Could he truly once have been that man?

"It is the name of your true self," Luke's gaze bore steadily down on the cloaked figure. "You have only forgotten. I know there is good in you. The Emperor hasn't driven it fully away." He molded with his voice, tried to form the potential reality with the strength of his belief. "That's why you could not destroy me. That's why you won't take me to your Emperor now."

Vader seemed almost to smile through his mask at his son's use of Jedi voice-manipulation. He looked down at the lightsaber the captain had given him—Luke's lightsaber. So the boy was truly a Jedi now. A man grown. He held the lightsaber up. "You have constructed another."

"This one is mine," Luke said quietly. "I no longer use yours."

Vader ignited the blade, examined its humming, brilliant light, like an admiring craftsman. "Your skills are complete. Indeed, you are as powerful as the Emperor has foreseen."

They stood there for a moment, the lightsaber between them. Sparks dove in and out of the cutting edge: photons pushed to the brink by the energy pulsing between these two warriors.

"Come with me, Father."

Vader shook his head. "Ben once thought as you do—"

"Don't blame Ben for your fall—" Luke took a step closer, then stopped.

Vader did not move. "You don't know the power of the dark side. I must obey my master."

"I will not turn—you will be forced to destroy me."

"If that is your destiny." This was not his wish, but the boy was strong—if it came, at last, to blows, yes, he would destroy Luke. He could no longer afford to hold back, as he once had.

"Search your feelings, Father. You can't do this. I feel the conflict within you. Let go of your hate."

But Vader hated no one; he only lusted too blindly. "Someone has filled your mind with foolish ideas, young one. The Emperor will show you the true nature of the Force. He is your master, now."

Vader signaled to a squad of distant stormtroopers as he extinguished Luke's lightsaber. The guards approached. Luke and the Dark Lord faced one another for a long, searching moment. Vader spoke just before the guards arrived.

"It is too late for me, Son."

"Then my father is truly dead," answered Luke. So what was to stop him from killing the Evil One who stood before him now? he wondered.

Nothing, perhaps.

The vast Rebel fleet hung poised in space, ready to strike. It was hundreds of light-years from the Death Star—but in hyperspace, all time was a moment, and the deadliness of an attack was measured not in distance but in precision.

Ships changed in formation from corner to side, creating a faceted diamond shape to the armada—as if, like a cobra, the fleet was spreading its hood.

The calculations required to launch such a meticulously coordinated offensive at lightspeed made it necessary to fix on a stationary point—that is, stationary relative to the point of re-entry from hyperspace. The point chosen by the Rebel command was a small, blue planet of the Sullust system. The armada was positioned around it, now, this unblinking cerulean world. It looked like the eye of the serpent.

The *Millennium Falcon* finished its rounds of the fleet's perimeter, checking final positions, then pulled into place beneath the flagship. The time had come.

Lando was at the controls of the *Falcon*. Beside him, his copilot, Nien Nunb—a jowled, mouse-eyed creature from Sullust—flipped switches, monitored readouts, and made final preparations for the jump to hyperspace.

Lando set his comlink to war channel. Last hand of the night, his deal, a table full of high rollers—his favorite kind of game. With dry mouth, he made his summary report to Ackbar on the command ship. "Admiral, we're in position. All fighters are accounted for."

Ackbar's voice crackled back over the headset. "Proceed with the countdown. All groups assume attack coordinates."

Lando turned to his copilot with a quick smile. "Don't worry, my friends are down there, they'll have that shield down on time . . ." He turned back to his instruments, saying under his breath: "Or this will be the shortest offensive of all time."

"Gzhung Zhgodio," the copilot commented.

"All right," Lando grunted. "Stand by, then." He patted the control panel for good luck, even though his deepest belief was that a good gambler made his own luck. Still, that's what Han's job was this time, and Han had almost never let Lando down. Just once—and that was a long time ago, in a star system far, far away.

This time was different. This time they were going to redefine luck, and call it Lando. He smiled, and patted the panel one more time . . . just right.

Up on the bridge of the Star Cruiser command ship, Ackbar paused, looked around at his generals: all was ready.

"Are all groups in their attack coordinates?" he asked. He knew they were.

"Affirmative, Admiral."

Ackbar gazed out his view-window meditatively at the starfield, for perhaps the last reflective moment he would ever have. He spoke finally into the comlink war channel. "All craft will begin the jump to hyperspace on my mark. May the Force be with us."

He reached forward to the signal button.

In the *Falcon*, Lando stared at the identical galactic ocean, with the same sense of grand moment; but also with foreboding. They were doing what a guerrilla force must never do: engage the enemy like a traditional army. The Imperial army, fighting the Rebellion's guerrilla war, was always losing—unless it won. The Rebels, by contrast, were always winning—unless they lost. And now, here was the most dangerous situation—the Alliance drawn into the open, to fight on the Empire's terms: if the Rebels lost this battle, they lost the war.

Suddenly the signal light flashed on the control panel: Ackbar's mark. The attack was commenced.

Lando pulled back the conversion switch and opened up the throttle. Outside the cockpit, the stars began streaking by. The streaks grew brighter, and longer, as the ships of the fleet roared, in large segments, at lightspeed, keeping pace first with the very photons of the radiant stars in the vicinity, and then soaring through the warp into hyperspace itself—and disappearing in the flash of a muon.

The blue crystal planet hovered in space alone, once again; staring, unseeing, into the void.

The strike squad crouched behind a woodsy ridge overlooking the Imperial outpost. Leia viewed the area through a small electronic scanner.

Two shuttles were being off-loaded on the landing platform

docking ramp. Several walkers were parked nearby. Troops stood around, helped with construction, took watch, carried supplies. The massive shield generator hummed off to the side.

Flattened down in the bushes on the ridge with the strike force were several Ewoks, including Wicket, Paploo, Teebo, and Warwick. The rest stayed lower, behind the knoll, out of sight.

Leia put down the scanner and scuttled back to the others. "The entrance is on the far side of that landing platform. This isn't going to be easy."

"Ahrck grah rahr hrowrowhr," Chewbacca agreed.

"Oh, come on, Chewie," Han gave the Wookiee a pained look. "We've gotten into more heavily guarded places than that—"

"Frowh rahgh rahrahraff vrawgh gr," Chewie countered with a dismissing gesture.

Han thought for a second. "Well, the spice vaults of Gargon, for one."

"Krahghrowf," Chewbacca shook his head.

"Of course I'm right—now if I could just remember how I did it . . ." Han scratched his head, poking his memory.

Suddenly Paploo began chattering away, pointing, squealing. He garbled something to Wicket.

"What's he saying, Threepio?" Leia asked.

The golden droid exchanged a few terse sentences with Paploo; then Wicket turned to Leia with a hopeful grin.

Threepio, too, now looked at the Princess. "Apparently Wicket knows about a back entrance to this installation."

Han perked up at that. "A back door? That's it! That's how we did it!"

Four Imperial scouts kept watch over the entrance to the bunker that half-emerged from the earth far to the rear of the main section of the shield generator complex. Their rocket bikes were parked nearby.

In the undergrowth beyond, the Rebel strike squad lay in wait.

"Grrr, rowf rrrhl brhnnnh," Chewbacca observed slowly.

"You're right, Chewie," Solo agreed, "with just those guards this should be easier than breaking a Bantha."

"It only takes one to sound the alarm," Leia cautioned.

Han grinned, a bit overselfconfidently. "Then we'll have to do this real quietlike. If Luke can just keep Vader off our backs, like you said he said he would, this oughta be no sweat. Just gotta hit those guards fast and quiet . . ."

Threepio whispered to Teebo and Paploo, explaining the problem and the objective. The Ewoks babbled giddily a moment, then Paploo jumped up and raced through the underbrush.

Leia checked the instrument on her wrist. "We're running out of time. The fleet's in hyperspace by now."

Threepio muttered a question to Teebo and received a short reply. "Oh, dear," Threepio replied, starting to rise, to look into the clearing beside the bunker.

"Stay down!" rasped Solo.

"What is it, Threepio?" Leia demanded.

"I'm afraid our furry companion has gone and done something rash." The droid hoped *he* wasn't to be blamed for this.

"What are you talking about?" Leia's voice cut with an edge of fear.

"Oh, no. Look."

Paploo had scampered down through the bushes to where the scouts' bikes were parked. Now, with the sickening horror of inevitability, the Rebel leaders watched the little ball of fur swing his pudgy body up onto one of the bikes, and begin flipping switches at random. Before anyone could do anything, the bike's engines ignited with a rumbling roar. The four scouts looked over in surprise. Paploo grinned madly, and continued flipping switches.

Leia held her forehead. "Oh, no, no, no."

Chewie barked. Han nodded. "So much for our surprise attack."

The Imperial scouts raced toward Paploo just as the forward drive engaged, zooming the little teddy bear into the forest. He had all he could do just to hang on to the handlebar with his stubby paws. Three of the guards jumped on their own bikes, and sped off in pursuit of the hotrod Ewok. The fourth scout stayed at his post, near the door of the bunker.

Leia was delighted, if a bit incredulous.

"Not bad for a ball of fuzz," Han admired. He nodded at Chewie, and the two of them slipped down toward the bunker.

Paploo, meanwhile, was sailing through the trees, more lucky than in control. He was going at fairly low velocity for what the bike could do—but in Ewok-time, Paploo was absolutely dizzy with speed and excitement. It was terrifying; but he loved it. He would talk about this ride until the end of his life, and then his children would tell their children, and it would get faster with each generation.

For now, though, the Imperial scouts were already pulling in sight behind him. When, a moment later, they began firing laser bolts at him, he decided he'd finally had enough. As he rounded the next tree, just out of their sight, he grabbed a vine and swung up into the branches. Several seconds later the three scouts tore by underneath him, pressing their pursuit to the limit. He giggled furiously.

Back at the bunker, the last scout was undone. Subdued by Chewbacca, bound, stripped of his suit, he was being carried into the woods now by two other members of the strike team. The rest of the squad silently crouched, forming a perimeter around the entrance.

Han stood at the door, checking the stolen code against the digits on the bunker's control panel. With natural speed he punched a series of buttons on the panel. Silently, the door opened.

Leia peeked inside. No sign of life. She motioned the others, and entered the bunker. Han and Chewie followed close on her heels. Soon the entire team was huddled inside the otherwise empty steel corridor, leaving one lookout outside, dressed in the unconscious scout's uniform. Han pushed a series of buttons on the inner panel, closing the door behind them.

Leia thought briefly of Luke—she hoped he could detain Vader at least long enough to allow her to destroy this shield generator; she hoped even more dearly he could avoid such a confrontation altogether. For she feared Vader was the stronger of the two.

Furtively she led the way down the dark and low-beamed tunnel.

Vader's shuttle settled onto the docking bay of the Death Star, like a black, wingless carrion-eating bird; like a nightmare insect. Luke and the Dark Lord emerged from the snout of the beast with a small escort of stormtroopers, and walked rapidly across the cavernous main bay to the Emperor's tower elevator.

Royal guards awaited them there, flanking the shaft, bathed in a carmine glow. They opened the elevator door. Luke stepped forward.

His mind was buzzing with what to do. It was the Emperor he was being taken to, now. The Emperor! If Luke could but focus, keep his mind clear to see what must be done—and do it.

A great noise filled his head, though, like an underground wind.

He hoped Leia deactivated the deflector shield quickly, and destroyed the Death Star—now, while all three of them were here, before anything else happened. For the closer Luke came to the Emperor, the more *anythings* he feared *would* happen. A black storm raged inside him. He wanted to kill the Emperor, but then what? Confront Vader? What would his father do? And what if Luke faced his father first, faced him and—destroyed him. The thought was at once repugnant and compelling. Destroy Vader—and then what. For the first time, Luke had a brief murky image of himself, standing on his father's body, holding his father's blazing power, and sitting at the Emperor's right hand.

He squeezed his eyes shut against this thought, but it left a cold sweat on his brow, as if Death's hand had brushed him there and left its shallow imprint.

The elevator door opened. Luke and Vader walked out into the throne room alone, across the unlit ante-chamber, up the grated stairs, to stand before the throne: father and son, side by side, both dressed in black, one masked and one exposed, beneath the gaze of the malignant Emperor.

Vader bowed to his master. The Emperor motioned him to rise, though; the Dark Lord did his master's bidding.

"Welcome, young Skywalker," the Evil One smiled graciously. "I have been expecting you."

Luke stared back brazenly at the bent, hooded figure. Defiantly. The Emperor's smile grew even softer, though; even more fatherly. He looked at Luke's manacles.

"You no longer need these," he added with *noblesse oblige*—and made the slightest motion with his finger in the direction of Luke's wrists. At that, Luke's binders simply fell away, clattering noisily to the floor.

Luke looked at his own hands—free, now, to reach out for the Emperor's throat, to crush his windpipe in an instant . .

Yet the Emperor seemed gentle. Had he not just let Luke free? But he was devious, too, Luke knew. Do not be fooled by appearances, Ben had told him. The Emperor was unarmed. He could still strike. But wasn't aggression part of the dark side? Mustn't he avoid that at all costs? Or could he use darkness judiciously, and then put it away? He stared at his free hands . . . he could have ended it all right there—or could he? He had total freedom to choose what to do now; yet he could not choose.

Choice, the double-edge sword. He could kill the Emperor, he could succumb to the Emperor's arguments. He could kill Vader . . . and then he could even become Vader. Again this thought laughed at him like a broken clown, until he pushed it back into a black corner of his brain.

The Emperor sat before him, smiling. The moment was convulsive with possibilities . . .

The moment passed. He did nothing.

"Tell me, young Skywalker," the Emperor said when he saw Luke's first struggle had taken its course. "Who has been involved in your training until now?" The smile was thin, openmouthed, hollow.

Luke was silent. He would reveal nothing.

"Oh, I know it was Obi-Wan Kenobi at first," the wicked ruler continued, rubbing his fingers together as if trying to remember. Then pausing, his lips creased into a sneer. "Of course, we are familiar with the talent Obi-Wan Kenobi had, when it came to training Jedi." He nodded politely in Vader's direction, indicating Obi-Wan's previous star pupil. Vader stood without responding, without moving.

Luke tensed with fury at the Emperor's defamation of Ben— though, of course, to the Emperor it was praise. And he bridled even more, knowing the Emperor was so nearly right. He tried to bring his anger under control, though, for it seemed to please the malevolent dictator greatly.

Palpatine noted the emotions on Luke's face and chuckled. "So, in your early training you have followed your father's path, it would seem. But alas, Obi-Wan is now dead, I believe; his elder student, here, saw to that—" again, he made a hand motion toward Vader. "So tell me, young Skywalker—who continued your training?"

That smile, again, like a knife. Luke held silent, struggling to regain his composure.

The Emperor tapped his fingers on the arm of the throne, recalling. "There was one called . . . Yoda. An aged Master Jed . . . Ah, I see by your countenance I have hit a chord, a resonant chord indeed. Yoda, then."

Luke flashed with anger at himself, now, to have revealed so much, unwillingly, unwittingly. Anger and self-doubt. He strove to calm himself—to see all, to show nothing; only to be.

"This Yoda," the Emperor mused. "Lives he still?"

Luke focused on the emptiness of space beyond the window behind the Emperor's chair. The deep void, where nothing was.

Nothing. He filled his mind with this black nothing. Opaque, save for the occasional flickering of starlight that filtered through the ether.

"Ah," cried Emperor Palpatine. "He lives not. Very good, young Skywalker, you almost hid this from me. But you could not. And you can not. Your deepest flickerings are to me apparent. Your nakedest soul. That is my first lesson to you." He beamed.

Luke wilted—but a moment. In the very faltering, he found strength. Thus had Ben and Yoda both instructed him: when you are attacked, fall. Let your opponent's power buffet you as a strong wind topples the grass. In time, he will expend himself, and you will still be upright.

The Emperor watched Luke's face with cunning. "I'm sure Yoda taught you to use the Force with great skill."

The taunt had its desired effect—Luke's face flushed, his muscles flexed.

He saw the Emperor actually lick his lips at the sight of Luke's reaction. Lick his lips and laugh from the bottom of his throat, the bottom of his soul.

Luke paused, for he saw something else, as well; something he hadn't seen before in the Emperor. Fear.

Luke saw fear in the Emperor—fear of Luke. Fear of Luke's power, fear that this power could be turned on him—on the Emperor—in the same way Vader had turned it on Obi-Wan Kenobi. Luke saw this fear in the Emperor—and he knew, now, the odds had shifted slightly. He had glimpsed the Emperor's nakedest self.

With sudden absolute calm, Luke stood upright. He stared directly into the malign ruler's hood.

Palpatine said nothing for a few moments, returning the young Jedi's gaze, assessing his strengths and weaknesses. He sat back at last, pleased with this first confrontation. "I look forward to completing your training, young Skywalker. In time, you will call me Master."

For the first time, Luke felt steady enough to speak. "You're gravely mistaken. You will not convert me as you did my father."

"No, my young Jedi," the Emperor leaned forward, gloating, "you will find that it is you who are mistaken . . . about a great many things."

Palpatine suddenly stood, came down from his throne, walked up very close to Luke, stared venomously into the boy's eyes.

At last, Luke saw the entire face within the hood: eyes, sunken like tombs; the flesh decayed beneath skin weathered by virulent storms, lined by holocaust; the grin, a death's-grin; the breath, corrupt.

Vader extended a gloved hand toward the Emperor, holding out Luke's lightsaber. The Emperor took it with a slow sort of glee, then walked with it across the room to the huge circular view-window. The Death Star had been revolving slowly, so the Sanctuary Moon was now visible at the window's curving margin.

Palpatine looked at Endor, then back at the lightsaber in his hand. "Ah, yes, a Jedi's weapon. Much like your father's." He faced Luke directly. "By now you must know your father can never be turned from the dark side. So will it be with you."

"Never. Soon I will die, and you with me." Luke was confident of that now. He allowed himself the luxury of a boast.

The Emperor laughed, a vile laugh. "Perhaps you refer to the imminent attack of your Rebel fleet." Luke had a thick, reeling moment, then steadied himself. The Emperor went on. "I assure you, we are quite safe from your friends here."

Vader walked toward the Emperor, stood at his side, looking at Luke.

Luke felt increasingly raw. "Your overconfidence is your weakness," he challenged them.

"Your faith in your friends is yours." The Emperor began smiling; but then his mouth turned down, his voice grew angry. "Everything that has transpired has done so according to *my* design. Your friends up there on the Sanctuary Moon—they're walking into a trap. And so is your Rebel fleet!"

Luke's face twitched visibly. The Emperor saw this, and really began to foam. "It was *I* who allowed the Alliance to know the location of the shield generator. It is quite safe from your pitiful little band—an entire legion of my troops awaits them there."

Luke's eyes darted from the Emperor, to Vader, and finally to the lightsaber in the Emperor's hand. His mind quivered with alternatives; suddenly everything was out of control again. He could count on nothing but himself. And on himself, his hold was tenuous.

The Emperor kept rattling on imperiously. "I'm afraid the deflector shield will be quite operational when your fleet arrives. And that is only the beginning of my surprise—but of course I don't wish to spoil it for you."

The situation was degenerating fast, from Luke's perspective. Defeat after defeat was being piled on his head. How much could he take? And now another surprise coming? There seemed to be no end to the rank deeds Palpatine could carry out against the galaxy. Slowly, infinitesimally, Luke raised his hand in the direction of the lightsaber.

The Emperor continued. "From here, young Skywalker, you will witness the final destruction of the Alliance—and the end of your insignificant rebellion."

Luke was in torment. He raised his hand further. He realized both Palpatine and Vader were watching him. He lowered his hand, lowered his level of anger, tried to restore his previous calm, to find his center to see what it was he needed to do.

The Emperor smiled, a thin dry smile. He offered the lightsaber to Luke. "You want this, don't you? The hate is swelling in you, now. Very good, take your Jedi weapon. Use it. I am unarmed. Strike me down with it. Give in to your anger. With each passing moment you make yourself more my servant."

His rasping laughter echoed off the walls like desert wind. Vader continued staring at Luke.

Luke tried to hide his agony. "No, never." He thought desperately of Ben and Yoda. They were part of the Force, now, part of the energy that shaped it. Was it possible for them to distort the Emperor's vision by their presence? No one was infallible, Ben had told him—surely the Emperor couldn't see everything, couldn't know every future, twist every reality to suit his gluttony. *Ben*, thought Luke, *if ever I needed your guidance, it is now. Where can I take this, that it will not lead me to ruin?*

As if in answer, the Emperor leered, and put the lightsaber down on the control chair near Luke's hand. "It is unavoidable," the Emperor said quietly. "It is your destiny. You, like your father, are now . . . mine."

Luke had never felt so lost.

Han, Chewie, Leia, and a dozen commandos made their way down the labyrinthine corridors toward the area where the shield generator room was marked on the stolen map. Yellow lights illuminated the low rafters, casting long shadows at each intersection. At the first three turnings, all remained quiet; they saw no guard or worker.

At the fourth cross-corridor, six Imperial stormtroopers stood a wary watch.

There was no way around; the section had to be traversed.

Han and Leia looked at each other and shrugged; there was nothing for it but to fight.

With pistols drawn, they barged into the entryway. Almost as if they'd been expecting an attack, the guards instantly crouched and began firing their own weapons. A barrage of laserbolts followed, ricocheting from girder to floor. Two stormtroopers were hit immediately. A third lost his gun; pinned behind a refrigerator console, he was unable to do much but stay low.

Two more stood behind a fire door, though, and blasted each commando who tried to get through. Four went down. The guards were virtually impregnable behind their vulcanized shield—but *virtually* didn't account for Wookiees.

Chewbacca rushed the door, physically dislodging it on top of the two stormtroopers. They were crushed.

Leia shot the sixth guard as he stood to draw a bead on Chewie. The trooper who'd been crouching beneath the refrigeration unit suddenly bolted, to go for help. Han raced after him a few long strides and brought him down with a flying tackle. He was out cold.

They checked themselves over, accounted for casualties. Not too bad—but it had been noisy. They'd have to hurry now, before a general alarm was set. The power center that controlled the shield generator was very near. And there would be no second chances.

The Rebel fleet broke out of hyperspace with an awesome roar. Amid glistening streamers of light, battalion after battalion emerged in formation, to fire off toward the Death Star and its Sanctuary Moon hovering brightly in the close distance. Soon the entire navy was bearing down on its target, the *Millennium Falcon* in the lead.

Lando was worried from the moment they came out of hyperspace. He checked his screen, reversed polarities, queried the computer.

The copilot was perplexed, as well. "Zhng ahzi gngnohzh. Dzhy lyhz!"

"But how could that be?" Lando demanded. "We've got to be able to get *some* kind of reading on the shield, up or down." Who was conning whom on this raid?

Nien Nunb pointed at the control panel, shaking his head. "Dzhmbd."

"Jammed? How could they be jamming us if they don't know we're . . . coming."

He grimaced at the onrushing Death Star, as the implications of what he'd just said sank in. This was not a surprise attack, after all. It was a spider web.

He hit the switch on his comlink. "Break off the attack! The shield's still up!"

Red Leader's voice shouted back over the headphones. "I get no reading, are you sure?"

"Pull up!" Lando commanded. "All craft pull up!"

He banked hard to the left, the fighters of the Red Squad veering close on his tail.

Some didn't make it. Three flanking X-wings nicked the invisible deflector shield, spinning out of control, exploding in flames along the shield surface. None of the others paused to look back.

On the Rebel Star Cruiser bridge, alarms were screaming, lights flashing, klaxons blaring, as the mammoth space cruiser abruptly altered its momentum, trying to change course in time to avoid collision with the shield. Officers were running from battle stations to navigation controls; other ships in the fleet could be seen through the view-screens, careening wildly in a hundred directions, some slowing, some speeding up.

Admiral Ackbar spoke urgently but quietly into the comlink. "Take evasive action. Green Group steer course for Holding Sector. MG-7 Blue group—"

A Mon Calamari controller, across the bridge, called out to Ackbar with grave excitement. "Admiral, we have enemy ships at Sector RT-23 and PB-4."

The large central view-screen was coming alive. It was no longer just the Death Star and the green moon behind it, floating isolated in space. Now the massive Imperial fleet could be seen flying in perfect, regimental formation, out from behind Endor in two behemoth flanking waves—heading to surround the Rebel fleet from both sides, like the pincers of a deadly scorpion.

And the shield barricaded the Alliance in front. They had nowhere to go.

Ackbar spoke desperately into the comlink. "It's a trap. Prepare for attack."

An anonymous fighter pilot's voice came back over the radio. "Fighters coming in! Here we go!"

The attack began. The battle was joined.

TIE fighters, first—they were much faster than the bulky Imperial cruisers, so they were the first to make contact with the

Rebel invaders. Savage dogfights ensued, and soon the black sky was aglow with ruby explosions.

An aide approached Ackbar. "We've added power to the forward shield, Admiral."

"Good. Double power on the main battery, and—"

Suddenly the Star Cruiser was rocked by thermonuclear fireworks outside the observation window.

"Gold Wing is hit hard!" another officer shouted, stumbling up to the bridge.

"Give them cover!" Ackbar ordered. "We must have time!" He spoke again into the comlink, as yet another detonation rumbled the frigate. "All ships, stand your position. Wait for my command to return!"

It was far too late for Lando and his attack squadrons to heed that order, though. They were already way ahead of the pack, heading straight for the oncoming Imperial fleet.

Wedge Antilles, Luke's old buddy from the first campaign, led the X-wings that accompanied the *Falcon*. As they drew near the Imperial defenders, his voice came over the comlink, calm and experienced. "Lock X-foils in attack positions."

The wings split like dragonfly gossamers, poised for increased maneuvering and power.

"All wings report in," said Lando.

"Red Leader standing by," Wedge replied.

"Green Leader standing by."

"Blue Leader standing by."

"Gray Leader—"

This last transmission was interrupted by a display of pyrotechnics that completely disintegrated Gray Wing.

"Here they come," Wedge commented.

"Accelerate to attack speed," Lando ordered. "Draw fire away from our cruisers as long as possible."

"Copy, Gold Leader," Wedge responded. "We're moving to point three across the axis—"

"Two of them coming in at twenty degrees—" someone advised.

"I see them," noted Wedge. "Cut left, I'll take the leader."

"Watch yourself, Wedge, three from above."

"Yeah, I—"

"I'm on it, Red Leader."

"There's too many of them—"

"You're taking a lot of fire, back off—"

"Red Four, watch out!"

"I'm hit!"

The X-wing spun, sparking, across the starfield, out of power, into the void.

"You've picked one up, watch it!" Red Six yelled at Wedge.

"My scope's negative, where is he?"

"Red Six, a squadron of fighters has broken through—"

"They're heading for the Medical Frigate! After them!"

"Go ahead," Lando agreed. "I'm going in. There're four marks at point three five. Cover me!"

"Right behind you, Gold Leader. Red Two, Red Three, pull in—"

"Hang on, back there."

"Close up formations, Blue Group."

"Good shooting, Red Two."

"Not bad," said Lando. "I'll take out the other three . . ."

Calrissian steered the *Falcon* into the complete flip, as his crew fired at the Imperial fighters from the belly guns. Two were direct hits, the third a glancing blow that caused the TIE fighter to tumble into another of its own squads. The heavens were absolutely thick with them, but the *Falcon* was faster by half than anything else that flew.

Within a matter of minutes, the battlefield was a diffuse red glow, spotted with puffs of smoke, blazing fireballs, whirling spark showers, spinning debris, rumbling implosions, shafts of light, tumbling machinery, space-frozen corpses, wells of blackness, electron storms.

It was a grim and dazzling spectacle. And only beginning.

Nien Nunb made a guttural aside to Lando.

"You're right," the pilot frowned. "Only their fighters are attacking. What are those Star Destroyers waiting for?" Looked like the Emperor was trying to get the Rebels to buy some real estate he wasn't intending to sell.

"Dahng nhng," the copilot warned, as another squadron of TIE fighters swooped down from above.

"I see 'em. We're sure in the middle of it, now." He took a second to glance at Endor, floating peacefully off to his right. "Come on, Han old buddy, don't let me down."

Han pressed the button on his wrist-unit and covered his head: the reinforced door to the main control room blew into melted pieces. The Rebel squad stormed through the gaping portal.

The stormtroopers inside seemed taken completely by surprise. A few were injured by the exploding door; the rest gawked in dismay as the Rebels rushed them with guns drawn. Han took the lead, Leia right behind; Chewie covered the rear.

They herded all the personnel into one corner of the bunker. Three commandos guarded them there, three more covered the exits. The rest began placing the explosive charges.

Leia studied one of the screens on the control panel. "Hurry, Han, look! The fleet's being attacked!"

Solo looked over at the screen. "Blast it! With the shield still up, they're backed against the wall."

"That is correct," came a voice from the rear of the room. "Just as *you* are."

Han and Leia spun around to find dozens of Imperial guns trained on them; an entire legion had been hiding in the wall compartments of the bunker. Now, in a single moment, the Rebels were surrounded—nowhere to run, far too many stormtroopers to fight. Completely surrounded.

More Imperial troops charged through the door, roughly disarming the stunned commandos.

Han, Chewie, and Leia exchanged helpless, hopeless looks. They'd been the Rebellion's last chance.

They'd failed.

Some distance from the main area of battle, coasting safely in the center of the blanket of ships that constituted the Imperial fleet, was the flagship super Star Destroyer. On the bridge, Admiral Piett watched the war through the enormous observation window—curious, as if viewing an elaborate demonstration, or an entertainment.

Two fleet captains stood behind him, respectfully silent; also learning the elegant designs of their Emperor.

"Have the fleet hold here," Admiral Piett ordered.

The first captain hurried to carry out the order. The second stepped up to the window, beside the admiral. "We aren't going to attack?"

Piett smirked. "I have my orders from the Emperor himself. He has something special planned for this Rebel scum." He accented the specialness with a long pause, for the inquisitive captain to savor. "We are only to keep them from escaping."

The Emperor, Lord Vader, and Luke watched the aerial battle rage from the safety of the throne room in the Death Star.

It was a scene of pandemonium. Silent, crystalline explosions surrounded by green, violet, or magenta auras. Wildly vicious dogfights. Gracefully floating crags of melted steel; icicle sprays that might have been blood.

Luke watched in horror, as another Rebel ship toppled against the unseeable deflector shield, exploding in a fiery concussion.

Vader watched Luke. His boy was powerful, stronger than he'd imagined. And still pliable. Not lost yet—either to the sickening, weakly side of the Force, that had to beg for everything it received; or to the Emperor, who feared Luke with reason.

There was yet time to take Luke for his own—to retake him. To join with him in dark majesty. To rule the galaxy together. It would only take patience and a little wizardry, to show Luke the exquisite satisfactions of the dark way and to pry him from the Emperor's terrified clutch.

Vader knew Luke had seen it, too—the Emperor's fear. He was a clever boy, young Luke, Vader smiled grimly to himself. He was his father's son.

The Emperor interrupted Vader's contemplation with a cackled remark to Luke. "As you can see, my young apprentice, the deflector shield is still in place. Your friends have failed! And now . . ." he raised his spindly hand above his head to mark this moment: "Witness the power of this fully armed and operational battle station." He walked over to the comlink and spoke in a gravelly whisper, as if to a lover. "Fire at will, Commander."

In shock, and in foreknowledge, Luke looked out across the surface of the Death Star, to the space battle beyond and to the bulk of the Rebel fleet beyond that.

Down in the bowels of the Death Star, Commander Jerjerrod gave an order. It was with mixed feelings that he issued the command, because it meant the final destruction of the Rebel insurrectionists—which meant an end to the state of war, which Jerjerrod cherished above all things. But second to ongoing war itself Jerjerrod loved total annihilation; so while tempered with regret, this order was not entirely without thrill.

At Jerjerrod's instruction, a controller pulled a switch, which ignited a blinking panel. Two hooded Imperial soldiers pushed a series of buttons. A thick beam of light slowly pulsed from a long, heavily blockaded shaft. On the outer surface of the completed half of the Death Star, a giant laser dish began to glow.

Luke watched in impotent horror, as the unbelievably huge laser beam radiated out from the muzzle of the Death Star. It touched—for only an instant—one of the Rebel Star Cruisers that was surging in the midst of the heaviest fighting. And in the next instant, the Star Cruiser was vaporized. Blown to dust. Returned to its most elemental particles, in a single burst of light.

In the numbing grip of despair, with the hollowest of voids devouring his heart, Luke's eyes, alone, glinted—for he saw, again, his lightsaber, lying unattended on the throne. And in this bleak and livid moment, the dark side was much with him.

VIII

ADMIRAL Ackbar stood on the bridge in stunned disbelief, looking out the observation window at the place where, a moment before, the Rebel Star Cruiser *Liberty* had just been engaged in a furious long-range battle. Now, there was nothing. Only empty space, powdered with a fine dust that sparkled in the light of more distant explosions. Ackbar stared in silence.

Around him, confusion was rampant. Flustered controllers were still trying to contact the *Liberty*, while fleet captains ran from screen to port, shouting, directing, misdirecting.

An aide handed Ackbar the comlink. General Calrissian's voice was coming through.

"Home-One, this is Gold Leader. That blast came from the Death Star! Repeat, the Death Star is operational!"

"We saw it," Ackbar answered wearily. "All craft prepare to retreat."

"I'm not going to give up and run!" Lando shouted back. He'd come a long way to be in this game.

"We have no choice, General Calrissian. Our cruisers can't repel firepower of that magnitude!"

"You won't get a second chance at this, Admiral. Han will have that shield down—we've got to give him more time. Head for those Star Destroyers."

Ackbar looked around him. A huge charge of flak rumbled

the ship, painting a brief, waxen light over the window. Calrissian was right: there would be no second chance. It was now, or it was the end.

He turned to his First Star captain. "Move the fleet forward."

"Yes, sir." The man paused. "Sir, we don't stand much of a chance against those Star Destroyers. They out-gun us, and they're more heavily armored."

"I know," Ackbar said softly.

The captain left. An aide approached.

"Forward ships have made contact with the Imperial fleet, sir."

"Concentrate your fire on their power generators. If we can knock out their shields, our fighters might stand a chance against them."

The ship was rocked by another explosion—a laserbolt hit to one of the aft gyrostabilizers.

"Intensify auxiliary shields!" someone yelled.

The pitch of the battle augmented another notch.

Beyond the window of the throne room, the Rebel fleet was being decimated in the soundless vacuum of space, while inside, the only sound was the Emperor's thready cackle. Luke continued his spiral into desperation as the Death Star laser beam incinerated ship after ship.

The Emperor hissed. "Your fleet is lost—and your friends on the Endor Moon will not survive . . ." He pushed a comlink button on the arm of his throne and spoke into it with relish. "Commander Jerjerrod, should the Rebels manage to blow up the shield generator, you will turn this battle station onto the Endor Moon and destroy it."

"Yes, Your Highness," came the voice over the receiver, "but we have several battalions stationed on—"

"You will destroy it!" the Emperor's whisper was more final than any scream.

"Yes, Your Highness."

Palpatine turned back to Luke—the former, shaking with glee; the latter, with outrage.

"There is no escape, my young pupil. The Alliance will die—as will your friends."

Luke's face was contorted, reflecting his spirit. Vader watched him carefully, as did the Emperor. The lightsaber began to shake on its resting place. The young Jedi's hand was trembling, his lips pulled back in grimace, his teeth grinding.

The Emperor smiled. "Good. I can feel your anger. I am defenseless—take your weapon. Strike me down with all of your hatred, and your journey toward the dark side will be complete." He laughed, and laughed.

Luke was able to resist no longer. The lightsaber rattled violently on the throne a moment, then flew into his hand, impelled by the Force. He ignited it a moment later and swung it with his full weight downward toward the Emperor's skull.

In that instant, Vader's blade flashed into view, parrying Luke's attack an inch above the Emperor's head. Sparks flew like forging steel, bathing Palpatine's grinning face in a hellish glare.

Luke jumped back, and turned, lightsaber upraised, to face his father. Vader extended his own blade, poised to do battle.

The Emperor sighed with pleasure and sat in his throne, facing the combatants—the sole audience to this dire, aggrieved contest.

Han, Leia, Chewbacca, and the rest of the strike team were escorted out of the bunker by their captors. The sight that greeted them was substantially different from the way the grassy area had appeared when they'd entered. The clearing was now filled with Imperial troops.

Hundreds of them, in white or black armor—some standing at ease, some viewing the scene from atop their two-legged walkers, some leaning on their speeder bikes. If the situation had appeared hopeless inside the bunker, it looked even worse now.

Han and Leia turned to each other full of feeling. All they'd struggled for, all they'd dreamed of—gone, now. Even so, they'd had each other for a short while at least. They'd come together from opposite ends of a wasteland of emotional isolation: Han had never known love, so enamored of himself was he; Leia had never known love, so wrapped up in social upheaval was she, so intent on embracing all of humanity. And somewhere between his glassy infatuation for the one, and her glowing fervor for the all, they'd found a shady place where two could huddle, grow, even feel nourished.

But that, too, was cut short, now. The end seemed near. So much was there to say, they couldn't find a single word. Instead, they only joined hands, speaking through their fingers in these final minutes of companionship.

That's when Threepio and Artoo jauntily entered the clearing, beeping and jabbering excitedly to each other. They stopped

cold in their tracks when they saw what the clearing had become
. . . and found all eyes suddenly focused on them.

"Oh, dear," Threepio whimpered. In a second, he and Artoo
had turned around and run right back into the woods from which
they'd just come. Six stormtroopers charged in after them.

The Imperial soldiers were in time to see the two droids duck
behind a large tree, some twenty yards into the forest. They
rushed after the robots. As they rounded the tree, they found
Artoo and Threepio standing there quietly, waiting to be taken.
The guards moved to take them. They moved too slowly.

Fifteen Ewoks dropped out of the overhanging branches,
quickly overpowering the Imperial troops with rocks and clubs.
At that, Teebo—perched in another tree—raised a ram's horn to
his lips and sounded three long blasts from its bell. That was
the signal for the Ewoks to attack.

Hundreds of them descended upon the clearing from all sides,
throwing themselves against the might of the Imperial army with
unrestrained zeal. The scene was unabridged chaos.

Stormtroopers fired their laser pistols at the furry creatures,
killing or wounding many—only to be overrun by dozens more
in their place. Biker scouts chased squealing Ewoks into the
woods—and were knocked from their bikes by volleys of rocks
launched from the trees.

In the first confused moments of the attack, Chewie dove into
the foliage, while Han and Leia hit the dirt in the cover of the
arches that flanked the bunker door. Explosions all around kept
them pinned from leaving; the bunker door itself was closed
again, and locked.

Han punched out the stolen code on the control panel beyond—
but this time, the door didn't open. It had been reprogrammed
as soon as they'd been caught. "The terminal doesn't work
now," he muttered.

Leia stretched for a laser pistol lying in the dirt, just out of
reach, beside a felled stormtrooper. Shots were crisscrossing
from every direction, though.

"We need Artoo," she shouted.

Han nodded, took out his comlink, pushed the sequence that
signaled the little droid and reached for the weapon Leia couldn't
get as the fighting stormed all around them.

Artoo and Threepio were huddled behind a log when Artoo
got the message. He suddenly blurted out an excited whistle and
shot off toward the battlefield.

"Artoo!" Threepio shouted. "Where are you going? Wait for

me!'' Nearly beside himself, the golden droid tore off after his best friend.

Biker scouts raced over and around the scurrying droids, blasting away at the Ewoks who grew fiercer every time their fur was scorched. The little bears were hanging on the legs of the Imperial walkers, hobbling the appendages with lengths of vine, or injuring the joint mechanisms by forcing pebbles and twigs into the hinges. They were knocking scouts off their bikes, by stringing vine between trees at throat level. They were throwing rocks, jumping out of trees, impaling with spears, entangling with nets. They were everywhere.

Scores of them rallied behind Chewbacca, who had grown rather fond of them during the course of the previous night. He'd become their mascot; and they, his little country cousins. So it was with a special ferocity, now, that they came to each other's aid. Chewie was flinging stormtroopers left and right, in a self-less Wookiee frenzy, any time he saw them physically harming his small friends. The Ewoks, for their part, formed equally self-sacrificing cadres to do nothing but follow Chewbacca and throw themselves upon any soldiers who started getting the upper hand with him.

It was a wild, strange battle.

Artoo and Threepio finally made it to the bunker door. Han and Leia provided cover fire with guns they'd finally managed to scrounge. Artoo moved quickly to the terminal, plugged in his computer arm, began scanning. Before he'd even computed the weather codes, though, a laser bolt explosion ripped the entranceway, disengaging Artoo's cable arm, spilling him to the dirt.

His head began to smolder, his fittings to leak. All of a sudden every compartment sprang open, every nozzle gushed or smoked, every wheel spun—and then stopped. Threepio rushed to his wounded companion, as Han examined the bunker terminal.

"Maybe I can hotwire this thing," Solo mumbled.

Meanwhile the Ewoks had erected a primitive catapult at the other side of the field. They fired a large boulder at one of the walkers—the machine vibrated seriously, but did not topple. It turned, and headed for the catapult, laser cannon firing. The Ewoks scattered. When the walker was ten feet away, the Ewoks chopped a mass of restraining vines, and two huge, balanced trunks crashed down on top of the Imperial war wagon, halting it for good.

The next phase of the assault began. Ewoks in kite-like animal-skin hang-gliders started dropping rocks on the stormtroopers, or dive-bombing with spears. Teebo, who led the attack, was hit in the wing with laser fire during the first volley and crashed into a gnarled root. A charging walker clumped forward to crush him, but Wicket swooped down just in time, yanking Teebo to safety. In swerving out of the walker's way, though, Wicket smashed into a racing speeder bike—they all went tumbling into the dense foliage.

And so it went.

The casualties mounted.

High above, it was no different. A thousand deadly dogfights and cannon bombardments were erupting all over the skies, while the Death Star laser beam methodically disintegrated the Rebel ships.

In the *Millennium Falcon*, Lando steered like a maniac through an obstacle course of the giant, floating Imperial Star Destroyers—trading laser bolts with them, dodging flak, outracing TIE fighters.

Desperately, he was shouting into his comlink, over the noise of continuous explosions, talking to Ackbar in the Alliance command ship. "I said *closer*! Move in as close as you can and engage the Star Destroyers at point blank range—that way the Death Star won't be able to fire at us without knocking out its own ships!"

"But no one's ever gone nose to nose at that range, between supervessels like their Destroyers and our Cruisers!" Ackbar fumed at the unthinkable—but their options were running out.

"Great!" yelled Lando, skimming over the surface of the Destroyer. "Then we're inventing a new kind of combat!"

"We know nothing about the tactics of such a confrontation!" Ackbar protested.

"We know as much as *they* do!" Lando hollered. "And they'll *think* we know more!" Bluffing was always dangerous in the last hand: but sometimes, when all your money was in the pot, it was the only way to win—and Lando never played to lose.

"At that close range, we won't last long against Star Destroyers." Ackbar was already feeling giddy with resignation.

"We'll last longer than we will against that Death Star and we might just take a few of them with us!" Lando whooped. With a jolt, one of his forward guns was blown away. He put the *Falcon* into a controlled spin, and careened around the belly of the Imperial leviathan.

With little else to lose, Ackbar decided to try Calrissian's strategy. In the next minutes, dozens of Rebel Cruisers moved in astronomically close to the Imperial Star Destroyers—and the colossal antagonists began blasting away at each other, like tanks at twenty paces, while hundreds of tiny fighters raced across their surfaces, zipping between laser bolts as they chased around the massive hulls.

Slowly, Luke and Vader circled. Lightsaber high above his head, Luke readied his attack from classic first-position; the Dark Lord held a lateral stance, in classic answer. Without announcement, Luke brought his blade straight down—then, when Vader moved to parry, Luke feinted and cut low. Vader counterparried, let the impact direct his sword toward Luke's throat . . . but Luke met the riposte and stepped back. The first blows, traded without injury. Again, they circled.

Vader was impressed with Luke's speed. Pleased, even. It was a pity, almost, he couldn't let the boy kill the Emperor yet. Luke wasn't ready for that, emotionally. There was still a chance Luke would return to his friends if he destroyed the Emperor now. He needed more extensive tutelage, first—training by both Vader *and* Palpatine—before he'd be ready to assume his place at Vader's right hand, ruling the galaxy.

So Vader had to shepherd the boy through periods like this, stop him from doing damage in the wrong places—or in the right places prematurely.

Before Vader could gather his thoughts much further, though, Luke attacked again—much more aggressively. He advanced in a flurry of lunges, each met with a loud crack of Vader's phosphorescent saber. The Dark Lord retreated a step at every slash, swiveling once to bring his cutting beam up viciously—but Luke batted it away, pushing Vader back yet again. The Lord of the Sith momentarily lost his footing on the stairs and tumbled to his knees.

Luke stood above him, at the top of the staircase, heady with his own power. It was in his hands, now, he knew it was: he could take Vader. Take his blade, take his life. Take his place at the Emperor's side. Yes, even that. Luke didn't bury the thought, this time; he gloried in it. He engorged himself with its juices, felt its power tingle his cheeks. It made him feverish, this thought, with lust so overpowering as to totally obliterate all other considerations.

He had the power; the choice was his.

And then another thought emerged, slowly compulsive as an ardent lover: he could destroy the Emperor, too. Destroy them both, and rule the galaxy. Avenge and conquer.

It was a profound moment for Luke. Dizzying. Yet he did not swoon. Nor did he recoil.

He took one step forward.

For the first time, the thought entered Vader's consciousness that his son might best him. He was astounded by the strength Luke had acquired since their last duel, in the Cloud City—not to mention the boy's timing, which was honed to a thought's-breadth. This was an unexpected circumstance. Unexpected and unwelcome. Vader felt humiliation crawling in on the tail of his first reaction, which was surprise, and his second, which was fear. And then the edge of the humiliation curled up, to reveal bald anger. And now he wanted revenge.

These things were mirrored, each facet, by the young Jedi who now towered above him. The Emperor, watching joyously, saw this, and goaded Luke on to revel in his Darkness. "Use your aggressive feelings, boy! Yes! Let the hate flow through you! Become one with it, let it nourish you!"

Luke faltered a moment —then realized what was happening. He was suddenly confused again. What did he want? What should he do? His brief exultation, his microsecond of dark clarity—gone, now, in a wash of indecision, veiled enigma. Cold awakening from a passionate flirtation.

He took a step back, lowered his sword, relaxed, and tried to drive the hatred from his being.

In that instant, Vader attacked. He lunged half up the stairs, forcing Luke to reverse defensively. He bound the boy's blade with his own, but Luke disengaged and leaped to the safety of an overhead gantry. Vader jumped over the railing to the floor beneath the platform on which Luke stood.

"I will not fight you, Father," Luke stated.

"You are unwise to lower your defenses," Vader warned. His anger was layered, now—he did not want to win if the boy was not battling to the fullest. But if winning meant he had to kill a boy who wouldn't fight . . . then he could do that, too. Only he wanted Luke to be aware of those consequences. He wanted Luke to know this was no longer just a game. This was Darkness.

Luke heard something else, though. "Your thoughts betray you, Father. I feel the good in you . . . the conflict. You could not bring yourself to kill me before—and you won't destroy me now." Twice before, in fact—to Luke's recollection—Vader could have killed him, but didn't. In the dogfight over the first Death Star, and later in the lightsaber duel on Bespin. He thought of Leia, briefly now, too—of how Vader had had *her* in his clutches once, had even tortured her . . . but didn't kill her. He winced to think of her agony, but quickly pushed that from his mind. The point was clear to him, now, though so often so murky: there was still good in his father.

This accusation *really* made Vader angry. He could tolerate much from the insolent child, but this was insufferable. He must teach this boy a lesson he would never forget, or die learning. "Once again, you underestimate the power of the dark side . . ."

Vader threw his scintillating blade—it sliced through the supports holding up the gantry on which Luke was perched, then swept around and flew back into Vader's hand. Luke tumbled to the ground, then rolled down another level, under the tilting platform. In the shadow of the darkened overhang, he was out of sight. Vader paced the area like a cat, seeking the boy; but he wouldn't enter the shadows of the overhang.

"You cannot hide forever, Luke."

"You'll have to come in and get me," replied the disembodied voice.

"I will not give you the advantage that easily." Vader felt his intentions increasingly ambiguous in this conflict; the purity of his evil was being compromised. The boy was clever indeed—Vader knew he must move with extreme caution now.

"I wish no advantage, father. I will not fight you. Here . . . take my weapon." Luke knew full well this might be his end, but so be it. He would not use Darkness to fight Darkness. Perhaps it would be left to Leia, after all, to carry on the struggle, without him. Perhaps she would know a way he didn't know; perhaps she could find a path. For now, though, he could see only two paths, and one was into Darkness; and one was not.

Luke put his lightsaber on the ground, and rolled it along the floor toward Vader. It stopped halfway between them, in the middle of the low overhead area. The Dark Lord reached out his hand—Luke's lightsaber jumped into it. He hooked it to his belt and, with grave uncertainty, entered the shadowy overhang.

He was picking up additional feelings from Luke, now, new

crosscurrents of doubt. Remorse, regret, abandonment. Shades of pain. But somehow not directly related to Vader. To others, to . . . Endor. Ah, that was it—the Sanctuary Moon where his friends would soon die. Luke would learn soon enough: friendship was different on the dark side. A different thing altogether.

"Give yourself to the dark side, Luke," he entreated. "It is the only way you can save your friends. Yes, your thoughts betray you, son. Your feelings for them are strong, especially for—"

Vader stopped. He sensed something.

Luke withdrew further into shadow. He tried to hide, but there was no way to hide what was in his mind—Leia was in pain. Her agony cried to him now, and his spirit cried with her. He tried to shut it out, to shut it up, but the cry was loud, and he couldn't stifle it, couldn't leave it alone, had to cradle it openly, to give it solace.

Vader's consciousness invaded that private place.

"No!" screamed Luke.

Vader was incredulous. "Sister? Sister!" he bellowed. "Your feelings have now betrayed her, too . . . Twins!" he roared triumphantly. "Obi-Wan was wise to hide her, but now his failure is complete." His smile was clear to Luke, through the mask, through the shadows, through all the realms of Darkness. "If you will not turn to the Dark Side, perhaps she will."

This, then, was Luke's breaking point. For Leia was everyone's last unflagging hope. If Vader turned his twisted, misguided cravings on her . . .

"Never!" he screamed. His lightsaber flew off Vader's belt into his own hand, igniting as it came to him.

He rushed to his father with a frenzy he'd never known. Nor had Vader. The gladiators battled fiercely, sparks flying from the clash of their radiant weapons, but it was soon evident that the advantage was all Luke's. And he was pressing it. They locked swords, body to body. When Luke pushed Vader back to break the clinch, the Dark Lord hit his head on an overhanging beam in the cramped space. He stumbled backward even farther, out of the low-hanging area. Luke pursued him relentlessly.

Blow upon blow, Luke forced Vader to retreat—back, onto the bridge that crossed the vast, seemingly bottomless shaft to the power core. Each stroke of Luke's saber pummeled Vader, like accusations, like screams, like shards of hate.

The Dark Lord was driven to his knees. He raised his blade

to block yet another onslaught—and Luke slashed Vader's right hand off at the wrist.

The hand, along with bits of metal, wires, and electronic devices, clattered uselessly away while Vader's lightsaber tumbled over the edge of the span, into the endless shaft below, without a trace.

Luke stared at his father's twitching, severed, mechanical hand—and then at his own black-gloved artificial part—and realized suddenly just how much he'd become like his father. Like the man he hated.

Trembling, he stood above Vader, the point of his glowing blade at the Dark Lord's throat. He wanted to destroy this thing of Darkness, this thing that was once his father, this thing that was . . . him.

Suddenly the Emperor was there, looking on, chuckling with uncontrollable, pleased agitation. "Good! Kill him! Your hate has made you powerful! Now, fulfill your destiny and take your father's place at my side!"

Luke stared at his father beneath him, then at the Emperor, then back at Vader. This was Darkness—and it was the *Darkness* he hated. Not his father, not even the Emperor. But the Darkness *in* them. In them, and in himself.

And the only way to destroy the Darkness was to renounce it. For good and all. He stood suddenly erect, and made the decision for which he'd spent his life in preparation.

He hurled his lightsaber away. "Never! Never will I turn to the dark side! You have failed, Palpatine. I am a Jedi, as my father was before me."

The Emperor's glee turned to a sullen rage. "So be it, Jedi. If you will not be turned, you will be destroyed."

Palpatine raised his spidery arms toward Luke: blinding white bolts of energy coruscated from his fingers, shot across the room like sorcerous lightning, and tore through the boy's insides, looking for ground. The young Jedi was at once confounded and in agony—he'd never heard of such a power, such a corruption of the Force, let alone experienced it.

But if it was Force-generated, it could be Force-repelled. Luke raised his arms to deflect the bolts. Initially, he was successful—the lightning rebounded from his touch, harmlessly into the walls. Soon, though, the shocks came with such speed and power, they coursed over and into him, and he could only shrink before them, convulsed with pain, his knees buckling, his powers at ebb.

Vader crawled, like a wounded animal, to his Emperor's side.

On Endor, the battle of the bunker continued. Stormtroopers kept irradiating Ewoks with sophisticated weaponry, while the fuzzy little warriors bashed away at the Imperial troops with clubs, tumbled walkers with logpiles and vine trip-wires, lassoed speeder bikes with vine-ropes and net-traps.

They felled trees on their foes. They dug pits which they covered with branches, and then lured the walkers to chase them until the clumsy armored vehicles toppled into the dug-outs. They started rockslides. They dammed a small, nearby stream, and then opened the floodgates, deluging a host of troops and two more walkers. They ganged up, and then ran away. They jumped on top of walkers from high branches, and poured pouches of burning lizard-oil in the gun-slits. They used knives, and spears, and slings, and made scary war-shrieks to confound and dismay the enemy. They were fearless opponents.

Their example made even Chewie bolder than was his wont. He started having so much fun swinging on vines and bashing heads, he nearly forgot about his laser pistol.

He swung onto the roof of a Walker at one point, with Teebo and Wicket clinging to his back. They landed with a thud atop the lurching contraption, then made such a banging racket trying to hang on, one of the stormtroopers inside opened the top hatch to see what was happening. Before he could fire his gun, Chewie plucked him out and dashed him to the ground—Wicket and Teebo immediately dove into the hatch and subdued the other trooper.

Ewoks drive an Imperial Walker much the way they drive speeder bikes—terribly but with exhilaration. Chewie was almost thrown off the top several times, but even barking angrily down into the cockpit didn't seem to have much effect—the Ewoks just giggled, squealed, and careened into another speeder bike.

Chewie climbed down inside. It took him half a minute to master the controls—Imperial technology was pretty standardized. And then, methodically, one by one, he began approaching the other, unsuspecting, Imperial Walkers, and blasting them to dust. Most had no idea what was happening.

As the giant war-machines began going up in flames, the Ewoks were reinspired. They rallied behind Chewie's Walker. The Wookiee was turning the tide of battle.

Han, meanwhile, was still working furiously at the control

panel. Wires sparked each time he refastened another connection, but the door kept not opening. Leia crouched at his back, firing her laser pistol, giving him cover.

He motioned her at last. "Give me a hand, I think I've got it figured out. Hold this."

He handed her one of the wires. She holstered her weapon, took the wire he gave her, and held it in position as he brought two others over from opposite ends of the panel.

"Here goes nothing," he said.

The three wires sparked; the connection was made. There was a sudden loud WHUMP, as a second blast door crashed down in front of the first, doubling the impregnable barrier.

"Great. Now we have two doors to get through," Leia muttered.

At that moment, she was hit in the arm by a laser bolt, and knocked to the ground.

Han rushed over to her. "Leia, no!" he cried, trying to stop the bleeding.

"Princess Leia, are you all right?" Threepio fretted.

"It's not bad," she shook her head. "It's—"

"Hold it!" shouted a voice. "One move and you're both dead!"

They froze, looked up. Two stormtroopers stood before them, weapons leveled, unwavering.

"Stand up," one ordered. "Hands raised."

Han and Leia looked at each other, fixed their gazes deep in each other's eyes, swam there in the wells of their souls for a suspended, eternal moment, during which all was felt, understood, touched, shared.

Solo's gaze was drawn down to Leia's holster—she'd surreptitiously eased out her gun, and was holding it now at the ready. The action was hidden from the troopers, because Han was standing in front of Leia, half-blocking their view.

He looked again into her eyes, comprehending. With a last, heartfelt smile, he whispered, "I love you."

"I know," she answered simply.

Then the moment was over; and at an unspoken, instantaneous signal, Han whirled out of the line of fire as Leia blasted at the stormtroopers.

The air was filled with laser fire—a glinting orange-pink haze, like an electron storm, buffeted the area, sheared by intense flares.

As the smoke cleared, a giant Imperial Walker approached,

stood before him, and stopped. Han looked up to see its laser cannons aimed directly in his face. He raised his arms, and took a tentative step forward. He wasn't really sure what he was going to do. "Stay back," he said quietly to Leia, measuring the distance to the machine, in his mind.

That was when the hatch on top of the Walker popped open and Chewbacca stuck his head out with an ingratiating smile.

"Ahr Rahr!" barked the Wookiee.

Solo could have kissed him. "Chewie! Get down here! She's wounded!" He started forward to greet his partner, then stopped in mid-stride. "No, wait. I've got an idea."

IX

THE two space armadas, like their sea-bound counterparts of another time and galaxy, sat floating, ship to ship, trading broadsides with each other in point-blank confrontation.

Heroic, sometimes suicidal, maneuvers marked the day. A Rebel cruiser, its back alive with fires and explosions, limped into direct contact with an Imperial Star Destroyer before exploding completely—taking the Star Destroyer with it. Cargo ships loaded with charge were set on collision courses with fortress-vessels, their crews abandoning ships to fates that were uncertain, at best.

Lando, Wedge, Blue Leader, and Green Wing went in to take out one of the larger Destroyers—the Empire's main communications ship. It had already been disabled by direct cannonade from the Rebel cruiser it had subsequently destroyed; but its damages were reparable—so the Rebels had to strike while it was still licking its wounds.

Lando's squadron went in low—rock-throwing low—this prevented the Destroyer from using its bigger guns. It also made the fighters invisible until they were directly visualized.

"Increase power on the front deflector shields," Lando radioed his group. "We're going in."

"I'm right with you," answered Wedge. "Close up formations, team."

They went into a high-speed power-dive, perpendicular to the long axis of the Imperial vessel—vertical drops were hard to track. Fifty feet from the surface, they pulled out at ninety degrees, and raced along the gunmetal hull, taking laserfire from every port.

"Starting attack run on the main power tree," Lando advised.

"I copy," answered Green Wing. "Moving into position."

"Stay clear of their front batteries," warned Blue Leader.

"It's a heavy fire zone down there."

"I'm in range."

"She's hurt bad on the left of the tower," Wedge noted. "Concentrate on that side."

"Right with you."

Green Wing was hit. "I'm losing power!"

"Get clear, you're going to blow!"

Green Wing took it down like riding a rocket, into the Destroyer's front batteries. Tremendous explosions rumbled the port bow.

"Thanks," Blue Leader said quietly to the conflagration.

"That opens it up for us!" yelled Wedge. "Cut over. The power reactors are just inside that cargo bay."

"Follow me!" Lando called, pulling the *Falcon* into a sharp bank that caught the horrified reactor personnel by surprise. Wedge and Blue followed suit. They all did their worst.

"Direct hit!" Lando shouted.

"There she goes!"

"Pull up, pull up!"

They pulled up hard and fast, as the Destroyer was enveloped in a series of ever-increasing explosions, until it looked finally just like one more small star. Blue Leader was caught by the shock wave, and thrown horribly against the side of a smaller Imperial ship, which also exploded. Lando and Wedge escaped.

On the Rebel command ship bridge, smoke and shouts filled the air.

Ackbar reached Calrissian on the comlink. "The jamming has stopped. We have a reading on the shield."

"Is it still up?" Lando responded with desperate anticipation in his voice.

"I'm afraid so. It looks like General Solo's unit didn't make it."

"Until they've destroyed our last ship, there's still hope," replied Lando. Han wouldn't fail. He couldn't—they still had to pick off that annoying Death Star.

On the Death Star, Luke was nearly unconscious beneath the continuing assault of the Emperor's lightning. Tormented beyond reason, betaken of a weakness that drained his very essence, he hoped for nothing more than to submit to the nothingness toward which he was drifting.

The Emperor smiled down at the enfeebled young Jedi, as Vader struggled to his feet beside his master.

"Young fool!" Palpatine rasped at Luke. "Only now at the end, do you understand. Your puerile skills are no match for the power of the dark side. You have paid a price for your lack of vision. Now, young Skywalker, you will pay the price in full. You will die!"

He laughed maniacally; and although it would not have seemed possible to Luke, the outpouring of bolts from the Emperor's fingers actually increased in intensity. The sound screamed through the room, the murderous brightness of the flashes was overwhelming.

Luke's body slowed, wilted, finally crumpled under the hideous barrage. He stopped moving altogether. At last, he appeared totally lifeless. The Emperor hissed maliciously.

At that instant, Vader sprang up and grabbed the Emperor from behind, pinning Palpatine's upper arms to his torso. Weaker than he'd ever been, Vader had lain still these last few minutes, focusing his every fiber of being on this one, concentrated act—the only action possible; his last, if he failed. Ignoring pain, ignoring his shame and his weaknesses, ignoring the bone-crushing noise in his head, he focused solely and sightlessly on his will—his will to defeat the evil embodied in the Emperor.

Palpatine struggled in the grip of Vader's unfeeling embrace, his hands still shooting bolts of malign energy out in all directions. In his wild flailing, the lightning ripped across the room, tearing into Vader. The Dark Lord fell again, electric currents crackling down his helmet, over his cape, into his heart.

Vader stumbled with his load to the middle of the bridge over the black chasm leading to the power core. He held the wailing despot high over his head, and with a final spasm of strength, hurled him into the abyss.

Palpatine's body, still spewing bolts of light, spun out of control, into the void, bouncing back and forth off the sides of the shaft as it fell. It disappeared at last; but then, a few seconds later, a distant explosion could be heard, far down at the core. A rush of air billowed out the shaft, into the throne room.

The wind whipped at Lord Vader's cape, as he staggered and collapsed toward the hole, trying to follow his master to the end. Luke crawled to his father's side, though, and pulled the Dark Lord away from the edge of the chasm, to safety.

Both of them lay on the floor, entwined in each other, too weak to move, too moved to speak.

Inside the bunker on Endor, Imperial controllers watched the main view-screen of the Ewok battle just outside. Though the image was clogged with static, the fighting seemed to be winding down. About time, since they'd initially been told that the locals on this moon were harmless nonbelligerents.

The interference seemed to worsen—probably another antenna damaged in the fighting—when suddenly a walker pilot appeared on the screen, waving excitedly.

"It's over, Commander! The Rebels have been routed, and are fleeing with the bear-creatures into the woods. We need reinforcements to continue the pursuit."

The bunker personnel all cheered. The shield was safe.

"Open the main door!" ordered the commander. "Send three squads to help."

The bunker door opened, the Imperial troops came rushing out only to find themselves surrounded by Rebels and Ewoks, looking bloody and mean. The Imperial troops surrendered without a fight.

Han, Chewie, and five others ran into the bunker with the explosive charges. They placed the timed devices at eleven strategic points in and around the power generator, then ran out again as fast as they could.

Leia, still in great pain from her wounds, lay in the sheltered comfort of some distant bushes. She was shouting orders to the Ewoks, to gather their prisoners on the far side of the clearing, away from the bunker when Han and Chewie tore out, racing for cover. In the next moment, the bunker went.

It was a spectacular display, explosion after explosion sending a wall of fire hundreds of feet into the air, creating a shock wave that knocked every living creature off its feet, and charred all the greenery that faced the clearing.

The bunker was destroyed.

* * *

A captain ran up to Admiral Ackbar, his voice tremulous. "Sir, the shield around the Death Star has lost its power."

Ackbar looked at the view-screen; the electronically generated web was gone. The moon, and the Death Star, now floated in black, empty, unprotected space.

"They did it," Ackbar whispered.

He rushed over to the comlink and shouted into the multifrequency war channel. "All fighters commence attack on the Death Star's main reactor. The deflector shield is down. Repeat. The deflector shield is down!"

Lando's voice was the next one heard. "I see it. We're on our way. Red group! Gold group! Blue Squad! All fighters follow me!" That's my man, Han. Now it's my turn.

The *Falcon* plunged to the surface of the Death Star, followed by hordes of Rebel fighters, followed by a still-massing but disorganized array of Imperial TIE fighters—while three Rebel Star Cruisers headed for the huge Imperial Super Star Destroyer, Vader's flagship, which seemed to be having difficulties with its guidance system.

Lando and the first wave of X-wings headed for the unfinished portion of the Death Star, skimming low over the curving surface of the completed side.

"Stay low until we get to the unfinished side," Wedge told his squad. Nobody needed to be told.

"Squadron of enemy fighters coming—"

"Blue Wing," called Lando, "take your group and draw the TIE fighters away—"

"I'll do what I can."

"I'm picking up interference . . . the Death Star's jamming us, I think—"

"More fighters coming at ten o'clock—"

"There's the superstructure," Lando called. "Watch for the main reactor shaft."

He turned hard into the unfinished side, and began weaving dramatically among protruding girders, half-built towers, maze-like channels, temporary scaffolding, sporadic floodlights. The antiaircraft defenses weren't nearly as well developed here yet— they'd been depending completely on the deflector shield for protection. Consequently the major sources of worry for the Rebels were the physical jeopardies of the structure itself, and the Imperial TIE fighters on their tails. "I see it—the power-channel system," Wedge radioed. "I'm going in."

"I see it, too," agreed Lando. "Here goes nothing."

"This isn't going to be easy—"

Over a tower and under a bridge—and suddenly they were flying at top speed inside a deep shaft that was barely wide enough for three fighters, wing to wing. Moreover, it was pierced, along its entire twisting length, by myriad feeding shafts and tunnels, alternate forks, and dead-end caverns; and spiked, in addition, with an alarming number of obstacles *within* the shaft itself: heavy machinery, structural elements, power cables, floating stairways, barrier half-walls, piled debris.

A score of Rebel fighters made the first turn-off into the power shaft, followed by twice that number of TIEs. Two X-wings lost it right away, careening into a derrick to avoid the first volley of laser fire.

The chase was on.

"Where are we going, Gold Leader?" Wedge called out gaily. A laserbolt hit the shaft above him, showering his window with sparks.

"Lock onto the strongest power source," Lando suggested. "It should be the generator."

"Red Wing, stay alert—we could run out of space real fast."

They quickly strung out into single and double file, as it started becoming apparent that the shaft was not only pocked with side-vents and protruding obstacles, but also narrowing across its width at every turn.

TIE fighters hit another Rebel, who exploded in flames. Then another TIE fighter hit a piece of machinery, with a similar result.

"I've got a reading on a major shaft obstruction ahead," Lando announced.

"Just picked it up. Will you make it?"

"Going to be a tight squeeze."

It was a tight squeeze. It was a heat-wall occluding three fourths of the tunnel, with a dip in the shaft at the same level to make up a little room. Lando had to spin the *Falcon* through 360 degrees while rising, falling, and accelerating. Luckily, the X-wings and Y-wings weren't quite as bulky. Still, two more of them didn't make it on the downside. The smaller TIEs drew closer.

Suddenly coarse white static blanketed all the viewscreens.

"My scope's gone!" yelled Wedge.

"Cut speed," cautioned Lando. "Some kind of power discharge causing interference."

"Switch to visual scanning."

"That's useless at these velocities—we'll have to fly nearly blind."

Two blind X-wings hit the wall as the shaft narrowed again. A third was blown apart by the gaining Imperial fighters.

"Green Leader!" called Lando.

"Copy, Gold Leader."

"Split off and head back to the surface—Home-one just called for a fighter, and you might draw some fire off us."

Green Leader and his cohort peeled off, out of the power shaft, back up to the cruiser battle. One TIE fighter followed, firing continuously.

Ackbar's voice came in over the comlink. "The Death Star is turning away from the fleet—looks like it's repositioning to destroy the Endor Moon."

"How long before it's in position?" Lando asked.

"Point oh three."

"That's not enough time! We're running out of time."

Wedge broke in the transmission. "Well, we're running out of shaft, too."

At that instant the *Falcon* scraped through an even smaller opening, this time injuring her auxiliary thrusters.

"That was too close," muttered Calrissian.

"Gdzhng dzn," nodded the copilot.

Ackbar stared wild-eyed out the observation window. He was looking down onto the deck of the Super Star Destroyer; only miles away. Fires burst over the entire stern, and the Imperial warship was listing badly to starboard.

"We've knocked out their forward shields," Ackbar said into the comlink. "Fire at the bridge."

Green Leader's group swooped in low, from bottomside, up from the Death Star

"Glad to help out, Home-One," called Green Leader.

"Firing proton torpedoes," Green Wing advised.

The bridge was hit, with kaleidoscopic results. A rapid chain reaction got set off, from power station to power station along the middle third of the huge Destroyer, producing a dazzling rainbow of explosions that buckled the ship at right angles, and started it spinning like a pinwheel toward the Death Star.

The first bridge explosion took Green Leader with it; the subsequent uncontrolled joyride snagged ten more fighters, two cruisers, and an ordnance vessel. By the time the whole exothermic conglomerate finally crashed into the side of the Death

Star, the impact was momentous enough to actually jolt the battle station, setting off internal explosions and thunderings all through its network of reactors, munitions, and halls.

For the first time, the Death Star rocked. The collision with the exploding Destroyer was only the beginning, leading to various systems breakdowns, which led to reactor meltdowns, which led to personnel panic, abandonment of posts, further malfunctions, and general chaos.

Smoke was everywhere, substantial rumblings came from all directions at once, people were running and shouting. Electrical fires, steam explosions, cabin depressurizations, disruption of chain-of-command. Added to this, the continued bombardments by Rebel cruisers—smelling fear in the enemy—merely heightened the sense of hysteria that was already pervasive.

For the Emperor was dead. The central, powerful evil that had been the cohesive force to the Empire was gone; and when the dark side was this diffused, this nondirected—this was simply where it led.

Confusion.

Desperation.

Damp fear.

In the midst of this uproar, Luke had made it, somehow, to the main docking bay—where he was trying to carry the hulking deadweight of his father's weakening body toward an Imperial shuttle. Halfway there, his strength finally gave out, though; and he collapsed under the strain.

Slowly he rose again. Like an automaton, he hoisted his father's body over his shoulder and stumbled toward one of the last remaining shuttles.

Luke rested his father on the ground, trying to collect strength one last time, as explosions grew louder all around them. Sparks hissed in the rafters; one of the walls buckled, and smoke poured through a gaping fissure. The floor shook.

Vader motioned Luke closer to him. "Luke, help me take this mask off."

Luke shook his head. "You'll die."

The Dark Lord's voice was weary. "Nothing can stop that now. Just once let me face you without it. Let me look on you with my own eyes."

Luke was afraid. Afraid to see his father as he really was. Afraid to see what person could have become so dark—the same person who'd fathered Luke, and Leia. Afraid to know the Ana-kin Skywalker who lived inside Darth Vader.

Vader, too, was afraid—to let his son see him, to remove this armored mask that had been between them so long. The black, armored mask that had been his only means of existing for over twenty years. It had been his voice, and his breath, and his invisibility—his shield against all human contact. But now he would remove it; for he would see his son before he died.

Together they lifted the heavy helmet from Vader's head—inside the mask portion, a complicated breathing apparatus had to be disentangled, a speaking modulator and view-screen detached from the power unit in back. But when the mask was finally off and set aside, Luke gazed on his father's face.

It was the sad, benign face of an old man. Bald, beardless, with a mighty scar running from the top of his head to the back of the scalp, he had unfocused, deepset, dark eyes, and his skin was pasty white, for it had not seen the sun in two decades. The old man smiled weakly; tears glazed his eyes, now. For a moment, he looked not too unlike Ben.

It was a face full of meanings, that Luke would forever recall. Regret, he saw most plainly. And shame. Memories could be seen flashing across it . . . memories of rich times. And horrors. And love, too.

It was a face that hadn't touched the world in a lifetime. In Luke's lifetime. He saw the wizened nostrils twitch, as they tested a first, tentative smell. He saw the head tilt imperceptibly to listen—for the first time without electronic auditory amplification. Luke felt a pang of remorse that the only sounds now to be heard were those of explosions, the only smells, the pungent sting of electrical fires. Still, it was a touch. Palpable, unfiltered

He saw the old eyes focus on him. Tears burned Luke's cheeks, fell on his father's lips. His father smiled at the taste.

It was a face that had not seen itself in twenty years.

Vader saw his son crying, and knew it must have been at the horror of the face the boy beheld.

It intensified, momentarily, Vader's own sense of anguish—to his crimes, now, he added guilt at the imagined repugnance of his appearance. But then this brought him to mind of the way he used to look—striking, and grand, with a wry tilt to his brow that hinted of invincibility and took in all of life with a wink. Yes, that was how he'd looked once.

And this memory brought a wave of other memories with it.

Memories of brotherhood, and home. His dear wife. The freedom of deep space. Obi-Wan.

Obi-Wan, his friend . . . and how that friendship had turned. Turned, he knew not how—but got injected, nonetheless, with some uncaring virulence that festered, until . . . hold. These were memories he wanted none of, not now. Memories of molten lava, crawling up his back . . . no.

This boy had pulled him from that pit—here, now, with this act. This boy was good.

The boy was good, and the boy had come from *him*—so there must have been good in *him*, too. He smiled up again at his son, and for the first time, loved him. And for the first time in many long years, loved himself again, as well.

Suddenly he smelled something—flared his nostrils, sniffed once more. Wildflowers, that was what it was. Just blooming; it must be spring.

And there was thunder—he cocked his head, strained his ears. Yes, spring thunder, for a spring rain. To make the flowers bloom.

Yes, there . . . he felt a raindrop on his lips. He licked the delicate droplet . . . but wait, it wasn't sweetwater, it was salty, it was . . . a teardrop.

He focused on Luke once again, and saw his son was crying. Yes that was it, he was tasting his boy's grief—because he looked so horrible; because he *was* so horrible.

But he wanted to make it all right for Luke, he wanted Luke to know he wasn't really ugly like this, not deep inside, not all together. With a little self-deprecatory smile, he shook his head at Luke, explaining away the unsightly beast his son saw. "Luminous beings are we, Luke—not this crude matter."

Luke shook his head, too—to tell his father it was all right, to dismiss the old man's shame, to tell him nothing mattered now. And everything—but he couldn't talk.

Vader spoke again, even weaker—almost inaudible. "Go, my son. Leave me."

At that, Luke found his voice. "No. You're coming with me. I'll not leave you here. I've got to save you."

"You already have, Luke," he whispered. He wished, briefly, he'd met Yoda, to thank the old Jedi for the training he'd given Luke . . . but perhaps he'd be with Yoda soon, now, in the ethereal oneness of the Force. And with Obi-Wan.

"Father, I won't leave you," Luke protested. Explosions jarred the docking bay in earnest, crumbling one entire wall, splitting the ceiling. A jet of blue flame shot from a gas nozzle nearby. Just beneath it the floor began to melt.

Vader pulled Luke very close, spoke into his ear. "Luke, you were right . . . and you were right about me . . . Tell your sister . . . you were right."

With that, he closed his eyes, and Darth Vader—Anakin Skywalker—died.

A tremendous explosion filled the back of the bay with fire, knocking Luke flat to the ground. Slowly, he rose again; and like an automaton, stumbled toward one of the last remaining shuttles.

The *Millennium Falcon* continued its swerving race through the labyrinth of power channels, inching ever-closer to the hub of the giant sphere—the main reactor. The Rebel cruisers were unloading a continuous bombardment on the exposed, unfinished superstructure of the Death Star, now, each hit causing a resonating shudder in the immense battle station, and a new series of catastrophic events within.

Commander Jerjerrod sat, brooding, in the control room of the Death Star, watching all about him crumble. Half of his crew were dead, wounded, or run off—where they hoped to find sanctuary was unclear, if not insane. The rest wandered ineffectually, or railed at the enemy ships, or fired all their guns at all sectors, or shouted orders, or focused desperately on a single task, as if that would save them. Or, like Jerjerrod, simply brooded.

He couldn't fathom what he'd done wrong. He'd been patient, he'd been loyal, he'd been clever, he'd been hard. He was the commander of the greatest battle station ever built. Or, at least, almost built. He hated this Rebel Alliance, now, with a child's hate, untempered. He'd loved it once—it had been the small boy he could bully, the winged baby animal he could torture. But the boy had grown up now; it knew how to fight back effectively. It had broken its bonds.

Jerjerrod hated it now.

Yet there seemed to be little he could do at this point. Except, of course, destroy Endor—he could do that. It was a small act, a token really—to incinerate something green and living, gratuitously, meanly, toward no end but that of wanton destruction. A small act, but deliciously satisfying.

An aide ran up to him. "The Rebel fleet is closing, sir."

"Concentrate all fire in that sector," he answered distractedly. A console on the far wall burst into flame.

"The fighters in the superstructure are eluding our defense system, Commander. Shouldn't we—"

"Flood sectors 304 and 138. That should slow them up." He arched his eyebrows at the aide.

This made little sense to the aide, who had cause to wonder at the commander's grasp of the situation. "But sir . . ."

"What is the rotation factor to firing range on the Endor Moon?"

The aide checked the compuscreen. "Point oh two to moon target, sir. Commander, the fleet—"

"Accelerate rotation until moon is in range, and then fire on my mark."

"Yes, sir." The aide pulled a bank of switches. "Rotation accelerating, sir. Point oh one to moon target, sir. Sixty seconds to firing range. Sir, good-bye, sir." The aide saluted, put the firing switch in Jerjerrod's hand as another explosion shook the control room, and ran out the door.

Jerjerrod smiled calmly at the view-screen. Endor was starting to come out of the Death Star's eclipse. He fondled the detonation switch in his hand. Point oh oh five to moon target. Screams erupted in the next room.

Thirty seconds to firing.

Lando was homing in on the reactor core shaft. Else only Wedge was left, flying just ahead of him, and Gold Wing, just behind. Several TIE fighters still trailed.

These central twistings were barely two planes wide, and turned sharply every five or ten seconds at the speeds Lando was reaching. Another Imperial jet exploded against a wall; another shot down Gold Wing.

And then there were two.

Lando's tail-gunners kept the remaining TIE fighters jumping in the narrow space, until at last the main reactor shaft came into view. They'd never seen a reactor that awesome.

"It's too big, Gold Leader," yelled Wedge. "My proton torpedoes won't even dent that."

"Go for the power regulator on the north tower," Lando directed. "I'll take the main reactor. We're carrying concussion missiles—they should penetrate. Once I let them go, we won't have much time to get out of here, though."

"I'm already on my way out," Wedge exclaimed.

He fired his torpedoes with a Corellian war-cry, hitting both sides of the north tower, and peeled off, accelerating.

The *Falcon* waited three dangerous seconds longer, then loosed its concussion missiles with a powerful roar. For another second the flash was too bright to see what had happened. And then the whole reactor began to go.

"Direct hit!" shouted Lando. "Now comes the hard part."

The shaft was already caving in on top of him, creating a tunnel effect. The *Falcon* maneuvered through the twisting outlet, through walls of flame, and through moving shafts, always just ahead of the continuing chain of explosions.

Wedge tore out of the superstructure at barely sublight speed, whipped around the near side of Endor, and coasted into deep space, slowing slowly in a gentle arc, to return to the safety of the moon.

A moment later, in a destabilized Imperial shuttle, Luke escaped the main docking bay, just as that section began to blow apart completely. His wobbling craft, too, headed for the green sanctuary in the near distance.

And finally, as if being spit out of the very flames of the conflagration, the *Millennium Falcon* shot toward Endor, only moments before the Death Star flared into brilliant oblivion, like a fulminant supernova.

Han was binding Leia's arm-wound in a ferri-deli when the Death Star blew. It captured everyone's attention, wherever they happened to be—Ewoks, stormtrooper prisoners, Rebel troops—this final, turbulent, flash of self-destruction, incandescent in the evening sky. The Rebels cheered.

Leia touched Han's cheek. He leaned over, and kissed her, then sat back, seeing her eyes focused on the starry sky.

"Hey," he jostled, "I'll bet Luke got off that thing before it blew."

She nodded. "He did. I can feel it." Her brother's living presence touched her, through the Force. She reached out to answer the touch, to reassure Luke she was all right. Everything was all right.

Han looked at her with deep love, special love. For she was a special woman. A princess not by title, but by heart. Her fortitude astounded him, yet she held herself so lightly. Once, he'd wanted whatever he wanted, for himself, because he wanted it. Now he wanted everything for her. *Her* everythings. And one thing he could see she wanted dearly, was Luke.

"You really care for him, don't you?"

She nodded, scanning the sky. He was alive, Luke was alive. And the other—the Dark One—was dead.

"Well, listen," Han went on, "I understand. When he gets back, I won't stand in your way . . ."

She squinted at him, suddenly aware they were crossing wires, having different conversations. "What are you talking about?" she said. Then she realized what he was talking about. "Oh, no. No," she laughed, "it's not like that at all—Luke is my *brother*."

Han was successively stunned, embarrassed, and elated. This made *everything* fine, just fine.

He took her in his arms, embraced her, lowered her back down into the ferns . . . and being extra careful of her wounded arm, lay down there beside her, under the waning glow of the burning Star.

Luke stood in a forest clearing before a great pile of logs and branches. Lying, still and robed, atop the mound, was the lifeless body of Darth Vader. Luke set a torch to the kindling.

As the flames enveloped the corpse, smoke rose from the vents in the mask, almost like a black spirit, finally freed. Luke stared with a fierce sorrow at the conflagration. Silently, he said his last goodbye. He, alone, had believed in the small speck of humanity remaining in his father. That redemption rose, now, with these flames, into the night.

Luke followed the blazing embers as they sailed to the sky. They mixed, there, in his vision, with the fireworks the Rebel fighters were setting off in victory celebration. And these, in turn, mingled with the bonfires that speckled the woods and the Ewoks village—fires of elation, of comfort and triumph. He could hear the drums beating, the music weaving in the firelight, the cheers of brave reunion. Luke's cheer was mute as he gazed into the fires of his own victory and loss.

A huge bonfire blazed in the center of the Ewok village square for the celebration that night. Rebels and Ewoks rejoiced in the warm firelight of the cool evening—singing, dancing, and laughing, in the communal language of liberation. Even Teebo and Artoo had reconciled, and were going a little jig together, as others clapped in time to the music. Threepio, his regal days in this village over, was content to sit near the spinning little droid who was his best friend in the universe. He thanked the Maker that Captain Solo had been able to fix Artoo, not to mention Mistress Leia—for a man without protocol, Solo did have his moments. And he thanked the Maker this bloody war was over.

The prisoners had been sent on shuttles to what was left of the Imperial Fleet—the Rebel Star Cruisers were dealing with all that. Up there, somewhere. The Death Star had burned itself out.

Han, Leia, and Chewbacca stood off a short way from the revelers. They stayed close to each other, not talking; periodically glancing at the path that led into the village. Half waiting, half trying not to wait; unable to do anything else.

Until, at last, their patience was rewarded: Luke and Lando, exhausted but happy, stumbled down the path, out of the darkness, into the light. The friends rushed to greet them. They all embraced, cheered, jumped about, fell over, and finally just huddled, still wordless, content with the comfort of each other's touch.

In a while, the two droids sidled over as well, to stand beside their dearest comrades.

The fuzzy Ewoks continued in wild jubilation, far into the night, while this small company of gallant adventurers watched on from the sidelines

For an evanescent moment, looking into the bonfire, Luke thought he saw faces dancing—Yoda, Ben; was it his father? He drew away from his companions, to try to see what the faces were saying; they were ephemeral, and spoke only to the shadows of the flames, and then disappeared altogether.

It gave Luke a momentary sadness but then Leia took his hand, and drew him back close to her and to the others, back into their circle of warmth, and camaraderie; and love.

The Empire was dead.

Long live the Alliance.

Lisa McInerney

Lisa McInerney is from Galway and is the author of the award-winning blog 'Arse End of Ireland'. The *Irish Times* has called her 'arguably the most talented writer at work in Ireland today'. Her mother remains unimpressed.

Praise for *The Glorious Heresies*

'A punchy, edgy, sexy, fizzing feast of a debut novel from an immensely skilled storyteller with a glorious passion for words. I loved it'
Joseph O'Connor

'Here's a writer who's totally and unmistakably the real deal and whose every page pulses with vim and vitality and mad twisty insights and terrific description and with real tenderness, too' Kevin Barry

'A gripping and often riotously funny tale . . . McInerney gifts us a memorable cast that are tough as nails, savagely articulate, and helplessly human' Colin Barrett

'A real stunner; a wild ride of a read' Donal Ryan

'This is, joyously, in that tiny sliver of books I read every year that I press on to people and insist they read . . . I hope I read a better Irish novel this year but I'm not sure I will' Rick O'Shea

'A spectacular debut . . . Tough and tender, gothic and lyrical, it is a head-spinning, stomach-churning state-of-the-nation novel about a nation falling apart' *Daily Telegraph*

'An accomplished, seriously enjoyable and high-octane morality tale, full of empathy, feeling and soul' *Irish Times*

'A remarkable novel . . . Sound the trumpets. Or perhaps the harp. *The Glorious Heresies* heralds the arrival of a glorious, foul-mouthed, fizzing new talent' *Sunday Times*

The Glorious Heresies

Lisa McInerney

JOHN MURRAY

First published in Great Britain in 2015 by John Murray (Publishers)
An Hachette UK Company

First published in paperback in 2016

8

A CIP catalogue record for this title is available from the British Library

ISBN 978-1-444-79888-3
Ebook ISBN 978-1-444-79887-6

Typeset in Sabon MT by Hewer Text UK Ltd, Edinburgh

Printed and bound by Clays Ltd, St Ives plc

John Murray policy is to use papers that are natural, renewable
and recyclable products and made from wood grown in sustainable
forests. The logging and manufacturing processes are expected to
conform to the environmental regulations of the country of origin.

John Murray (Publishers)
Carmelite House
50 Victoria Embankment
London EC4Y 0DZ

www.johnmurray.co.uk

This, like everything else, is for John

The Dead Man

I

He left the boy outside its own front door. Farewell to it, and good luck to it. He wasn't going to feed it anymore; from here on in it would be squared shoulders and jaws, and strong arms and best feet forward. He left the boy a pile of mangled, skinny limbs and stepped through the door a newborn man, stinging a little in the sights of the sprite guiding his metamorphosis. Karine D'Arcy was her name. She was fifteen and a bit and had been in his class for the past three years. Outside of school she consistently outclassed him, and yet here she was, standing in his hall on a Monday lunchtime. And so the boy had to go, what was left of him, what hadn't been flayed away by her hands and her kisses.

'You're sure your dad won't come home?' she said.

'He won't,' he said, though his father was a law unto himself and couldn't be trusted to follow reason. This morning he'd warned that he'd be out and about, so the kids would have to make their own dinner, though he'd be back later, trailing divilment and, knowing the kindness of the pit, a foul temper.

'What if he does, though?'

He took his hand from hers and slipped it round her waist.

'I don't know,' he said. Oh, the truth was raw, as raw as you could get, unrehearsed words from a brand-new throat.

He was fifteen, only just. If she'd asked him the same question back before they'd crossed this threshold he would have answered according to fifteen years' build-up of boyish bravado, but now that everything had changed he couldn't remember how to showboat.

'It'll be my fault anyway,' he said. 'Not yours.'

They were supposed to be in school, and even his dad would know it. If he came home now, *if*, all lopsided with defeat, the worse for wear because of drink, or poker or whatever the fuck, it'd still take him only a moment to figure out that his son was on the lang, and for one reason only.

'Here it'd be yours,' she said. 'But what if he told my mam and dad?'

'He wouldn't.' It was as certain as the floor beneath them. His father was many things, but none of them responsible. Or bold. Or righteous.

'Are you sure?'

'The only people my dad talks to live here,' he said. 'No one else would have him.'

'So what do we do now?'

The name of this brave new man, still stinging from the possibilities whipping his flesh and pushing down on his shoulders, was Ryan. In truth, his adult form wasn't all that different to the gawky corpse he'd left outside; he was still black-haired and pale-skinned and ink-eyed. 'You look like you're *possessed*,' shivered one of the girls who'd gotten close enough to judge; she then declared her intent to try sucking the demon out through his tongue. He was stretching these past few months. *Too slow, too steady*, his nonna had sighed, the last time she'd perused his Facebook photos. She was adamant he'd never hit six feet. His mother was four years dead and his father was a wreck who slept as often on the couch as he did in his own bed. Ryan was the oldest of the wreck's children. He tiptoed around his father and made up for it around everyone else.

Something didn't fit about that. Of course, men of any age were entitled to flake around the place giving digs to anyone who looked like they might slight them, and that was certainly how the wreck behaved: hollow but for hot, cheap rage, dancing between glory and drying-out sessions in miserable rehab centres a million miles from anywhere. Even when Ryan dredged up the frenzies required by teachers' scorn or challenges thrown down by bigger kids, he knew there was something very empty in the way the lot of them encouraged him to fight. He'd been on the lookout for something to dare him to get out of bed in the morning, but he'd never thought it could have been her.

She was part of that group of girls who wore their skirts the shortest and who commandeered the radiator perches before every class and who could glide between impertinence and saccharine familiarity with teachers. He'd never thought she would look at him as anything but a scrapper, though he'd been asking her to, silently, behind his closed mouth and downturned eyes, for *fucking years*.

Three weeks before, on the night of his birthday, she had let him kiss her.

He'd been in one of his friends' cars – they were older than him, contemporaries of his sixteen-year-old cousin Joseph, who knew enough about Ryan to excuse his age – when he'd spotted her standing outside the doors of the community centre disco, laughing and trembling in a long black top and white shorts. He'd leant up from the back seat and called her from the passenger window, and he didn't even have to coax to get her clambering in beside him. Dumb luck that she was in the mood for a spin. And yet, a leap in his chest that tempted him to believe that maybe it was more again: dumb luck and trust. She trusted him. She – Jesus! – *liked* him.

They'd gone gatting. There were a couple of cans and a couple of joints and a cold, fair wind that brought her closer to his side. When he'd realised he couldn't medicate the nerves, he'd owned up to how he felt about her by chancing a hand left on the small of her back, counting to twenty or thirty or eighty before accepting she wasn't going to move away, taking her hand to steady his own and then finally, finally, over the great distance of thirty centimetres, he caught her mouth on his and kissed her.

In the days that followed they had covered miles of new ground and decided to chance making a go of it. They had gone to the pictures, they had eaten ice cream, they had meandered at the end of each meeting back to her road, holding hands. And lest they laid foundations too wholesome, they had found quiet spaces and dark corners in which to crumble that friendship, his palms recording the difference between the skin on her waist and on her breasts, his body pushing against hers so he could remember how her every hollow fit him.

Now, in his hall on a Monday lunchtime, he answered with a question.

'What do you want to do?'

She stepped into the sitting room and spun on one foot, taking it all in. He didn't need to stick his head through the frame to know that the view was found wanting. His father's ineptitude had preserved the place as a museum to his mother's homemaking skills, and she had been as effective with clutter as the wind was with blades of grass.

'I've never been in your house,' she said. 'It's weird.'

She meant her presence in it, and not the house itself. Though she wouldn't have been far wrong; it was weird. It was a three-bedroom terrace so cavernous without his mother he could barely stand it. It echoed shit he didn't want to think about in chasms that shouldn't have been there. It was a roof over his head. It was a fire hazard, in that he thought sometimes he could douse it in fuel and take a match to it and watch it take the night sky with it.

She knew the score. He'd admitted his circumstances in a brave move only a couple of days before, terrified that she'd lose it and dump him, and yet desperate to tell her that not every rumour about his father was true. On the back steps of the school, curled together on cold concrete, he'd confessed that yeah, he clashed with his dad, but no, not in the way that some of the more spiteful storytellers hinted at. *He's an eejit, girl, there's only the weight in him to stay upright when he's saturated, but he's not . . . He's . . . I've heard shit that people have said but he's not warped, girl. He's just . . . fucking . . . I don't know.*

She hadn't run off and she hadn't told anyone. It was both a load off and the worst play he could have made, for it cemented his place on his belly on the ground in front of her. On one hand he didn't mind because he knew she was better than him – she was whip-smart and as beautiful as morning and each time he saw her he felt with dizzying clarity the blood in his veins and the air in his lungs and his heart beating strong in his chest – but then it pissed him off that he couldn't approach her on his own two feet. That he was no more upright now than his father. That uselessness was hereditary.

There was no anger now, though. He had left it outside the front door with his wilting remains.

She held out her hand for his.

'You gonna play for me?'

His mam's piano stood by the wall, behind the door. It could just as easily have been his. He'd put the hours in, while she fought with his dad or threatened great career changes or fought with the neighbours or threatened to gather him and his siblings and stalk back to her parents. She used to pop him onto the piano stool whenever she needed space to indulge her cranky fancies, and in so doing had left him with ambidexterity and the ability to read sheet music. Not many people knew that about him, because they'd never have guessed.

He could play for Karine D'Arcy, if he wanted to. Some classical piece he could pretend was more than just a practice exercise, or maybe one of the pop songs his mother had taught him when she was finding sporadic employment with wedding bands and singing in hotel lobbies during shitty little arts festivals. It might even work. Karine might be so overwhelmed that she might take all her clothes off and let him fuck her right there on the sitting-room floor.

Something empty about that fantasy, too. The reality is that she was here in his house on a Monday lunchtime, a million zillion years from morphing into a horny stripper. That's what he had to deal with: Karine D'Arcy really-really being here.

He didn't want to play for her. Anticipation would make knuckles of his fingertips.

'I might do later,' he said.

'Later?'

He might have looked deep into her eyes and crooned *Yeah*,

later, if he'd had more time to get used to his new frame. Instead he smiled and looked away and muddled together *Later* and *After* in his head. *I might do After. We have this whole house to ourselves to make better.* There was going to be an After. He knew it.

She walked past him and out into the kitchen, and looked out the back window at the garden and its dock-leafed lawn laid out between stubby walls of concrete block. She flexed her hands against the sink, and pushed back her shoulders as she stretched onto tiptoes.

'It's weird,' she said again. 'To have never been in this house until now. You and me have been friends for so long, like.'

It had been an anxious kind of friendship. There were school projects and parties and play-fighting and one time a real fight during which he had accused her of only hanging out with him to get access to those parties. It was during that outburst of impotent temper, between off-white walls in a wide school corridor, that he realised their closeness amounted to years of her dragging him along like a piece of broken rock in a comet's tail.

It hit him like a midwife's slap that if it wasn't for his house being so cavernous, if it wasn't for his dad traipsing the city looking for cheap drink and indifferent company, if it wasn't for the fact that scrappers cared little for mitching off school, she wouldn't be here with him now, offering him the possibility of removing the burden of friendship and at least some of his clothes. Karine D'Arcy looked back at him with one hand on the draining board, rearranging the kitchen by way of chemical reaction, bleak snapshots fizzling against her butter-blonde hair and popping like soap bubbles against the hem of her grey school skirt. The house looked different with her here, on his side. She didn't know the history in every room and every jagged edge. The bottom step of the stairs. The coffee table that was always there, just so, to trip him up whenever he was shoved into the front room. The kitchen wall, the spot by the back door, where he'd watched the light switch from an inch away with one cheek pressed against eggshell blue and his dad's weight condensed into a hand flat on his left temple trying to push him right through the plaster.

'You're beautiful,' he told her, and she laughed and blinked and said, 'God, where did that come from?'

'You are,' he said. 'What are you doing here?'

She nestled against his neck. *Missing Geography*, she might have said. But she didn't say anything and the longer her silence went on the closer they got to the stairs, to his bed, to whatever came after that.

He hated his bedroom marginally less than he hated the rest of the house. He shared it with his brothers Cian and Cathal, who were messier than he was. The space was laid out in a Venn diagram; no matter how loudly he roared or how gingerly he protected what was his from what was theirs, they always managed to arrange an overlap. She sat on his bed – gratifying that she knew which was his – and he kicked his way around the floor, sending Dinky cars and Lego and inside-out pyjama bottoms under beds and into corners.

She was sitting on her hands and so when they kissed it was as if they'd never kissed before and weren't entirely sure whether they'd like it. The second one was better. She reached to cradle his face. The side of her finger brushed against the back of his ear. He pushed her school jumper over her breasts and when she pulled back to take it off he copied her.

'Maybe,' she said, three buttons down, 'like, we should close out the door. Just in case.'

'I could pull one of the beds in front of it?'

'Yeah.'

He pulled the curtains too. They lay on his bed and held each other, and kissed, and more clothes came off, and all the way along he kept thinking that she was going to withdraw her approval, that his hands would betray him here as he worried they would on the piano keys.

She didn't. She kissed him back and pressed against him and helped him. And he wondered, if he could do this with her in every room would it sanctify the place, exorcise it of the echoes of words spat and each jarring thump recorded against each solid surface?

He wondered if he should stop wondering, when a wandering mind was heresy.

'Just be careful,' she whispered. 'Oh please, Ryan, be careful.'

She clasped her hands around his neck and he found his right hand on her left knee, gently pushing out and oh fuck, that was it, he was totally done for.

Cork City isn't going to notice the first brave steps of a resolute little man. The city runs on the macro: traffic jams, All-Ireland finals, drug busts, general elections. Shit to complain about: the economy, the Dáil, whatever shaving of Ireland's integrity they were auctioning off to mainland Europe this week.

But Monday lunchtime was the whole world to one new man, and probably a thousand more besides, people who spent those couple of hours getting promotions or pregnancy tests or keys to their brand-new second-hand cars. There were people dying, too. That's the way of the city: one new man to take the place of another, bleeding out on a polished kitchen floor.

Maureen had just killed a man.

She didn't mean to do it. She'd barely need to prove that, she thought; no one would look at a fifty-nine-year-old slip of a whip like her and see a killer. When you saw them on the telly, the broken ones who tore asunder all around them, they always looked a bit off. Too much attention from handsy uncles, too few green vegetables. Faces like bags of triangles and eyes like buttons on sticks. Pass one on the street and you'd be straight into the Gardaí, suggesting that they tail the lurching loon if they were looking for a promotion to bring home to the mammy in Ballygobackwards. Well, not Maureen. Her face had a habit of sliding into a scowl between intentional expressions, but looking like a string of piss wasn't enough to have Gardaí probing your perversions. There'd have been no scandals in the Church at all, she thought, if the Gardaí had ever had minds honed so.

She looked at the man face-down on the tiles. There was blood under him. It gunged into the grout. It'd need wire wool.

Bicarbonate of soda. Bleach. Probably something stronger; she wasn't an expert. She didn't usually go around on cat feet surprising intruders with blunt force trauma. This was a first for her.

She was shit at cleaning, too. Homemaking skills were for good girls and it was forty years since anyone had told her she was one of them.

He was definitely dead, whoever he was. He wore a once-black jumper and a pair of shiny tracksuit bottoms. The back of his head was cracked and his hair matted, but it had been foxy before that. A tall man, a skinny rake, another string of piss, now departed. She hadn't gotten a look at his face before she flaked him with the Holy Stone and she couldn't bring herself to turn him over. It'd be like turning a chop on a grill, the thought of which turned her stomach. She'd hardly eat now. What if his eyes were still open?

There was no question of ringing for the guards. She did think – her face by now halfway to her ankles – that it might be jolly to ring for a priest, just to see how God and his bandits felt about it. Maybe they'd try to clean the kitchen floor by blessing it, *by the power vested in me*. But she didn't think she'd be able for inviting one of them fellas over the threshold. Two invasions in a day? She didn't have the bleach.

She turned from the dead man to pick up her phone.

Jimmy had drawn priests down upon her like seagulls to the bridge in bad weather. He was sin, poor thing, conceived in it and then the mark of it, growing like all bad secrets until he stretched her into a shape no one could shut their eyes to.

If she'd been born a decade earlier, she reckoned giving birth out of wedlock would have landed her a life sentence scrubbing linens in a chemical haze, hard labour twice over to placate women of God and feather their nests. But there was enough space in the seventies to allow her room to turn on her heel and head for England, where she was, on and off, until the terrible deed she'd named James tracked her down again with his own burden to show her.

Some women had illegitimate babies who grew up to be

11

accountants, or teachers, or heirs to considerable acres of good ground in the midlands. Not Maureen.

She frowned at the blood on the floor and dialled. Jimmy would know what to do. This was exactly the kind of thing he was good at.

2

The man on the street, the scut in the back corner of the pub, and the burnt-out girl on the quay all said the same: it was better to run alongside Jimmy Phelan than have him run over you. In short pants he was king of the terrace; in an Iron Maiden T-shirt he was Merchant General of the catchment area. He'd sold fags and dope and cans of lager, and then heroin and women and munitions. He'd won over and killed cops and robbers both. He'd been married. He'd attended parent-teacher meetings. He'd done deals and time and half the world twice over. There wasn't much left that Jimmy Phelan hadn't had a good go of and yet it was only very recently he'd owned up to the notion that inside him was a void kept raw and weeping for want of a family tree. It turned out, though, that Jimmy Phelan's eyes were bigger than his belly, and that applied to anything he had a yearning for: imported flesh, Cognac, his long-lost mother.

The bint had only gone and killed someone. He supposed it was appropriate carry-on for the block he was chipped from, but it didn't make it any less of an arseache. Jimmy liked to leave himself room for manoeuvre in his diary, but 'Clean up after your mother offs someone' was a much more significant task than he'd ever have thought to factor in.

He had set aside an apartment by the river for Maureen's use. With his being such a captain of industry, it had never been the plan to have her living with him, even if it hadn't turned out that she was crazier than a dustbin fox. It hadn't really been the plan to bring her home in the first place – all he'd aimed for was to track her down and give her the lowdown on her grandchildren

– but he'd had to re-strategise when he'd found her living amongst shuffling addicts and weird bachelors in a London tenement. He'd heard enough nationalist rants to know that leaving an Irish person in poverty in England was leaving them behind enemy lines, and it had been well within his capacity to take her home. She'd dug her heels in, but there was no one who could draw away from Jimmy Phelan's insistence, no matter how much pride or how many limbs they looked set to lose.

He'd bought the building for a song because a bunch of Vietnamese had been using it as a grow house and the guards had left it with more holes in the walls than there were cunts down in Crosser. If there had been any Vietnamese left he might have sold it back to them, on the 'lightning strikes' adage, but they'd gathered their skirts and scurried down to Waterford, or so he'd heard, so he'd used it as a brothel for a while, and might do again once he found somewhere less draughty to store his mother. He'd left her in the ground-floor flat, convalescing from her emigration, and had a few part-time part-tradesmen making structural improvements to the floors above, but he'd thought it had been secure. Maybe susceptible to punters lost and roaming, but she'd been under strict instructions not to open the door to anyone, and it had been a while since they'd begun redirecting appointments to the newer venue.

So how Maureen had managed to kill an intruder was beyond him. How did the weasel get in? Had the Vietnamese forgotten him? Had the guards not noticed him tucked away in the attic? Was he a john whose longtime kink was climbing in through skylights?

Whoever he was, he was dead now, and it turned out he probably wouldn't have been an open casket job even if he'd reached his natural expiration date. In fact, looking at him, he'd clearly been in the process of hurrying that along.

'What the fuck did you do to him?' Jimmy asked Maureen, as she sat at the kitchen table making faces at her cigarette. She was a dour little thing. Lacking height himself, he'd resorted to growing outwards to achieve the bulk demanded by his

14

vocation. Even now at forty he was mostly muscle, softened only very lately by a languid habit of eating out and drinking well. Maureen was whittled straight and had a glare just as pointed. They didn't look alike.

'Belted him,' she said. 'With the Holy Stone. I wasn't giving up the upper hand on the off-chance he was Santy Claus.'

'What Holy Stone?'

She gestured towards the sink.

For every Renaissance masterpiece there were a million geegaws cobbled together from the scrapheap, and this was awful even by that standard. A flat rock, about a fistful, painted gold and mounted on polished wood, with a picture of the Virgin Mary holding Chubby Toddler Jesus printed on one side in bright Celtic colours, and the bloody essences of the dead man on the kitchen floor smeared and knotted on top.

'Where the fuck did you get this?' If it wasn't for the fact it was mounted on that plinth, he'd have assumed some opportunistic crackpot had painted it for a car boot sale. He turned it over in his hand. The Blessed Virgin stared guzz-eyed back at him.

'I've had that a long time.'

'I didn't take you for a Holy Josephine.'

'You wouldn't want to, because I'm not.'

'You just collect bulky religious souvenirs to use as murder weapons, is it? No one ever suspects the heavy hand of the Lord. *Repent, repent, or Jesus might take the head off yeh!* How did you even swing this thing, Maureen? Did you take a run at him from the front door?'

'The Lord works in mysterious ways,' she said.

'I know a few lords like that all right.' He ran the Holy Stone under the tap and looked back at the dead man. 'You have no idea what he wanted?'

'Isn't it funny; I didn't think to ask.'

The body was weedy, its clothes shabby, even before the chap's blood had glued them to his frame. He had nothing in his pockets but a balled-up tissue and two-fifty in coins.

'Some junkie, maybe, looking for cash. I don't know the face,

He looks Irish. Or maybe a Sasanach. Rooted down in West Cork with the rest of the chin-wobblers.'

She sniffed. 'Dirty tramp. Robbing all around them. I'm just the type they target.'

'He's no one I know. And if he had any local knowledge at all he wouldn't have dared come near this house.'

He tossed the Holy Stone from one hand to the other. 'Dame Maureen, in the kitchen, with the rock o' Knock. We'll get rid of him for you.'

'The floor will need scrubbing.'

'And someone to clean the floor.'

'The grout will need replacing.'

'We'll get you a new floor, then.'

'You'll get me out of here. Who'd want to stay in a place a man died?'

'Oh, you'd want to watch out for vengeful spirits. He'll be in every mirror now, Maureen. He'll be coming up at you from the floor when you're trying to make the tay.'

'You can grin all you like, boy,' she said, 'but it's not right to leave a woman alone in a house like this.'

'It's you who made it like this,' he said. 'But point taken. I'll get you a cat.'

She threw daggers.

'First thing's first,' he said. 'I'll hire some hands. After that we'll look at living arrangements. I have nowhere else for you at the moment. I'll figure something out, but it won't be tonight.'

'It will. I'm not staying here.'

'You are until I find somewhere else for you.'

'I'm not. I'll sit outside for the night.'

'And you'll freeze and then there'll be two corpses and I tell you what, girl, I've only the patience for digging one grave.'

'You should have left me in London,' she said. 'Poor interest you have in me, at the end of the day.'

'That's right, Maureen. Poor interest. That's why it's me standing here, being fucking munificent with my fingerprints, instead of the state pathologist and Anglesea Street's finest.'

'I'm not staying here,' she said.

'First things first, I said. Will you stay here till I get back? Will you at least do that much for me?'

She tipped ash onto the tabletop. 'I'm not staying here with a corpse.'

'And whose fault is it that he's a corpse?'

'I don't know yet,' she said.

He met the challenge and it went right through him.

'Fine,' he said. 'Fine. Come on. Sure Deirdre'll be thrilled to see you.'

Maureen wasn't officially living in Jimmy Phelan's building. The building didn't officially belong to Jimmy Phelan. Even so, he didn't want to use his nearest and dearest men for this job. There was something off about the whole thing. He wasn't convinced that the foxy-haired intruder was just some gowl hunting desperately for spare change. Jimmy Phelan trusted his gut, and now he felt it howling.

The job had to be done. There was a body on his mother's kitchen floor, and it wasn't going to get up and leave of its own accord. Ordinarily he'd have swiftly handpicked a few decent sorts – at the very least his right-hand man Dougan, whose brutish dexterity and wicked sense of humour would be just right for the occasion – but that would suggest that he had a designated clean-up crew, and he couldn't be sure how Maureen would take it.

Or how Dougan and the boys would take her. They knew scraps of the story: that he had tracked down his birth mother and brought her home. They didn't know she was such an odd fish as to be capable of impromptu executions. Their respect for him, and for his lineage, could well be mangled by news of her little rampage. He bristled at the thought of it. He was sore where he'd grafted on this brand-new past.

Deirdre Allen was as stubborn as she was tough, which may have sounded like an admirable mix, but as far as Jimmy could tell it simply meant she was too stupid to know when she was wrong and too slow to notice the consequences. She was still dyeing her hair jet-black, still smoking twenty a day, still insisting that if he funded her expedition into real estate, he'd get his money back and doubled again. Still thinking there was opportunity on the right side of the euro. Still believing the recession was a sag in Ireland's fabric, stretched as far as it could go and on the point of bouncing upwards.

That pig-headedness was what had taken her so long to leave him. She had sailed through nearly a decade of his debasing their marital vows before she'd run aground. He hadn't made a habit of affairs; there were plenty of girls he could fuck without having to fork out for extras. Even so, there were so many all-nighters, so many week-long absences that any other woman would have read the warnings. By the time Deirdre noticed, it was much too late to draw boundaries. Jimmy gave her the house and wondered if one day she'd chalk their collaborative fuck-up down to experience. For now, she still laid claim to the title of Jimmy Phelan's Wife. She didn't want him in her bed anymore, but she was too stubborn and too tough to give up what she thought were the perks of his infamy.

'I want to get the kids a piano,' she said, dispatching a cup of tea in Maureen's general direction, wrinkling her nose. She hadn't asked how Maureen took her tea, but Deirdre had long assumed, incorrectly, that she had a knack for hostessing. 'I've always regretted not learning an instrument. I don't want them saying the same thing in ten years' time.'

'Are you having me on, girl? They'd have no more interest in learning the piano than they did in anything else you demanded I foist on them. It's you who wants the piano. A front-room centrepiece. Something to rest a vase on.'

'You can be a very thick man, Jimmy.'

'Maybe it's because I never learned to tickle the ivories. There's no art in me.'

'You'd deny your children the opportunity to learn a skill so? Just because there's a chance they might not stick with it? Is it depressed you are, or just plain mean?'

Maureen took her mug and walked out onto the back decking.

'Ah, she's thrilled you found her,' sneered Deirdre.

'I'm glad you know her so well, girl, because she's staying here with you tonight.'

'What?'

'The flat's getting cleaned. Industrial shit. No way can I have her stay there overnight, and I have too much on to offer her my bed. Long and short of it: you're stuck with her till tomorrow.'

'I am in me shit, Jimmy,' she hissed. 'You can't leave that loon here.'

'You've got a spare room. And she's been wanting to spend more time with her grandchildren. At least until she starts knowing them from the next pair of spoiled brats.'

'The cheek of you, boy. That woman, wherever you found her, might have ties to you but she doesn't to *my* children.'

'That's a failure of the most basic concept of human biology, Deirdre.'

'You know what I mean, Jimmy. There's a lot more to family than . . .' She waved a hand and grimaced. 'Fluids. Genetics. Whatever you want to call it.'

Maureen wasn't moving but to bring cigarette to mouth. She stared out across the lawn, serene as a cud-chewing cow. Just the right demeanour for the city's newest reaper: taking the scythe in her stride. Jimmy hadn't met many new murderers who weren't bent double by the aftermath, who didn't puke on their shoes as an epilogue.

'Well look, I'll tell you what I'll do,' he said to Deirdre. 'I'll find you a piano and you can honky-tonk your musical regrets away to your heart's content. I won't even ask why Ellie and Conor's fingers are still pudgy as pigs' trotters in a year's time. And all you have to do is mind my mammy for the night.'

'Ah, in fairness, Jimmy . . .'

'You should try talking to her. She's got your children's history knotted up inside that wizened head of hers. She's got Ireland's history in there. She's a very interesting woman.'

'A bit too interesting. Don't you think I've had it up to here with how interesting you can be?'

'A piano for sanctuary,' he said. 'You'd deny your children the opportunity to learn a skill just because there's a chance my dear mum will leave smudges on your furniture? Don't be plain mean, Deirdre. Aren't you better than me and my ancestry?'

He went out onto the deck and closed the door behind him.

'You're to stay with Deirdre tonight, Maureen. Say nothing about yer manno. We'll have him scooped up and out in no time. Who knows, you might even fall in love with the new floor.'

'I won't go back there,' she said. 'It's not safe.'

'Yeah. Well. We'll talk about it after.'

He took care of some chores after leaving Maureen in the reluctant hands of the daughter-in-law she'd missed out on, but as day stretched into evening there was still a human sacrifice on his mother's kitchen floor, one with a dent in the back of its head made by Ireland's ignorance of fine art and penchant for cut-price religious iconography.

He wondered where Maureen had gotten the Holy Stone. Had someone pressed it on her when she was reeling from childbirth? Had they assumed that even that crude image of the world's ultimate single mother would provide solace in hard times? Were they just blind, deaf and dumb to style?

Jimmy Phelan was raised by his grandparents, not unwillingly, but awkwardly nevertheless. They brought him to Knock once and offered him up to the wall once favoured by apparitions as a living paradigm of their piety. He'd been very bored, but afterwards they'd taken a jaunt through the town and he remembered gift shop after gift shop, gift shops as far as an eight-year-old eye could see, stocked to the rafters with baubles. Rows of Virgin Mary barometers; her fuzzy cloak would change colour depending on the weather, which was very miraculous. Toy cameras with preloaded images of the shrine; you clicked through them, holding the flimsy yokey up to the light. And so many sticks of rock. You could have built a whole other shrine out of sticks of rock.

Maureen's Holy Stone wouldn't have looked far out of place. Maybe his grandparents had purchased it. Maybe it was his speeding around this wonderland of faith-based kitsch, jacked up on neon-pink rock and too many bags of Taytos, that advised them of its relevance.

And so supposing the Holy Stone symbolised something to Maureen. Repentance. Humility. New beginnings. Supposing smashing it off the skull of an intruder set her back forty years. How much healing did a fallen woman require, if she had the whole of Ireland's fucked up psyche weighing her down to purgatory?

Evening was drawing in and there was a corpse drawing flies back in the flat, and no one yet nominated to move it.

He stopped at a Centra and bought himself a sausage sandwich and a coffee, and sat in his car to eat and think.

It felt wrong to be hiding from Dougan the source of a problem the man would have to fix. Jimmy wasn't used to this kind of isolation. His mother – the woman he tentatively thought of as his mother, as a rickety leg-up to understanding the blood that ran in his veins – had fucked up, and for once in his life, Jimmy felt a weak spot.

He was mulling this over when he spotted someone, ten feet away from his car. The figure was vaguely familiar. A dark, tousled head bent over an outstretched palm, opposite fingers picking through coins as one would for a parking meter. Thickset running thin, in a navy hoodie and blue jeans that had both been through the wash ten-too-many times. Jimmy balled up the sandwich wrapper, stuck it in his empty coffee cup, and stepped out of the car. Between the bin and his mark, he chanced, 'Cusack?'

The other looked up. It was him all right. More than a few years older, though Jimmy would have sworn it had been only months since they last spoke.

'J.P., boy,' he said, still with his palm out.

'Cusack. You're looking well.'

It was a disingenuous greeting but the only alternative was the most brutal honesty. *The absolute state a' yeh, Cusack! If there's a whore you've been visiting, it might be worth sprinkling her with holy water and commanding her back to the fiery depths, because you look like someone's tapped you for fluids.*

21

The desiccated accepted the salutation with a mournful nod.

'It's been a while,' said Jimmy.

'I suppose it has.' His voice was thick. Drunk? It looked more possible than anything else that had demanded his analysis today.

Back when Jimmy was in Iron Maiden T-shirts, Tony Cusack had been the useful kind of scamp, eager to prove he could hang around with the big boys by virtue of his keen eye and malleable morals. He'd been Jimmy's messenger when he was small enough to be fleet, but as he got bigger they'd drink together, or get stoned, and shoot the breeze about easy women and anarchy. When Jimmy was twenty-four, a coagulation of bad luck convinced him to head to London for a while, where he could carry on as before only with a shiny coat of anonymity, and, having fuck all else to do, Cusack had gone with him.

London had been good to Jimmy. It had given him cause to aim high. London had been good too to Tony, in its own way. He'd met a beour, impregnated her and brought her home with him, instead of staying put where the sun was shining.

His path had seldom crossed Jimmy's since. Christmases, here and there, they'd spotted each other in pubs. Jimmy had been known to send over a drink, but he'd taken care not to be too inviting. The charming laziness that had once defined Tony Cusack had morphed into dusty apathy; as a thirtysomething he was clumsy and morose, taxidermy reanimated. It was no secret that Cusack had pissed away what good London had given him. Even while his wife – had he even married her? – had been around, he had been steadily eroding his liver and the goodwill of every vintner in the city.

There wasn't much Jimmy didn't know about the city's vintners. Or its moneylenders, or dealers, or bookies. Cusack didn't have a reputation, as such, for that would be assuming that people bothered thinking about him, but if his demeanour didn't warn off investors then there were plenty of people able to cure their myopia.

Jimmy Phelan had a reputation. Tony Cusack had more of a stench. Forlorn and forgotten, cast out . . .

Perversely, that made him a good man for secrets, for who'd believe him if he talked? Who'd even listen to him?

'Are you busy? Jimmy asked, though he'd already anticipated the answer, and had already settled on the bribe.

Cusack wasn't busy. He wasn't a man used to being busy, and took the detour as a short holiday from whatever freeform tedium was routine to him. Jimmy gave him the bones of the brief – frightened woman, dead burglar, no suitable hands to complete the deed – and Cusack flinched, and puffed out his cheeks as if he was considering bolting, but Jimmy was OK with that. Fear was a quality he looked for in part-timers, though it was strange to encourage that attribute in a man he might once have called his friend, back, way back, when Jimmy had neither mother nor need for one.

When they got to the flat Cusack needed a minute on his haunches with his back turned, but after the rebellion inside him had been quashed, he dutifully found a ratty carpet on one of the upper floors, pulled up as part of the redecoration project, and helped Jimmy roll the dead man like a cigar. The tradesmen had left behind some cleaning tools; Jimmy and Tony scrubbed up as best they could, given the length of time the stranger had had to tattoo the floor. Maureen was right; they'd need to lay a new one. There was more to this job than the lick of a mop.

'How are you with tiling?' Jimmy asked.

'I did the bathroom of my own gaff,' said Tony. He'd sobered up, of course. 'Floor to ceiling. Put down tiles in the kitchen too, but that was a while ago.'

'Do a job here for me and I'll give you a few bob. I don't want to have to bring anyone else in on this now. What are you at tomorrow?'

'Nothing.'

'I'd a feeling you'd say that.'

In the absence of another vehicle, Jimmy drove his Volvo around to the back gate, at one end of a weathered brick alley garlanded deliberately with creepers and weeds. They flattened the back seat and laid the carpet cigar on a diagonal line: what once had been a breathing, thinking head to the back of the

23

passenger seat, what once had been trespassing feet to the opposite corner. They arranged empty paint cans and a ladder on one side, and on the other the double-bagged rags and brushes they'd used to clean up the blood.

Jimmy handed Tony a set of keys and notes enough to buy tiles and bleach.

'You've a car?'

'I do,' said Tony.

'Go with quarry tiles.' And then, because custom suggested, he said, 'What have you been up to anyway, Cusack? You're not working?'

'Here and there. Best anyone can manage now, I think.'

'You're probably right, boy. Even this is a one-off; I have more than enough mouths to feed.'

'I know that.' Tony shifted his weight. 'I know that, boy.'

'Speaking of mouths, how many little Cusacks are there?'

There was a ghost of a smile; it set on and escaped Tony's mouth in a snap second. It was the first time in a long time Jimmy had noticed something approximating life in the old dog.

'Six.'

'Six? You'd want to tie a knot in it.'

Six made leverage plenty.

They stood by the back of the car, still enough to let birds continue their evening rituals in the greenery around them, flitting in and out of bushes, darting shadows moving on walls the height-and-a-half of Jimmy.

'There's one job I'll have coming up,' said Jimmy. 'Nothing big and certainly nothing worth what I'll pay you, but you've done me a turn today. I'll be getting my hands on a piano sooner or later. The ex is looking for one for the kids. If you're around you can help move it in.'

'What kind of piano?'

'Worried for your back, are you? Not one of them long ones, if that's what you mean.'

'No, I mean what kind are you looking for? I have one I'm trying to gct shot of.'

24

'You? Where'd you get your grabbies on a piano, boy?'

Tony clucked and shook his head. 'Not like that,' he said. 'I own one. It's a few years old but it was bought new. It's a beauty, but all it's doing in my gaff is taking up space.'

'Is that the kind of thing that has to go, Cusack, when a man's got six kids?'

Tony shrugged. 'I can't play,' he said, though it sounded petulant, a tone not right for business deals, even on a day when reason had made way for blood, ties and tide.

Before they locked up Jimmy retrieved the Holy Stone and laid it carefully on the rolled-up shape of his mother's second greatest mistake.

Big Words, Little Man

'I'm just saying,' she says, 'that it's weird, like, that you can be so distant with someone you're actually in a proper relationship with.'

God though, tell you what but she's fucking beautiful when she's pissed off, even if it's pissed off with me. She's gone pink-cheeked and her eyes are flashing hazel to black and she's even standing with her arms folded and her chin sticking out. And all around her you get people moving from here to there in the school yard like dancers in formation, like snowflakes in the sky, like shitty little bangers around a falling star.

She's all like 'My friends think it's mean' and 'My friends say it's a really bad sign' and it's not like I'm whipped or nothing but what her friends think means a fuck of a lot more to me than she knows because you know the way ould dolls are, it's all fucking crowdsourced. But I go, 'Look, it shouldn't matter what your friends think, it should matter only what you think,' and she goes, 'Well it is about what I think, Ryan, and I think it's awful because I've done everything for you, you know?' By 'everything' she means she's let me fuck her and she's not even being over the top with that; it was everything, it was the whole world. She doesn't know that though. She only says 'everything' because she doesn't want every Tom, Dick and Harry hearing her say the word 'sex' coz you don't get away with words like that in the middle of the yard in the middle of lunchtime with every kid in this school sporting lugs the size of Leitrim. Which is funny because what she's pushing me to say is a whole lot bigger.

I say, 'You know how I feel about you, though.'

She says, 'How would I know it?'

I say, 'Coz don't I show you?'

And she says, 'Eh, the only thing I see shown is how much I let you get away with and what if it's all for nothing, like?'

And I smile and she goes, 'It's not funny, Ryan!' and looks like she might cry, and the thing is I know exactly what to do and I want to do it, believe me, I'm gagging to, only sometimes you have the right words in your mouth in the right order but it's such a big thing and a big fright that you're not sure if you can open up wide enough to get it out.

She says, 'Coz this is such a big deal, Ryan,' and looks away and shakes her head. 'And if you don't, well, it just means I'm stupid for letting you after only a couple of weeks. And I wouldn't ever again then.'

'That's not the way it is,' I tell her.

'What way is it?'

I get all mortified and look at the tarmac between my feet and she says, 'Oh my God. Fine so,' and turns away and I know she doesn't realise what a weird thing this is for me, because this isn't shit I've heard or said since I was a small fella, and I wince and she gets further away from me and I call, 'Hey, D'Arcy,' and she turns around, blazing, and I shrug and say, 'I loves yeh,' and the whole yard reels with her and shouts Oooooh! and I go bright. Fucking. Red.

But she smiles, and brings her hand to her mouth and gives me the eyes, because she knows there's no way I would have made a total gobshite of myself in front of everyone if I didn't totally mean it.

3

Georgie met Robbie when she was fifteen and he was twenty-two. He admitted to twenty-two; she admitted to nothing, not age nor origin nor the fact that she didn't have a fucking clue what she was doing. She was a runaway and he was wandering, and it happened that they found each other.

She lost him abruptly one April week, six years later. She couldn't say what day because there were often absences. She'd be working or he'd be climbing a wall somewhere, trying to come down before he fell down. So she didn't panic when she arrived home one day and he wasn't there, or start chewing her nails when he didn't pick up his mobile; he lost phones in perpetuity, sometimes quite intentionally. She phoned around the few friends they had but no one had seen him. On the third day she started to worry.

Georgie, small-town wild child and intermittent claustrophobic, self-styled, was into drugs well before she met Robbie. She wouldn't have met him at all if it wasn't for that shared interest: they kept bumping into each other on the same couches, doing the same drugs to the same end. He had sea-grey eyes and hair the colour of a muted sunset. Coasting on borrowed intelligence, they spoke about all manner of insubstantialities.

At one party, he told her that he had a room in a flat, and that she could sleep there, if she wanted.

'It's only a mattress on the floor,' he said. 'But it's better than couch-surfing or . . .' He blinked. '. . . moving from party to party, if you know what I mean.'

She went with him and twenty minutes later lay staring at the flaking wood on the inside of a white sash window, wincing as he shoved and stuck inside her, an invasion she'd sanctioned because she was spiralling and indebted. That was how Georgie lost her virginity: in a negotiation for mattress space.

After that he produced some more coke.

'You can stay as long as you like,' he said. 'I mean . . . that was really good of you.'

'No problem,' she replied.

His dick looked smaller than it had any right to feel when it had been inside her. He handed her his T-shirt and she bunched it between her legs.

She did another line and when she straightened up she noticed he was staring at her tits, gawping, like he hadn't seen a naked girl in years.

'No, it was really, really good of you,' he said.

Silence for a moment, and then, 'Do you like me?'

'Yeah. Course I do.'

He didn't believe her. 'I like you,' he said. 'Have done, too. For ages. You can stay as long as you like. I mean it.'

You can stay for six years, he could have said, and Georgie would have believed his offer but not in her ability to put up with him for that long. But that was it, wasn't it? You don't know your own strength till you need it.

Outside of their appetite for inebriation, Georgie and Robbie had little to hold them together, and there were more photogenic couples. He looked jointed enough to be folded away when not in use, and it wasn't often anyone had use for him. She was short and freckled, prone to weight where it wasn't wanted. The size of her breasts had made her barrel-like in her school jumper; ould fellas had breathed rough suggestions when they passed her on the street.

First she told Robbie that she'd moved to the city after her Leaving Cert to party. The longer she slept on his mattress, the heavier the lie felt, until she was too exhausted by its heft to be comfortable under it. She told him when she was sure he wouldn't baulk: she was fifteen and she'd run away but no one was looking for her because she'd told her parents she was just fine. Rang them every fortnight, actually, and evidently the guards weren't interested in tracking down a girl who was doing just fine. She was still here to party, she insisted.

Robbie took it exactly as she'd predicted. He scratched the back of his neck and puffed his cheeks out. 'Whoa,' he said, and reached no further than that. By then it was too late for him to demur, even if he had the guts for it. He had already walked her into an agreement with the guy he rented the room from; the landlord fucked her, now and then, in part-payment for another month of indoor binges and insubstantialities.

After that it was their dealer, and then a night's worth of punters around the back of the college while Robbie patrolled and parleyed, maybe once a week, maybe more than that. And Robbie, of course, though that was for free.

Birthdays passed, coke passed, crises passed. He patched her up when she needed it, she put her body against his debts when he needed it. She got pregnant but it didn't work out. Later, maybe. In the interim they stopped going to parties. They sat in, where he suffered death after death on his Xbox, and she sank into novels about dogged detectives and murderers who hid in plain sight.

She went to work indoors, at his insistence. Maybe he was just ridding himself of the responsibility of minding her, but he swore it was because the men who bought her in brothels would be less worrisome than the ones who trawled the streets.

He was wrong.

Up to that point she'd defined her time with Robbie in lively terms: *fighting*, *fucking*, *breathing*, *being*. After that point she was mostly concerned with death. The men who prearranged their time ensured that she was aware, every moment, of how many moments she might have left. By and large they were vicious, much more so than the last-minute trawlers. Maybe it was that these punters had time to stew in their contempt; it was often bubbling over by the time they got to their ordained girl. When she wasn't working she took solace in serial killers, and watched

Robbie bleed out on the TV screen a hundred times a day, until at last the irony started to sting.

One Sunday she got Robbie to borrow a car and drive her to her parents' house, where she waited, parked up the hill, until they'd gone to Mass.

Between brown walls, behind windows too close to sagging trees, underneath the tick-tock of wall clocks in sync, Georgie took in the scent of marrowfat peas and wet clay. She knew now how much worse things could be, and yet she still felt it: the hours lost and opportunities turned stale in the country air, the feeling that if she didn't get up and march out she'd grow roots down through the thin carpet, down through the foundations, down into the soil, the dirt, the rock, and trap herself there until her brain turned to jelly and thick hairs sprouted on her chin. Her parents were born of the land and stalled by the land, and Georgie was an alien. She'd taken off because there didn't seem to be any other way to go. Similarly, there was no way back now.

She stole one of her father's shirts from the back of the wardrobe and from the bedroom windowsill her mother's scapular. Because Home was something denied to her, she took only what bits of it wouldn't be missed. They served as bittersweet reminders of how badly she'd fucked up.

After that, every time she went to work she wound the scapular around the handle of the bedside table drawer. She eyed it as if to challenge it to produce salvation. Bleed out an angry Jesus. Call forth the wrath of his da.

These ecstasies kept her preoccupied, and it was a rare punter who noticed. Punters weren't equipped to notice such things, though they were clear-eyed enough when it came to her worldly being. Lack of enthusiasm for their libido usually provoked punishment in the form of thrusting hips or fists clenched around her hair, but sometimes they'd be passive aggressive and only take it out on her afterwards, sitting prim in front of their laptops, typing her into a hiding.

She'd a face on her like a slapped arse and an arse on her like a bag of Doritos . . .

The brothel moved to a new premises about a month before Robbie disappeared, and when the men came with the furniture the bedside table and its scapular was missing, and Georgie was too mortified by the shape of her sentimentality that she said nothing, except deep into Robbie's shoulder back in their flat.

So it wasn't that she feared that Robbie might be dead, because his death was the first logical conclusion. He wouldn't have run away because he had no one left to run to; they were, in all sorts of ways, the last two people on earth.

She looked for his corpse with determined detachment. If she found him bloodied or bloated that'd be something to deal with, but right now all she needed to do was her duty. She hunted for him. Alleyways, doorways, up the ways, down the ways. Nothing. It was like he'd been plucked out of existence, the way you'd flick a crumb off your shirt.

She reported him missing, and the guard taking her statement leaned back with his biro tapping out a march on the fleshy bit between his thumb and first finger, and stared as if she'd invented Robbie from scraps of punters and a fever-dream of wishful thinking. He sent her on her way with undisguised disgust and a flimsy promise to keep her updated.

If there had been a body, her grief wouldn't have felt so form-less. As it was, the fact that Robbie had been there one day and gone the next, leaving behind nothing but second-hand jumpers and foodstuffs she didn't like, left her suspended between mourning and wired impatience. He was there, then he was gone, and wherever he'd gone to he'd taken six years of Georgie with him.

The practicalities inherent in suddenly finding herself inde-pendent were many and unfortunate. She could support herself – there was money in prostitution, not a huge amount, but enough to make up the rent and keep her smashed – but . . . Well, there had been things she hadn't had to worry about when Robbie was around. Like he'd make sure the heating was on, or he'd go do the various errands that kept the coke and smoke topped up, or whatever. And now there were all of these *whatevers* and Georgie without the wherewithal to get through them.

Maybe I'm depressed, she wondered, idly, as she stood in the shower, thirty minutes at a time and sometimes noticing at the end that she was still in her knickers or that she'd forgotten to take her hair down. What little peace she had made with her circumstances when he was around to encourage it disappeared. She supposed the sudden six-year gap was making her sick. She was sick of the brothel and sick of the pimp and neither the promise of a roof over her head nor having someone to handle her appointments was doing it for her.

She could have just walked out, but that would have created more problems than it solved; the pimp could have had her for loss of earnings and might have insisted she stay on to work off debts he'd conjured out of bloated waffle. Instead she drank her way out. Punters arrived for appointments and she belched her disapproval at them, which they tried to pound out of her. Then the pimp tried to beat it out of her. He tried to hammer her straight, when being hammered was her problem. He wasn't a very smart man, in fairness. He was running the brothel for someone else, which was all in all a pretty stupid career move.

A few days of belching and beatings and Georgie was out on her ear. She went home and cleaned herself up and was back on the streets the next day. Sure, she had to worry now about the guards, but that seemed very much the lesser of two evils, especially when she could point out to them that they should have been searching for Robbie, and not stunting her earnings by booking her for solicitation or taking blowjob bribes in a back street off the quay. Oh yeah, a man was a man, when he was there.

And so that led her, in the week after her gin-soaked dismissal, to search for another kind of man.

Georgie had felt Tara Duane was a construct from the first day she'd met her, though of a positive sort, back then, a slice of luck given form by some propitious celestial alignment. Tara had found her around the back of the college, pockmarked by pebbledash and bad weather. She'd brought her a sandwich and a coffee and, later on, a vodka in one of the pubs off Oliver Plunkett Street; Georgie couldn't remember which. Sixteen years old and getting into cars with married men, and yet Cork City remained a mystery, the expanse of it forbidden to people like her, a soirée to which she held no invitation.

Tara swore she'd done her time in sex work, and that after having brazened out her trials she felt it her duty to offer support to the girls still involved in the trade. Winningly she implied she understood better than anyone the circumstances pinning Georgie down. It quickly became apparent that being pinned down was, in Tara's opinion, nothing to be ashamed of in these recessionary times. Ireland in a tailspin? Who could blame the girls on the street for their choices! Georgie didn't remember making a choice and she felt uncomfortable having it so neatly abridged by this uninvited proponent, if it was there at all.

As a rule the other girls in the trade were as supportive as they had room to be. The oldest women – the ones too far gone with booze or smack to operate on anything but instinct – were best avoided. They had quicker fists than a cast eye would assume. But, in general, Georgie found she had little to fear from her peers, and that there were times when it was wisest to trust them, and when more than one of them told her she was better off ignoring the wandering affections of Tara Duane, she listened.

The more she listened, the more cracks appeared on that alabaster mug. Tara always knew where the pimps and the dealers were, which knocking shops were looking for staff, who was facilitating the cam work. Some of the girls whispered that she was the city's most devious madam, taking pay from all manner of third parties as she spun the streets. Georgie wasn't sure Tara was practical enough to be a madam. Instead she wondered if she wasn't just a creep, feigning aid like she feigned smiles.

The activism Tara Duane purported to fill her time with usually amounted to handing out home-made sandwiches to the destitute. So it was tonight. Georgie spotted her on the opposite end of the quay, filling plastic cups for a couple of the old junkies from a flask out of the boot of her car.

It was just after ten, and between the street lights and the river, damp shadows ran up Georgie's limbs and pressed springtime chills against her chest; every breath was a gasper.

Tara noticed her from fifty yards away, and broke into one of her cracked-mirror smiles as soon as she was sure Georgie was close enough to get the full-frontal benefit.

'Georgie! Hey, girl, how are you? I haven't seen you in so long; what have you been up to, hon?'

Georgie said, 'I need a dealer.'

Tara pursed her lips and tried out a couple of different faces until she settled on one approaching concern, but the flickers of the sides of her eyes, and the twisting to-and-fro of her lips, betrayed the connections whirring through her head. She pulled her ponytail tighter. 'Well, you know I wouldn't condone it, Georgie. I mean God knows you have enough on your plate.'

'My plate's swept clean,' Georgie said. 'That's the problem, Tara.'

Hmm. 'Would Robbie not know someone?'

'Robbie's not home yet.' She felt that one. Unexpected, a pang in her abdomen like a knifepoint, or the warning signs of a life about to be lost on a public bathroom floor.

Tara made another face.

'Not yet?' she sighed. 'Oh, poor Robbie. I hope he's OK, girl, I really do. I mean even if he'd left you; to know is to heal, pet.'

Georgie pulled her jacket across her belly. 'Yeah,' she said. 'In the meantime, though . . .'

'A dealer,' said Tara, thoughtfully. 'Of course, I don't like to enable it.'

'Oh sure yeah. You don't partake at all, do you, Tara?'

Stern now, Tara said, 'Well, there's a difference between a smoke and the class As, Georgie.'

'Who said I'm after class As?'

'I'm not insinuating anything. Just history, Georgie, you know yourself. What about . . .' She lowered her voice, though the old junkies had shuffled on, and there was no one to hear them. 'Work? Would they not provide?'

'I'm not working there anymore, Tara. I thought you'd have heard?'

Of course she would have heard. Tara Duane heard everything. She knew the city like a spectre of many hundreds of years, even though she couldn't have been more than thirty-five; she wafted into lives, poking and prodding, and listening, mostly listening. Maybe the toll due for a coffee was a rumour and a sandwich cost a story half verified. Maybe she did relief work around the city's brothels – not in the bedrooms, but answering their phones, keeping the doors locked, washing the towels, peeping through keyholes . . .

Maybe she had lovers in the criminal fraternity, though Georgie wondered who'd have her. She was wraith-like in stature, with long, pale hair and eyes wide as open graves. And the forged sincerity. Couldn't you just see it? Tara Duane's tongue circling some gangster's distended cock, imbibing his rage and the shapes he threw at the city from his back, his massive belly rising and falling against her forehead as he blathered all his secrets into her ears. Maybe they passed her around like a virus, and that's how she harvested specifics and conjecture both.

'Have you moved on?' Tara frowned, and then smiled widely and suddenly like she'd possessed another woman's face. 'Would you like a coffee?'

'I'm grand for coffee. And yeah. Moved on. Back on the street.'

'That's very dangerous,' said Tara, who had started to pour a coffee anyway. 'You know you're better off indoors. Clean, no Gardaí, vetted clients . . .'

Georgie took the coffee. 'That doesn't always work out as it should,' she said, carefully.

'Were you drinking?' asked Tara. Her face had turned solemn.

'And how would you know that?' Georgie said.

'I don't know that. At least I didn't.'

'Ah no,' said Georgie. 'Lucky guess.'

'I might have heard something,' Tara conceded.

'Have you heard, then, where I can find a dealer who's not up to his bollocks in the same swamp I was just fucked out of?'

'All right,' said Tara. 'I might know someone who'd suit. A young fella. We're close, so he'll look after you if I tell him to.'

This delivered with a sickening simper, an invitation to empathise that was ill-advised but unchecked; Tara was too pleased with herself. She might well take lovers from the criminal fraternity but rumour had it that she preferred younger men, and eyewitnesses suggested the effect intensified with every lay. Certainly she didn't discriminate between genders when it came to extolling the benefits of sex work. Georgie had been on the game for six years and in that time she'd learned plenty about the stranger tastes men developed. She had theories: that sex was everywhere, and so what was once titillating was now everyday and so men required boosters personal to them. Or that the entitlement natural to purchase of service made them savage with unchecked lust. Or that they'd all been diddled by priests. Whatever the reason, she'd seen plenty outside the remit of the freakiest girlfriend, but even so, she couldn't get her head around a young fella wanting to get close to Tara Duane, no matter how overpowering his MILF fantasies. The woman wore hunger like a second skin.

'You know young fellas,' Tara went on. 'They can be so very keen.'

'Yeah,' Georgie said, weakly. 'Take what you can get.'

'What's that mean?'

She was frowning. Georgie shook her head.

'That came out wrong,' she said. 'I didn't mean you'd have to take what you were given, only, like, seizing opportunities or whatever.'

Tara relaxed. She gestured for Georgie's mobile and entered a number.

'Be gentle with him,' she said. And though the joke begat a smirk, Georgie flinched, and felt unease swell and break from her belly to the hot points at the back of her ears and the fine tips of the hair on her arms.

*

See, people are afraid of dealers. Prostitutes are objectionable; you wouldn't want them tottering in their knee-highs for trade on your street. But dealers? Oh no. Abject terror, then. Dealers have guns and vendettas. They might target your children and kick down your door.

Georgie couldn't deny that there was some validity in that, though she wasn't afraid of the merchants, not as a general breed. Some of them were too keen to get into other forms of capitalism and looked working girls up and down the way you would a horse at a town fair. They were obvious as landslides and a clever girl kept her distance. Most of them, though, were but a slightly sharper edge on pathetic. A lot of them stocked up only to feed their habits, and lost a little up their noses and into their veins with each transaction, buying their way into slavery.

The smart ones fell somewhere between both categories; their efforts at expansion stayed within the realms of pills and powder, and their noses remained intact. When Georgie had worked indoors, there hadn't been a shortage of inlets for numbing substances, all but essential when you were fucked for a living. Otherwise it had been Robbie's responsibility, and he had hooked into the same network in recent months. Breaking away from brothel employment didn't mean that she was forbidden to tap her sources for coke, but there were within that network people that she never wanted to see again for the rest of her life.

Tara Duane's own dealer was not the ideal. Georgie went down to the corner and asked a couple of the other girls for contacts, but the market they frequented was practically a monopoly, and every avenue led Georgie back to ground she'd walked before.

Eventually it came to an impasse, so she buried Tara's smirk, and dialled.

'Yeah?'

'Hey. I got this number from a friend of yours. I'm looking for a bit; can you help?'

'What friend?'

'A girl named Tara.'

'Tara who?'

Obviously this one had little regard for the lugs of the law. Georgie hesitated. 'Tara Duane.'

'Oh,' he said. And there was a pause and then, 'I dunno. Where are you?'

'In town.'

'Coz I'm not.'

'I can go to you if needs be but "needs be" right now is a need-to-know,' she said.

'That's fucking poetry,' he said. 'You're lucky I'm stoned. All right. What is it you're after?'

In the lull between placing her order and making the collection, she managed to turn over a couple of punters, one fearful and unfit and sweating like a pig because of both, the other after a blowjob which failed to cure his boredom. That gave her enough to pay for what she wanted from the merchant, but not enough to go home on. Provided he was a decent skin who wasn't about to rip her off with ground up aspirin wrapped in tinfoil – and who knew what kind of person she was foisting upon herself on Tara Duane's recommendation – she would at least get a bump before getting herself back out there. Maybe conjure the scapular from behind closed eyes, and hope she didn't gush blood onto the client's neck.

It's stigmata, baby. I just blew my lord.

She didn't see him at first. She got back to the end of the quay and he was a little ways in behind a parked car, sitting on a bollard. He made her jump and she really hated that.

'You Georgie?' he said.

'Jesus.'

'Naw,' he said. 'Not even close. Ryan.'

He was sitting with his legs insolently stretched, but his shoulders were hunched and his hands deep into his pockets. He was feeling the cold. No wonder; he was wearing a school uniform, no jacket, just a thin maroon V neck over a grey shirt it wouldn't have become him to button up.

4

First it occurred to Tony Cusack that he needed to track down Robbie O'Donovan's family and tell them that the poor divil was dead. Then it occurred to him that behaving anywhere approximating worthy would only land him in a hell of his own making. There'd be guards. The plaintive wailing of sisters and mothers. Above all there'd be Jimmy Phelan. Above all, looming like Godzilla, with a face on him like an old quarry.

Tony hadn't had much regard for Robbie when he was alive, but then it was rare Tony attracted the kind of company that demanded or deserved it. Robbie used to drink in the same local. Another daytime guzzler, he'd come in with his betting slips and a *Star* folded under his arm and his mobile phone, and he'd sit at the bar, looking up at the telly, and down at his slips, and then to the paper and then to his phone. Not much of a conversationalist, even when steaming, but Tony had never been concerned with that. He knew of him more than he knew him, even with hours spent on parallel stools, drinking in sync in the afternoon hum.

Finding the craitur all caved in on the floor of Jimmy Phelan's flat, though, had turned Tony's gut inside out. There was, of course, the ugliness of it, in a practical sense. Smashed egg physics, enough to turn all the stomachs of a cow. Then there was the fact that Tony knew the bloke, and that he hadn't expected to, and that he needed to yank tight his instincts in front of J.P. before that recognition gushed right out of him and all over the floor. That was physically exerting; Tony wasn't cut out to be an actor.

But more than that again. There was something of sickly camaraderie between Tony Cusack and the faces he saw, blurred and

40

blubbering, haloed around him on a daily basis. Robbie O'Donovan got it on the back of the head and Robbie O'Donovan wasn't all that different to him. And what was the difference, really, if a man was going to meet a sticky end? The universe didn't care whether he was a gangly ginger or a dusty-haired chunk, if it was in the mood for killing off wasters. Fuck, like. It could have been him. It could have been any of them.

And if it had been him, would he not want his mother to know about it?

He'd gone home from the clean-up with a roll of J.P.'s money in his pocket and a headache that started somewhere below his shoulders and pulled a hood of churning colours down over his eyes. Sat in the kitchen with a bottle of Jameson and an empty glass. He'd wanted the drink, but it had taken him time and effort to get the whiskey from the bottle to the glass and then from the glass past his teeth. A few hours in the company of a corpse would do that to a man still living. And that state was hardly guaranteed, with his having duped J.P. into thinking he didn't know who the dead man was.

Maybe he should have told him. Maybe it would have worked out. *Eh, Jimmy boy, I know this feen.*

And maybe J.P. would have taken it as an invitation to drive Tony's head back into his shoulders. You don't go around telling wrought-iron hard men that you know who they've been offing. Otherwise they go around wearing your skin as a cravat.

It was such an insignificant thing, when he thought about it. He knew a guy, and he neglected to disclose it. That's all. A small fucking thing to be in fear of your life over. Forget to move your tongue and suddenly you're driven to drink with piddle dribbling down your trouser leg at your kitchen table.

He dragged himself between each conclusion for days stretching into weeks: read the death notice on the O'Donovan doorstep, or bend under Jimmy's shadow and wait for the guilt to wither. He was harsher with the kids because of it. Everything they did wrecked his head. He hid in the kitchen when they were watching TV, in his bedroom when they were eating, in the pub when he could afford it. He went over his potential revelation from various angles, and from each perspective it ended badly – with O'Donovan's family riotously questioning and him at a gaping loss.

Missus O'Donovan? I'm sorry to catch you unawares . . . Poor bitch. . . . *but your son is dead as a fucking dodo.*

And how would you know that, you bedraggled old fuck?

Cue J.P. screeching in just as the guards finished their questioning and blowing him out of this life and into the next, as if Tony Cusack's existence held only the durability of plastic sheeting stretched tight on an old door frame.

Tony and Maria had gotten married as a postscript; sure weren't they already bound together by offspring and his parents' disapproval? Maria had mentioned it as something that ought to be done at some stage after they got the keys to the house. Tile the bathroom. Adopt a puppy. Get hitched, I suppose, in fairness like.

He brought her home to Naples so that they could say their vows. The reception was held on the terrace of a restaurant chosen, decorated and, more importantly, paid for by her parents. He hadn't a clue what any of them were saying but they looked relatively jolly. Keen to provide an alternative to the Italians' frolics, his parents had spent the day wrinkling their noses as if, roused by foreign tradition, each of their new in-laws had lined up to cordially shit on the cake.

It got to him; first that the Irish party was so scrubby-thin, and then that it was in such foul form. The language barrier wasn't helping. Nor was Maria, floating around the place as Princess Mammy, a toddler under each arm while her décolletage was muddied with sugary thumbprints and white chocolate. She let the Italians monopolise the baby talk and kept her tanned back to her old enemy, her new mother-in-law, who sat sipping her G&T, scowling, sour, making a holy show of him right there on the edge of the dance floor.

Maria put down their small fella to adjust her neckline and

Tony scooped him up again, walked with him to the bar, and bought a Nastro Azzurro and a Coke.

'You having fun, Rocky?'

His son looked at him with the dopey, Disney-brown eyes the Italians had tried to claim credit for, and Tony pressed his lips against the curls on his little forehead and said, 'Coz I'm fucking not.'

He cowered between choices until the decision was made for him.

It was midday on a Thursday, some Thursdays after the deed. He'd been on the go since seven, and not for entirely wholesome reasons; the ugly favour he'd done Phelan had left him with episodic insomnia and an unwelcome tendency to rise early. This morning there had been copybooks to locate, shoelaces to tie, slices of toast to butter, teenagers to bellow out of bed. Once the brood had loped off to school he'd tidied away the topmost stratum of jumble, put on the first of two loads of washing, and made his way to the supermarket for milk, bread and whiskey. He was on his way home again when his mobile rang.

The thing with Cork having been built on a slope was the further out you got from the hub, the better the views were. Tony put the bag of groceries on the footpath and reached into his jeans pocket for the phone. Below him, his city spread in soft mounds and hollows, like a duvet dropped into a well.

The breeze and the elevation made the city feel emptier than it had the right to feign. Less than a mile further out the estates would lose to green fields and hedgerows; it was calm here, as if the residents had flowed sleepily down the hill to pool in the streets around the Lee. Else they were indoors drinking tea and quietly dying. Tony leaned on a dustbin sporting three of the same sticker, a guide in aggressive bold letters to rejecting the authority of the Irish courts and the banks they slyly served. Not for the first time, he was glad he'd never bought a house. The country had gone to shit and the desperate were growing mad.

When he turned his phone over in his hand there was J.P.'s

number, fresh in his contact list from their collaboration, bright and brash on the screen.

Tony Cusack felt a bolt of fear shoot down his throat and out his arse.

He hit the answer button.

'Are you busy, Cusack?'

'No,' Tony said. 'No, boy. No, I'm not.'

There was a gap, as J.P. considered the triplicated guarantee and Tony caught his tongue between his teeth.

'D'you remember that tiling job you did for me?' J.P. said.

'I do.'

'You're going to have to redo it.'

At the end of the quay, where the river curved and the traffic quietened and the grand Georgian facades were smudged and flaking and tagged black and blue in unsure, ugly hands, stood the house in which Tony was expected to replicate his own hard work.

He knocked and the door was opened by an ould wan, about his mother's age, dressed like a chilblained scarecrow with a face that would have reversed the course of the Grand National.

'You're Tony?' she asked.

'Yeah. I understand there's a problem with the floor?'

'I bet you do,' she said. 'You understand more than you're letting on.'

She stalked down the hall, and Tony picked his way after her like he was stepping around landmines, which, fuck it, he might as well have been, considering she was capable of knocking the stuffing out of him.

He watched her narrow back for signs of pole-shift. Fuck, he watched her narrow back for signs of brutality of any depth, for how could a pisawn the size and shape of a bog wisp kill someone? And how then could a stout man of thirty-seven, a father of six with the courage to roll up a corpse in a carpet, feel afraid of her?

He followed her into the kitchen and she gestured at the tiles with a floppy wrist and a childish lip.

She'd made a mosaic out of them. The squares he'd put down

in rows neater than any he'd thought his own home worthy of had been scattered in overlapping clumps, broken into shards, maybe by a hammer, maybe by the same force that had smashed Robbie O'Donovan's head like a jam jar.

'Holy fuck,' he said.

She sniffed.

He didn't want to ask. Afraid of the answer, maybe, but something beyond that too, basic as the gawks rising in his throat; he didn't want to acknowledge the presence of this ghoul in a cardie. In this space occupied by just the pair of them he felt his body seize up; first his neck, then the backs of his arms, then his waist. Like the horror-movie victim who'd just noticed the shadow at his elbow.

'What did you do?' The arse of the question formed a tuck in his throat; he swallowed, but it bobbed there, and grew.

'Ha?' she said.

He coughed.

'What did you do?'

'I told him I wasn't staying here. And his answer is to throw down a new floor and tell me that makes a new house?'

He didn't know what to say so he let her statement hang there, counted solemn breaths and said, 'D'you have black bags, or . . .'

She produced a roll of flimsy bin liners.

'That won't do,' he said. 'I'll look upstairs.'

He left her by her protest piece and hastened to the next floor. He went from room to room – shells of rooms now, bare floorboards and stripped-down walls. The floor echoed under each footfall. Here, he was alone. Downstairs, everything was wrong. The pall of the act and its cover-up. The little lady with the violent streak.

The fresh air of Cork spread out before him seemed a long way back now. Tony paused for breath and wiped his hands off his thighs.

One of the rooms had been set aside as a store for the workmen's rubble. Tony spotted a dustpan and brush with a roll of bin bags on top of an old bedside table.

He moved to the window and looked down to the street. J.P. had phoned in his orders over an hour ago. He was surely on the way over.

Outside, the Lee lay still and glistened green.

Tony turned his back to the river and looked at the piled furniture.

There was something knotted around the handle of the bedside table from which he'd plucked the clean-up tools. He ran his fingers over it. Fabric. Like a shoelace, only with square cloth tags bound up in it at intervals.

He unwound it from the handle for want of something else to do.

Tony made a home with Maria once they were given four walls to contain it, and he spread out and grew older around the clutter of a life lived in sweeping strokes and splash damage. One night, and one fight too many, she drove away from it all, cursing it loud enough for the whole terrace to hear, leaving Tony on their landing with the colour rushing to his stinging left cheek.

Her insistence on cultivating an independent social life and his disdain of the dawn-to-dusk jobs both their mothers claimed suitable for him were pretty stupid things to fight about, but Tony and Maria could draw a fight from nothing, if they were drunk enough. She had a bottle of red wine in her and blood stoked to madness, and all he could do was wait for the Gardaí to show up on his doorstep with their caps off. Didn't stop him hoping, though. That she'd swing awkwardly into the driveway – taking the gate with it if she liked, he didn't care – and hammer an aria up the stairs. Or that she'd phone him from a ditch, bruised but breathing. But she didn't. She drove from home right into the grave, with the shadow of his hands on the steering wheel.

The Gardaí sat with him at the kitchen table. His oldest son, eleven then and the soft curls well gone from his forehead, appeared at the door with wide-eyed gumption and Tony snapped 'Get out' at him, and then, when the lad didn't move, 'Get out!' again, having risen to his feet, and Jesus Christ but he regretted that afterwards. You can't blame yourself for your reactions when you're in a state; he knew that. But if he could have gone back to that moment for another shot at it he would have held his arms out and cradled the young fella and maybe stopped the whole thing going to shit from there on in.

'What's that?'

Tony stepped backwards, catching a toe off its opposite heel and snagging the end of the brown material as it came with him. The woman strode towards him. She held out her hand.

'What?'

'The yoke you're after ripping off that small table. Let me see.'

'It's nothing,' he said, and held it over her palm. 'Just a thing. I don't know what kind of thing.'

'It's a scapular,' she said. 'A churchy yoke. See? The Virgin Mary there, looking out at you . . .'

'What's she looking at me for?' he said, and put his hands in his pockets and the ould wan stared at him and said, 'It was an accident, you know.'

'What?'

She said, 'What happened here.'

'Oh.' She was no mind reader.

'I see you looking at me like I might crack you open too, but I'm telling you, 'twasn't the way I'd planned to spend my morning.'

'Course not,' he muttered.

'Maureen is my name,' she said.

'Oh. Yeah. Tony.'

'Tony what?'

'Cusack.'

'And which Cusack are you?'

There wasn't exactly a rake of Cusacks in Cork. 'Up Mayfield.'

'John,' she said. 'And Noreen. And you're the only boy. Ah, I know you now.'

A knack for geographical pinpointing was, at least, an expected trait in an ould wan.

'It wasn't intentional,' she said. 'I'm living alone, you know,

What would you do, if you're half the size of the fridge and there's a fella in front of it as wide as he's tall?'

'A skinny yoke, wasn't he?' Tony said, weakly.

She sniffed again. 'Sure perspective is the first to go when your arse is against the wall.'

She bunched the scapular into one of her pockets.

'Was it yours?' Tony asked.

'Indeed it was not.'

'Funny thing to find here,' he said. 'What did you call it? A scalpula?'

'A scapular. Why is it a funny thing to find here?'

It occurred to him that it probably wasn't the ex-madam he was talking to.

'No reason,' he said.

She frowned.

'No,' she said, 'why is it a funny thing to find here, Tony Cusack? Because it's a holy thing and there's something wrong in this building, is it? Because a man died, and artefacts of God no longer belong? Is that your line of thinking, is it?'

'No. Not at all,' he said, though the sound came out as *No, not that tat all.* 'Just . . . y'know, workmen aren't known for taking prayer breaks.'

'That's not what you were getting at,' she said. 'You think I've sullied the place.'

'I don't.'

'That's what it is.'

'It's not.'

'You think I've blood on my hands.'

He seized the dustpan and brush and made to walk out of the room, but she caught his left arm and hung on, weight in her now like a bag of coal and his head suddenly humming with the thirst.

She did have blood on her hands. And so did he. For the short moment both his breath and arm were held, he considered telling her that.

'The state of your hands is none of my business,' he said

48

instead. 'This place used to be a whorehouse. That's what I meant. Funny to have a Holy Mary chattyboo here then, see?'

'This used to be a whorehouse?'

'Not so long ago too,' he conceded.

She paused.

'Dirty little bollocks,' she said, but she was looking down through the floor, so Tony knew it wasn't meant for him.

'I probably shouldn't have said that so?' he chanced.

'You probably shouldn't,' she replied. 'Not that it matters to you, my lad, because even if it wasn't my transgression you were referencing . . .' She stepped forward and he stepped back. '. . . you're still warped in thinking that a whore has no right to be religious. Haven't you heard of Mary Magdalene?'

'I didn't say that.'

'You did, boy, loud and clear. Funny thing to find a scapular in a place like this, because the only people worthy of grace are the people who've done the least to need it, hmm?'

The sun broke through outside the window, and a shaft of light appeared across the floor and opened up the room. Off the sage green walls it cast a spotlight on Maureen's head, making her, for just a second, the bulb off the Wicked Witch of the West.

'I've no problem with anyone getting religious,' he said.

'You do, and it's buried so deep inside you . . .' She poked his belly. '. . . that you can't even see yourself for the bigot you are.'

'Jesus, I was—'

'Ah, and now you're taking the Lord's name in vain.'

'Look,' he said. 'Clearly you're into all that, and I'm sorry if I offended you—'

'I'm not into any of it. I'm just pulling you up on assuming your right to religion if you're going to deny it to whores.'

'What? I'm not . . . I'm just . . . Jesus Christ.'

'And you're only saying *Sorry if I offended you* because you think the power of Christ might compel me to compel you to the next life, isn't that it?'

'Well listen, girl, whatever poor Robbie O'Donovan did to you, I want to avoid it.'

'Robbie O'Donovan,' she said.

Downstairs the door opened, and J.P. rolled his name out of his maw.

'Cusack? C'mere timme and get these tiles! Maureen? Maureen! Did that fella not get here yet at all?'

Tony looked at the gleeful old dear, and turned, and walked downstairs to J.P. like a boy moving towards a principal sworn to mete out reprimand, screaming protest in his head and yet feeling the loss of will like a punch to the gut as his feet kept inching forward.

'Nice one,' said J.P., spotting the dustpan and the bin bags, and Tony sank to his haunches and started sweeping up the broken tiles.

'I don't know how she did it,' J.P. said. 'I swear to God, that woman wrecks all around her.'

'It's coz she doesn't want to stay here,' Tony said.

'And yet here she'll stay, because she doesn't have anything to bargain with,' J.P. replied.

Tony Cusack swept the tiles into the black bag, stood up and faced Jimmy Phelan, and from his thin dry lips he said, 'C'mere, are you ever going to be ready for that piano, boy?'

The dew was heavy on the grass by the time he got home. He crossed the green towards his gate and the damp stretched from the blades to his jeans and up onto his calves.

She stood at her front door, hanging on to the jamb with a bare foot hooked round its opposite ankle.

'Evening, Tony!'

His estate was an ugly thing – near thirty houses bordering a scruffy green, a couple more rows behind each terrace. *You can't look a gift house in the mouth*, his sister once said under a wrinkled nose; he found that funny. It was home, at this stage. It wasn't perfect, nor had it been long before his family outgrew it, but it was cheap and they weren't going to be kicked out, barring his deciding to start dealing drugs out of the place or running a knocking shop in the box room.

The drawback was that there was no way of knowing what kind of degenerate would become your neighbour, seeing as the whims of the Corporation were rickety as a city of sticks and the only trait required in its tenants was a wallet full of moths. For a couple of years Tony had lived between the McDaids, who were coolly pleasant, and the Healys, who couldn't wait to get out of there. The Healys made a break for it and in their place the Corporation installed Tara Duane, who he remembered vaguely from his own schooldays. She'd gotten knocked up by some Scottish fella and her lone sprog granted her placement in a house the same size as his own.

She was frail and bug-eyed, but he knew his mother hoped that one day they'd knock through the dividing wall; a single mother and a doleful widower, sure why not, sure no one wants to die alone in a double bed. For a while Tara seemed to have subscribed to this line of thinking, and her conversations would coast between flat jokes and forced intimacy.

It was bad enough suffering this breathy plámásing, but then she took an interest in his kids.

Kelly first, because her young wan was Kelly's age and so naturally they became buddies. It wasn't such a problem with Kelly. She was like her mother: a pretty face and a vicious bitch. Ryan then, and that bothered him a lot more, because boys will be boys and this boy was easily led and, occasionally, startlingly sentimental. There were indications that she'd been playing the mammy with him. There was a flaunted familiarity with his quirks; a slight, sickening competitiveness; a proper little devil in the details.

'Nights are getting shorter,' she beamed.

He grunted. The kids hadn't closed the curtains. Every light in the house on again, and the place wide open to inspection. The idea of every biddy in the estate rubbernecking dismayed him, but there was no talking to his six; the darkening glass on the four walls didn't prompt in them self serving instinct, not yet anyway.

Through the sitting-room window he watched a lurid parade of TV cartoons and school jumpers and various projectiles

'And sure Ryan won't feel it till the Junior Cert,' Tara went on.

Tony's shoulders drooped. He closed his eyes.

'Sure he'll fly through it,' said Tara.

Even with the best will in the world Tony couldn't play friends with Tara Duane, but her trilling was part of this landscape, and this landscape was his, boring and all as it was, sodden and all as he made it.

C'mon, boy. What would Jimmy Phelan want with this?

Laser Light

She's grand for half an hour and the next thing she is totally off her game. I'm waiting for it, so it's not a surprise.

We're out at a Junior Cert results party in town which in fairness I'd otherwise have avoided like the plague but she was mad to go; there's two floors and two DJs and kids here from every side of the city. I've been sitting by the bar all night and there's been a few people coolly wandering over because they've heard I've got yokes. They sit down beside me with their hand awkwardly curled on the seat cushion by my arse and I exchange tablets for tenners.

Karine's wearing hotpants and a tight top and a scalding pink bra and her heels are so tall they bring her right up to my height, and so she's all legs and shoulders and skin. She's sitting on my lap shouting over the music at her buddy Louise. I've got my arms around her and my mouth pressed to the back of her neck, coasting a boner that just won't go away. Not that she minds. She's figuring that if she stays sitting on my lap she'll shield me from customers' funny looks. It's her sitting on my lap in fucking hotpants that's doing the damage but no way am I telling her that.

I've popped a yoke and I've given her a half. She's never done one before.

So one minute she's talking to Louise and the next she's turning around to me saying, 'I think it's happening,' and I hold on tight as the wave hits her. I put my hand under her top, flat on her tummy, and every breath she takes is deeper than the one before.

I turn her so she's leaning against my shoulder and I put my hand between her thighs and into her ear I say, 'Y'alright?'

She nods and smiles and her eyes are flying saucers.

There's a laser show on the dance floor. Green beams chase over the ceiling and dip onto hands held high, everyone's hollering. I hold on to my girlfriend and press my cheek against her shoulder; she hooks her arm around my neck and strokes my ear and says, 'Oh God, Ryan. Oh God.'

'Is it good?'

'Oh my God, this is amaaaazing.'

She's floating. She leans her head back and though my buzz is climbing as fast as my dick is waning I catch her and push her back onto my shoulder, and she says Mmm and I laugh and tell her to be careful, because there's stewards all over the place looking out for wasted kids.

She kisses me then, long and slow, and doesn't open her eyes again afterwards, just smiles and sighs as if she's coming. And I just hold her and keep holding her and the lasers make a web in the air over our heads, pull it apart and build it again, make stars to fall down on us.

She's all over me.

The thing is, every girl in this place is all over some fella, so we don't look special, but we are. We're plugged into the lights and plugged into each other and I had no fucking idea it was possible to love someone as much as I love her right now.

5

So it was during a class on Newton's Laws of Motion that Ryan had an epiphany. Third Law, as it happened, and probably his third epiphany that month. Maybe even that day, if he was to scale epiphanies down to their basest elements. Small truths. Snatches of caught breath as playback skipped just enough for him to grab on to something new. Maybe that was just growing up, though no one around Ryan seemed to suffer the same sudden expansions of consciousness. He was a bright kid. A bit too fucking bright, it had been said.

There's no force in the universe, said his teacher (Mr O'Reilly, whose designer spectacles were betrayed by a face mired in 1985), which doesn't have an opposing force to balance it. Action and reaction, push and pull. That's the Law, now, kids. Sir Isaac Newton came up with that one. That's knowledge that came before you and so defines your lives without as much as a by-your-leave. Shit happens, then more shit happens.

Ah, but shit happens right up to the point where it's happening in the face of someone who doesn't want to see it. That was the truth and the truth had fuck all respect for Sir Isaac Newton and his axioms. So here, Ryan realised, was a case of the pig-headedness of people versus the Laws of Physics, and while flesh and bones have to obey the push and pull of the universe the real meat of men, their thoughts and actions and utter arrogance, ignores the processes the universe has run on for aeons.

We're all gods when we fucking feel like it.

There were a number of tiny holes on the surface of his desk, made months or years ago by students with compass points and short attention spans. Ryan jammed his biro into one, pushed down on it, circled the crater with ballpoint ink and swept an awkward black trail across to the next.

Mr O'Reilly liked to sing to the back of the room, and Ryan was right up the tippy-top, under his nose, where, it was said, he could do less damage. Ryan rested his thumb on the top of his pen, balancing it between his touch and the pre-punched holes in the desk, and looked up Mr O'Reilly's snout. There was a wedge of soft grey gunk caught in the hairs at his left nostril.

Plenty of damage Ryan could do to people's noses, directly or through encouraging lack of self-control. Did Mr O'Reilly ever take a line of coke? In his life? In college when he was learning to be a physics teacher? Between courses at dinner parties, his moustache brushing the cistern as he hunched over in the under-stairs toilet of some cunt he was only pretending to like? Before he came to work every weekday?

Ryan had a baggie in his pocket that he didn't yet have a buyer for. He wouldn't usually have brought it someplace like school, but his dad was mid-episode and hanging for trouble, so it had struck Ryan as being a better idea to take it hidden on his person than leave it where Greedyguts might get at it. And who knew, teachers might be a great market to tap into. God knows they needed an edge.

He let the biro rattle loose and Mr O'Reilly's moustache twitched.

He picked up the biro again and moved on to another little hole.

Balanced it on its tip, let it fall . . .

Mr O'Reilly leaned over his desk with his neck arched, like he was doing a push-up.

'Is there something *wrong* with you, Ryan?'

Ryan looked down at the biro. 'Gravity I'd say, sir.'

His nearest neighbour sniggered. O'Reilly glanced over and the sniggering was sucked back behind pursed lips.

'Look at your desk! School property and it's covered in black marks . . .'

There were marks on Ryan's face this week. Not black. One, kind of greening, on his cheekbone, cradling his left eye like the organic sprouting of a superhero mask. The other, purple and red-dashed, across the top of his forehead where he'd had it whacked off the lip of a step four from the bottom of the stairs. He knew that there were marks on his face because he had felt them applied and he had examined them extensively in the three days he'd spent at home convalescing under the wide eye of a father both ashamed and peevish. They were gaudy blotches, not easily missed.

More Laws there too, he reckoned. The Law of Unavoidable Contusion, where blunt force trauma drew the blood from his capillaries into the tissue around them. The Law of Here, Have a Splash of Ugly that stated that every run-in with his father had to be recorded on his face. Yeah, the Law of Fuck You, Ryan that rendered everyone around him oblivious. Like, he wanted people to see, just for fucking once, and at the same time didn't want them to notice it at all, and it was the latter that people seized on, to the extent where a moustachioed keeper of the peace could stand not six inches from him and not see the fact that his whole fucking head was bawling out for someone to say, 'Jesus, boy, whatever kind of little cunt you are I'm sure you didn't ask for that one.'

'Now that you've made that mess, what are you going to do about it?' snapped Mr O'Reilly.

Ryan rolled his tongue around his mouth and looked down at the holes and the ink and spat on them.

He looked up at O'Reilly and O'Reilly had a head on him like a salmon rolled into a hot press.

'Wipe that up,' he said.

There wasn't much moisture there to wipe. Ryan's mouth was dry. It had been for days.

He dragged his sleeve off the desk.

'Office,' said O'Reilly.

Ryan's chair clattered to the floor and he kicked it backwards and marched out of the room, carrying his classmates' stares and

O'Reilly's dogged impassiveness across his shoulders until the door slammed shut behind him.

Karine asked him all the time why he felt the need to act the maggot. Did it not exhaust him to have to explain himself to teachers? There couldn't be any peace in demanding to be thrown out of class. Even if he was in terrible form, would it not be the easier option to sit there pretending to listen than to make a show of his repulsion?

Ryan couldn't answer her. It wasn't boredom, though he'd heard teachers hypothesise that his intellect made him susceptible to impatience. It wasn't political, for he had no problem in theory with authority figures. Just . . . sometimes he was sick over it. The burden of it. Himself. All the bits of Ryan were just clumps invented by his father and moulded into an uncomfortable whole by his mother's birth exertions. Not able to get away from them, not able to get away from himself. Sometimes he thought it was driving him crazy.

A door closed further down the corridor, and there was brief adult laughter from the assembly area, but otherwise there was no sound but the duff pounding of his runners on the carpet. He was such a small thing here, like a marble rolling around in an empty bath.

He hovered outside Room 18. Annie Connelly in the front row spotted him through the glass rectangle over the door handle, and he mouthed 'Karine' at her.

She didn't have to be a lip-reader. She knew what he was saying. Any of them would.

He ducked into one of the locker alcoves.

Karine came out a couple of minutes later, hair piled onto her head in lackadaisical perfection, the sleeves of her school jumper pulled down over her fists.

'Hey,' she whispered. She was shaken still. The revelations of the week had drawn tears enough to break her boyfriend's heart, and yet she only knew the half of it.

'C'mere,' he whispered back.

'I am here.'

'More here.'

He held her and pressed his lips to her neck and she hooked her hands around the back of his head.

'Let's go away,' he told her neck. 'Deadly serious; let's take off.'

'Ah, I don't think that's going to work when I've just told Miss Fallon that I'm going to the toilet.'

'Era fuck her.'

She must have felt the heat building, because she pulled back and said, 'What's up with you, boy? You're not all right.'

One spider-leg eyelash had fallen onto her cheek. He pressed his thumb against it and the lash cushioned itself in the warmth of his skin and came away with his hand.

'You shouldn't have come back to school yet,' she said.

'The choice wasn't there this morning.'

'Even so. You could have gone somewhere else. I'd have come to you.' She paused. 'What did you do?'

'Now? Bad form. It just poured out of me. And I'm on my way to the office. For a stern talking to.'

He rested his forehead against hers.

'Everything's wrong, Karine. If I can feel it then why can't they see it?'

'You want them to see it?'

'I don't know. I honest to fuck don't know.'

She put her hand on his chest and pushed him back just enough to look into his eyes. Hers were sticky-lined with black pencil, smudged out at one corner by a stray yawn. 'I can force it, you know. I can say something.'

'And think of the trouble you'd get into. That's the thing anyway, girl. I don't want to have to instigate it. It's the same thing if I get you to do it. Fuck 'em. I don't want any of them knowing my . . . Ah fuck it.'

She winced as he dragged his knuckles off the wall. 'Don't do that,' she said, and she caught his wrist.

'I think I'm cracking up, like. They can't see it and look at you, girl, you can't see it either. Coz I'm all kinds of fucked up and you haven't noticed yet.'

'Because you're not fucked up; shit around you is fucked up. I know that coz I know you. And you know me, and we have each other, right?'

He could have cried. 'Right,' he said.

'And I'm here,' she said. 'For you, like. And I will be, too. You don't need to worry about that.'

'D'you love me?'

'More than anything.'

'It's "everything" for me. More than everything. Like the whole lot put together.'

She kissed him. A proper kiss, too, one that would have gotten her into heaps of trouble if a teacher were to come along and interrupt her. 'Maybe we *should* take off,' she told him. 'What kind of girlfriend would I be if I left you feeling shit?'

'A sensible one.' He tightened his grip on her waist and swung her around. 'Naw, it's OK. I'll face the music. I'll conduct the fucking orchestra. Whatever they've got to throw at me, I'll soak it up the way I soak up everything else.'

'I want you to be OK.'

'I will be. I'm just . . . Bad week.'

'Just don't . . .' She paused, and frowned. '. . . give them any excuse. In the office. Just say you're sorry. For once, Ryan. Please.'

'But I'm not sorry.'

'Pretend you're sorry.'

'Like they pretend my face is the right colour, yeah?'

He waited until she was back in her classroom before he continued on.

He imagined himself saying sorry. Imagined the run-up to it: the headmaster's sighs and solemn pontificating (he'd given up bawling him out long ago), the requests for clarification on motive and psychosis, and, worst of all then, the lecture on a lost future and oh, the miasma of potential he swore he could barely see Ryan through. Maybe that was the reason no one could see the clatter pattern on his face. His being too enveloped in opaque promise, choking the faculty with it. Eyes streaming and throats constricted with the noxious concentrate of Cork's great post-millennial hope. Oh God, that was it. Ryan was all tied up in nasty knots of his own smothering competence.

Don't you want to be an engineer? Or an architect? Or a scientist or a programmer or, God help us, a doctor? Don't you want to be something, Ryan? Oh go on. Fucking be something.

The apology would fit most naturally there, but Ryan knew the words wouldn't come, not even if they tried beating them out of him.

It was different with Karine. He had every reason to apologise to her, but she didn't know that. He'd mean every syllable but it wouldn't matter. Where he'd need forgiveness he wouldn't get it.

He turned into the final stretch before the principal's office.

Past the chaplain's room, and the first action in the chain.

It had started months back. One sticky, airless Saturday, dull as any clump of empty hours and charged with potential because of it.

He woke to muffled thumps and muttered direction.

He lay there for a bit, on his side, blinking at the wall, coming round to the cacophony. When he'd made sense out of it he galloped down the stairs and there was his dad and this other fella, hoisting his piano out the door.

'What are you at?' he asked, and his sister Kelly, inflated with knowledge and bobbing into sight from behind the piano case, said, 'What does it look like?'

'Dad,' he said. 'Dad, you can't. You can't take the piano.'

His father said, 'You don't need it now your practical exam's done. You don't even play anymore.'

'I play when you're not here.'

'Oh, you do, yeah.' There was a pause as they stared each other down and his father blurted, 'It's doing nobody any good having that thing here. Don't you tell me you still play!'

But he did. When there was no one around to hear him he did, even though it felt increasingly weird to sit on the piano stool and stretch his fingers and watch them fly over keys like they belonged to another boy entirely. A couple of times he'd played for Karine and that was even weirder, when they weren't his hands and his hands had done so much to her. And she'd said, *Oh my GOD Ryan, you're really good*, but he hadn't been; everything he'd played for her had been stilted, because he was so desperate for it to sound the way it did when he knew there was no one else in the house to hear it and nothing to prove even to himself because he already knew it was there, the music, in his head and in his belly and in his hands. And he'd presumed, *Well, one day I'll be able to do that for her, too, because I won't be freaking the fuck out about how she thinks of me*, but now that day wasn't going to come, was it, now that his useless cunt father had stolen his piano from him.

Oh, you fucking gom, boy, for fuck's sake, it's only a fucking piano, it wasn't your knob you lost.

Now he crossed the assembly area, taking care to plant a foot on the thin blue cushion of the nearest of the benches laid out in rows, pushing off each to land with mock jubilant grace in front of the next.

Only hours after the theft he told Karine, even though he knew what would happen once he lost the confession from his gritted teeth to her ears. He told her up in his bedroom as she lay happy and naked on top of him; he always got chatty Afterwards, in a stupid *Here's my soul, why don't you shit on it?* kind of way.

'My dad sold the piano.'

That bit was easy, but then she raised her head from his chest and he realised that none of the other things he wanted to tell her – how the piano meant this much to him and fuck all to his father, how it wasn't fair that they didn't just sell the telly if they needed the money, even though he knew the telly was worth a fraction of what his dad got for the piano, proceeds he was probably soaking in right now, having followed the piano out the door – that none of those things had to be pushed past his throat because she already knew. Instead he fought to keep his eyes unfocused and fought to not look at her and started losing the fight and feeling that horrible juddering weakness begin in his tummy and work its way up to his face. So he pulled his arm over his eyes and sucked air through his teeth.

'Aw, baby boy,' she said.

Still with his eyes screwed up, he put his arms back around her and pressed her against him so that she'd stop his heart leaping out of his mouth, and she lay there until he was able to breathe again.

She lifted her head, and said, 'I'm sorry.'

'It's all right.'

His phone was on the floor beside the bed. He reached down to get it, and started thumbing the screen, blinking at menus.

She smoothed the corners of his eyes with a fingertip.

'I want to make you feel better,' she said. 'Will I give you a blowjob?' and he thought how lucky he was, really, no matter what else kept landing on him, and he said, 'Yes please.'

He didn't bother announcing his transgression when he got to the office. He sat himself in a grey plastic chair facing the secretaries and the saggy one, Mrs Cronin, looked up at him and said, 'For God's sake, Ryan.'

He folded his arms and stretched out his legs and stared at the floor beyond his runners.

Karine had heard plenty warning about allowing a boy to keep compromising images of her on his phone, because boys are cruel and the moment any of them see your tits is the moment you lose all value in their piggy eyes. Yeah, yeah. But she trusted Ryan, and he trusted her, and the two-minute video of her looking up doe-eyed while she sucked him off was something he knew he would never show to anyone else. Never. It would have ruined it.

He watched it a couple of times late at night, with the lights off and his dad passed out and his brothers snoring. OK, a fuck of a lot more than a couple of times, but he didn't feel anyone could blame him. Even Karine was OK with it still being on his phone weeks and weeks after. Any time she'd texted him something sexy before, she insisted on nominating use-by dates, and went through his phone afterwards just to be sure. The video was different. Maybe it was that she could see the same thing in her upturned eyes that he could. Maybe it was because she knew that there was something missing from his life now, but something he chose to think of as a necessary loss as he transitioned to a better future. No piano, but who needs pianos anyway? That was something he did as a boy. At night he looked at the nymph on the screen and let his hand close tighter and his chest rise and fall and thought, *Yeah, well, she's something I do as a man, isn't she?*

The thief's guilt was manifest. There'd been more drink taken than usual; Tony Cusack clearly felt the loss of the piano in the back of his mouth. He was irritable and when he was irritable he was to be avoided – everything was everyone else's fault when he was on the skite.

The neighbours knew. Why wouldn't they know? It takes persistence and dedication to remain oblivious to violent noise in a small terrace, and if there was work in the bed Ryan was sure most of his neighbours would sleep on the floor.

Last Saturday night he got a nice black eye over something Kelly had done. God forbid his dad would ever smack Kelly – Tony didn't hit girls, oh sure girls were precious altogether – so Ryan had to take it like a good big brother, a puck into the left eye administered after closing time.

The shiner was a map left for Tony to read on the Sunday morning, and it put him in even worse form. He went out in the afternoon and Ryan stayed in his room, tripping between seething and sadness and smoke. When Tony arrived back that night his son counted his steps and paid heed to the drumbeat of cabinets and doors, and when Tony settled in the sitting room Ryan pulled his runners on and went out into the back garden and sat on the wall. He did that plenty, on the nights he knew that even a glance could nudge his father back onto the warpath. Tony would be asleep soon enough.

And then out scuttled Tara Duane.

With only a hollow wall between her house and theirs, Tara

knew the score better than anyone, and she never pretended other-wise. Sometimes Ryan sold her a bit of dope and sometimes she invited him to come in and skin up with her and sometimes if it was raining he complied, because sometimes anywhere was better than home, even if sometimes the stupid bitch tried to pay him in prescription drug leftovers and sometimes she even tried it on with him, with her dainty bone-fingers climbing up his leg to see if they could charm a hard-on.

'You don't have to go through this alone, pet,' she said.

It wasn't raining but he took her up on the offer anyway.

Afterwards he asked the mirror, *What the fuck were you thinking, boy?* His reflection suggested, Well, maybe the loss of the piano had shattered his common sense. Or maybe the video had made him cocky. Maybe this, maybe that, maybe the other. Whatever it was he was desperately sorry.

See, there was a cup of tea and a shot of whiskey in the cup of tea. Then there were a couple of joints and a couple of cans of lager and the fact that he'd been smoking earlier on made him especially susceptible to being blasted, he supposed, though wasn't hindsight twenty-twenty?

All he knew was that he'd drunk too much and smoked too much and lost control, which was the wrong thing to do because c'mon, fucking hell, he knew she had a bit of a thing for the young fellas, everyone knew she had a bit of a thing for the young fellas. He remembered her telling him the back story to the show she was watching on the telly, and he remembered her laughing at some piss-weak anecdote he couldn't give two shits for, and then he remembered . . .

He didn't feel like remembering it even now, days after the fact and not even the worst thing that had happened that week.

The principal's name was Mr Stephen Barry. He came out into the corridor, in his shirtsleeves, like he was going to have a go and all.

'I was planning on having a chat with you today, Ryan,' he sighed, 'but not like this.'

He remembered waking up in his own bed on Monday morning, the house mercifully still, his siblings long dragged off to school. He was sick as a small hospital. He sent Karine a text, telling her he had caught the flu or something, got up and puked his ring out, went back to bed and put his head under the pillow and watched what was left of the night before jump and fade and bleed in over his eyes.

Piss-weak anecdotes and carefully pitched laughter, and Tara Duane standing then with her arms folded as he pulled his tracksuit pants back up, saying: 'You have a girlfriend.' Putting him straight, with her knickers crumpled on the floor beside the couch.

Tony called up the stairs around midday, saying that he was heading out but that he'd be back soon, and Ryan couldn't answer except under his breath: *I don't care if you never come home, you prick; look what's after happening.* He curled into terror and tears.

Tara *fucking* Duane.

If Karine found out, she'd never forgive him.

But I'm sorry, he told her, and she a mile away in a classroom and utterly oblivious. *I'm so fucking sorry. I fucked up. I didn't mean it.*

Kelly came home at half past four and popped her head in the door and screeched, 'You must be *dying*, boy. You were a mess last night. I'd to let you in at three in the morning and you fell down twice and it was Un. Fucking. Real.'

'Yeah,' he said. He rolled onto his belly and closed his eyes; the sheet smelled of sweat and sick. 'I pulled a whitey I guess.'

'Where were you, anyway?'

'Nowhere,' he said. 'Leave me alone.'

'You've been out for three days, Ryan. Is it too much to ask that you sit quietly for three hours on your return?' said Mr Stephen Barry, Principal.

Ryan said, 'I might as well. I'm fucking invisible anyway.'

*

The penance was swift and as deserved as its supplier was ill-chosen. When his dad got back on Monday evening he let a roar out of him that ricocheted off each of the four walls in turn.

'Ryan!'

He inched into the kitchen. Tony was leaning on the sink, his lips and eyes bulging. 'Gimme your phone.'

Ryan handed it over.

He assumed his dad needed the phone to make a call, because Tony was as often lacking credit as he was lacking everything else. He stood waiting for it to be handed back; that's why he was only an outstretched arm away when the phone played out the soundtrack to Karine's salve. The floor plunged under his feet and his blood pushed through pallor; Tony said, 'What the fuck, Ryan? What the *fuck*?' and the first slap landed, on his left cheek, and he breathed in the shock and the whiskey stench and willed himself hard not to cry.

'I'm sorry.'

'You're sorry? You're fucking sorry?'

'It's just a video, Dad. Just a stupid thing.'

'You're proud of it, aren't you?'

There was nothing new in his father's intent to wreck his head inside and out; whiskey had never agreed with Tony, no matter how convincing his arguments. Ryan puckered his brow. 'What?'

'Who else has seen this?'

'No one.'

'Then why the fuck did Tara Duane just tell me to go looking for it?'

'What?' Ryan said again.

Didn't matter how many whats he managed; those bits of the night before he needed to access had been erased by shots and dope and bile. Gone. Slipped down the back of Tara Duane's couch, on which he'd spent just one too many nights getting stoned for the sake of having something to do. Had he shown her the film he was so privately proud of? Had his traitorous dick been fuelled by her reaction? There was no room for remembering in any case; he was being slapped back out into the hall, pinned to the wall by the front door, cuffed between accusations.

'How did that bitch know it was there?'

'I don't know.'

'You don't know? Is she fucking psychic, is she?'

'I don't know.'

'Ryan . . . Do you think I'm fucking stupid?'

This is how he knew he was in the biggest trouble of his life; his dad was crying. He grabbed Ryan's neck and slid two clammy thumbs up to his cheekbones. 'Where were you last night?' he howled. *Nowhere* wouldn't do; Ryan started into it by loose instinct, and Tony shook him. 'Where!'

'Next door,' Ryan whimpered.

'What were you doing next door?'

Hiding out coz you were fucking langers, you useless, bitter prick.

None of the truth for Tony Cusack. Instead Ryan blubbered, 'I'm sorry, Dad. I didn't mean to. She started it. I was really, really drunk.'

'What the fuck does that mean?'

Ryan was pushed onto the stairs. His forehead clattered the fourth step. His father continued the interrogation with one knee between his son's knees and both hands down hard on his back. *You didn't mean to what?* Ryan shut his eyes and coughed out brackish remorse. Tony wasn't happy with rescinded answers from a spineless child. And sure why would he be? Why should he be?

'What the fuck do I do with you, boy? What the fuck else can I do?'

'You are going to have to calm down,' said Barry. 'Into the office here. We'll talk over it.'

'We'll talk over it, will we, boy?' Ryan said. 'What'll we talk over?'

Mrs Cronin wasn't even bothering to hide her interest. She stood by the photocopier with her outrage hung on the set of her mouth.

'We'll talk over your behaviour,' said Barry. 'We'll talk over what it is that's compelling you to spit in the face of your potential, Ryan. And the best place to do it is behind closed doors, don't you think?'

'Fuckton that happens behind closed doors, don't you think, sir?'

'Watch your language.'

'I will,' said Ryan. 'When you start watching. When you start opening your fucking eyes.'

'Fill me in, then. I'm on your side, Ryan. Tell me what I'm missing.'

Ryan's fingers, which had the grace for concertos so long as there was no one there to hear them, closed around the baggie in his pocket and he fucked it at his headmaster, and it fluttered to his feet, inconsequential and shining bright.

'You see that, I bet. You see that all right.'

Mr Barry looked down at the offering and said, 'What. Is that?'

'That's cocaine, sir.'

The principal looked up again, and for once in his eyes, proper fury; not disappointment, but something Ryan could deal with.

'You're a fucking stupid boy, Ryan Cusack,' he said.

The Initiate

6

The city isn't going to notice the first brave steps of a little free-man, especially one emancipated only by tearing down all around him, but all the same, Ryan Cusack walked on like he was being watched.

That was an easy strut. Chest out, shoulders back, the heavy gatch of a lad whose balls hung low. Locomotive chicanery for after the tears had dried up. Once school had finished for him he'd had one last run-in with his father, anticlimactic in that there wasn't room in his throat, past the gawks and the hot mass of babyish misery, to force the words up from his belly. Then he'd left home, followed (courtesy of his cousin Joseph) by his hobo's kerchief of personal effects: socks and jocks and a tooth-brush. A brief spell of sleeping on strange couches and, twice, town centre doorways, and he conceded and approached his boss for extra work.

'I'm just saying that if you need any bit more, boy, I'm at a loose end.'

Hanging from it.

His boss's name was Dan Kane. He was a well-turned-out brute in his early thirties: mild-eyed, going grey, accent dampened, intentionally harmless up to the point his hands closed round your throat and his spit bubbled through a growl only an inch from your empty pleas. He was an anomaly in the underworld, a little monolith in a city held on blood bonds. Ryan had been sell-ing for him indirectly before Kane copped on and decreed it hilar-ious; there weren't many teenagers who could move quantities. Dan had made kind of a pet of him – allowed him tick and engaged him in grinning debate on ethics and best practices – but better a pet than the leech that drew blood from Tony Cusack's knuckles.

Dan had work for him. More than he could spare. He possessed the keys to a couple of apartments which he used as walk-in safes for stashes of shifting size. He installed Ryan in one to keep an eye on things – the four walls, mostly. On the first night they sat at the bare kitchen table and talked fathers, and Dan slapped him on the back and grimaced in sympathy. He had an arctic disposition punctuated by explosions of lurid temper, but a heart too, when it suited him.

Ryan didn't bother trying to make himself at home. He knew he'd be moved on soon enough. Dan Kane's flat was a place to sleep: that would have to be sufficient.

He wasn't fond of being alone. This apartment, climate-controlled for the benefit of the stash, was as clean and as cold as the cavity in his chest. He had a telly, an Xbox and a laptop, and a fridge for beer, and a double bed with a duvet heavy enough to keep his girlfriend warm. That only helped a little. He missed home and this failing kept him up at night. He missed the terrace and the green outside it and the shortcuts and gatting spots that had marked the boundaries of his world. He missed his brothers' snoring and the banging on the bathroom door and the blaring of non-stop *Simpsons* episodes from the sitting room. A couple of times he thought he might miss his father, kind of like you'd miss a bad tooth, or a gangrenous arm.

He guessed that it was just the hangover of being from a big family. And like any hangover, he could only deal with it by getting through it and avoiding the source until he forgot how much it hurt.

Beside his father's house was the scene of the crime, tended by a treacherous curator, preserved without his collusion. One day he knew he'd want to see his dad again, and that shame would line the path home. He'd seen enough of Tara Duane to last him till perdition, in her sickly back garden come-ons, in her half-dressed admonishment, in the crippling late-night replays he conducted alone in his borrowed apartment. She had turned him on to turn him in, and though he'd folded up the memory and folded it again, it flared on dark occasion, and he couldn't get his head around it.

It was April. A surf of cloud broke grey over the streets and Ryan walked through a city where debris stuck in damp clumps in every dirty corner. He was alone, still feeling out the expanse of it. There was hint of Dan coming around later on to evaluate his reserves, which wouldn't take long with a bit of luck, because Karine had a dance class she intended to mitch from so she could come up to the flat and get naked.

They had celebrated their first anniversary in March, on his sixteenth birthday. There was another anniversary today, and he wasn't sure whether it'd be a good idea to mention it. It had been a year since they'd first had sex. Would she go for that, he wondered? Some alcohol, maybe a smidge of Dan Kane's coke, and fuck right through the everyday and into something new to make another anniversary of?

He trotted on, chest out, shoulders back, for an audience oblivious.

He was headed for a service station, which by a perverse twist would probably employ the people with the fewest fucks to give, but there was an off-licence on the way, and it was worth a shot. He ducked in out of the drizzle and stood back from the counter, behind a half-sized, snuffling woman intent on procuring a kind of liquor that neither he nor the thin-smigged clown at the till had ever heard of.

'This is the only ice wine we stock,' said the fella behind the counter. 'It's Canadian. That's probably the one.'

The woman spun her wrist like she was winding a crank.

'That's not it either,' she said. Her voice was thick and deep; she cleared her throat. 'Maybe it's like a schnapps thing? Or a brandy even.'

'What fruit?'

'I can't remember. I'll know it when I see it.'

Ryan picked a couple of bags of Taytos from a lopsided display and gawped at the ceiling. It made sense to cloak himself in the inertia of a musty shop interior if his success depended on his not looking like he was on a great adventure. No adventure to doing the shopping, was there? Grabbing a naggin, heading home, doing the washing or his taxes or whatever the fuck. Ryan Cusack was a grown-up and grown-ups were always bored.

That left just one person in the off-licence who wasn't a grown-up, and she appeared to be the dithering woman's child. A doonshie wan of no more than four stood back by the beer fridge, her baby finger in her mouth. Her mother postulated that the alcohol she sought was cherry-based. The assistant turned to the shelves behind him and the child stuck her paws into the beer fridge and picked up four tins and ran out the door of the off-licence as quick as her matchstick legs would carry her.

'D'you know what?' said the scrawny woman. 'I'll leave it. I'll check the name of it and be back to you.'

She didn't look at Ryan as she went past. Through the window he watched her join the tiny thief and a man as bony as she was, and the man picked up the cans and she picked up the child, and they darted over the wet streets like the city was being ripped out from under them.

'Can I help you?' said the guy behind the counter.

If there had been a bit more enthusiasm in his offer, Ryan might have warned him to look out for repeat visits. Instead he threw the Taytos on the counter and said, 'A naggin of Smirnoff and a naggin of Jameson.'

'Have you ID?' snapped yer man.

'Nope.'

'Well, what age are you?'

'Sixteen, boy.'

The sarcastic feigning of sarcasm proved too dense a barrier to cut through and, besides, it was during the school day, and Ryan was in civvies. The vendor twitched and turned.

'Bring some ID next time,' he said, knocking the bottles off the counter.

They had a dog at home. Nero. A mongrel with a touch of

Labrador to him and a habit, in his old age, of sleeping underneath the kitchen table, farting at intervals with such gusto that it
was a wonder there was varnish left on the legs. He'd come home
with Tony when Ryan was five – too young to teach his puppy any
tricks. When he was old enough to have given it a shot, he no
longer wanted to. It was as though in teaching the little fucker to
fetch, he would have been corrupting him. Changing his lolling
doggy nature to suit a movie mandate.

It was pretty fucked up to do the same to a kid.

He gathered his purchases and went in the direction the matchstick trio had taken.

Here's your trick, Junior. When Mammy's in her hour of need
and the guardian's back is turned, you stick your hands into the
icebox and retrieve the medicine. When Daddy needs it and he
can't drag his arse out of bed to get it, you dash down to the offy
with your blankest-ever face and wait till Missus Horgan's cleared
her weepy eyes enough to hand over the whiskey. And maybe
Matchstick Mammy will drink up and get warm and happy, and
cover you with cuddles and confirmation of your preciousness, or
maybe Splintered Daddy will turn on you and accuse you of judging him or having the wrong kind of face, and maybe all you'll get
from it is a clatter headache. Either way just do the trick and shut
up.

He found them preparing to cross the road. The man's eyes met
Ryan's as he approached, but there was no flicker until Ryan said,
'C'mere, what d'you think you're doing?'

At which the man said, 'What?'

'I said what the fuck do you think you're doing?'

The man stood in front of the woman and the child – more by
accident than instinct. He was wearing a baggy green hoodie. He
looked like he'd shrunk in the wash. Or maybe he'd swiped the
hoodie like he'd swiped the gatt; maybe he flung his little accom-
plice over garden walls in the sunshine so she could harvest washing lines for him. Whatever it was, he was a mismatched nothing
with sticky eyes; Ryan knew his sort.

'Getting a small wan to steal your drink for you while your ould doll throws fairy stories at the shopkeeper. And you outside with your hands down your trousers. Aw stop, aren't you the fucking berries?'

'Listen—' said the man.

'You fucking listen,' said Ryan, 'because people obviously don't tell you you're a scumbag half enough.'

'Sorry, who died and made you Chief Inspector?'

'I couldn't give two shits if you went in there and cleared the gaff, boy. What you do with your grubby paws is nawthin' to me. But you get a kid to do it for you, that's low, boy. That's creepy low.'

'Here, mind your own business,' said the woman, throwing shapes from behind her fella.

'If you were doing the same we wouldn't be having this rírá,' said Ryan.

'You'd want to scoot on,' said the man.

'Or what? Or what, boy? You going to take me on, yeh little mockeeah man, yeh? You are, yeah.'

'And you're hardly going to swing for me if you're so worried about the small wan, are you?' the man sneered. 'Isn't that right? So keep walking.'

'Yeh brat, yeh,' said the woman.

Ryan grinned. It'd be all too easy to take this pair by the scruff and toss them onto the street. They wouldn't have weighed fifteen stone between them. They were right, though; he'd bound his fists on this one.

'I'm not going to bate you,' he said, 'unless I see you again, like. Though that said, I'd say you bring the small wan with you everywhere, do you? Stand behind her out of harm's way, right? Is she yours, boy? Because you're some waste of a pair of testicles.'

The child looked put out, but not as much as either of her guardians. She had a long way to go before she hit sixteen and was able to take off from home and find herself a safehouse stash to babysit. Ryan winked at her.

'Tell your mam and dad to steal their own tins. Do.'

'Don't you dare talk to my daughter,' said the woman.

'I hope she's taken off you,' Ryan said, and crossed the road ahead of them.

He tried to think of other things on the way home – whiskey, anniversaries, his girlfriend's tits – but something like that happens and it fucks up your innards, belly to brain. He sated his temper with fantasy, and beat the man in the green hoodie to a pink and cream pulp between the river and Dan Kane's flat, and when the door shut behind him he put the naggins and the Taytos on the table and sat on the leather two-seater opposite and stared at them, and then at his watch.

After a while he thought, *I'm never going to be like that.*

Too big and too bold now to be the stooge, and too smart to put his roots down in the shade of his family tree.

It was a year to the day since he'd become a man and already he'd progressed beyond Green Hoodie's sorry state.

He rolled a joint and looked at his watch again.

Maureen was seeking redemption.

Not for herself. You don't just kill someone and get forgiven; they'd hang you for a lot less. No, she was seeking redemption like a pig sniffs for truffles: rooting it out, turning it over, mad for the taste of it, resigned to giving it up.

Robbie O'Donovan, said her conscience. *Poor craitur. Had a name once, and a body, before you offered both to the worms.* How easy it was to kill someone, really, much easier than it had any right to be. One day they're occupying space in a living city and the next they're six feet under – or wherever it was Jimmy stowed his leftovers – and out of sight, out of mind. Because no one came looking for Robbie O'Donovan. No guards, no wives, no mammies. Poor craitur.

He inhabited the old brothel with her now, out of harm's way and anyone else's eye line. He watched her from the stairs. He waited to one side of the kitchen table while she ate, avoiding the spot of his ebbing. He stood at the end of the bed, right at the middle of the footboard, staring down at her when she couldn't sleep.

'Is it any wonder I can't with you here?' she used to say to him.

He didn't reply. His mouth wasn't made for it. His face shifted with her guesswork and never settled long enough to answer back. Sometimes he had blue eyes and luminescent white skin. Sometimes he had thin lips and hollow cheeks. Sometimes he smiled, or formed a wide O in belated horror. He never had teeth.

The cape of sticky crimson spread over his right shoulder and weighted his faded black jumper so it clung to him, exactly as it had in his final moments.

She sought redemption in him first. She lay awake at night and explained herself to him, first her actions, then her history, in case it would provide background against which he could shape his acceptance. But his mouth wouldn't stay put to confirm it. She told him again, fleshing it out where she thought he might want it. His sometime-face refused to engage.

'Will I tell you a story, Robbie O'Donovan?'

His blue eyes smeared across his sockets and onto his cheeks. Black substitutes flowed into position.

'When I was eighteen I met a man. He was twenty-four and from out Cobh direction, he wore a beard and beads; you wouldn't know the type, Robbie O'Donovan, because it was long before your time, but he was a catch and all the girls said so. His name was Dominic Looney, so it's a good job I didn't marry him. I was a skinny minnie – I used to wear pants up to my ears with bottoms on them wide enough to sweep the streets, and I had a head of hair on me like a mushroom cloud, so between the trousers and the fluffy *ceann* I don't know how he saw enough of me to want what he thought was on offer. But there you go: you fellas are strange. He thought I was a lasher and I didn't deny him the chance to keep telling me. So we were doing a line. We'd go out to Crosshaven for the dances and he'd get me drunk on shandy, which will tell you, Robbie O'Donovan, how small I was back then.

'We didn't go out for that long but it must have looked fairly serious because there was an assumption amongst the girls I worked with that we'd get married. And we pretended to be married enough times; we went for weekends away and told the Mary-Anns in the B&Bs that we were Mr and Mrs Looney and only married a year. And you can imagine what went on after that, can't you? Not that it'd do you any good imagining it now; I don't cut the figure I used to.

'Of course, it's different nowadays, but back then being a trollop was full of occupational hazards. No doubt the Mary-Anns would have called it my own fault and gloated at my situation – and that's what they used to call it then, Robbie O'Donovan; a situation, or a problem, oh, something vague and fateful. *What are we going to do about Maureen's problem?* Well, the first thing I did was arrange a shotgun wedding in my head. I was to wear a floating cream dress, and he'd have his beard and a suit, and we'd be in a house of our own before my belly escaped from bondage and made a whore and a charlatan out of the pair of us.

'But that wasn't to be, for as soon as Dom Looney got wind of it he was out the gap, flapping like a chicken trying to outrun a fox.

'So what do you think happened then, Robbie O'Donovan?' The apparition's face flickered.

'Then I was sent away. For the neighbours' benefit I was gone away to work, but really I was being watched as I grew and grew and grew and the faces around me got longer and longer and longer. And then when I had the baby my mother – God rest her soul and say hello to her if you see her – fell head over heels for him and so it was decided that I give him up in atonement so that my mother and father could raise him in the stable and proper home that had given rise to the likes of me.

'So you tell me this, Robbie O'Donovan, when your face stops fading in and out and your mouth fixes in whatever shape your parents gave it: why was I asked to redeem myself for something my mother ended up coveting? Hmm? And if I've done all my redeeming, forty bleddy years of it, why in God's name do you think I should be seeking redemption for you?'

Lacking the necessary equipment to answer, the ghost of Robbie O'Donovan said nothing.

'I'll atone,' grumbled Maureen, 'but I'm not taking any more punishment. Up to me oxters in punishment I was, for doing feck all. Do you hear me?'

Her thirst for redemption unquenched by the wraith's sullen insubstantiality, Maureen was left picking through more indirect routes.

The church seemed like the obvious place to start. The clergy were self-professed experts in bestowing grace on behalf of the absentee landlord. Then there was the notion of being pre-cleared of the burden of Robbie O'Donovan's death by dint of her suffering years of penitence with no sin to show for it. Was that not a thing with the Holy Roman Empire? Didn't they tend to make up these kind of dirt-kicking assurances whenever anyone sufficiently gold-laden came to them dragging a sack of their indiscretions? If the church that condemned her to childless banishment forty years ago could offer her something in the way of a consolation prize, well, she was interested in hearing it.

The church nearest her was across the river and ten minutes down the quays. The morning after she told Robbie O'Donovan his bedtime story, she took a walk.

It had been a nasty April so far, the weather weak and wet, and bitter. She had wanted to wear white for the occasion, but the rain dissuaded her; she swapped white trousers for a black pair, and her sandals for sturdy dark shoes, and her cream cardigan and white shirt gave her the look of someone who'd only sinned from the waist down, which was generally where it manifested on nineteen-year-olds in the seventies.

It was an old church, imposing in a way they'd discourage now that the country was wide to their private flamboyances. Maureen strode up the steps and through the colossal doors and inside spied grandeur good-oh. Gold and marble and wall-mounted speakers so as to better hear the word of the Law-Di-Daw. She chortled, loud enough to upset a couple of biddies sitting in one of the end pews.

There were confession boxes in the corner. She ran her hands over the outside of the left-hand door. Hardwood, varnished over and over again; all veneer at this stage, she thought. There was a black grille on the top half. The priest's station in the middle was hung with a velvet curtain.

Maureen slipped inside and stood in the dark, remembering all that time ago, when you'd be waiting on the priest to slide the hatch open, enjoying the stuffiness, the pomp of the ritual, even the smell of the thing, rich and musty, something of the bygones . . .

The hatch slid to the side and a voice said, 'We're not scheduled for confessions now, but I saw you come in.'

'Jesus Christ!'

' "Bless me father for I have sinned" is the customary salutation.'

She shoved the door open and hurried to the exit, and behind her the priest, bespectacled and white-haired as uniform dictated, opened the door of the confessional and hung out on one foot.

'I didn't mean to startle you,' he called.

Robbie O'Donovan was waiting for her when she banged shut the door of the brothel. His face, elongated this time, mouthless and sallow, stared her down from the end of the corridor. He was standing at the kitchen door, blocking entry.

'I'll get them,' she said. 'Not today, obviously. But you'll see at the end of it: you, my lad, have no right to be here.'

She wanted a cup of tea and to sit down, and so she blinked hard, and when she opened her eyes again he was gone.

7

Maureen sat on it like a bird of prey fluffed up on an egg. She guarded it closely at first, but as soon as Jimmy gratefully consigned the deed to history the air around her turned viscous with her glee, and Jimmy watched it bubble into thick sighs and snorts and unspent exclamations until she decided it was time to tell him what she'd learned; it wasn't good.

That gowl Cusack had let slip the name of the corpse.

What harm? Dougan might have asked, if he'd been let in at all, and he hadn't. The worst of all possible outcomes had already happened; the fool was dead. What difference did it make if Maureen knew the name of the man she'd killed?

Without Dougan, though, Jimmy Phelan was a mess of what-ifs and how-dares.

The name of the corpse was a complication. Maureen made casual references to a ghost who'd popped into existence as soon as she had a name to give it, and the breeziness bothered him. No manifestation of guilt, this. Who knew what else the witch could do with a name?

It had been a season of extremes. The sun, when it shined, crisped everything it caught, but it never appeared except in a bruise of cumulus clouds. Showers kept the children indoors. The air was thick with fuming wasps.

Jimmy drove up to Cusack's house to beat out of him what in fuck's name he thought he was doing telling Maureen who the dead man was. He drove up to beat sense into him. He drove up to gauge his unruliness, and to find out whether there was more to this fuck-up than insubordination. Jimmy Phelan thought himself a great judge of character, and Cusack hadn't seemed like he knew the corpse's identity on the day they'd removed it from Maureen's floor. There was a possibility the fucker had conducted his own investigation, and carried the results back to Maureen for her to do with as she pleased. Jimmy didn't know.

He didn't know!

Tony Cusack's terrace was only one of dozens flung out in a lattice of reluctant socialism. There was always some brat lighting bonfires on the green, or a lout with a belly out to next Friday being drunkenly ejected from his home (with a measure of screaming fishwife fucked in for good luck), or squad cars or teenage squeals or gibbering dogs. Jimmy parked and grabbed a passing urchin for exactitudes.

Tony's house was in the middle of a short terrace facing the green. There was a silver Scenic in the stubby driveway, but the curtains were closed on both floors and there were no signs of life behind the frosted glass on the front door. Jimmy knocked anyway, and knocked harder when he didn't get an answer. How many children did the man say he'd sired? Six? Jimmy turned. The lawn was overgrown, the garden didn't sport anything in the way of ornamental hedges or flowerbeds, and the only indication of children was the couple of sweet wrappers caught between the corner of the lawn and the pebble-dashed front wall.

He stepped onto the drive and leaned against the car bonnet.

'Where are you, you little maggot?'

He cast his eyes to the end of the terrace, where figures shrank behind cars and walls and rosebushes, then looked the other way and caught a familiar face diving behind a curtain in the house next door.

That would do.

He began to whistle as he crossed from this driveway into the next. When he rapped on the door she opened it only a couple of inches and allowed him her eyes and her forehead.

'Can I help you?'

'For fuck's sake, Tara. You're not playing oblivious, are you?'

He clapped the door again, and it bumped off her nose.

'I'm not playing oblivious,' she said.

'Good girl. Because I don't have the patience for your play-acting. Are you going to let me in?'

'My daughter's in bed.'

'That's not an answer.'

She winced and sniffed as she stood aside and let him into her hall.

The sitting-room curtains were drawn. The room was illuminated by the glow from a laptop on the coffee table, supplemented by rolling sunlight from the sundered summer sky. Jimmy sat on the couch, spreading his arms across the back and crossing his left leg over his right and Tara Duane hovered by her own sitting-room door like a burglar made to face the music.

She was a poisonous runt, Duane. She drifted on the edges of the city's real meat, feeding on its carcasses for a kind of sustenance he couldn't get his head around. Villains he could harness, but this one . . . He'd never met a villain so convinced of its own virtue.

She'd fancied herself a madam once, and approached one of his underlings for collaboration. The ugliness of the work had stunned her, and she'd spent more time wringing her hands over the ashes of her Munster Moulin Rouge than exerting herself, so she'd been deposed, and the collaborating subordinate given a slap around the chops. Since then she'd learned conversational Russian and had assumed a position as a kind of guide for girls whose penury pointed them towards sex work. She still fancied herself a madam, only now she believed her freelance status allowed her an attractive impartiality and an air of great benevolence. A whore had once told Jimmy that Tara kept unhealthy hours online, employing sockpuppet accounts to argue with anti-prostitution campaigners and cribbing about Catholic Ireland. That had tickled him. He was happy to give her delusions free rein; his managers used her on occasion as a finder or a go-between.

Her front room was poky. There were magazines stacked on the shelves, clashing art on the walls. Beside the laptop on the coffee table was a mug with a delicate paper label hanging down the side. There was a chat window open on the laptop screen.

Of course hunni xxx Dont worry. My mom's just come home brb. Don't start without me plz luv u.

Don let her get to u baby. B strong.

'Online chat?' he said. 'I thought your daughter was in bed?'

'She was up a while ago, like.'

He grinned and leaned forward. 'Her "mom" just came home and sent her to bed, was it? Was she up all night talking to nobbers? And drinking tea with labels on it; ah, she's pure sophisticated.'

'Can I help you with something, Jimmy?'

'Probably,' he said.

She went to fold her arms and changed her mind, for one brief moment falling into the chicken dance.

'Tara,' he said.

'Yes?'

'I'm obviously looking for someone.'

'Yes.'

'Do you know where the fuck he is?'

'Tony Cusack?'

'That'd be the man. I have the right house so.'

'Why are you looking for Tony Cusack?'

'Why are you asking me?'

Her hands made fists. She tucked each into its opposite armpit.

'Seriously, Tara? Trying to ascertain what I know before choosing your best answer is only going to make me very pissy.'

She pouted. 'He's drying out.'

'He's what?'

'Drying out. You know. Some residential programme. The kids are with his sisters and he hasn't been home in weeks.'

'I didn't see Cusack as the health conscious type,' he said.

'He's not,' she said. 'It was court-ordered.'

'Court-ordered? Fuck me – what did he do to deserve that?'

'What didn't he do to deserve it?'

'Seems a harmless sort, is all.'

She seethed. 'He's not harmless. He's a horrible man. Violent. Very violent.'

'We are talking about the right Tony Cusack, aren't we? Scruffy fella, big brown peepers, married a dago lasher with knockers out to here?'

'Some people are just bad,' she said. 'No matter how often you get lost in their eyes.'

Her peevishness tickled him. 'That doesn't sound like the bleeding-heart Tara Duane I know.'

'He's a child abuser.'

'Holy fuck, anything else?'

'Yeah, actually. He put my front window in. With a hurley. Beat the glass through. And I have to live beside him after all that and I frightened of me life of him.'

'Tony Cusack put your front window in.'

'Yeah. So I'd advise you to have nothing to do with him.'

'Why'd he put your window in?'

'Why do you care?' she said.

'I don't.' He leaned forward, elbows on knees. 'Lovers' tiff?' he asked. 'Were you fucking him, Tara?'

'Excuse me, I was not.'

'Why else would a man blow your house down? Did you put the wrong tags on the bins? Stay up too late bawling along to ABBA? Come on, Tara. Why'd you fall out with him?'

'Are you looking for him or questioning me?'

'First one, then the other.'

The light from the laptop screen dimmed as it switched to screensaver. Jimmy stretched and shifted back on the couch.

'His oldest is a boy,' Tara said. 'Sixteen. He thought I was . . .'

It was pause enough to draw out his laughter.

'Jesus Christ, Tara. You're fucking children now?'

'I am not,' she hissed. 'He's paranoid with the drink and the drugs. You'd want to be, wouldn't you, to accuse a young mum of something like that? Especially one like me.'

'One like you?'

'I'm a good person!' she snapped. 'And that man is a nutjob.'

'If he caught you with your legs round his young fella's ears I'd say he had good reason.'

'Don't be disgusting.'

He was close to paroxysms. 'Oh come on, Tara. I work at a conveyer belt of deviants and I know for a fact you failed quality control. The man knocked your window in because you've been playing Hide the Underage Sausage.'

'I didn't! I did not! I tried offering the kid a friendly ear and he obviously took it the wrong way, all right? And I had to offer that friendly ear because his father's a lunatic and living beside him has lopped years off my life.'

'If only living *with* him put years *on*, eh?'

'Yeah, getting back to it, OK? I don't know where he is,' she said. 'Drying out. Court-ordered.'

'For what?'

'Drunk and disorderly. So taking into account his unprovoked attack on my glazing, that was enough for a judge to decide he had a problem. He's got too many kids for gaol, I guess.'

'That part sounds like Cusack,' he said.

'It all sounds like Cusack. You obviously don't know him very well.'

'I don't,' Jimmy said, and clucked his tongue, and put his hands on the couch, readying himself to get up again. Tara thought to exhale. He laughed.

'Christ, Tara. You'd swear you were the one up to no good.'

She sucked her lips in.

'I'll be on my way,' he said. 'You've been useless. Still, I get you have more important things to be doing, like pretending to Mr Internet there that you're his little wet dream soulmate. Sorry I haven't been a better *mom* to you.'

She followed him to the front door.

The pavement glistened under a sky indigo and low. Jimmy rolled his shoulders.

'One more question,' he said. 'Do you know a fella by the name of Robbie O'Donovan?'

Her eyes widened. 'No.'

'Think now. He'd know Cusack.'

She shook her head.

'Maybe thirty. Foxy hair. A right hand-me-down-the-moon. You couldn't miss him, but that's of no benefit to sore eyes.'

'I guess that's what you want Tony for?'

Jimmy stepped out the door and onto the driveway.

'So much guesswork, Tara. I'll take my leave of you. Stay weird.'

He walked towards the front gate. Wasted journeys tended to put him in bad form, and he could see that mass ahead of him, maybe five minutes into his future, maybe ten, a private tantrum that would fuck the rest of his afternoon. He had things to be doing. Much bigger things than chasing Tony Cusack around the city.

Behind him, Tara Duane called 'Wait!'

He turned.

She was nodding. 'Robbie O'Donovan. A tall ginger guy, whippet-thin, no great shakes, yeah, yeah.'

'Oh, it's come to you! Tell me: what do you know about him?'

She stepped onto the driveway and closed out the door behind her. Beyond her front wall, two bickering girls played on scooters, oblivious to the building pressure above them, the carillon hum of the imminent squall.

'He's with one of the . . . working girls,' she said. 'You know.'

'One of the whores? Which whore?'

'I don't know what she calls herself but I know her as Georgie Fitzsimons.'

'Irish?'

'They do exist,' she said.

'And where does she work? What does she look like?'

'Oh, she's one of the unfortunates. She's on the streets. Not hard to miss; she's usually down the quay. She's short but, y'know, chesty.' She gestured extravagantly. 'Dark hair down her back. Skinny now, like, but she was pretty once. I think the term is "gone to shit".'

'I know the sort.'

'She used to work for you,' she said. 'In the house at the end of Bachelor's Quay.'

'Really.' Well, now the langer's being there made sense. The insignificant other of one of the whores, probably a junkie, probably thinking the house was empty, probably looking to rip the copper out of the walls or the carpet up. Probably the kind of company that eejit Tony Cusack was used to keeping. The issue of the corpse's exposed identity quickly shrivelled.

'Does he owe you money or something?' Tara asked.

'Who?'

'Robbie O'Donovan. I get the feeling he skipped town, is all.'

Jimmy chewed the air.

'You ask too many questions, Tara.'

'I'm just trying to help . . .'

'It'd be more in your line to try zipping your trap, because the day will come when someone will solder it shut for you.'

'OK. Jesus,' she said, and held on to the wall dividing her property from Cusack's, and put her other hand to her chest.

'Just a pointer.' He dismissed her with a casual wave and returned to his car.

She reappeared at her front window, peeked out from behind the curtain, disappeared as soon as she saw him watching. He snorted.

One of the squabbling girls pushed her companion off her scooter. The deposed one screamed. Tara Duane glimpsed out again. Jimmy considered another wave.

The distraught girl's screams were met and matched by a yowl from one of the gardens across the way. A man with gym-sculpted shoulders pitched towards them, snarling at Sarah or Sasha or whoever she was. Jimmy couldn't tell whether it was the victim or the perpetrator that had drawn out the yowls, but the chap was coming for them, hard, and when he reached them he picked up the screaming one with one hand and slapped the offender with the other. The one who'd been pushed was set upright. The culpable one was spun around by her wrist. She went white with shock. The judgement kept coming.

Hot day, though. Short tempers.

A woman in lilac with a stretched-out seahorse tattoo waddled towards the scene. She stood back from the spitting man, the bawling children, and threatened to call the guards. The man raised his hand.

Still there was no rain. Jimmy smiled out at the olive light and the drama and drew Tony Cusack's indiscretion from catastrophe to conspiracy to clanger.

Boyfriends

We're going out later. Nothing much happening, but we're going to get some cans and go gatting with Joseph and the lads, have a few smokes, a bit of a laugh. Karine, though, she'd get dolled up for the opening of an eye. We're up in Dan Kane's stash house and she's 'getting ready'. Getting ready, like. So that if she pulls a whitey at least she'll look gorgeous gawking all over my runners.

I'm at the bottom of the bed, rolling a joint, and she's sitting up against the pillows watching telly and painting her toenails baby-blue.

It's one of them dancing competition shows that's on. She loves them. She does hip hop twice a week and enters competitions with a proper crew and everything. She can do the splits. She can rest her calves on my shoulders. Yeah, it's fucking awesome.

'Your manno's amazing,' she says, all goo-eyed at this fella lepping around in front of the judges in a pair of leggings.

'Yeah?'

'Yeah, he's got moves like.'

She's completely gripped. She finishes her toenails and leans back, a finger in her mouth as she stares at the screen. I hold the joint up in invitation but she pays me no heed.

Her toes are splayed in case she ruins the paint job.

I take a pinch of tobacco and slowly, slowly stretch over

She sighs as the judges give a standing ovation. She gets very wrapped up in the feelgoods.

I sprinkle some of the loose tobacco over the nails on her right foot and it sticks to the polish, flecking it baby-blue and bog-water brown.

She doesn't notice.

I do the other foot. She pulls her knees towards her just as I finish.

'He is like super talented,' she says.

I spark up.

She looks over at me, mouth open, ready to tell me something else mind-blowing about the steamer on the screen when she lamps her piebald toes.

'Oh my God! Ryan!'

I'm breaking my hole laughing.

'Ryan Cusack, you are fucking LOUSY!' She jumps up and throws a pillow at me and practically has a fit right there on the floor. 'You gowl! I don't even have varnish remover with me, like. They're ruined! What am I gonna do? Oh my God, you break my melt, d'you know that?'

She is beetroot with fury but I can't say anything, I'm choked.

She stomps into the bathroom and just before she slams the door she screams, 'I wish I was a fucking LESBIAN!'

On the screen yer man in leggings is standing with his hands joined in a silent prayer. I wipe the tears from my eyes. The judges call yer man's name and he jumps out onto the stage like he's got a wazzie down his drawers.

She comes out again a couple of minutes later.

'Your boyfriend got through,' I tell her.

She scowls. 'My boyfriend better get his jacket on coz he's going to get me nail polish remover right now. I honestly don't know why I put up with you, Ryan. You're such a child.'

8

It was beautiful down at the lakeside in the early morning. The air was cold, stripped of the fragments it had picked up the day before, though it would be stale by midday and offering mouthfuls of flies by dusk.

Georgie had made a habit out of coming down to the water before breakfast. In the great expanse of hill and sky, it stayed early for longer. Back in the city there was traffic and torment from dawn. Out here, so long as the air held that chill, the limbo between then and now stretched as far as she needed.

She sat on a flat rock by the water's edge and closed her eyes to the milky-blue sky, and the breeze that coaxed tresses onto her cheeks and over her lashes. The birds could be raucous near the water, but this morning their song was spiralling light. Beyond that, nothing. Later, when duties began, there'd be car engines and noises of cooperation as people grouped off to deny the devil idle hands.

David's voice, behind her: 'You weren't wrong.'

She neither turned nor opened her eyes. 'You're so negative, David. *You weren't wrong*. You could have said instead, *You were right*. Turn the negative into the positive, remember? Break free of sour processes. Turn that frown. Upside down.'

His shoes crunched on the shingle. When she opened her eyes, he was standing at the water's edge, his back to her, hands on his hips.

'You look like you're appraising the plantation,' she said. 'Lord and Master of all you survey.'

'Only one Lord,' he said. 'And no possessions. Isn't that right?'

She laughed, and he turned to smile. He was neatly proportioned, moulded by good fortune rather than hard work. He had a trimmed beard, which tickled, and eyes blue as the mountain sky.

'I didn't think you were one for getting up early,' she teased.

'You said it would be worth my while,' he said.

Gambling was David's vice. He used to hole himself up for entire weeks, just him and his laptop, losing shirt after shirt in landscapes of flashing lights and vivid green. You wouldn't think it to look at him. He seemed more like the lead in an IKEA ad. When his parents got divorced, his father had turned to pastors new, which was how his youngest son had ended up at a lakeside refuge run by Christian soldiers whose military tactics amounted to communal porridge pots and long walks in the woods.

Georgie's first thought had been that it was all very American, but the mission leader was Irish. William Tobin was his name and he called his organisation CAIL, which she had since discovered, with a hastily stifled snigger, stood for Christians Active In Light. Try as she might she couldn't find an ulterior motive to William's decency; he was too gentle a soul for trickery. He had a grey ponytail and a wife called Clover to whom he displayed a very noncultlike monogamous devotion. He had found Georgie in need and had given freely.

What that need had been was nobody else's business. William had told her that what she disclosed to his knot of volunteers was entirely up to her. So she'd told them she was an alcoholic, which was probably true, even if it was the least of her problems.

It wasn't rehab in the traditional sense. William Tobin's West Cork property was more drop-out than check-in. Bed and board in exchange for a little light farming and daily sermons about the loving grace of Jesus Christ. Georgie hadn't yet found the Lord – in His defence, she hadn't been looking very hard – but they seemed an honest bunch, she had always liked porridge and she loved the lakeside air.

'You're sure you're set for later?' David said.

'Oh yeah. That won't be a problem.'

'I guess it's handy they're bringing you.'

'They must trust me not to run off into the nearest pub, scream-ing for a Jägerbomb.'

'You think they're right to trust you?' he smiled.

'Please. Booze is so last month.'

He sat beside her on her boulder perch and as he stretched an arm around her he looked back, in the direction of the centre, just in case.

William and Clover didn't like to make rules not already enshrined in the teachings of Himself, but He probably wasn't keen on fraternisation and, if Georgie remembered her religion classes correctly, thought fallen women only handy for washing His trotters. The fact that she had embarked on a quiet affair with David would no doubt have been a deal-breaker, at the very least an incitement to proper spluttering Bible-thumping.

But there was something so perversely pure about it. Georgie hadn't told David about the career path that brought her to William's door, and his blind attraction was quite the aphrodis-iac. And though she had long lost the notion that she would be dragged out of perdition by the clammy hands of a man, there was something therapeutic in the nature of their bond. The secrecy reminded her of the first few stolen kisses as a girl back at home; furtive pecks at the back of the hurling pitch, the fluttering excitement of a hand sliding under her top. So there was a kind of rebirth to it, she supposed.

She leaned into David's shoulder and they kissed.

The first time had been a revelation. They had been talking late in the common room about his converted father and her stub-bornly pious mother. Without warning he'd lunched forward, an action as clumsy as its resulting kiss was tender, and as his mouth worked hers open she'd felt heat spreading, belly to hips to thighs. Like a blossoming, a poet might have said, but at the time she had linked it to the idea of an opening tomb. Something that would stir a pharaoh's wrath and unleash a plague of locusts. It had been a diversion from genuine butterflies.

That night they'd had sex on the bench Clover used to fold sheets. She thought afterwards that she probably shouldn't have, on the basis that it wasn't good for her rehabilitation, but actually wanting to was novelty enough to carry her.

If Robbie were to come home now, would he find her willing and born anew?

If Robbie were to come home now he wouldn't find her at all.

David slipped his hand down the front of her dress, teasing taut a nipple.

'D'you think we have time . . .' he said.

'I doubt it.'

But David was a gambling man.

She had leaned against a parked car and heaved.

You could never be safe, even though you'd be so careful and smart, leaning in through car windows to slyly sniff their breath for signs of riled drunkenness, reading the tics and faces pulled to gauge violent intent. A few would always get through, and the ones you couldn't interpret were the worst of the lot, the real evil bastards, the ones who hid behind stony facades the rage, the frustration, the deep-seated mammy issues they were only dying to take out on you. You, the dirty whore. You, representing in living, breathing audacity everything that was wrong with them.

This one had accepted the terms of the sale, then decided, once she was in his car, that the terms of the sale were unacceptable.

When she protested, he punched her. When she shouted, he walked around the side of the car to the passenger door, took her hair in his fist and dragged her out. He pushed her onto the bonnet and raped her. Then he punched her again and spat into her face and hair and told her that she disgusted him, and left her at the side of the road, and from there she began walking back into town, and a host of the oblivious walked and drove past until by luck or as he might have put it, divine intervention, William Tobin found her.

He was driving home from the hall he maintained in the city for prayer services and Bible study groups.

'You poor child!' he exclaimed, tearfully. 'God is here for you. You have only to let him in.'

She had been asked to return to the prayer hall in the city now with William and Clover and a couple of the converted: Saskia, a girl of near thirty who'd been raised in bohemian carelessness down in Kerry by her German parents and all of their hangers-on; and Martin, a bearded giant in his forties who had spent years in prison for some crime only darkly alluded to. William drove the minibus, and Georgie balanced her chin in her hand and watched the countryside drift by as Saskia wondered aloud if Ireland was, in its heathenism, doomed to suffer the fate of ancient Rome.

The four were to attend some public meeting about political non-compliance, or the threat of feminism, or knitting jumpers for Jesus or something. Her role was to prep the hall for their return; sweep the floor, arrange the chairs, make the sandwiches.

She had been looking forward to the excursion since William had mentioned it, three days before. It wasn't just because of the plan she'd hatched with David to bring back some goodies for a midnight feast, though that was most of it; giggling with David behind the backs of the brethren made her ache for childish pursuits. She had also been looking forward to some time away from the serenity of the lakeside. To feel something real again, and in its contact make certain that she was entitled to it this time out. Because sometimes she felt that the earnest faith of William and his disciples, the cleansing chill of the lakeside air, even the sanctified secrecy of her encounters with David – all were fragments of someone else's bedtime story, lost in the aether and erroneously granted her.

The 'hall' was a poky thing. There was a keyboard by the back wall, and a few books of sheet music, and enough faux-leather-bound Bibles to make a fort. Once she'd set up the circle of plastic chairs and the trestle tables, and pulled out the lectern from the corner, there seemed a dangerous shortage of the room necessary to keep breathing an assembly of Christians all equally afire with the faith. Still, the first part of her job was done. She locked the door behind her and walked to the Centra on the next street over. She had sliced pan to buy, and a plan to put in motion.

'I'm sorry to ask,' she said, as the girl behind the counter scanned the provisions, 'but is there a phone I could use?'

There was no provision given for call credit at the centre. Mobile phones were a distraction, William said, a link to the outside world that had chewed them up and puked them out. That had made perfect sense at the time, because Georgie had been sure that nobody needed or wanted a call from her while she was getting sober or realigning her principles or whatever you fancied calling it. She hadn't taken her phone out of the bedside table drawer in weeks.

She remembered his number, all the same. It was one of those numbers you never forgot. 999, your parents' house, your dealer.

'*What* is going on with you?' he asked, in charmed incredulity, when she opened the door.

'What, the rig out?' She twirled. 'Better than freezing your arse off in a greyhound skirt, isn't it?'

'It's a bit wholesome, like.'

'It's a long-sleeved maxi dress, not a burqa! Modesty is the whore's kryptonite. Besides, it's kind of a condition of this whole thing.' She gestured at the hall, and he stepped in and looked around and said, 'Jesus Christ, Georgie. You're hardly trying to convert me.'

'Could you be converted, Ryan?'

'Not without a skinful of acid.'

'Well *phew* for the pair of us, coz they haven't gotten me yet either.'

'Clearly not if you're calling me down. Where've you been anyway, girl?'

'Getting saved,' she said, and he smiled at her, and she was pleased to note that his smile lacked the mercantile cunning she had worried the missing months would give him. 'Down in West Cork. They have this commune.'

'A cult, like?'

'No! Unless you mean it in the Christian sense. But I bet you're a good Catholic boy so you can't really talk.'

She handed over the money she'd put together with David, and Ryan produced a couple of wraps, one of which she tucked into her bra.

'Don't get them wet,' he said.

'I'm not lactating, for God's sake.'

He looked put out. 'If they get damp they're fucked altogether.'

'I'll mind them. Anyway, they're not yours anymore, so relax.'

She sat in the circle of chairs and opened the second wrap.

'Have you got anything to chop this with?'

He was wearing combat-style jeans; folds and compartments enough for the one-man band. He reached into a pocket and produced a small knife.

'Aren't you ever worried you'll be stopped and searched? Drugs and weapons on you; it's like something out of *The Wire*.'

'That's not a weapon,' he said.

'Yeah, I'm sure the guards would see it that way. Here, pass me one of them Bibles.'

The faux leather wasn't the ideal chopping platform; she'd have to wash the cover after. She opened the wrap.

'Sit down,' she said, and he did, across from her.

'Your congregation aren't on the way back for you so?'

'They'll be a couple of hours yet,' she said. 'I told them I was going to visit my mam and dad.'

'But you're from Millstreet.'

'Exactly.'

She was glad to see him. It wasn't wise to get too fond of your dealer, and the likelihood of one of that breed gaining her approval had never come up before. It's just that Ryan was . . . well, young. And though his existence was proof that they were learning the dark arts prematurely these days, she still felt safer in his company than she had done with any other dealer.

'Is it good?' she asked as she chopped, and he said, 'It's unreal,

Seriously, Georgie, you could get ten lines out of that, especially if you've been dry this past while.'

'As a bone,' she said.

She wished she had figured out sooner that young merchants were the way to go.

Maybe, too, young punters.

It was a bad thought to come roaring in after two months of Christian healing in the arse end of nowhere; she hadn't killed off the whore, not entirely. She told herself she had yet to bring her thinking back in sync with the rest of the world. The longer she stayed out of sight in flowing garments in West Cork, the more likely the stench of sin would be obfuscated by contrition's perfume, until repentance diluted her history, until all but lupine senses were confused by her spick, span self.

But the thought was there now and the ghost of who she was an hour ago bleated its dissent.

She'd heard of fathers bringing their sons out for a taster, and wasn't Hollywood always eking out the comedic charm in golden-hearted hookers and the desperate young virgins who found more than surrender in their welcoming depths? Oh yeah, it was really noble. Popping cherries all around her, that would have been the way to go. Charging them fifty quid to bob, red and tearstained, on top of her with her sworn guarantee she wouldn't laugh at the size of their winkies. Ridding them of the burden of inexperience so they didn't make fools of themselves when their pretty little girlfriends finally granted them entry. Before they fixed on their own perversions and started getting grabby.

She bent over the Bible with a rolled-up fiver and snorted her line.

What difference would it make to get them young? They were animals soon enough.

She passed the Good Book to Ryan, and as code dictated he accepted.

'Never did one off a Bible before,' he said, pinching his nostrils and blinking.

She took the book back. 'Mass produced and made of dead trees; there's nothing special about them.'

'It's a bit mean though, isn't it?'

'What?'

'Snorting coke off your Christians' favourite book?'

'It's not like they'll ever know.' She tucked up the wrap and dotted the residue from the book's cover with a licked thumb.

'Are they not nice to you?' he asked.

'Eh?'

'The Christians, like.' He gestured at the book. 'There's a bang of vengeance off that.'

'That's not it at all,' she said. 'I didn't even think, to be honest.'

'So they're not bad to you,' he said. 'They're not asking you to change anything but your wardrobe.'

'Well, and my wanton ways.'

He pushed the chair onto its back legs, folded his arms and looked at the ceiling.

'That's it, though,' he said. 'All the judging. Doesn't that put you off?'

'They're not really judgemental,' she said. 'They're meek and mild and shapeless. They think God has a plan and that all they need to do with their lives is follow it. Live in the country and milk goats.'

'No wonder you were aching for a bump.'

'I wasn't, really. I was convalescing. Coke doesn't go with convalescing; I needed my feelings, you know?'

'You don't anymore?'

'I'm sick of having feelings.'

She was joking, and he smiled as he should have, but he said, 'Seriously though, Georgie. You're looking well, like. Don't fuck it up.'

'Oh my God. A dealer's telling me to stop doing drugs.'

'Dealing doesn't automatically make someone a cunt, is all.'

'Unlike whoring.'

The cocaine hadn't kicked in yet, of course, and the line she'd given herself was more a taster than a parade, but she had always found the ritual very encouraging of conversation.

'I don't know how judgemental they'd be,' she said. 'Truthfully,

Only the leader guy knows that I was on the game. The rest of them just think I'm a souse. But even if they knew and hated me, well, more to forgive, right?'

'I didn't mean you in particular,' he said. 'It's just judgey bollocks all round, isn't it? That's the whole point.'

'That's not very fair,' she said.

He shrugged.

'They've been really decent to me. Free accommodation and all the veggies I can eat and all I have to do is renounce bikinis and not look bored when they're going on about Jesus.'

'And they've no ulterior motive?'

'*That's* the motive. Saving my soul. And let them think they're saving my soul, because in doing that they're saving me from being abused by bastards who think they have a right to rape me.'

He winced.

'It's true,' she said. 'It's not as if Mr Punter Man's bothered whether I enjoy it. And he can't be a nasty, angry prick to his girl-friend so he hires a woman to pound his cock into instead. So if some cooperative of Jesus freaks want to give me an extended holiday that's fine, and if they're only doing it to hook me into their prayer circle that's fine, let them; it has to be better than the alternative, doesn't it?'

He looked at her.

'But what if you don't think you've done anything wrong?'

'I have done something wrong. And I suppose I'd be directed to show Christian forgiveness to you for not knowing that because a: you're male and b: you're never going to be in a situation where you're made cannon fodder for the appetites of people better off than you.'

'All right,' he said. 'All right. Leave it.'

He stood up, making, she thought, to leave, but instead of heading for the door he went the other way, towards the lectern and the keyboard and the stacks of unsullied Bibles.

'I know it's not like I should expect you to care,' she said.

'It's OK.'

'It's just, y'know, the Christians might be daft but they're trying to do the right thing.'

'Yeah, I get that.'

'They might think short skirts are slutty but at least they've come up with an alternative.'

He picked up one of the books of sheet music.

'You wouldn't use a prostitute, would you?' she asked.

It was a funny thing to ask a kid, even if he was your dealer. She chased this grown-up disquiet with ugly reminiscence: the younger men, booked in groups to sate the gang-bang fantasies unearthed by porn habits that stretched from pre-teen curiosity right up to the stoked cruelty of adulthood; the ones who were never satisfied; the ones whose displeasure reverberated in slaps and misspelt jibes.

'I have a girlfriend.'

'That's not an answer.'

'It is,' he said. 'I wouldn't because I have a girlfriend.'

'That doesn't stop your typical punter,' she said. 'Girlfriends have nothing to do with it.'

'That's as may be,' he said. 'I have a girlfriend. I'm not interested in anyone else.'

'How long have you been with her?'

'Year and a half.'

'Jesus.' And then a nasty thought, as she remembered their initial introduction. 'It's not Tara Duane, is it?'

He looked like he'd come down Christmas morning to find a box of bees under the tree.

'What?'

'The night she gave me your number, she let on that there was history between you. Which is partly why I got some fright when you rocked up in your school *geansaí*.'

'That's sick.'

'She's not your sugar mammy, then?'

'That's fucking sick, Georgie.'

'I've seen weirder.'

He placed the sheet-music book on the stand over the keys and said, 'If I'd seen weirder I would have gouged my fucking eyes out.'

'So where did she get your number?'

'She's my dad's next-door-neighbour. Happy? Seriously, Georgie, you're giving me the gawks.'

'Weren't you her dealer?'

'Once upon a time. I've gotten picky with age.'

'Couldn't be too picky, if you're coming into Christian retreats to sell me coke.'

'Maybe I don't find you half as creepy, Georgie.'

'That's a compliment, is it?'

'Statement of fact. Even with your new cult.'

She started to protest, but he hushed her with the first few notes from the keyboard; startling, in that she didn't expect it, and certainly not from him. She didn't know what it was, except that it was played with fluidity and grace, and she gawped, and tried to shout over it, but he ignored her, and by the time he got to the end of the piece she was muted but good, yes, getting there, feeling good.

'Did you play that just to shut me up?'

'It's awful,' he said. 'Lazy, simple bollocks. But it's the only instrumental in here.'

'You don't look like a musician.'

'You don't look like a God-botherer.'

He put the music book back where he had found it, and walked to the door, hands in his jeans pockets.

'What's your girlfriend's name?' Georgie asked.

For a moment he looked like he wasn't going to tell her. He narrowed his eyes, and considered her, and conceded. 'Karine.'

'What's she like?'

'Stunning.'

'So what would she say if she knew you were doing coke in a Christian prayer hall with a prostitute?'

'I've done worse.'

'So she's a saint.'

'Highcr up than that, I'd say.'

'So where do I get one of those?'

'You don't,' he said. 'She's one of a kind.'

He stepped onto the path and hesitated. 'Take care of yourself,' he said. 'Seriously.'

She gave him an awkward smile. 'Don't buy prostitutes. Seriously. If I can't change any hearts in virtuous Christian chests then at least I can change yours.'

'I told you. Not going to happen.'

'Good. And Ryan?'

He looked back.

'You should probably avoid that Tara Duane, too.'

'Give me fucking strength. Anything else?'

'Go in peace?'

'Go and fuck off for yourself,' he said, and he was gone.

The day had gone without a hitch. She'd gotten to the city, she'd called a dealer who wasn't a bullying bastard to bring her blow she had both mind and money for, she'd helped her new friends conduct their Bible study without yap-yap-yapping her true colours into their Christian ears. And when she got back to the farm in the late evening, David was delighted to see her, and over tea and biscuits in the common room she demonstrated, by way of smiles and winks, that she had been successful in her quest, that their midnight feast could go ahead.

David crept to her room when the others were asleep and as she watched him snort a line in childish glee, the day's leftovers tangled in her head.

The rush in chopping up the lines, the unintended sacrilege of a hastily adapted base on which to do it. The thoughts that had come on considering her dealer's frame: that she'd been doing it wrong all those years on the street and in the back bedrooms of crumbling townhouses, that boyhood was a state on which to take pre-emptive revenge.

Then as David came over to lie beside her, murmuring tactile promises on her skin, she knew, suddenly, lucidly, that what she was doing was a curse. She was the succubus aiding his fall. He'd come here, wide-eyed and broken, to mine some life from the depths of his failure and she was bringing him coke and pretty falsehoods.

This community, this flaky citadel of do-gooders, had been poisoned by her presence. The meagre rules of William Tobin, smashed with pitiless zeal. *Respect your body*; here she was on her back again, for some man she hardly knew. *Respect your friends*; here she was, having brought cocaine into their cocoon.

'I need to get out of here,' she said to David, who shrugged it off as he spread her legs. 'I don't belong here.'

'*Ssh*, baby; can't let them hear us.'

'Get off me,' she said, and then, 'Get off me!'

She pushed him off and pulled on her dress as he spluttered disbelief, and ran through the deep shadows of a house she had just begun to know and out onto the yard, down the woodland path to the water, her feet bruised by the shingle, the hem of her ridiculous dress floating as the mud hindered her.

'Georgie!' David was behind her; she didn't turn to look. 'What are you doing, Georgie? Jesus, you'll drown!'

No fear of that; the water, cold and still as the morning air, didn't have the depth to either baptise or kill her. So she stood up to her waist in it, and cried at the shadow shore opposite, for how could good intentions so easily dishonoured ever stand a chance of saving her?

9

They held it up as a Get Out of Jail Free card when it was just another yellow star. Tony lay in the dark in a residential treatment centre in the middle of a vast nowhere. Here, he was to be crumbled to dust and put back together. Here, he was to admit his failings and submit to something of greater import and headier influence. At the end of it he would be a more humble man with drier balls. And sober! Yes, he'd be sober; the Law decreed it. Inside, he succumbed to the horrors doled out by their programme and sobriety stretched in front of him like miles of broken glass.

It had been a stipulation of his admittance that he completed detox before they began his re-education. Even so, his frailty punished him. Getting to sleep was no longer something accomplished by design, but by some Fates' trick: he lay sweating and watching shadows, harrowed over fleeting agonies until he began to dream. The dreams were vivid to the point of cruelty, and he would wake up and have to start all over again. His shell cracked and splintered. His stomach heaved; his muscles sagged; toxins oozed from every pore.

Every time he broke the bottle the period of adjustment was longer and harsher. They kept hanging him out to dry before he was ready to come out of the brine. Next time round it would probably be the DTs. Hallucinations, fever and death. But that'd suit them fine, wouldn't it? They always lumped for the option least bothersome to them. If they'd really given a fuck about his drinking they'd have asked him, *Why? Why, Mr Cusack, did you feel the need to medicate yourself into such a state? It was in effect an overdose. To what end, boy? To what fucking end?*

He turned on his side. His watch, flung onto his bedside table two days ago when it had begun to itch, flashed 3.17. He had been sleeping. He'd dreamt he was drinking again. In therapy sessions he had kept that recurrence to himself, thinking it a sign of ill intent the staff would take badly, but his fellow inmates had mentioned similar delusions. Horrors to them; they were in it for the long haul.

Well, the why is an interesting thing, Mr Bleeding Heart Bastard. Maybe not everyone in here drinks out of Neanderthal instinct.

Interesting, Mr Cusack. Do go on.

She denied it, the venomous bitch. She struck her chest and made a speech about trust and breach of trust and how she had offered his son nothing but a shoulder to cry on. 'And why the fuck would you think he'd need to cry?' Tony snapped, to which Tara cocked her head and wept through narrowed eyes, 'Oh, we both know you're struggling, Tony, there's no shame in admitting that you're struggling.'

He attempted to hound the truth out of her by demonstrating his rage on her windowpane, but all he'd ended up with was a legal obligation to reimburse her and a neighbour who spent her days by the new glass with her curtains bunched into her fist and who skittered up and down her driveway like a spider making a dash across the kitchen floor.

Ryan, then. Tony might have asked him about the night in Duane's, his half-confession, about what perversion had prompted his sharing his home-made porn with the pasty witch, but he'd been so fucked from pilfered flashbacks that the thought of holding a conference had riled him into atrophy. He stewed for days. Then he let the boy go to school in an attempt to win back breathing space. The boy threw a bag of cocaine at his headmaster.

Too much to ask for Ryan to have explained this act of self-sabotage before he took off from home. Temper. Revenge. Something foreign and intangible. When threatened, the boy went mute as Father Mathew himself.

So why did you threaten him at all, Mr Cusack? Don't you think The Demon had something to do with that?

Tony didn't ever set out to lose the rag with Ryan but in no way did the young fella ever quell the rising tide; God forbid he use the term 'asking for it' . . .

Asking for it would be entirely the wrong turn of phrase.

Well, far be it from him, then, to suggest the boy was asking for it but they certainly seemed to have locked themselves into rounds. Tony would attempt to admonish the lad, the lad would go still as a rock, and the boy's silence drove Tony like a whip.

That he was driven to drink by a taciturn child was as good a reason as being defective in spirit and in genetics, but the counsellors preferred internal triggers and vague spiritual shortcomings to logical grounds for needing the poison. In one of last week's sessions he'd explained it: the cruelty of his progeny was what had left him in this shitheap.

'I got into trouble because the woman next door was up to no good with my kid. If that wouldn't drive you to drink then I don't know what would.'

'Did you not find your drinking to be an issue before this?'

'It's not an issue at all,' Tony said. 'I'm here because the court would rather punish me than prosecute that psychotic whore.'

'Jesus, what age is your kid?' said one of his fellow losers.

'Fifteen at the time. And she's my age. And I put her window in and suddenly the problem is my relationship with alcohol and not her relationship with my bloody child.'

He could have killed her. He had practice now in getting rid of bodies, didn't he? He could have killed her and then J.P. would have been obliged to help him turn her to fertiliser, owing him a favour and all. He could have kicked her door in and bludgeoned her, literally knocked the smile off her face, smashed her to pieces. But didn't she have the devil's own luck; he wasn't that kind of man. His rage manifested in muttered oaths. He took out her window instead. He could have killed her but instead he was stuck here, gelded, talking shit in circles so that vultures with clipboards could pick over his compulsions while his children were fed and watered by better people and his son was out there alone being fucked and fucked over.

There were no locks on the windows or doors. Part of the insidiousness of this dungeon was that the only thing keeping him there was torpor. But they didn't make it easy for you; oh no. They had built their covered hellhole in the middle of a postcard vista: miles from the main road and miles from there to anywhere else.

It was boldly functional. White block walls, blue carpet, big windows which left the place airy and bright and cold and exposed. He supposed the intent was to provide a stark alternative to whatever stuffy sets they'd come from, but he was the participant with the most children – the next to him had only three – and so the contrast hurt him worst of all. He yearned for all of it: the crusts on the worktop, the empty toilet roll tubes, the plates under beds and on shelves and, one time last month, on the bathroom windowsill. The triumphant complaints from Kelly on yet another infringement of her teenage right to languor. A mound of socks tumbled onto the kitchen table for Ronan and Niamh to match into pairs. The modish disdain for schoolday outerwear. Him in the middle of it all, dazed sometimes by the whirligig colours and cacophony, but operating nonetheless, handing out lunches, putting on dinners, emptying bins. He couldn't think of home as a space that demanded his reconstruction. There was nothing wrong with it. He was not in here because once in a while he forgot to empty the washing machine or get up on time on Mondays.

He turned again and eyed his bedroom window. Where would he go, if he cranked it wide and made a run for it? Even if it was, defiantly, to one of the pubs peppered over the countryside, he'd be waiting until late morning for them to open. Even if it was back to the city, he'd be sitting in the shell of his home, taunted by echoes and prepping himself for Garda custody. The choice was no choice at all.

From the outside world he heard someone cry.

Such sounds had no right to be anomalous in the dry asylum. Tony stared at the window. The cries were faint, but tormented; this was no fellow inmate indulging themselves with a sneaky wah, but someone further afield, across the lake, in one of the bordering copses. There were other buildings viewable from his window with a daytime squint, but they were either farms or piles of stone and glass belonging to Cork's upper crust. These cries could not have belonged in those places.

No words he could make out.

He got out of the bed and stood by the window with his palms against the glass.

It had been a while since he'd had mind for ghost stories.

The wind rushed the plaintive sounds over the water toward him. He thought about closing the window. Some childhood memory warned him to put the eras between himself and the echo, to make a barrier of modern glazing, or window locks, or a set of headphones. Or was it that you were fucked altogether if you heard the banshee's wail? Maybe there was no escape; it was an omen stirred in blood.

Shrieking, then silence.

Maybe she had come for someone else and he hadn't been meant to hear it.

It was an unusual curse and he only barely had room to nestle it with all the others. He stood at the window looking into umbral immensity, waiting for the screech that confirmed his surveillance had been noted, but he heard no more after that.

'I don't think you should go in,' said Joseph, 'but that's only me, and I'm a lot less forgiving than you are. Whatever I think, I know for a cold hard fact that if you don't go in, you'll regret it.'

They were sitting in the teeming car park of Solidarity House on a Wednesday morning in August. There were vans making deliveries, official sorts carrying folders, visitors doing what Ryan was doing now – hesitating behind their windscreens and tying their fingers up in knots. Ryan's legs were leaden. His shoulders were fused to the back of the seat.

He'd been badgered into attending by his aunt Fiona, Joseph's mother. His dad's twin was as coolly insincere as her counterpart was reckless and thick; the evidence pointed towards her having requisitioned more than her share of nutrients in utero. Her having bullied him into turning up at Solidarity House's 'family day', in which loved ones were roped into the rehabilitant's long-term recovery plan, had been recognised and assuaged by Joseph, who offered to cadge a car so that Ryan wouldn't have to suffer Fiona's pontificating on the journey down. It was a small comfort.

'What d'you think is going to happen in there?' Ryan asked.

'What did they tell you? You get a chance to talk about how his drinking affects you, and then you all learn coping strategies.'

'How his drinking affected me,' Ryan grunted. He doubted they'd welcome the answer: *Physically*.

'And then you all hug or some shit and Tony goes home to resume gargling himself into the ground. Great craic.'

'If I don't show up though I'll be the biggest cunt on the planet.'

'You shouldn't care whether anyone else thinks you're a cunt. What are they going to say to you, anyway? *Oh Ryan, you're a bold, bold boy with no regard for your daddy's disease*. Fuck off. Like six weeks in the country's going to cure Tony.'

'Stranger things have happened.'

From the corner of his eye Ryan saw Joseph consider him.

'Maybe you're right, boy. He's your dad. I get it, you know. I have a dad too.' And then, 'Are you going to have that joint or what?'

Ryan had crafted a fat spliff before they had set off from the city. First, he was going to smoke it on the way down – it'd provide a nice rollover from the one he'd had at breakfast – and then he changed his mind and decided he'd smoke it when he got there. Now he didn't want it at all.

'Feels wrong,' he said. 'Can't go into a place like this stoned, can you?'

'Why not? It's not you making a hames of clean living. They'd probably spot it, mind you. Deprivation can make you very fucking perceptive.'

Ryan shook his head. 'It's just wrong.'

'It's not a church, boy.'

'It's not far off it.'

Fiona's car glinted across the gravel. It was empty, because it was five past the hour and the session had already started.

'I better go in,' Ryan said.

'You know you don't have to, boy? You know he doesn't deserve the steam off your piss?'

'I know that.'

'So why're you doing it, then? What's making you go through that door and into a meeting that's just going to wreck your head? Fifteen minutes, boy, and we could be in Clon, buying a box of beer for a day at Inchydoney. Give this a couple of hours and it'll be baking. Fucking bikini weather and all the lashers down sunning themselves. How bad?'

Ryan let the scene play through his head – the sand, the beers, the sunshine, the flat tummies and the perky arses and necks flowing into shoulders and shoulders pouring into soft curves – and was sorry for it as soon as it faded away. *No harm in perusing the goods*, Joseph might have said, if Ryan had confessed the periodic crises that turned him from red-blooded man to cowering penitent. Or maybe he'd have said, *What the fuck is wrong with you, boy? Are you that whipped?*

Once his pause weighed what reverence Joseph's suggestion demanded he gave his cousin a joyless smile and opened the car door.

Tony waited in the meeting room, chewing his knuckles. His mother was due down to catalogue her myriad disappointments. His father had been invited, of course, but wouldn't Father Mathew have made the trek before him? And then there was Fiona, who had arrived in the world seven minutes before him and so was very saddened she was so frequently dismissed as a font of knowledge. She lived in Dublin, but had driven down for the brouhaha and custard creams.

Tony's counsellor had recommended his older children attend, and so Fiona had roped in Cian and Kelly, and vowed that she'd track down Ryan. On the face of it that wouldn't have been hard; the boy and Fiona's own son were thick as thieves. In reality, Tony knew that getting Joseph to divulge such a touchy secret would have been like asking the Pope where the bodies were. And yet when the door opened there he was, the brat, bringing up the rear and then, when the door was closed, hanging by the wall as if welded to it.

His mother asked Tony how he was. Fiona positioned herself directly across from the counsellor. Cian smiled at him because he was a generous kid – always had been. Kelly smacked her arse onto the chair nearest the door. Ryan stayed by the wall, his hands behind him and his fingers flexed on the brickwork, not meeting his father's eyes, not meeting anyone's.

'Do you want to take a seat?' the counsellor chanced.

The boy said, 'I'm grand.'

'If you take a seat we can get started.'

'I'm all right a minute.'

The counsellor was stumped.

'Yeah, keep standing there,' said Kelly. 'G'wan, make everything about you.'

On any other day her barb may have been snatched mid-air and flung back in her face, but the surroundings had sucked the fight out of the lad, just as it had Tony, who late at night stood staring for *sídhe* and willing them to whip the skin from his bones.

The counsellor smiled as Ryan detached himself from the wall. There were two chairs left: one beside Tony, the other between Cian and Kelly. He took the one between his siblings, and Tony looked at them, sitting in a row as if ordered to file into the formation most likely to bother their father's conscience. When you haven't seen your children in weeks, and for so long before that only through a medicated haze, to have them organised so neatly was a bit of an eye-opener. All three had shot up like weeds.

'Our focus today isn't on mediation or family therapy,' intoned the counsellor. 'We have a specific task and that is to deal with the addiction. So what's helpful at this juncture is for each of you to tell Tony, honestly, how his drinking affected you, and that will provide a solid foundation on which to build a strategy unique to this family. Yeah? *This* family. Everyone has a different story.'

'I can start,' said Fiona.

'Oh. Yeah. Yup. Sure.'

The charade took each of them in turn. Fiona spoke about losing her connection with her twin, conveniently leaving out her globetrotting, and how her resulting affectations made her as popular as a Guinness fart in a snug. His mother said something about the shame of having birthed a professional noodeenaw. Tony watched his children. Kelly feigned boredom, but she was all ears under that leonine mop. Cian kept patting his pockets. Ryan hunched over, staring at his shoes. Black rubber dollies with the thick white sole; there was a name for them, but Tony couldn't remember it. The lad was never out of them. God knows where he got them, because they weren't a brand Tony had the money for.

It could have been Tara Duane. The bitch had always maintained she didn't have a bob to her name but with only one kid and a frame that suggested she only ate on Thursdays, it was obvious she was hawking the poor mouth. She could have been spending her money on fancy footwear for his son; he wouldn't have guessed. How would he have guessed? The concept was too fucked up to take a decent run at. He cast back to see if he could hit on a time when Ryan had had anything but those fucking plimsolls on his feet but nothing came. He'd been a runt of a thing till he was fourteen. Maybe then. Tony's fingers hooked under his seat. His nails scraped off plastic.

Cian looked mortified but managed something about homework and bedtimes and proper breakfasts.

But sure what could you do about it? Fucking nothing. If you called the guards what were they going to do? Arrest her? They would in their shit. They'd have come stomping in all over him, as if he had been the one offering cause to the child to run to that bitch's flapping teabag bosom.

Kelly launched into a gleeful speech about how she had to do everything around the house, and got a dig in too at her older brother for having left her there up to her elbows in the ware and the washing, and Ryan ignored her and Tony ignored her too until it came down to it, when the counsellor turned in his chair to face the boy.

117

'Ryan?'

He didn't look up. 'I don't have anything to say.'

'Nothing at all?'

'No.'

'Your father's drinking didn't affect you at all?'

'I can't think of anything.'

'Oh my God,' said Kelly. 'Like, seriously, Ryan? Fucking seriously?'

Her grandmother said, 'Kelly! Watch your language.'

'Are you for real, boy? Oh, it didn't affect you at all, is it? Just the rest of us and we're all making a fuss. You're such an enabler!'

'Well,' said the counsellor, 'that may well be an avenue worth exploring when we talk tactics, but right now it's an unhelpful label.'

The girl was on a roll. 'I bet I'm not supposed to know that word, like. *Enabler*. Yeah, I couldn't possibly be able to look this shit up on the Internet before I get here. Fine, I can spill the beans on his behalf. My dad's drinking has affected my brother in the following ways: he doesn't rat him out and he doesn't hit him back and he sure as shit doesn't take responsibility when he drives my dad so crazy he smashes our neighbour's windows. Do you know . . .' She made a great show of lowering her voice. '. . . why my brother can't live—'

'How my dad's drinking affects me,' Ryan said, and he stretched back in his seat, instantly claiming his due space in the room as if by a magician's trick. 'I can't remember a time my dad wasn't drinking so I can't tell you.'

'Oh my God, such bullshit,' sang Kelly.

'So if my dad's always drinking, how am I supposed to tell you how it affects me? How would I know?'

The counsellor shrugged to concede the point, but Kelly snorted, and the cretin let her wade back in.

'He's just changing the subject,' she said, 'because he knows it's his fault Dad's here.'

Her brother snapped, 'Will you ever mind your own business?'

'This is my business, Ryan. This couldn't be more my business.'

118

'I don't make my dad drink.'

'You make him break Tara Duane's windows.'

'We could frame this a lot more constructively,' tried the counsellor.

Tony's mother folded her arms. 'What's all this about?'

'Ask your grandson,' Tony said.

'That's right, Dad. It's all my fault. It's always my fucking fault.'

Tony's mother made to say something but Fiona gripped her arm, and by no small miracle the damn woman shut her trap again.

'Ne'er a truer word,' Tony said. 'I'm not in here because the guards found too many empties in my bins, am I? I'm in here because I smashed Tara Duane's window. I'm in here on the tack because that's a hell of a lot easier for the State to deal with than your gallivanting.'

'I didn't ask you to put her fucking windows in, Dad!'

'I wasn't going to wait for you to fucking ask me. Don't think I don't know what went on.'

'Nothing went on.'

'Didn't you tell me yourself?'

'I told you nothing.'

'Just to interject here,' said the counsellor. 'Tony, you're not here at Solidarity House on criminal charges, only as a condition of your parole, because the judge felt that alcohol was a considerable factor in . . .'

It was drink. Oh, look, no denying that. Course it was drink, but it was drink because circumstances required saturation, and again, this bullshit chatter was only blaming the medicine instead of rooting out the tumour.

Ryan looked at his father now with an off-kilter malice Tony wasn't used to seeing from him.

'You told me half a story,' Tony said. 'Why won't you tell me the rest of it?'

'Coz you're dangerous enough with half a story, aren't you?'

'And you think telling me lies is the answer?'

119

'I'm not lying.' Even in the lie he offered the truth. He shook his head, then bowed it, and started on his nails.

Tony heard his mother hiss *What in the name of God?* at Fiona, who shushed her yet again as the counsellor cleared his throat and Cian folded in on himself like a paper fan.

'You're lying to me because you're a fucking liar, Ryan. Brought up in two fucking languages; of course you are. So what were you up to with her, then? Teaching her Italian? Or selling her smoke? Ah, that's it and part of it,' off his son's set jaw, 'dealing drugs at your age. You should be in here, not me. Eh? D'you want to tell your grandmother that?'

'I knew this was going to happen,' Kelly chanted at the counsellor.

'I knew it too,' Ryan said, and up he sprang, making his sister jump. 'I knew nothing would have changed and still I let them talk me into it. Like drying you out would make a blind bit of difference.'

He went for the door, and Tony would have gotten up and knocked his head clean off his shoulders if it wasn't for the fact his mother was there, and the counsellor, a right old man's arse in a skinny shirt and a nose only just long enough to look down.

'That's your answer when I say you're no angel, is it? Walk away?'

Ryan turned back. 'You didn't even ask me where I was, boy. *Where're you staying, Ryan? Who are you with? What're you up to?* Nawthin'. Is it that you couldn't give two shits or you're afraid I'll start talking about what drove me there?'

'You think I don't give two shits? I'm in here for you, you little bollocks.'

'You're in here and you're supposed to be getting better when you're still damn sure there's fuck all wrong with you.' His eyes were shining; the chin was starting to go. 'And d'you know what? I never told no one. About you. And if I had done, where would you be? Not in here complaining coz you're sober; you'd be behind the fucking high walls.'

The door rattled on its hinges as he slammed it.

'Does anyone want to go after him?' asked the counsellor.

'Oh, trust me,' said Kelly, 'he won't be part of the recovery.'

Back out into the car park, one foot after another and blinking desperately, as if every drop squeezed was poison. Ryan had just cleared his vision when he reached Joseph and the car, but he was still sniffing salt and slime back down his throat as if his life depended on their sustenance. Oh fuck, that was no good at all. Not when the very act of leaving home was meant to cure him of that childish weakness that only his father could twist out of him. He could build a customer base whose appetite for smoke, coke and yokes was matched only by their inability to keep their wallets shut; he could live on his own and trick sales assistants into giving him naggins of whiskey; he could strip his girlfriend gently and fuck her hard but for the life of him he couldn't figure out how to move his triggers so his father wouldn't know how to yank them.

'Jesus Christ,' Joseph said, as he got back into the car.

Ryan took the spliff out of the glove compartment and stuck it in his gob.

'He'll never change,' he choked. 'He'll never fucking change.'

Gold Digger

Joseph is on Paul Street, busking. That lad has balls, like. He just toddles down there with his guitar and lays the case on the ground in front of him and off he goes, belting out anything from rebel songs to shit that's in the charts. I don't know how he does it. I'd be mortified just singing in the shower.

It's Saturday lunchtime and town is jointed. I go in with Karine and we get milkshakes in Maccy D's and then slink round the corner to watch him. He's doing a cover of 'Gold Digger'. He's got a daycent voice and there are a couple of girls shaking their arses and giving the air the old sexy one-two. The sun's out. One of the girls removes her jacket and whoops, provoking the evil eye in an ould fella shuffling past. If I was being a prick I'd tell her that Joseph's ould doll has just had a baby girl and that there's no point waving her tits at him coz he's too fucking tired to notice.

Leigh, they called the baby. The christening's next month. I'm gonna be the godfather. Joseph swears he didn't just ask me because I'm half Italian.

Karine stands in front of me and backs her arse right up against me so I take my hands out of my pockets and join them round her waist.

'He gets better every time I hear him,' she says.

There's a bunch of people sitting outside the pubs and outside Tesco. Some of them are singing along. There'll be a few bob made today.

'Did y'ever think of coming down with him?' Karine says, and she twists in my arms to stare at me.

'Me?'

'No, the fella behind you. Yeah you!'

'With Joseph? Busking? G'way outta that. All I play is piano and I don't think they'd let me drag one of them out into the square.'

'You could sing. You're way better than he is.'

'I am in me shit.'

'You're really good. You're a proper musician, like. I don't know what you're doing selling dope. You could go for X Factor.'

'You're shaming me now,' I tell her.

'Hasn't he asked you?' she says. I slide my hands up along her arms and down again and press up against her arse in a fit of gall; I'm wearing trackies, though, so it's probably not a good idea to think too hard about her arse.

'He's said it a couple of times, like.'

'And what did you say?'

'What d'you think I said? I said what I'm saying to you now.'

'You were really good at music at school, is all.'

'Can you imagine me?' I tell her. 'Caterwauling away and lads I do business with rubbing their eyes and wondering who put what in their weed? Imagine what Dan Kane'd say to that?'

The joke flatlines. 'I like to think there's more to you than Dan Kane.'

'There is,' I tell her. 'Loads more.'

'Oh, you reckon so too, do you? For a while there I was thinking it was only me.'

'Well it's not, all right? I'm just . . .' But I can't think of what to say. Joseph finishes the song. People cheer. He catches my eye and I give him the thumbs up and then quietly I go, 'There's no choice, like. I either do a bit for Dan or I go home, and I can't go home.'

'Jesus, Ryan, d'you really think you need to explain that to me? I know that, like! That's not what I'm saying.'

'You're saying I don't fucking sing enough?'

'I'm saying I didn't start going out with you because you could get yokes.'

There's frost now. It's like I've said the wrong thing and it's like she's said the wrong thing and we're just a bit out of whack, just

enough to notice but not enough to fight over. She folds her arms.
I move my hands back down to her belly but I don't let go; there'll
be a real fight now if I let go.

'Bless me, Father, for I have sinned. It's been decades since my last confession.'

'Decades?'

'Oh, aeons. Can you imagine what a burden it's been, Father? Carrying all that sin around, like saddlebags on the back of an ass?'

'Well . . . You're here now. It's the contrition itself that's important, after all.'

'Yes, and there's sins here I'm only dying to be rid of. Ready?'

'Go ahead.'

'I killed a man.'

'. . . Are you joking?'

'Do I sound like I'm joking? What do I sound like? A sixty-year-old woman, if your ears are sound, forgive the pun. Do you think that's how the bingo brigade get their kicks? Confessing crimes to priests?'

'When did this happen? How did this happen?'

'It was a long time ago. Didn't I tell you I hadn't been in decades?'

'But it's playing on your mind now.'

'I live on my own and one day a man broke into my flat, I crept up behind him and hit him in the head with a religious ornament. So first I suppose God would have to forgive me for killing one of his creatures and then he'd have to forgive me for defiling one of his keepsakes.'

'And did you involve the Gardaí?'

'Indeed I did not. You'll have to add another Hail Mary on for that. I didn't involve the Gardaí at all; instead I called up my son and he cleaned up the mess on my behalf.'

'He contacted the Gardaí?'

'No. He has his own ways of dealing with things, I've discovered. And that would be his sin on the face of it but unfortunately it looks like we can attribute that to me too. Another Hail Mary! Will I tell you all about it, from a mother to a Father?'

'If you are truly repentant, God is always here to hear you.'

'God is great that way. He has massive ears and a mouth sewn shut.'

'Well, that doesn't sound in the least bit contrite.'

'I've always had an attitude, Father; you'll have to forgive me for that yourself. It was my attitude that brought me all the way up to your lovely old-fashioned confessional here today. You see, I had a son. But I had him illegitimately because I had an attitude and therefore no respect for myself. He was reared by my mother and father who were very much in cahoots with the Man Above so between my bad attitude and my parents' piety the poor lad was spent, and so now he has no morals at all and he's turned to a life of crime. And you might say that's his own sin, Father, but surely his circumstances had something to do with it?'

'Well . . . Well I suppose we never act entirely alone. Our actions are informed by everything around us. And there is much temptation in the modern world.'

'Temptation that leads young girls into sin, you could say.'

'Times change. There are unique challenges for God's children in every age.'

'Oh indeed there are. And I suppose God was challenging me to deny my son's father his hole. But the Trickster was having none of it, so off my drawers came.'

'This is entirely the wrong tone for the confessional! You must be respectful . . . this is a Sacrament!'

'Is the Sacrament as revered in God's house as the miracle of birth?'

'Well, one is divine, and the other very much an earthly thing . . .'

126

'So do you think God could accept my contrition when all I've done is put to ground one of his earthly things? I killed a man, Father. Now surely that's a story fit to stretch the Seal of Confession?'

'Nothing can break the Seal of Confession. All I can do is encourage you to approach the authorities; it is the moral thing to do. Not doing so would only add another sin and call into question your remorse for the first.'

'So you won't absolve me unless I go to the guards.'

'I cannot put stipulations on God's grace. You will know yourself what should be done.'

'It's a funny thing that the ritual is more powerful than the killing. What's tied to the earth is less important than what's tied to the heavens. You're crosser about my language in the confessional than you are about the fact that I killed a man. An unpleasant man, a waster man at best. A man maybe as born in sin as my son was and therefore an expendable man. Who knows?'

'I sense you're struggling with guilt, and again I must tell you that while God will absolve all who repent with an honest heart, perhaps the only way for you to find peace is to tell your story to the Gardaí.'

'Ah, Jaysus, they must have you on commission or something. No, I'm not going to go to the guards. Not a condition of my telling God how sorry I am.'

'You don't sound very sorry.'

'Well look, Father. There are a lot of things I'm sorry for. Indeed, when I think about it, it feels like I've been sorry all my life. First I was supposed to be sorry for having a child out of wedlock – and if it weren't for the Magdalene Laundry being on its last, bleached-boiled legs I would have been up there scrubbing sheets for the county. Instead I was exiled. I went away to have the baby and then I gave him up as my penance and was sent away again. Your kind had my mother and father's ears; I didn't stand a chance. So if many, many years later my son has found me and brought me home, only he's turned into a thug and my hands are so shaky I accidentally kill fellas, don't the amends I've already made mean anything to the Man Above?'

'It seems you don't want to be absolved at all.'

'Of course I do. Why wouldn't I? I have a son; why wouldn't I feel bad about taking another woman's? I was a wretch; why wouldn't I feel bad about doing in one of my own?'

'Are you really asking me if the punitive measures you felt were forced on you back when you had your child exempt you from guilt now that you've done something you feel is worth God's attention? We are all born in sin; no one gets respite from the nature of their soul.'

'I found out his name, Father. The poor eejit I killed. That was accidental, too, but it was something I held on to, like rosary beads. When I got the chance to tell my son what the man's name was, I seized it, because I couldn't wait to see the look on his face. Oh, Father; he was livid. He has no mercy in him. He wasn't made to examine his actions by the fact the corpse had a name; he was furious that the name provided a complication. He doesn't want to have to deal with his mother's conscience. He's a pup, Father. And who's to say I couldn't have raised him right? Propriety did nothing for him.'

'Well, times were different—'

'Oh, they were. Times were tough and the people were harsh and the clergy were cruel – cruel, and you know it! The most natural thing in the world is giving birth; you built your whole religion around it. And yet you poured pitch on girls like me and sold us into slavery and took our humanity from us twice, a third time, as often as you could. I was lucky, Father. I was only sent away. A decade earlier and where would I have been? I might have died in your asylums, me with the smart mouth. I killed one man but you would have killed me in the name of your god, wouldn't you? How many did you kill? How many lives did you destroy with your morality and your Seal of Confession and your lies? Now. For the absolution. Once God knows you're sorry he lets you off the hook, isn't that right?'

'How can I believe that you're sorry when you're—'

128

'Me? Oh, Father. I know I'm sorry. What about you? *Bless me, Ireland, for I have sinned*. Go on, boy. No wonder you say Holy God is brimming with the clemency; for how else would any of you bastards sleep at night?'

The Echo

II

The weatherman said that this April had been warmer than usual, but as the charcoal canopy was wrung out over the city and the hem of her dress sucked up the residue of a hundred days' winter, no one could have convinced Georgie that it was balmier than Himself had intended. She stood on the corner of the Maltings and the Mardyke; not the first time she'd been standing on street corners in dismal weather, but this time she was accompanied by Clover, which discouraged bitter memories.

They had had a busy morning. They'd been up at the Lough going door to door to spread the Good Word, Clover with calm determination, Georgie in abject mortification. Clover had insisted on their returning to town via the university, where she managed to pass on a few leaflets outside the back gate. Most of the students who took a leaflet immediately bunched it up and carried it just as far as the next dustbin, but a few had absent-mindedly stuck them into pockets of rain jackets or baggy tracksuit bottoms. If only one of them was moved, Clover pointed out, that would be worth the whole excursion. Georgie thought that if only one of the students was moved it would be a waste of their very meagre printing budget, but she kept it to herself.

They had carried on down the Western Road and towards the Coal Quay, where William had parked up the minibus for his own mission across the river on Shandon Street – and excited he was about it too, 'So many Africans!' he'd enthused, mysteriously. It was on the Mardyke, just around the time a relieved Georgie could once again taste sweetness in the air, that Clover got the notion they should visit the few houses in and around the quay

So they stood on the corner, Clover running over the strategy, Georgie exhausted and close to tears. She'd already been told to fuck off, to get off the doorstep before the dog was called, to get a life, to burn in hell, and to stick her propaganda up her shapely hole. She had no mind to repeat the process.

Especially not around here. The old brothel was only around the corner; she was nervous, even though it had been two years, even though the enterprise had moved on since. Jesus, it may have moved only in a loop; the building couldn't have been sold in the interim, not in that dilapidated row, not in this dilapidated economy.

'Well, look,' said Clover. 'Let's split up. That way we'll get through them faster and then we can have a well-earned rest. Hmm?'

'We haven't earned a rest yet?' Georgie despaired.

'Come on, Georgie, what would Jesus do? Besides, we can't meet William with so many flyers left.'

'Throw them in a bin then,' Georgie said. 'He'll never know.'

Clover darkened. 'William's not omnipresent. The Lord is.'

'Fine,' said Georgie. 'I'll go around the front here and meet you at the other end.'

She'd made a mistake in suggesting they dump the flyers. Clover was as rotund and twinkling as a fairy godmother, but she treated Georgie like a puppy she'd brought home from the pound for the sole reason that the authorities would otherwise have put her down.

'I should go with you,' she said, 'seeing as you're so tired.'

'I can manage. It's the shorter route, you know?'

'I'll come with you,' Clover decided, and marched on, with Georgie waddling after.

They deposited some of the flyers into the limp hands of those fretting outside the hospital, and while Clover was explaining her mission to a bemused pensioner with a Westie on a leash, Georgie desperately demonstrated intrepid spirit by dropping some of the leaflets into the communal postbox of an apartment complex.

Between that and the delay brought about by the pensioner's

heedlessness, Clover seemed more reluctant to continue her chaperoning. She stood with Georgie on the corner of the quay, only a couple of doors away from the old brothel, and relented, as if shrinking in the rain.

'Maybe it would be quicker if I went the other way,' she said.

'It would be.'

'Maybe if you continue along the quay and meet me halfway.'

'Sure.'

'Go on then,' said Clover, and pointed towards the first door.

In Georgie's day the house next door was empty. She moved towards it, doubtfully, and Clover stood where she was and watched.

'I can do this, Clover.'

'But what if they have questions?'

'But what about the time?'

Another mistake. Clover frowned.

'I'll just make sure you're grand with the first few here,' she said.

'Clover,' Georgie cried, 'let me do this. Honest, I can!'

The older woman's aversion had not come from nowhere. Georgie knew she'd let them down time and time again; they had allowed ball lightning into their nest. Breakdowns and escapes and more than one interlude where she claimed not to care about what she was doing to them, the poor, gullible eejits; any other collective would have been tested up to and over the line, but William and his disciples were either made of more resilient stuff than she'd accounted for, or they had never encountered ball lightning before and as such hadn't a clue what to do with it.

She had been sure her last blunder would have guaranteed her exile, but that wouldn't have been their style. These days there was so much more of her to save.

There was no answer at the first door.

'Just drop a couple of leaflets through the letterbox and move on,' Clover advised. 'Maybe they're apartments. Try the next one.'

'That'll probably be the same.'

'Try it anyway.'

The door had been painted; the front windows looked new. The intercom, which had once signalled appointments with gutting regularity, was gone. The building seemed to have been reassigned. Apartments now, maybe, housing underpaid professionals who ambled round ignorant to the shadows. God, maybe even young families.

She stood in the archway and tapped on the door.

'They won't have heard that,' Clover said, from the corner. 'Give it a good rap.'

'I don't think anyone's home.'

'Oh come on, Georgie,' said Clover, and moved as if to join her, so Georgie gave it another go; she rapped on the door and stood back and felt tears even under the damp on her lashes. She couldn't explain this to Clover, though there was little doubt that William had divulged her origin to his wife. There were some parts of her story that she could simply not vocalise, held to silence by shame and by expectation of judgement, and, really, William's group were accommodating but they operated entirely on judgement; who can forgive what they haven't already judged? Ryan had been right – their grace could only come from a pitying verdict.

So when the door opened she could neither bolt nor smile.

The resident was a woman in her sixties or so, too dishevelled to make an apposite gatekeeper, but healthier than the nubile corpses who'd toiled here two years ago. Her hair, still thick but hued entirely in shale and snow, came most of the way down her neck and stood out in waves. She said nothing, and scowled.

'I'm here . . .' Georgie said, and faltered, and the woman raised her eyebrows.

'Have I been expecting you?' Her voice was a tart growl.

To her right, Clover made to move.

'I'm here,' Georgie began again. 'To spread the word of . . . of Jesus Christ.'

'You'd think He'd send someone less scatty,' said the woman. 'But fine. What has He got to say for Himself?'

Georgie thrust one of the leaflets at the woman. Clover shifted her weight.

'Oh, He's written it down for you,' said the woman. 'Handy.'

'He says . . . He says: *Go unto . . . go into the world and proclaim the gospel to . . . creation. Whoever believes and is baptised will be saved, but whoever does not believe will be condemned.*'

'Harsh fecker, isn't He?'

'He's loving,' said Georgie. 'He's . . . *We love because he first loved us.*'

'What a pile of shite,' said the woman.

Georgie wilted and Clover beckoned her away, but the woman said, 'What are you doing out preaching on a day like this, anyway? And in your condition? What are you doing? Walking off your sins?'

'We have prayer meetings every week—' Georgie began.

'Era, balls to your prayer meetings,' said the woman. 'You want to convert me, you better do it now, because this missive is going in the bin as soon as I close the door. Do you want to talk to me about the Lord God Almighty or not?'

Georgie looked at Clover, who gestured towards the door.

'I'm not an expert,' Georgie admitted.

'Let me tell you this,' said the woman, 'neither is yer wanno there. Anyone who claims to be an expert in the mysterious waftings of Himself is talking through their high hoop. Are you coming in or not?'

Clover nodded.

'There's so much in the leaflet,' Georgie said.

'Are you going to deny an old lady her consultation, little preacher? Who goes door-to-door and declines the first invitation they get to pontificate?'

'I don't know what I could answer,' Georgie said.

'Give it a go.'

The woman turned and walked back into the building. Clover came to Georgie's side, and said, softly, 'I know she seems a little off but think of it as good practice, and if I don't see you by the time I've covered the rest of the houses I'll come back and get you, how's that?' She walked on before Georgie could answer, and so she went through the door and into the hall in which she used to hear her heart snap, every single time.

The place had been done up. Even from her tiptoed spot in the downstairs hall she could see that. The walls had been painted cream and there was a new floor; when she closed out the door behind her, gingerly, she noted that it had been painted on the inside, too, and the old bolts and chains removed for a single, modern lock.

'Come through,' called the woman, and Georgie followed her voice into a downstairs kitchen, a room she'd never seen when she'd worked there, as her company had only been required in the bedrooms upstairs.

The kitchen was new, too. Cream units around a sleek oven and hood, a breakfast bar, a shining sink before a window that looked into a quaint, ivy-draped yard. The design was defied in magnificent fashion by the proliferation of religious keepsakes on the windowsills, on the shelves and in the corners of the worktops: crosses, statues, rosary beads and sombre brass busts.

The woman clicked on the kettle and took two mugs from one of the presses. 'Tea, I assume?'

'Oh, I'm grand.'

'You'll have tea. And for God's sake will you sit yourself down?'

She sat at the table, and the woman stared over with one hand on the counter and the other on her hip.

'You haven't a clue about the Good Book, have you?' she said.

'I told you,' said Georgie. 'I'm not an expert.'

'You're an actress is what you are, and you haven't learned your lines. What's your name?'

'. . . Georgie.'

'Mine's Maureen,' said the woman. 'And, Georgie, what are you doing wandering around Cork trying to convert people when you haven't completed the process yourself?'

'I haven't been doing this long.'

'That's not what I asked.'

Georgie faltered. 'It's that obvious, is it?'

'I just don't know what your pudgy friend was at, letting you doorstop heathens when your words don't have a backbone. Not to mention how tired you must be.'

'They think the Lord appreciates physical labour.'

'You'll be going into labour if they're not careful. Who are they, anyway?' She turned over the leaflet. 'Christians Active In Light. Ha! Christians Active In Lumbago.'

'They've been really good to me.'

'Is that before or after you blossomed out to here,' she said, with a flamboyant gesture. 'How long are you gone, anyway?'

'Six months.'

'You're big for six months. I suppose you're very short, though. I was the same. So when did they recruit you? With sin or without?'

'Ten months or so ago.'

'Lord almighty. A sex cult, are they? Christians Active In Lovemaking? How did you manage to get into trouble if your soul had been saved? Married off already?'

'No.'

Maureen dropped teabags into the mugs. 'Milk? Sugar?'

'Yes, please. One.'

'Christians Active In Lactose,' Maureen muttered, and Georgie said, 'Are you going to keep doing that?'

'Up until it stops amusing me.'

She got a spoon and started jamming the teabags against the sides of their mugs.

'I met a man through them,' Georgie said. 'That's how.'

'One of their number? I take it they approved.'

'They didn't. He left and I had nowhere to go.'

'And does he know?'

'Yes, he knows. He's from a well-to-do background. It'd be awkward if I went with him. He'll be back to me once he sorts things out.'

'Are they still telling the girls those stories?'

'He will,' said Georgie. 'It's complicated. He's in recovery too. So . . . It was just decided it would be damaging to both of us to deal with this together. We can't focus on our recovery if we're focused on each other.'

'How practical. And what are you recovering from, if it's not virginity?'

'Drugs,' Georgie said. She was too tired to snap.

'What kind of drugs?'

'I don't mean to be rude, but what's it to you?'

Maureen placed the tea in front of her. 'Would you rather we talked about the Lord Jesus Christ, so? We can do. I fell out with Him myself.'

Georgie cupped her hands around the mug and slumped.

'I don't know much. They say you have to be open to letting Him in. They say that He makes everything clearer. That you get a purpose. That it's . . . I guess that it's a load off. I haven't found Him yet.'

'Have you checked under the bed?'

'I'm trying to take this seriously.'

'And yet something's telling you it's not worth taking seriously. Maybe that's a thing with us short women: hands too small to grasp at straws.'

'You sound like a preacher yourself.'

Maureen snorted. 'Oh, I wouldn't know a soapbox if it was bubbling. I have as much time for the Man Upstairs as he does for me. Take a breather and finish your tea; you'll do no converting here.'

The mention of the Man Upstairs made Georgie start and glance upwards, and Maureen noticed and smiled a thin smile.

'Did you know,' she said, leaning conspiratorially, 'this house was once a brothel?'

Georgie's feet were sore, her back ached, she hadn't taken a full breath in weeks. If she had been just a bit further along, just a bit more drained, she might have come clean to the supernatural quickness of her hostess. Instead she swallowed and feigned interest.

'I didn't know that,' she said. 'Like, in a historic sense?'

'Try a couple of years.'

'Oh, are you serious?'

'The lines are coming easier now, aren't they?' said Maureen, and she straightened. 'Yes, I am serious. A place of vice in twenty-first century Ireland. Have you ever heard the like?'

Georgie wanted to ask *What lines?* She took a sip of her tea and scalded out the objection.

'It might have been a brothel historically too,' Maureen continued. 'But not to my knowledge. You don't need the eras echoing to feel the weight of this place.'

Georgie rested her chin on a trembling hand. 'Did you buy it cheap, so?'

'Indeed I did not. It belongs to my son. It's belonged to my son this long time.'

'How long?'

'Long enough,' Maureen said, 'for him to direct its activities.'

Georgie stood up, prompting groans of discord from her feet, her thighs, her back. 'C'mere, thanks so much for the tea. You're really kind, but I better be going now.'

Maureen said, 'Would he even recognise you?'

Georgie sat down again. *I don't know what you mean,* she tried, but the statement struggled to leave her mouth, and what words she managed wilted in the air.

'I'm guessing he wouldn't,' Maureen said. 'He doesn't strike me as the kind who shits where he sleeps.'

Georgie said, 'I owe nobody anything,' and started to cry, quietly; she brushed the tears away with a brittle sweep. 'Don't think you've caught a runaway because you haven't. That was a long time ago.'

'There's a shadow on you,' said Maureen. 'Dripping black and miserable. It was there when I opened the door. I knew you didn't want to come in and that you hadn't a clue what you were supposed to be doing and that some sanctimonious prig had convinced you that you had something to atone for. You either need to accept the past as the building blocks that brought you right up to today, or you need to be a better liar. The world is full of girls like you.'

'You're J.P.'s mother? He puts his mother in a place like this?'

'I'd like to think your tears are for pitying me. Yes, he put me in a place like this. He's a bit too pragmatic, that boy. Hollow with it. I didn't want to stay here at first, but once I learnt the history of the place, something told me it was my duty to remain, in case he drowned it again in squalor. Now he can't get me to move. I'm sure it'll come to his barging in and wheeling me out one of the days, but for now I'm happy. It has whispers, like I said. It has ghosts.'

Georgie gulped and hung on to the tabletop. Maureen brought over a roll of kitchen paper. It was beyond Georgie to ask what the ghosts were doing.

'Do you think,' Maureen said, when Georgie had calmed, 'that this will save you?'

She gestured towards Georgie's belly, and Georgie clasped her hands over the bump and said, 'Why do you think I need saving?'

'I don't. I figured you thought it, seeing as you're in the company of zealots. Whatever way you want to look at it, I hope it works for you. Take it I have an interest. Take it that you're the anti me. Take it pregnancy's awful transformative.'

'I didn't think it was even possible,' Georgie said.

'Then you were probably in the wrong line of work.'

'I mean . . . I didn't think I was . . . entitled to this. This is my second. I lost the first.'

'I'm sorry,' Maureen said.

'You don't get it. It was my fault. I was on drugs, I was drinking . . .'

'Maybe that's so, maybe it's not. You don't know with these things. Pointless to work yourself into a lather wondering about it.'

'I keep thinking this one'll leave me as well.'

'Yeah, well it might if you don't put your feet up and stop trying to cure the lepers. You tell your Nazarenes that; their path to Heaven isn't flattened out by you shoving your boulder in front of them.'

'They're not bad people.'

'How very gracious of them.'

Maureen took Georgie's mug from the table, brought it over to the counter and refreshed it. Georgie sniffed and wiped her eyes

142

and straightened in her seat. She looked towards the kitchen door and at the ceiling. She strained for the whispers and the ghosts.

'You can look around if you like,' Maureen said.

'I don't think I want to.'

'Maybe it'll be good for you. You can scrub the shit off absolutely anything, maybe. This can be your metaphor. Maybe.'

The endeavour to reduce a pile of bricks seeping shadow into a thimble of symbolism didn't appeal to Georgie, but neither did the idea of entering into another conversation with the seer Missus Phelan. Caught between gratitude and flesh-rucking unease, she chose gratitude, accepted the topped-up mug, smiled weakly at Maureen and skittered into the hallway, where she stood by the banister and stared up at the landing.

'Go ahead,' Maureen said, from the kitchen door.

The rooms upstairs had been gutted. Where there was once the colour of lazy decay were clean walls and restored wooden floors. The beds and furniture were gone, as was the telephone on the wall. The makeshift kitchen where the girls had stashed their inebriants had been ripped out and smoothed over.

Maureen was standing behind her. Georgie turned and said, 'Did you find things here? Were you here when they were doing the work?'

'I was in once the downstairs flat was done. They were working away up here after that. Why, what are you missing?'

'Nothing. It's just that the place looks so empty.'

'There were a couple of trinkets. I have them in a drawer downstairs. Let me go and look; you'd never know. That said, if it's a bra you lost I have them well fecked out.'

Georgie frowned, but Maureen had turned away.

She continued through the other rooms, but they were pretty much the same: their darkened corners ripped away, insignificant to the quest Maureen had given her. She tried to reconcile this shell with flashes of a past she had mind for only late at night: being shoved onto her belly, hot breath on her cheek, semen on her breasts, on her face, in her hair, like they were dogs pissing all over their territory. These flares made her shrink into herself – her

143

nails dug into her palms and she hunched her shoulders – but they were still very far away, as if they had taken place not just in her past, but in another country. A lick of paint and she felt no connection to this place.

In one of the rooms on the second floor, there was a small pile of paper and a notebook on the window ledge. A pen made up the accoutrements of the writing space. The ledge was deep, and the room looked onto the Lee. Today the river was swollen, and cars moved either side of it like a lava of litter. But on sunny days, when the light was glinting from the water and the steel, she was sure it would have made a much more inspiring perch. She moved the papers towards the pane, carefully, and sat down with her back to the wall, looking over her shoulder and onto the street.

Two storeys down, she could hear Maureen opening drawers.

She picked up a couple of sheets of the paper on the sill. It was hardly likely that the beast Jimmy Phelan had come from a mother sharpened on art; she had had no run-ins with him, for he had directed their movements only through the pimp, but his legend was monstrous both in reach and report.

The first page appeared to be the start of a letter to a priest.

Bless me Father for I have sinned. Or is Dear Father all right with you, pitter-pater?

Georgie slid this sheet under the other, and read:

Robbie O'Donovan was here.

She should have dropped it. In doing so she'd have given the poor guy some sort of regard, after the fact. Instead she turned it over, as if on the back she'd find an explanation of how his name had scrawled its own clue into the palm of her hand, but the rest of the page was blank. She turned it over again, and reread it: *Robbie O'Donovan was here.* in the same hand as the priest letter. Her breath caught. She sat suspended in voicelessness, as if the sudden stasis of her lungs could make her float, bounce off the walls, up to the ceiling.

Maureen came back into the room with an armful of leftovers.

'Robbie O'Donovan was here,' said Georgie. The air escaped her throat.

'Oh, him?' Maureen clucked. 'Don't mind *him*. He won't touch you. He just stands around.'

'He just stands around?'

Maureen's eyes narrowed, and she smiled. 'Did you know him? He died here.'

Georgie dropped the paper and darted past the woman and down the stairs. Her shoes slipped on the last step; she grasped the banister, and cried out, and scrambled for the door. The lock wouldn't budge on her first go. She found the clasp and the bolt sprang back and she ran out onto the street, where Clover was approaching, only a few yards to her left.

'What's wrong, Georgie?'

'I'm just feeling sick, Clover, really sick. Please let's go.'

'OK,' Clover said. 'We can do that.' She put her arm around Georgie, and Georgie clung to her, sniffing and retching. They had gone only a couple of hundred metres when Georgie heard a voice behind her, calling her name, and Clover slowed but Georgie begged, 'I'll be sick, Clover, I'll be sick!', but it wasn't the matriarch Maureen closing in on them. The voice had that unmistakable ringing whine, the musicality of shattering glass. Georgie turned and Tara Duane waved at her, hurrying forwards on stiletto boots that cast her to the left and right as if she was dancing on a listing deck.

'Georgie! Wait up! Oh my God, it's so great to see you! Where have you been?'

'This one's not a good one,' Georgie said to Clover, who nodded and squeezed her arm, but stayed otherwise stupidly solid to watch the scrag advance.

12

Karine arrived over with a bag stuffed with goodies: two chicken salad rolls, four packets of Taytos, handfuls of chocolate bars, tobacco and Rizla, a two-litre bottle of Coke and, best of the lot, a bag of pick 'n' mix as big as a baby's head.

Ryan said, 'You absolute lasher, D'Arcy,' and she rolled her eyes and said, 'You better remember this when you're rich and famous.'

The curtains were closed, because there wasn't light worth letting in. It was damp and miserable and balls-shrinkingly chilly. There wasn't much to look at, in any case; Ryan was in his father's house, and all he could see from his bedroom window was other people's back gardens, sodden from the pitiless April march. Next door and almost a week ago, Tara Duane had dragged a plastic airer outside and draped a number of towels over it, either from desperation or bloated optimism.

He hadn't meant to spot her, afraid that if she looked up and saw him watching she'd take it as a favourable sign. It was anything but. He'd sunk behind the curtain and sat on his bed, elbows on knees, hands joined and eyes to the floor. There were tons of drawbacks to being home again, but none that frightened him like she did. Two years might have diluted her story to the point where it would sound, to Karine's ears, reedy and fanciful. That was the best possible scenario and even that could ruin him. Karine might not want to share him, even in secret thought, with someone like Tara Duane.

'Ew, like she was hollowed out and sewn back together,' she'd whispered one time, years back, when Duane had offered to do an offy run for the underagers.

Tara's airer had toppled and the towels had fallen to the ground. They were still there today, rumpled in the mud.

Karine slipped her shoes off, smoothed her school skirt and climbed onto the bed beside him.

'Pass me my roll there,' she said, and he retrieved the tobacco and started rolling a joint as she tucked in.

'Where'd you get the smoke?' she asked.

'Dan the Man posted it to me.'

'He *posted* it to you?'

'Swear to God. He has me spoiled.'

'Eat your roll first,' she said. 'There's warm chicken in that.'

'All right, Mammy.'

He finished rolling the joint and tucked it behind the curtain on the windowsill, and they sat together, munching into the picnic in their cobalt cave. When he was a couple of bites from the end she reached into her schoolbag and produced a pen, pad and her maths book.

'Where are you supposed to be, anyway?' he asked.

'Maths grind,' she said, and placed the things on his lap.

'You're funny.'

She buried her head in the bag again. 'Come on, Ryan,' she said, once she emerged. 'Be sensible. The sooner I get my homework done the sooner we can relax.'

'I'm already relaxed.'

'Unrelax yourself, then. Page 57, questions 11 to 20. And I'll do my French while you're doing that and if you're really, really good, you might even get a blowjob at the end of it.'

'I'll get a blowjob anyway.'

'And you're haunted, aren't you?' she said. 'You think you'd be more inclined to help your girlfriend out with her homework, so? When she's so nice to you?'

She placed her French book primly on her lap and brushed a strand back from her face and he started laughing and she said, 'What?' in mock indignation.

'It's just funny.'

'What's just funny?'

147

'You're just funny.'

'D'you know what's not funny?'

'What?'

'The fact that you haven't started my homework.'

He opened the book. 'You can't keep doing this to me,' he said.

'Yeah? What are you going to do about it?'

He *was* haunted; plenty of fellas would confirm it. His girl-friend liked giving him blowjobs. There was only the fact of his required passivity to sully the act. As a precursor to sex a blowjob was a hundred per cent awesome, but occasionally – only very occasionally, he wasn't a total loss – if she was going down on him just for the hell of it, there was a shade of submission that maybe knocked that hundred per cent down to ninety-five. He tried to reframe it as something which put him in the driver's seat, but it wasn't easy to claim control when he was putting his cock in someone else's mouth. There was something of la Bocca della Verità about it.

He knew what was wrong. He knew that on the occasions that last five per cent was taken from him it was because of a flash-back, not to a scene – there was little of the memory left – but to a feeling of losing the run of himself, and making stupid mistakes for no good reason.

There was a time they filmed it and it was a hundred and ten per cent, fucking perfect.

Now there was a half-hour of quiet, punctuated by the odd remark about something that had happened in school, various text messages, the sounds of his father opening and shutting the living-room door, of Niamh and Cathal bickering about who had authority over the remaining Coco Pops. He finished the maths before she'd done her French and lay back on the bed, and when she'd caught up she put away the books and pens and lay with him.

As was custom in the years before, he had pushed Cian's bed in front of the door after she'd come in. It was a strange thing to be back where every second was bloated with the possibility of ambush. They kissed for a while; she was fine with removing her school jumper and letting him unbutton her shirt but when he went to remove it she hunched her shoulders and whispered, 'Oh God, Ryan, I'm so scared he's going to come up the stairs. I don't know how we ever did it like this.'

'Necessity is the mother of invention.'

'Eh, you'd want to invent something more convincing than that!'

'He won't come up,' Ryan said. 'He's been avoiding me like the fucking plague since I got here. Like he thinks I'll drive him back to drink.'

'I guess it's awkward because you were away so long.'

'It's awkward coz he doesn't know what to do with me. I came back here and I wasn't a kid anymore . . . He knows anyway.'

She winced in agreement. 'I know that video was more than a year ago, boy, but I'm still cringing.'

'Me and all, but . . . It means he knows. And that, plus the fact that he spends his days pretending there's nothing wrong from his fort in the sitting room, means he's not coming near us, girl. And even if he did come up, he can't get in.'

'I suppose not.'

'Are you gonna let *me* in then?' He kissed the spot where her neck joined her shoulder and she arched her back and sat up with him. He slid her shirt from her shoulders and she pulled his T-shirt up and off and when they were a lot less decent they dived under his duvet.

He framed her against the sheet, skin-blush to blue shadow. She kissed his neck and traced his spine but both as reactions to his actions, because that's what he wanted, today and anymore. After a while she put her hands on his shoulders, wordlessly suggesting he roll onto his back to accept the promised blowjob. He kissed her; she pushed at him again and he resisted again, and she pulled back and smiled and whispered, 'Don't you want me to go down on you?'

'It's just . . . I dunno . . . I could go down on you?'

She gave him her most pained smile, the kind she usually reserved for instances where she had to cry off on a date, or guilt

149

him into a shopping trip, or indeed, turn down his offer of cunnilingus.

'I don't *know*,' she sighed, which generally meant *Not in a fit, but I don't want you to feel bad about it.*

'You go down on me all the time,' he said.

'I know, but you love it.'

'But you might love this.'

'I don't *know*.'

'We're two years together, like. I don't know anyone who's been together longer than we have. And I've never gone down on you.'

'You might not like it.'

'It's supposed to be about you, though.'

'Why are you so mad for it, then?'

'Coz I want to do it for you.'

She sighed again, and smiled and looked away, and he inched back the duvet and said, 'Seriously, girl, you're the most beautiful thing I've ever seen in my life,' and she tutted and he said, 'You're the most beautiful place I've ever been in my life, too.'

'Ryan!'

'It's true.'

He traced his finger from her mouth over her neck, between her breasts, down her belly, between her legs.

'You let me do that,' he said.

'That's your finger.'

'You like my finger, and my finger's all rough and I bite my nails and it's not nice, really.'

She giggled. 'It's not the same and you know it.'

'Yeah . . . I think my mouth'd be better.'

'Ryan!'

'Seriously though. Seriously. What is it about this that's putting you off?'

'I'd be embarrassed.'

'Why? With me? After two years you'd be embarrassed?'

'Look,' she said. 'You're probably thinking it's going to be a certain way and then it mightn't be and you might hate it and then I'd die.'

'What d'you mean, a certain way?'

'Like . . . you know. Like in porn.'

'You been watching porn, D'Arcy?'

She stroked his neck. 'No. You have.'

'No I haven't.'

'Have.'

'Haven't.'

'Course you have! All boys do. And you're probably thinking it'll be bland and rubbery like . . . like plastic fruit and you'll get a terrible land.'

'You must think I'm an awful gom.'

'No . . . I just think . . . I don't *know*.'

'You think this is something you're doing for me?'

She frowned. 'What?'

'Sex.'

'No. Of course not. Don't even think that.'

'It's just . . . I want you to love it, like.'

'I do.'

'Well . . . if you love it, and you're not embarrassed when I lie here and look at you, or when I kiss you or finger you or when you come or when you go down on me, why should you be embarrassed about me going down on you?'

'It's different for boys,' she said.

He felt his shoulders tighten. He said, 'No it's not. Why should it be?'

She looked away and smiled, and he watched the smile twitch at the corners of her mouth like a living thing, growing, fading, taking root.

'Haven't you ever thought about it?'

She didn't answer.

'Listen,' he said. 'We're together two years. And we'll be together two more. And another two after that and on and on and on because I'm that sure that this is it for me and you, that this is it entirely. So I don't want you to hold anything back because you're afraid of what I might think; that's just wrong, girl. I love you. That's what love is supposed to be.'

151

She said, 'You say the deepest things when you're trying to get your own way,' but she was teasing, and she reciprocated when he kissed her.

'Please, Karine.'

She threw the playful smile back out into the expanse of their sanctuary.

'Please?'

Still no reply. He kissed her breasts, back up to her neck, along her jaw and said, 'I'm not going to do it until you tell me yes, girl. Has to be a yes, not just a *not no*.'

'If you don't like it, it's all your own fault, though. OK?'

'Totally.'

'*Mmm* . . . Yes, then.'

She wouldn't kiss him afterwards. She made him brush his teeth. He went for a piss while he was in the bathroom and leaned one hand flat on the tiles to keep himself upright.

Weak at the knees for my girlfriend's cunt.

As an attempt at a statement of fact, it felt ridiculous, but intoxicating. It was something new. It constituted a nail in the coffin of the memory.

All on his own, he allowed himself a jagged sigh.

When he returned to the bedroom she was wearing her skirt and his Napoli jersey, rummaging through the bag of pick 'n' mix.

'D'you think your dad would twig it if I had a shower?'

He lay on the bed and put an arm around her waist. 'No. Yes. Maybe. Who cares?'

'I care.'

'I don't. It's none of his business.'

'Yeah I know, but . . . D'you wanna white mouse?'

'I've just brushed my teeth, remember?'

'All part of my diabolical plan.'

'Here, if you eat all the cola bottles I'll kill you.'

She chewed, and stuck a finger in her mouth to dislodge a jelly, and said, 'Well? Was it OK?'

He sat up with her and she gave him a stern look, one more

suited to *Did you just write with my eyeliner again?* than *Did you enjoy the act of oral pleasure, you selfless tongue champion?*

'I loved it,' he said.

'Really, though?'

'Really. You have no idea. Did you like it?'

She made a face.

'I know you did,' he said. 'I could taste it.'

'Oh my God, you're so disgusting.'

'Why is that disgusting?'

She made a big deal out of dismissing the question – clucking, rolling her eyes, giving him a playful slap – but she understood, she accepted it, she was fucking delighted.

She went off to have her shower and while he waited he opened the bedroom window and started on the joint. Beneath the clouds his estate lay still as the rain uncovered brilliant shades of green on the trees, and the ivy, and the weeds growing along the back wall.

She came back in with her hair in a towel turban and he handed her the joint. She took his place by the window and shivered dramatically, so he got one of his hoodies and she snuggled into it.

'That's tasty,' she said, exhaling.

'Yeah. It's handsome.'

'I can't believe he posted it to you.'

'Yeah. He's not such a bad guy, really.'

'And yet here you are . . .'

'You know what I mean, girl. I was bricking it. I thought he was going to kill me. And yeah, for a while he was pissy beyond, and I thought *That's it, boy, he is gonna flake into you*, but he knows I'm not going to say anything and . . . Like, he trusts me not to blab and it's not even because I know he'd slaughter me otherwise.'

'Maybe he realises you wouldn't be in this mess if it wasn't for him?'

'But I probably would be, girl. I have two previous convictions and they were before I even met Dan.'

'Yeah, but . . .' She passed the joint back. 'It was his coke. This is his mess. And you're the one in trouble for it.'

He shrugged.

'I don't know how you can be so OK with it, Ryan.'

'I'm not OK with it.'

'You are. And you don't seem to realise you don't have to be. Sometimes it really is someone else's fault.'

'It's how things go, is all. Risks and stuff. You make an educated guess as to whether you'll get away with something but at the end of the day it's just a guess. It got me out of the house for a year and it got me out from under my dad's feet, so it was worth it.'

'I don't mean to take that from you,' she said. 'I know you had to get away from your dad. But this shouldn't be the price you pay.'

'It probably won't work out all that pricey.'

'What if it does, though? I mean, who gets a twenty-four-hour curfew? That's off the wall; you said so yourself.'

'I guess coz I wasn't living at home, they thought this was the best way of keeping tabs on me. If I had been living at home I'd probably have gotten your common-or-garden bail. *Turn up on April twenty-first for your hearing, sonny Jim. And no drugging while you're waiting.*'

She plucked the joint from between his fingers.

'Well, it sucks,' she said.

'I know it sucks. Being here with him sucks. I mean, he's on the dry and he's trying not to be a prick but . . . I dunno. Too much water under the bridge. For both of us.'

'Oh my God, whatever about Dan, everything that happened with your dad is his fault only.'

'Is it, though?'

'Jesus! Yes!'

She handed back the last drag, and he turned to watch her return to the bed. She slid her legs under the duvet and pulled his hoodie across her chest.

He knocked out the joint on the sill outside and closed the window.

'Look, there's more to what went on between me and my dad than . . .'

'Abuse?'

'Don't say that.'

'Is there a better word or something?'

'Look,' he said. 'I don't want to talk about my dad. Not now. Not after what we just did. Coz that was lovely and . . . amazing and . . .'

'Yeah well, I'm scared, Ryan.'

'What are you scared of?'

'Ah, the judge? The judge doesn't know you, like.'

'It'll be grand. Honestly. The solicitor said. I'm pleading guilty, I'm not going to break the curfew, I'm being good as gold. We tell the judge that, y'know, I did OK at school and that I'm looking into going back and stuff.'

She considered him. 'Are you serious?'

'Why wouldn't I be?'

'You're gonna stop dealing.'

'If I tell the judge I'm going back to school, I'll have to go back to school, right?'

He slipped into bed beside her and she rested her head on his chest. Her towel turban scratched his cheek and flopped open on the pillow behind them.

'It'd mean more of this, though,' he whispered. 'Me living here with my dad, me and you having to do it all stuffy-quiet in the middle of the day. The last year of freedom, it'd be gone.'

'It'd be worth it in the end, wouldn't it?'

She slid a hand underneath his T-shirt and thumbed the skin around his bellybutton.

'I like the idea of Ryan going back to school,' she said. 'And Ryan going to university. And then Ryan getting a nice job and buying me lots of shoes.'

'Hey! Buy your own shoes.'

'I never said I wouldn't buy you shoes too. A pair of Cons for every day of the week.'

He stroked her shoulder, and she nestled in the crook of his arm

'You think we'll still be together then?' she said.

'Told you that earlier, didn't I?'

'Really though?'

'Yeah. I can't imagine it any other way. If I had another joint right now I'd see the whole decade out before me and every minute would have you in it.'

'And what would we be doing?'

'The usual, I suppose. Buying a gaff. Getting married. Popping sprogs.'

'How many sprogs?'

'Dunno. Four or five?'

'Jesus, I hope you can buy them in Tesco by then or you're going to be very disappointed.'

'I won't be disappointed. There's no disappointment in it. It's all good. Every second of it.'

He raised his head. Her eyes were closed. He kissed her forehead, and stared up at the ceiling as she started dreaming, and he watched the world spread out in front of him, corner to corner, flush with colour and glowing like the sunrise.

Downstairs, there was a gentle knock on the front door, as if even the visitor was wary of interrupting them.

13

The next step was getting a job. It wasn't a step of his own design, but shaped by so many gloating well-wishers that Tony was stuck with it.

The woman at the Social was as helpful as he wanted her to be. He brought up youthful summers working on fishing boats, with pointed references to cutbacks at the Port of Cork. She passed him the details for a deli assistant position. He told her he had six children under eighteen and frying builders' rashers at 6.30 a.m. was a welcome impossibility. She recommended he try an internship. He asked her if she thought he was fucking crazy.

Springtime held another challenge when the Law, consistent as it was in its pointed cruelty, dropped Ryan back into his lap. Silly gosser had only gotten himself caught with enough cocaine on him to be done for possession with intent. Again.

He'd run from them. That was his undoing. The guards had stopped him on the street when he had a couple of baggies on him, and once he felt their questions were snowballing, he bolted. *Stupid thing to do*, Tony had groaned; the boy had responded tetchily that they would have searched him anyway, and so he had to chance flight. If one of the guards hadn't been a young muck-savage swift as he was zealous, he might well have gotten away with it.

The amount they'd caught him with wasn't enough to threaten him with gaol; he was small fry, and they were trying to squeeze names and dates out of him. Tony noted wryly that the last thing on God's green earth Ryan Cusack was likely to do was talk. The cops didn't know that. His capture had been a waste of their time and when they cottoned on to that there might well be hell to pay. Tony didn't mind that. A bit of intimidation might do the lad good. Maybe the guards would find, through spite, a way to bully him straight.

At the first hearing the judge had imposed a twenty-four-hour curfew, remanding the kid in the custody of a father newly dry and squeaky clean. Between himself and Cian there wasn't room to swing a cat, but Ryan seemed content to shut himself off in his bedroom, black buds jammed in his ears and a laptop screen as his mask.

An effervescent liar from the phone company had sold Tony a broadband subscription, which had had the effect of lobotomising his three teenagers and giving him the cold comfort of meditative silence. Once a week Kelly commandeered the laptop and went through the jobs website with her father, and between them they figured out which posts were worth procuring rejection letters from. Sometimes he got an email back that thanked him for his efforts but denied the existence of suitable positions. When he was so blessed he showed them to his probation officer. The job hunt was going well.

April had come around in a vicious funk, summoning snowstorms in Dublin and floods in Fermoy. Tony ordered home heating oil earlier than he'd presumed he'd need to, and he'd handed over the fee before it had occurred to him that he'd done, without wheedling procrastination, something of equal import and expense. It was a fine thing to be sober, sometimes. It hadn't been pointed out in rehab: *When you're sober, you'll buy home heating oil when you actually need it and it'll feel like a fucking miracle.* It was the small things.

It was the big things that threatened him, though: the loss of routine and the awkward jettison of bad habits and old pals, the boredom, the claustrophobia. Small victories he stockpiled, and yet the barricade was flimsy and dangerously stunted. Sometimes he sat halfway up the stairs when the kids were in school and watched the world warp through the frosted sidelight of the front door. On occasion he rested his head against the wall that separated his territory from the grabby púca Duane's, and listened with dour intent as one would to penance given as the world outside splintered his front door and chipped away at the plaster. Even purer than that, sometimes: he really wanted a drink. The physical addiction had been dismantled, but the compulsion grew unchecked without its frame. *I want a drink*, he thought. *I want a drink*. He would grip the armrests on his living-room furniture as the longing threw a whirlwind around him. *Just one. Just one, for Jesus's sake. I want a fucking drink.*

That's why they were so keen on jobs, the therapists and the probation officers and the mammies and the sisters. They kept telling him: a job to replace an addiction.

Cian brought the *Echo* home from school and Tony sat in the living room, in front of the telly, and went through the jobs page for opportunities for which he was underqualified. The kitchen, designated as a homework hub, shook with his squabbling brood. Young Karine had arrived over a couple of hours ago and made great haste to wall herself up with Ryan in the back bedroom, where, no doubt, they were getting into divilment, though he'd take that over Duane's insinuating guilt any day of the week.

Through a lull in the kitchen mayhem he caught the last taps of a half-hearted knock on his front door, and he rose. Too feeble for any of the kids' friends, and far too gentle a sound for anyone trying to flog a leather three-piece suite.

He opened the door to a young woman blatantly pregnant.

Without protection from the rain, her hair had sprung into a wiry halo; she clasped one hand to her forehead and squinted.

'Tony?'

'That's right.' He thought she might be a new caseworker. They had a habit of shapeshifting, though he'd never had one come to the door wearing her incompetence on her head before.

She was dressed in a denim jacket and some measure of patterned tent, befitting her fecundity if not the miserable weather.

'I'm sorry,' she said. 'I don't know how to say this but . . . Do you know Robbie O'Donovan?'

The name pushed past Tony and into his hall, wheeled around

his head, clung to and coloured his walls, a shadow for every letter.

'Who are you?' he asked. 'Sorry, what's this about?'

'My name's Georgie,' she said. 'I was told you knew Robbie O'Donovan. I'm sorry, this is . . . Do you think I could come in?'

'I don't know any Robbie O'Donovans,' he said.

'Maybe if you think back? He was my boyfriend, and he went missing a couple of years ago . . . Look, if I could come in? I'm pregnant, you see.'

'After a couple of years?'

'I'm tired. And it's raining. I'm really sorry to ambush you like this but I think maybe if I go through a few bits with you, you might remember him?'

'There's a lot of kids in the house.'

'I'm only six months gone,' she said. 'I won't be adding to them.'

Behind him, the kitchen door opened and Niamh's dark head popped out to pry. Over his shoulder, he said, 'Get back in there a minute.'

An offended tut from his nine-year-old busybody and the door was closed again.

Outside, the young woman stood, pained and wringing.

Tony moved aside and she accepted the invitation gratefully. He gestured towards the living room and she stepped in and sat at the edge of the sofa.

'D'you need a towel?' He nodded at her hair.

'Oh! That would be so great.'

He climbed the stairs and retrieved a towel from the hot press. The break didn't provide time enough to think. *Robbie O'Donovan – how do you know him?* Drinking buddy? Gambling buddy? You don't know him at all? *Jesus Christ, Cusack; pick one.*

Who'd think he knew Robbie O'Donovan? Had the lass gone sniffing out bones in the pub they used to drink in? Had Maureen Phelan sent her?

His blood fizzed. The balls of his feet found dips in the carpet beneath him.

160

He'd given J.P.'s mother the gift of a name and she'd accepted it like a child accepts a mound of sweets and the promise of sticky hands. Had he thought, in the months of eerie silence that followed, that she'd forget his slip-up, or clutch it jealously? No. Sure why would she?

Stupid fucker, Tony. Stupid. Stupid.

He closed the hot press as the door next to it opened and his firstborn gawped out at him.

'Who's that, Dad?'

'Just someone looking for someone. It's nothing.'

'Looking for who?'

'No one, Ryan.'

Back in the living room the sodden visitor accepted the towel and attempted a smile. Tony stood by the fireplace and said, 'Georgie who?'

'Fitzsimons. I don't think I've met you before.'

He shook his head. 'You're looking for some ex-boyfriend?'

'Robbie O'Donovan. I know this sounds very strange. He disappeared just over two years ago now. I reported him missing at the time but the guards have had no luck. He was kinda hard to miss, though. He was around six foot two, red hair, really skinny.'

'I don't know anyone like that. Someone's after telling you I do, though.'

'Yeah, there's a girl that lives up around here, she said that you might be the man to ask. Her name is Tara. Tara Duane?'

Tony bit his cheeks and rubbed his palms off his thighs. Georgie turned the towel over and ran it through her hair again.

'She's my next-door neighbour.'

'Oh. I didn't know that.'

'Why the fuck would she tell you I'd know where your ex ran off to?'

The expletive hit hard. 'I don't know . . . I met her in town the other day. She flagged me down and said if I was still in the dark as to where Robbie went that you might know.'

'She flagged you down?'

'Yeah . . .'

'I don't get along with her. Suppose she neglected to mention that. She's trying to drop me into something. She's a vindictive bitch.'

Georgie clutched the towel.

'Drop you into something? No, she just said you were a mate of his, and I thought maybe . . .'

Too late, Tony found the meagre details in the girl's few statements and concluded she had little reason to be suspicious before he'd opened his mouth. He sagged and the mantelshelf pushed into his lower back.

'Look,' stammered Georgie. 'I'm not usually in the habit of annoying strangers over something as dodgy as one of Tara Duane's notions. I wouldn't have come up here, not in a fit, but it wasn't like Robbie to run off. If I told you half of it you wouldn't believe a quarter—'

'Listen, girl, I don't know any fella called Robbie O'Donovan. I'm sorry but there you go. I do know a woman called Tara Duane and I've had my run-ins with her. I'm thinking maybe she's stitched you up to stitch me up or something but I had nothing to do with your fella going walkabout. I've enough of me own problems!'

'I just want to know where he is,' she whimpered. 'I would have been grand but only a few days ago this started up again. Someone told me he was dead . . .'

'Duane?'

'No, not Tara. Meeting Tara was a coincidence . . .'

Tony thumped his fist on the mantel. Coincidences followed Duane like rats after the piper. Once he tore through the conspiracy he'd tear through her, consequences or no consequences.

'Well ask whoever told you, then!' he barked.

'I can't. You don't understand . . .' Georgie's countenance had changed; her chin was quivering. 'I can't bring it up with them again, I can't go to the guards . . . Tara just told me you knew Robbie. I really didn't think I'd be upsetting you like this, or I'd never have come here . . . Oh God!'

'Here,' Tony said, desperate as the tears intensified and the hubbub from the kitchen died down. 'I feel for you, girl, don't get me wrong, but I don't know the fella you're on about, and I've a house full of kids and a working pair of ears on all of them. You're going to have to take this up with Duane.'

The girl wiped her cheeks with the flat of her hand. She was short and raven-haired, pudgy around the cheeks, and, it seemed, in the process of completely losing it right there on his couch. Tony endeavoured to make sense of her fit. Tara Duane's name rose a fog in him. He sank into the armchair across from the crying woman and blinked.

How the fuck would Tara Duane know he had anything to do with Robbie O'Donovan? How the fuck, how the fuck . . . He found himself mirroring Georgie's actions, pinching the corners of his eyes, running his hands over his head.

The girl's chest heaved in an exaggerated hiccup and she knotted her hands over her belly.

'You're going to have to leave,' Tony tried, but she sat up straight, mouth open under her shining eyes, and said, 'Shit, you're Ryan's dad.'

'What?'

'You're Ryan's dad! If Tara Duane lives next door to you . . . I *knew* I knew you from somewhere.'

'You don't know me at all.'

'He's the bulb off you. It's unreal. Are you trying to tell me you're not Ryan's dad?'

'I haven't a notion of talking about my children with some girl who's just accused me of burying a man I never met.'

'Look, I'm sorry. This past week has just been throwing the weirdest shit at me . . . I don't know what I'm doing here.' She started sobbing again.

'Stay here a second,' Tony snapped, and bounded up the stairs and onto the landing, where he knocked an elbow off the boy's bedroom door.

Ryan came out far too wide-eyed.

'Who the fuck is yer wan downstairs?' Tony hissed.

'Who?'

'Don't fuck with me, Ryan. That's why you came sidling out

when I was up here at the hot press; there's a fucking woman downstairs claiming to know you and flinging some serious shit at me.'

'Who's she looking for?'

'Me, for some fucking reason. Why is that?'

'I don't know.'

'Ryan, for fuck's sake. Not this now. Of all times, not now.'

The lad . . . could he even call him that anymore? He'd left the homestead in a haze of his father's regret and he'd done so as such a narrow thing. He'd come home again with a couple more inches on him and a trim muscularity his father could track most easily down his back, across his shoulders. Maria's brothers were sinewy and tall. It was disconcerting to spot that in his own son.

The lad, what was left of him, said, 'I know her from a couple of years ago but I haven't a notion why she's up here.'

'How? How'd you know her?'

'Jesus, Dad . . . How d'you think? I used to sell her a bit of dope. That's all. She's not my buddy or anything.'

'She's a grown woman, Ryan! How in Christ's name were you selling her dope?'

Ryan paused. 'She's a pal of yer wan next door.'

'Oh, fuck me. And?'

'And yer wan gave her my number.'

Tara Duane was a hex neither of them had given name to since the boy's return. 'Tara Duane,' said Tony, and Ryan looked away. 'Every time I hear that cunt's name it shaves years off my life . . . Get rid of yer wan downstairs, Ryan.'

'But what's she want with you?'

'Don't fucking talk to me, boy, just get fucking rid of her.'

He followed Ryan down the stairs and hovered then in the kitchen doorway, listening to the hum of his son's words and the shrill, to lowing, to wet return he was getting from the stranger.

'Who's that, Dad?' Ronan had gotten a slick of butter on one of his cuffs. Tony beckoned him to the sink and swiped at it with a damp J-Cloth. 'Who's that?' Ronan said again. He was only seven, friendly and guileless.

164

'No one,' Tony said.

'Is she sad coz she's fat?'

'Yeah.' He caught Cian's eye. The boy snorted.

After ten minutes he returned to the living room. Ryan was standing in front of the fireplace. The crying woman was holding the towel on her lap, twisting it in her hands, wringing salt out of it. From the kitchen there came a crash, then a clamour of moving chairs and giggling.

'You only need to hop the front wall,' Tony told Georgie, 'if you want to take it up with the person you really have a problem with. I told you I can't help you.'

'I'm sorry,' she said. 'I'm desperate.'

'I don't care how desperate you are; this is intimidation.'

'Dad,' Ryan winced.

'What? It is. On the behest of that crazy bitch Duane you're coming to my home and telling me ghost stories.'

'It is a ghost story,' Georgie said. 'That's exactly it. Two years on and suddenly I'm hearing his name everywhere.'

'If it's everywhere that means there's a ton of other places you can haul your lunacy. I'm a single father, for fuck's sake. Crackawlies instructed to hold seances in my sitting room while my kids are doing their homework . . . This is all wrong.'

'Georgie,' said Ryan, 'why did Tara tell you my dad would know where your fella went?'

'She just asked if I knew him and when I said I didn't she said I should speak to him. She said that he'd have known Robbie well.'

'You didn't ask her how she knew that?'

'Why would I?' Georgie cried. 'I just thought maybe they were friends or something. Ryan . . . you know I'm not crazy.'

Ryan said, 'I don't know you at all, Georgie,' whether through honest affirmation or a clumsy sidestep, his father couldn't tell.

'You know me well enough! So if I tell you that this is the second time in a week someone's mentioned Robbie to me and the first time I was told he was dead, you know I'm not making it up.'

'This is bullshit,' Tony said. 'Bullshit, and you need to get the fuck out of my house.'

He flung open the front door and clambered over the dividing wall, marking his hands with the mossy slime of a barrier unkempt for its significance. He pounded on Tara Duane's door but it stayed closed. He pounded on it so hard that it looked like giving underneath his fists. He came back into the house and the girl Georgie was standing up, still crying, with Ryan beside her looking for once in his little life like he had encyclopaedias in his gob lined up and ready to be recited.

'The bitch isn't home to shed light on this,' said Tony. 'And the last time I tried busting in there to drag her arse out for an inquisition I got done for it. In the absence of her mediation, you're going to have to jog on. And do it quick, girl. Heavy and all as you are you don't want to push me.'

Georgie said, 'I'm sorry. But you have to understand—'

'I understand you're unhinged. I understand you're only familiar with my son because you were using him to get your drugs for you, and I understand you're associated in some way with that toxic whore next door. I don't have to understand anything more than that. Leave now, stay away from me, and stay away from my kids. Do you understand?'

She left. She closed the door out gently behind her and made her way down the driveway – as he noted when he looked out to make sure of her trajectory – with shaking shoulders and a gait to match. There was a pang of sympathy, involuntary. Tony clasped his right hand around his neck to choke it down. Every time Maria had been pregnant it had built in him what her wild nature had eroded. He was a whole man when biology had required it. Six times he'd watched her blossom and it had been the making of him, as well as of his children.

The first of them, his sullen antagonist, his bravest soldier, stood waiting for his father to grill or dismiss him.

'What the fuck, Ryan?' Redundant, repetitive, and frail, and what else could he manage?

'I swear to God, Dad, I haven't a clue what that was about.'

'Never mind what it was about! Jesus!' He pushed his hands over his forehead, walked to the far wall and knocked the flat of his fist against the plaster. His son stood his ground, though even Tony wasn't sure whether this spat could escalate according to precedent.

A sober man now, he felt the months tug at him.

'Why would you have anything to do with these people?' he said, and Ryan looked away; they both knew it wasn't just the visitor he was referring to.

'I wouldn't now,' he said. 'That was years ago.'

'How many years ago?'

The pause had him well told before his son confirmed it: 'I dunno. A couple.'

'And we know what you were up to a couple of years ago.'

This was old ground, overgrown. There was more laughter from the kitchen, reminding him he could choose just as easily to push forward, to send Ryan back upstairs to the charming little tyrant to whom he was sweetly indentured.

He brought his forehead to his fist.

'Is it the mother thing?' he asked, and turned then, and said, 'Is that what drives you to people like that?'

'No, Dad . . .'

'Coz every time I think I'm making progress, something happens to remind me that I've fucked up with you. The reason you're home. The reason you knew that bloody woman.'

'Dope is the only reason I know her,' Ryan said, softly.

Tony assumed he was worried about eavesdroppers and retribution.

'Whatever it is or was,' he said, 'you'd hardly tell me. And I'm supposed to be protecting you. Isn't it desperate? Even if I wasn't shit at it, you wouldn't let me, would you? Why would you? Go back up to Karine.' He shook his head. 'I won't say anything.'

How could he tell J.P.? There was no telling with J.P.

Tony returned to his *Evening Echo* and the lies of his sobriety. Ryan went back upstairs and the rest of them trotted in and out of the kitchen in turns, losing interest as he batted away their questions. The interruption was largely forgotten by dinnertime.

He ran through a confession in his head, and forecast a bloody nose and a march on his home, threats flung at his children, and an interrogation that would expose Ryan's minor role. What then? The lad would be quizzed on Georgie's background. Maybe it'd go well. What then? J.P. would track the girl down and grill her. What then? There would be a mess to be tidied. Maybe the girl would be disposed of; maybe she'd be encouraged towards amnesia. Tony pondered taking that chance. She was pregnant. He couldn't risk it.

She might go to the guards, despite her assertions to the contrary. If someone had let slip to her that Robbie O'Donovan was dead, then chances were good that she knew better than to take it to the cops. Even so. If the cops got wind at all, he was fucked. All the more reason to tell J.P. about the visit.

But then what of Ryan? If J.P. was involved, Ryan would know there was something up. The woman had turned up talking about ghosts and suddenly the meanest cunt in the city – and it was all but guaranteed that Ryan knew who J.P. was, seeing as how he was knee-deep in the runoff – shows up on the doorstep asking after her? Tony's declarations of ignorance would be examined and judged as bollocks.

Fucking stupid kid. Fucking involved in everything he shouldn't be. If the girl had turned up on the doorstep and the boy hadn't recognised her, well, wouldn't that have been something? Wouldn't that have been too much to fucking ask?

If Tony said nothing about his afternoon visit, J.P. would remain at arm's length and maybe the bitch next door would spill sense. There was only one woman looking for Robbie, and judging by her belly she'd moved on. Maybe there was fuck all to worry about but happenstance and his shrunken city.

The rain cleared off in the evening. Tony walked down to the off-licence and stood outside it like a child with tuppence to his name outside the toy shop. If he pressed his nose to the glass, he may well have been able to smell it. The heady warmth of the thought seeped through his shell and into his bones and lifted him onto his toes and rose off him like holy water off the devil's shoulders.

The twenty-first of April was as miserable as the rest of the month had been, and it came round before Tony had made his decision. The last ninety-six hours he'd spent in airless languor. He had tried Tara Duane's door every morning and every evening, but there wasn't a peep out of her, and Kelly had eventually thought to tell him that young Linda was temporarily staying with a buddy while her mam ran up and down the garden path with some sap in Dublin; whatever the destination, it seemed that Tara Duane had thought it a good time to go on the missing list.

The courthouse was packed. Ryan's hearing was set for 2.30, along with everyone else who'd been summoned to the afternoon sitting. The newcomers mingled with the dregs of the morning's session, who had commandeered the seats in the stuffy green waiting room. Parents sat gloomy and still, like rows of turnips in a grocer's box. Their little criminals sat with them, tapping LOLs on their phones, or milled in the yard outside stinking of Lynx and taut nonchalance. Solicitors strode in and out in a twist of slacks and briefcases.

They called him shortly before four. Tony ducked out of the waiting room and found him standing with McEvoy, the solicitor. He gestured them both inside.

McEvoy was a decent chap who had taken more care with Ryan's case than they'd enjoyed with previous representatives. He hadn't taken instruction so much as informed his own brief. They were blessed with him; Tony hadn't wanted to use the same one who'd failed to save him from six weeks in Solidarity House.

They were blessed with a different judge, too. Mary Mullen. McEvoy said she was smart and thorough. *Is she OK, though?* Tony had asked, and McEvoy had replied, *You could do a lot worse.*

She spoke to the solicitor. It was a rare judge who bothered with the pleasantries. Tony leaned forward. They could be over so quickly, these hearings.

'And what do you think yourself, Mr McEvoy,' said the judge, 'about where he goes from here, if he's not in school?'

'My client intends to return to school in September. He got excellent results in his Junior Certificate and knows that was the better path to be on.'

'What kind of excellent results?'

'He shows a great aptitude for music and mathematics, both of which earned him an A grade in Higher Level. University, rather than training, is clearly the right way to go and the boy is taking steps to—'

'And, Mr McEvoy, how do you suppose he'll stay out of trouble?'

'I believe that a probation bond would be the most suitable response, Judge. Given the circumstances—'

'I've heard the circumstances.' She straightened, and looked over at Ryan, and said, 'Let me tell you something, young man. Are you listening?'

'Yes, Judge.'

'There's a very specific kind of boy I see whenever I come here. A lot of them have no family support; a lot of them have no education; a lot of them have been, most likely, led astray. But you are not like my typical young offender. Mr McEvoy has shown me that you're intelligent, that you've got a good father, that you did well in school, that when you apply yourself to something you achieve it without struggle. Would you say that's accurate, Ryan's father?'

Tony cleared his throat. 'Yes, Judge.'

She looked back again at the boy. 'And, Ryan, this is what frightens me about you. You are smart, and you do apply yourself. And you have no qualms about pointing your brains or your determination in the wrong direction entirely. When I see boys coming up here before me, there's a fair amount of them who don't know any better. Genuinely. They don't know any better. But you do. And Mr McEvoy tells me that you have learned the error of your ways and that if I apply conditions to your parole, I won't see you here again. I don't have any faith in that.

'I have to bear in mind that you refused to cooperate with the Gardaí who questioned you and that every time you've appeared in this court, it was for the same offence. And what worries me, Ryan, what really worries me, is that you don't seem to be learning anything except how to do this better.

'What is he like at home, Mr Cusack?'

Tony went to stand up, stopped, gripped the back of the seat in front of him. 'Your typical teenager, I suppose.'

'What I'm concerned about is how easily he can switch between being your typical teenager and your not-so-typical criminal. Other than the loss of his mother, are there any family circumstances that could be contributing towards this behaviour?'

Tony said, 'No.'

'Do you feel you have any measure of control over him?'

To which arose, unbidden, an image of Jimmy Phelan bellowing for answers, seizing the boy for a search of the city, sending him into drug dens and tenements to flush out the Georgie girl, having her dealt with, having him dealt with, uncovering ugly truths and dismantling whatever peace they'd forged during the curfew.

'Oh, God,' he breathed.

'Mr Cusack?'

'I don't have any control over him,' said Tony.

The boy turned in his seat and said, 'Dad . . .', and Tony looked down as the judge hushed them, and directed Ryan to look at her, and said, 'In light of the circumstances, and in light of the seriousness of this crime, something it's clear you are gravely and deliberately underestimating, I feel the best sentence is one of nine months' detention in Saint Patrick's Institution, wherein, my lad, you'll find a school to blaze a trail through.'

On the Cheap Midweek Flights

It's supposed to look like a shopping trip. My mam spins it as a pre-exam treat, in case any of the neighbours twig.

On Tuesday morning, instead of putting on my uniform, I go with her into town to the airport bus. She's trying to talk to me but I don't feel like talking. Everything she says is slapped back. I guess I'm sulking. I dunno.

We buy our tickets and walk around by the side of the station and she sees them before I do and I hear her go, 'Oh dear Jesus.'

There's four of them, two men and two women. They've set up a trestle table and they've got big signs saying 'Abortion stops a human heart from beating' and 'For unto us a child is born' and this picture of a haloed foetus and you'd think my heart would fly up my throat and out my mouth or something but instead I am just instantly raging.

My mam is horrified. Like, she doesn't know where to look. I call over at them and she grabs my arm but it's too late, the words are flowing. 'You sick bastards,' I say. 'You sick, shaming fucks. Why can't you mind your own business and keep your glorious mysteries to yourselves?'

The two fellas and one of the women are old as balls but the second girl is only in her twenties I'd say, and you'd think at that age she'd know better. She's sitting behind the trestle table. When I get close I see why. She's pregnant. Massively pregnant. She's like a blimp pregnant. So I say to her, 'You're down here shaming when you're having your own baby and you don't see anything wrong with that?'

And she's like, 'Well, we're just campaigning for—'

But I stop her because honestly, I could hop off her. 'How many girls walking past here might have had to terminate even though they don't even want to? What about the ladies whose babies have no brains and stuff? What about girls who were raped? Oh, my God, you know what you are? You're fucking evil. You're a fucking evil cow.'

The oldest guy, the one with a grey ponytail and big stupid eyes too close together, says, 'Please move along, this is a peaceful protest.'

'You should be moved along, you miserable bastards.'

But my mam is dragging me away and I'm letting her, because the rage is making me cry. I hate that: when you get so angry you start crying and then people think they've beaten you when in reality you're just so wound up you can't stop yourself. My mam stops in front of our bus; it's not boarding yet. 'Don't mind that now,' she hisses. 'Don't think about it.'

'When am I allowed to think about it? On the plane home again?'

I wished she hadn't noticed this mess in the first place but that's what mams are for, isn't it? Noticing.

They were the worst two weeks of my life. At the beginning I get a call from Ryan's phone and I answer it all, 'Oh hey, baby boy, go on, what happened?' and it's his bloody dad, not him and I'm crying even before he tells me: 'He got nine months, girl, I'm sorry, he's gone, they took him straight up.' I couldn't eat for days I was stressing so much, and everything I did eat I threw up again, till my mam came into my room one morning and shut the door behind her and said, 'I know you say you're sick from stress, hon, but . . .'

And she was right. The second she noticed she made it real. And I wish she hadn't noticed, I really wish she hadn't, because then I might have been too far gone to talk out of it, I dunno. Stupid to think that, isn't it? Ryan would do the entire time inside, away from me. Yeah, nine bloody months. And how would I cope with that? I've never been this long away from him and I cry every night because I miss him and I'm scared for him and I want to fucking kill him.

My mam said, 'Can you not see what a bad match you are? A time when you needed him and he's in prison, Karine. Prison!' My dad was way harsher but only because I've never seen him so close to bawling. 'That's the kind of waster he is, girl, gets you into trouble and fucks off. How much school and grinds did you miss for this fucker in a fucking exam year? And there you go now, isn't it a roaring lesson for you?' He's always hated Ryan.

And you know what? They're right. I did need him and look what happened. I could be here with him now, working this out, deciding how to manage because if he was around I'd be keeping this baby but he's not, is he? He's not around and if he keeps dealing he'll never be around and if I can't trust him how can I have his baby for him?

The driver opens the door and my mam and me get on.

She sits near the front but I walk a few rows back from her and sit by the window with my iPod turned all the way up.

As the bus pulls off I put my hand on my tummy. It's still flat, because what's in there is only the size of a grain of rice, it's not a baby yet and it never will be and I'm crying again, because I know this is the right thing but I'm so cross that I have to do it, cross with my mam and dad and cross with Ryan and missing him and hating him and loving him and I'm scared, above all. I'm so fucking scared.

14

Frank Cotter: they called him General Franko. He had a head of curly black hair and wind-tanned skin; he looked like a lighthouse keeper, or a shepherd, something that spent its days in the elements rather than in the back rooms of shuttered casinos, breaking fingers and cracking skulls.

He was waiting in the yard when Jimmy arrived, the waves on his head lifting with the coastline bluster, dressed in a faded jumper and jeans, dirt on his shoes and a gleam in his eye.

'Thanks for meeting me, Franko.'

'No bother, boy. You know me. I'm not afraid of hard work.'

From his jacket pocket Jimmy fished a pair of black gloves and pulled them on as he rounded the other side of the Volvo.

Though cleaned from his chin and lips and philtrum, the blood had caked around Tony Cusack's nostrils; Jimmy guessed he'd decided not to spend his last hours picking his nose. When he opened the door Cusack chanced weight on legs unable to hold it. He flopped out of the car and onto the dirt, then got to his knees, holding on to the inner fittings of the door to steady himself.

'Come on, Cusack,' Jimmy offered. 'Jellyleggedness is so unbecoming in a grown man. And father of six.'

'Why are we here?' Cusack croaked.

'Because I can't trust you. And those I can't trust I don't keep around.'

Cusack started keening his own wake. He put his hands to his face and his fingers dragged at the skin under his eyes. 'Oh God,' he said. 'Oh God.' Jimmy gestured to Franko and he came around the car and pulled Cusack upright. 'Oh God,' he said, again, and then for variety's sake, 'Oh Jesus.'

The yard was trimmed with nets and rope, the substantiation of a forsaken hobby or a career left to rust in old age. Later on, when Dougan arrived, they would take the boat out. They would wrap the body in rope and weigh it down with shale and quarry blocks. They'd drop it where it would never wash up again.

Jimmy Phelan hadn't been able to swim in the sea for many years.

'I don't know this one,' Franko said. 'What's he done on you?'

'Why would you think I'd answer that?' Jimmy said.

'Ah, I'm only asking. It'd be a rare time you wouldn't know the feen, is all.'

'You're all mouth, Franko.'

Cotter simpered.

The yard was at the bottom of a boreen bordered by overgrown hedges and divided by a thick ridge of thriving grass. Sometimes you got dog-walkers and joggers chancing the stretch; they never got close enough to worry about. Half a mile along the wild shoreline, over flaking gates and on a path beaten only by shuffling gangsters when there was an undesirable trussed up to use as pollock bait, you reached the little harbour, and the dinghy that would take you out to the fishing boat. It was a good spot. Jimmy and his boys had used it for a couple of years, longer than he was comfortable with, but the yard was a hard habit to break.

Besides, he liked getting out of the city.

'Right,' said Franko. He pulled Cusack forward, to a tearful yelp.

Jimmy shook his head. Cowardice was nobody's darling. So much of a man was stripped away when notice was given of his demise; it was no surprise to see them cry and beg and empty their bladder all over their shoes, but it was an ugly thing. What use was a man who couldn't stand up straight to face his mortality?

He saw Cusack clearly now, a prolific weakling, a creature at his peak in his teens who'd been steadily sinking since.

Franko had begun the prep. The tarpaulin was laid flat. The hose was extended to sluice the inevitable mess from the concrete; they were promised rain later, too. Jimmy raised an eyebrow, and Franko produced the prearranged weapon and handed it over.

Jimmy crooked a finger around the trigger. It had been years since he'd taken on a job himself, but he had the same good reason for keeping Cusack from his crew now as he'd had when the waster had first clawed at his patience. Dougan knew nothing about the O'Donovan corpse and the brief maternal glitch that had produced it. It followed that he couldn't be told about Cusack's flapping insurrection, his spilling the dead man's name in front of Maureen. It followed then that he couldn't be told about Cusack's reluctant reveal of yet another damned aggravation: a visit from a panicked ex-girlfriend on the direction of that ridiculous cunt Duane. For what could Jimmy tell Dougan on that cock-up? That his mother was a loon and that his attempts to provide a smokescreen had backfired and left him blind and gasping?

It was a skit of the highest fucking order.

Franko stood Cusack in the middle of the yard, shaded his eyes, and searched the skies.

'Why are you here, Cusack?' asked Jimmy, and his old friend whined, 'This isn't something that needs to happen, boy. You know I'm no danger to you. I'm a father, for fuck's sake. They're already missing a mam; don't do this to them.'

'D'you know your problem?' Jimmy brooded. 'You don't know when to stop. I asked you why you were here and you went off on a tangent. I don't know what Maureen asked you but you went off on a tangent there, too. So many angles are bound to ride your arse eventually. Why are you here, Cusack?'

'Because of a fucking accident, boy, a stupid slip-up, a name and a surname is all, dear God.'

'You'd think that'd be all, but what happened? You left it unchecked because you thought Maureen might neglect to tell me. You retreated to your hovel on the hill and quaked into a bottle and you let your slip up grow and grow until there was a whore prying at your door for a dead man. See what happens when you think shit'll just work itself out?'

'I get it, I get it.' There were two colours a man could turn out here, apart from the pervading yellow backdrop: ashen or dribbling puce. Cusack was white from forehead to knuckles. 'But I'm not the problem, boy. All I did was make a mistake. I'm no danger to you. Why can't you see that? Why can't you . . .' Whatever force had fed his voice ran dry.

'You're a waste of space, Cusack.'

'I was there when you needed me,' Tony rasped.

'And look where that brought me.'

He'd been sniffling even when he'd come crawling to Jimmy. Panic about a mourning girl turning up on his doorstep, two years after he'd done his good deed for his old friend, compounded by the fact she'd been directed there by Tara Duane. *It might just be one of Duane's notions*, he'd said, flaccid and wheedling. *She may have only just remembered that we used to drink in the same pub, some shit like that.* Jimmy had cursed the bitch under his breath, warned Cusack to let him handle her, and assuaged his anxiety through gritted teeth.

Alone in the aftermath he'd wondered if Tim Dougan was his good-luck charm. It had been decades since he'd tried unpicking complications without his old buddy's help, and his efforts had double-knotted the thing and bound his hands with it.

This morning he'd determined to have a final lash of it, called General Franko, hounded the retching Cusack into his car and made for West Cork.

By the time Dougan showed up Cusack would be gone and Franko certainly wouldn't be talking.

Cusack got a second wind and launched into another petition he'd cobbled together on behalf of his little darlings. Jimmy held up his hand.

'Nothing you say's going to change my mind that you're a maggot and my mistake.'

'Jesus, Jimmy, do you want me to fucking beg?' Cusack sobbed.

'You are begging.'

178

'Six kids, Jim. Four boys and two girls. Seven to seventeen. What d'you think is going to happen to them? We're so brittle as it is. I've one in prison, I need to be around for them . . . You have kids of your own!'

Jimmy said, 'I have to show you what happens to people who I can't trust, Cusack.'

'Please! Please, for fuck's sake—'

The gunshot shut him up. The second made him wail. Jimmy stood over the little General Franko and put a final bullet in his head.

Tony was on his knees. He heaved. Saliva anchored his head to the ground.

'You see?' Jimmy said.

Cusack said nothing. He was crying.

'One mistake can bring the whole city down around me, Cusack. I take mistakes more seriously than you think. Don't for a second believe that if it had made sense to, I wouldn't have wiped you the fuck out.'

'What did he do?' Cusack blubbered.

'Him?' Jimmy waved a wrist at the former general and his fragments and fluids. 'He talked too much. More than you do, even.'

He stepped over to his old friend and caught the back of his head, twisting him on his hands and knees so he could face another future.

'Don't let what happened to him happen to you, Cusack.'

Cusack dispatched to wait in a pub five miles back, Jimmy relaxed in his car with a well-earned cigarette and half a playthrough of *Against the Grain*. On the other side of the yard, beyond the concrete wall and over the rutted sea, cloud begat cloud and the air turned damp and grey. Where Frank Cotter's blood had washed into the muck the flies danced, intoxicated.

Dougan arrived a couple of hours post-mortem. Jimmy watched from the car as he approached the tarpaulin and surveyed the glittering concrete. He was a bulldog of a man: squat, muscular, and stern. He had a stomach lined with iron and a pragmatism that extended to murder and murder's horizon.

He flopped onto the passenger seat and said, 'JimBob, you started without me.'

'I was feeling old and fat, Timothy. I thought it was time I got busy again.'

'And how was it?'

'Overrated. We should bring the boat out soon. Rain later. The water'll be choppy.'

Dougan said, 'You were down here a lot earlier than you said you'd be, boy.'

'Yeah.'

'Always your plan to do it yourself, was it?'

'Yeah. I suppose I was being a bit snakey about it.'

There was a pause. Dougan considered the tarpaulin. Jimmy watched the clouds.

'Has it happened to you yet,' Jimmy said, 'that you thought going into a job that you might feel a bit too old for this carry-on after, that you thought, *Well, this'll be the one to herald my retirement*, and yet when it came down to it you felt the same old familiar nothing?'

'Being honest, boy, I never expect to feel anything, and I remain unsurprised.'

'Twenty years ago this shit used to rise bile. You get used to it, then you wait for a time you'll lose the knack for it. I hadn't pulled a trigger in years up to today. And look at that; I'm still a killer.'

Such blunt language was exceptional, even between old friends. Dougan frowned, but raised his eyebrows nearly as quick, thought about the infraction, let it slide.

'Were you expecting ascension?'

'I was expecting to be older than I am.'

This is how it was usually done. A man would commit an unforgiveable transgression. Maybe he'd screw the wrong fella over, maybe he'd be found in a position where ratting out his betters might seem the only option, maybe his jaw was gaping and clumsy, as General Franko's had become. A decision would be made. Most of the time there was a good run-up to the action. A call would be made, a favour called in or loaned out to a contact in the UK. Someone would fly over, find the problem and snuff it out. It was all very neat. Everyone had an alibi. The assassin wouldn't be in Ireland long enough to shit and wipe his arse.

General Franko's demise might have been arranged this way, if Jimmy hadn't found himself with an extra thorn to pluck from his paw.

He doubted that there'd be harm done in having Franko sorted the traditional way. In fact, he was banking on it being constructive. He was still capable of rash decisions if his temper was so stoked; beware of the dog. And if this Robbie O'Donovan thing came to light – the whore had to be found and he didn't think Cusack capable of the task – he wanted there to be no illusion as to the boss's mental faculties. When he needed to be ruthless he was.

'Let's go fishing,' he said.

Cusack phoned him up two days after.

'She's home,' he said.

'Since when?'

'I dunno. The last half hour or so. I didn't see her come back but I can hear her moving around in there.'

Like a rat in the walls. Jimmy went straight over. He parked at the bottom of Cusack's driveway, blocking him in for the divilment of it, and hopped the wall to Duane's front door, where he knocked with polite restraint and waited, one hand resting on the sidelight.

Her bottom lip started quivering as soon as she opened. Her hair was arranged in two childish plaits hanging over her shoulders; he reached out and tugged one, and said, 'What's wrong, Tara; aren't you pleased to see me?'

'I'm only just home,' she said. 'What, I don't even get an hour's peace?'

He stepped in and she stepped back.

'How was your holiday, Tara?'

'I was only in Dublin,' she said. 'Visiting my sister. She's not well.'

'Is she not? Ah, Jesus, that's awful.'

He closed the door behind him and she said, 'I don't even have milk in the house or anything.'

'It's OK. I'm not after tea.'

'Well what do you want, then?'

'Oh, just to follow up on the last time I saw you. Remember? I asked whether you knew of a fella called Robbie O'Donovan.'

She held on to the banister and pursed her lips. 'Yeah. You said he was a buddy of Tony Cusack's.'

'Did I?'

'Yeah. And like I told you, he's on the missing list, so I—'

'You told his girlfriend and now the whore's been up here nosing around. Did I fucking ask you to befriend his fucking next-of-kin, did I? *Tara, will you ever go and tell Robbie O'Donovan's ould doll that Tony Cusack knows where he is.* Did I say that at any stage, did I? Did you hear me do it?'

'You didn't tell me I wasn't to say anything about it!'

'Well fuck me, I didn't think I'd have to spell out to you that you weren't to give the floozie the idea O'Donovan was dead!'

'He's dead?'

'The only person who seems to know for sure is the fucking call girl, and you're the only one who's been talking to her.'

'I didn't tell her he was dead!'

'Well, how'd she get the idea then?'

'Maybe because he looks the sort?'

'He looks the sort to die?'

'He looks like a junkie! Junkies die! Junkies die all the fucking time! I didn't make him overdose; it's not my fault!'

He reached for her, but she ducked and dashed into her kitchen, where she avoided his second grasp by swinging a chair between them and then diving under the table, to which he could only stand and laugh.

'Come out from under the table, Tara.'

She was bawling. 'Leave me alone! Leave me alone!'

'Do you really think I can't get in there after you?'

'I tried to help you! It's not my fault you didn't make clear it was a huge big secret!'

'It is your fault, Tara. You're a fucking cretin.'

'I have a daughter!' she shrieked.

'What is it with assholes trying to hide behind their offspring when they think they're getting a clatter?'

He sank to his haunches and made a grab for her, and she batted his hand away and cried out.

'Jesus Christ, it really is like trying to catch rats in the walls.'

He grabbed again and managed to catch one of her plaits, and he pulled her across the floor as she kicked out behind her. She ended up faceplanting in front of her fridge; he stood over her and pulled her upright, and she whined and spat like a small child throwing down in the biscuit aisle.

'Why is it so far past your grasp, Tara, that you shouldn't be sticking your nose where it isn't wanted?' he growled. 'Why are you so fucking dense that in asking you a simple question I run the risk of you summoning apocalyptic shit-storms?'

'How was I to know?' she gasped.

'Well you can forget you knew, or I'll have more than words to batter you with next time. But before you scrub your broken brain clean, tell me where I can find this whore who's so desperate to tell the city her boyfriend's dead.'

'I don't know where Georgie is! She's not around anymore. I was shocked to run into her.'

'If anyone can track the drifting bitch, it's you. You like to suckle the lifeless, don't you?'

He let her go.

'Find the whore,' he told her. 'Get an address and deliver it straight to me. Don't talk to the whore and don't talk to Cusack. Don't even talk to your fucking self if you can manage it. Does that make sense?'

'I was only trying to help,' she cried. The lasso plait had come loose into a soft kink. Her face burned red with the exertion of playing wounded.

'Sure that's you all over, Tara. Only trying to help when you stir up shit that didn't need stirring. Only trying to help when you herd the whores. Only trying to help, I bet, when you stuck your rickety claws down the front of Tony Cusack's young fella's jocks. Is he the one in prison? I assume so.'

'In prison? What?'

'Didn't he tell you he was going away, Tara? Did he not put your name down on the visitor's scroll so you could go press your tits against the Plexiglas for him every fortnight?'

'You're not funny,' she said.

'Fucking remember that,' he replied. 'I'm not.'

There was a piano recital that evening. Deirdre had phoned him twice to ensure he didn't forget, and so he showed up in the stuffy auditorium of the old community hall and sat with Deirdre and smiled encouragingly at Ellie as she spread her fingers and plodded over the keys. Ellie looked worse than her exertions sounded. She frowned all the way through the piece and then turned and faced her audience like she'd been instructed to do so by a voice in her head which intended later to encourage her to burn down an orphanage.

And how they clapped, those munificent blenchers, tucked into their bitter rows, thinking about *EastEnders* or the match or the tubby lovers whose grunts they were missing to cosset the egos of their neighbours' dumplings. They clapped like their escape depended on the rhythm. Swollen with forged pride, they jostled each other and muttered in empty approval as one bored child after another took to the stage to play out their dues. The smell was intolerable; perspiration, ancient stage curtains, slippery arse cheeks, perfume.

Jimmy Phelan was not at home in such a crowd, but who was? Some of their number looked more comfortable than others – the women, mostly, whose painted smiles hid well their boredom – but they were not happy to be here. There was no camaraderie, no real regard. Jimmy's parents had enjoyed a sense of community. The city was a smaller place then, and the people's expectations matched. Now the world had burst its banks and no one had anything in common with anyone anymore.

All day he'd had that anxiety festering again at the back of his skull: that his mother's streak of madness took him out of the society he'd built, that the lads he turned the clock with would catch wind of his genetic defects and abandon him, betray him, give tribute to a new chief. They were not tied to his character, only to the qualities they found use for.

He would give Tara Duane a chance to quietly find the whore. But he thought he'd have to make it all disappear then: the whore, Duane, and Cusack too, whether or not he wanted to.

15

When she was small, they said she liked to toy with things. That she enjoyed making babies of dogs, people of woodlice, pets of dying birds. That things existed for her amusement, whether they were lacquered wood or flesh around a beating heart.

Maureen Phelan's mother had been brainwashed beautifully. There had never been a question of her choosing her gender over her church; she pandered to the vestments as if by debasing herself she could avoid the stain of her sex. Her own daughters she saw as treacherous vixens. Puberty marked their descent. She hated the hair under their arms, their sloping waists, the blood that confirmed they were ready for sin. She was a vicious and stupid woman. Some combination. Her name was Una.

Una's parents lived just up the hill from the Industrial School and Laundry, where, she told her daughters, all the bad girls went. She seemed both deathly afraid of the place and satisfied it was there at all, in the same way she was full sure of hell and content that it wasn't for the likes of her. She announced that the Laundry's inmates would therein learn the humility they were sorely lacking. Every girl with a fashionable hemline, every girl who had notions about herself, was fit for nowhere but *behind the high walls*. Boys she had less of a problem with; they were dumb creatures whose animal whims were to be carefully managed.

Maureen was the middle child of seven; despite her efforts, Una's management of her husband's impulses hadn't followed her austere ideal.

Una Phelan was a frightened hag, comfortable in a dying Ireland and snapping feverishly at its future. For her there was no authority but the Holy Trinity: the priests, the nuns and the neighbours. Hers was the first generation of the new Republic, the crowd hand-reared on Dev and Archbishop McQuaid, the genuflectors.

When Maureen figured out that not only was she pregnant, but pregnant and abandoned by a coward, it was both horrifying and vaguely freeing, like hitting bedrock. She considered her options: the stairs, the coat hanger, the boiling baths. It didn't take her long to reject them. There was something to be said for fulfilling the destiny her mother had kept harping on about.

So she flounced into the kitchen and announced her misdeed with the bravado of scientific detachment. She watched the colour drain from her parents' cheeks, and the emotions that betrayed their humanity cross their faces like clouds on an October sky. She was nineteen but they were still the authority; she prepared for their punishment with frosty curiosity. One thing she knew: she wasn't doing her penance up to her elbows in soap and steam in the Laundry. She would have killed them both first.

She had brought the devil into the family home and so all hell broke loose. *Behind the high walls* seemed her mother's preferred choice, but in the 1970s the tide was turning. Giving up a daughter to appease sour-faced nuns no longer seemed the only thing to do, and the third leaf of Una's Holy Trinity was beginning to wilt and fall. A second cousin was found in Dublin willing to take in the slattern.

James Dominic Phelan was born in Holles Street and clutched to his mother's breast 'like a doll', according to the scowling grandmother, while the grown-ups debated what to do with him. In the end they decided the shame of raising him themselves was the lesser shame. He was taken from Maureen, whose childish wont would otherwise have been to make a plaything of him, and this was no time for games. He was installed as the baby, twelve years younger than his youngest uncle, and Maureen was sent to a hastily procured position in a London office.

She started three weeks after giving birth.

'No toys there,' Una announced, triumphantly. She was wrong.

There were plenty of things to toy with in London, but the joy had been taken right out of it.

Ten minutes walk from her front door and she was at the entrance to the old Laundry. If there was someone at the gate lodge, or the newer building near the entrance, they didn't bother her. She walked up the path. Overgrown now, the city reclaiming its darker monuments.

There were cracked stone steps leading up to the building, but the building itself was only a shell, the red brick, the arches, the iron crosses on its towers, all stained and falling down. She walked a little way along the front of the place, and spotted the space behind the facade; it had been gutted.

Statues everywhere. Some of them defaced. Here was a shepherd with a twirling black moustache, a lichened maiden with an alien name daubed on her robes. They stood in silent guard, oblivious to the unchecked march of the branches, grasses and fronds. Oblivious to Maureen. Relics of the past, swallowed by a world expanding.

Christ, it was silent. Maureen stood, her back to the barren brick, and looked out towards the river.

There were plenty of other Irish exiles in London back in the 1970s. Maureen had met her share; they rushed together like streams of the same mercurial poison. She'd known a number of women who'd spent their girlhoods in places like this, two who had been right here. Both had had baby boys. One of them had reared hers until he was twenty-one months old. The nuns had come in one day and informed her that he was being adopted, and that was it; she said her goodbyes and never saw him again. The other had only had five months with hers before he was taken away at an hour's notice; she had sat on her cot, she told Maureen, her breasts still heavy with milk, clawing at her face, rocking, sure now that this was the end, that she'd never be out of the place. There was talk of surrendering her to the asylum, but the action was abandoned when she came to her senses and her elbow grease became profitable again. Born only around the corner, Una Phelan was damn glad of the nuns' service.

To think of the babies, when they grew old enough to wonder! James Phelan had been told with dignity stiff and cold that Maureen-in-London was his real mother, and that he should think no more of it, but still he'd come after her once Una had given up her grip on the world and expired in her marital bed for an audience of effeminate printed Jesuses. So many other boys and girls grew up with holes in their chests gaping as wide as the Christian fissure that had spat them into the world. Maureen had read about it in recent years, once the tabloids had tested the value of Magdalene anguish. Hordes of Irish children – American, too; the exported generation – digging through Catholic detritus to find out who they were. Their searches were, more often than not, fruitless. Natural mothers had died, returned unto dust by the chemicals in the laundries. Documentation had been scant and useless. Women who'd moved on refused to remember and denied their flesh and blood their closure. Sometimes the mothers had just disappeared, as their country had designed.

In the shadow of the landmark, Maureen Phelan picked her way through thickets and thorns, enduring memories, even the ones that were not hers.

When she rounded the corner at the end of the building there was a man sitting in the grass, more interested in the weight of his bottle than he was in the walls before him. He spotted her but seemed indifferent, then testily, as she approached, he brought the bottle to his lips.

He was a vagrant, much younger than her, though his beard hid it well. He wore jeans and scuffed boots and was sitting on a pair of waterproofs. His baseball hat displayed the name of a Florida golf club; underneath its peak he scowled.

'D'you want something?' he said. He wasn't American.

'What do you know about this place?' she asked.

'What? G'way with you.'

'Just how you can sit here getting merry and looking up at that ruin. Admirable.'

'Do I look merry?' he said.

'No. I assumed you were giving it a lash, though.'

'Fuck off.'

'I'm about to. I didn't come up here to talk to you, sunshine.'

'Grand, so . . .' His wit failed him. He took another drink. 'Jog on.'

'D'you know this place used to be a Magdalene Laundry?'

'Course I did. Fuck off.'

'D'you know what happened to it?'

'Are you not going to fuck off?'

'When I'm good and ready.'

He considered the bottle, then frowned at her. 'It burned down. Twice. Now fuck off.'

'Twice?'

'Grudges everywhere, up here,' he said. 'One for every brick.'

'Is it possible to get in?'

'Missus, the grudges stuck because it's impossible to get out. Why the fuck would you want to get in?'

'To set another fire,' she said.

He smiled. He was missing a tooth on the top, right in the middle. 'You don't look like a woman who'd set fires, in fairness. I was reckoning you were walking a dog. A bitching-freeze or chi-wow-wow or something. The last thing I needed.'

'No dog,' she said.

He raised the bottle again, and stared at her between the peak of his cap and the vicious slope of the glass. When he'd finished, he said, 'Are you one of them?'

She looked back up at the crumbling brick. 'No.'

'So you're not going to set any fires, then.'

She grimaced.

'Me neither,' he said. 'There's not much left of it to burn. Still, though. Nothing as cleansing as a fire. This heap turned the air black but d'you know what? Everyone felt cleaner after it.'

'That so?'

'That's the job, I'm telling you.'

She found a tenner and gave it to him and he thanked her for not fucking off sooner. And even knowing he was there watching the walls for her, she felt uneasy walking away, like the heat of a pointed stare was burning up her shoulders, like the bitterness soldered to the past and to the ground the past was built on had touched her, and marked her. There were places this city wanted no one to tread.

Hidden Messages

It's Tuesday morning, the place is baking, and I'm stuck in writing you a letter. Melting, I am. Neapolitan blood will only get you so far. Only wearing prison-issue trackies and socks in my cell and I'm wringing. Tough on me, eh? S'pose next time I'll try not getting into trouble and see how far that gets me. Until then I just have to deal with it.

Prison is shit. Prison is very very shit. Of course it's supposed to be shit. Still, it's some land. Every day I get up I have to deal with the fact I'm only another day closer to getting out. Destination all the ways over there in January and January seems like a million miles away when you're stuck gasping hot in the middle of a heatwave. This is the absolute worst place you can possibly be when all you can think about is going down to Fountainstown for the day and balming out.

On top of everything else school is out for the summer, which I totally get the irony of because when I was at home I'd have done anything to not go to school. Weird what you miss. Really considering getting back into all that once I'm done here. It wouldn't be that hard. There's loads of schools in town. Except I guess Barry'd have to tell them I was expelled. There's no way I'd get away with that one.

Have a load of books taken out from the library over the past few weeks instead. It's funny how sick you get of reading when that's all you can do. Seriously, I was down there flaking through books thinking I'd never be bored again but a couple of days later I'm sick to death of them. Obvious irony is obvious.

Pretty much lost for things to tell you. Every day's the same. Nothing new happens. Least of my worries I guess.

'You like prison, Ryan?'

'Bored as fuck in there I was.'

'Eh, isn't that the point? Can't make it into a holiday camp for you, can they? Arts and crafts you're after? Ukulele? Surfing? Elephant polo? Tell me you're for real, boy. Here's a slap of reality. Eventually you'll get out and you can go surfing then. Shut up and put up in the meantime.'

Christ, I went off on one there, didn't I? Really, there's so little to tell you I'm waffling. Education through reading is noble but not the stuff of brilliant letters home. What about if I focus on the stuff I'm going to do when I get out? Seriously, here's the plan.

Ryan gets out of prison. Ecstatic, he dives into a whole new life. And he sticks to it. Determined, wiser and with a whole head full of book-learning, he finds some course to do, gets a job and even goes busking with Joseph. Eventually, he atones for fucking things up with his girlfriend and she forgives him. Very very slowly, but she gets there. Each day then is better than the day before. Ryan buys her tons and tons of shoes. Yup, he knows he said he wouldn't but he's changed his mind. There aren't enough shoes in the world for Karine D'Arcy. Heels five inches high, slipper flats, Cons, boots, whatever she wants. It's shoe central around her gaff. Now her mam can't even get through her bedroom door for shoes. 'Girl, your boyfriend must be loaded if he keeps buying you all these shoes,' she'll say. And you'll say yeah, he is, he got himself together, he's totally worthy now. Next thing Ryan knows, Jackie D'Arcy has invited him in for dinner and is telling him what a daycent son-in-law he is with daycent taste in shoes.

Does me good, that little dream.

Cian came up with Dad last time and said one of the McDaids next door to us emigrated last month. Australia. Now there's a gaff I wouldn't mind dipping my toes into. Melbourne, did he say? Adelaide? Karine, I don't remember but let's write them all down as possible destinations. Even the poison spiders would be worth it. There's more things that can kill you in Australia than anywhere else on the planet. Heard it on a documentary on the telly in the cell a few days ago but it didn't put me off.

193

I probably shouldn't have told you about the poison spiders, should I? Now you'll probably never go. Get over the poison spiders. Sun, sea, sand and surfing. There's no way we wouldn't love it. Of course, they're always looking for nurses there so maybe we could go once you're qualified. Until then though I guess I can cope with Fountainstown.

Guess who sent me a letter? Head-wrecker general herself, Tara Duane. I know. Freaky. The woman's actually off her game. How she'd think I'd want to hear from her I don't know. Even reading it gave me the wobblies. You know she lives in cuckoo land. There's rumours about her, like. Heard stuff like she told Con Harrington's ould doll that they were having an affair and poor Con hadn't gone next nor near her. It's insane what some people make up. No way is she to be trusted and no way do I want letters from her. Keep well away, like.

Yesterday it came. Opened it up in front of the officer because you always open letters in front of officers and he said my face could have turned milk sour. Unreal, in fairness. Restless all morning waiting for the post to come around and when it does it's a letter from a raving loon. Excitement wilting into nothing in the space of five seconds. Like you'd ask yourself if she really thinks I'm wasting one of my letters writing back to her? Obviously not.

She had nothing to say either. It's very quiet on the terrace, my dad's grand, my brothers and sisters are grand and she's sure they all miss me. No shit Sherlock, thanks for the update. God almighty like. I know I'm bored but I'm not that desperate. The silly bitch even hinted that I should stick her name down on the visitor's thing and she'd travel up to see me. Batshit! Up the walls of the cave batshit!

The thing is, I know it's not easy for you to come up and see me but your name is down as a visitor, like. I know I'm kinda clutching at straws on that one. Can't imagine your mam and dad would be too keen. And I know that I really let you down when I did what I did and ended up here. Never thought you'd even write for a while. Thought you'd be furious. But I guess you're even more amazing than I thought you were, aren't you? Really, you didn't have to be as nice about this as you've been. Every time I think about it it shames me. All I can say is that I don't deserve you.

That's the sad truth, isn't it? How I let you down. Even though the worst thing I could think of was being away from you I let it happen. When I get out I'll make it up to you.

I could do a hundred of these stints and if you read one letter for every one of those sentences I'd consider myself lucky.

That's about all for this letter I'd say. How to end these things I never know. Only to say I love you I suppose. Understand? There's nothing more true in the whole entire world.

Yeah, that's a pretty soppy ending.

Off I go.

Until January.

Ryan.

Kindling

16

Tony got the call at a most inconvenient time, halfway down his second pint with Catherine Barrett's hand halfway up his thigh, to which she'd progressed following a friendly pinch of his knee maybe ten minutes back.

He didn't get up to answer. 'Hello?' Eyes on his conquest, who smirked with easy confidence, welcoming even. She was married but on bad terms with her fella, who'd been sniping at her from England for the last four months. She had cropped dark hair, laughing eyes and a great wide mouth like a sock puppet; no looker, but she had a soft spot for Tony, and he'd learned to manage with a lot less.

'Am I speaking to Tony Cusack?'

'You are.'

'Hello, Mr Cusack; it's Michael Tynan here.'

It was the governor. The fucking governor, at whose voice Tony became immediately enfeebled. He had always been inept in his dealings with authority figures, even when they weren't his own.

'The car isn't on the road so I can't get up there,' he said, and Catherine Barrett returned to her glass of beer with the careful grace of a spurned braggart. 'But I could send my sister? My sister lives in Dublin. She could pick him up.'

'The usual arrangement would be to give him his train ticket,' said the governor, 'but with him not being eighteen yet, I'd prefer to have him picked up. If your sister is available that would do.'

'Yeah, of course, yeah. I'll get her to meet him.' He paused. 'I thought he'd be another week.'

He'd counted wrong, or they'd been messing with the dates again up there. They did that. Tony was confused by the process, but then it was made to be confusing, was it not? They were trained to make a monkey out of you. Over the past nine months he'd visited, written, received phone calls which were recorded and often, whether by design or shoddy apparatus, cut ridiculously short. Every time there was communication facilitated by these people they made Tony feel like a shit-flinger.

The visits were the worst. It was like going back to school. The same impatient courtesy, the same hot mass settling at the back of his tongue.

For the second call he made his way out to the smoking area, ignoring the woman Barrett with whom he might otherwise have enjoyed an ugly but crucial ride.

'Fiona? You'd never do me a favour, girl?'

'Jesus. What's he need now?'

'A lift to the station?'

January, and his lungs were full of fog and soot. January was a cunt at the best of times, pissing ice down upon a crowd damp to their bones. Sudden room in the shops after the Christmas eruption, cold space in the pubs and the cheer sucked back out and up the chimney.

This January reeked of vengeance. Tony had suffered a Christmas subdued for his recharged addiction and the absence of his oldest son, and then a dose that confined him to the bed for a week. In the horrors, he'd had to plead with his mother to buy him a few naggins, citing the DTs, the sickness, his weakness, his failures, until she'd angrily relented. Then he'd curled on his side under the duvet, clammy and gulping.

He deserved it, oh, he knew it well. He'd turned in the pregnant girl, he'd watched a man die, he'd broken his sobriety, he'd betrayed his son.

Now and then J.P. took his recreation at the terrace, watching him or watching Duane or neither; he didn't know. His children, oblivious, had walked past the Volvo on the way home from school. They had been in the house when J.P. had barged in for unscheduled one-to-ones. He'd even turned up on Christmas Day with a bottle of Jameson, gift-wrapped but only half full.

200

Tony attempted to show his belly and hoped that it would prove too pathetic for the invader's sense of pride. The rolling over stung. Late at night, between hallucinated gunshots in a concrete bay and his next nightmare, he remembered J.P.'s sneer about jellylegged dads, and the shame burned down his gullet and summoned sweat. Feeling keenly the gaps in his character, he wept alone.

He had betrayed his son but his son was the forgiving sort and Tony Cusack was deeply sorry. The rationale had stood up to scrutiny; little doubt the boy thought he could handle himself, but wandering into Jimmy Phelan's field of vision was a life-changing experience, as Tony knew too well. Even so. Seventeen was no age to be locked up. Tony's family had intimated he deserved it. Gurriers tied to you were still gurriers.

During their visits the boy had been reticent to the point of silence but that was nothing to wonder about, not when the visiting room had been so full. Roaring mammies and young fellas screeching 'HA?' down the phones; who could have a conversation in that environment? Ryan had always been soft-spoken.

Tony had a quick cigarette under the wind-rippled canopy and went back into the bar.

Catherine Barrett was sending a text. When she saw him on the way back over she smiled, and her mouth split her face in two.

'I thought you'd gone and left me!' she cawed.

He saw her plan in her twinkling eyes. They would drink up, drink up a couple more, she'd get frisky and they'd go back to her house and have a joyless fuck on her living-room couch, provided he could get it up and she didn't throw up over the edge of the armrest.

It was half an hour shy of midday. The barwoman continued with the clean-up from the night before, stretching out in the narcoleptic presence of her early drinkers: Tony; Catherine Barrett; Seamie O'Driscoll with the bent, bulbous nose; a couple of flushed ould fellas on whose pints the heads had turned the colour of straw; one crumpled ould wan whose name Tony had never learned, sitting alone at the end of the bar with a glass of crème de menthe. Tony had taken care with his disguise since his tumble from the wagon; today he was clean-shaven, fragrant and ironed. He was close to charming the knickers off Catherine Barrett, whose long coral nails and ornate necklace made a decent equivalent to his get-up. He was a morning drinker, but of a different kind to the horde. He could have been heading to a wedding, or a business meeting.

He drained his glass, and Catherine Barrett looked at him with vicious dismay.

'Have to go, Kitty Cat,' he said, and she tried a cartoonish pout and said, 'Ah, Tony. But weren't we having the craic?'

'Another time,' and he considered adding *Something's come up*, but he didn't think he could bear the innuendo.

Tony arrived home with a slab of lager and a bag of rubbish – crisps, chocolate, fags. What else would the young fella need? Nothing, sure; he'd left the place in such a State-enforced hurry that he'd not even packed himself a bag, knowledge that had hit his father like a knock to the neck when he'd returned from the court. After that first weekend he'd made the trip to Dublin with the few things the lad was allowed and the shock still hadn't rolled off him. The kid had pretty much stayed in that state for the whole nine months, as far as Tony could tell. He'd banked on it; once he'd fallen for the Demon again, he'd fretted about Ryan twigging it on visits.

Later on there'd be words, if it still mattered to the young fella. Tony was hoping to circumvent that. Share a couple of pints with him, rip away the hard feelings.

He opened a can while he cleaned the house.

Bedrooms, bathroom, hall. He cleaned out the fridge and made space for the lager. He retrieved the laptop from Kelly's room and left it back on Ryan's bed. He hoovered the stairs. He had a second can while he rang his mother; she had received word already, through Fiona, that the boy had been released. A text message confirmed that Fiona had met Ryan at the prison and was taking him for something to eat before dropping him to his train. And that was it – nine months passed in the blink of an eye, and all that could happen within.

He texted back: *Is he OK?*

Fiona's reply: *Not a bother on him. All he wants is a Big Mac.*

Tony was, like the gaff, in tip-top shape by the time Ronan, Niamh and Cathal arrived in from school, and, off their reactions, in even better form by the time Cian and Kelly wandered in an hour later. He met them in the hall. Kelly dropped her bag by the door and glared at him, giddy in the kitchen door frame with a third can snapped open in celebration.

'Your brother's on the way home.'

She curled her lip and said, 'I'm sure he's only desperate to see you.'

'Do you ever take a day off, Kelly?'

Cian waited until his sister had stalked away and cheered, 'That's pure brilliant!'

'It is, isn't it?'

Cian reflected, 'It flew.'

'Ask your brother whether it flew and I'm sure we'll get a different story.'

There were plans to be made. Dinners: there had been a quiet complaint about boiled spuds and cheap chops, so none of that muck. Should he ferry the lad over to see his grandparents? Maybe tomorrow; they'd likely nag but he might get a present of twenty quid out of it, and that'd keep him going for phone credit at least. It might have been an idea to put together a list of schools that might take him in, if he were to return to do his Leaving Cert. What else, what else? He didn't know. The drink was going down well.

The train was due at 5.30. He pulled on his coat and stood in the hall. Did Ryan have a coat with him? Had he been wearing one for court? Funny how memories you'd swear burnt tattoos on you dissolved into nothing when you needed to examine them. He remembered the judge, disastrously businesslike; the solicitor, who'd turned magenta with the indignity of having been so fuck-ing wrong. He remembered Ryan, turning to face him, eyes like dinner plates, going, 'Dad . . .' but as to what he was wearing, his father couldn't remember.

What had Maria been wearing the night she had sworn to take her children to the other side? Those were the details he didn't wish to remember, they were of no practical purpose. Here she was though, in the hall with him, threatening to wake the lot of them up and leave him in an empty shell. She went for the stairs, he dragged her back. She kicked his shin, he made a grab for her ankle and missed, he caught her only at the bedroom door where she was heading for chubby little Ronan, he slapped her, he caught her wrists, she screamed in rage. Black jeans, a trim grey Nike T-shirt, ivory ballet slippers dirty and worn, her hair kinked from heat and fury.

He came back to himself and shook his head like a swimmer dislodging a trickle.

He hunted through the coats under the stairs and found Ryan's hooded jacket, which he balled up under his own. He left the house distended and frightened Tara Duane, who was coming out her front door at the same time.

'Tony!'

He set his jaw and started down his driveway, but she hurried to reach the gate and hopped out in front of him.

'Tony, please stop.'

He stepped off the footpath to swing around her and she babbled, 'I know we haven't spoken in months and months, Tony, but now that all that unpleasantness has died down I thought we could mend some bridges.'

He stopped. 'What's died down?' he snarled. 'Your fucking paedophilia?'

'Jesus, that is so insulting. I tried to be *pleasant* to Ryan – to all of your children – because we're neighbours. What's wrong with you that you have to twist that?'

'Get away from me, Duane.'

'You smashed my front window, Tony. You terrorised me. You embarrassed me in front of the whole terrace for giving you a friendly heads-up about Ryan's advances. And I'm the one trying to make peace; will you not even give me credit for that?'

'You're full of shit and I hope you die roaring,' he said. 'And no fucking unpleasantness has *died down*; if you think I'm ever going to forget what you did with that girl . . .'

He shoved past and she threw her arms up and marched alongside.

'What girl, Tony?'

'You know what girl,' he said. 'The pregnant girl. The one you sent up here on a watery promise that Tony Cusack would know where her boyfriend had gone. The one that came into my house and accused me of killing the prick in front of my fucking kids!'

'I had nothing to do with that, Tony, I swear.'

'If you had nothing to do with it, Duane, then why was the girl so sure that you did? Where'd she get your name? She string it out of her arse? Must be the same place she got my son's name when she was looking for a bit of dope, isn't that right?'

'I resent that. All I told Georgie, who I've known for *years*, was that you may have seen her boyfriend before he went missing. He was a drinker.'

'What's that supposed to mean?'

'You know,' she said, lowering her voice, 'like yourself.'

'The day,' he said, 'that I take lifestyle pointers from you . . .' He shook his head and dug his fingernails into his palms. 'You stay away from me, Duane. I don't know what you've done or said to that poor girl but I'm sticking to what J.P. tells me and he can deal with you.'

'How are you so cosy with J.P. anyway?' she said.

'None of your fucking business.'

'Because if you had nothing to hide you wouldn't have involved him, would you? I tell Georgie that you knew her boyfriend and the next thing I know Jimmy Phelan is at my door looking for Georgie's address. Why is that, Tony?'

He exhaled.

Shit, he thought. *Fuck. Fuck shit fuck.*

The therapist down at Solidarity House once said, in a moment of rare candour, that the problem with functioning on even low, steady levels of alcohol was that it makes you thick as shit. For J.P.

to have dealt with Duane as he'd said he did would have meant explaining to the bitch that namedropping Tony Cusack in conversation with the dead man's ex-girlfriend was inadvisable. Therefore, that there was a real connection between Tony Cusack and the dead man, forged in steel by J.P.'s insistence that Duane forget all about it. To have missed that could only be attributed to the Demon. Ta-dah. A couple in the morning and three afternoon cans made him thick as fucking shit.

Same as thinking about the night his wife's drunken stubbornness killed her off on the day their firstborn got out of juvenile detention. Same as getting involved at all with Phelan, who he'd run with as a kid, for fuck's sake, who'd dragged him as a grown-up into murder after murder and Jesus, what was Tony Cusack, only a grown-up with the cop on of a twelve-year-old?

He tried to exude menace but his voice came out croaking.

'You need to stop talking, Tara.'

'I see. The shady bully thinks I'm not good enough to be his ally.'

'Get fucked.' How he wished he hadn't said that. *Get fucked*, as she stripped off in front of his kid and worked at him till he was able for her bony thighs to straddle his. Now he jabbed both elbows backwards, on the chance that it might maim the bitch; it fucking didn't.

'I've hit a nerve,' she marvelled. 'Call Tony Cusack a lot of things, but don't call him a bully, even when the evidence stacks. Even when he's running around after Jimmy Phelan.'

She grabbed his wrist and dragged back, and he whirled around, fist in the air and ready, so close to it he could feel the air thicken between his fist and her head.

'Or running to him!' she gasped. 'Setting him on me. Is that because when Georgie got up here she said Robbie was dead? Is he dead? That's it, isn't it, Tony? Robbie O'Donovan's dead. Don't worry; I'm not going to tell. Why would I drop you in it on the day Ryan's home from prison?'

'You don't fucking mention my son!'

'Kelly just texted Melinda and said he was coming home –
that's why I thought now would be the time to make peace.'

'Stay the fuck away from him.'

'It's funny, you kill someone and he goes to gaol.'

She dropped his wrist and put her face in her hands. Beneath
the tresses, underneath her fingers, from the utter depths she
made a gurgling sound that could have been laughter or tears or
some mad chant. Tony jumped away and she came to again,
smiled and said, 'Don't worry, Tony. J.P. asked me to track down
the girl. See, I'm just as close to J.P. as you are. We're on the same
team, for God's sake.'

What did he expect? That he wouldn't need a drink?

He arrived down at twenty past and ducked into the pub across
from Kent station for a pint of Guinness – medicinal, respectable
– and a short, straight Jameson.

He took a seat by the window and when the traffic in and out
of the station evened he asked the barman to watch his pint and
jogged across the road.

There had been one open visit, one opportunity to hold his son
in nine months, and that had passed with a kind of apologetic
awkwardness, the boy taciturn perhaps because of the screw
sitting there all eyes and ears, or maybe because he'd decided, in
the long hours of lockdown, to try holding a grudge for a change.

So it had been a while. And there was no guarantee that there
would be any contact now, awkward or otherwise, with all that had
gone between them, with the courtroom betrayal, and the drink,
and the fact that he'd grown way up and all behind Tony's back . . .

He was standing at the door of the station with his bag on the
ground beside him, wearing his court date clothes. Tony saw it
now: the courtroom, the polished wood of the row ahead that
he'd gripped when the judge had called him to speak, the black
and white checked shirt . . . Funny how you forget shit, even when
it's something like that, even when it involves your own baby.

Ryan tried a smile when he spotted his father, in fairness to
him.

Tony pulled the hooded jacket out from under his coat and held it out.

'Thanks, Dad.'

'No bother. How are you, boy?'

A shrug.

'How was the . . .' Tony started, and then, by dint of that shot of whiskey, broke off and found a lump in his throat and reached out and pulled his son into an embrace, caught the back of his neck and pressed his head onto his shoulder and held on until he felt him exhale, until the rigidity across his back and down his arms melted into brief, beautiful amnesty.

He held Ryan then at arm's length, gritted his teeth and said, 'You've grown again, I'd swear.'

The boy smiled in bitter defeat. He looked over his father's shoulder and said, 'You've been drinking.'

'Only a splash. Only coz you're home. It's a celebration, isn't it? I've a pint sitting across the road; come on over, I'll get you one. Bet you were mad for one, weren't you?'

'But you're not supposed to be. I thought.'

Tony swung into step beside his son, one arm around his shoulder, and said, 'It's all under control now, though. No difference anymore between me and the next man,' and they walked together towards the entrance, back in the direction of his pint, towards an interlude in which Tony swore there'd be no thinking about J.P., none at all about Duane, not while this harmony lasted.

Homecoming

Joseph wants to cart me over to his gaff the night I come home and I'm all for it, because my dad's half cut and it's weird to see him like that after he's been dry so long. In fairness, I'm half cut too. Two pints and my knees are going like the Shaky Bridge. We leave my dad nodding in the blue glow of the telly and we swing by the bottom of Karine's road to pick her up.

I get out of the car when I see her approaching.

Nine months. She's more beautiful than she was when I left her. She's in college now so maybe that's it. She's eighteen. She's a grown-up. I dunno, she's just delicious. And I get weirdly shy, and it's as if we have to start all over again because I feel like a stranger in front of her.

'Hey girl.'

She slams into me and puts her arms around my neck and presses her head against my shoulder. I put my arms around her waist and fold over enough to bury my head against her neck, and after a few minutes she pulls away and looks up at me, and places a silk soft hand either side of my face and I kiss her, and she opens her mouth to me, and I'm so relieved I think I could cry.

'You can breathe now,' she whispers.

We go back to Joseph's. He's only just broken up with his ould doll, so the house is kind of scanty. He's got some grass and a box of Corona in the fridge. I sit on the couch, and Karine sits beside me with her legs over mine, and we listen to him blether on about his new band, and how my god-daughter's doing, and what's been on telly, and what albums have been out and on and on and on and you'd think I'd be bored off my nut but you'd be wrong. Spend nine months inside and you come out just starved for your mates, for the banter.

For your girlfriend.

It's kind of coming up to it and I don't know what to do.

In the end Joseph very mildly says he's going to hit the hay and that if we want to stay over that's grand, there's a duvet on the bed in the second bedroom.

I go all shy again. We kind of hang around for fifteen minutes after Joseph goes to bed, talking around it, and then I say, 'D'you want to stay here, like?' and she shrugs; she's shy too. So I take her hand and lead her up to the second bedroom and we sit on the bed.

There's nothing in the way of mood lighting up here; there's the overhead or the dim glow of the city outside the curtains. I move against her until she lies back and she hooks her hands around my neck and brings me with her. The bulb's like a million watts and the room is practically bare. It's not too far off a cell, I guess.

So we do it, eventually. It takes ages because we're both kind of waiting to see where the other leads; I only want to do what she seems to want me to do, and she's very quiet and very timid, and so we get undressed in fits and starts, and I've still got my jeans on when we get under the covers. All the way through I'm thinking she'll stop me and tell me she doesn't want this now that I've done time; I'm so scared I'm fingering her like I'm trying to pull a hair out of a bowl of soup.

And it's the strangest thing. Like it's probably the worst fuck we ever had because we're both so anxious, but at the same time it's the best feeling in the world, better than the first time even. Despite the pure awkwardness she's so wet I slide right in and pretty much come straight away. It's a mixture of having a nine-month horn and being overwhelmed with relief. She doesn't mind.

Once I've come it's immediately better. Like there's a weight off. She snuggles onto my chest and doesn't ask for tissue or a T-shirt or anything. I get used to the air in my lungs and she talks to me till I'm ready to go again.

17

Dan Kane might as well have carried him out of the prison on his shoulders. The day after he'd come home, Ryan had contacted him, nervous as fuck, really, coz the man might have thought he was tainted or something now, who knew? But Dan had been even more pleased to see him than his father was, and that was saying something. It was nice to get a welcome home. Blew Ryan's mind, if he was honest.

On the second night of freedom Dan brought him out to dinner. It seemed a rather formal gesture, the mere notion of it pompous and off-putting, but once they were there it was grand. Dan had lumped for a bistro filled with large, loud groups. There was nothing out of place about the pair of them. Ryan wore a T-shirt and a new pair of jeans. He had grown, only an inch or so, but enough to air his ankles in his pre-prison clothes. Funny really; he would have sworn he'd shrunk in there, hunched down to maybe half the size he should have been, homunculus to his own sentence.

Dan said, 'Order anything you want, boy. Order the fucking lot if you like.'

Ryan grinned and Dan said, 'I mean that. You did nine months for me, little man.'

'What else was I gonna do, boy?'

'Lot of things you could have done and didn't; you're a fucking lion, d'you know that? Do you drink red? I'm getting a bottle. Have the steak, for fuck's sake.'

Ryan ordered lasagne and went through it like a chainsaw through chopsticks. He'd been ravenous since he'd left St Pat's. When Fiona had collected him she'd brought him for a Big

Mac and a milkshake, which he'd been hanging for all week. When he arrived home, he'd had a couple of pints with his father that left him vexingly woozy, eaten three Tayto sandwiches and a jar of pesto, washed that down with a bottle of Coke and then almost gawked the lot out the back door. Hunger had been one prison universal; he ate everything he was given, but there was never enough. He'd thought the liberty to make a pig of himself might take some getting used to. He was wrong. Wrong and famished.

'Yeah, yeah, put it away,' said Dan. 'You'll hit my age and suddenly everything over a ham sandwich will give you a paunch.'

Ryan sat back and rubbed his belly.

'It's the odd time I remember you're only a cub,' smirked Dan.

'It's just nice to get a bit of decent grub, is all.'

Dan leaned back, arms folded, and smiled.

'So,' he said. 'How bad was it?'

Around them the hubbub continued. Birthday shout-outs slapped the air; cakes went past, sparkling; girls tugging at ambitious hemlines trooped to the toilet in twos and threes; ould fellas, their faces wrinkled with mirth, howled.

'Worse than I thought it'd be,' Ryan said. 'And I thought it was gonna be hell.'

He hadn't said this to his father when he'd been asked. He'd said, *It was grand, Dad*, or *It was doable, like, you keep your head down*. Joseph, on the doorstep as soon as Ryan had crossed it, had pried but Ryan had pleaded with him to change the subject; he wasn't ready for stories, his thoughts were fucked as far as the rafters.

'I was there myself,' said Dan. 'Just before the millennium. I did three months for nicking a car. It was shit then; I can't imagine it's changed much since the nineties.'

'I don't think it's changed since the 1890s.'

'So what was so bad? The other fellas? The screws? The boredom?'

'Everything. The whole fucking lot.'

The screws had placed him first night in one of the committal cells. He'd stood waiting for the sound of the door slamming shut behind him, expecting some significant, gut-wrenching crash. It was quieter than he'd predicted and then he stood wondering if that was it, and if he shouldn't holler out at them to do it again, because he hadn't felt it hard enough the first time. He didn't cop right away but realised eventually that he was playing out the echo in his head. The door shut behind him. And shut behind him again. It looped and looped and he was sitting on the bed staring at the wall with his hands in his pockets, retching with the bleak and absolute scale of it.

The screw who processed him in the morning had asked, 'Did you phone home?'

Ryan hadn't been given the option.

'You could have,' the screw had shrugged. 'You probably should have. Called your mam at least.'

The seventeen-year-olds had been kept separate from the older lads and the screw had said he was lucky. There were only twenty-one other seventeen-year-olds in there with him. No overcrowding in their wing, separate facilities, spoiled little bastards.

The first month they'd had him on lockdown for, they said, his own protection. He was only a couple of days clear of that when one of the Dubs had volunteered to cut his throat. Ryan had told him to just fucking try it. Back on lockdown. Three months in, and back on the wing, he'd realised that he'd done only a third of his time, and the enormity had crushed him. You didn't tell them if you were feeling in any way down, whether it was because you'd stubbed your toe or wanted to hang yourself – you just fucking didn't, not in a fit, you kept your mouth shut because you knew what was waiting for you otherwise. One morning had come around when he just couldn't get out of bed. The screws had pulled him out, dragged him to the observation cell, stripped him and left him there.

How do you tell your dad something like that?

The other prisoners were cretinous or vicious or in most cases, both. When he was on the wing he hung around with a couple of lads from Waterford. One of them was due to hit eighteen and would be transferred down to Cork, and Ryan assumed he was looking for influence to bring in there with him; Ryan being banged up for possession with intent was, yer manno hoped, a bankable connection. Ryan had little time for either of them, and less time for the Dublin jackeens, and though Dan had various connections in the capital he didn't wish to find where to plant an affiliation. The Dubs spent most of the time throwing shapes and attempting to kill one another. Ryan was too busy gasping for air to want in on that.

Now, back in the real world, Dan said, 'It's no joke, I know that.'

'It's grand.'

'We both know it's not. Shit like that you don't forget in a hurry. That's a burden you carried for me.'

'Well look . . . It's over now.'

Dan grimaced. 'Hard to say this to you now, Ryan, but it's not over until you get your head around it. It stays with you. You'll think of it when you're meant to be doing anything but thinking of it. That's what the system's for – to break you down. And it works. Believe me.'

A girl, maybe Ryan's age, maybe a bit older, came in from the smoking area. She was wearing a royal-blue dress that wrapped around her fleshy thighs and barely covered her arse. She smiled at him, and he felt an urge to jump up, follow that smile to the back of the restaurant and convince her to cross her ankles behind his waist. He supposed if you've been surrounded by nothing but smelly, dopey fellas for nine months it whet your appetite for the ould dolls.

'I'm just glad to be home,' he told Dan, who leaned forward.

'I'm just saying to you, little man, the methods they use inside are designed to control you even after you get out. They want to fuck you. They want to fuck you so hard you forget what it was like to live without a cock up your arse. Don't let them take your autonomy from you. Don't bury Pat's. Because this won't be the last time the Law will look to lube you up and remembering how they work is the first step to fighting them off.'

He sat back again, sucked his teeth and sighed.

'This is only the start of it, little man.'

Joseph had broken up with his girlfriend and she'd gone home to her mam and dad with their baby daughter and left him in need of a housemate. On Dan's promise of more lucrative employment, Ryan volunteered, so only a week after coming home he was out of there again, hobo's kerchief and all.

Tony went over for an ineffectual root around.

'I didn't think you'd leave again so soon,' he mumbled and Ryan, halfway in behind the television with the Xbox cable bunched in his fist, matched the wounded tone and said, 'I'm eighteen, Dad.'

'Not for a couple of months you're not.'

Ryan came out from behind the telly and concentrated on pointing the remote at the screen.

'So much shit you don't know yet,' Tony said.

'So much shit I do, as well. I've been to prison for fuck's sake.'

'You were too young for that, too.'

Ryan could have turned to face his father. What harm? Accept the hint and stare him down. Instead he put the remote on the couch and hunted around for something that wasn't there.

'You're still only a kid.'

'I'm not.'

'You should be at home.'

Ryan pulled out the couch and looked behind it.

'I don't want to see you making any more stupid mistakes, Rocky.'

Ryan sank to his haunches and rested his head against the back of the couch, giving himself the chance to exhale, to close his fists, to screw up his eyes.

Are you going back to school, boy?

Ryan wasn't. Not in twenty fits. Where would he be going at almost eighteen? Back into another fucking uniform to sit under the gaze of another fucking moron who knew nothing about anything? It was all bollocks anyway. They'd said he could do school in St Pat's and there was nothing even like a fucking school up there: arts and fucking crafts and fucking cooking, what good was that to anyone? He'd learned more sitting on his arse staring at the four walls. Some of the lads he'd been in with couldn't count to twenty without taking off their socks. Learning? No fucking learning in there, unless you were learning how to watch your back or how to get out of a fucking headlock.

So if he went back to school now, at almost eighteen, back into fifth year with all the sixteen-year-olds as his girlfriend danced through university, yeah, well, he'd find himself on the scrapheap before long, wouldn't he?

Oh Karine, where's your boyfriend tonight?

He couldn't come out, girl, he had homework to do.

Not a fucking hope. If he was old enough to throw in a padded cell, he was old enough to make his own way.

What could they teach him anyway? The country was fucked. If he took the straight decision it would be between the airport and the dole queue.

What hadn't they fucking taught him already? How to be fucking blind and deaf, how to apply the rules that suited them, how to deal with awkward problems: lock them the fuck away. *Oh, having trouble with your dad, Ryan? Having trouble with this jackeen scrote? Having trouble with your fucking brain, tangled up in thoughts that your girlfriend, the one fucking good thing in this whole fucking world, is out there finding a better man to fuck? Ah, we have solutions for you, boy.* Clang. Another fucking door locks behind you.

Fuck the lot of them.

Dan Kane's main man was nicknamed Shakespeare, because he was as verbose a thug as you could find. His real name was Shane O'Sullivan, though it had taken Ryan two and a half years of dealing with him to figure that out. He was absurdly wiry for an enforcer; his success stemmed from the fact that there was barely enough of him to punch back. Ryan had heard it intimated that Dan Kane kept him in a spaghetti jar.

The first time Ryan had met him, it was because the order he'd placed with his usual contact was too big to proceed without notice. Shakespeare had come to investigate. Ryan was fourteen, pre-Karine, quick-tempered and unafraid to pay the price for it. Shakespeare hadn't looked very amused but had apparently reported back that the whole thing was quite the hoot. Kane hadn't been looking for a protégé but the opportunity to take one had tickled him too much to turn down.

And of course there were parallels. Dan Kane had had a shit time with his own father. Dan Kane had been to St Pat's.

Shakespeare wouldn't tell you whether or not he'd been inside. He liked puns and proverbs, but he was as blank a professional as the archetype; you worked with Shakespeare, never with Shane.

Ryan was going on a job with him.

He hadn't received all of the details and Shakespeare certainly had no mind for filling him in. Dan had nominated him as backup for a recovery operation – some waster who owed a few bob and had a deeper mouth than pockets. This was learning. This was a practical.

Shakespeare picked him up at the end of Ryan's new road. There had been frost in the morning but now it was foggy and silent. Headlamps moved in the mist like the lanterns of the lost. The stereo played a techno set so tight as to be practically feature-less. It was headphone music. Relegated to the background, its rhythm was unsettling and relentless.

'How are you in a scrap?' Shakespeare asked.

Ryan shrugged. 'I can handle myself, like.'

'And how are you initiating a scrap?'

'What d'you mean, boy?'

Shakespeare frowned. He had a precise goatee, a slender nose and narrow eyes; his face sharpened into a sparse sketch of geometric shapes.

'You can handle yourself, grand, but can you start aggro when you have to?'

'I suppose so.'

'You suppose so?'

'It's not something I do all that often. I don't go around raking up shit, like.'

'And usually I'd say life's too short but sometimes you've got to throw down, d'you know what I mean? Our troublemaker today isn't going to flake into you, but nor are they going to listen to reason. If I said, *Here, slap this cunt*, would you do it?'

They stopped at traffic lights. Ryan fixed on the red glow and said, 'Yeah. I would.'

'You're pure obedient, aren't you? You'd have made a great guard. Can you drive yet?'

'Yeah.'

'Have you a car?'

'Not yet.'

'Have you your licence?'

'Not yet.'

'I'd stick that on the To Do list if I were you,' said Shakespeare.

He followed Shakespeare's instructions with the same robotic deference that had inspired the enforcer to sneer about a vocation in An Garda Síochána; what else could he do?

He did the knocking, Shakespeare barged in. He pulled the curtains and checked the gaff for hangers-on, Shakespeare kicked his target down the darkened hallway. He found their quarry's phone and purse, Shakespeare hissed and grumbled as she expelled choked promises for deaf ears.

'C'mere!' Shakespeare snapped, and Ryan came into the hallway just as Shakespeare smashed the woman's forehead off the kitchen door sill.

'Show me that purse.'

Ryan handed it over and Shakespeare, one runner jammed over the woman's right wrist, rifled through it, pulling out cards and receipts. A couple of twenty euro notes fluttered to the floor.

Shakespeare flicked a small photo in front of her nose and said, 'What age is the small wan? Four? Five? Nearly time to collect her,

I suppose,' and Ryan's eyes flickered onto the crying debtor, a dumpy girl with a weak chin and a belly halved by an elasticated waist, whose curls plastered to the skin under her eyes, whose top lip was split and bleeding.

'I don't understand people who drag their kids into this shit,' said Shakespeare. 'You'd think if your fella was snapping tempers all over the town you'd send the child to live with someone a bit more organised. You think you wouldn't expose your smallies to your failings. One thing that drives me mental, like.'

He opened the door under the stairs, slapping it off the debtor's head.

'I'm going for a slash,' he said. 'Don't let her get up.'

His back to the wall, Ryan slipped into the living room. He shut his eyes tight and swallowed, opened them again and caught snapshots of a life scattered around him. An orange striped mug on the coffee table, the TV tuned to a chat show in which a procession of slobs tried to snarl tears out of each other, on the mantel a photograph of a doleful tot in a roomy blue and grey school uniform. The smell of fresh toast, wafting from the kitchen.

All against the steady stream of Shakespeare's piss hitting the bowl.

Ryan rolled around, forehead to the plaster.

This woman's partner could owe Dan thousands. He could have stolen from him. She could have threatened to involve the guards; they were likely to do that, he supposed, the ould dolls.

'Fucking disgusting,' Shakespeare said.

Ryan stood back into the hall. Shakespeare was in the doorway to the toilet, curling his lip.

'Smells like a wino's drawers in here. Jesus Christ, it wouldn't kill you to sluice the place out once in a fucking blue one.'

She whimpered. Shakespeare grabbed her hair at the back of the neck, dragged her onto her knees and pulled her into the bathroom.

'Lookit! Fucking bog roll and everything still in the bowl. You don't even flush, you scab.'

Louder tears now, then a scream. Ryan caught a grunt in his chest.

'Are you just going to fucking leave it there?'

'Please,' she said. 'Oh God, please . . .'

'Pick it up. Go on.'

Ryan had assumed a male target and had prepped for fists swung. Instead Shakespeare had settled for intimidating the sinner's woman, not as a consolation prize, but because the task didn't call for finesse. Perhaps Shakespeare would have claimed its ugliness was the mark of any entry-level mission. Didn't matter. It was a jolt no matter how Ryan defended it.

He sat on the stairs, facing the front door, his head in his hands.

'Put it to your nose and take a good sniff and tell me, girl, that that's any way to keep a house.'

The woman retched, and Ryan echoed her.

If there was one thing Joseph O'Donnell loved, outside of starting shouting matches with political conservatives in old-man pubs, it was launching short-lived bands. When Ryan arrived back there were three other blokes sprawling with his cousin in the living room, guitars abandoned in corners to make room for the migration of a couple of chunky joints.

'Cusack Cusack Cusack, do you have anything nice for me?'

'I might do,' Ryan said. He'd put aside an eighth for Joseph. He wasn't keen on flashing it about. Fuck knows who any of these dudes were, and open season on dealers lasted the whole twelve months with double points on bank holiday weekends. Joseph acknowledged his glare, tutted, and made his way out into the hall. 'They're all sound,' he said, 'honest to fuck. I know you're a bit . . . y'know.'

'You know the way the "sound" ones get once they get wind of a dealer. There'd be girlfriends less possessive.'

'Like you'd fucking know. You're only one step up from "virgin".'

Ryan winced and Joseph took it as confirmation.

The lads were watching *Family Guy* clips on Joseph's laptop.

Ryan sat on the armrest of the couch and was introduced – 'This is Darragh, this is Graham, this is Barry, we call him Bobo, don't ask' – but he'd left his mind back with Dan Kane, who'd been glib and jovial about the mission and who'd peeled Ryan's reluctance from his vacant answers and labelled it a temporary blip.

'It's a lesson, little man. You've got to be tough. If you're a soft touch in this game you'll get steamrollered, and you can't call the cops when you're shafted, can you?'

What the fuck was the game? The playing field expanded with every step he took; he was always at the middle of it.

Dan Kane had caught his shoulder and laughed and given him a handy hundred quid.

A hundred quid, you silly panicking fuck, and just for sitting on the stairs with the gawks while Shakespeare made a cokehead suck his piss from a handful of bog roll.

A joke went around his new front room, and he missed it. Bobo reached for the laptop and said, 'This one's my favourite,' and there was Peter Griffin, standing in the doorway of a young fella's bedroom, trying to talk to him about bullying, losing the rag altogether with the brat and lashing out with trademark brutality. The lads howled.

What was it, ten seconds? If that? Ten fucking seconds of a cartoon man punching a cartoon kid, and it stretched into a wound.

Ryan gave the congregation a swift thumbs-up and went to his bedroom.

A cartoon man beat up a cartoon boy. One pile of pixels laid into another. Same thing as blasting through bots on the Xbox, and you didn't see Ryan Cusack falling to pieces over virtual casualties for the sake of a couple of overwound heartstrings. Nor should you see him seizing the corners of his mattress and gulping back the sniffles over something as fucking stupid as seeing Peter Griffin fly into a rage.

Ryan pulled out his own stash, found the book he'd requisitioned for the task – one of Joseph's, a hardback boasting a hundred essential chords – and rolled a spliff. He sparked it, opened the window and leant against the sill staring into the silver evening fog; he breathed deep, willing the thoughts drowned, but they persisted. Of course they did. The weight of his psychosis dwarfed a piddling fucking eighth.

As contrite as Tony was there was history in his fists and a thirst on him that couldn't be quelled by God or son. Peter Griffin had straddled that cartoon boy and knocked a string of pucks into his jaw; that's the position you needed to be in to be broken, prone on the floor while a row of knuckles knocked red-flecked spit out of the side of your mouth and onto the carpet beside you. Prone again while the screws barged into your cell for your own fucking good, took an arm each and dragged when the enforced crouch failed your legs, three of them, big fucking men weren't they, cutting every stitch off you if you so much as kicked out, and sure why wouldn't you? Of course you'd kick out, for fuck's sake, mechanically if anything, out of fear and shame and what pride you had left.

Who didn't like a good fight now and again? Who didn't like to stretch their muscles and throw their body into the fray? It made you feel alive, wasn't that it? Ah, just the job. Go beat up some young mammy somewhere because you could do with the exercise and after all, she owes you a few bob.

You had to get off on it. They all got off on it. That's why your shelves were full of *Call of Duty* games and box sets of *The Sopranos*. That's why you could crowd around picking out your favourite bits from *Family Guy*, because you hadn't been fucked irrevocably by shit that isn't even supposed to upset you.

Karine was at home finishing an essay. He was of the conviction that she could have finished her essay just as easily in his gaff, but he'd let it slide. She had stayed with him nearly every other night this week, and they were making up for lost time. He couldn't get enough of her. Shoulders, breasts, navel, cunt. Everything else too: laugh, smile, voice, breath. Funny thing then that he hadn't yet given it to her hard. When they'd done it in the past couple of weeks it had been slow and gentle. He'd wanted to savour it, fuck her like a princess should be fucked. Now he worried that his laziness had been born of anxiety, not generosity.

The spark of a brief connection was enough to freak him out. He grabbed his laptop, opened PornHub, and went for everything on the front page: threesomes, cumshots, gangbangs, anal, whatever. The fellas had donkey dicks and dead eyes; the girls glared. Any other day there would have been a ton of shit he would have gotten into, and here he was after nine months of celibacy with barely a semi for the lot of them. Every pounded ass, every rough hand grasping blonde extensions, every 'bitch' and 'whore' was a weight on his chest. He opened his jeans and coaxed a hard-on but he couldn't come, didn't know why either, except that everything looked like humiliation, everything looked like plunder.

In the end he snapped the laptop shut and lay staring at the ceiling. How he managed to start crying with his dick still in his hand he didn't know, but there you go.

This was only the start of it.

He felt a lot better in the morning. Miles better. Fucktons. Dan phoned and told him to come over for a slice of a delivery. The coke had been cut and divided into grams, and Dan was generous with a payment plan. 'Get shot of it and pay me then,' he said. 'No rush. Don't I know you're good for it?'

That evening he and Karine went down to the local, The Relic, which was, converse to its name, one of the lively pubs his dad chose not to frequent. She, eighteen since November, went in ahead of him, so by the time he reached the table she'd procured him a pint and herself a vodka and Coke.

'Told you you'd come in handy one day,' he said, and she replied with tart grace, 'Fuck off.'

It was Friday night and he was two weeks out of St Pat's. Karine was all dolled up in a white dress and towering sequinned heels, smoky eyes, pale pink lips. Tresses of her hair, styled into loose curls, fell over her shoulders; he teased one around his first finger and said, 'You look so fucking hot.'

'I know that.'

'Grand so. How do I look?'

'Tall! When did you get so tall, like? I'm wearing five-inch heels and you're still all the ways up there.'

'I'm five eleven, Karine, not the BF fucking G.'

'You couldn't be,' she mused. 'Coz I'm five five.'

'You are in your shit five five.'

'My mam's five five and I'm the height of my mam.'

'Your mam's a munchkin.'

'Yeah well at least I have a mam.'

He choked on his pint, swallowed, coughed, wiped his mouth and then his eyes.

'You're some bitch, D'Arcy.'

She bit down on her smile and when he'd recovered she rested her head on his chest; he put an arm around her and kissed her forehead, and she said, 'I can hear your heart.'

'How's it sound?'

'Steady.'

The plan was to have Joseph and his sometime band meet them in a couple of hours, do some shots, neck some pills, and go into town to meet Karine's posse. For the time being they shared a stillness. The staff played R&B over the PA system for a sparse crowd too sober to sway. Karine sat up and stretched, and checked his shirt for the powdered residue of her affection.

He thought about asking her to set aside her plans for the night and head back to bed with him, though he knew what the answer would be. Being allowed into nightclubs was a novelty to her, three months legal and only out of school. He felt a twinge for the partying he'd already missed.

'Karine?'

'What?' She was playing with her curls, fluffing them carefully before letting them tumble through her fingers.

'Can I tell you something?'

'Only if it follows "You're amazing and I love you."'

Pfft. 'Obviously.'

'Go on so.'

'When you're inside,' he said, 'you feel like your life is over. Like

224

even though you know you're only doing so many months or whatever, it stretches out beyond all logic, and you're so smothered by all that you forget what's going on outside. And I missed stuff for you, y'know? Birthday and Christmas and your Leaving and your Debs. I've been an asshole. I know it, like. I'll make it up to you.'

She touched his arm. 'Ryan . . .'

'Y'know, Dan thanked me for it. Doing the time for him. But while I was doing time for Dan you were out here waiting for me and I reckon that deserves thanks too.'

'That's just silly,' she said. 'Let's just get on with living, like. Gimme a tenner; I'll get a couple more drinks.'

He watched her walk to the bar on her killer heels and let his eyes travel from her calves to her thighs and then over the curve of her arse, running into the small of her back . . . The same way, he thought with a turn, that he'd been looking at the girl in the restaurant, except this time it was right that he wanted to slide his hands between her legs, push out her thighs.

He wasn't the only one. At the bar, a fella walking past grabbed a handful of her arse, and she started and yelped. The guy put his arm around her waist and that was as much as Ryan saw before he landed over beside them, going, 'Ah, what the fuck?'

It was a fella they'd gone to school with, a bloke Ryan had barely seen since. Niall Something, Coen? Vaughan. One of the hurlers. One of the sort that was never found hiding behind the fence at the back of the pitch, so stoned he could barely stand up.

'Fuck me,' said Niall Vaughan. 'Is that Ryan Cusack?'

'Is that my girlfriend's arse in your hand?'

'When did they let you out?' Vaughan asked.

'Fuck off and mind your own business.'

'Everyone was talking about it, is all. Y'know, you look at your Leaving Cert class and you remember who's missing and why'

'You'd want to say sorry to Karine,' Ryan said, stepping right up to Vaughan, chest to chest, and in fairness, the other didn't back away. There was a grin dancing on his face.

'Karine doesn't mind,' he said.

'Karine does,' snapped Karine.

'Oh God, sorry I grabbed your arse, your ladyship.'

Karine took her vodka from the bar counter, gestured towards Ryan's pint, and tugged at his arm. Ryan didn't move.

'You don't sound very fucking sorry,' he said.

Vaughan rolled his eyes. 'Jesus Christ, get over yourself.'

'Ryan,' Karine whinged, 'come *on*.'

'Come on, come on!' Vaughan echoed, pressing his hands together.

'I'm not convinced he's that bothered about being called on his bullshit,' Ryan said.

'Yeah, he's drunk? Can we leave it please?'

'I'm not drunk,' said Vaughan. 'I didn't know you were back together, did I? Y'know, grabbing your ex's arse shouldn't bother you.'

'She's not my ex,' Ryan said, moving close enough that he could snarl into Vaughan's ear. 'And if you touch her again I'll take you apart, yeah?'

'Sorry, Mr Breaking fucking Bad. Far be it from me to go back for seconds with you gawping at me. She's all yours.'

'Ryan!' snapped Karine. 'Come. On!'

Ryan frowned. 'What d'you mean, go back for seconds?'

'Seconds of her arse, like. Seconds of the rest of her.'

'What's he on about, Karine?'

'He's pissed and he's disgusting,' she said. 'Pick up your pint and get back to the table. Now.'

Niall Vaughan mimed a cracking whip.

'Ryan, honestly, if you're going to spend any more of tonight spatting with clowns . . .'

'Ah, Karine,' said Vaughan. 'Ah now. That's not nice.'

'Dickhead,' she muttered, turning away.

Ryan looked back at Vaughan, who pushed his bottom lip out.

'You don't have to be so aggressive, like,' he said. 'Or is that what happens in there? No, seriously? Like after a few dozen rapes in the shower?'

Ryan said, 'Whatever problem you have, d'you wanna take it outside?'

Vaughan held up his hands. 'Ah no. No, I couldn't do that to you.'

'Yeah,' said Ryan. 'I didn't think so.'

When he turned around Vaughan said, 'Not after I fucked your girlfriend.'

Ryan turned back.

'What'd you say to me?'

'I fucked your girlfriend. After the Debs. In fairness, boy, she was in fucking heat. If it hadn't been me it would have been some-one else.'

Ryan would have punched him. Not a bother; he would have levelled the fucker. What contest? The lad was barely able to stand up straight and he was asking for it, howling for it, taking out billboards up and down the motorway advertising his need for it.

But he wasn't lying. Ryan Cusack stared at his girlfriend of three years and the look on her face, her glistening eyes and her parted lips, told him that this was the rawest truth he was ever likely to hear.

On Cheating

*She's sitting on the bed, mascara smudged under her eyes, and I
stand as far away from her as I can get, over by the door, my hand
hovering onto the handle every so often as instinct tells me to get
away, get the fuck out, just run, boy, keep running. I have to make
myself stay. Every molecule is screaming against me being this
close to her and it's a feeling so alien I've already thrown up. I just
can't believe it, like. I can't fucking believe it. I just . . .*

She's crying and I'm crying.

'C'mere,' she implores, for the seventh or eighth time.

*I shake my head. I can't look at her. 'No,' I say. I fix on the
corner of the ceiling. My head is sliding left to right. I'm like
Churchill the fucking dog.*

*She's sniffing. My head feels like it's been scooped hollow. Then
the next minute it feels like my brain's been jammed up right
behind my eyeballs. Then the next it feels like the brain's dripping
down my throat and choking me.*

*You've no idea. You've just no idea. Like that's it. I'm done. I'm
finished.*

'Ryan, please, just talk to me.'

*She's already spilled her side of the story. It's the end of August,
I'm away in prison, she's got her Debs coming up, yer man asks
her, her mam and dad and sisters tell her she'll regret it someday
if she doesn't accept, she remembers what a prick I am for leaving
her, she drinks the bar dry and he fucks her in the car park. There
you go. I lost my girlfriend up the side of a fucking Ford Focus.*

'You have no idea what I went through,' she blubs.

'You, girl? You? What about me? All I fucking had in there was

the knowing I'd come home to you and you were spending your nights out whoring with fucking Niall fucking Vaughan!'

'You did come home to me, Ryan! I'm still here for you!'

'No. No you're not.'

'I am! One mistake, for God's sake. And where were you? In prison! You weren't thinking about me when you got yourself caught with someone else's cocaine, were you?'

'It's my fault, is it?'

'It's both our faults! Ryan, for fuck's sake. I love you.'

I cough out a laugh and drag my hand across my eyes.

'I do, Ryan.'

'No, you fucking don't.'

'I do. Oh for God's sake, I do!'

I'm fucking proper bawling now and I can't get the words out at all. Jesus fucking Christ. Jesus fucking Christ. I wheel around and kick the wall. I kick it again, and again, and knock my head off the plaster and she jumps up and hugs my back. I don't even push her away. I'm too exhausted. I don't know what I am.

A few minutes later I get the words out: 'Did he come inside you?'

I shake her off and she sits back on the bed and folds up like a poked slug.

'Did he, Karine?'

'He wore a condom, if that's what you mean.'

'How would you know if you were that fucking drunk?'

'Coz I made sure. Fuck you, Ryan. Because he wasn't you.'

'Did you go down on him?'

'Of course I didn't.'

'Why "of course you didn't," Karine? I'd have said up to two hours ago that of course you wouldn't cheat on me and here we fucking are.'

She puts her head in her hands. 'I didn't go down on him. I swear. It was just an ugly stupid fuck in a fucking car park.'

'Did you come?'

She says no and I really want to believe her. If the Lord God appeared right now and said, 'Here, Cusack, you can have either the promise of eternal life or the promise that your girlfriend didn't show her O-face to Niall Vaughan,' I'd take the second with both fucking hands.

So we sleep somehow. Both in our clothes, beside each other on the bed, fucking bate. And when we wake up, she starts kissing me, and saying sorry, and touching me and I'm getting hard despite myself and there's this sudden forked road and a signpost telling me if I don't fuck Karine D'Arcy right now I'll never fuck her again.

So I do. I have to. I can't lose her. I'm not able. I hold her down and fuck her like I'm exorcising her. An ugly fuck. That's how she wants it, isn't it?

And after I come I roll over and listen to her crying again, until I can't stand it anymore. I get up and go for a slash and when I come back to bed she looks at me all red-eyed and says, 'That's how it is now, is it? That's just how we're going to fuck from here on in?' and I can't answer her. I lie on my side with my back to her and stare instead at the fucking floor.

18

'You don't have the money to take this to a courtroom. You'll drag it out, you'll hurt everyone, and you know you'll fail well before the end. So let's be sensible and settle this now. For God's sake, isn't that the only thing we can do?'

Georgie was sitting on the couch in the living room of the CAIL centre. Flanking her, William and Clover Tobin. Across from her, elbows on his knees and staring at the floor, was David. His mother, a glacial thing in a thin cardigan, sat on the armrest of his chair, rubbing his back. Opposite and to Georgie's left sat David's father, Patrick Coughlan, CEO-turned-cultist. He had plump jowls so clean-shaven they seemed artificial. He looked like a melted bucket.

In Georgie's arms slept Harmony Faye Fitzsimons. Born on a Monday afternoon with a student midwife holding her mother's hand in her father's stead, she was, as all babies were, perfect. Her primitive demands invoked something similarly primal in her mother, but Georgie was careful not to indulge instinct. Though Clover said that Harmony should be breastfed and allowed to share the bed with her mother, Georgie chose bottles and a Moses basket. It had been ages since Georgie had done cocaine or touched a drop; being with child had proved a better deterrent than being with Christians. Still, the notion that she was contaminated by her past was a tough one to get shot of Harmony was too beautiful to risk blemishing.

Patrick Coughlan sighed.

'This isn't how we wanted things to go either,' he said.

'How did you want things to go?' asked Georgie. 'Did you hope

David would find a paragon of virtue so tolerant she wouldn't be turned off by his drugging and gambling?'

'Well, I tell you what we didn't want. Him to impregnate an addict when he was supposed to be tackling his own demons.'

William delivered a wobbly interjection. 'Is this going to resolve anything? This mud-flinging? This is a place of mercy.'

'It's a place of bloody vice!' snapped Coughlan. 'I'd hoped your adherence to the gospel would be enough to direct David, and look what happens! This woman is a damned vagrant. How did you even accept such a person? I sent David to you, William, because I thought he would be protected. And instead you fed his weaknesses.'

'All we can do is ask for your forgiveness,' said William.

Georgie shifted the weight in her arms and leaned forwards. She'd cried all her tears, and was left with a dull headache and stained cheeks.

David kept his eyes on the floor. He had spoken only to confirm his father's assertion that this takeover was his wish. They were at the centre because they wanted to take Harmony with them, and their logic was watertight.

William and Clover were anxious about the idea of raising a child on their land. They explained that they couldn't provide structure but were too spineless to admit the fear that Georgie would drag them into ignominy with her once again. In David's bid for custody he had complained how Georgie introduced him to cocaine, which she'd procured and brought to the centre under pretext of conversion during a city break. William and Clover were upset, but more again, they were frightened. Their lakeside retreat had crumbled into a mess of responsibility and risk. Their notion of bringing the world together under the Jesus banner hinted now at effort without recompense, and they hated it.

'It's clearly in the baby's best interests to be with her father,' Coughlan said. 'We can support him. She'll be safe with us. What has she otherwise?'

'She has her mother,' Georgie said.

'A "mother". Why do women think that word alone is enough?

Why should my granddaughter suffer while her "mother" gets her act together? Grand, you're clean, whatever. That's no guarantee that you won't relapse.'

'David could relapse just as fast!'

'If he does, he has his family there to stick him back on the straight and narrow. If you relapse, who's here for you?'

'I'm not alone down here.'

William sighed and sat forward off his wife's silence.

'We're not set up for looking after a baby,' he said. 'I'm sixty-two, Georgie.'

'You wouldn't have to look after her,' Georgie cried. 'I'm just saying it's not as if I don't have support. You know. For if things . . . If things don't . . .' She stood and turned to face William. He looked away. 'Things will be fine, actually,' said Georgie. 'Why wouldn't they be?'

'We can't support you both, Georgie,' said Clover.

'I'm not asking for charity.'

Coughlan said, 'Then what are you going to do, ha? Move out? Get a job? Go to college?'

'Other women manage. I'm not the only single mother on the planet. I've been fine up to now, haven't I? I never starved.'

William said, 'Georgie, the state you were in when I found you, how much worse would that have been if you'd had a baby at home?'

Harmony Faye pursed her lips. Georgie crooked her first finger and stroked her cheek and the little mouth opened.

'I didn't though,' said Georgie. 'Did I? I was looking after myself.'

'And you were failing.'

'I've grown up since.'

'Have you?' asked William. 'Look, Georgie, I know your heart's in the right place—'

'I thought that was enough? Belief and good nature and all that shit, am I right?'

'For God's sake this isn't a game, Georgie. You were a prosti-tute! You could have been killed and you didn't care!'

Forced to listen to her saviour's well-intentioned treachery as the faces around them turned white, Georgie fixed her gaze on her daughter, her perfect face, the even features yet to display allegiance to one parent or another. There was nothing she could say. William stammered and David's mother gasped.

Georgie had not yet been saved. The baby had to be given up. David looked up at last with round eyes and lips pulled back. Georgie managed a tear. It slid down her face and hung on her jawline; when she cuddled Harmony the tear fell and landed on her cheek.

She tried for a while, chasing salvation in hard work, except it was hard work in rounds and circles, and it never got her anywhere. She arranged a cut of the profits from the farmers' markets in return for her tending shoots and weeding, so that she could put some money away for a training course. But what was she left with, only pennies? William told her not to worry about funds while she was at CAIL; her leaving was no longer a priority, now that the baby was safely away.

David had left her an address and phone number. Whenever she called he would run through Harmony's development as if he kept milestones noted on a pad by the phone. Should she wish, at any stage, to acknowledge his selfless hard work he was available for praise and appreciation. Should she wish to revisit their arrangement, he warned, she would have to get herself a house, a job and a lawyer.

William and Clover and her fellow spiritual halfmen continued as normal. They got as far as pitying Georgie, for pity was easy enough.

'I don't know how you could have done that to me,' Georgie bawled to William, after the community indicated they'd wring their hands for her behind turned backs.

'You forced my hand, Georgie. What else could I do?'

'Oh, I don't know. What would Jesus have done?'

'The very same thing,' William frowned. 'You'll see that someday.'

Georgie left CAIL nine months after they'd given her daughter away.

'Left', like it was some proud stand? No. 'Stole away', months later, like it was a last resort. She went through her stuff in the witching hour and plucked out what remained of her old life, which was sweet fuck all after William had tried shaming the devil out of her wardrobe. She stuffed her world into a stolen knapsack and slipped out the back door, clambered over the fence at the back of the vegetable gardens, and tripped through wet grass in the black night until she had room to skirt around and come back to the road. From there she trudged, the bottom of her dress wringing, a deserter from Christ's army.

The road was bordered with brambles. She pushed into the hedgerow and dragged her arm along the thorns, and after seven miles of penance she found a bus stop and sat on the other side of the wall propping it up until morning.

Was there a more miserable month than February? Was there a less welcoming time to return to the streets?

Once off the bus at Parnell Place, Georgie realised she had nowhere to go. Her escape had been fuelled on the assumption that some way would open up as soon as she arrived, but she left the bag on the ground by her feet, bunched her hair behind her head, looked out over the Lee and that was as much as she got.

She had accumulated enough to rent a cheap hotel room. The receptionist directed her to the nearest Internet cafe, which was full of Spanish students attempting to stave off the damp by flailing loudly at one another from computers placed inconvenient yards apart. Georgie searched for one-bedroom flats and calculated deposits.

She got a takeaway for dinner and felt sick afterwards. In her hotel room, she fought a losing battle with the air conditioning and made herself a cup of instant coffee that twitched in her veins for an hour afterwards.

At eight thirty she got a phone call.

'William said you'd run off.'

It was David. He was peevish.

'I'm back in the city,' Georgie said. 'I'm going to get my life together and I'm going to come for Harmony then.'

'You're going to get your life together with what, Georgie?'

'Something more concrete than prayer.'

'Yeah? Well, if you think you can battle with me using ill-gotten gains, you're mistaken.'

'Ill-gotten gains? What the hell are you talking about, David?'

'You know what I'm talking about.'

Quivering with the effort of indirect accusation, he berated her for vague intent as she sat on the hotel bed and cried.

'I never said I was going back to that, David. I've moved on. I'm only sorry that William Tobin didn't have the decency to see that and keep his stupid hippy mouth shut.'

'See, that's what's poisonous about you, Georgie. After all he did for you, you're insulting him. If it wasn't for William Tobin you'd probably be dead in a ditch somewhere.'

'If it wasn't for William Tobin I wouldn't have met you, you mean.'

'If you cared about Harmony you'd never have said that.'

'I meant it for you! *You* think it would have been best if you'd never met me. Your parents think it!'

'I accept my trials,' he said.

'You're turning into one of Them, David. Is that how you're going to raise my daughter? As a judgemental little prig?'

'Something tells me you won't be around to find out.'

She paid for two nights in the hotel and for two nights she lay awake and fancied ways out of the rut. One time she was passing out CVs and getting called for interviews. In the next vision she was awarded an emergency payment from the social welfare, enough to put down a deposit on a flat. Each dream slid with the encroaching midnight stupor into stark prophesies of straddling punters in the back seats of their cars, and Robbie O'Donovan was a shroud over it all.

She had tried to put his insinuated demise out of her head, she

236

really had. It was difficult to draw up murder mysteries in the last trimester, and after that she'd been distracted, wholly, by David's invasion and conquest. Robbie's ghost hadn't followed her down to the West Cork lakeside. Now she was back in the city and his memory jabbed at her.

She left the hotel on the third morning.

Her sums were sound and they told her that if she chose another night in a rented bed she'd be cutting her newfound sovereignty short. She had no wish to rush back to William and Clover's awkward embrace and, really, what were the odds they'd even want her to? She'd burnt bridges in dashing off under moonlight. In the daytime this shore was inhospitable, but she was stuck here.

What she was about to do frightened her. She walked through the mist, the knapsack dragging on her shoulders and her dress hanging limp, and considered running away blindly, or going to the Gardaí with her hazy lead or even jumping off a bridge and into the river, where the water might make a balloon from her skirt and take her out to sea. Her feet pushed her forward. From the mist before her loomed the footbridge. She walked over it, tracing her fingers against the steel, and stopped halfway to stare downriver at the choking white and the city that rose from the murk in blocks and sharp angles. She could clamber onto the parapet and no one would see her. She could flutter below and no one would stop her. It was a fine day for drowning and a fine bridge for jumping from.

What rest would Robbie have then, if the only one around to remember him dashed instead to meet him?

Across the bridge, she stood at the door to the old brothel and raised her hand.

A beat, a deep breath, and she rapped on the door.

She had felt the same fluttering terror when she'd knocked at the man Tony's door, back before Harmony, when she was closer to a whole person. What an experience that had been. Anger and accusation welded together in punch-drunk avowal and a stern direction to take complaints to the liar Duane. And then for her little dealer to arrive down the stairs and act as buffer between the

237

noxious allegation and his father's declarations! It might well have proved the weirdest day of Georgie's life, if she'd followed the lead back to Tara Duane's front door and demanded an explanation. As it was she got out of there and hurried back to William and Clover, flushed at having fallen for Duane's ploy and equally so at disturbing her dealer in his own home and seeing how young he really was. There with a daddy and baby pictures on the mantelpiece and toys scattered on the living-room floor. Domesticity wrapped around a boy she'd done lines with in the middle of the day.

There was no answer now from the old brothel door. She breathed.

She stood back and watched the windows, and on getting no glimpse of life walked around and tried the back gate. It was locked, but there was a foothold on the brickwork beside it, and the lakeside air had made her agile. She climbed.

There were plenty of bits in the back yard to assist her return to the top of the wall: builders' rubbish in the process of being reclaimed by the ivy, a wheelie bin on the other side of the gate. She was about to drop down to check the back door when she noticed a toplight left open on a first-floor window.

No doubt she could be seen, easily too, if anyone were to take this moment to gaze out of their bedroom window. She reminded herself that no burglar went around wearing maxi dresses. She'd look more like a granddaughter attempting to help out after the doddering dear left her keys on the dresser. She padded along the top of the wall and reached the window, grabbed the toplight and hauled herself onto the sill. The room had no curtains, and it was as bare now as it had been the day she'd been told of the ghost.

She lifted the skirt of her dress, tucked it around her legs, kneeled on the sill holding on to the toplight and reached inside to open the casement.

Maureen still lived here. The downstairs apartment was warm and messy; she had gone out, and Georgie estimated it wouldn't be for very long. She went to the top floor and to the sill on which she'd spotted Robbie's name. The writing implements were gone, the pages missing. The rooms on the two upper floors were completely bare.

She returned to the ground-floor apartment. There was a bedroom at the front of the house, and she stood in its doorway and thought about ransacking it for a slip of paper that was likely scrapped or burned. It might have been the dregs of Christian charity clinging to sinner skin or the fact that Georgie felt deeply stupid considering looting an older woman's nest, but she knew she wouldn't be tearing the place asunder. She looked into the bathroom, in case she'd find a horror message written in steam on the mirror, and then in the kitchen, where she drummed her nails on the breakfast bar.

What now, after engaging in some light breaking and entering for the memory of a missing swain?

Georgie pulled out the kitchen drawers. In the first, cutlery, string, scissors, candles, all in a heap. In the second, tea towels and a roll of kitchen paper.

In the third, a tangle of relics.

A couple of pens, a couple of notebooks with faded names on the pages. The old phone from the desk upstairs. A necklace. A foundation compact. Two lipsticks. An old business card, blank except for a mobile number and a busty silhouette. A scapular.

Georgie closed her fingers around the brown cloth. A lipstick, wound in its bands, dropped back into the drawer as she lifted it; she bunched the scapular in her fist, shut the drawer, and leaned against the breakfast bar with her hand held against her breastbone.

Robbie O'Donovan. Did you know him? He died here.

Georgie sat upstairs in the middle of the old brothel floor.

On the ground floor, Maureen moved about, clinking cups, rustling newspaper.

Outside, the fog had lifted from the Lee in time for the night to fall down upon it.

Georgie thought, *Did he come back for this?*

It was contentious in its absurdity, but when she spread it flat it made a kind of sense. She had pinned too much meaning to the scapular. She had complained about its loss. He was useless in almost every conceivable way, Robbie, but it would have been just like him to throw his weight into something as maudlin and pointless as recovering the bloody thing.

He died here.

He'd broken in. He'd arrived in the middle of the night and surprised Maureen, who had only just been installed by her wicked son, and she had called the gangster Phelan and he'd done away with Robbie because frightening his mother was a much bigger crime than stealing away a scrap of cloth.

Such a simple story. Alongside it, Tara Duane's tip-offs knotted into sinister futility. Knowing that Georgie had misplaced her dud boyfriend she'd taken the opportunity to implicate her neighbour in a crime predicted on an educated guess. Tara Duane had almost certainly seen shit like this before, and she wasn't the kind of person you could trust with an opportunity. Even alone, Georgie flushed. That she had played her part and upset her dealer's father for Duane's smirking benefit was its own ugly burden.

Downstairs, the front door opened and she heard a deep voice call out to its mother's low answer.

'Where?'

And then there were footsteps on the stairs.

Georgie didn't have time to make for the window. On Maureen's return she had chosen to stay still and wait for the woman's bedtime; she had nowhere else to go. Logic had intimated that no one would make for the bare rooms above. She had thought herself safe so long as she stayed silent.

Panicked, she slid behind the door, and when it opened it was with such force that the door slammed against her and rebounded on the intruder. She cried out as Jimmy Phelan rounded on her. He caught her arm and dragged her upright, and hit her, with an open palm, so hard it spun her almost out of his grasp.

'You're the whore,' he said. 'Aren't you? There I was sending the whole of the city out hunting for you when all I had to do was wait for you to crawl back to me. What a fucking stupid bitch you are.'

His palm came round again and caught her between her jaw and throat. She spluttered and as her knees went from under her Phelan closed his fist around her neck and snarled, 'You know, I get a hard-on from offing bitch messes and you, my girl, have caused me no end of trouble in the past year.'

Georgie choked and he slapped her again, and Maureen came into the room and said, 'You'd want to stop that, Jimmy, or you'll regret it.'

'Stay the fuck out of this, Maureen.'

'This house has killed before and it's generally the stronger of the pairing that gets it. I'm only warning you.'

Georgie was allowed to crumple.

Through tears she saw her subjugators: Phelan, puce, wet-lipped and oh, so massive, taking up the whole middle of the floor, the span from shoulder to shoulder packing muscle and wrath. Beside him stood Maureen, only half his size, cold-eyed and calm. She crouched and plucked the scapular from the floor.

'I thought you were born again, my dear?'

Phelan pulled a phone from his pocket, but Maureen held her hand over it. 'Who are you calling?'

'I'm getting rid of this whore, Maureen.'

'That's no way to speak about a woman, especially one that used to make you money.' She stared down at Georgie and said, 'She's only looking for Robbie O'Donovan, aren't you?'

'Shut your mouth, Maureen.'

'You don't talk to your mother like that either.'

Phelan scoffed. 'That's not likely to work on me, girl.'

'Ah, sure you were brought up by Una Phelan; no wonder you're the way you are. I'd not be happy to see you hurt this girl, Jimmy.'

'Your happiness, Maureen, is exactly why she needs to be gotten rid of.'

'I'll never be happy again, so.' To Georgie, she said, 'You're not going to say anything, are you? Sure all you want to know is where Robbie O'Donovan went. And if I tell you, you won't breathe a word, will you?'

'Maureen, this is not how this is going to go,' stated Phelan, but his mother shushed him, and said, 'Of course it is. There's one dead already because of me and I don't want that number added to.'

'She's going to die,' said Phelan.

'She won't die,' said Maureen. 'And she won't disappear again either. Isn't that right, Georgie? Haven't you enough to be worrying about without telling great big secrets?' And she laid a kindly hand on Georgie's flat stomach, and smiled.

19

Oh, he wasn't an easy man to bargain with, James Dominic Phelan. He took after his stand-in mama in that sense – ignorant as the day was long and stubborn as an ass. Maureen worked a way around him, but only just. One ghost, she explained, was bad enough. Two? She'd never sleep again. Especially if they were thick as thieves. Robbie O'Donovan nodded mournfully from the corner. He didn't want Georgie's company.

Jimmy was all, *Oh Maureen, Oh Maureen, you don't understand*. The world was an orgy of disquiet once you'd killed someone. Those who might suspect you needed to be controlled. The penalties for lenience were harsh and so lenience was no option.

Era go on outta that, said Maureen. What harm in the sparrow? She was hardly going to tell anyone. She had no influence in Jimmy's world; what was she, only a pisawn whore? Who would believe her? Was she not an addict and a victim? Did she not have a history of joining cults?

Was she not a mother?

'Where's the baby?' Jimmy asked. The girl cried and said the child was in care.

'No one', said Maureen, 'steps out of line once you're holding that over them.' Hadn't Jimmy been only a baby when she'd been banished? Maureen knew what Georgie would and wouldn't do, and she wouldn't be telling tales, no she wouldn't.

'If you step out of line,' Jimmy told the weeping slip, 'I will kill you. And I'll take what I'm owed from the child.'

He made sure the windows were jammed tight and left the girl in the room, asked Maureen to join him in the kitchen, stood on Robbie O'Donovan's ebbing place and snarled, 'Now, Maureen, d'you want to tell me how that whore knows your ould buddy Robbie is dead?'

Serendipity. Coincidence. Religious intercession.

One day, Maureen told James Dominic Phelan, when she was feeling the presence of Robbie O'Donovan with oh, very particular keenness, a fallen angel came to the door, looking to earn back her wings by paying strident homage to the Good Lord Almighty.

'What the fuck does that mean?'

It meant that she'd taken the form of a little Magdalene, with a bellyful of sins. The trickster God had directed her exactly where she needed to be. She came into the brothel, and she was right at home and in great misery because of it. Maureen had at first been taken by her mangling of the gospels and she'd invited her past the threshold for larks. Then she was charmed by the stench of the girl's past. It had been pushed beyond doubt when Maureen had mentioned her son the brothel keeper and the fallen angel had stood as if to bolt.

'Why the fuck would you tell her such a thing, Maureen? Jesus, are you in the habit of telling all your visitors that I'm so fucking specific a disappointment?'

That wasn't all Maureen had told her. The Magdalene had started to cry out the truth. She hadn't wanted to cross the threshold because she'd been a whore in that very building. She'd been plucked from grace by Maureen's bastard son. Maureen had invited her to retread the shadows and the girl had reluctantly complied. On the way up the stairs she'd met the ghost. He whispered in her ear and suddenly she was all-knowing. 'Robbie O'Donovan was here!' she exclaimed. 'Ah, it's true,' said Maureen. 'He died here.' And the Magdalene had flown out the door, wings latched on to her by a truth bigger than either of them.

'Jesus Christ,' said Jimmy. He paced the floor of the kitchen and stabbed the air above his head. 'You mean *you* told the whore

244

O'Donovan was dead? Jesus Christ, Maureen. Why didn't you take a stroll down to the sty and tell the Law you'd knocked some junkie's block off while you were at it?'

Maureen said, 'I'm not a fool, you know.'

'Oh, you're not, naw. Jesus, Maureen. I thought Cusack telling you the name of the corpse was a slip-up I could forgive but you soaked it up only to spit it out. Who else have you confessed your sins to?'

'I hope you're not going to barney with that nice Cusack man, Jimmy.'

'I'll rip his spine out his arse is what I'll do!'

'You probably wouldn't have known them, but he's John and Noreen's boy. She's a thundering bitch and he's a drunk but I wouldn't deprive either of them of their only son. That can do terrible things to a person.'

'You think,' said Jimmy, 'you can punt at me all sly-like, but you don't have room to swing from, not this time. Have you told anyone else?'

Maureen said, 'Indeed I have not.'

'Don't you understand what would happen? Not only would you be carted off to the loony bin, but I'd be done for disposing of your rubbish and my whole life here, Maureen, this whole fucking city, runs on a cowboy's foundation. I'd be ruined.'

'Do you not think it'd be time for you?'

Jimmy stopped pacing. He welded his fingers round the corner of the breakfast bar.

'Do you think', said Maureen, 'it was wrong of you to bring me home?'

'Was it a mistake, you mean? Clearly it fucking was.'

'Not just a mistake, Jimmy. Wrong. A boundary broken. An action taken that you can never claw back from.'

'To take you home from London . , ,'

'What's home, though?'

'This is home, Maureen. This is your city. To take you home again was the least I could do and I waited forty years to do it.'

'But who said I wanted to come home?'

245

'Isn't that how we sort anything out, Maureen? We come home?'

Maureen smiled. 'What have I to sort out, Jimmy? Whether I die here or there makes no odds to me. You brought me home because you thought it'd make you feel better.'

'I brought you home because I thought it'd be one right in a history of wrongs.'

He leaned against the breakfast bar and his head lolled forwards. He sighed. Maureen studied his shape cut rough from the air. He was broad, grown-up James. There was nothing of Dominic Looney to him. He was instead the spit of her own father, in his bullish weight and the grey stubble creeping over the folds on the back of his neck . . . grey to pink in a strange soft frailty, like his baby head as she held him to her breast.

See how the world turns?

'What do I do with you, Maureen?'

It amazed her that he was talking at all. He'd popped out sticky and cribbing, and in the next instant he was a giant in a leather jacket with his very own lifetime of words learned. She picked up a cardigan from the back of the dining chair and pulled it over her shoulders. From the back window she said, 'I don't want you to hurt the girl. It's my fault. I told her.'

'I know it's your fault. That's another cross for you to bear, you and your massive trap.'

'Would you do that to me, Jimmy?'

'I owe you nothing,' he said, 'except my existence, but if I was missing that I wouldn't know it. You don't get a say, Maureen. All you did was squeeze me out.'

'A life for a life,' she said. 'All she did was listen.'

'See how the world turns?' Maureen said to Georgie later that same evening. 'All you wanted was your religious die-dee back. And now you owe Jimmy your life simply because he could be convinced not to take it from you.'

Georgie was still sitting in the middle of the floor. She had a fine purple blotch rising on her cheek and eyes swollen pink.

246

Maureen had given her the cardigan and a blanket but she was still quaking like a bowl of jelly. Her hair matted down her back.

'Would you like a hairbrush?' Maureen offered.

The girl gulped.

'You can calm down,' said Maureen. 'He's not going to kill you. I told him not to and you know, I'm his mother.'

Georgie said, 'I didn't mean to frighten you.'

'Frighten me? It'd take something a bit bigger and bolder to bother me, girl.'

'I just wanted to know what had happened to Robbie.'

'You wanted your wee scapular back, sure.'

Maureen crossed the floor and sat facing Georgie, and leaned out and grasped her ankle, gave it a little shake.

'Why would a whore care about the Church?'

'It was my mother's . . .'

'Ah for feck's sake altogether. Another religious mother. You'd have to ask yourself what's wrong with this country at all that it can't stop birthing virtuous ould bags. And what would your mammy say, Miss Georgie, if she knew you'd done your time here?'

'I haven't seen her in years.'

'How many years?'

'Almost ten.'

'Almost ten? Sure if you landed home now it'd be like you'd never been away. The Holy Ghost would have carted you back again. She could take a rest on the novenas. I didn't see Jimmy for two decades before I came back to this hole. Can you imagine that? I came home one Christmas when he was twenty and he bought me a brandy. The next time I saw him he was forty and the size of a small shed.'

Georgie squeaked, brushed tears from her cheeks and wiped her hands on her dress. 'Why didn't you see him in twenty years?' she asked. 'What happened?'

Maureen paused. The bleached room provided nothing in the way of prop or inspiration, and it was such a massive story, a story too big for four walls.

'We'll go for a walk,' she said. 'I have something I could do with showing you.'

'There were girls I knew in London,' Maureen said. 'Girls like yourself. Strumpets with scarlet smiles.'

They were walking the night streets past students on the tear, eighteen-year-olds laughing in drainpipe jeans and wispy beards, crying revolution from phone screens, through bottles of beer. Dominic Looney could well have been among them, in his beads, his head full of mutiny and lust. Fashion came round in cycles. Shitehawks, she guessed, stayed the same.

Georgie stared at the ground. Maureen felt her fear as keenly as the chill. She guessed the girl would stay docile through dread of vengeance, as if Maureen might turn around and snap her neck on bad-blood whim, and it irked her. She needed engagement for the lesson to work.

Ah, but could she blame her? The girl was a shell. The only thing left in her was fear.

'I'm not judging you,' Maureen said. 'I know what made you.'

A laughing girl reeled round the corner and straight into Georgie. They both stumbled. The girl apologised. Her friends, following thick, shrieked in glee. The girl tottered on, bellowing her mortification to her posse. *Did you see her face*, one of them gasped.

'Most of them,' Maureen said, as one of the girls, yards away now, lurched on her heels and grabbed the arm of the dolly next to her, 'most of them got out of the game, but only one I remember did so intact. The rest of them were hags after their stint. They trusted no one. They drank like sluts. They beat their children.'

'I'd have made a good mother,' Georgie said, but there was no conviction behind the proclamation.

'Well you might have,' Maureen said. 'And I hope you get to find out. Me, it's not like I could have done a worse job, so they should have let me try. Look at the state of him!'

'Where are we going?'

248

Maureen clucked. 'I told you. I need to show you something.'

'I can't face him again tonight.'

'Who? Jimmy? I'm not taking you back to Jimmy. Or back to anywhere. I'm taking you forward. Lookit.'

They turned the corner to face the church, and Maureen flicked a thumb at it and pressed forward locked arm in arm with her fellow pilgrim.

'You're taking me to Mass?'

'Mass? I am not.'

The church was hewn from rock and the city around it built from twigs. Maureen brought Georgie along the side of the building. Above them stained-glass windows dripped dark and the hush of consecrated ground heavied their steps and made prowlers of the pair of them.

'I've always hated these places,' said Maureen.

They went round the back of the church to the priest's house, a two-storey block for a celibate man and his ghosts. Maureen didn't approve. She had never approved. She had never understood, as a child, why the priest had a bigger house than she did. Surely Holy Intangible God left room enough to walk around?

She and her brothers and sisters often played in the grounds of churches after Masses, celebrations, funerals, the litany of a faithful life. You could stretch your legs as the adults congratulated or commiserated or condemned, but every so often you'd run round the corner and get collared by the holy man white-lipped with rage over your impudence. It seemed a shame to grant such a pretty garden to the whims of a miserable old goat. It seemed a shame to tend such a pretty garden in the shadow of a grim theatre. There were always tidy lawns, flower beds, maybe even a grotto if you were lucky. It was the one green spot she'd never seen the tinkers graze their horses.

Now she brought Georgie to the shrubbery which looked onto the priest's side door. Georgie murmured protest but Maureen shushed her, and tucked her between plants with confident hands. Georgie was confused. In the weak orange light from the side door, she seemed ready, again, to cry.

'See the cars?' Maureen pointed.

'Yeah . . .'

'There are people meeting with the priest. Every night. They're always working, the priests.'

'What kind of people?'

Maureen studied her.

'Boys and girls getting married. Mammies getting Mass cards. Daddies looking for validation. Just the flock.'

'Why are we here? I don't get it.'

Maureen crouched and turned. Behind her, Georgie's eyes, downcast, searched the dirt for sense. She wouldn't find it there, but it wasn't a bad start. Born of dust and raised in stony soil, wasn't that it? The girls had no more changed than the beaded boys, one enabling the other.

'It was a wheyface by the name of Dominic Looney that led me into sin and left me there,' Maureen said. 'I had Jimmy when I was nineteen. My parents wouldn't let me keep him. It was far too shameful, you see. Those were the days. I lived in England and he grew up here. I worked in offices for a while, but I could no more hold a job than a hot poker. Did a bit of housekeeping. Worked in kitchens. Drank in the clubs with the rest of the Irish, made a few friends and stepped out with a few fellas but I wouldn't settle down. Couldn't, I think sometimes. What was the point? How do you build a life from bones? I only came home when Jimmy got the whim to bring me. There's too much passed now for us to be anything but strangers. That's why I know what's bothering you, and you having lost your little baby.'

Georgie let out a sob. She left her hands on the dirt to steady herself.

'Your Robbie O'Donovan,' Maureen said, soft as the light from the door, 'wasn't meant to die. It was an accident.'

'He meant something, you know. He might not have looked it but he did. And you had no right . . . You had no right to take him and no right to hide him then.'

'I know that,' said Maureen.

'What did you do with him?'

'Because it was an accident, Jimmy made it go away. And so Robbie's body was taken from the brothel floor, but there's the rest of him still there. I guess I'm stuck with him. You don't believe in ghosts, do you?'

Georgie said nothing.

'I wouldn't blame you,' Maureen said. 'I wouldn't believe in them but they've been following me around all my life. He came for your mother's scapular, wasn't that it? What if I told you you're not all that different to your mother?'

'What, because we're standing in a shrubbery outside a church? Is that going to cleanse me, is it?'

Maureen said, 'Do you like being a prostitute?'

Georgie stiffened. A flash of umbrage crossed her broken face, just a flash, but enough for Maureen to grasp.

'Do you think I'd do it if I didn't have to?' Georgie said. 'Do you think anyone would?'

'So why do girls do it?'

'Money.'

'They're fond of money?'

'They need money.'

'Exactly. They're in need of something and so they'll fold up under a spoiled man to stay alive, isn't that it?'

Georgie dabbed her eyes with the inside of her wrist.

'So they divide up the women into categories,' said Maureen. 'The mammies. The bitches. The wives. The girlfriends. The whores. Women are all for it too, so long as they fall into the right class. They all look down on the whores. There but for the grace of God.'

'God had nothing to do with it.'

'The point is there's a class of women put aside for the basest of man's instincts. That's your type and by Jesus you better play to it.'

'All men? Are they all like that?'

'Ha! They're divided up just as neatly, didn't you know? Saints and sinners. Masters and slaves. The good guys and the bad guys. Like my Jimmy. Hasn't he a role too? No one gets to the top if he hasn't a mound of bodies to climb.'

'What's that got to do with my mother?'

'She's religious, isn't she? They don't sell scapulars in Tesco.'

'Yeah . . .'

'She's on her knees for the higher power. The Church craves power above all things, power above all of the living. The Church has an ideal and it'll raze all in its way to achieve it. The Church needs its blind devout. Your mother, my mother, the people in there plumping Father Fiddler's ego, they're all for it. They've been given a class and they're clutching it. The Church creates its sinners so it has something to save. Your mother's a Magdalene for her Christ.'

The door opened. Maureen placed a hand on Georgie's back, willing her still.

A young couple came out into the yard, turned back and shook the priest's hand. There was laughter. The hall glow spilled onto the steps and cast an amber circle on the ground beneath the disciples and, from the shadows, the Magdalenes watched their heaving backs.

'Look at him,' spat Maureen. 'Look close. Handing out indoctrination, keeping them faithful, keeping them hooked.'

20

She had hair black as outer space and eyes startling and dark blue. The only thing about her that wasn't magazine perfect was her long nose, of which she was ashamed, but he loved that too, and the flashes of humility it provoked in front of mirrors; he used to kiss it when he thought he could get away with it.

She was supposed to get a white shirt for work but was too vain for anything functional. Instead she wore one that hugged her waist and barely covered her midriff and had to be held together with safety pins if she didn't want a button taking anyone's eye out halfway through her shift. She'd told him to meet her at the cafe. She made him a BLT when he arrived and as he munched she poked at a salad and made faces.

'I have something to tell you,' she said.

He thought she was getting shot of him. She said she loved his eyes and his up-and-down accent – 'Just like the hills at home,' he told her – but there was only so far you could go on that, and he didn't have much to offer otherwise. He had been labouring on a site off White Hart Lane but everything he earned he spent on Ecstasy and booze. She was supposed to be putting herself through Goldsmiths but still seemed to be spending the GNP of an island nation on weekend parties and shopping trips. If they made a good couple it was gauged entirely on lack of financial cop on.

The BLT stopped two inches from his mouth.

'This is such a surprise to me,' she shrugged.

It was the middle of August and sweltering. London hadn't slept in days and it showed. Small children poked about in patches of melting tar. Old women slumped on park benches as their Scottish terriers panted beneath the slats. There were two fans going in the cafe with the door wide open. Everyone was sticky and sluggish.

'You're surprised why?' he asked.

Behind them, an enormous man in a wifebeater dropped his teaspoon onto his newspaper and swore.

'You see,' she said, 'it turns out . . . I . . . am pregnant.'

The man in the wifebeater hadn't noticed but Tony Cusack had just been turned inside out.

'You're what?'

She shrugged again.

A wasp drifted towards them and he batted it away. It persisted. Tony grabbed a discarded *Sun* from the table closest the door and crushed the insect against the windowpane. Maria Cattaneo cocked her head and ran her fingers through her hair and when he came back to the table she raised her eyebrows as if to say *Your move, bucko.*

He looked down at the half-eaten BLT.

'Well,' he said. 'That's . . . ah . . . What d'you want to do about it?'

She raised eyes to heaven. 'God, you're romantic,' she said.

When Tony was eighteen a girl he'd been with said she thought she was pregnant, but it turned out she wasn't, news so good it knocked his knees from under him because she'd been his first, he'd pulled out and he didn't really like the beour in the first place. This was different. He was four years older. He was crazy about Maria Cattaneo. He prodded at the toast with studied indifference but in his head there was a brass band and a parade of tumbling cheerleaders.

'Just making sure you're OK with it, like,' he said.

'I love babies. You're handsome . . .' She made a popping sound with her mouth. '. . . handsome babies.'

'OK then.'

'OK.'

'Have you been to the doctor?'

254

She nodded. 'It looks like March. Springtime. Like the lambs.'

He jumped up and leaned across the table and kissed her and the man in the wifebeater said, 'Steady on, son, I'm trying to eat here.'

Nineteen years later Tony Cusack occupied himself in sluggish reminiscence. There was sunlight snaking through the curtains in his sitting room, showing up a carpet flecked with loose tobacco and cracker crumbs. The hoover was on the blink.

He was out of booze and in no shape to get more; he was logey from the heat and too caught in the kaleidoscope of memories to want to leave the house. The kids had scattered in the sunshine. The small ones were out on the green playing. Cian had headed off in high spirits and would no doubt return trying to hide his drunkenness behind his mobile phone. Kelly had folded up a couple of towels and said she was heading to Myrtleville with her buddies. They had lives, the little Cusacks, more than he'd given them. They left their father sifting through scenes beginning to wilt around the edges.

He'd come back to Cork with a pregnant nineteen-year-old whose desire to isolate herself from her middle-class lineage had spotted her vision. Friends and family alike had asked *How in fuck's name did you get your paws on her?* and he couldn't answer them, because he sure as shit didn't know.

They lived with his mam and dad for a while and when they got the house they got married and once they got married they started killing each other in earnest and the casualties – oh! the fucking casualties – they were piled high but it was worth every last bruise.

He had proved shit at absolutely everything except giving her beautiful children. She was no different. They both drank. Neither worked with any regularity. They had matching tempers. They lived in a fleapit and fought on the street. But at the end of the day he had six children out of it, six dark-haired, dark-eyed wonders with his blood in their veins and maybe that was enough.

He watched the minutes die on the Sky menu and the thirst spread until he could bear it no more.

He kept his head down in the off-licence, aware, just below the surface of his single-mindedness, that he was one of the idiots who kept the place open seven days a week. He grabbed a six-pack from the display at the back, where they stocked the cheap shit. The shop interior was lit by strip fluorescents and fridges; on display, he blinked and hurried. He made for the till, a tenner bunched damp in his fist.

His name snaked after him.

'Tony! Tony, stop a sec!'

The sunshine had brought out the slapper in Tara Duane. She was in a yellow bolero and black shorts so small they'd have scarcely made underwear. She'd piled her hair on her head and off her neck. From there down it was all bones. No tits at all. She was a mother and she couldn't have looked less like one. She'd starved herself back to her teens.

His having holed himself up while his children ran out into the world meant he'd escaped seeing too much of Duane. Occasionally he'd spotted her from the windows. A couple of times they'd narrowly missed each other hanging out clothes in the back garden. She seemed to have lost interest in orchestrating encounters since Ryan had come home only to move straight out again; Tony grasped the correlation, substantiated it and then hoped his logic was faulty. The last time she'd collared him, in the driveway, months ago now, had been to tell him that J.P. had enlisted her to conduct the hunt for the doomed girl. Tara Duane was made an ally without his consent. You'd think that'd be a thing worth challenging. It wasn't. It was a thing to be accepted and shelved.

Sure what could he do about it? Confront the bastard?

Two days after Maria Cattaneo had changed his life, Tony sat in a pub with Jimmy Phelan. Surrounded by wood panelling and echoing football commentary, he was getting congratulated and smashed with equal aplomb.

'You couldn't have done much better for yourself without a hanky soaked in chloroform,' said Jimmy. 'Are you going to shack up with her?'

'I'm going home with her.'

'Home to Italy? With your pasty Irish arse?'

'No, boy. Home to Cork.'

'Home to *Cork*? Jesus Christ, Cusack, you're only just out of it!'

'My son's gonna be born in Cork, boy. Wouldn't be mine otherwise.'

Jimmy laughed. 'When are you heading, so?'

'Dunno. A couple of months, probably. It's early yet.'

'And have you told your mam?'

'Eh, I'll arrive home "for a visit" and I'll tell her then.'

'One cute hoor, aren't you?' Jimmy beckoned a barmaid and said, 'A couple more there, love. And a couple shorts too. What's your best Scotch? This fella here is going to be a daddy in the spring.'

'Oh wow!' she said. She was carrying a tower of glasses that reached from her belly to her chin. She shifted its weight and tilted her head round it and smiled. Her eyes were heavily made up and the colours coagulated in the heat. 'Congratulations!'

Tony smiled back and she gave him an extra shot in his Scotch.

'It's a boy so, is it?' asked Jimmy, his nose in the tumbler.

Tony shrugged. 'Too early to tell officially, like, but it's a small fella, of course it is.'

'What the fuck do you want now?'

Tara Duane was momentarily and lavishly upset. Her eyes swung toward the ceiling. Her jaw dropped. 'Is that any way to greet your next door neighbour?' she gasped.

'That's not a connection by choice,' Tony snapped.

'You think I like living beside you when every kindness I brought to your door was met with scorn and fury?'

'I don't give a fuck what you like or don't like,' he said. 'If that's why you stopped me, let's cut this short. I have better things to be doing.'

'Oh I know you do.' She gestured. 'They come in cans.'

He turned away, but there were a couple of young men at the till, holding slabs and pointing at naggins. He was captive.

'I didn't stop you just to insult you,' she said, alongside.

'Oh, brilliant.'

'I stopped you because I've been doing a lot of thinking. About J.P., and how he's made pawns of the pair of us, and how we both need to move on.'

'You think we need fucking counselling?'

She grabbed his arm with a hand that had made shit of his relationship with his son, and he shook her off with an energy reserved for pests he chased around the kitchen to crush between the tiles and the sole of his shoe.

'Don't touch me, Duane!'

'Why not? What do you think you could possibly catch?'

'It's not about catching something,' he said. 'It's about not wanting to give you the satisfaction—'

'What, of laying my hands on a nasty, violent drunk? You have a swollen opinion of yourself, don't you?'

'What did you call me?'

'I know,' she whispered, 'that you beat your kids.'

One of the men at the till broke into raucous laughter. Oblivious to the conversation that had winded Tony, he slapped the top of his lager slab.

Tara said, 'It's a skit, isn't it? You're full sure I had something with Ryan and you go on about it and on about it as if you actually cared about him. When the reality is you beat him. You humiliated him. He used to sit out on the back garden wall in the cold and the dark waiting for you to go to bed so he'd be safe in his own home. You're obsessed with the idea that I might have slept with him. Why's that, Tony? Would that make you jealous, Tony?'

He said, 'You're crazy. Fuck you, fuck J.P.—'

'Fuck Ryan.'

He inhaled, let his body go still, pushed the poison out through his lips in a cool, wordless stream.

'Cards on the table, Tony. I think you're a piece of shit. I tried and tried with you but the only way you deal with people is abuse them. I know you hate me, because you think there was more to my asking your little boy black-and-blue into my home so he could sleep off the pain of your discipline. Whatever way you used to dole it out.'

The jovial men cleared the counter and walked out of the shop, their arms full. The assistant looked towards Tony and Tara, then down at a clipboard by her till. She started marking words off with a black pen. There was an ink smudge marking her thumbprint, and another smear across two of her knuckles.

'Remember Georgie?' Tara said.

Tony swapped the cans to his other hand. He didn't reply.

'Of course you do,' Tara said. 'I couldn't find her for love nor money—'

'That's nothing to do with me.'

'Please. It's everything to do with you.'

The girl at the till began to sing a song. In an uneven jumble of breath and flat melody she forced on Tony a broken musical accompaniment.

'I couldn't find her,' Tara went on, 'but she turned up of her own accord. A few months back. J.P.'s done whatever he had to do—'

'What's that mean?'

She scoffed. 'She's fine. I'm not. Do you realise how useless we look to J.P. now?'

'I don't look like anything to J.P. I've got nothing to do with him.'

'Oh Jesus, give it up! I do a bit for him myself. I know the score.'

'You know nothing, Duane.'

'Fine. I know nothing, you know nothing.' She rolled her eyes and mimed chattering jaws with her hands. 'But while you're convincing me of your ignorance, J.P. is realising what a pair of losers we are. If there's one thing worse than being the go-to for favours, it's becoming the go-to for framing. I need to get out of the city. Go down West Cork or something, start again.'

'Go then.'

'You might not have noticed, Tony, but I'm not exactly rolling in it.'

'If you're trying to convince me that that's my problem—'

She cut him off. 'I went to the Council. Told them I was sick from stress. I asked them to move me. They wouldn't. My issues with you weren't serious enough, even though you smashed my window and intimidated me. It's classed as antisocial behaviour and the Council would be playing rounds of musical chairs all day and night if they gave a shit about that.'

She looked away, adjusted her jacket and exhaled.

'Don't think I'm not aware of how dangerous you are. You beat your son and you kill your drinking buddies.'

'You're crazy, I said.'

'Save it, she can't hear us.' She brushed hair from her face. 'I don't want to live beside you anymore, Tony. I don't want J.P. knowing my address. Help me get out of here. That way we're both happy. Pay for your medicine. I'll meet you outside. I want to tell you something and you will hear it.'

In the early afternoon brilliance of high summer, on a day earmarked for fond reminiscence, she relayed to him the details of a plan concocted over high and white spirits. She wanted him to burn her out.

This was the plan, pulled from the addled head of the lunatic, imparted on the path outside the off-licence in matter-of-fact tones broken of emotion and repellent to passing snoops. She had determined that the best way for the Corporation to take her seriously would be to demonstrate a serious problem. She wanted Tony the Drunk to serve up a Molotov cocktail and throw it through her back door some prearranged night. The authorities would move her on. As for Tony Cusack, she'd vouch for him. He'd hardly try and smoke her out when his house joined hers.

'You're fucking serious,' Tony said, and Duane joined her hands and said, 'I know it sounds mad, but I've thought about it and thought about it and it really does seem like the right solution for both of us. I'll say I've had trouble with Jimmy Phelan and the cops will drop it fierce fast. They're scared of him.'

Tony said, 'I left school when I was sixteen and I haven't read a book since, but I know a stupid notion when I hear one. You're warped, Duane. You're either trying to trick me because you think I'm thick as the hairs on a gorilla's hole or you actually think that I'll commit arson to get you a country cottage.'

'Right.' She fell back. 'So you're not going to help me.'

'Will I put my kids in danger because you've lost the plot? Let me think now. No.'

'I'll do it anyway,' she said. 'I'll do it without your input and how are you going to know when to get out then?'

'You think I'm not going to go right to the guards about this?'

'No. Because if you do I'll tell them you killed Robbie O'Donovan. And then when my house goes up in flames I'll tell them Ryan did it. Spurned lovers at that age. You just don't know what they're capable of.'

He reached for her but she leapt back and wagged her finger, gasping, 'Ah ah ah!' Tony pushed back against the wall. The streets were alive, even in the heat. Across the road, a girl pushing a bare-legged toddler in a buggy stared.

Tony said, 'I'll have to bring this back to J.P. then, won't I?'

'But you won't,' said Tara Duane. 'Even if he cared enough to do something about it, you know if anything happens to me he'll just pin it back on you, because that's what dopes like you are there for.'

In her shorts pocket, her phone trilled.

'Have a think about it,' she said, taking out the handset. 'I wouldn't want to move on it for a while yet, anyway. Melinda's going off to live with her dad soon. No date set but she can't stay in Ireland much longer, sitting on her bum. The country's banjaxed, sure she's as well off out of it.'

She smiled. 'I suppose yours will move on soon enough too. Nothing hurts as much as losing a child, though.'

She left him speechless and blinking in the sun.

On Cheating II

Joseph goes into the bedroom with the other wan so I'm left in the kitchen with the green-eyed girl and she's approaching like a tsunami.

Look, don't get me wrong. She's unreal. She's wearing this black and gold patterned dress that sets off her olive skin, she's got long wavy hair just made for bunching in your hand while you shift her, she's got the absolute lot. We've been cordoned off in a corner talking all night because I'm that starved of Italian I'd wear a wire for la Guardia di Finanza if all they were promising was stammered conversation with camorristi. Her name's Elena. She's from Salerno. She keeps finishing my sentences. It's the fucking berries.

But I know she's expecting something in return. She's dead right, of course. I mean, me and Joseph came all the way back to their apartment to do more than admire a pair of living dictionaries. The other wan, Sofia, started mauling the face off Joe as soon as he got in the door; they're heading home in couple of days and I guess she's mad to go out on a high. The bedroom door closes. So there's me and Elena and she's giving me eyes and stroking her cleavage and here she comes, across the tiled floor, and I'm gonna have to, you know.

First girl I ever kissed was Lauren Sheehan. I was eleven. She was twelve. It was two days before my mam died.

I haven't kissed anyone but Karine in years, and I hadn't planned this.

Elena flicks her tongue against mine and all the blood rushes out of my face and down.

She pulls back with her hands on my chest, and says she won't tell my girlfriend if I don't.

Only last night me and Karine were out for a munch and then to one of her fancy pubs so she could drink cocktails and tell me how hot I am as I screwed up my eyes and tried to drink Niall Vaughan out of my head. She tells me there's nothing to forgive so I have to focus on forgetting. Her actions beg my pardon, though. She's so attentive. She's so fucking into me. She wants to spoil me and the truth is she's wasting her energy. I'm carrying anger around like a sack of wailing kittens; I'm not able to drown it. Like, this thing we have is so deep, and so brittle because of my mistakes, and my mistakes are so massive and glowing so bright I'm scared to set them down. And it turns out Karine's a reprobate too. I can't get my head around it. I'm angry, and relieved, and angry again because I'm relieved, and it's in my head, fucking pulsating, day and night, no matter what I do and I've room only for that and for nothing else so I don't even feel like me anymore. And I'm putting myself through that because I love Karine D'Arcy and it's no good, I can't bear to be without her.

Elena kisses me again, longer, softer, and my hands move down over the hill of her arse to the hem of her dress.

It's like . . . I dunno. Like something's pulling me forwards but it's splitting me in two doing it because there's a part of me completely unwilling to go with it. My fingers push her dress up and reach in and there's just this damp piece of fabric between me and her cunt. I'm pushing against her with my cock and she moans and goes for the top button of my jeans and I can hear bone splintering and wind howling and my whole entire soul shouting at me to stop, stop, two wrongs don't make a right, boy, stoppit! *but I'm gonna do it, I'm gonna fuck her, why shouldn't I fuck her? That's how it goes, isn't it? I'm out with friends and I got drunk and I'm coked up nicely and my dick's gonna do whatever it wants to do. What's the point fighting it if Karine won't bother either?*

Elena bucks onto the table, pulls her dress over her head, clasps her heels around my waist and pulls me over. She slides her hands over my shoulders and I wince because she's gone straight onto the scar.

There's a brushstoke dragon across my shoulders, flicking down onto my arms. It's a week old. It hurt like hell for seven days and now it's a burning ache. Probably because it was inked on bone but maybe too because I got the artist to add an extra stroke, a K at the bottom of my dragon's tail, right on my spine.

It hurt, but it didn't stop me.

All the Stones Turned

21

Across the skyline of his city, the modest heights other men's ambitions had carved from the marshy hamlet, Tony tracked his losses and kept watch for his damnation.

Sobriety became a memory that glimmered only in his children's disappointment. Ronan and Niamh stretched past the point of coddling. Cathal turned thirteen and moody. Cian talked of pursuing an apprenticeship. Kelly entered her Leaving Cert year. Their father's failures weighed on them less and less as they fixed on their own futures. His home was peopled by the shades of the one life he had worth living. His one-time assertion that he was a father above all things burned in Tara Duane's fluorescent vision. He hid in his front room and conjured resolutions; they crisped up and withered into ash with the first lungful breathed into them.

He watched the boy Ryan burn himself out. From a distant plain he tried calling armistice but whatever it was that Ryan had become didn't need it.

One dank November morning he arrived up in a ten-year-old Golf and Tony went out to kick tyres and mutter approvingly. He didn't know from whom Ryan had learned to drive. It wasn't lost on him that the teaching was a task for a boy's father.

'Are you set for Christmas?' Ryan asked, one hand clasped to the back of his neck and wincing like he'd cupped a wasp. 'D'you need a few quid, like.'

Tony barely jibbed. His son gave him a roll of notes. He closed his hands around the gift and said, 'Where did you get this?' and his son stared into the distance like a mariner mourning the fleet and said, 'A bit of work, that's all,' and Tony knew then what he'd birthed.

Briefly, he considered asking this new Ryan what to do about Tara Duane, but wouldn't that give wings to an ugly truth? The conversation turned back to the car. Tony thought of histories etched on his son's skin and felt sick. He watched Duane's house, imagining her peeking from behind the sitting-room curtains, plotting how she was going to stitch them both up. Ryan said, 'I'm saving for a GTI but this'll do for getting Karine to and from the shops in the meantime,' and his father patted the bonnet and laughed weakly.

As Christmas rushed him he thought of Jimmy Phelan's visit the year before, the half-drained bottle of whiskey he'd brought as a fuck you. Three December evenings in a row he contemplated picking up the phone and asking J.P. for help. Each time he stopped himself with bitter rationale. Jimmy Phelan wasn't his friend. He had slung his sins around Tony's neck and Tony had bowed and let him.

Two days before Christmas, the house from which he and Jimmy had removed poor Robbie O'Donovan went up in flames.

He only realised when he saw the photos on the front of the *Echo*. Two engines blocking the quay, the dampened smoke smothering the river, the sky above, stained. He read the report and was relieved to find there had been no one in the house at the time and no one hurt in the buildings around it. Preliminary investigations suggested faulty wiring – the property was ancient, after all – so the guards had ruled out foul play. Tony knew better. He had grown cynical enough to assume that the guards knew better too.

He supposed the fire turned the page on a black chapter of his life.

But he wasn't the same man who had stumbled onto J.P.'s path nearly four years before. The tidy removal of the crime scene couldn't draw a line under what had happened. Robbie O'Donovan was still dead. Tony Cusack had still washed his blood off the floor. Tara Duane had still used the wound as leverage.

On Christmas Day young Linda came over to compare presents with Kelly. Can in hand, Tony asked after her plans for the new year. She said she'd organised to continue her training in a salon in Glasgow, where her dad lived. She said she'd be leaving in the second week of January.

Kelly said, 'Think of all your mam can get up to with you out from under her feet,' and Linda shuddered treacherously.

Pallid in the glow of the Christmas tree lights, Ryan stared straight at the telly, feigning apathy.

Tony made up his mind.

The day before the scheduled blaze Tara Duane was all zest and merriment, as if she was relaying instructions for a supermarket sweep.

'So what'll happen,' she said, placing a mug of milky tea on the table in front of him, 'is that I'll leave the house at six o'clock, and take care to be seen here and there in town, and I won't come home until you phone me to tell me that there's been a terrible incident, or . . .' and she winked, 'that the job is done.'

Tony hooked his fingers around the handle of the mug. He'd watched her make the tea and was satisfied she'd neither drugged nor spat in it. Still didn't make it any way appetising.

They were sitting in her kitchen. Efforts had been made to emphasise its owner's nonconformity – colourful, mismatched crockery, tea towels with cheeky slogans, holiday knick-knacks arranged on the windowsill – but the baubles didn't mask the decay. Piles of clothes had been set on the table and left for so long they'd become musty. The wall behind the dustbin was streaked brown and grey. The top of the cooker was thick with old grease. It was as if the resident had died months ago. Tony watched Tara Duane prep her own tea. She could easily have been a shade, remembering nothing but the most twisted flashes of what she once was.

'You don't need to worry at all,' she enthused, sitting across from him. 'I've thought of absolutely everything. I've sold off some valuables because Melinda's just left and I've taken that opportunity to sort my stuff out. See? Makes total sense. You're going to throw the bottle into the kitchen leaving the key in the door behind you – I'll give it to you now, so we won't be seen together tomorrow – and it'll be like I simply forgot to lock it before going out. You know what a bad idea that is in a neighbourhood like this. You call me straight away because we're neighbours and you noticed the smell of smoke. And if anyone sees you leaving by my back door it's really easy to say, *Well yeah, I stuck my head in and realised the fire was out of control and I immediately called Tara and then the fire brigade*, yeah? And then I tell the Council I was right all along and they move me out of here. And that's that!'

No bother on her at all that she was explaining an elaborate ruse to a man only involved because of his incurable hatred.

'Best for all of us, I think you'll agree,' she said. 'This house has always been too big for me and Melinda. There are families who need it more than I do. So! Any questions?'

Tony remembered the banshee by the lake. He shook his head.

'Great!' she said. 'Oh, have a biscuit, for God's sake. Do me a favour. I'm watching my figure!'

He hadn't planned to have a couple beforehand but he was no more able to stop himself drinking than he was to stop the act itself.

He lay in his bed and wept the poison out in preparatory ritual. Thought, *Am I even able to see this through? Will I get caught?* and then, *What will my kids think of me?* They wouldn't understand. What's a father to them, except someone who makes their dinners and ensures the house doesn't fall down around their ears? *Not even that, Tony Cusack.* What's a father to them, except someone who boozes and stumbles and fights and spews? They wouldn't understand that this was something he had to do, and he could never make them.

Every now and then he picked up his mobile and checked the hour and at 3 a.m. he slid out of the bed and stood by the front window and looked out at the estate.

It was raining. Wind shook the shrubs and hedges in neighbouring gardens, banged a gate somewhere across the way, slapped the windowpane. There were no lights on in the houses directly across the green. Nothing stirred but the night's own breath.

He stood there for ten, maybe fifteen minutes, then found his feet.

Even if one of his children woke up they would pay no mind to his nocturnal roving; it wouldn't be the first time insomnia had tortured him. He dressed and went downstairs to the kitchen, opened the back door, and looked out. No lights in the houses backing onto his, either, except the usual glow from some of the neighbours' bathrooms.

It was the kind of night that could go on forever.

The key turned in Duane's back door. He stood for a moment in her kitchen, inhaling the scent of air freshener coiled through stale smoke and grease. Then he picked his way through the darkness into her hall, the layout identical to his own heap, checked the sitting room for signs of life, and crept up the stairs. The bathroom light was on and its door left ajar.

A creak on the step third from the top. He wondered what he'd say if she woke and caught him. If he claimed to have been overcome by night-time fervours and desperate for the loving touch of a spindly bitch, would she believe him? Would she cast him aside, his being all grown up and therefore way too fucking old for her?

He tried the door to the front bedroom and was momentarily bewildered by the decor, fittings and fragrances. His eyes tuned into the dark and he made sense of the shapes around him. Posters, perfumes on the dressing table, the Playboy bunny on the bedclothes. The bed was empty. This was the daughter's room.

He stepped back out into the landing and considered the mistake as a lifeline. How easy it would be to skulk back down the stairs and return to his own home without having left anything but his uneven breath.

But what of tomorrow? What of her rage once he backed out of her plan? What of her informant's mouth?

He slipped into the back bedroom and closed the door out

silently behind him as quickly as he could, and Duane stirred in the bed, sighed and turned onto her back.

He wiped his mouth with his sleeve and stepped over to stand by her body, and bit down on his lip so that the pain would chase away thoughts of this bedroom having hosted his boy, and crossed himself for a god he didn't really believe was there, and straddled her and put his hands to her neck and leaned down and closed his eyes. She thrashed and gurgled. Her hands flapped against his. Her knee curled behind him, he felt her thigh against his back and then nothing, but he kept pushing down and kept his eyes closed and afterwards told himself she'd barely been conscious at all.

He remembered the way more from his journey home than his own death march, so he had to navigate in reverse.

He had no torch in the car but he told himself he'd be better off, not wanting to be noticed from land or from sea. It was an awkward task. He found a sheet of tarpaulin and tucked her up tight. She looked light as a feather but dead weight was dead weight.

The walk along the overgrown path to the old quay, pointed out by J.P. on Tony's first visit, was harder than he had imagined. The ground was wet, the flora overgrown, the light non-existent and his burden enormous. He imagined himself losing footing and sliding into the black water below to be found alongside his enemy's body three or four days later. He imagined what his children would think. He imagined the traitor Jimmy Phelan, livid as the scandal threw light on his butcher's yard. He imagined his investigation. He imagined him coming face-to-face with Ryan and trying to bleed out the boy's ignorance.

The water churned as he rowed out to J.P.'s fishing boat. He didn't think he'd make it. It was dark, the wind was vicious, his arms sang as soon as he set them to work, and he thought he might not deserve to make it either, no matter his reasons, no matter how far he was backed into the corner . . . But he got there. He sat for ten minutes in the bobbing dinghy wondering how in Christ's name he was going to get her into the boat. He managed it through the devil's favour. He found rope and trussed the dinghy tight to the stern and dragged her into the fishing boat through strength of desperation. And then he left the rowing boat to its buoy and set sail, believing with every passing second that he was heading to his doom, to the unforgiving open sea, to the end maybe, but at least he was taking her with him.

Spinning

This is what it boils down to: image. And not like wearing designer sunglasses and jeans so tight they melt your balls. Just in general. What you give out, what people see in you when they first meet you.

I don't play piano.

I haven't forgotten it; you don't forget something you've been doing since you were three years of age. No, it's like . . . I started dealing and I fucked it up. Doing what I do for a living in and around playing the piano would be fucking ridiculous; I'd either be seen as a precious cunt or worse again, I'd be transparent. So I don't play piano. Not so's you'd notice, anyway.

The music won't go away, though. You learn that language and you're pretty much stuck shouting in it. So I fake it. I put my fingers to a set of decks and I learned to mix. That image works. People are comfortable with stereotypes; they want to think they have a handle on their merchant. You gift them an image so you can keep earning and you jettison whatever bit of yourself doesn't fit. That's just how it is.

Me and Karine go off to a gig on Saturday night and when it wraps up we get invited back to a party. I get to talking technique with one of the DJs and he tells me to throw a couple of tunes together. So I do. And he goes a bit googly-eyed because he thought I was talking out my hole.

Mixing's easy to me. I'm a bit nerdy about the science of sound, and those few months of Leaving Cert Physics and Maths stood to me, I suppose. 'Let the dealer DJ,' the partygoers think, and then it shifts to 'Why's that DJ dealing?' I don't stay on that long. I want a bump.

Karine comes over before I've even taken the headphones off and she says, 'I'm bursting.'

'I'm sure they have a toilet, like.'

'They do, but they don't have a lock.'

I go with her and keep the door shut and she hitches up the dress and sits down.

'D'you need another yoke?' I ask her.

She makes a face. 'I don't want to be dying Monday morning.'

'Have half a one.'

She makes another face.

'Go on,' I tell her. 'I need a top up anyway.'

I take a pill from my pocket and bite it in two and suck my half down. I wait for her to get up again. She washes her hands and takes her half from me.

I take a piss while she checks her fake eyelashes.

When we leave the bathroom there's another girl standing waiting and she smiles at me and says, 'Do I know you from somewhere?'

Karine steps past to retrieve her drink and so I get to smile back. 'I don't think so,' I say.

'I'm sure I do.' The other girl is tall, athletic, you know the type. She's wearing a tight, short dress and spike heels and she has a dark bob that swings when she cocks her head. She steams into a cascade of places she thinks she might know me from and you know what? They're all gig-related. Like, she sees me as the DJ, not as the dealer. She's wrong on every geographical guess and she's wrong about my professional position too but her attention is light and warm and, all right, a bit touchy-feely because she's fuckerooed but I could do with it, I'm swelling up in it, it's fucking lovely.

And of course she makes the mistake of touching my chest and Karine is catapulted back over.

'D'you mind?' she says to the athletic girl.

'Sorry?'

'D'you mind keeping your big orangutan hands to yourself?'

There's a quarrel that fizzles like a damp match because the athletic girl is too high to want to respond, apart from a short, 'Girls like you give us all a bad name,' and because I'm catching Karine's wrists and pushing her gently backwards out the front door, catching each spat accusation with a headshake and a smile. There's a car parked outside and I keep walking her backwards until her arse bumps against it, and she's protesting but I push up against her and put her wrists around my neck and then my hands on her thighs and ask her what in God's name she's doing.

'Oh, you know that Mister DJ,' she says. 'All the girls love him.'

'Let's not do this now,' I say. I'm conscious of the top-up yoke, and the mood inside so essential to its success.

'Am I wrecking your buzz?' she says, accusingly.

'You *are* my fucking buzz, D'Arcy.'

'So on that basis I'm not supposed to mind you flirting Bigfoot's knickers off?'

'I'm not flirting.'

'You are flirting. And they all know in there that I'm your girl-friend and it's making me look, like, so tragic.'

'Bollocks,' I tell her. I slide my hands around under her arse cheeks and push harder against her. 'Besides, wouldn't you rather be going out with Mister DJ than Mister Dealer?'

'I'd rather be going out with a fella who could keep his eyes on his girlfriend.'

It's funny, because I can actually hear a voice, ringing clear and true, as if it was someone else's trapped inside my own head, saying Don't do it, Ryan, You'll only make things worse, but it's too late, my mouth is opening and I'm saying 'I'd rather be going out with an ould doll who could keep her knickers on at her Debs' and she slaps me, she fucking clatters me, and starts marching off down the footpath in her tiny dress and her wobbly heels and when I readjust my jaw and follow she spins around and screeches, 'Oh my God, OH MY GOD, you have no right to say that to me after you fucked that tourist, Oh my God I had AN EXCUSE, you were IN PRISON' and well, that's shattered the shit, hasn't it? And I walk behind her and tell her I'm sorry, sorry, fucking sorry and the top-up comes up on me and catches her shortly afterwards and we end up shifting the faces off each other by a pebble-dashed wall at the side of the road at five o'clock in the morning, and whether that's something a dealer or a DJ does I don't fucking know.

'Ryan,' she says, 'Ryan.'

'Mmm?'

'You know this is like, "it" for me?' Her jaw is going ninety.

'Mmm.' My teeth have Velcroed.

'Let's have a baby,' she says.

I go, 'Ha?' but all of a sudden she's teared up, and where I thought I'd laugh and tell her to come down off her yoke before making any life-changing decisions, I end up pulling her onto my shoulder and rocking her back and forth and telling her, Whatever you want and whenever you want it, *and usually I'd chalk this silliness down to the night, the shots and the Ecstasy, but there's something different this time, and even in my wastedness I can feel it. I hold on to her and tell her I love her and tell her I'll do anything she wants me to do but beyond my words and her weight in my arms there's the knowing we fucked this up. There was something beautiful here once.*

22

Easier get a taste for arson than murder.

Maureen accidentally-on-purpose left the candles by the curtains and burned her house down. It had, at the time, been a means to an end but she'd really enjoyed the spectacle once it got going.

With murder she found a definite crossed line, and it was hairbreadth. One second there was life, the next it was gone. The ultimate in finality. Once you cross over you can never go back.

Arson was a different thing and a glorious thing. It was a monument to its own ritual. Once the fire caught it etched a statement into the sky. There was time to savour it and time, too, to quench it, if second thoughts were your thing.

She watched the brothel burn from a broken doorstep across the river. The fire brigade was almost as punctual as the amateur photographers. There was a reverent hush and she longed to cross the bridge to tell the rubberneckers that there was no one inside, no one had died, no one would die, but she had to stay still and discreet. Modest, even. It was her handiwork but there would be no medals.

She watched as Jimmy turned up in his car – even across the river he was conspicuous as an invading army – and sprinted towards the firemen, and felt a little warmth herself, from a safe distance. There was something in the way of regard for her, then. Maybe it wasn't fondness but the idea of her dying of smoke inhalation clearly perturbed him. It was either that or he was stricken at the loss of the kitchen tiles.

Of course, he was rather heated in his own way, once he

realised she wasn't dead. He called her every name under the sun and nearly combusted listing all of the ways her insanity had inconvenienced him. To which she coolly replied, 'Don't you have insurance?' and sent him spitting out the door.

He swore to her that she wouldn't get away with trying the same trick twice, but her new dwelling, a ground-floor apartment in a gated city centre development called Larne Court, didn't deserve the punishment meted out to its antecedent. It was a modest place and she slept better without all that history weighing her down.

Robbie O'Donovan hadn't come with her. She didn't like to think of him being trapped where he'd fallen by thick black smoke but sure, he was dead already and she could hardly kill him again. She did wonder where he had taken himself, but she didn't miss him.

The vagrant up at the Laundry, a year and a half ago now, had told her there was nothing as cleansing as a good fire. Maureen had assumed to test the hypothesis, but while ridding the city of the brothel had made her feel better, it hadn't resonated, at least not in the chords she was attuned to. She had done it for Robbie and for young Georgie, but, she realised, nine months afterwards and analysing her failings, she hadn't done it for herself.

So in the sunny September, she rectified that.

You couldn't go wrong with hippies. Their philosophy hinged on their empathy and Maureen had tried sons and priests and whores and had come away without a dash of castigation. Maybe her sinless exile really had depleted the universe's urge to shit on her. She wanted to be sure.

Out of her new gate and a hundred yards to the right there was a newsagent's, and outside of the newsagent's on most mornings sat a pasty beggar in baggy jeans and plastic runners. She usually bought him a cup of tea and a sandwich and stopped to ask how he was, because he fascinated her. He was young enough to have a mammy somewhere. There was a two-week period in August when he was missing from his pew, but he'd returned before anyone's worry could be moved to action, and told Maureen he'd gone to stay with some kindly dropouts outside Mitchelstown. It had been a bid to cleanse himself of smack and it hadn't worked. Still, he was appreciative of the dropouts' conviction.

'Mitchelstown,' she mused.

'Yeah. There's this girl called Ruby Dea. She's got a farm above and she has the gates open to any ould gowl she takes pity on. Place is full of caravans and wigwams. She used to be in one of those cults.'

Maureen sniffed. 'The Catholic Church?'

He enunciated carefully. 'No. A cult. She doesn't talk much about it, but she has more than a few ex-believers up there. Ex-believers of all sorts.'

And sure how could Maureen Phelan resist that? Only hours after gorging on the beggar's tale she converted, and became Mo Looney, wife to the man Dominic Looney would have been. She draped herself in sorrow and headed up to Mitchelstown to find the girl called Ruby Dea, who turned out to be less of a girl and more of a matron, all skirts and woolly cardigans.

At first Ruby Dea thought Maureen was an irate mammy coming to claim back a loafer and blanched accordingly, but it wasn't long before she accepted Mo Looney as another casualty of faith, and lent her a two-man tent to knock out a space in a fallow field.

There were, as the beggar had promised, others. There was one twentysomething with a couple of small children and a ramshackle mobile home, who kept to herself in the bottom corner of the same field. 'Hiding from a husband,' Ruby Dea confided. There was a jittery youth whom Maureen was sure couldn't last the night from whatever longing had leached into his marrow. But the rest of the residents were friendly. Maureen was the oldest and they treated her as some Biddy Early come to set them straight. She took advantage, getting a man named Peadar to put up her tent and a girl named Saskia to make her some dinner.

It was her intent to stay only for the weekend, but come Sunday evening the hippies had spilled nothing but tobacco leaf and quinoa down their fronts, and Maureen wasn't in the mood for holding it against them.

She sat on the grass outside her borrowed tent and watched the sun set. Across the way, Saskia waved and eventually came to sit beside her, and Maureen gave her a beatific smile and patted her knee. As the dew formed they got to talking. Saskia told Maureen about her upbringing down in Kerry – 'Not too different to this, if you can believe it' – and Maureen listened with polite patience as crane flies skimmed the blades in front of them and faraway engines swept the roads.

'It was so unstructured, so *sloppy*, my childhood,' said Saskia. 'No rules, no pressure, and I rebelled in all sorts of oddly conservative ways. Everything my parents believed in, I condemned. Consider they believed in personal freedom and you get a snapshot of a real buttoned-up brat. I studied hard and went to university to spite them, not to suit myself. Graduated a virgin and found myself at a loose end because I had absolutely no interest in my law degree. So what did I do? Ran off and joined a cult.'

'A cult?'

There was something more on Saskia's face now, threaded through sun-darkened freckles and crows' feet. Disgust. It lit her up the way a smile should. Maureen winced in solidarity as the younger woman's voice continued, cracked, 'Well, when you look at Christianity that's essentially what it is, isn't it? Sorry, Mo. I hope you're not offended by that, but it's what I really think.'

'I'm not offended,' Maureen said, mildly.

'I was baptised by a real shower of freaks. The kind that hate absolutely everything: men are masters to be obeyed, women are dangerous sluts, sexuality has to be controlled to the nth. I lived with them for a couple of years until I remembered that Jesus wasn't supposed to be a subjugating bastard. I ran, and ended up with another bunch of Christians, but the doddering, smiley kind. But they had money and they had space, so I stayed with them and tried to live the life and be a decent disciple. Five years. Would you believe that?'

'So what happened?'

'Sudden disillusionment. A whole life swept away in the blink of an eye. We're pretty fragile, you know?'

She was staring straight ahead. Maureen mimicked her. They divided the washed-out evening light between them. On the other side of the field, the hermit mother held one of the children at arm's length to brush burs off its back and legs.

'There was another girl down there with us for the last couple of years,' Saskia continued. 'Had problems with alcohol, wandered into the light pissed. She had a relationship with one of the men and she got pregnant. All that Christian love just melted away. The guy's family muscled in and insisted on custody of the baby. Poor girl, she was distraught. The Christians refused to back her up. Told the guy's family that they were right to assume guardianship because the girl had been on the game before she'd turned to Jesus. They waited for their opportunity to stitch her up and by God, did they take it. She ran off; who knows where she is now? About a week later I took off too.'

Small world, thought Maureen, but she said nothing.

'I hope she's OK,' said Saskia.

'And are you OK?'

'I'm getting there.'

'I thought I needed a confessor,' said Maureen. 'One time. Took me a while to realise but in the end it came to me . . .' And she paused, let the thought permeate, like a bead of brilliant colour dropped into a glass of water. 'There's nothing there. No confessor, no penitent, no sin, no sacrament. Just actions to be burned away.'

'Burned? Strong word.'

'Nothing as cleansing as a fire,' Maureen said.

Ryan knew it was going to be a disaster before they'd even packed the car. He stood in the sitting room with Joseph and stared down at the provisions with despair and affection; Karine, in the bathroom at the top of the stairs checking her festival braids, had stacked her life's effects in the middle of the floor. Two bags of clothes. An inflatable mattress. Three pillows. A mirror. A toiletries case in which you could fit half-a-dozen small appliances. A pair of pink wellington boots with a faux fur trim, her knock-off Uggs and two pairs of flats. A duvet.

'A fucking duvet, Cusack.'

'I know.'

'You're going to have to talk to her.'

'I know.'

She hadn't wanted to go in the first place, so the notion of having to chastise her before they'd even left the house struck him as counter-productive. Karine loved music but Ryan could imagine occasional furniture more outdoorsy. Joseph had demanded a wingman for Electric Picnic and Ryan had been more than happy to oblige, but Karine would be damned if she was letting him go drinking for a weekend without a chaperone. She didn't trust him. And he was glad she was coming with him because he didn't fucking trust her either.

She'd tried to persuade him to select one of the 'glamping' options – some colossal wigwam that cost a grand to rent for the three days and came with its own monkey butler, he assumed – but he'd told her it wasn't right to two-tier their party. They'd camp in the main grounds with Joseph and his buddies. She had pouted. He had told her she didn't have to come at all. They had had an almighty row about it that had lasted a whole week.

'A fucking duvet,' Joseph said again.

Karine came down the stairs rooting in her bag and started when she saw them.

'What's the matter?' she said, brightly, but her eyes were steel-set. Half past eight in the morning and she was raring for round two.

Joseph said, 'We're going to look like we've been looting.'

'What?'

'Seriously, Karine. There's less shit in the Argos catalogue.'

'What do you propose I leave behind?' she said, folding her arms.

Ryan raised his eyebrows at Joseph, who met the challenge and scowled back.

'Tell her,' he said.

'Tell her what, boy?'

'Tell her this is too much stuff.'

Ryan sat back onto the couch and ran his hands over his head. Joseph took the car keys from the coffee table and bumbled around the installation and out of the room, tutting. Karine's nails, specially painted black with neon rainbow stripes, drummed against her upper arms.

'There's got to be some stuff you don't need,' Ryan said.

'What,' she enunciated, 'do you. Propose. I leave behind?'

'I don't know. Most of the shoes? A metric tonne of the make-up? We're going to a festival, girl, not searching for Doctor fuck-ing Livingstone.'

'You're being mean to me already,' was her reply.

'I'm not being mean to you already.'

'You are,' she said. 'You never wanted me to come.'

'Don't be daft.'

'It's true. You've been trying to put me off for weeks. You'd much rather be up there on your own, wouldn't you? You could fuck whatever slut you liked then.'

The words were caustic and he deserved them; Elena from Salerno had been the kick-off of a really bad habit. He looked up at Karine and she stared back at him, flushed, and maybe it was just because it was early morning or the start of a potentially great weekend or maybe even because he was a bit hungover, but he didn't want to fight with her, couldn't see the justification tucked into that pile of superfluous wossnames.

She identified the change in him and reeled back the tantrum.

'I just don't want to be uncomfortable, Ryan.'

'But you won't be, girl.'

'I will be! I hate being mucky and I hate not having anywhere to shower and . . . and you know the girls he'll have around him. Joseph. You know his mates. They'll be all these ripped tights rocker bitches and that's not me at all and . . .' She exhaled. 'They're all gonna hate me.'

'It's not even possible to hate you, girl.'

286

'They'll think I'm a slut and I just want to be pretty for you.'

He got up, stepped over two of the pillows and the make-up case and held her.

'You don't need to be anything for me,' he said, and she shied away from his kisses and flexed her shoulders and said, 'I do, though, Ryan. I'm not good enough.'

'Oh God, please don't say that. Please.'

'It's true, isn't it?'

'None of it is your fault. None of it. I'm a dickhead who can't believe his luck.'

'Are you only saying that because you want me to leave half this stuff behind, though?'

'No.' He wrapped his arms tighter around her. 'Bring all of it. Bring your whole fucking bedroom in a trailer if you like.'

She rubbed her cheek against his chest like a cat and said, 'Tell Joseph.'

Elena. Sasha Carey who was friends with Joseph's ex-girlfriend. Rachel O'Riordan; she worked behind the bar in Room, a night club in town. Christina whatever-the-fuck-her-surname-was, at that party in Ballincollig; she of the lacklustre blowjobs. Triona Neville who booked session musicians down in the Union studios; she was at least twenty-three but what the fuck. Kasia . . . yeah, he didn't know her surname either, back at Bobo's gaff, and that was only last week. Was he finished yet? He didn't know. He hoped so.

Betrayal was a miserable salve and he was not at all cut out for it. It had started with a beautiful tourist, a goddess come to his sphere specifically to grant him justice; it should have ended there too. Beautiful as Elena was, she wasn't what he wanted. What he wanted was to go back in time and stop himself getting caught with Dan Kane's coke so that Karine would never have cheated on him. Even if he could only go as far back as the night he met Niall Vaughan in The Relic, just to walk the fuck away when Karine told him to. What he wanted, Ryan Cusack, was Karine D'Arcy, all of her body, soul and intent.

That denied to him, he tried revenge, and the more he pushed it the harder it punished him. The ease at which he coaxed opportunity was a gilded curse. His life had become a gauntlet run of parties, negotiations, car parks, VIP rooms. He'd done more cocaine in the last year and a half than he was comfortable thinking about, and that's what it had come to: cocaine, money, pills, women.

Oh, very fucking glamorous. It wasn't glamour that kept him sleepless and dry-mouthed, or prompted the big deals and the big reprisals. And what had he become, in his travels through the underworld? Just another cheating cunt in a city of cheating cunts. It had started when he was fifteen and he was stupid for thinking he could hold it back. The predictability of his transformation hurt him terribly. He hated it. He hated the girls who came on to him at parties and his inability to say no to a nice smile and a fresh slice. He hated it all, he hated himself, he hated Dan, he hated Karine; it was all just hate hate hate, a cacophony, a blizzard, line after line after line.

The first night was a dream, more than just figuratively. Having pitched tents and torn open slabs of lager, they dropped a few yokes and crowded around each other at the backs of the big tops that housed the star performances, dancing and drinking, shouting and wading chin-deep into conversations of a hazy and numinous quality.

The day after had been stuffed into a timetable and suffered for it. Ryan had acts he wanted to see and a girlfriend who wanted placating. They walked the breadth of the arena, their tempers slipping. Twice there was a proper, thunderous row which made shit of the moods of the people around them. Once, Joseph took him aside and told him to rein it the fuck in, but though Ryan took the words as wise and heartfelt, they weren't gospel, and he couldn't heed them. After the second row Karine said fuck it, she was going home, and had gotten halfway to the main gates before he caved in and dashed after her. But sure what could he do? They were now as they would always be: splintered but desperate, in love and worn out.

Karine retired just after midnight but he was nowhere near ready for sleep, thanks to the double-drop he'd sneaked only an hour back. There was a discussion at the door of Joseph's tent. Joseph was mucky-stoned – 'I couldn't get up if I climbed your fucking leg, Cusack' – but Ryan was itching for a distraction, and in the end he wandered off to the rave in the woods with Joseph's friend Izzy, who played lead guitar in a punk outfit called Scruffy The Janitor and taught a contemporary dance class on Thursdays. She wore lots of eyeliner, but never any lipstick. Joseph was desperately in love with her, and proved it by pretending very badly that he wasn't.

There was no dancing. Ryan blamed himself because the pills were the best he'd had all year and he'd known before he'd even arrived at the Picnic that he'd be blasted. He sat instead on the grass, back from the dancers, with his arms hooked round his shins and, from time to time, his forehead on his knees.

Izzy bounced over. 'You're no craic.'

'I am usually. I'm just *fffffucked*.'

'You're no craic all day. You or Carly.'

'Karine.'

'That's right,' she said. She pulled her hair over her shoulders and started plaiting it. Around them the tree trunks blazed neon green and pink, and the beats crashed.

'Why are you guys even together if you don't like each other?' she shouted.

Ryan was getting rushes up the inside of his arms, so he stretched, and put his hands flat on the ground behind him, and let his head loll backwards. Izzy sat beside him.

'How long are you going out, like?'

'Years and years. Since the night of my fifteenth.'

'Oh right. So it's a bad habit, hard to break.'

'No, no.'

'Look,' yelled Izzy. 'It's kind of obvious. You keep her all the ways up here . . .' She stretched an arm over her head and walked her fingers along the underside of the canopy far above. 'And she doesn't deserve it. I mean that with kindness and love, by the way.

It's a shit thing to be someone else's religion. And you know, even you've got issues with it and it's coming out in all sorts of shitty little ways. Like, Joseph was telling me the story. First she did the dirt on you and now you can't stop doing the dirt on her. And still you're wearing her like a hair shirt. It's fucking tragic. As in, it's sad *and* it's pathetic.'

'She didn't.'

'She didn't what?'

'She didn't do the dirt on me first. I did it first.' He didn't leave Izzy time enough to soak it in. He turned to her and said, 'Joe doesn't know that and neither does she.'

'Shit,' she said.

As the beats ebbed into a breakdown, the voices around them came back to a roar. There was a chorus of whistles and cheers. Izzy moved closer.

'You're not to tell either of them,' he said.

'Obviously.'

'Because it'd end me.'

'Cross my heart and all that.'

He rolled out the confession. The yokes swam through him. He could see himself: sitting on the ground beside his nodding acquaintance, eyes perfect circles and jaw slipping in and out of alignment. He got to the end of his story and it meant nothing. No weight off. He still felt like a cunt.

'You know what it is?' shouted Izzy. 'You set up this whole relationship as this picture-perfect penance for something stupid you did when you were fifteen and you're pissed off now that Carly . . . Karine . . .' She raised her eyes to the lights. '. . . didn't follow the script.'

'No. I love her. That's all.'

'So why'd you keep cheating on her?'

'Because. I dunno.' An epiphany. God, he remembered epiphanies. 'Because I can.'

'Oh man. That's such a shitty thing to say.'

'No, I mean . . . Because I didn't want to the first time. Or I didn't mean to, and so now at least . . . Fuck. You know.'

'You didn't mean to, like, you feel Missus MILF had all the power or something?'

'I don't even fucking remember. It's just . . . Yeah. Probably. I dunno. I don't know why I did it and it kills me.'

'Ever think you're being too hard on yourself? We all did stupid shit when we were kids, like. I was into shoplifting and I only got caught once and I'm still morto. And fifteen-year-old boys are just . . . all dick, like. So, maybe it was just hormonal. Adolescent craziness. Maybe fucking *own* it. Face up to it, own it, and let it go.'

'How do I own it? I didn't want it. Hence the last few ould dolls I fucked. If I'm going to be hung for it, it might as well be for shit I actually wanted to do. Every fuck improves the ratio.'

A girl walking behind them stood on his fingers. He examined them as she came down to his level, put her arm around his shoulder and bawled an apology into his ear. Ryan smiled forgiveness. The girl kissed his cheek.

'That is seriously fucked up!' Izzy shouted, once the clumsy girl had barrelled on. 'Dude, I love you wholly right now, but you have issues. Like I think you need to see someone.'

Ryan stared at his muddy fingers.

'But you're not going to do that, are you?' Izzy went on. 'Because you're too fucking male or something. Well, you know what I think you should do? I think you should go talk to Missus MILF. Ask her for the gory details. This is a part of your story you can't even remember and it's turned you into a control freak.'

'I can't do that either,' Ryan said. 'She took off a few months back. Left a ton of debt behind her, locked the doors and high-tailed it. Even her daughter doesn't know where she is.'

'This is insane!' Saskia hissed. 'Mo, I am totally on your team in terms of philosophy, absolutely, one hundred per cent, you are right and I should know, I've been looking for truth long enough. But this? This is morally wrong. *Criminally* wrong. I can't be part of it. I can't *blah blah blah blah blah.*'

Maureen stood at the gable end of the church, her back to

291

rolling, sightless countryside. She had already broken a stained-glass window, partly to take the first step and partly to check whether the place was alarmed. It wasn't. It was probably too small. This was the thing with the countryside parishes; you were attacking something of minor import and massive sentimental value.

'Mo, listen . . .' reasoned Saskia; she did not make as good a pupil as her ex cult-mate. 'You have a bone to pick with the Catholic Church; I get that. I'm Irish as well, you know. We all harbour resentment. But this is criminal damage! You'll spend the rest of your life in prison!'

'Jesus, how old do you think I am?'

'I can't be a part of this. The Gardaí will follow this back to the commune. Think of the others. Everyone's trying to deal with their own issues. Causing havoc will impinge on them.'

'Era, it's not like we're family.'

'You can't come back, then. This kind of mischief is at total odds with how we're trying to live!'

'Mischief me arse,' cried Maureen. 'How you're trying to live . . . don't make me cough up a lung! Wasters and dropouts and dregs, hiding in fields in the arse end of Ireland, oh! don't stick your heads out of the trenches anyway, for fear, for fear.'

'Oh right! Right! So we're just not being active enough. And what in God's name is this going to achieve? D'you think this is anarchy? This isn't anarchy!'

'It's what you make of it.' Maureen turned, her back to the stone, and held the night sky in her outstretched arms. 'And you should run with it, because they can't catch me, you know. I've done my time. Everything after that is my bonus to spend as I wish. Take advantage if you want to make your mark.'

'What, and follow you? Mo, this is insane because *you* are insane, and I've copped preachers a lot more cunning than you.'

'Grand,' said Maureen. 'Off you go. Tell Scooby Doo thanks for everything.'

'Oh my God. You have no respect.'

'Scoot along, Saskia. And for Jesus's sake will you learn to stand on your own pair? Commune to commune – get a fecking job!'

Well, that had done it. Maureen had banked on having an ally, and Shattered Saskia had seemed a damn good candidate, in the absence of tried-and-tested serfs. It certainly looked as if she was going to tell tales, which was probably to be expected in an off-the-wagon born-again. She hadn't even waited long enough to hear blinding reason: the smoke would belch into the air but everyone would feel cleaner after it. It had worked for the Laundry, it had worked for Jimmy's brothel, and it would work for the Catholic Church.

As Saskia stalked away, Maureen lifted onto tiptoes and peered in through the splintered glass. Not much to see but varnished shadows, and varnish likes to burn.

Three days of Carling cans, dropping nodges, woodland confessions and curry cheese chips left Ryan in a haze bordering incoherence, but Joseph was working on the Monday evening and so he'd promised to drive him home immediately after the closing gigs. They packed up their gear on the Sunday afternoon and Ryan and Joseph carried it back to the car park, twenty minutes away, in two trips, while Karine went gatting in the dell with a bunch of college friends. They all met up again, Joseph got off with one of the college girls, Karine had a minor meltdown over having left her facial wipes in the wrong bag, and Ryan popped his final yoke from the stash tucked down his balls and lay back on the grass and tried, gamely but unsuccessfully, to let the lot float off and pop in the sticky autumn air.

They made for the arena a couple of hours later to catch the last of the lily-hitters. Joseph had some experimental guitarist he wanted to see; he brought Karine's college friend with him. Ryan and Karine headed to the main stage. They found a patch of grass near the back and away from the main thoroughfare, and sat down, and she positioned herself in front of him so as to secure rueful cuddles without having to speak to him. He put his arms around her, pulled her back against his chest, put his nose against her bare shoulder and closed his eyes as the sediment of his last pill settled onto the pit of his stomach.

How they had managed to barney away the sweet evenings of the dying summer he didn't know. It felt like they'd been fighting forever. Stuff he'd said, stuff she'd said, wound upon wound ripped of their stitches. He remembered something of Niall Vaughan, and something of Elena from Salerno whose scent Karine had identified on her boyfriend's body after he'd laid stammered clues at her feet, like a cat bringing corpses to its mistress. He remembered his conversation with Izzy.

'I'm sorry,' he said.

She turned her head. 'What are you sorry for?'

'Everything.'

Directly across from him a mammy wearing face paint and fairy wings held a joggling toddler at arm's length and brushed unseen contaminants off its back and legs.

Karine waited until he took his head from her shoulder and let him kiss her. A quarter of a mile away, a figure lost on a mammoth stage invited a thunderstorm of approval. Karine took a sip from her drink. 'Is it sad that I just wanna go home now?' she asked, and he kissed her again and told her no, course it wasn't, it had been a crazy weekend, he was just as keen for a shower and his bed.

They set off from the car park at two in the morning, with Joseph's new squeeze in tow. Ryan had a fag coming back through Stradbally, another when he hit the motorway. In the back seat the girls nodded. Joseph, still buzzing, blethered on about the experimental guitarist, the inspiration he was bringing home with him, the whole experience. 'We're *definitely* coming back next year,' he said. In the rear-view mirror Ryan watched Karine's nose twitch and her mouth fall open. Mist dashed the window behind her and for a moment it felt like there was something in pursuit. His luck catching up with him, maybe. The moment washed over him and dissipated before he could get a handle on it. Maybe the only thing following him was a mighty hangover. He shook his head.

He stopped at Urlingford for a coffee and a Moro and pulled

off the motorway again just outside Mitchelstown for a slash and it was there, pissing onto the ditch off the hard shoulder, that he noticed the fire.

He went back to the car and said to Joseph, 'D'you see that?'

They climbed the ditch and stared into the dark. It was a fire, no doubt about it. Maybe five, six miles in.

'It must have been called already,' said Joseph. 'I'll ring them just to be sure.' He phoned 999 with one finger in his ear and relayed vague coordinates to the person at the other end as cars slid past them from one acre of pitch to another.

'D'you reckon we could find it?' Ryan said.

He did wonder why, as he exited the motorway and drove down winding regional roads, but what answer could he conjure, except he was curious and oddly loath to return home, tired and all as he was? Neither girl in the backseat stirred. Joseph went quiet and furrowed his brow, as invested in the mystery now as his cousin, though out of jovial drunken recklessness beside Ryan's bitter focus. There was no Internet to get maps up and what were they marching towards anyway? They kept spotting the flare, losing it behind copses, twisting away from it as the road tangled like a knotted snake. As the clock crept to four, they shared a glance and silently agreed to let it go.

Ryan pulled over and got out. A gate led into a wide, thin field, bordered by a line of trees, then a low hill and beyond that, they could see the orange glow of the relinquished beacon and smell its acrid smoke.

'If we made off now,' joked Joseph, 'over the hill there, like the intrepid bastards we are, we'd pin that gaff down in fifteen minutes. But who'd mind the women?'

'I hope it's not a house,' Ryan said.

'Nah.' Joseph caught his shoulder. 'It's probably some barn or something.'

'So fucking quiet here.'

'It'd drive me mental living in a place like this. Sensory deprivation. No wonder the boggers are always seeing ghosts.'

'Are they?'

'Yeah. Shades of dead people on the sides of the road, lads there since the Rising. The devil picking his teeth at the cross-roads. Weird shit. We've more history than we're able for.'

Joseph turned to go back to the car but Ryan stayed where he was, watching the fire. His cousin came back, caught his shoulder again, knocked his head against his back and said, 'What's up with you, Cuse?'

'Just coming down, is all.'

'Dunno about that. Told you you shouldn't have brought her, man. You need room to breathe, the pair of you.'

'That's not it.'

'No? Coz it's obvious you're crumbling, you and her.'

'Going up in flames, you mean.'

'Maybe,' said Joseph. 'Maybe.'

'And nothing grows from ashes.'

'You're going ending it?'

More lights now, more smoke. Wherever it was, someone was tackling it.

'No,' Ryan said. 'I can't.'

Unsettled by ghosts and confession, he went back to the car.

23

Georgie liked to compose letters to David she was never going to write.

Dear priggish David mama's boy Coughlan,
How is my daughter? You don't need to answer, so unzip your prissy mouth and let yourself breathe. I'm coming for her. I'm nearly there. I have more money now than you'd be able to fathom. How did I get it? Oh, nefarious ways. I was wicked as the wickedest woman, and you know how we are, David, wicked as wicked can be. But it's all your fault. You made me a whore, so what harm charging premium rates for others to do the same? At least they won't knock me up then condemn me for it. All the shuffling horns of the city are better than your limp prick. I hope your Christian girlfriend chokes on it.
   Enjoy your never-ending poker tournament/wanking cycle, you beardod creep.
   Your pal, Georgie.

She didn't have half as much money as she wanted him to think she did, but it wasn't as if he'd find out either way, if she never got round to writing those letters. She hoped the strength of her bitterness was enough to carry it back to him as an edge to the wind, or a nagging pain that kept him up at night. Fuck the letters. Fuck David. She owed him nothing. He owed her a universe.

The notion of debt had been pressed on her and she learned to open her hands and allow its weight to pull her down. J.P. had put her earning after the debacle with his mother; he said she owed him a favour. She did six months' penance in a house where she was the only Irish girl. She reckoned she'd been brought in as a substitute for some unfortunate who'd run off or been offed. When there were better girls to choose from he let her go again. 'Don't get any ideas about telling tall tales, either,' he said. 'Coz in this world, girl, you're just a scrapheap bit, and no one's going to believe you.'

Scrapheap or not, she was the sergeant at last and this was the drill: she got up, made tea, sat around thinking of the money she'd made and lost and the money she'd make again, and did a bit of work, when she was able to.

In order to get Harmony back she needed money. In order to make money she needed to continue doing the only thing she was good for. In order to continue doing the only thing she was good for she needed medication. Living expenses, taken from her nest egg. She used the brothel contacts, even after they'd let her leave; the path of least resistance would do fine now that she had a destination. In her head she told David she was wiping her arse with fifty euro notes but the real world bled her. She was doing far too much, but she had to be muddled for the graft or the graft would never get done. She tried alternatives but nothing worked as well. There was reason in it, no matter how unpleasant the logic.

Night was when the trouble started. She didn't sleep. She didn't feel threatened as such, just restless, stuck in some cosmic halfway house, just a little out of whack and waiting for her number to be called and the process explained anew. Twenty-six was just like being twenty-one. It was nothing like being twenty-three. Georgie felt the dichotomy and it confused her. How could you be two people in five years? How could you undergo such a metamorphosis – whore to saint – and paint the slattern back over the scar tissue only a few short years later?

She lost interest in her detective novels. They were long-winded and she didn't have the time for cheesy gasbaggery. Instead she sat up reading true crime files on the Internet, nauseous and lost, following link after link until the morning came and it was time to start over. Sometimes she went to the

Missing Persons site because Robbie's picture was still there, staring out of a photograph she hadn't provided. Must have been his mother, if he had one. She'd pay her a visit one day. Tell her to quench the home fires.

'You think you'd notify *someone*,' Robbie chastised. 'After you telling the old woman I mattered, and all.'

'Oh, you mattered,' Georgie replied. 'It's your fault I'm in this mess. Bad habits you taught me. Bad habits from a bad man.'

'Yeah, blame a man and not yourself, Georgie.'

'Men are all the fucking same! Maybe you *didn't* matter, Robbie O'Donovan. There's a million more out there just like you.'

She never lost focus on the goal, even when her strategies shrivelled to husks of ideas, the residue of forgotten escape plans.

Though Maureen's words circled, she kept the scapular knotted around her wrist.

One Saturday night in April, Georgie turned a trick with a bloke who dropped her at the wrong end of the city centre. She made her way back to her usual spot slowly, shaken — he had seemed like an OK chap until he'd finished and then his disgust was tangible. She swung into an off-licence that was just shutting and bought a naggin of vodka and drank a third of it in the toilets at McDonald's before continuing on her way. The alcohol kicked in and circled the fear, gave it warmth and made it greater.

Alcohol was not going to fix this, but God never closed a door without opening a window.

For a moment she couldn't think who he was. Plenty of familiar faces crossed her path, of course. All day and night she spotted ones who'd paid for her, and for a moment she assumed he was another, punters were as likely to be tall and dark and good-looking as they were to be sweaty, squat clichés. He was walking down the street with a couple of other guys, all in their early twenties or so, jostling, lively types. Ryan. She hadn't seen him in such a long time. He was a grown-up now, all legs and cheekbones. She called after him and one of his companions jogged his arm and gestured backwards and he waited, God bless him, as she hurried over.

'Ryan. It's been a while.'

'Jesus fucking Christ, Georgie.'

She flushed. She had lost weight, she knew. It might have been what she was wearing: a mini dress, black heels, but in that there was no difference between her and the chattering girls out dancing tonight, except intent. Maybe not even that.

'It's good to see you,' she offered.

It was cold for April. There was frost settling while the city partied; it clarified the air, outlined the orange street lights, the glow from pub windows, the neon signs outside of the nightclubs. He was wearing a heavy jacket, dark jeans and thick white skate shoes, and even so he had rammed his hands into his pockets and was throwing his weight from foot to foot.

'I wish I could say the same thing,' he said. 'What the fuck happened to you?'

There was no point in pretending she'd simply found her thighs again after a few years of Christian body-policing. She shook her head.

'Really?' she joked, feebly. 'I got that old-looking?'

'Have you even been eating?'

'You're not a bit saucy! Of course I've been eating.'

'When? Last fucking summer? Jesus.'

She was needled. *What if I'd had an eating disorder*, she thought. *Or cancer? Or lost a parent and was wasting away with grief?* She chose to ignore his tetchiness. 'How are you keeping?' she said. 'I think the last time I saw you was . . .'

Up at his father's house. When she was pregnant with Harmony, and searching for Robbie, hormones backed into her brain, making her brave and crazy. Up in that poky council house, only a paper wall between them and Tara Duane, with Ryan's father asserting his ignorance and exposing the frailty of the lead with statements she only understood months afterwards; his anger that she'd disturbed his children, and threatened his status. She tried to put it out of her mind, and Ryan picked up on the pitch and cut her off: 'Did you find your fella?'

'No,' Georgie said. 'He died.'

She might have expected commiseration under different circumstances. Instead she got exactly what she expected; he flinched, and changed the subject.

'You had your kid, then.'

'Yeah,' said Georgie. 'A little girl. Harmony. Isn't that pretty?'

He nodded and looked over her shoulder and down the street.

Off his discomfort she conceded, 'I didn't just stop you to say hello.'

'No?'

'No.' She asked his shoes, 'Are you still dealing?'

'Are you still on the game?'

'Why?' she snapped; the force of his rejoinder had surprised her. 'Are you up for doing a swap?'

'Funny,' he said. He slouched and there was an echo of compromise to the action, but she wasn't finished, freewheeling on the vodka burn and the echoes of their last meeting. 'What business is it of yours?' she said. 'Are you going to save me?'

He neither answered nor moved.

'*Judgey bollocks*,' she quoted. 'Isn't that what you said?'

'What d'you want, Georgie?'

'I need something,' she said. 'I just wanted to know if you're still in the habit of selling.'

'Not on the fucking street I'm not.'

She felt the statement for an edge, but couldn't determine if he meant to cut her. 'What's that mean?'

'It means I've moved up in the world, girl. I don't carry shit around with me.'

'You don't deal anymore?'

He paused. 'Just what I said, girl. I don't carry shit around with me.'

'Oh.' The chance of instant gratification faded into another night of hurried phone calls and bitten nails. 'I'm kinda hanging, like.'

A group of girls skirted around them. Ryan moved back against the wall and Georgie stepped towards him; he put his hand up.

'Hanging,' he said. 'Back fucking hanging again.'

'It's just a turn of phrase, for God's sake. Fine, I'm not hanging. It's Saturday. I'm just a bit bored, OK?'

He gestured tersely at the moving streets. 'That's Saturday boredom, Georgie. You're wasting away. You're not asking me for help with your night out.'

'I'm not wasting away!'

'Fucking look in a fucking mirror!'

'What's it to you? It's not like you know me at all, is it?'

He remembered the words. 'I don't know you from Adam,' he said, head back against the wall, staring again over her shoulder, like a bouncer, she thought, or a guard. 'That doesn't mean I'm stockpiling the crazy shit just to spite you.'

'A dealer with a conscience,' she said. 'That's rich. You weren't so bothered about selling me shit when I was supposed to be in recovery.'

'You weren't doing such a good impression of a corpse at the time.'

'Judgey bollocks,' she said, stepping away, backwards for a few beats to watch for signs of concession, turning when she saw nothing of the sort. 'You've changed,' she said, over her shoulder. 'What happened to you? What happened to that decent kid?'

'You killed him off with your custom,' he barked. 'Get your fucking act together, Georgie.'

She marched between groups of revellers and strolling couples, holding her arms tight against the chill. Then he was beside her again. He caught her arm, she yelped, and it must have looked bad, it must have, he was bearing over her, one fist bunched around her arm and the other at an angle as if he was going to swing for her, but she knew that even on the street on a Saturday night he wouldn't be challenged on it, no one wants to interfere, never fucking interfere . . .

'Where's your kid?' he said.

Her lips moved to whimper and he snapped, 'Where's your kid, Georgie?' and she didn't dare snap back, she cried, 'I don't have her, she doesn't live with me, OK?'

'Who has her then?'

'Her dad. All right?'

He dropped her arm and stood chewing air and she took a chance on his new demeanour and pleaded, 'Look, I'm gagging, Ryan, if you can even give me a number . . .'

'I told you, that's not me anymore.'

'Like, even someone in your network or whatever, even someone from another crew, I don't mind.'

'Can't help you,' he said, and then, softer, 'Jesus, Georgie, you had your shit together.'

'What, hanging out with Cork's slackest cult?'

'Yeah, and now? It's like an episode of *The Walking Dead*, Georgie!'

'Look, I know I've slimmed down a bit . . .'

'It's not that. You look like shit.'

'This coming from a guy who makes people look like shit for a living?'

It wasn't a worthy comeback but it seemed to have done the trick. He fell back. 'There's a difference,' he said, and she replied, 'You'd hardly do what I do sober.'

'I'd hardly do what you do full stop.'

'And aren't you lucky you were born a boy, then? All you have to do is sell drugs.'

He looked down at the footpath, shaking his head.

'It's not like I want this,' Georgie said.

'Remember . . .' he said, slowly, and then he took her arm again, and escorted her to the edge of the path and the cold stone walls of their city centre. 'Remember the time I came down to you in that weird chapel place?'

The prayer hall. 'Yeah.'

'Remember you told me never to buy a prostitute?'

She remembered.

'But if I ask you to stop buying coke it wouldn't work.'

'That's sweet,' she said. Her voice cracked.

'If I told you that lads like me end up inside over shit you buy, would that stop you?'

There was nothing earnest to his expression. He seemed pained, impatient and resentful, all in one oddly beautiful tic.

She faltered. 'You don't know my life . . .'

'You don't give a fuck for mine,' he said, and took his hand away. She pushed her fingers over the spot he'd held, instinctively. And for the beat before he wordlessly left her she grasped something of what he was trying to say. And that it might have been nice to have someone like him, someone on the outside too, someone who got it, someone who might have stood by her and bawled her out of it when she stepped out of line.

When she made it home, two tricks later, she went online and deleted the bookmark for Robbie's Missing Person page, but found herself visiting him again later that night, and again, three times in total as the clock ticked on and she sat in her rented room, looking deep into Robbie's frozen eyes for something they might once have shared, but all she found was resentment, coming from inside her, rising up her throat.

24

'You are fucking joking me,' Jimmy choked, one day in the coldest April the city had seen in decades.

Maureen was like a lunatic. Not 'like', he thought. *Was* a lunatic. Right now, in her kitchen in the new apartment at Larne Court, she was doing a very passable impression of a maniacal beast, spitting, tutting, pacing.

'I'm not joking you,' she said.

Beside them, on the polished pine table, lay a copy of the *Echo*. Its front-page headline read 'Repairs Completed On North Cork Church' and underneath, '*No arrests made in nightmare arson attack*'.

'Well then why the fuck aren't you joking me?'

She stopped pacing and crinkled her nose as if she'd caught a whiff of decay. 'It was a statement,' she said.

'What kind of statement? "I'm off my fucking meds?" "I don't think my son's suffered enough?" "I'm suffering delusions of demonic grandeur?"'

.'That's the problem with your generation,' she said. 'You're politically apathetic.'

'Oh? And what damn purpose does this kind of madness serve, Maureen? You burn a country church down? Up in fucking Mitchelstown, of all places?'

She slapped the table 'It's a pyre, isn't it? For *that* Ireland. For *their* nonsense. For the yoke they stuck round our necks.'

'Jesus Christ, what are you on about? What, you wanted to make a metaphor of the horizon, was it? And you expected the buffers above to get that? Jesus, Maureen, have you any idea what they could have done over this? You're damn lucky they didn't root out some black-pantsed fourteen-year-old twerp and nail him to a fucking cross!'

'Well they didn't, did they?' she said. 'They did nothing. Why would they, sure? They've taken so much from me there's nothing left of me to see. I can do what I like and go where I like and all I get is a blind eye turned. It's ridiculous.'

'You want to get caught, Maureen? You want to spend a few years above in Limerick?'

'I can't get caught,' she said. 'Churches and brothels and Robbie O'Donovan, and not a climbing wisp of fault for any of them.'

'Oh, mother of Jesus.' He hung on to the back of the nearest kitchen chair and pinched his forehead. 'Maureen. Listen to yourself. You're not nine years old. You know this shit. Nothing goes unnoticed. You might think you got away with this and that, but people paid, and paid fucking dearly, for your messing.'

'Your insurance premium went up, I suppose.'

'You think you can burn buildings and kill gawky bayturs with impunity? Oh fuck me. Just because you don't see the stains doesn't mean you didn't make shit of things!'

There wasn't much more he could say. She refused to be moved. He couldn't tell whether anything was getting through, and in her madness he saw his city snap and tumble down and in the long years of his complicity he saw his weakness, as man and monster.

She felt she could do what she liked now. That much was clear to him. In burning down the brothel he had thought she'd made her decisive point and once he'd exhibited his rage he'd decided he could stand to grant her that last folly. He had stupidly assumed that was that. But the headline proved he couldn't trust her around loose ends. If a name lost from the lips of Tony Cusack could catch fire, then what could Maureen do with a living whore and a dented know-all like Duane?

Jimmy had watched the city long enough to know that it would right itself, sooner or later, and that the silence following Robbie O'Donovan's death was just a long, caught breath.

306

He extracted her promise that she wasn't going to get up to divilment as soon as the door shut behind him, and hurried to reinforce what he could before she got mind to break it.

Months back he'd been brought a mystery.

He hadn't had reason to bring the boat out in a while, but at the end of the summer he'd taken a day down at the yard, where he'd rolled up his sleeves and engaged in some therapeutic maintenance.

There was an ould fella who lived a couple of miles from the opposite end of the quay – Mike Costello, a gentleman bachelor, whose face was scored from coastline winds and disapproval at the unremitting advance of 'feckin' Japanese' technology. He had his own boat, though Jimmy rarely saw him do anything with it. More often he engaged in the lightly infuriating habit of sitting around on the quay with his Border Collie, smoking Players and offering unsolicited advice on the sea and sky. On this day, with the sun making sheets of blinding light from the puddles on the concrete, he approached Jimmy with customary solemnity, and asked after his plans for the vessel.

'I'll dock it this winter,' Jimmy said. 'It took a bit of a hammering last year.'

'Of course it did,' said Mike. 'And bringing it out in all weather, too. What you were at in January I don't know. Lucky you weren't mangled.'

'When was that?'

'January. In the rake of bad weather. Only the one time I saw you, in the early morning, but wasn't once enough? Ah sure, you do it for pleasure and you don't know what you're at; aren't you only a city boy? Dock it this winter and don't go making a widow of your good lady.'

Jimmy took this first exactly as he was tempted: he assumed Mike was mistaken. Hallucinating, even. Poking the ashes out of boredom and the malice boredom can call up. The image wouldn't leave him, though, and Jimmy wouldn't be where he was and who he was if he wasn't open-minded to cloaked dangers. He made delicate enquiries amongst his own, and no one had taken the boat out. He checked the dinghy and the boat itself for signs of mischief, and concluded there was no one tapping him for fuel and kicks on the high seas.

He didn't immediately suspect Tony Cusack, because suspicious as Jimmy was, he wasn't bloody insane. But there was an inkling, one day, driving into the wretch's terrace on unrelated business. Alongside Cusack's pile was Tara Duane's, boarded up. Jimmy asked his boys: *Did Duane take off?* It got back to him that she'd gone wandering, and that no one had any clue where; cops, drifters or the motherless chicks that lay for their sins under him.

You'd want to be stupid, he told himself, as he unwound the mystery. Tony Cusack knew where the boat was kept and where he'd been promised a watery grave. Tony Cusack had a set on Tara Duane. But Tara was a flighty fuck-up and Cusack a weeping fool. Most likely one of Jimmy's own had been moonlighting, and lying to him.

Still, though.

Still.

Jimmy did his sums.

Good clean murder was art, and that was reflected in its price. He could do the done thing and call in a professional, but even with favours recalled there'd be a cash penalty, and he baulked at the notion of spending five-figure sums tying loose ends on what was essentially a domestic spat. Five damn years he'd been taming this cock-up.

You're getting old, sneered the city. *Old and fat and soft and soft-headed.*

With Duane's disappearance he was left with two superfluous players.

Oh, far from soft-headed, he snapped.

With Duane's disappearance he wondered if he could line up his targets.

One to fall and take the other.

Against this backdrop, he re-examined the mystery of his borrowed boat and went with his gut.

He drove up to the estates on the hill and tried the handle of Cusack's front door. It opened. He let himself in.

Cusack was sitting at his kitchen table, a torn white envelope in one hand and a bill of some sort in the other. In granting himself access, Jimmy had not been quiet. But that was the thing, up where they had nothing worth stealing and five or six kids apiece. Privacy was neither granted nor expected.

Tony looked up and Jimmy watched his expression change.

'Afternoon, Anthony.'

He walked to the kitchen table and pressed his knuckles against its surface. Cusack gawped. The possibility that he thought their acquaintance suspended once more suggested itself to Jimmy, but he didn't derive the amusement from it he would otherwise have made use of. Cusack looked . . . fucking old.

'I need you to do something for me,' Jimmy said.

Cusack laid the bill on the table, and made a mask of his left hand. Jimmy looked over his head. The kitchen window was weather-splashed and smeared by little fingers writing lines in condensation, little palms wiping them off. The sill held the miscellanea of the poor bugger's life: coins and phone chargers and birthday cards soiled by the wet glass.

'You remember the whore,' Jimmy said.

Cusack said nothing, but looked down at the table and then back at Jimmy when his silence was matched. Jimmy took the eye contact as affirmation.

'She never stopped asking questions. Time's up on that bullshit. I want her gone.'

'Gone,' echoed Cusack. He took his hand from his mouth and said, 'What d'you mean, asking questions?'

'What d'you think I mean, Cusack? Come on, the ould brain isn't that mushed, is it? Asking fucking questions. Making fucking noise.'

'It's been years.'

'Years enough for your brood to grow up? No.'

Cusack came round to it. 'So you need what from me?'

'I need you to make her disappear.'

Jimmy pushed himself off the table and paced. Over at the sink, he flicked through forks drip-drying in a grey plastic caddy. Over at the drawers, he rifled through tea towels and school timetables. 'I need you to clean up another mess,' he said, evenly. 'I need you to do me one last turn. That's not so hard, is it, Cusack? For your own sake? For your kids'? I need you to end the whore so we can finally draw a line under this.'

Cusack said, 'I'm sure you have lads better qualified for this kind of craic' in a voice no match for his meaning.

'How would that be, Cusack? How would I have lads better qualified? This is our issue, and one I'm not keen on compounding. I'm not offering it up to anyone else. What do I look like? Fuck's sake.'

'Isn't this compounding it?'

'No. It's drawing a line under it. I told you already.'

Cusack managed to get to his feet. 'Jimmy,' he said. 'Jimmy', and his old friend stopped thumbing through the dregs and raised his eyebrows. 'What are you trying to do to me?' Cusack said. His voice was a testament to conviction lost. 'Jimmy . . . I helped. That's all I'm good for. Being given directions. Even then I get lost. You saw it yourself. This isn't something I'm even capable of doing. Think about what you're asking me.'

'Capable,' said Jimmy, and laughed. 'Oh, Tony. What's that they say? "You don't know your own strength till you're pushed?"'

Cusack shook his head. 'No point pushing. I can't do this.'

'You did Duane, didn't you?'

Tony sat down again. He put his face in his hands.

Jimmy waited.

'I don't know where Duane is,' Tony said.

'I can't imagine you do. It's been a long time since you sank her.'

'I had nothing to do with her taking off.'

'You did,' Jimmy said.

310

He returned to the side of the kitchen table and grasped Cusack's shoulder.

'She's no loss,' he said, mildly. 'And men do what they have to do, don't they? Bit of a vampire to that wan. She wasn't very good at masking it. And sure, didn't she fuck your young fella?'

'Where the fuck did you get that idea?'

'Aw, come off it. Straight from the gee-gee's mouth. That's why you put her window in. That's why you've been holding a grudge. Shattered glass, shattered bones . . . it's a slippery slope.'

It was a good fifteen seconds before Cusack responded.

'If you thought I had something to do with her running off, you'd hardly be saying shit like that to me.'

'What, because you think I'd be afraid of you? Oh Christ, you're hardly that naive.'

He let go of Cusack's shoulder and leaned back onto the table. It wouldn't matter what was said now. The man looked like a child in a dentist's chair. Jimmy shook his head. A spark was a complication, but out of deference to a shared past he wanted Cusack to show him something. Even a raised vein. A twitch, or narrowed eyes. Not this watery supplication.

'I don't blame you,' he said. 'My young fella is thirteen in the summer. If anyone interfered with him I'd rain down fire and fucking brimstone. So it was your right, Cusack.'

He leaned closer.

'And it was my fucking boat.'

'So you're saying I owe you?'

'So you're admitting you did it?' Jimmy straightened. 'I'm not saying you owe me, Cusack, not at all. This is your mess as much as it's mine. One of us has to get this sorted. It can't be me. You're a nobody. That's why it's you. You got away with the last one, didn't you?'

'I don't know where Duane went,' Tony said.

'Yeah, you said,' Jimmy went for the kitchen door. 'Let's say till Friday to find the girl and do the deed. If you need to go boating

I'll let you off one more time. Give me a buzz when you're finished and I swear to the Lord Above that we'll be done with this.'

'How do I know that?'

'What? You don't believe me?'

Cusack stood up. He leaned on the table, lost his nerve and looked down. 'How do I know you won't pin this on me? Isn't that why you roped me into the Robbie O'Donovan thing? That's what dopes like me are there for.'

Jimmy smiled, and jovially slapped his hands off the worktop. 'Putting two and two together, are we? And what fucking ridiculous number are we coming up with?'

'What would you want with this,' Tony said, 'except a place to pin the blame?'

Jimmy paused to weigh the violation.

'That could be it,' he said. 'And so what if it is?'

Cusack looked up.

'Just like that, Jimmy?'

'Just like that.'

'I did you a good turn, boy.'

'And what d'you want? A fucking medal? Cusack, if we lived in a world where good deeds meant anything I'd have played along, but this isn't that kind of world, and this isn't that kind of fuck-up.'

'You dragged me into this.'

'I did.'

'And how do I know I'm going to get out of it at all?'

'Coz I fucking said so. We're going round in circles, Cusack.'

He moved back towards his old friend, and felt – and was astonished at it; it was something he'd taken for granted for far too long – the sickly satisfaction at seeing the other flinch and then cower. His guts twisted. He caught Tony's shoulder again. Half a man, halved.

Jimmy spat, 'Don't think I'm completely black-hearted, Cusack. We have history. I respect that. Do this and we're square. Don't do this, and . . . Well. You know you're going to do it because you don't have a choice, do you? Father-of-how-many, knock-kneed killer.'

The front door slammed.

Jimmy turned, hand still on Tony's shoulder, and into the kitchen came, he guessed, the little prince.

'What's going on?'

Jimmy pinched Tony's shoulder and said, 'Well, fuck me. They grow up so fast.'

The kid was the spit of his ould lad. A touch taller and missing the gut, the benefit of his mother's genes in these and other refinements; a good-looking lad, Jimmy thought, not your typical scut. He was out of the scut's uniform, too, in a smart jacket and black jeans instead of the tracksuit and sovereigns combo. 'Ryan,' Jimmy said. 'I'm right, amn't I? The heir to the Cusack fortune. Well, how are you today?'

'Can I help you with something?'

'That's not a very helpful tone.'

'Well let me re-fucking-calibrate. D'you want something?'

Jimmy whistled.

'Not so much a chip-off-the-ould-block as he looks, is he?' he said to Tony. 'Fire in him, though this town'll have something to say about that eventually.' Back at Ryan he said, 'I do want something, and I got it. Don't worry your pretty little head about it.'

He released Tony.

'Friday,' he said. 'I'll talk to you then.'

The son moved out of the way as he walked past and back into the cluttered hallway, back out through the grubby door, back down the driveway lined with ragwort and dandelion, back onto the street outside and its concrete footpaths dashed with gum and bird shit.

He wondered, as he walked, about the sprained turns that made a man a murderer. Jimmy didn't consider himself a member of that family; no, there was something sicker to murder than pragmatic judgement, which is all he ever engaged in. Tony Cusack was one kind of man: shuffling from one weak comfort to the next. What darkness was in him had been so well buried Tony himself likely didn't know it was there to call on, when his position as man and father and household god was threatened.

313

But then maybe he did. And maybe the boat was a tool seized to carry out another task in a long schedule. You just don't know, do you?

He unlocked his car door and as his fingers closed around the handle a voice caught him and spun him back again.

'Hey!'

It was the young lad. Murderer or not, Tony Cusack wasn't bold enough to bellow dissent.

Ryan Cusack strode right up and stopped just short enough to leave room for swinging fists.

'What the fuck was that about?' he said.

Jimmy laughed. 'Excuse me?'

'You. My dad. In my dad's house. Just now. What the fuck was that about?'

Jimmy closed the gap between them.

'None of your fucking business, pup.'

There was a height difference. Jimmy thought: *A good gut-punch will sort that out if necessary.*

'Watch me make it my fucking business,' said the boy.

'Aw, stop,' sneered Jimmy. 'I know what you're at and I appreciate it, I do. Showing off your baby claws is how you little fuckers learn. But you don't practise your play-acting on me, because I will put you in the ground. And your daddy after you.'

He meant to turn away. He didn't. There was, all of a stark sudden, too much there to turn away from.

Beyond Ryan's shoulder was a heavy stone sky and the dark, thick green of overgrown grass, and between both the reds and greys and browns of the suburban terraces. The boy was dark as his father, but lacking the ruddy palate of these hills and their rusted air. Here was a changeling who'd laid claim to the landscape and the place had grown up around him. Jimmy curled his lip.

Ryan said, 'You don't come into my house, and threaten my father, without giving me the chance to put you back in your box.'

Jimmy pushed against him; Ryan stood solid.

'If you had any idea who you were talking to,' Jimmy said, 'you'd be cleaving out your tongue on your fucking knees. Boy.'

'I know full well who I'm talking to. Phelan.'

Jimmy bared his teeth.

'Well, look at the fucking balls on you. That must be the Neapolitan talking, because it sure as shit isn't your father.'

'Funny that, isn't it?'

'Fucking hilarious. All I had left to know about you was how you spoke to your betters. Part-time half-grown dealer scum, Ryan Cusack. Kicked out of school, time under your belt already and a future bright as a bruise.'

'Spot on, boy. And your problem with my dad is what?'

'Hoho! Like a dog with a bone. Why don't you ask him?'

'Because I'm asking you.'

'The question is, Ryan, would you like it if I told you?'

Jimmy stepped back again, leaned against the Volvo and folded his arms. The boy's fingers curled into fists. Fifty feet away, Tony Cusack hovered at his hall door. Jimmy nodded towards him.

'He's afraid for you, Ryan, but more afraid for himself. Watch him.'

'Maybe he's not afraid for me at all.'

'No, he is. Always thinking about you. Oh, you've no fucking idea. But he won't come out here after you, because you've gone and gotten yourself into deep, deep shit. Didn't he warn you, when you went rushing out the door after me?'

Ryan snorted. 'There's a problem, I sort it.'

'What, you think getting banged up in borstal qualifies you to butt heads with me?'

'You bothering my father in my kitchen qualifies me to butt heads with you. You want something, talk to me about it. My dad's no good to you. And you fucking know it.'

'Oh, hark at this! Are you falling on your sword, kid?'

'Maybe.'

Jimmy nodded at the house again.

'What did he tell you?'

'Nothing.'

'And you don't reckon that's because he doesn't want you sticking your oar in?'

'I doubt it.'

'Does he normally get you to do his dirty work, Ryan?'

'If there's dirty work needs doing.'

In the doorway, Tony Cusack pushed his hand over his forehead.

Aloud, Jimmy wondered, 'After all he's done, the man throws his boy to the fucking wolves.'

Ryan said, 'So. What the fuck was that about?'

Jimmy swiftly measured outcomes. In front of him, the young avenger waited, a sharp twist to the corner of his mouth. Tony Cusack never once looked like coming over the threshold to reclaim him.

'All right,' said Jimmy.

Underneath logic and strategy, he was burning. Anger, more than was reasonable, caught his breath and quickened his pulse. He had no time to put a name to it, but he recognised its tincture from the same processes that had fucked his place in the world he'd made since he'd brought Maureen home from London. There were more out there like Ryan Cusack, boys half Jimmy's age for whom reputation was a thing to be taken from someone else.

'There's a problem your father and I share. I want it gone. It has a name: Georgie Fitzsimons. It shouldn't be hard to find because it circles this town like a bad penny. Take the thing out of circulation and I'm square with your piece-of-shit father. Let this go one step further and I'll make orphans of your siblings and hang you over the Lee in a fucking gibbet. You got that?'

He smiled.

'Bet you're sorry you asked now, aren't you?'

The boy said, 'Is that it?'

'It's in the smart mouth you betray yourself, kid. You have till Friday.'

He got back into his car unimpeded and drove out of the estate.

Mission accomplished, he supposed.

The nights were getting shorter, and once the weather cleared they'd see the sky, the lot of them, and feel the vastness above the city; the air, the wind and the world. They just had the April to suffer first. The walls of Jimmy's city inched towards the sides of his car as he drove. The lamp posts bent over him.

It would right itself, sooner or later. He just needed to be prepared.

25

Tony was at the kitchen sink, one hand on the draining board, the other in a tight fist by his side, bled out from his forehead to his knuckles, but still standing.

His father used to be a giant but as Ryan had stretched he'd shrunk to frailty, and his stature was only part of the story. All those rages, distilled by time down to petty tantrums. The good moods Ryan used to pray for, reclassified as desperate shows of learned affection. And that fucking strength, ha? Where was the bruiser now? Ryan could take him. He could do more than take him. He could kill him. Even with his bare hands. Catch him by his mop, knock his head off the wall, slam his face off the draining board, run him onto the stairs, slip his belt off, whip the old fucker.

Instead he walked over to the table and picked up the electricity bill.

'Ouch,' he said.

He counted out the fee, then a fifty on top of it, and put it on the table. He'd brought an eighth of grass too, a good poky smoke, and as such one he was considering leaving in his pocket and laying into with extreme prejudice once he got home. He left the baggie by the bill.

'Better for you,' he said.

He looked back at his father and Tony swallowed and looked at the floor.

'Rocky . . .'

'And you say I make stupid mistakes, Dad.'

'You don't understand.'

'No.' For a moment his stance matched his father's, and then he tossed his head and looked up again and said, 'Make me understand.'

Tony came over to the table. He sat down, awkwardly pulled a packet of cigarettes from his jeans pocket, and slit one open. Ryan put his Rizla on the table. Tony rolled a joint. His hands were shaking.

'What did he say to you?' he mumbled, once he'd sparked up.

Ryan sat down. 'Nothing that made any sense.'

Tony exhaled and rested his forehead on his wrist. His fingers scratched at his hairline.

'He wants that girl killed,' Ryan said. He coughed out a laugh. 'Like, fucking hell.'

'That's the long and short of it,' Tony said.

'Eh, no it fucking isn't, Dad. That's the bare bones. The girl who came up here asking after her fella is a problem you share with Jimmy Phelan. And somehow he thinks you're capable of pulling shit like that and you're not, Dad. How could you be? What the fuck is he on?'

Tony looked up. 'I couldn't,' he said. 'You know that. See? You know that but he doesn't. Or he does and he doesn't care. But you're right, Rocky – I couldn't be like that and I'm not.' There were tears in his eyes.

'How's Georgie a problem you share with Jimmy Phelan?'

'I didn't mean for any of this to happen. I was walked into it. That young wan's fella . . . he was killed.'

'Oh, fuck me.' Ryan leaned back in his chair.

Georgie had said as much the previous Saturday. *Did you find your fella? No. He died.*

There were threads of dusted web drifting gently round the shade above him.

'I met her in town, last Saturday,' he said. 'First time since she was here in your sitting room, Dad. She looked like shit, y'know. Like a skeleton in a dress. She said the feen was dead. I guess that's why Jimmy Phelan's talking out contracts on her.'

'She's a buddy of yours—'

319

'No. I fucking told you she wasn't. She's someone I used to sell dope to.' He gestured at the baggie in front of his father. 'See? Just like that. Aw, fuck me!'

He pushed the chair back and paced over to the worktop, and brought a fist to the surface between the hob and the dirty mugs.

It needed saying.

'Did you kill him, Dad?'

'No,' Tony said.

He was staring at the table. 'Phelan crossed my path one day, five years ago now. He said he needed a favour. I had no clue what it was until I was landed in front of it – the fella, dead on the floor up in one of Phelan's gaffs. A total accident, he said. I was to help him clean it up. And I did it. You don't say no to Jimmy and at that stage . . . I couldn't have said no. That's Jimmy. He shoves you off the cliff and as you're falling he shouts after you: *No way back now, boy!* I didn't know the girl'd come looking for him and I didn't know she'd come up here. I don't know why she never learned to shut her mouth. Whatever madness drove her to piss him off, it's done now. And because I'm the only one who knew about the first one, he says I have to . . . to do the second.'

'How do you even know Jimmy bloody Phelan?'

'From years back. Before you were born. Before I was your age, even. We went to London together.'

'That's how he knew about my mam, so.'

'What did he say about your mam?'

'Oh, fuck all, for Jesus's sake.'

Ryan's phone beeped. He took it out of his pocket and stared down at the screen. It was a text from Karine. She'd be on her lunch break by now, back there in the real world. He turned the phone over in his palm and closed his fingers round it.

'So what did Tara Duane know about all this?'

Tony inhaled, sharply, making a sound somewhere between a hiccup and a bleat.

'What d'you mean, boy?' he said.

'She sent Georgie up here, didn't she? Telling her you'd know where her fella went?'

'Twist of fate, I suppose. She was late remembering that I knew the poor fella.'

'So you did know him.'

Tony closed his eyes. 'Yeah.'

'How'd you know him?'

'Pub. That's all. I couldn't tell her that, though, not after what had happened.'

'And Tara just landed on that one, did she?'

'Why couldn't she? We both know, don't we? The world marked that wan for divilment. Why else would she have . . .' He flinched.

'. . . With you.'

'Are you still going on about that?' Ryan snapped.

'You were fifteen, Ryan.'

'Yeah, well. Fifteen-year-olds are all dick, aren't they?'

He put his phone on the worktop, placed both hands flat on either side, then sank onto his elbows and covered his head with his hands.

'I didn't have a choice,' his father stressed feebly, from behind him.

'There's always a choice,' Ryan said.

'If it makes you feel better to believe that.'

Ryan straightened.

'Right,' he said.

He put his hands on his head and moved to the window, and let his eyes drift from clothesline to back wall to lawn.

'Rocky, listen—'

'Don't fucking talk to me a minute!'

He'd seen it splashed and screaming on her face: Georgie was fucked anyway. Her cheeks sunken, her eyes like holes punched in paper; fated to expire in a gutter after ODing or being choked out by the wrong punter and there was nothing Ryan Cusack could do about that. Child already taken off her. Slipping from salvation to the street. Hanging.

'Aw, fuck,' he breathed.

Tony tried again.

'Ryan, I—'

321

'I'll sort this,' Ryan said. He went back to the worktop and picked up his phone. Tony shook his head. His mouth warped and changed his grimace into something faintly ludicrous, like the painted melancholy of an old clown.

'How "sort it", boy? What's that mean?'

'It means I'm going to fucking sort it, Dad.'

'Ryan, you can't bargain with Jimmy Phelan—'

'I'm not going to bargain with him.'

'Aw Jesus Christ—'

'Aw Jesus Christ what, Dad? What? It has to be sorted, doesn't it?'

Tony got to his feet.

'Ryan . . . I can't let you do this.'

'That's grand coz I amn't asking your permission, am I?'

He turned back at the hall door.

'Don't bring this up with me again,' he said.

He watched his father's pallor wash out against the smudged eggshell blue of the kitchen walls, and couldn't decide whether it was the right tone at last that had done it, or the right words or the right height or the right criminal trajectory. Or the right emergency. What the name of the magic trick was that turned Tony Cusack from one kind of man to no man at all.

He made the decision but it sat with him for a while, and he ended up driving from one end of the city to the other, smoking, and asking himself who the fuck he was.

He picked up Karine at the hospital at clocking-off time and she jumped into the passenger seat with the post-work high she denied and he was addicted to.

'Hey, baby boy!'

There was an even blanket of mist over the city. Karine shivered. 'So dark,' she complained, turning up the heat. 'It's like December.' Out of the corner of his eye he noticed her narrow hers and smile. 'You're cranky, are you?'

'Not really,' he said.

'You OK?'

'Course I am.' They were at the car park exit; he leaned over the steering wheel and stared into the traffic. 'How was work?' he said.

'Mental. Like, we're supposed to be learning and the only thing they're teaching us is how not to explode with stress. I swear to God, that's the number one nursing skill.'

'Someone's got to do it,' he said.

She shimmied in her seat. 'Yeah! Someone's gotta patch 'em all up.'

It wasn't a dig at him. It might have looked perverse to the uninitiated, him doing what he did for money and her being nearly-a-nurse, but they both knew, well, you've got to be realistic. Someone's got to do it: the mantra applied to both paths. He was glad of that shared pragmatism, though when he was hungover he worried that it was as down to rebelling against her parents, who hated him, as it was to her urban ethics.

He dropped her home to her parents' terrace, and she leaned over and into a slow kiss.

'Will you come and get me later?' she whispered.

'Yeah.'

'Don't be too long.'

Before she pulled away he framed her face in an open hand.

'Tell me you love me,' he said.

'Duh, I love you.'

'Really, though?'

'Oh my God, is my word not good enough?' She smiled, then the smile faded, and she cocked her head. 'Have you done something?'

'No.'

'You're talking like you've done something.'

'I haven't.'

'Coz I'm all done forgiving you, Ryan.'

'I know.'

She let him kiss her again. 'I'm just a bit off,' he said. 'I was up with my dad earlier. You know how it goes. He gives me the emos.'

'I should have guessed.'

'I've a small job to do. I'll be back later for you. We'll go to mine. Watch a film or something. Listen to some tunes. I dunno. Have fucking tea and Jaffa Cakes.'

'OK,' she said, soft as the rain.

'And you can tell me about work,' he said. 'Tell me plans, and tell me stories.'

He crossed the river for the fifth time and turned onto the quay, and traffic lights quivered through the mist on the windscreen.

She was there. He pulled up alongside her and rolled down the window. *If I'm caught doing this*, he thought, *how the fuck will I ever explain it?*

'Get in, Georgie.'

She looked at him like a cornered teenager, slid towards the passenger door, and slouched in.

'What?' she said.

The mist had teased her hair into a tangle, and its volume made her face even more gaunt. She pulled her jacket sleeves over her fists. Her skirt was short and her legs bare; he'd had the GTI only a month, and was still obsessively odd about anything dirtying the seats. He recognised his revulsion to her naked skin as irrational. Possibly essential, if he was going to be smart about it. He pulled back onto the road and drove towards the Mall. 'How the mighty have fallen,' Georgie muttered.

Over her right wrist she was wearing a piece of brown cloth, wound and knotted; it kept catching as she yanked at her sleeve.

'That's the best you can come up with?' he said. 'Mumbling something snippy to shame me? Fucking hell, Georgie. You've no fight in you.'

'I'm supposed to fight you?'

'You think I'm a hypocrite, don't you? You think I've some nerve picking you up after what happened Saturday. You think it all boils down to whether or not I'm horny.' He snorted. 'And you get in anyway, and you'd let me, wouldn't you? After everything.'

'See, that's what happened to the decent kid,' she said. 'He turned into a man.'

'But you'd let him fuck you, though.'

'It's a job, Ryan. It's not personal.'

'No,' he said. 'It's not.'

He had to contact his father afterwards for Jimmy Phelan's number, and he could only do so via text; he didn't want to talk to Tony. He didn't want to talk to anyone, but he managed it with Phelan. A quick introduction and a quick confirmation. Phelan wasn't satisfied.

'Come meet with me,' he said.

So Ryan did, down in the cellar of a Barrack Street pub with a facade that had not so much seen better days as decayed the street on which it stood. They weren't alone down there, though he doubted a man like Jimmy Phelan was used to being alone. There were a number of lads in the far corner playing cards, one of them Tim Dougan, whose legend had long served Ryan both as warning and inspiration. Though Phelan kept him standing near the door and talking to the floor, he had no doubt the men around them were all ears. They glanced up at intervals, sniffing, scowling, sucking their teeth.

The room was lit by two low, bare bulbs. This was for function and for show, and Ryan was just as scared as he should have been.

'You had two days,' said Phelan.

'Couldn't put something like that off,' Ryan said.

'No? Plenty who would. Though I don't recommend it myself.'

Phelan's words, low, smooth and cold, crept up on him like a trippy pill. He flushed, felt the sweat break on his forehead, and the butterflies push against the walls of his stomach. Two of the card players turned to stare. Ryan looked away. There was a point of pain, suddenly, on each side of his nose. He pinched the bridge.

'Am I supposed to just take for granted that you came through for me?' Phelan said.

'Pretty much.'

'What if I ask you for proof?'

'What d'you want, a fucking photograph? Are you assuming I

wasn't taking you seriously in the first place? With my father's neck on the line?'

Phelan smiled thinly. 'Did you ever ask yourself, Ryan, if he doesn't deserve you?'

Ryan said, 'Are we done here?'

Phelan looked away. 'I did my research a long time back, of course. How's the apprenticeship going? How's Dan Kane treating you?'

'Am I supposed to answer that?'

'I heard he's pure fond of you,' said Phelan.

Ryan's phone started buzzing in his jeans pocket. He assumed it was Karine. He was late. Very late. It was bedtime-late. There was the doghouse, and there was the cellar. He exhaled, quietly. Having practised now for years he knew his face was hard as the stone walls around him, and almost as blank as the man he was standing in front of. But behind it all he was crumbling, and desperate to get out of here, and mad to crawl back to the doghouse on his belly and wait for her to forgive him yet again. He didn't think that edginess could break through. No. No, he knew it couldn't. And that was nearly as bad.

Phelan said, 'I hardly need to tell you that what happened between me and you and that broken fool who fucked your mother is no one's business but ours. Dan Kane is not to hear of this.'

'It isn't my proudest moment,' Ryan said.

'Ah, but you're a good boy. Dan Kane knows it. I know it. Let's say I'm done with Tony Cusack. I am not done with you. Not by a long shot.'

'You are,' Ryan said.

Phelan smiled and caught his shoulders. 'You don't get to decide that, boy,' he said.

Beneath the powder-blue sky of a new Sunday morning, Ryan sat smoking on someone else's balcony. Behind the sliding door Joseph and a couple of other lads sat around a table, doing lines and drinking beer. Karine had gone for a snooze in one of the bedrooms. Ryan needed lungfuls of sharp air and a break from boisterous conversation. He had a head full of coke and thoughts as cold and clear and even as the new sky above him.

It wasn't his fault. He knew it wasn't his fault. It was something bigger.

His 'job' – nothing personal – entailed purchasing quantities of intoxicants, cutting them and selling them at a profit to people who were, as Georgie's terminology stated, 'dealing'. Taking precedent over how he made his money was how he proved his loyalty to Dan Kane: stepping in as his representative in cases where he deemed it necessary. Negotiations with fellas further down the chain. Retribution against those same fellas if the negotiations didn't pan out. He'd gotten his fists bruised. He'd gotten his head around it. This was his part in the story. This was what he boiled down to, flesh, guts and bones.

'I'm the bad guy,' he said.

The city didn't heed him. He looked down on rooftops, the corrugated shell of thousands of lives, all with their own part to play, fitting together like cogs, keeping the wheels turning. Doctors, dockers, dancers and dealers.

He'd been twenty years coming to this point. There probably hadn't ever been another way.

From his back pocket, his business mobile rang. He shifted his weight and dug it out. He changed the SIM every few weeks. He had authority, at least, over which people he sold to. If there were any clients he needed to drop he simply didn't give them his new contact. They faded from his life without protesting their relegation. Such things weren't questioned. Ryan Cusack had that much autonomy.

He answered the phone. 'Yeah?'

Donnelly's voice. 'I got that.'

'Oh, good stuff.'

'Yeah, hassle free. I'll see you later so. What are we looking at?'

Ryan narrowed his eyes and took another drag. His mind was racing. He snapped it back. 'Six G,' he said.

'No problemo.'

Ryan hung up. He opened the browser, screencapped a map

327

and sent it on. Later he'd meet Donnelly at the mapped address, once he'd had a medicated snooze. He wasn't coming down for a while. He'd been flying fucked for two days straight.

Hereditary

'You're a prick is all you are!'

She's sitting on my bed in her knickers, and I'm standing at the foot with my jeans still unbuttoned, and the room's saturated with the sweat and musk of what we've just done . . . How do we manage to fight in something that heady? This is how it ends? We've become so allergic, the smell of each other's bodies is raising welts and driving us insane?

'Yeah, I'm a prick, that's what it is, Karine, I'm a fucking prick.'

We've been out since midday, had a couple of glasses of wine with the lunch, and pints after that. We came home for a snooze before heading out for the night, and when we woke there was murmuring and giggles and her turning round and pushing against me and asking me for it, and all of a sudden we have the spitting start of World War fucking III.

It's Halloween, so that's an excuse for her to go out wearing a ladybird costume that amounts to a spotty mini dress and black thigh-high stockings and a pair of glittery wings. The female population of the city will be baring their legs and their tummies and the very tops of their thighs and I'm not supposed to look at any of them because she knows I'm a pathetic twisted cheat. She can go out in a dress right up to her arse and just fucking ask to be groped but I'm to blind myself in case I accidentally exchange a look with one of her number. This is the kind of shit Karine can dredge up without even having to think about it: vicious hypocrisy dressed up in timidity and thrown back in my face if I dare question her. I'm so close now to walking out of here and getting my nose into a mound of coke and my cock up the first girl that smiles at me.

329

My shirt is on the floor beside her and I don't want to lean over her to pick it up.

'You don't get to tell me what to do, Ryan. You're a liar and you're a cheat and you do not get the high ground here.'

'I haven't touched another girl in fucking God knows how long.'

'Oh, yeah. God knows how long. Never mind all of them that you touched before God started keeping tabs, they're not supposed to count.'

'They don't count any more than Niall Vaughan counts.'

She stomps over and jabs a finger on my chest.

'Bring up Niall again,' she says. 'Go on, dig deeper. Because one minute you're all "Oh, when I cheat it doesn't matter but when you cheat it's because you were infatuated," so if you're equating Niall Vaughan, who you believe I was madly in lust with, with your gamut of sluts, then you're admitting that you were infatuated with all of them, aren't you?'

She's hurting my head.

Alongside the ugly little hangover, warming up for the relay as my lunchtime drunkenness collapses.

'Are you for fucking real?' *I ask her.*

'Are you, boy? Are you for fucking real?'

I don't know how this happened. One minute we're coming together and the next she's accusing me of emotional infidelity, and OK, listen, I've fucked other girls and I'm not proud of it. But it's not like I loved any of them. It's not like it's even possible for me to love anyone else. It's a deficiency and I know it. I feel it. It wrecks my head, it ties my tongue, it hobbles me.

'Do you have to keep pulling me inside out with this shit, Karine? You know full well you're the only one who's ever meant anything to me and what did it matter when I couldn't trust you as far as I could throw you?'

'Oh my God,' *she says.* 'You're so full of shit.'

'How is that full of shit? You fucked Niall Vaughan when I was—'

'In prison! You have no idea what that was like for me! You

weren't there and I needed you. I couldn't trust you not to get banged up and you're still doing the same thing, aren't you? Yeah, talking shit about Australia and you and me leaving this dump and making something of ourselves when you know full well that's not going to happen with your record. We're stuck here and it's all your fault.'

'Aw yeah, see, I'm your prison, am I?'

'Something like that, Ryan. You cheat on me and lie to me and I'm stupid for letting you . . . and the absolute kicker? You haven't a notion of ever quitting. I've never been as important to you as Dan Kane. The next time you get caught you'll get ten years and where will I be then?'

'I'm not going to get fucking caught.'

'How do you know? You were stupid enough to get caught in the first place.'

'All right, so I'm a cheat and a liar and I'm a cage and I'm fucking stupid. Anything else you want to say?'

'Oh,' she hisses, 'there's plenty else I could say.'

'Fucking say it, then!'

I can see the poison rising, filling her out as it climbs, a wave of hatred coming from her belly to her jaw. 'You have no idea what you put me through when you got caught with Dan Kane's coke,' she says. 'And I am going to make you suffer for it.'

'Fucking Niall Vaughan wasn't revenge enough, then? In a fucking car park? Like a fucking whore?'

She thumps my chest so I push her, all the way back to the wall. I stand over her and she struggles and kicks out and gets my shin with her bare foot and this is the thing, it doesn't even hurt, but it doesn't have to hurt because this is just a reflex: I lift my fist to her.

I lift my fist to her.

And she shrieks, 'Oh my God! Oh my God, you were going to hit me! You pig, you were going to hit me!' and I can't stop it, I lash out and knock my fist off the wall beside her head and then again, and again, and I've got my hand on her throat beating the fuck out of the wall and her legs go from under her.

331

I let her fall and she crumples to the floor and I stagger backwards and end up on my arse.

'Oh my God,' she says.

'I didn't touch you,' I say, but whatever it was has been knocked out of me; all I can do is whisper.

'I knew this would happen someday,' she sobs. 'I've been watching this coming for months.'

My chest's hammering. 'I'm sorry,' I say. 'I'm really sorry. I didn't mean to scare you, girl. I fucking love you; I'd never hurt you.'

'No?' Her eyes are red, her hair teased rough from sweat and sex and now this, oh Jesus Christ, where did this come from? 'Then what the fuck was that?'

26

It was the worst time to be in the A&E – Saturday drinking time, when the city's youth drowned standing up. It was compounded by the coming bank holiday, and the place was predictably jointed. Pale girls in their weekend finery sat dumb with swollen knees, drunks bellowed at nurses who carried the scars of their vocation on their faces . . . ould fellas, ould wans, stern mammies holding teenage boys who looked like they might burst into tears, trolleys, coffee cups, televisions no one could hear . . . Jimmy took it all in with the astonishment of a child who'd pulled a rock off the soil to see the woodlice scatter underneath.

He had other things to be doing, but – the realisation was made luminescent by the white lights of the waiting room – Maureen didn't have anyone else to accompany her. It was late in his life to feel a son's duty. His stand-in siblings had been so much older than him that he'd never felt pressure to obey, tend to or bolster. This was new, and what positive novelty did he expect to find in life at his age? From here on in it should be nothing but challengers and traitors.

Maureen sat on the plastic chair beside his, surly under the lights and the pain of her injured wrist. She had climbed up on the worktop in her apartment that afternoon to clean cupboard shelves, and had fallen. After two cups of tea and a few hours grumbling didn't cure her, she called the doctor, who sent her into A&E for an X-ray. She didn't appear to have wanted to call Jimmy. She did anyway. And so they sat together.

He tried, though where the compulsion came from he wasn't sure. 'D'you want a cup of tea?' he said. 'D'you want a newspaper?' In between staring at the weekend casualties and fantasising about getting head from that one good-looking nurse, he provided what his mother needed.

'How the A&E in this piddling hole is slower than the ones in London I'll never figure out,' Maureen groused. She had given up on her newspaper, having found it difficult to turn pages with only one hand. Now she sat with her legs crossed, holding on to her paper cup, making evil eyes at the opposite wall. A man who'd taken the seat below the spot she was directing her attention squirmed.

'Every A&E is the same on Saturday nights,' Jimmy offered.

'Bloody government,' she responded.

Jimmy smiled.

'D'you need to go out for a cigarette or anything?' he asked.

'And what if they call me? And what if I miss it and they end up sticking me back on the arse of the queue?'

'Sure I'll go out and get you.'

'Oh, stop fussing.'

To this he couldn't help but laugh. 'Fussing? Me? You're off your fucking game if you think that's fussing.'

'You're like an old hen,' she said.

Here in the vivid light, he was exposed and wrong-footed. On a Saturday night he might otherwise have been holding court in the *síbín* he ran on Barrack Street. Shadows might have cloaked him and kept him on his track.

'This is odd,' he told Maureen.

'What's odd?'

'This place, and me in it. This isn't usually my scene.'

'What? D'you think it's out jiving you are? This isn't anyone's scene.'

'That's not what I meant,' he said, and he cast his eye round again, and caught jaded porters, and threadbare corners, and footage of county floods scrolling on the TV screen on the wall. He meant normality. This was outside of his usual trajectory and yet home to all of these lifeforms who snapped and bled and shattered and had nothing but their country to fix them again. He got a sudden vision of a doppelgänger walking around, shaking hands, accepting their welcomes, like one of America's rock star presidents come to grace the spud-gobblers with his urbane presence.

His guide said, impatiently, 'Well, what did you mean?'

A nurse stood at the corridor and called, 'Maureen Phelan?'

'They'd shame you,' Maureen muttered. She rose and Jimmy alongside her. 'Are you coming too?' she asked, surprised, and he said, 'Why wouldn't I, Maureen? Is that not what I'm here for?'

They sat outside of the X-ray room and what he'd said obviously nagged at her, because she came out with, 'I'm probably not what you expected in a mother.'

He shrugged. 'I'm probably not what you expected in a son,' he said, but only because he felt he had to. That he wasn't what anyone would expect in a son was not a revelation. She was right, though. Maybe you get the mother you deserve.

He examined his hands and looked from there down the length of his legs. Alien or not, he was most certainly here, and he wouldn't have been if it wasn't for her youthful indiscretion. He glanced at Maureen and wondered how it was even possible to have come from her body and to have grown up into . . . whatever he was. It was an unpleasant sensation. His just being alive had ruined her life.

Well, he'd been called the Antichrist more than once.

She got her wrist X-rayed and was directed back to the waiting room. Their seats had been taken, so they walked around to find another pair.

Tony sat in the shadow of an enormous doctor as an exhausted climber with half a mountain yet to go. The doctor was young, calm and distracted. He had the chart in his hand but even as he spoke he was looking around at other notes, at his computer screen, at some diagnosis he had yet to make a call on. Tony felt light-headed. He held on tight.

'You'll keep him in, then?' he asked.

'Oh God, yeah,' said the doctor. 'For observation, first of all.

We've cleaned him out but, y'know, we're still talking alcohol intoxication, cocaine intoxication . . .' He squinted down at the chart. Tony flinched. 'Preliminary bloods suggest he didn't get as much paracetamol into him as we feared, but hepatotoxicity is still a concern. We'll do bloods again in two, three hours. When he's back with us I'd like someone from Psychiatry to speak to him.'

'Psychiatry?'

'Yes, Mr . . . ah. Cusack?'

'Cusack,' said Tony, miserably.

'Combined drug intoxication is usually accidental but both you and his . . . ah, housemate have indicated that this was deliberate. Better safe than sorry, eh? We don't want him in here again.'

'No.'

'So we'll move him to the unit in a bit and you can see him then, all right? I'll send a porter out to you.'

The doctor rose, and as he turned to hold the door open Tony took his hand and squeezed it. *Jesus*, he thought. *I'm like those gobshites who clap when the plane lands.*

'Thank you,' he said. 'I know these young fellas must break your melt. I know you have better things to be doing.'

The doctor furrowed his brow and smiled. 'It's what we're here for. Don't worry about it.' He allowed Tony to hold his hand for another second. 'He'll be fine,' he said.

Tony went back out to the waiting room. Kelly, Joseph and Karine were where he had left them. Joseph had draped an arm around Karine, who'd folded herself into a ball. There had been a fight earlier, apparently. She'd left Ryan and had gone into town to her friends. He'd followed, and it had culminated in a screaming match on the Grand Parade, '. . . but there's no way I thought he'd do something like this,' she wept. 'I'd never have fought with him if I'd have known . . . Oh God, this is all my fault.'

She'd confessed a variety of incidents and run-ins in the hours they'd sat in the waiting room. The past six months had exhausted her. She'd told Ryan three times that she couldn't do it anymore and each warning had developed into nothing more than a short detox: they spent a week apart and faltered, and after the second

336

time their friends stopped remarking on it. In the meantime there were parties. 'He's DJing more,' she said and, almost as if it wasn't his father she was talking to, blurted, 'and you know what that means. Coke isn't as forgiving as we are.'

She'd stopped crying. Tony stood in front of her and she looked up, red around the nose and panda-eyed. She was a beautiful thing, still, and he thought that Ryan must be fucked altogether if he could hurt her time and time over.

He relayed the doctor's update. 'He'll be fine,' he said. None of them believed it.

'How could he be fine,' Karine squeaked, 'when I don't know who he is anymore?'

Joseph squeezed her arm. 'Hey,' he said. 'This is where it starts getting better, OK? You'll see.'

Tony went outside for a cigarette. He curled his hand around the flame of the lighter; the wind got at it anyway. He turned to the wall and tried again. An ambulance pulled into the bay to his left and paramedics removed a creature on a stretcher. They were joking. Just another night for them. Just another fucking casualty.

Jimmy Phelan stepped up beside him and said, 'Jesus, the whole of Cork City must be in A&E tonight.'

Tony's cigarette caught. He had little mind for running.

'What do you want?' he asked.

J.P. scowled. 'Is that any way to greet an old friend?' he said.

It had been months. J.P. was as good as his word. It had been months between visits before, too, but this time was different, and Tony felt it in his son's distance. The girl was gone and his association with Jimmy Phelan consigned once more to history, but the cost was all around him tonight, in white faces and Karine's tears.

'Probably not,' he said, 'but we haven't been close in a while, have we, Jimmy?'

And yet the fucker had jumbled Tony into junk.

'I suppose we haven't,' J.P. conceded. He lit his own cigarette and raised his eyebrows. *Continue*, he invited. Tony did.

'You didn't have to involve my young fella,' he said. The cigarette smoke was noxious as his very first lungful; he was nauseated, dizzy. 'Whatever he said to you. He's only a boy.'

J.P. said, 'He involved himself, Tony.'

'Are you trying to tell me he knew what he was doing? He's twenty years of age, Jimmy.'

J.P. took a drag and shook his head. 'You're dredging up some old shit there, Cusack,' he warned.

'So what?' said Tony. 'We're old shit. Aren't we?'

'Meaning?'

'Meaning we were buddies one time. Meaning you were the first person to buy me a drink when I found out he was on the way.'

Tony finished his cigarette and stood with the butt between his fingers. In front of them, the car park hosted a drowsy light show as vehicles inched in and out, swung around tight corners, searched for space in the cramped dark. Crises from one end of the county to another. What was Tony's, only another one?

'Who told you I was the sentimental type?' said J.P., mildly.

'Yeah. That's a mistake I made, for thinking there was still a man in there underneath the bullshit.'

Phelan turned. He backed Tony up against the wall.

'No one talks to me like that, Cusack.'

'I fucking know that,' Tony snapped. 'I know it better than most! Bear that in mind, will you, boy? I know what you're capable of. I've seen it and I've fucking felt it. You took my son from me. You've nothing left to take.'

'I'm sure I could find something.'

'Let me save you the trouble of looking – you couldn't. If you're going to kill me, fucking kill me. I've had enough. It's all coming away under me.'

'Why would I want to kill you, Cusack? You're not dangerous.'

Tony thought, *I didn't used to be.*

J.P. said, 'Are you finished?'

Tony exhaled.

338

J.P. said, 'Our friend Robbie . . . Well, it wasn't you I was worried about talking, Cusack.'

The automatic doors opened to their right and a couple came out. They stood at the other side of the doors and lit up. J.P. looked over, gauged intent and spoke again, so quietly that Tony had to strain to hear him over the autumn wind and the car park hum and the living, breathing, dying moments playing out in the building behind them.

'Consider yourself told only because we are old shit, Cusack, very old shit indeed. If it had come out about our friend Robbie, what d'you think would have happened? She's an old woman. She keeps putting herself in harm's way and it's my job to keep pulling her back again. You do what you have to for family. Absorb that one, and let the old shit go.'

'You ruined my family while you were saving your own.'

'No,' said J.P. 'I didn't. The state of you, Tony. I didn't do that to you, and you know it. You can stand here in the dark harping on about your family and your boy and your badly faked innocence, but it's just me and you here, and I see right through you. You can whinge about what needed doing, but it was nothing new to your young fella.'

'You don't know that,' said Tony.

'Yeah I do. Open your eyes, Cusack. Your young lad was well able for it. He's already twice the man you are.'

'Good news,' said the doctor. 'It's just a sprain. You'll be hurling again before you know it, Maureen.'

'Oh, mighty,' she sniffed. 'And I here all night.'

The doctor brushed off the gibe. 'Could be worse,' he said, looking over his glasses at the waiting room. He presented her with a prescription. 'Painkillers,' he said. 'Three a day, with food. Look after yourself.'

'And that's your lot,' grumbled Maureen. She stood by their seats as Jimmy retrieved the newspaper and their coats. 'What are you giving out about?' he said. 'You got to go home to bed now. If it had been broken they'd be setting it and you'd be here another four hours.'

'Sure amn't I institutionalised at this stage?'

'Well what did you expect with your messing?'

'Last time I try to clean anything, so,' she said. 'You can get me a housekeeper.'

They moved towards the doors. Across the room, Maureen spotted a familiar dark mop, and she paused.

'Everyone's in this place tonight,' she said.

'That's just what I thought,' said Jimmy.

Tony Cusack looked up at them. Maureen raised her good hand, but he didn't acknowledge it.

'What's wrong with him?' she said.

Jimmy touched her arm and shrugged towards the door.

His world wasn't something his mother had a great interest in sharing, but across from Tony Cusack she felt a connection to Jimmy's deeds. 'What's he in for?' she asked Jimmy, to another shrug. 'What?' she said. 'You didn't ask?'

'Why would I ask?'

'That's a kind of sad way to be,' she mused.

'You don't mix business and pleasure,' Jimmy said. 'It's as simple as that.'

Maureen frowned. 'I'm going to ask him,' she said.

'Do no such thing, Maureen.'

She snorted. 'Are you going to stop me? The man did a lot for us, Jimmy.'

'As I'm sure he's keen to forget.' He took her by the arm. 'I get what you're saying, Maureen. Honest to God I do. But just because you have a tie to someone doesn't mean you have to double-knot it.'

The parallel was enough to render her pliant. She let him lead her into the car park.

He opened the car door for her. She settled in and took a deep breath; the interior smelled so very like him, the grown-up him, a long way travelled between the soft perfume of his baby head and the smoke and cologne and metal and leather she associated with him now.

He relented. 'Tony Cusack was a decent sort,' he admitted,

sitting in beside her. 'Bit of a langer as a kid; I grew up with him. Sank into a bottle in his teens and never came out again. He's exactly the kind of person you'd use for such an awkward task as the one you set me, Maureen. In need of a few bob, innate mistrust of guards, too much to lose to consider talking.'

'What's "too much to lose?"'

'Kids,' he said. 'A hape of them. He met an Italian girl in London, brought her home and had six smallies with her. Then she went off and died on him. Fucking car accident. His oldest is twenty now. Young fella, criminal record acquired already. Ryan. Tony was a Man United man.' He laughed. 'His kids mustn't be so laddish, mind. I bought Ellie's piano from him. He had a house of little musicians. No wonder he didn't know what to do with them.'

'You threaten a man's kids?'

'No. The implication is enough. You ask how many he has. No more needs to be said.'

'It's a nasty way of holding someone,' she chided.

'It's a nasty world,' Jimmy said. 'What else was I going to do? You went on a rampage with your Holy Stone. Someone had to clean it up. If you don't want to hear truths like that don't go around forcing them.'

She was silent. The city slid around them and Jimmy navigated as a bright-eyed captain on a sleeping sea.

Tony sent Kelly home with Joseph but Karine refused to leave, even after the doctor had insisted that Ryan was in no danger. It took her mother, arriving down bleary-eyed at four in the morning, to drag her away, and even then it was a slog.

'You don't understand,' she bawled. 'It's my fault.'

'It's not your fault,' Tony offered, and Jackie D'Arcy glared at him, as if his input was detrimental to her daughter's return to sanity. He knew what the mother was thinking. She was a nurse herself. *Histrionic bully boy making a point with a packet of painkillers.* Maybe she was right, but here wasn't the time or the place.

'Am I upsetting you?' Tony snapped, and she jumped. 'She's crying but he's unconscious, so maybe just keep the high and mightiness to a minimum, all right?'

'I wasn't being high and mighty,' said Mrs D'Arcy, feigning injury.

'It's all right, Mam,' said Karine. 'We're just all a bit tired and stressed out.'

Jackie coaxed her down the corridor and out into the car, and that left Tony, alone in a thinning crowd, with no son yet to show for it.

Once they'd moved Ryan into the unit, he was allowed to go in. He hung back for just a moment before taking his place in the chair by the bedside.

He seemed fine. It would have made Tony feel a lot better if a nurse had popped her head around to say 'He's only sleeping it off' or 'He'll have some head in the morning' but they weren't treating this with comforting levity. He'd complicated everything, apparently. The alcohol was one thing, the cocaine another, the paracetamol a further. The treatment was a problem to be worked out. And then at the end of it they'd whistle and a psychiatrist would swoop down from the rafters with a prescription book and a big red stamp with which to brand Tony Cusack Cork's greatest fuck-up.

'What did you do that for, Rocky?' Tony whispered.

He rested his head against the mattress.

'What am I gonna do with you?'

Still with his forehead to the bed, he reached for his son's hand. His skin was warm. Tony ran his thumb over his knuckles and in his sleep Ryan took a deep breath.

'You're not going to die on me anyway.'

There was room and time to talk. Mouth pressed against hospital sheets in case anyone heard him, Tony confessed to his sleeping son. 'I didn't mean it,' he said. 'I didn't mean any of it. They said down in Solidarity House you lash out at the ones you love the most, you know? If you'd just talked to me more often . . .' He paused. Medical staff drifted past the cubicle. Murmured diagnoses were met with shaky questions.

'I know this is my fault,' he said. 'I know I fucked up. I know you stepped in and I know I should have stopped you. So if this is a point you wanted to make, you've made it. You frightened me. Whatever about me; you frightened Karine. Karine doesn't know who you are anymore. D'you hear that, boy? Are you listening to me?'

He sat up straight and looked at his son. Dark lashes rested on dark circles. The bulb off his ould fella.

'And yet with all your mam's faults, yeah. It's not enough for you to feel, boy, no. You have to feel everything ten times harder.'

Time had smoothed out the chubby cheeks, straightened the curls, sharpened the jaw line, but he could see the baby still in his son's face.

'Your mam would never have let you do this.'

Tony was tired. He could do with a bottle of water, a couple of Solpadeine and his bed.

'I shouldn't have let you, either. It wasn't right. But fuck, Ryan. None of it was right. This city's fucking rotten, falling down around us.'

The dark pool around Robbie O'Donovan's head spread on the floor of the cubicle. The tiles he'd replaced for Maureen Phelan ran patterns through his vision. The deep throb of the boat engine under his seat made him gag.

'I killed her, Ryan. Oh God help me. I killed her.'

The tears were falling and his son was blind to them.

'You need to understand,' Tony said. 'Whatever punishment comes for me I'll take it as long as you know . . . I did it for you. For the very same reason you did what you did: you do what you have to for family. How can I be sorry, then? How can I be sorry when I did it for you?'

Elegy

There's a piano in the lobby. I spot it when we're walking in and then it grows and grows until it's all I can think about. I'm not usually waylaid by pianos on nights out. I don't spend every second social occasion fantasising about enormous inanimate objects that one time used to mean something to me. But I've been fucked these past three weeks. I've been sick, and tired, and dizzy, and dead. And so that fucking piano is taunting parts of me I kept well covered until temporary madness stripped back the skin and left me beaten and bleeding. You couldn't play me now, *it* says. Your fingers have fused, your mind's gone grey, you're deaf, you're blind, you're dumb. You're nothing.

It's Karine's twenty-first birthday.

Her mam and dad have organised this serious shindig. Hotel, bar extension, DJ, canapés, cocktails, everyone she's ever met in her fucking life, this cake with white chocolate flowers all over it that I swear to God would kill someone if it fell on them. She's got everyone dressed in either black or white so she's the only one wearing colour. She's flitting about in this turquoise dress, making sure everyone's all right, that they're all having fun, that they know everyone they're supposed to know. And what am I doing? I'm stuck to the railing of the terrace outside, smoking over the river, dead to it all but that piano in the lobby and the dirge it's playing for everything I'm not.

I don't want to be here. Today is the first day I left the house since they discharged me from the hospital, three weeks ago. Karine had to cry to get me moving and even then I registered the tears with . . . I don't know. I don't want to make her cry. I'm sick of making her cry. But it's like I don't have any real will to stop it. I can hear her and I want to reach for her and hold her in my arms and tell her I'm sorry and that I'll snap out of it but I can't, because I'm a million miles away, lost in the dark, and I can't get to her.

But I can breathe. I can move around. I can eat and sleep and watch telly. Sometimes I can't believe it. I'll be three spoons into a bowl of Weetabix and suddenly I'll ask myself, Well, how'd you do that, boy? How'd you get here?

Y'know how many times I've fucked Karine since that night? Twice. In three fucking weeks. And only because she insisted that making me hard would cure me. She stripped for me, she sucked me, she whispered I could have it any way I wanted it . . . and it was grand, once I got going. But once it was done I was back underground. Like, Oh, that was nice, but it's not for the likes of me. I don't deserve it. Worse, I don't want it.

Maybe it's guilt, for Georgie. Slow-burn kind of guilt. Maybe the adrenalin was always supposed to take six months to bleed me out.

Maybe it's just that I did so much coke I wasted all my feelings. A whole lifetime of emotion honked through in a couple of years.

Maybe it's just that I'm so wrapped up in replaying the day I nearly hit my girlfriend that I can't feel anything else, like I've been rolled up in a bit of old carpet and dropped into the sea.

But then surely all she'd need to do to cure me is forgive me? And she has. She has because she thinks I tried to kill myself at Halloween, with a bottle of tablets and a bottle of Jameson, like an ould hag.

No. Coz if I'd wanted to kill myself I would have just shot myself.

Joseph comes out to me on the terrace.

'It's pussy central in there,' he gasps.

I might be a corpse but I've noticed him chatting up one of the other nurses for the past hour. Karine's best mate Louise is usually Joseph's fuckbuddy. There'll be drama there before long.

All I can say is 'Yeah.'

'You all right, boy?'

'Yeah.'

'You don't look all right.'

'I'm OK,' I tell him, but he's hovering, so after I finish my smoke I go inside with him, and the place is hopping, really hopping. I go to the bar and order a beer.

Karine is back over beside me. 'I thought you weren't drinking?'

I'm not supposed to be. I told her I'd knock it on the head for a while and see if that helps me stop making a total arse of myself in front of the entire city. I don't particularly want a drink, as it happens, but the whole place is staring at me. The whole fucking place.

'It's only one,' I tell her.

'Yeah, I know, but . . .' She's fixing the collar of my suit jacket, and I know there's nothing wrong with it. 'Y'know, maybe you shouldn't. Maybe you should give yourself a chance to . . . I dunno, come back to yourself.'

Yeah, maybe. And in the meantime the vultures are circling and the eyes on Mammy and Daddy D'Arcy are turning into pinpricks of hate and the room is whispering Poor Ryan, poor poor Ryan, don't you know he tried to top himself? Para-fucking-cetamol, like an amateur. But you know about him, don't you? You know his mother drove drunk into a ditch. Vehicular suicide. Imagine. Poor Ryan. Look at him not drinking, he can't drink anymore, like, can't be trusted with it, neither his dad nor his mam could be trusted with it.

'It's all under control now, though,' I tell Karine. 'No difference anymore between me and the next man.'

'OK,' says Karine. 'Just be careful, though.'

I take a sip and walk away. Careful, like. I know what she means. Don't lose the temper and don't lose hope. No chance of that now. It's lost and gone and her boyfriend's empty.

By the door I turn back. The dance floor is full. Joseph's shifting the nurse. Someone's rubbing Louise's back. Gary D'Arcy is watching me over his pint. Karine is twirling in her turquoise dress and her subjects are moving around her like dancers in *formation, like snowflakes in the sky, like shitty little bangers around a falling star. And I don't deserve her. I can't feel sad about that, because I've broken myself, but I know it because it's that sharp and true.*

I put the beer on the ledge behind me and walk out of the function room and down to the lobby and approach that vicious fuck of a piano as it goads me, You couldn't do it, boy, the music's stopped, *and I walk past it as my throat closes up, as the last of the fight goes out of me,* You waster, Cusack, you piece of shit, your girlfriend's twenty-first and you're walking out, she'll never forgive you for this, *I get to the door and out into the winter,* Pathetic, fucking pathetic, why'd you even bother trying to kill yourself, don't you know you killed yourself years and years ago, when you stopped hearing the music and started listening to the city . . .

I'm nearly home by the time she calls me.

'Where'd you go, boy?' She's worried.

'I just had to go, girl. I shouldn't have come at all. I can't do this.'

'But I need you here. Don't do this to me tonight, Ryan. Please!'

I could be back there in half an hour, at her side, holding her up when she got tipsy, giving her the first and the last of her twenty-one kisses. I could be there for her but I won't be. I can't. It's done. My city stretches in the dark, and I can no more go back than go forward.

What Ryan Did

It's a shithole, but of course it is, because it's cheap and Georgie doesn't work long enough or hard enough to afford anything else. Not since the first landlord, in her illustrious career as fucker and fuckee, has she had someone back to her own space, but she has already thought it through and accepted that Ryan's different. And besides, he's intimated that there will be cocaine, and a little party, and as weird as the whole thing is – and it is weird, because she's known him since he was a boy – she reckons he'll make it worth her while. Look, she should have known better than to try to shame morals into him. She thinks that a few decent lines will cushion the blow of reality winning out, yet again.

Ryan looks around him and notes that reality: ugly floral curtains; a coffee table stained with grey rings and round black burns; cream-coloured walls on which shadows have been made permanent through her negligence. There's a low, olive-green couch with wooden armrests; he sits down and clears crumbs and ash off the tabletop with an open palm.

'It's not like I was expecting anyone,' Georgie says.

'Don't worry about it.'

'You know, no one is ever let back here, Ryan.'

'Lucky me then.'

He takes a baggie out of his pocket and starts lining up.

'D'you want a drink or something?' she says.

'No.'

'I want a drink.'

She comes back as he finishes raking out, holding a glass of vodka or gin or whatever it is.

'OK, well, there's no point being coy,' she says. 'What are you after?'

He continues staring at the lines. There's a beat in his head, echoing loud. He feels as if the control he has over his own body is about to give in, and that he'll puke, or cry, or snap or faint or fucking something; he's afraid of that, first of all. He can be afraid of consequences later.

'I don't know what I'm after,' he says.

'They usually know.' She takes a sip. 'Did you fight with your girlfriend or something? Is that why you're here? You know, without your judge's wig on?'

'Don't,' he says.

'It's just that . . . *something's* changed.'

And she's just going to accept that, isn't she? Something's changed but she's not going to rethink her complicity. He's angry now, on top of everything else. It's beyond him how Georgie had the nerve to march up to his dad's front door barking questions, but not the nerve to find her way home again.

'I'm sure you have a price list,' he says. 'You tell me.'

'Am I still allowed to think it's weird?' she says.

'I thought you said it was just a job?'

'It is. Still, though. We have history, you and me.'

She's sorry she said it as soon as it's out of her mouth. He looks up from the bars he's drawn on her table, and his top lip twitches at the corner as a snarl is caught and turned inwards. *He's going to be one of them,* she thinks. For a moment she considers telling him she's changed her mind, and that he's going to have to leave. She wants to preserve what she thinks he showed her on Saturday last. But she decides it's worth taking a chance on and even then she knows she's wrong, deep down, buried with the rest of her cunning.

She finishes her vodka.

'OK,' she says. 'Well, when I go somewhere with a guy it's fifty for the hour. And that's, like, oral and whatever position. Not anal though.'

'That's extra, is it?'

She looks back down at the lines. 'Yeah, I guess.'

'Fuck's sake,' he says.

He's glowering, and she's surprised it turned so soon. 'If you're going to be a dick about it,' she says, 'it's going to be horrible for both of us. You know? I mean, you're the one asking for it, you don't get to judge.'

'Take your line,' he says. 'Before the fucking eyes fall out of your head.'

She kneels in front of the table. 'I'm just saying,' she says. 'I'm disappointed in you too, Ryan.'

She closes her eyes and as she snorts she hears the gentle clunk of something being placed on the table beside her.

She sits on her haunches, staring at the gun out of the corner of her eye, as he leans back on the couch and grinds out noises of disbelief and regret.

It's a while before he accepts she hasn't got a damn thing to say, so he says it for her.

'I'm not here to fuck you, Georgie.'

He leans forward.

'Why would I be? Didn't you tell me before I was never to buy a prostitute? If you really think your words are that weak, I suppose it explains why you couldn't stop asking Jimmy Phelan questions.'

'I don't work for J.P. anymore,' she whispers.

'He wants you dead,' Ryan says.

She twists her hands on her lap and looks at him with sinkhole eyes.

'How does he want me dead, Ryan? I've done everything he asked me to do. I haven't said anything. I haven't asked questions in years.'

'I don't know, Georgie.'

'J.P. told me the whole story. I accepted it. I let it go. I did! I did what he told me . . . It's been years, Ryan.'

Ryan shakes his head.

Georgie says, 'Why you?'

'It's just a job.'

She says nothing for a long time and he has no more mind for leading her. He watches her quake and he hates her for it. He watches his gun on the table in front of her and he hates himself for having it. Most of all he hates what he's about to do but he knows there's no way around it.

He bows his head and sighs.

Georgie is in the horrors.

She sits on her haunches on the floor of her rented one-bed, crying, and distracting herself on and off with the stupidest of notions. *Sniff. Sob. That's it, it ends here. Gulp. Cough. Look how dirty the carpet is. I wish I had a hoover. I should have bought a hoover. Bit late for thinking this now but Oh! To have a hoover! Vacuuming used to be my favourite chore, back when I had a mam and dad and not just old pieces of cloth holding my memories together. Sniff. I'm going to die.*

The fear-sweat leaves her shaking cold. She pulls her arms around herself.

She's sick knowing it won't work but still she tries. 'But me and you, Ryan . . . We're friends. Aren't we?'

He picks up the gun.

'What makes you think I have friends?'

'I saw you with them, on Saturday. All walking down the street, going out or whatever. You have friends because you're a normal guy. You're not . . . this.'

He's standing up. She doesn't move. She cries onto her lap and he moves around the table and over to the window.

'This is normality,' he snaps. The volume makes her jump. She blinks and he comes back into focus; he's staring, hard, his brow furrowed and his lips trembling. 'People do what they have to do. But not me. Fuck this, not me!'

He doesn't raise the gun. He cradles it against his right thigh. With his left hand he covers his eyes.

Ryan's failed and he knows he's not going to get away with it, even here where God fucking damn it, it could still be fixed, if he had the balls for it.

She's weeping with fright, and he feeds off it, pacing so he takes up as much air as he can, here in her dingy set.

He's pushed her into her bedroom and she stands with a bag and her passport. He's booked a flight. The next one out of Cork is to London Stansted. It'll do.

'Ryan,' she blubs. 'I can't. My daughter's here. All of this is so that I can get her back. You telling me I can't see her again is just insanity—'

'Me leaving you live is fucking insanity!'

He's right. He's giving her his life instead of taking her worthless one. He's offering his father to her whims. His gaudy rage stops him crying. He really wants to cry.

'I'm a mother,' Georgie insists. 'What about my daughter?'

'What about her!' He points at her, his mobile clutched tight in his hand like another useless weapon. 'She's better off, isn't she? You're no mother, Georgie. Mothers don't go around getting fucked for coke money!'

'That's not fair, Ryan; how else am I going to get by? There are no jobs out there, there's no way I can go to college . . . Be realistic! This is all I'm able to do right now. I'll get it together!'

'You haven't a notion of getting it together! Don't try this one on me, girl. My mam was taken off me so I know what that's like and I wouldn't wish it on anyone so don't for a second think this is because I'm being sentimental about you and your kid; she's better off without you and I don't say that lightly.'

'What if I go home? Back to my mam and dad's. It's in the middle of nowhere, Ryan. No one'll ever see me again. I won't ever come to the city, I swear it!'

'Only now you're thinking of going home, girl? You couldn't go home before you fucked my life up, no? Fuck you. You're going. You're gone.'

Georgie crumples.

'You're not saving me, Ryan. You're killing me.'

352

'I'm counting on it,' he says. 'And if you come back here, fucking ever, *ever* Georgie, you'll find me a lot less cowardly about putting one in your brain. And your daughter's. And your mam and dad in Millstreet. D'you hear me?'

She holds a hand over her mouth and the tears fall onto it and over her knuckles and slide onto the brown cloth over her wrist.

'I will do it,' he says. 'The only thing wrong with me can be fixed by growing up a bit. You're just damn lucky you caught me when I was too stupid to pull the trigger. You're just damn lucky Jimmy Phelan got me to do the job.'

'I'm not lucky,' she cries. 'This isn't fair—'

'I know it's not fair, girl. But that's the way of things in this rotten city. I barely know what this fuck-up is about, but it's going to take someone. And it's gonna have to be you.'

Ryan has to contact his father afterwards for Jimmy Phelan's number, and he can only do so via text; he realises, up in his old estate, parked thirty feet from his old driveway, that he doesn't want to talk to Tony.

When the reply comes through he puts his hand back on the key in the ignition and freezes.

He's not sure why he didn't notice it – perhaps because he's not been around enough for the alternative to become the norm – but there are lights on in Tara Duane's house, and Tara hasn't been there in ages. She took off the Christmas before last. Someone said she was seeing this Indian guy so she probably ran off to become a Hindu. Tara was flighty that way, and she's done shit like that before, so even her daughter Linda can't call bullshit on the theory.

For a moment he thinks: *She's back.*

After a while the facts begin to settle. The car in the driveway isn't Tara's. There are no curtains or blinds up in the front room, and he can see people, none of whom he recognises, walking past the window. He realises that someone's moving in.

It's been months since Joseph's friend Izzy recommended he seek answers from Tara.

He's conducted the conversation in his head a dozen times but it's made a poor substitute. In fairness, he hasn't cheated on Karine since that neon-lit conversation in the living woods, so it hasn't escaped him that Izzy was right. He's been trying to own it, trying hard, reclassifying it as an indulgent mistake made by a new man driven temporarily mad with the possibilities.

He tells himself, sitting in his car down from his father's house with worse deeds now to his name, that what happened in Tara Duane's house five years ago doesn't matter, not in the grand, fucking dark scheme of things.

He imagines it now again anyway, seeing as she's never coming back.

In her sitting room she hands him a mug of tea and sits there with her vacant smile as he tells her *Hey, I fucked you. I did it. I wanted to. That's what happened, OK?*

It kills him, though. He knows it shouldn't but he feels it like a kick to the gut now that he realises she's gone and his chance for making sense of it's gone with her.

I just want her to confirm it, he thinks; his lips move with it. *Tell me I went for it, that I wanted it, let me have this one, oh God, please, give me this one.*

He starts the car. He has Jimmy Phelan to lie to yet.

Georgie finds her feet. She doesn't know how. It just kind of happens.

She just kind of happens now. From one end of the street to the next. She exists.

London is a massive place and she's frequently lost, and even thinking of it as a collection of towns all jumbled together doesn't help. She is lucky, in that she's happened upon almost straight away by an Irish couple who offer to help her find where she's going. Of course she has no destination. She tells them, tearing up, that she had to leave Cork because of an abusive boyfriend. She tells the Irish couple that she has friends in London but she hasn't seen them in years and claims that the address she has for them is out of date, oh, what is she to do? They find her a guesthouse. She thinks that's about it but the next day the woman from the couple comes to the guesthouse to see her. She gives her the name of a friend in Islington who's got a downstairs flat to rent. It turns out to be no great shakes but no one pays any attention, least of all Georgie. Her desperation is a potent scent and though she never sees the Irish do-gooders again, just that stroke of luck is enough.

She finds an agency. It's not difficult; her ground-floor flat is surrounded by the domiciles of shuffling addicts and weird bachelors, and they know where the action is. She meets a bright-eyed Russian woman in a cafe on Holloway Road. She tells her she's older than is usually asked for, unless she goes into specialised stuff. More lucrative, she says. Georgie shakes her head. Whoring isn't her calling, for fuck's sake. The woman gives her the number of another agency, which provides much cheaper lays.

She has found a place in which to exist, outside of reality, as a glitch in someone else's world.

She thinks about exacting her revenge, but it's too soon, and she's not sure where to direct it. Concocting plans around Jimmy Phelan strikes her as futile, like marching on Heaven and demanding God's resignation.

She thinks about Ryan, and one day making him see what he did to her.

One day, she thinks, *God willing*.

She might die in the meantime. She hasn't made up her mind yet.

While she's waiting she posts the scapular back to whatever's left standing on Bachelor's Quay. She addresses the envelope to Robbie O'Donovan.

What Tara Did

Young Ryan is out on the back wall. Tara spots him from her kitchen window. It's a quarter to eleven and it's a Sunday night. He really shouldn't be there at this hour. She figures he's been driven out again. She determines to offer her sympathies. No harm; Melinda's away. Her dad has taken her to Dublin for a few days, to see the sights. Tara would like to be lonely without her, but she's glad of the peace and quiet. Melinda is very demanding.

Boys are demanding too. Ryan, like all boys, is usually cheeky and funny but tonight he's quiet as a mouse. There's a nasty bruise around his left eye. 'Oh, darling,' Tara says. She sits beside him on the wall and presses up against him; he's shivering. No one in their right mind would sit out in the cold without good reason. The night is damp to its very breath. Ryan has problems with his father. Tara knows because she hears the boor's convulsions. There's no privacy on this terrace. Quite rightly. If there was then the poor boy would have to suffer alone.

'Come inside,' she coaxes, 'and we'll have a lovely cup of tea.'

At first he resists because he doesn't want to trouble her. She assures him that she wants to look after him. She rests a friendly hand on his knee and when he doesn't flinch she skims gently up to his thigh and squeezes. 'You don't have to go through this alone,' she says.

If he was any other boy on this terrace she wouldn't be so insistent because some of them are only brutes in the making. They follow her down the street and whoop obscenities. They make loud remarks on the bus. Ryan is different. He has grown up very fast, the one positive from his father's cruelty. He has wrested some independence by doing a little bit of dealing to his friends. It's naughty, but sometimes Tara enjoys smoking with him. He's getting taller and broader by the day. He's almost sixteen.

She leads him inside and puts the kettle on.

'Tell you what I'll do,' she says. 'I'll put a drop of whiskey into your tea for you. It's beautiful stuff; I got it at Christmas and I've been saving it for a special occasion. Aged. Have you ever had aged whiskey?'

The boy says he's fine.

'Don't be silly,' Tara blusters. 'It'll warm you right up!'

The whiskey she has isn't old at all but she thinks it's best if he gets a good drop down him and she doesn't want him complaining about the taste in the tea. She makes it fairly strong. It is very cold outside.

'Come into the sitting room,' she says. 'And we'll have a chat. And you know what? If you don't want to talk about your dad we don't have to. We can just watch telly and talk about that instead. Do you like *True Blood*? I have a few of them lined up in the Sky Box.'

When Ryan gets into the sitting room he sheepishly produces a baggie of grass and asks if she wants some. He knows the propriety of barter. She smiles. She lets him skin up and sits cross-legged beside him on the couch and shares the joint with him.

'You roll another,' she tells him, after they finish, 'and I'll make another cuppa.'

She doesn't have a second drop herself; she doesn't need it.

He sits on the couch only half watching Bill and Sookie and messing with his phone. He's as taut as a guitar string; she thinks if she touched him now he'd sing for her. They can be so jittery at his age.

'What are you going to do later?' she asks.

'Go home, I suppose.' His voice is so very low; he probably doesn't want his father to know he's next door. Perhaps it's not allowed. Perhaps his father knows the damage a boy can do, especially when the woman next door is on her own. *Ryan knows he's being bold,* she thinks.

'Don't worry,' she soothes. 'You can stay here on the couch. I'll bring you down a blanket and pillow.'

On the way back to the sitting room she grabs a couple of cans from the fridge.

'Here,' she says. 'I've already given you my loveliest whiskey, so we might as well keep going.'

He drinks up as he's told.

Still so quiet. She tries to get him to talk but he's brooding. She sits back beside him on the couch and tells him if there's anything he needs to get off his chest, she's here for him. He says he's fine, but, mouth a bit more liberated now, he expresses thanks for giving him somewhere to sit while he waits for his dad to calm down. 'Calm down?' says Tara, eyes wide. Ryan shrugs. Tara says, 'Oh, sweetheart.' She holds him. He doesn't know how to handle that. He freezes. She puts a hand on the back of his neck and guides him to her breast. 'It's OK,' she says. 'It's going to be OK.'

He pulls away and tells her he needs to use the bathroom. While he's gone she dashes into the kitchen and gets him another can. He doesn't seem so keen when he returns. 'I kinda shouldn't,' he says. 'Oh, darling,' she replies. 'When life gives you lemons, make a gin and tonic. How much worse could tonight possibly get?'

Well, he is langers altogether once he gets to the end of the can and she laughs and gets him another. He's chattier but he's starting to slur. She wonders if he's had a few joints already tonight. By the end of the next can she's able to hug him a lot easier. 'Poor baby,' she says, and kisses the top of his head. She can feel his breath on her chest.

One more and he's done altogether. He lies back on the couch and she continues talking to him, telling him that he's worth more than his father knows and that the world is full of good friends if you only learn how to open the door. She realises halfway through one of her favourite anecdotes that he's asleep. She leans over him. 'Ryan?' she murmurs. He doesn't move. She sits at the end of the couch and puts his head in her lap and strokes his hair while she watches the end of her episodes.

He starts to snore.

Tara reaches for his phone and goes through it. She makes sure her number is in his contacts. It's saved under 'T.D.'. Maybe he's worried his dad will see but it's too impersonal, so she changes it to 'Tara x'. She opens the Facebook app and considers writing a jokey status update but concludes that it would be inappropriate. She goes through his photos. They're mostly of him and his little girlfriend. Tara rolls her eyes.

There's a video in the library. It's frozen on blurred skin tones. She presses play and holds her hand tight over the speakers.

It's the girlfriend. For a moment Tara doesn't recognise her because she's sucking on a cock and the angle shows only her lips and her downturned eyes, but when the trollop looks up she realises. The girl is naked. The camera occasionally glides the length of her body. Tara figures it's Ryan holding the camera.

'Well,' she says, softly.

The video stops when he comes. Tara watches it a couple more times.

She gets up carefully and leaves Ryan's head back on the couch.

'You're even naughtier than I thought you were,' she tells him. He doesn't stir.

She crouches by the couch and looks at him. He's wearing a pair of grey cotton tracksuit bottoms and a stripy polo shirt in lemon and grey. He's got a stud in one ear and – she gently tugs his collar down – one of those leather necklace things. He doesn't move when she touches his collar so she traces her fingers down his chest slowly.

'You're so fucked I better sit with you,' she tells him, 'in case you throw up, and then where would we be?'

She starts at his neck again

'So fucked,' she says. There's a song to it. 'You're so, so fucked.'

This time she works a little way into the waistband of his pants, just to see. Black underwear. 'Classy,' she tells him. She strokes his tummy, under his shirt. She touches the thin dark ridge below his bellybutton and slides her finger down. His dick twitches.

'Are you even asleep?' she teases.

She touches his crotch on the outside of his tracksuit bottoms and says, 'Ryan? Ryan?' but he doesn't answer. She strokes until his dick is hard enough for her to close her hand around it.

She makes a decision. She straddles him, very gently, and leans down so her head is on his chest, and she listens to his heart beating. 'Ryan?' she tries again. His dick is still hard against her. 'You might be asleep but your body's wide awake,' she tells him. 'Don't you think that's odd?'

No response. She brushes her middle finger against his bottom lip.

'A girl told me recently,' she confides, 'that I should take what I can get. Which I thought sounded a bit ugly, but now I wonder if she just wasn't well-read enough to have heard the term "*carpe diem*". And *clearly* . . .' She laughs. 'Clearly you don't mind.'

She gets up again. She slides her knickers off, kneels by the couch, works his clothes down to his thighs and nuzzles against him for a while, eyes fixed on his face. Then she opens her mouth and holds his dick between her lips and licks and sucks him till she's ready to get back on top. She's wet and it's stupidly easy. She holds his dick and slides over him and starts to ride and eventually he blinks and groans and she's too far gone to want his input or to want to start all over so she cuddles against his chest again, still rocking, almost there, and says 'Sssh, baby, go back to sleep' and he does, how easy, how well his mind knows to stay out of this and just let his body have its fun, how fucking easy . . .

But his hands are grasping her arms, and then there's a rude tumble and she's on the floor, and she skins her elbow on the carpet and clutches it and allows her eyes to water with the shock.

'Ryan, that really hurt!'

He's curled up at one end of the couch, gasping and swallowing like he's had a desperate nightmare.

'That was not very nice,' she chides, back on her feet and fixing her dress.

He stands up, and she feels too wounded to offer an arm as he wobbles and pulls his tracksuit pants back up and peeps like a baby bird.

She folds her arms. 'What's wrong?'

And sure he can barely speak, the stupid boy. 'No,' he says. 'Coz it's not . . . I have a girlfriend.'

'Well, you better not tell her, so!'

He's very, very drunk, because he starts crying.

'Oh for God's sake,' says Tara. She's careful to look stern because in his foolish, showy blubbering she sees trouble enough to catch in her throat.

'You can't tell her,' Ryan says.

Tara moves towards him but he backs away, and knocks against the sitting-room door frame, and has to grab the banister to keep himself upright. 'Why would I tell her?' Tara says, carefully, trying out a smile, finding a foothold. 'She wouldn't understand. It's OK, I get what you're telling me. This'll be our secret, I promise.'

She watches him fumble with the front door lock.

She frets about it the next day. She really likes Ryan. He's a pleasant young man. She doesn't want to fall out with him. But she can't be so complacent as to trust his perception of the previous night's events; he drank too much, and he'd clearly been stoned before he'd even come onto her property. No, she'll have to do a little damage limitation. She can't risk him broadcasting his half-remembered misgivings, not with her history. People are far too quick to judge these days.

In the early evening she spots his father walking up the driveway and she steels herself and runs out to catch him.

Tony Cusack hates her. She doesn't mind that; he's pathetic, the kind of man whose favoured publican lives for Children's Allowance day. 'What?' he says. Tara's not at all bothered by his tone. Weak-kneed malingerers don't frighten her.

'Just a quick word,' she says. 'Ryan was around at mine last night. I don't think he was entirely sober.'

'What was he doing at yours?'

'He says he came by to see Melinda, but . . . Well look, Tony. I really don't like to get him into trouble, but his behaviour was inappropriate. It became rather clear that he has . . . well, fixated on me. He seems to think there's something between us.'

'Does he now? And where would he get that idea?'

She bristles. 'I'm hardly leading him on!'

'So you're telling me that my fifteen-year-old, who can't go ten fucking minutes without texting his girlfriend, is suddenly infatuated with you? What the fuck are you getting at?'

She scowls. He's pronounced it 'infactuated'.

'You're being needlessly hostile,' she says. 'I'm only trying to help. I'm so aware of the fact that he lost his mother and so it's hardly surprising that he's acting out with older girls, is it? He showed me a video, on his phone. I think you need to watch it,' she smiles, 'and just inform yourself as to what he's up to.'

26

The frame around which one builds one's life is a brittle thing, and in a city of souls connected one snapped beam can threaten the spikes and shadows of the skyline.

Robbie O'Donovan died hunting for sentiment to bring home to a girl he refused to save and in his expiration made shit of structures he'd never seen. Small houses. Small sanctuaries. Small lives. The city runs on the macro, but what's that, except the breathing, beating, swallowing, sweating agonies and ecstasies of a hundred thousand little lives?

Cork City isn't going to notice the last faltering steps of a lost little man. All those lives, all those beams, crisscrossed into the grandest of structures . . . the city won't see the snapping sticks, or feel the first sparks.

So scale it down. Zoom in. Look closer.

Fighting cats in the courtyard outside woke Maureen at 4 a.m. She couldn't get back to sleep so she travelled through time.

She was well aware that she lived in the past but, she decided, it was because she'd been left there. Decisions taken on her behalf forty years ago had anchored her to a moment doomed to repeat itself, over and over. Here's the piss-licking face of Una Phelan. Here's her husband, a sheep in wolf's clothing. Here are the clergy, gathered outside the maternity ward like an unkindness of ravens, grasping every perch they were and weren't entitled to. Ireland, the clouds outside. *And shame on you, Ireland,* thought Maureen, four full decades later. *You think you'd at least look after your own?*

She got out of bed and stood at the window. The cats were well gone. In the apartment directly across from hers, a Christmas tree twinkled between heavy curtains. *Bad idea*, she thought idly. *The place could go up in flames*.

Her own vengeance lay festering under piles of sodden ash in Mitchelstown, and what use was it, at the end of the day? Without a perpetrator the Gardaí had no motive and without the platform of culpability Maureen had no audience at which to shout it. The papers had said the Gardaí were looking for a woman to assist with their enquiries, so that hoyden Saskia had obviously blabbed. They hadn't found this woman because she'd never existed. In the meantime people blamed unruly youths and assumed no political motivation.

She wrote a letter to the *Indo* hinting that the person who'd set fire to the church up in Mitchelstown had, perhaps, been making a bold statement, and that maybe Ireland should expect more in the way of this kind of carry-on if it wasn't going to learn its history lessons. The *Indo* hadn't published it. What kind of Ireland had she inherited at all, when the *Indo* wouldn't even publish crackpot woe-betides?

She put the kettle on.

In Holles Street four decades past a midwife lay a wriggling mound on her stomach.

And that was all she got.

She didn't miss Robbie O'Donovan and though at the time she'd been sure it had been the flames that had taken him, she wondered now, wringing out a teabag in the middle of the winter dark, if it hadn't simply been time for him to feck off. Hadn't his demise been his own fault? He had crept in through a window on the latch and skulked though her home looking for relics, and had been knocked into his grave by the kind of woman no one thought still worthy of blame.

She sat at her kitchen table. Around her the debris stacked. She hadn't done any housework in the six weeks since she'd sprained her wrist. That was Jimmy's job and he'd failed to provide a decent solution. She assumed his interest in his mother had waned now that she was no longer causing him trouble. The girl Georgie had disappeared off the face of the earth, her lips sealed and her mind at last honed by Maureen's generous wisdom. The man Tony had been threatened to keep his mouth shut. Robbie had gone up in smoke. Maureen had been left redundant and Jimmy had other things to worry about, in his line of work.

Spraining her wrist had slowed her down, and she'd stopped hunting for redemption, or what measure of it the charlatans sold wrapped in hymn and waffle. She was finished toying with swindlers, either by laughing at their convictions or burning down their temples. She had no energy left for divilment, not now she knew how much her son got up to on her behalf, behind her back.

She went for a walk.

It was just before five when she left the house and the city was a pyre too damp to take the flame. She wandered towards the Lee. Its forked tongue was probably the reason the place wouldn't burn.

What keeps this bloody city alive at all? she wondered.

It wasn't Jimmy; wasn't he too busy ruining it?

There was no stopping him now, and even if she found a way to vocalise it, to explain that he'd done his bit but her revenge was ultimately an empty thing, so he could stop now, and rest . . . Well, someone else would take his place. Some other scoundrel bent out of shape by the twisted streets of this pirate's city. Jimmy's fall would birth another, and another, and another, and Maureen would be matriarch of all.

Too late for Jimmy. That's why she time-travelled. If she could have caught him that Christmas he bought her a brandy, when he was twenty and she was dismissed as no longer threatening by the baseless piety of her stupid parents, who's to say what she could have done?

She walked along the Lee and towards the old brothel. On the water the reflections of street lights shimmered like sinking lanterns, golden and red on the black, and beautiful.

On the iron bridge across from the gutted brick there was a figure on the parapet, standing still and staring down.

Maureen wondered first, *Robbie O'Donovan?*, because the figure was tall and skinny and definitely male, and more again, because it was so frozen and so quiet that it seemed otherworldly. She managed to walk all the way onto the bridge without disturbing him.

The likeness was startling. For a moment she fancied she had time-travelled, but had managed to land beside the wrong son, John and Noreen's, the one whose fragility had been shaped to fit under her own boy's turpitude. But the fancy dissipated; this wasn't Tony. This one was taller and thinner, quite the wrong shape, but the dark hair, the jaw, the chin, the mouth, the bloody everything else was just the same. She whistled under her breath. Another boy who wasn't his mother's son.

Now that she was this much closer she realised he wasn't so silent. He was singing something in tuneful whispers, something to which he didn't know the words. He was quite lost in it, and lost in the will-o-the-wisp colours in the black water beneath them. No light to his song. She realised with a sickening start that he was set to jump, and so she snapped,

'What do you think you're doing?'

And he turned, and her breath caught as she saw him lose his balance, but he fell the right way, just a few feet away from her, whacking his head off the concrete.

She stood over him. His eyes met hers. Big black pools, as much as the river was below them.

He sat up, suddenly, against the parapet, and she sighed and repeated, 'What do you think you're doing?'

He pushed himself upright, dragging his back against the parapet, and when he was on his own two feet he dug into his pockets and produced a lighter and a cigarette, and three goes later he managed to drag deep enough to keep it lit.

'Well?' she snapped.

'Well what?'

'Well, what do you think you're doing?'

'Nothing.'

'Oh yes. Great times we're having, when you meet young fellas making eyes at the Lee in the early hours. Doing *nothing*. What would your mother say?'

The Italian girl, the prematurely departed. Maureen wondered how happy she could have been in this city, surrounded by the insular and the suspicious, and their faith, and their fallen.

Her son stood with one hand clasped to the back of his head. His jaw rolled. Maureen assumed that he'd knocked it on his graceless descent, but moments passed and he didn't speak up, so she peered closer, through the night, through the ancestry fixed on his features, and wondered if it wasn't half out of his tree he was, and if his balancing act hadn't been born of synthetic bravado rather than the despair she thought she could spot in his stance. She didn't know the ins and outs of inebriation, outside of being able to diagnose every stage of drunkenness as dictated by her nationality; he was inebriated, though, and not pissed. It was in the size of his eyes, and she'd mistaken it for character.

'What's your name?' she asked.

He complied. 'Ryan,' he said, after a while gnawing the air in what seemed to her to be terror churned with a slight concussion, and she waited for him to elaborate until he followed up with 'Cusack.'

Of course it is, she wanted to say. *Isn't it nearly dripping off you?*

'What in God's name are you at, Ryan Cusack?'

Again, silence. He blew out his cheeks and looked over her shoulder. She cocked her head.

Under his breath, she thought she heard, 'Grandmaw, what big teeth you have . . .'

She scowled.

'Come on,' she said, turning around and walking back towards the city centre, away from the hollowed landmark, along by the indolent water, and she looked back twice and he was following her, as she knew he would, as she knew his father would too, once given a command voiced with appropriate authority, and she thought that this was how it should be. The parents cast the mould for the little ones and the little ones curved to fit.

Between the opera house and the gallery she found a stone block bench and waited for him to approach, and when he got close enough for her to see the fear and the loss she directed him to sit beside her and said,

'What are you on, then?'

He folded up and laid his head on his crossed arms. 'I dunno,' he said.

'You don't know? And what d'you think your mother would say to that? Winking at the river, having gobbled goodness knows what. Is that so you'll drown easier? Your poor father, Ryan Cusack.'

'Fuck him.' He rubbed his forehead off his forearm and raised his head.

'You look tired,' she said.

'I am tired.'

'How could you be tired? Fine lad like you. What must you be, twenty?'

'Yeah,' he said. 'Twenty-one in March.'

'Are you that afraid of twenty-one?'

'Maybe I just wanted to go swimming.'

'Aw, shite.' She leaned closer. 'Why are you afraid of twenty-one?'

'I'm not,' he said, and stared over the square, and she gave him time to figure out his mouth, and after a while he said, 'I am. I dunno. I dunno.'

'All these young fellas,' Maureen chided. She looked across the river. The Northside rose dotted in white and yellow lights, and she wondered how many of those lights denoted a young life yet to be dammed and diverted? How many of them could be another Jimmy?

She looked back at Tony's son and furrowed her brow.

'I think it's sad,' she said. 'You have a child and your child is the whole world. What did your father ever do that you'd want to take that from him?'

Ryan mumbled, 'Why docs it have to be about him?'

'He made you, didn't he?'

368

'You don't know him. He doesn't give a fuck.'

'Of course he does.' If he didn't, Jimmy wouldn't have spun his noose so easily.

'He doesn't,' said Ryan. He leaned back and looked up at the sky. 'If you knew him you'd know that. He's a prick and that's where I got it from.'

'Ah. You're suffering from something inherited, is it? Something that makes you want to take to the Lee only days before Christmas?'

Decades ago, a twenty-year-old Jimmy Phelan offered his mother a Christmas brandy and she took it and closed her hand briefly around his and smiled.

'What if I cured you?' she said, but Ryan didn't answer. She shuffled closer to him and held her hand out and he looked at it, blinked, and frowned. There was a light sheen on his face, even in the chill. She jerked her hand, and he sat up and held out his own and she grabbed it.

'Yours aren't workers' hands,' she said.

She turned his hand over in hers and traced from the tip of his index finger to his wrist.

'What do you do, Ryan? Are you in college?'

He shook his head.

'Well, what then?'

'A bit of this and that,' he said.

'A bit of this and that? Shady little fecker, aren't you?'

He put his head back onto his free arm.

'Pup,' she said.

He looked at her, his nose and mouth hidden in the crook of his arm.

'Easy know what you are,' she said.

'That easy?'

'Oh yes. And yet don't you have complicated eyes? Very dark. But then, your mother wasn't Irish.'

He closed his eyes and for a moment she wondered if he hadn't done so in self-preservation, but then he opened them again, and she watched them in focus until he was ready to say, 'How'd you know that?'

'I know things,' she said, confidently; more than the priests, more than the idiot savants down at Ruby Dea's ramshackle commune. 'You're the musician,' she stated. 'But you're not playing, are you?'

He sat straight and stared at her and his hand in hers turned heavy.

'Fuck,' he said. 'How'd you know that?'

'Coz I can see right through you,' she said. 'Coz you're as blatant as a burning church. Don't you think I know what's wrong with you? It's easy see what you're able for, and not able for, and despite what he tells me I know you're not able to play the little gangster.'

'What the fuck did you call me?'

'A little gangster. Isn't that all you are? Don't you think how you make your money has plenty to do with wanting to drown yourself?'

She'd hit the spot. He made to pull away, but she held on tight and he had neither the foundation nor the spite to drag her with him. He stopped pulling and she said, 'That river doesn't care who or what you are, but it will take you, boy, if you dare it to. Don't you know that?'

He wasn't able to answer.

'I should know. This city ruined me,' she confided. 'But the odd thing is, while it was ruining me I was ruining it, and I only figured that out when it was too late to stop it. What I did to this city, me and Dominic Looney, is something immeasurable and I see it in the faces of people I never should have met. And yet . . . maybe I can make it up to one man, at least. The city doesn't see me, but maybe I'm aiming too high.'

She rubbed her thumb over his skin again, taking him in, his father's face, his father's eyes, and a future all of his own to burn.

'Don't let the river take you,' she said. 'Promise me!'

She put her arms around him and his pulse leapt as she pressed the palms of her hands against his neck.

'Promise me, I said!'

She let him sit up and took his face in her hands.

'You don't understand,' he said. 'I'm a bad guy. Worse than you could fucking imagine.' His voice was choked with woozy torment; she rubbed her thumbs over his cheekbones, delirious. 'I've already done the damage. I had something good and I wrecked it, and ruined it and lost it. What am I without her? I'm turning into Him.'

'Not if I can help it.'

She tilted her head towards the city and smiled.

'Of course this place can pull you apart,' she said. 'But this country's done punishing me, and I can do what I like now, and so I choose to fix you, and by God this pile will let me. Don't mind that river, Ryan Cusack. Whatever's bad we'll burn it out; that's how it's done. If you want to take the fuckers with you, that can be arranged.'

Beyond them turned the world and the land and its sleeping city. Maureen felt giddy. Robbie O'Donovan had been a mistake Cork hadn't even noticed, but this one, this one she'd substitute, a life for a life, and she'd make damn sure the city knew it.

'I will put you right,' she said. 'Sure haven't I already saved your life?'

Acknowledgements

Heartfelt thanks are owed to Mark Richards for the advice and the tweaks and his patience with terrible jokes. And to Caro Westmore, Becky Walsh, Rosie Gailer and everyone at John Murray.

To the lion Ivan Mulcahy, to Sallyanne Sweeney and Stephanie Cohen for all of their help, and to the tirelessly wonderful Sinéad Gleeson.

To the brave souls who read and steered and bolstered me without ever realising how much it meant: John Green, Richard Fish, Arlene Hunt, Liam Daly, Damien Mulley, Julian Gough, Conor O'Neill, Haydn Shaughnessy and Sinéad Keogh.

To Kevin Barry, for shoving me where I needed to be, and to Sami Zahringer, for her immense generosity.

To my sprawling, intimidating, brilliant family, and to the friends who continue to put up with me, particularly to Ellen Brohan, Louise Lynskey, Kevin Lehane and his exceptional brain, and my partner-in-crime Caroline Naughton.

And most especially to Róisín, who has a writer instead of a mother and doesn't seem to mind, and to John, because there'd be nothing without John.

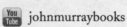
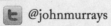
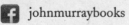